Chaotic Tranquility

Published by

Two Realms Publishing LLC

Irmo, SC 29063

https://tworealmspublishingllc.com

Cover Designer: Sweet 15 Designs

Interior Designer: Two Realms Publishing LLC

Editor: Cassandra Fear

Illustrator: Nicodemus Holroyd

Cartographer: Jog Brogzin

Ebook ISBN: 978-1-955106-11-5

Paperback ISBN (Amazon): 978-1-955106-12-2

Paperback ISBN (Worldwide): 978-1-955106-29-0

Printed in the United States of America

Content Warning

Welcome to Prisma Isle, a realm not for the faint of heart.

Humans may not exist, but that doesn't mean villages don't have any fucked up shit happening inside their walls. We would warn you of everything, except the list is extensive. And we could be here far longer than necessary. All you need to know is that shit gets bad and escape isn't always possible.

On the brighter side, because let's face it, there has to be one. There's a lot of sex to counteract all that dark.

Yes, we agree.

Balance is the necessity of life.

Chaotic Tranquility

Prisma Isle™ Series
Book Two

BRIGIT ROSÉ & NIKKI HARAS

TWO REALMS PUBLISHING LLC

TERMINOLOGY

Adolescent: term in shape shifter culture for children ten years of age to twenty years of age

Aphros [af-rows]: the second cycle of the Vernal Equinox (the spring)

Antekilio [ant-E-keel-oh]: library of the Sirens

Chicane Village: village of the guilers

Cycle: approximately one month or from one full moon to the next

Demeter [dee-MEE-ter]: the goddess of fertility, earth, and harvests; protector of marriage and social order; daughter of Cronos and Rhea; mother to Persephone; and creator of the sirens

Full-fledged: term in shape shifter culture for adults; those twenty years of age and older

Galenus [gah-LEE-nus]: male, canine shape shifter, deceased

Guiler [guy-lure]: a humanoid species with elemental abilities

Hades: the Greek god of the underworld; sometimes used as a sort-of curse word by the shape shifters

Informant: soldier to the shape shifter king, Markham

Julunna [jew-lew-na]: the first cycle of the Luminos Equinox (the summer)

Kriah [KREE-uh]: a female nymph who lives in Migas Village

Lacuna [la-KEW-na]: an hour of time

Luminos Equinox [lum-OH-nose]: summer

Marana: the second cycle (month) of the year

Métamorphe [met-a-mor-fey]: the shape shifter village

Migas Village [MEE-gahs]: the hidden hybrid village and a place of sanctuary

Mindlink: a telepathic connection between twins and some mates

Nestling: term in the shape shifter culture for children one year of age to five years of age

Newling: term in the shape shifter culture for newborns to one year of age

Penumbra(s) [pah-num-BRAH]: week(s)

Pteryina [ter-EEN-uh]: home of the sirens; adjacent to The Clouds

Seiphinx [SEF-IŋKS]: a creature with the head and front torso of a bird (sparrow), back torso and tail of a lion, and gold beak; they are battle-intense creatures created for the warriors of Migas Village

Solaris: year, which comprises sixteen cycles (months) for the inhabitants of Prisma Isle

Ta morá mou: My sweet one(s)

Umbra(s) [um-BRAH]: day(s)

Vasilia [vuh-SILL-ee-uh]: female siren that is the Elder of the sirens and lives in Pteryrina

Verdant Grove: home of the fae

Vernal Equinox [ver-NAL]: spring

Youngling: term in shape shifter culture for children five years of age to ten years of age

Zancle's Rock [Zan-kuls rock]: bar and restaurant in the marketplace run by Ambrosia; known for their venison stew

Chapter One

Julunna, Year 1027

Gavin felt Parthenia nearing the treehouse. His excitement and relief at seeing her again was overwhelming, but it wasn't enough to overpower his fear. She was walking, not flying, because it hurt too much to do so. They hadn't seen one another since the morning after they'd made their trip to the barrier. That had been nearly three days ago. Then, afterward, whatever had happened to her—he'd felt it all. As he'd sat at the top of the staircase, pining after her but unable to reach her, he'd sensed her wake and felt her excruciating pain. His mate's suffering had eased somewhat. Perhaps someone had tended to her. Parthenia had thought of him, and her body had relaxed. When she'd radiated calm, she'd fallen asleep. Though it had been a natural sleep that time, not her passing out. Gavin had stayed there for as long as he could until the sun had nearly set. Then he'd fled back to the village, arriving just in time.

She hadn't shown up to the treehouse the next day. Hadn't been able to move without pure agony assaulting her. Today the ache wasn't as great, but periodically he felt a searing sting lance his shoulders.

As her presence drew near, her yearning fluttered through him, to see him and to hear his voice. He longed for her just the same. The sensations grew more and more intense the closer she got. As her pain hit him anew, his eyes turned black. Squeezing them shut, he tried to calm the roaring rage inside and get his eyes to change back to their normal color. He didn't know what had happened to her. Nor did he know how badly she had gotten hurt.

Gavin took several deep breaths, but they did little. As she got within feet, he eyed his reflection in the silvered mirror Gabby had placed on a shelf. Nope. Black as charcoal. Gods, his body shook. He needed to calm down. *Now.*

It wouldn't happen. He was halfway down the tree before he'd even registered leaving. As he leaped the last ten feet onto the ground, he shifted to his humanoid form. Parthenia stood at the base of the tree in one of her white dresses. "You are hurt. What has happened?" Closing the distance between them, he went to take her into his arms and she winced away. He'd barely touched her shoulders. He snatched his arms back, letting them fall to his sides. "What has happened to you?"

As she stared into his eyes—which he knew were still jet black—he sensed the direction of her thoughts. She felt as though she shouldn't have come, injured as she was. But he could also sense how badly she'd wanted to see him. Parthenia swallowed, her throat working as he watched. It was still another moment before she formed words. "I was punished."

Gavin growled. "Punished?" He reached a hand out; despite the rage that coursed through him, the caress he gave her cheek was gentle. "Why?"

"I said some things to Fagonia I shouldn't have."

His jaws clenched tight together, and he barely held back a snarl. Though she said aloud that it was Fagonia, her thoughts pointed in a different direction altogether. Her mother. "I want to see. No. I need to see. Show me."

Showing him wouldn't change what had happened, and he could sense that Parthenia didn't think it was a good idea. All the same, she exhaled a soft breath and slowly turned around. Her dress hid most of what she'd endured, but it didn't hide all of it. With a grimace, she untied the top of the straps to her dress and let the back slide from her skin, gently clutching the front to her breasts. Although she tried, her wings didn't extend very far. It was enough that he could see.

Hot tears spilled from his black eyes as a loud roar emanated from him. Balling his hands into fists, he dug his claws deep into his palms. He felt nothing from them, not even when blood trickled through his fingers and dripped onto the ground. No. All the pain he felt right now came from her.

Large gashes that were still healing covered her back. On several spots lay angry, red welts. Something had ripped small chunks and holes from her wings, tearing out her feathers. "Whoever has done this to you ..." Oh, gods, he would lay them to waste. He couldn't get any more words out as his throat seized up. He faced the tree holding the treehouse. She had told him she'd brought more healing potions here. He needed to get her one immediately. Touching the trunk, he glanced over his shoulder at her. "Close your wings, love. Do not hurt yourself anymore. Stay right here, and I will be right back."

Letting her wings fold into one another, Parthenia shook her head. "I know what you're thinking, and no. I can't take the potion."

All he could do for a moment was stare at her. "Why would you not? You need it to heal. You are... you are in so much pain." He let out a growl, but his wrath wasn't towards her.

"Because she will see. I can't." A tear rolled down her cheek. "They will know I didn't stay put. If they find that out, they will never let me out of their sight. If I take the potion, then I cannot return, and we may never find all the answers we've been looking for. Gavin, we have spent *penumbras* pouring through books. I can't let that happen. I just can't."

With his body sagging a bit, he gripped the bark of the tree, leaving a gouge in the wood. His eyes clenched so tightly shut he felt as if they were trying to fuse. He let out a low, keening cry, his chest heaving as he tried to draw breath. "What can I..." He let out a deep, shuddering breath. Her pain and her tears were shattering him apart. "Can I tend to your wounds? If you cannot take the potion, may I at least do that for you?" Then he remembered. "Gabby. She brought more herbs here, the ones for pain. Let me give you those."

"Can you... can you retie my straps first, please?" she whispered.

Gavin could only nod. Blinking furiously to get his eyes to lighten to their normal hue, he pushed off the tree and went to her. He took great care as he re-tied her straps. Taking her face gently in his hands, he brushed her tears with his thumb. "Do you think you could hold on to my neck? I could take us up to the treehouse. I will go slow so as not to jostle you as much as possible." His voice was soft, but still strained. He fought to hold his anguish back. She didn't need to feel that from him, not now, but it was so difficult.

Her gaze held his for a minute. "I think so."

Turning his back to her, Gavin shifted to all fours. Putting his front paws on the trunk, he peered over his shoulder at her. "Put your arms around my neck, lock your fingers together, and grab my back legs with your talons. I will wrap my tail around your waist, too. I will not let you fall, beloved."

Briefly dipping her chin, she followed his instructions. With a small wince, she placed her arms around his neck and interlaced her fingers. Lifting one leg, she curled her talons around his leg, and then did the same with the other. The pull on her back was a bit more intense at that point, but it was tolerable.

"I will go slow," he reminded her. "Tell me if it hurts too much, and I can slow down." He brushed his cheek against hers as he wrapped his tail around her waist. She rested her head against him just a touch, and he inched up the tree. It was going to seem to take forever, but if it gave her a chance to rest until she had to go back, it would be worth it. "When we get up there, will you allow me to dress your wounds? Or is that not allowed either?" he asked through clenched teeth.

"They are only allowed to be cleaned to prevent infection."

He bit the inside of his cheek to stop the growl from coming out. He didn't want to risk her losing her grip if his body vibrated. Rage surged through him. "Do they need to be cleaned?"

"Likely. They have not been cleaned since yesterday."

"I will clean them after I have given you the herbs." He spoke no more words until they had gone further up the tree. Flickers of images from her reached his mind, but he could tell she was trying to keep the details from him. He had probably terrified her already with his eyes. Part of him didn't want to ask, but the other part of him needed to know. "Will you tell me what happened?"

"If you feel you truly must know, I will tell you, though not before we reach the top."

Gavin simply nodded and continued to climb. He wasn't sure how long it took before they reached the top. Moving over only so far as she would need to step off, he then stopped so she could dismount at her own pace.

It took several minutes, but she climbed off with minimal twinges. Parthenia stepped in further to give him room to climb in. After entering the treehouse the rest of the way, he shifted to his humanoid form, took her hand, and helped her lower herself to the floor. After pressing his forehead to her knuckles for a moment, Gavin made his way around the room. It took him a minute to find the herbs Gabby had left, and even longer to find what he'd need to clean her wounds. He grabbed a jar of water to mix the herbs in as well. With their texture, it was easier to drink them than to chew them. Not to mention, their taste left a lot to be desired.

Gavin glanced at the silvered mirror in passing. His eyes were still black. It was rare that his eyes changed like this, and they had never stayed dark for so long. But then again, he'd never been quite this livid. When he'd collected everything, he lowered himself to the floor in front of her. Keeping his eyes downcast, he worked on readying the herbs.

Parthenia inhaled a heavy breath. He flipped his gaze up to meet her stare, then turned back to his task. "Do not worry over me, my love. My anger will pass." Even when his eyes returned to normal, even when the trembling in his body settled, and the constriction in his chest lifted, he would never forget what had happened to her. When he was done with the herbs, he held the jar out to her. "Drink all of it, if you can. When they have worked and your pain has eased, I will do what I can for your wounds."

"I wish you didn't have to be angry, though I understand why you are." Gingerly, she picked up the jar from his hands and took a sip before taking a larger gulp.

The taste was horrid, but the herbs did the trick. His voice was still quiet and weary. "My mate has had violence done to her. I cannot go after the ones that harmed you right now, and I cannot do anything to take your injuries away. How could I not be angry?" Taking her free hand in his own, he stroked her palm and fingertips. He would wait until he sat behind her to ask her for the details. She was in enough agony, not to mention everything she would feel from him. His eyes were still black, but she didn't need to see his expression or his tears when she told him.

"I would've waited longer, but I missed you too much. I simply had to come." She drank the last of the remedy in the jar. It wouldn't take long for it to take effect.

As he moved his fingertips up and down her forearm, the touch of her skin allayed him a little. "I am glad to see you. I have missed you so much. That you are in pain, though..." He let out a breath. He could feel the ache in her body taper off. "Will you allow me to carry you home when you must return?"

He sensed the protest on the tip of her tongue but also that she really didn't want to turn his offer down. It would certainly be better than walking, and they would be able to further enjoy one another's company.

"Yes. I would like that. Thank you," Parthenia said.

"Of course, my love. I cannot do what I wish, so I will do what I can to keep you from further pain." He brought her wrist to his mouth and stroked it with his tongue. The last thing he wanted to do was cause her any more discomfort by touching her too much. "Let me know when you are ready for me to clean your wounds."

The tension further eased from her shoulders. Combined with the herbs, he could feel the first bit of relief he'd felt from her in days. A deep sigh left him. His trembling passed as her tension left. The constriction in his chest settled into a dull throb. He was too in his head to know if his eyes returned to their normal color or not.

"I am ready."

Gavin moved behind her, dragging the supplies to clean her wounds with him. Sitting cross-legged on the floor, his chest tightened again as he scanned all of her injuries. Lifting a shaking hand, he clenched it to steady himself. He inhaled and exhaled slow, deep breaths. In. Out. In. Out. Trying again, Gavin worked on her, keeping his touches as light as he could. "Will you tell me?"

Silence stretched between them. "Fagonia was outside the library when I returned after our trip to the barrier. She questioned me on my whereabouts. Somehow, it turned into a verbal fight. I said that her insistence that The Poppy Fields and The Reflection Pools had nothing to do with the isle was our downfall. Our argument drew everyone's attention. At which time, I called her a burden to our people. I may be right, but it was the wrong thing to say."

He was quiet for a minute once she'd finished speaking. "Perhaps, if they disliked the truth so much, they should have looked at the perpetrator. Not who called them out. Everyone should be allowed to speak the truth." What was he saying? No one in his village could do so either. "Why does Fagonia care so much where you go?"

"I am responsible for The Poppy Fields and The Reflection Pools. We continue to lose lots in the fields, and the second pool has lost water. They think I am being derelict in my duties. That instead of finding answers, I am causing more problems."

"What is happening with those is not your fault. Any more than what happens in my village is mine. We cannot grow crops within our boundaries since well before my birth. Trees grow even though they appear to be dying. But nothing else. And the difficulties with pregnancies." None of that had been anything he'd yet told her. Gavin shook his head. "What good does misplacing blame do? They should assist you in finding a solution, not chastising you for something that you have no control over."

Parthenia half glanced at him over her shoulder. "I do not believe we are the only ones suffering. The problems you've just stated in your village seem to confirm my suspicions. Something is happening on the isle. Something that is the true cause."

"If they are happening within the other species as well, Devin may know. She travels around the isle more than anyone I know, but I do not know if she speaks to the other species or not. What do you think the cause might be?" Neither of them had thought to ask her. Even if they could confirm suspicions, they'd be the only ones who knew. But at least it would allow them to focus on other areas.

"I have found none. But the more I study it, the more it feels as if the isle is losing its power." She paused. "Regardless, no one cares to hear my thoughts. And the argument with Fagonia was simply the ammunition my mother needed."

"If the isle is truly losing its power, it does not seem to have any effect on Markham. The village, yes, but not him. His power only appears to grow. Each *solaris*, it appears he is stronger." Which really made little sense unless there was something else at work with Markham. He couldn't have said what, though. Once he finished cleaning the wounds on her back, Gavin moved to her left wing. Her last words confirmed his thoughts from what he'd caught from her earlier. "So, your mother did this to you."

"Yes. I'm certain she has been looking for a reason over the last *cycle*. This simply presented her with the opportunity. And because of the nature of the argument, the punishment..." Her words trailed off. "It demanded to be public as well."

It felt as though fire burned within them. Gavin jerked his hands away from her wing as they curled into fists. "*What?*" he growled.

"It was..."

Images of her memories flickered through his head. Thoughts of the moment her mother and Fagonia had agreed to a public lashing. Her sister stepping forward to object. Her refusal to reveal his existence, even though it may have stopped her punishment.

Fury surged through him so much that his vision shorted out for a moment. He picked up one bottle of medicament in his hand and threw it against the wall. It shattered, covering the floor beneath it in liquid and shards of glass.

Parthenia jolted at the sound of the crash and cried out as a pang lanced through her shoulders, radiating down her wing. Tears rolled down her cheeks as she squeezed her eyes shut tight. She swallowed, taking shallow breaths as she tried to gain control of the erratic throbbing at the base of her wing. For a brief second, an image of a spiked metallic whip popped up in his head.

Oh, no. What had he done? Another keening cry, louder than the one he'd uttered on the ground, came forth from him. He couldn't have even said where such a sound came from. It was one he'd never uttered before today. His claws gripped the wood beneath him, and he leaned over until his forehead pressed against it. His chest heaved and fell, quick gasps leaving him. He couldn't breathe. He had caused her pain. His emotions and his anger were out of his control, and it hurt her. "I am... sorry. I am... oh, gods, I am so sorry," he sobbed out.

Parthenia reached out and stroked his back. "It's not your fault. Please, please, do not blame yourself."

The tremors through his body slowed as her fingers sifted through his fur. "It *is* my fault. I cannot seem to control myself. I have never been like this. Oh, Parthenia, I am so sorry. I should not have startled you. My action caused you pain. I would never..." Well, he couldn't say he *wouldn't* cause her pain because he just had. "I would never mean to cause you pain." Forcing himself upright, Gavin faced her. As gently as he could, he took her face in his hands, rubbing his thumbs over her cheeks where her tears had fallen. "I am so sorry," he whispered.

"I know you wouldn't." Closing her eyes, she pressed a tender kiss to the inside of his palm and lifted her gaze to his once again. "I don't blame you. The pain, until I fully heal, simply cannot be helped."

He stared into her eyes, his thumbs slowly caressing her cheeks. "I wish to hold you, but I know I cannot. Is there anymore I can do for you?"

Her gaze dropped to his broad chest and flicked back to his eyes. "I believe there is. Lay down, please."

"On my back? Or otherwise?"

"Yes, on your back. Just don't move until I am settled." Once he'd laid on the floor, she crawled on top of him bit by bit. He stayed utterly still as she adjusted herself. It took several minutes, but she lay atop him in a way that didn't cause her any discomfort. Her head rested just over his heart, her arms tucked in close, her wings and shoulders relaxed, and one knee right above his hip. "If you keep your hands on my hips, we should be fine."

He let out a contented sigh. Settling his hands on her hips, Gavin kept them still, but stroked her skin through the slits of her dress with his thumbs. Closing his eyes, he breathed in her scent that surrounded him, letting the beat of her heart resonate through him. "I wish there were a way for us to run away now." The words came out all on their own. Thinking about wishes that had no hope just yet of coming to fruition made his heart ache allover again. But it was too late to take them back. "One day, hopefully soon, I will whisk you away from all of this. And I will never allow harm to come to you, never again." He gently kissed the top of her head. They both wished for that more than anything.

"Yes, one day soon. We will leave and never look back."

There was a comfortable silence between them for a while before he spoke again. "I would like to have a family with you one day. Even if Markham is defeated, I would not want to stay here. I do not want to raise young here. There has been too much darkness." It was nice to speak about the future. Speak of what they believed would happen. Soon Devin would find the answers they needed to get past the barrier. And they would find the answers to their other issue. Not that it was the right word for it. Though, perhaps it was a good thing they couldn't take their lovemaking further. They still enjoyed and satisfied one another, but they needed to find a way off the isle before they brought young into their lives. So, not an issue, just a delay.

"I do as well, but I agree with you. This isn't the place to raise them. I'd like for us to find a place of love and acceptance. I believe that is where we should raise them."

"Our young, when they are born,"—Because he refused to believe that they wouldn't find the answers they sought; refused to believe that a true future for them wasn't possible—"will be free. To grow up in safety. Make their own choices. Speak their minds. Love who they wish for when that day comes. Without punishment. Without repercussions. They will have two parents who love them, and they will know our love knows no bounds. They will have my sister and her mate." A sudden tear pricked at the corner of his eye, but he didn't want to move his hands except for the soft strokes of his thumbs, so it stayed where it was, not yet traveling down his cheek. "They will have all of us to teach them right from wrong. To show them how things should be. To give them the life that they deserve. They will never know the pain we have."

"Yes, they will. They will have an abundance of love. As we all will." She shifted her arm just a touch. With her thumb, she gently caressed his chest. Unhurriedly, she inched her hand closer to his collarbone and continued to trace an indiscernible pattern through his fur. A quiet purr came out of him, and he tilted his head to the side to give her better access. "I do not wish you to get angry again, but I thought about you when it was happening. You gave me strength. I endured because of you."

That news gave him a strange sort of happiness. But the rest of what she said made him feel as if his heart were constricting again. The tear that had threatened slipped down his cheek, followed closely by another one. He still refused to move his hands. His throat tightened, and he swallowed hard to clear the lump. Gavin forced his thumbs to linger as they brushed against her hips. He felt unworthy to be touching her perfection at all. "You should never have had to endure that," he murmured. "I should have been able to come to you. I should have been able to put a stop to it."

"I know, my love. But I would have done whatever was necessary to keep you safe." Possibly keep them both safe, and be able to leave and still come down to see him. This was their current reality. Until they could change the outcome, this was what they had to do. Parthenia's fingers rosea little higher and gently ran the length of his neck.

"Mmm." He tilted his head a little more, his purr a little louder now. "I do not want you to feel like you have to sacrifice yourself for me. Endure pain because of me. But I would take every death blow thrown at me in order to protect you. So, I cannot fault you for that." Her fingers inched a little higher. "I love to feel that peace from within you."

"It's all your doing. Your purrs, the gentle beat of your heart. It's like the perfect lullaby."

The corners of his lips lifted just slightly. "Then we will stay like this for as long as we have."

"I very much like the sound of that."

He could feel how comfortable she was, the most she'd been in days, and he didn't want her to move any more than she did. He lightly nuzzled her head. "Do you know how long until you need to return?" As much as he despised she had to return at all, it was necessary.

"Before evening meal. Cipriana and Fantasia will come to my apothecary with dinner for me."

"If you would like to rest, I can wake you in enough time to get you back there." Before he'd even finished speaking, her fingers stilled, and she'd fallen asleep. He watched her as she slept. The slow rise and fall of her body with each breath she took. The feel of her on top of him, her hand against his neck, and the peacefulness he felt within her all helped keep his anger at bay. He kept his breathing slow and even, not moving his hands from her hips. Every once in a while, he would glance at the view of the sun that he could see out one window. While she slept, he enjoyed her dreams about a little girl with his emerald green eyes. There would come a day when that dream, as well as all their others, would become reality.

Chapter Two

Pierce didn't blame Jo for doing what she'd done. How could he? As he'd told her, that was her home, and those were people—her family—so that was where her duty lay. Oh, he knew all about duty, didn't he? He'd almost killed a member of her village. He'd had a good reason, and he didn't regret it. Not one bit. But it changed nothing about what he'd done. All actions came with consequences.

What position did that animal hold in her village? Did it matter? In his village, attacking—let alone killing—an Informant was punishable by death. He'd never escaped punishment, but he'd escaped death—purely because of his position, lineage, and because he was good at what he did. He could only imagine what the repercussions would be for his behavior.

If they killed him for this, who would care for and protect his sister? Gods, let Logan not forget about their sister. To all the gods, let him not leave her in that place.

Pierce couldn't bear to think of the true gravity of what this might mean. Beyond what would happen if Lilli got left in Métamorphe, he didn't want to look at Jocasta, knowing it might be the last time he ever saw her. He didn't want to see the tears he smelled, the ones that ripped his heart to shreds. He wanted to hold her, but if he held her now, he would never let her go. And he must.

As he went to what might be his death, he wanted to remember the sun on Jocasta's face. Droplets of water against her bare skin. Her laughter. The sounds she made when they made love. When she gasped his name. Her taste.

As they traveled to her village, neither of them spoke. They didn't touch each other. He didn't look at her. It killed him. Utterly destroyed his soul. But if he lowered the wall he'd thrown around himself, he would completely break. If he thought about saying goodbye to her, never touching or kissing her again, and never getting another chance to express his love to her, it would break him. If he stopped shielding himself from his emotions for even a fraction of a second, he would drop to the ground and shout to the gods, 'Do not take me away from her!'

But what had the gods ever done for him? They gave him a life of heartbreak and loss. Everything important, everything and everyone that meant anything—they had torn away from him time and time again. He'd gotten a brief gift of happiness—a fleeting glimpse of what it looked like for the sun to shine in his life.

Someone would rip it all away now. He should have expected nothing less.

As Jocasta led him through her village, he noticed nothing surrounding them—none of the sights, scents, and creatures staring at him.

Their path ended in front of a lone hut. "Just go inside."

Pierce wanted to say goodbye, tell her once more just how much he loved her. That she had changed everything for him. She had fixed him, made him a better male, taken away his anger, his feelings of worthlessness, and made him feel like he finally belonged somewhere. But he couldn't. If he did, he would run from this, and he ran from nothing. He never fled from duty, so he would do what was right. He would do this.

All actions had consequences, he repeated to himself. And he would take his.

Before Jocasta, the life he'd lived would have thrown him straight to Hades. At least now, he wouldn't go to his death with darkness in his soul. Perhaps that would make the difference, and maybe he would get to see his mother again.

Saying nothing, Pierce moved past her, stood just inside the door, and waited. A short female, only half his height, eyed him. With a minor dip of her chin, she led him further into the hut to the back room.

A male with fiery red hair kneeled on a mat. When he rose to his feet, he stood almost three feet shorter than Pierce, but his demeanor made him appear to tower over all. His bright yellow eyes shifted to the female. "Thank you, Delenia." With a bow of her head, she departed. "Come in, Pierce."

It didn't even seem strange that the male already knew his name. Of course he would. Did the ache in his heart reach his eyes? Perhaps not. He'd trained himself a long time ago not to show emotion. But he had not once felt quite like this.

Pierce took another step in. He would come no further until instructed, speak no words until he was told, and do nothing that might offend the Elder. That was not who he was. He rarely broke rules or laws. Not if he could help it. A few times over the course of his life, he had. Once when he'd tried to go to Logan and warn him about Markham—against Ailwin's orders—only to be forced to send Derrick instead. Then when he'd stolen Lilli away and made sure she kept her precious life. And when he attacked many to save her honor—what honor Ailwin had allowed her to keep. And he couldn't forget when he'd tried to kill that male to protect his mate.

Okay, so more than a few times.

But there was nothing he wouldn't do, nothing he wouldn't lose for the ones he loved. Not even his life.

"You may sit." The male gestured to the mat in front of him.

Pierce crossed the room slowly and kneeled as instructed, resting his rear on the heels of his feet. As his hands settled on his knees, his claws sank in. No, no. He could not break, *would* not break. He didn't fear death. Far from it. It was everything he'd finally found that he knew in his heart he was about to lose.

"Tell me of the incident with Leo the day past." The male didn't mince words, getting right to the key aspect.

Pierce inhaled a deep breath, exhaling slowly, then spoke.

He recounted everything—seeing Jocasta at Mosina Falls, their plan to meet that morning. The feeling he'd had all morning. Not that he meant to say that aloud, but it came out anyway. His eyes darkened to black. "I have known many males like *him*. I could smell his intentions, and I sensed how it would have ended had I not come upon the scene. It was not something I could allow. Would allow. Most especially, because..." His eyes shifted back to their natural ruby color as a vision of *her* filled his mind.

Because it had been her. It had been Jocasta. Because she was his, and he would never allow harm to come to her.

"She is your mate," the male stated matter-of-factly.

"Yes." The word left him in a hard rush. "Despite everything about who and what I am, she chose me."

The Elder slowly circled Pierce. "Would you change your decision to attack Leo? If given the choice?"

"No. I would not change what I did. I would make no other choice. Despite the repercussions, despite that it means death for me, I love Jocasta, and nothing will change that. Nothing. She is my everything. I would never allow harm to come to her." He looked up but didn't turn his head, only seeing the male when he came around. "I am not sorry."

Stopping in front of Pierce, the male stood there a moment. "Why do you believe it means your death?"

"Against my will, my King made me an Informant. That it was against my will makes no difference. Informants, more so than any of the other villagers, cannot mate unless he permits it. Doing so outside of our species is forbidden. I have broken one of our most sacred laws. But again, I am not sorry. I would alter nothing. She has changed everything for me."

"Then I would not blame you for protecting your mate." The male paused. "Tell me what your position as an Informant entails."

The male may not blame him, but punishment would still follow. And when word of all that had transpired reached Markham, Pierce's life was forfeit. "Leaving the village to live elsewhere is another thing in our village that is forbidden. The duties of Informants are to find—hunt down—those that have left, and Informants who have deserted. Locate those who go against any of our laws. Hunt hybrids. Break in the females who wish not to mate. Regardless of the duties I am given and how outwardly I may appear to follow orders, in reality, I do not. Although it is a risk, I work in the shadows. Often taking punishments to protect those who cannot protect themselves. While I have taken lives, I refuse to kill an innocent. I have never shed blood based on genetics." Oh, gods, the words were spilling out, and he couldn't stop them. "I have helped to fake the deaths and hide three hybrids that were fleeing from my King."

"Everything you have said aligns with the other statements I have collected. I am aware of Markham's rule. Based on requests made on your behalf, I will offer you sanctuary. We have but one law in our land. Should you accept sanctuary, you shall not commit a crime against another. Is this understood?"

His chest tightened. He couldn't breathe. There was a loud ringing in his ears. This could not be right. "What?"

"We do not punish with death. Nor do we punish those who have suffered wrongdoing. I will handle the matter of young Leo. I have heard nothing save truth from those I have spoken with, including you, my son."

The female that had escorted him into the room earlier reappeared. "Yes, Santos."

"Fetch Jocasta, please. I believe he will wish to speak with her again. She has returned to her mother's."

"Yes, Santos." The female left.

"I will ask you again. Do you understand our law?"

His head bobbed up and down so swiftly his brain rattled. Pierce swallowed the hard lump in his throat. "Yes. Absolutely. I understand." He cleared his throat. "I cannot accept your sanctuary just yet, though. I cannot leave my village until I free my little sister."

"Logan has spoken to me about Lillianna. I have already granted her sanctuary." Santos offered a brief acknowledgement to Pierce. "Now, I must tend to young Leo's statement and punishment." For a moment, his eyes changed color to a bright orange like fire. "Delenia will show you where you may speak with Jocasta." With that, he exited the room.

The male disappeared before Pierce could say *thank you*. Something wet dripped onto his lap. He swiped at his cheeks. When had he started crying?

A few minutes went by before the female returned. "Come with me, please."

Pushing himself to his feet, his head still reeling, Pierce followed her. He felt as if he would fall over from the shock. None of this had been anything like what he'd expected.

The female led him down the hall to another room two doors down. Opening the door, she stepped aside. He could feel it as Jo's heartbeat faltered. She'd been trying to clean up her face, but her tears still flowed. Entering the room, he fell to his knees before her, gathered her into his arms, and buried his face in her neck.

"I am so sorry, my love," he whispered. Gods, how could he have gotten this all wrong? How could he have treated her so harshly? The way he'd acted so cold and guarded toward her. He'd been unable to be any other way, though. On the other side now, as he held her in his arms, for the first time, genuine hope consumed him. Things might actually change. Lillianna would be safe. They could both become free.

Pulling back slightly, Pierce placed a kiss over her heart and kissed her tears away, and finally, her lips. "Sorry. I love you. I am so sorry." He couldn't stop saying it, couldn't stop holding her. And he never, ever wanted to let her go.

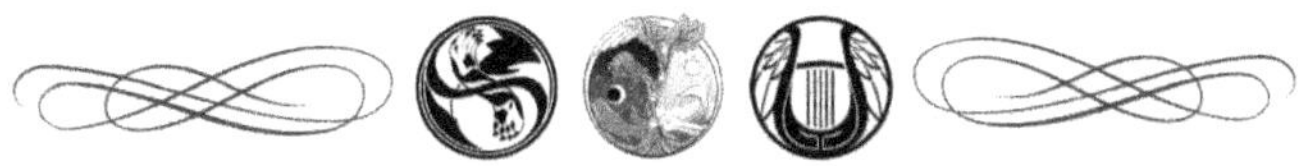

Jo was in his arms. Oh, gods. She was in his arms. Tears ran down her face as she hugged him tight and stroked the back of his head. It was an attempt to calm her racing heart as much as it was to comfort him.

Oh, gods. His apology and declaration just made her cry more. However, these were tears of joy. For a short time, she didn't think she'd see him again. Hear his voice, or those words from him. "I love you, too. I'm so sorry. Santos had to know. I had to tell him."

"It is okay. Everything is going to be okay." Pierce kissed her and then lifted her chin until their eyes met. "Santos has offered me sanctuary. I cannot accept until Lillianna is safe, and I told him so, but he has offered me sanctuary."

"Oh, thank the gods." She threw her arms back around Pierce's shoulders and peppered his face with kisses. Once she had covered his entire head, she kissed him on the lips.

"I was so afraid..." His voice was strained. "I was so afraid to be taken from you."

"He wouldn't kill you. I knew that. Not for what happened. He just wouldn't. But I had to tell him you were an Informant. And I didn't know..." Gods, she couldn't let him go. It was hard just to put any space between them. She finally withdrew enough to lock her gaze on him. Those beautiful ruby eyes she thought she'd never see again. "I didn't know if he'd give you sanctuary. I told him you weren't like the others. You were different. You were warm and loving. I just... even with Logan asking, I wasn't sure." Was she rambling? Possibly. But the words she couldn't form earlier had found their way forth. "Telling him felt horrible. I didn't want to. I was afraid if he knew, he wouldn't grant you sanctuary. And I just couldn't deal with that. I need you. I need you here, with me."

"Shh." He brushed a tender kiss across her lips. "It is alright. I was never angry at you. Not once did I blame you. I just did not want to lose you, lose this... what we have." He pressed his lips to hers again, where the kiss lingered. "I need you too, my queen. With everything in me, I need you. I would stay with you now, if not for my sister. I may not leave the village with her, and we barely get to speak. Markham is always watching, and when he is not, my father is. Hopefully, Derrick will speak to her soon. Then we can both leave and be free of that place forever. Once that day comes, I will never leave you again."

Gods, it had felt like she'd already lost him during that trek here. She never wanted to go through that kind of anguish. Jo pressed her forehead to his and inhaled a deep breath. He was everything to her. "I didn't want to lose you either. But I would never ask you to leave Lillianna. And I pray you can both be here soon."

The door opened, and Delenia poked her head in. "Your presence is required outside."

Pierce looked up at her and gave her a nod before getting to his feet. Jo watched as he scrubbed the tears from his face, wrapped an arm around her waist, and together, they followed Delenia through the empty corridor and exited the hut. Which gave her the chance to clear her tears away as well. There was no telling what this could be about, what they needed them for, but nothing could part them from one another right now.

Once they stepped outside, Delenia halted them just past the front door. Two guards escorted a shackled Leo through the clearing and disappeared with him through the maze of houses.

Santos walked toward them and stopped in front of the both of them. "We have formally charged Leo, and he is being taken to the prison. He will no longer be of concern. Thank you for coming forward." Santos bowed his head ever so slightly and started forward, but paused before leaving them. "Jocasta, if you wish it, we will find suitable housing for you and your mate for when he returns." He didn't give either of them a chance to respond before he departed.

They both stood there, silence stretching between them for a beat. "He is a male of honor, that one."

"Yes, he is." There was a reason he was their Elder. Not only could she feel relief wash over Pierce, but she was ever so grateful to Santos. It felt like he'd done more than just resolve an issue and ensure their safety. He'd given her a future with her mate.

Pierce dropped a kiss on her neck. "See, my love? Everything is going to be okay," he whispered in her ear.

Jo turned her face into Pierce's chest and hugged him tightly.

He held her against him, stroking her hair and her back, placing kiss after kiss against the top of her head and her canine ears.

"When do you have to go back?" Jo asked.

"Soon. Lillianna is… not well today. But I had to see you. I could not stay away. I am glad I did not."

"Me too." She leaned into him. "I'm sorry she's not feeling well. Hopefully, you can get her away from there soon, and that will be something less for you to worry over."

A moment passed before he uttered a single word. "I hope so too," he said, his voice tight.

There was something about the way he said it. Something that told her the female *needed* to get out. Sooner rather than later. "Would you like to walk around before you have to go?"

"Yes. I would love to see your village, your home."

"Soon to be ours." The corners of her mouth curled up as she thought of exactly where to take him first. Grasping his hand in her own, she tugged him toward the barns.

He laced their fingers together as she took the lead. "Yes. Soon to be ours."

Jo led Pierce back through the throng of homes and past the gardens. There were two large barns on one side, with the doors open. Across from them sat another one with the doors closed. Animals of a more basic nature filled the smaller of the two large structures. That had long ago built about twenty individual stalls into the massive barn. The size had been a necessity because of the physique of the spourgiffs.

She immediately went to the back of the barn. A few days had passed since her last visit, but she'd never stop coming to see them. They were beautiful creatures, with silky fur covering their rounded heads, taloned front feet, muscular bodies, and hooves for their back feet. That was without even considering their massive wings. "Several members of the village take them out daily so they can stretch their wings."

"That is probably a good thing. My mother told me once that they get cranky if confined too much."

"They do. It's why we do everything possible to treat them as we would treat another person."

"I am sure they appreciate that. Unfortunately, not everyone does so."

She strode to the last two booths. A low piece of wood separated the compartment so that the two spourgiffs could easily gain access to the other. A large spourgiff, seven-feet at the shoulder, stood in the right stall. His eyes were harsh but inquisitive. A smaller spourgiff, six-feet at the shoulder and covered in white, fine fur, stood in the left stall. The lighter-colored creature lowered its head to Jo. She reached up and stroked the top of her head.

"This is Grace. And this is Beast." She gestured to the creature to the right.

He smiled with appreciation at both of them. "She is beautiful. And she seems to like you." His eyes drew to Beast.

"I don't ride. One time was enough, but I come in to feed them." She crossed over to the wall, picked up a brown mesh bag of corn and grain, and returned to the female. Holding the morral out, Grace dipped her beak into the fibrous bag to feed. "They're mates. It's why we lowered the space between them."

"That is sweet. Why the piece of wood separating their stalls, though? Do they need their own space sometimes?" He walked over and got another of the nosebags. Getting closer to Beast's stall, but not closer than arm's length, he raised his eyebrows as he offered the bag. "Are you hungry?" Beast sniffed at him before dipping his head in the bag, but his gaze never left Pierce.

"Every couple does. It also makes it easier for them to be taken out separately." She continued to run her fingers along the top of Grace's head as she ate from the feed bag in her hand.

"Ah, that makes sense. I was not around just yet when the village had a few in captivity. My mother just told me stories." He grinned at Beast. "Do not worry. I will not touch you unless you wish it. You are magnificent, though."

A low chuckle left her mouth. His assumption was kind of adorable. As much as she didn't enjoy hearing of the spourgiffs in captivity, these creatures weren't much different from them regarding mates. "He'll let you touch him. Just don't come near Grace." Beast snorted as if in agreement.

"I can respect that." Holding the bag of food in one hand so Beast could continue eating, Pierce slowly extended his other and stroked the creature's head.

"He's the largest we've ever had. Most of them are all the same height."

"Is there a reason he grew larger than the others?"

"We honestly don't know. He's always eaten a little more than the others and gotten a bit more exercise, but it's just because he needed it. Our best guess, it's something in his parentage and their genes." The village had dedicated a lot of time to understanding the difference over the years, but they'd found nothing.

"Hm. Well, perhaps he is just special," he said, letting his hand trail the nape of Beast's neck.

"Oh, he's special, alright." Jo snickered. She shot a look at Beast. He'd been the first spourgiff she'd ever ridden. Talk about a disaster in the making. He was also the only spourgiff believed to be large enough and strong enough to carry the weight of a shape shifter. "When my dad was alive, he was the one who took Beast out for his flights."

"I can tell he would need a firm hand. He seems to have a dominant personality. Tolerant, though, at least at the moment." A quiet laugh slipped past his lips. "My mother told me she was not supposed to get close to the ones in the village. They did not permit it. She did so anyway, though." There was a brief tilt to his mouth. "Did you visit them here with your father?"

It didn't surprise her that his mother got close to the spourgiffs. They were beautiful creatures. The temptation to get near was simply too much to pass up. "I did. He always tried to encourage me to ride, but I wouldn't. It wasn't until *solaris* later I did. And once was enough. What about your mom? You said she got close to them. Did she ever try to ride one?"

"She said she did once, but that she got punished for it. Now her brother, apparently he let them out all the time." Pierce chuckled. "Why did you not want to ride them when you were younger?"

Yeah, life in his village. His village treated females differently than males. "They were big, and I was small." Okay, that wasn't entirely true. "You remember how I told you I tried to spook the keeper while in the pasture? I might have attempted to get closer to the spourgiffs when I was around three, I think."

"Oh, gods, that had to have been terrifying. They would seem enormous to anyone at that age."

"Oh, no, I was older when that happened. I learned to swim before I could walk, but as soon as I learned to walk, game on. I never stayed still. My parents lost track of me on more than one occasion. Needless to say, I made my way into the barn. I might have grabbed the wrong part..." A burst of mirth erupted from her, cutting off her words. She stepped back from Grace as the memory flooded her brain. Maybe she couldn't finish the story, but she'd given Pierce enough information to get the gist. Only her twin could've convinced her to try riding for the first time.

His eyes popped wide open. "Oh." He laughed out loud. "A little too inquisitive for your own good, love?"

It took her a second to get her fit of giggles under control. She wiped at the tears in the corners of her eyes. "You should've seen the look on my father's face when he found me. Shock. Amusement. Among other things. You think that makes me inquisitive? Wait until you meet my sister. You ever want to know anything going on in the village or the market? She's your go-to. I swear she always has one ear to the ground."

"That sounds like someone I know back in my village."

"Oh?"

"Derrick's sister."

He'd mentioned Derrick once before to her. Another Informant, but one he considered a friend. She lifted the bag back up for Grace. "Constantly listening and talking to those who would offer information."

"Yes. She seems to always know when someone around the village needs her." He paused. "She travels around the isle a lot as well. I think she breaks the rules more than she gets caught at it, but she does not seem to care much. If the good of the outcome outweighs the bad, the punishment is worth it to her." Keeping the food where Beast could reach it, he moved a little closer to the stall, allowing his hand to stroke lower onto Beast's back.

The female almost sounded like her mother, minus the traveling part. That was more like her sister. Jo adjusted her stance a bit as her gaze flicked to him. "Are you going to miss any of them?"

He was quiet for another minute, his fingers running down Beast's back some more. "Perhaps. But not enough to think of changing my course."

She didn't imagine it would. Nor would she want it to. Maybe that was selfish of her, but she always wanted to know he was safe. Have him in her arms whenever she desired. Fall asleep with him. Talk to when something bothered her. All the things they hadn't been able to do. Lowering the empty bag, she closed the distance between them and wrapped an arm around his waist.

His bag was empty now, too. He tucked her into his side. Bending down, he nuzzled her neck and breathed her scent in. She knew he didn't want to return to the village, nor did she want him to, but he would have to go before too long. His sister needed him. "I am glad that you brought me here. It was very enjoyable. One *umbra* soon, we will come here every *umbra* if you wish and feed them together."

Jo pressed her lips to his chest. "I'd like that. And maybe we can convince my sister to give you riding lessons." She snickered slightly, and a soft giggle escaped.

"What is funny, love? Do you not think I could ride?" he teased, tickling her side a bit, which only made her giggle more.

She playfully swatted at his hand. "Oh, no. I just thought it would amuse me."

"Oh, would it, now?"

"Oh, yes."

He tickled her again as he pressed his body into hers, moving them back toward the wall. As he did so, the best idea ever popped into her head. Although other shifters lived in the village, she'd had no one else to play with. They were all far older than her. And she'd guarantee they'd both have fun. Jo bit her bottom lip.

Reaching the wall, he gripped her ass with a rumble deep in his chest, almost as if he knew what danced across her brain, and lifted her. Automatically, her legs came around his waist. "I love when you bite your lip like that." He licked up her neck with a growl and nipped her ear.

Crossing her legs at the ankle, she tugged him closer. With a soft moan, she gripped his shoulders, biting her lips as she raked her nails down his back, through his fur. "I love when you growl at me like that."

"I cannot help myself around you, love. Especially when you do that." He kissed her. Another growl permeated the air as the corner of his mouth lifted. "I love your nails on me. I love every time that you are touching me."

Things probably shouldn't progress further, given their current location, but the chance of someone walking in on them heightened the blaze lighting her veins on fire. This was about so much more than the physical communion between their bodies. "Mmm, no more than I can help myself with you. Or how much I love when you grab my ass. Push me up against the wall. The way you feel on top of me. Against me." She trailed her fingers up and down the nape of his neck. "How much I love touching you." She brushed a soft kiss across his lips. "And I can't wait until you're here permanently, because I have some ideas I think we'll both enjoy."

"Oh?" He slid his hands up her arms, pinning them above her head. He teased her neck with licks and nips. "What ideas might those be, my queen?"

Her back arched as she ground against him ever so slightly. Angling her neck to the side, she offered better access and moaned. "I call it camouflage tag, and I've never had a playmate."

"Hmm, that sounds like it could be loads of fun." He sucked and licked at her neck as he moved her wrists to just one hand. Sliding his free hand along her curves, he pushed her shirt down, then palmed her breast. He massaged it, drawing a gasp out of her, and slid his hand lower. "Are you wearing anything under this skirt, love?"

For once, she was grateful she never wore undergarments except in the marketplace. Maybe she couldn't move her arms much, but she could use her mouth. She nibbled on his bottom lip. "Maybe you should find out."

Plunging his tongue into her mouth, entangling with hers, he slipped his hand between her thighs. The vibrating, thunderous sounds coming out of him intensified as he stroked her slit. "So wet for me already."

Oh gods, the things he did to her. Grinding her sex against his hand, she groaned. "Always."

A new rumble rose in his chest as his gaze fell across her face. "Do you want something, my queen?" He pinched her nub then went back to stroking her, harder this time.

Gods, yes. She wanted... no... needed to feel him. The tingling sensations served as a sharp reminder that they were alive and that what they'd found in one another was within reach. Something neither of them realized they desired. Her back arched as she ground her slick folds against his fingers. "More," she demanded. "More, my king."

"Say that again." He nipped her lower lip as his digits slid inside her, stroking the inner walls of her sex. "Call me your king."

"Oh, gods!" she cried out. Her eyes locked with his. Sometimes *I love you,* got expressed in a multitude of ways. Physical touch. Acts of thoughtfulness. Verbal communication. They were nothing more than two simple words strung together in a particular order, but their meaning went beyond their simplicity. They didn't just convey how she felt about him, but that she'd found something in him she hadn't known she was missing. Both of them had. That made these two words profound in her book. She swept her tongue along his lower lip and fused their mouths together. Releasing the deep kiss, she moaned those two precious words, "My king."

"That is right, love," he growled. "You are my queen, and I am your king." Their mouths crashed together, his tongue plunging deep inside. Pulling his fingers out of her, he gripped his cock, angled it up, and slid her down on it. A sharp hiss left him as her sex sheathed him completely and he drove into her. "You fit me so perfectly."

She cried out in ecstasy as he pistoned in and out of her. No matter how many times they came together, it always felt like the first time. Gods, she'd never get enough of him. He was right. They fit together perfectly. Her back arched as she met him thrust for thrust. "Oh, gods, yes, Pierce." Tightening the hold she had on his ass with her legs, her talons raked along the back of his thighs as they rocked against one another.

"I love it when you moan my name." He grabbed her ass in one hand as his thick cock pumped in and out of her. Fisting a palmful of her hair, he tugged on it and ran his tongue across her breasts. "You are mine. All mine."

A shiver ran up her spine as all of her synapses lit up. She clutched the back of his shoulders and dug her nails in deep as he pounded into her. Her thighs clenched, her body going into an exquisite and powerful freefall. She threw her head back and cried out, "All yours!"

He roared as his orgasm exploded out of him. Releasing her hair, he slapped his palm against the wall. As a shudder rolled through him, his claws curled, scrapping against the stone. A moment passed before his body stilled.

Her forehead dropped against his chest as she panted heavily. Slowly, Jo eased her fingernails from his flesh. She might have grabbed a hold of him a little harder than she intended, but she wouldn't change a thing about it. "Astounding," she uttered in a breathless whisper.

Pierce nuzzled her ears, then laid his head on top of hers. Ragged breaths burst out of him. "Every time with you is amazing. Every moment with you is amazing." He wrapped his arms around her, holding her close.

She shut her eyes. Gods, she loved when he did that. Just a gentle touch. There were no words she could come up with that would ever express how beautiful he made her feel with her furry, pointed canine ears. Her thundering heartbeat settled, as did her pulse and breathing. She brushed a tender kiss across his chest and enveloped his shoulders. "It's always...wonderful."

Lifting her chin, he gazed into her eyes. "You are perfect." Pierce pressed a soft kiss to her lips, lingering for a moment, then laid his head back on top of hers.

"So are you." Resting her head against his chest, she listened to the sound of his heart thundering behind his ribcage and inhaled his exquisite smoky aroma. "We were made for each other."

He stroked up and down her spine with his fingertips. Neither of them wanted to be parted from the other. Eventually, they wouldn't have to, but it couldn't come soon enough. "Yes, we were." He kissed the top of her head. "I love you, Jocasta."

"I love you, too, Pierce. More than I feel like I can ever show you." Though, maybe one day soon, she'd find the perfect way to express everything he meant to her.

"There are no words, no gestures, strong enough to express how much I care for you. How much I love you."

She had to disagree with him. Gently, she lifted her head and cupped his cheek. "I think you do. Every time you caress or nip at my ears. When you kiss me, slow and deep. Even when you just hold me. Or when we're in the quiet aftermath. I don't even know if you realized how many times you tenderly stroked my arm, back, or hip. Or held me close. Maybe we have shown each other, even if we didn't notice it."

Pierce beamed. "You have certainly shown me. When you kiss my chest over my heart, and lay your hand there. Anytime you run your fingers along my forearm, neck, and head. When you hold me and let me hold you. Every time you do not judge me for my thoughts. Or when my anger does not frighten you away but makes you come closer so you can comfort me." He nuzzled her nose with his. "You show me in so many more ways than you think you do as well."

"I'll keep showing you every *umbra* for the rest of my life. I can promise you that, Pierce. For the rest of my life, you will always be my one and only, my king." Pressing her forehead to his, she trailed her fingers along the nape of his neck.

"As will I. You will always be my one and only, my queen; every *umbra*, until my last *umbra*. There will not be one moment that I do not love you, take care of you, cherish you." He kissed her. It was languid and intense, speaking beyond their shared words. Then he dropped his forehead to hers.

She knew he had to go, and she could already feel the ache from both of their hearts because of it. "We'll be together soon, my love." It wouldn't be more than a few days apart. At least, that's what she prayed for. Nearly as much as she prayed, he returned to her safely. There was no going back.

"Yes, my queen. Soon. Not soon enough... but soon." His lips found hers. "I will pray to the gods that the time passes quickly."

"As will I." Kissing his chest one last time, she lifted her gaze to his and brushed a loving kiss across his lips. "I'll show you the front so that you can find your way back easier."

With a brief nod, he eased her down, letting out a groan as his cock slipped out of her. Once he re-situated her clothes, he wrapped his arm around her, tucking her into his side as they left the barn.

Jo took her time leading him back beyond the gardens and through the maze of houses. Someday soon, one of them would be theirs. Perhaps the one next to her sister and Logan. If she remembered correctly, it was empty. She thought about all the things that would need to be taken care of as they walked toward the clearing. They hadn't gone the most direct route, but it didn't stop the ache in her chest. Even the number of times she told herself it was temporary. Soon, he'd return, and their whole family would be together. Soon. Jo swallowed to wet her parched throat as they entered the clearing with Santos' hut to their left.

The closer to the entrance they got, the more unhurried their steps became. The heartache from him became more and more apparent with each footfall. Right before they reached the archway, Pierce stopped them and drew her into his arms. "This is not forever. This is only temporary.

Soon, we will be together again for good, and I will never have to leave you."

Right. Not forever. Temporary. She knew he said it as much for her as he did for himself. She needed a project. Something she could do until he returned, and she knew exactly what that was. Santos had offered it. Jo squeezed him tight. "How would you feel about living next to Ambrosia and Logan?"

"That sounds perfect. When I am here to stay, I want to be close to my family. Lillianna will want to be as well."

"Ambrosia and Logan have gotten a room ready for her with them."

"It will be nice when they finally meet and get to know each other. He was very close with our mother, and Lillianna looks just like her."

That would likely be an interesting meeting. Though Logan probably knew all of that. Then again, she hadn't heard it mentioned when the two males had spoken the day before. But she hadn't heard everything. She had truly done her best to give them privacy. "That had to have been shocking for you as she grew up."

"It was. Most of the time, it brought me joy. Sometimes, it was difficult."

"I can't even imagine." What he must have gone through. Happy to see her thrive, but sorrow at seeing the female look more and more like his mother every year.

Pierce tugged her closer and kissed her slowly. "I love you, my queen. I will see you soon." He stared into her eyes and caressed her cheek. "Each night we are apart, gaze at the moon. No matter where we are, no matter how far apart, I will look at the same moon, and soon we will stare at it together." He kissed her once more.

She leaned into the kiss and deepened it. It would be one she'd think about as she stared at the moon later. As she waited for nightfall, she'd get their new home in working order. A home they would share. Releasing the kiss, her gaze met his one final time. She glanced toward the treeline. The trees shifted, parting as the branches rearranged into an archway. Her eyes flicked back to his. "I'll watch the moon every night until you return to me."

"As will I. Until the night comes when I can hold you close to me as we sleep. That night and every night that follows." He kissed her, and then nuzzled her ears. Squeezing his eyes shut as the pain in his chest made it hard to draw breath, he moved away from her and shifted into his animal form. "I love you." He turned away, then took off through the archway and out of sight.

"I love you too. Be safe, my king," she whispered as the archway closed behind him.

Chapter Three

Devin had rather enjoyed her morning. More so than she had in a very long time. The meal the evening before had been delicious, and the conversation airy. With her stomach full, she had slept rather well in a bed that was a hundred times more comfortable than the pallet she slept on in their hut at home. Morning came with another meal and delicacies she'd never had before. More talk, and then Ambrosia had shown her around the village a bit. By afternoon, she knew she needed to go, but hadn't been able to pass up yet another meal. It had been on the lighter side, though just as filling. As Logan and Am led her to the archway they had entered through, she took in her surroundings. Who knew if she would ever see this place, or them, again? She was going to miss all of it. And, while in the confines of the village, it was just yet another thing she would have to make sure she didn't think about.

She hugged them both before leaving, thanked them for everything they'd done for her, then shifted and took off into the trees. She hadn't gone far, though, when her steps slowed down. Delaying her arrival wouldn't change anything. The punishment would be severe no matter what. The later she was, the more Informants there would probably be. But she'd handled up to five before. That had been the time she'd been near death. That had been after the day she'd gone the other direction from the marketplace. Met the hybrid empath, Atifah. Ended up spending two days with her without even realizing it. The memory brought a smile to her face.

The entire experience had been a wonderful distraction from reality, and she had made a good friend.

Traveling a roundabout way to get back to the boundaries, Devin skipped the market while avoiding the chimera village. When she got close to the boundary line, she veered off into a specific section of the forest. She couldn't take the star charts home. If found, Markham would use them for evil, or he would have them destroyed. As far as she knew, no one had a claim on this area. Métamorphe was on one side, and the chimera territory was on the other. She moved through the trees until she came to a rather unimpressive-looking hill. What appeared to be willow branches hung over it, covering the entrance. She made her way inside the cave and shifted to her humanoid form. To anyone else, it probably appeared empty. To her, she knew the rock walls weren't what they seemed.

A flat boulder sat against the back wall. It blended into the rest of the cave, but she had no problem finding it. She'd put it there. Rolling it aside, she made her way into the small room. Shelves lined the walls, filled with many supplies and trinkets she'd collected during her travels around the isle. Like she'd done in the past, there wasn't time to scour through everything. Ambrosia had given her a bag with a handle to carry the star chart scrolls in, and she put the entire thing on one shelf. Then reconsidered her decision. She moved it to a different shelf, farther back, and on the very top. It should be safe here. No one had ever found her hidden space.

Leaving the way she'd come, Devin returned the boulder, so it covered the entrance to the small room. Shifting to all fours, she left the cave, ensuring the willow branches fell back in place before she took off again.

As she crossed the boundary line into the shape shifter territory, it was as if the very air around her changed. There was darkness everywhere here. It all had to do with Markham. Whatever dark magic he possessed—because that was the only thing that made sense—had permeated every inch of their land. Even for those who were used to it, it could choke the senses and overwhelm one's faculties.

The sounds of leaves rustling reached her, not that she halted her steps. Nor did she run. Devin emerged into a small clearing at the same time others stepped out on the other side. Abaddon, Devland, and Runihara, standing in a row. All three were canine Informants. She stood where she was, and so did they. Despite the knowledge of what was to come, she refused to invite it. Dahlia strode through the trees behind the males. It was almost unnoticeable, but the female rubbed up against Runi as she passed, then took her time crossing the clearing. Devin might not have shown it, but she was ready for her.

When Dahlia lunged, she reared back. With their teeth and claws, they bit and scratched each other. It ultimately didn't matter, though. The female was bigger and stronger and was older than her by over ten years. The fight ended with Dahlia biting her neck and slamming her to the ground, holding her in place.

Three Informants lumbered over to where Dahlia held her down. One of them laughed—Runi. "Good job, Dahlia. Now shift, bitch."

Devin glared up at him, her chest heaving as she tried to catch her breath. "No." She yelped when Dahlia bit into her neck.

"I said shift, bitch. That is an order."

"Do you think I care about your orders?"

"I think you care about not having your throat ripped out." He jerked his head toward her, and Abaddon and Devland stationed themselves on either side of her. "Shift."

"No." She tried to claw at them, but each still got a hold of one of her front legs. They bit down, and she yelped.

Runi chuckled. "Last chance."

Devin said nothing, and he nodded at the other two. They bit down harder at the same time Dahlia did. Devin cried out in agony. Blood ran down her neck and front legs that had nothing to do with her fight with the female. Her body shifted to its humanoid form all on its own, and she watched Runi do the same. The hold that the other three had on her didn't lift, and blood continued to slide down through her fur. Movement from the corner of her eye had her glancing over with just her eyes. She didn't dare try to turn her head. She could barely swallow.

Cyrus, Jolon, and Set, all canine Informants as well, came across the clearing. As they neared her, they shifted to their humanoid forms. Runi's smirk radiated pure evil as he stared down at her. "You should not have been late. But I am so very glad you were."

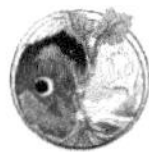

As Pierce headed home, his gut twisted into a sense of foreboding the closer he got to the territory. He hurried more quickly, worried about Lilli. What if something else had happened to her in his absence? As he crossed over the boundary line, he shook off the shudder that ran through him. He hated coming back here, but it was necessary for now.

His speed picked up of its own accord as he sprinted toward a small clearing about midway to the village. He became hypersensitive as his senses fine-tuned. His ears and nose twitched. The sounds of laughter and growls hit him. Then the scents of vomit and blood. He ran faster.

When he reached the clearing, the sight before him made his eyes flip jet black.

Devin was being held down on the ground in her humanoid form. Her eyes were closed, and she didn't appear to be breathing. When he focused on it, though, he saw her chest rise and fall, though her breaths were very shallow. Dahlia was at her neck, Abaddon and Devland at her arms. Blood was all over her. On Dahlia as well, so the two must have fought beforehand, not that it fazed his sister. Runi, Jolon, and Set stood around them. Cyrus was on top of her. Blood spots covered the clearing. There was vomit in one area, drag marks leading to another pile of vomit, and more drag marks leading to where they were now.

He snarled so loud it shook the leaves in the trees. Dahlia looked up first. She immediately released Devin's crimson-stained neck and stepped away, licking the blood from around her maw. Pierce glared at her, but out of his periphery he saw Set shove Cyrus's shoulder. Cyrus laughed as he climbed off of Devin and stood up. Abaddon and Devland released her arms. Blood covered the places their jaws had been, and blood coated her inner thighs.

"You had better get the fuck home, Dahlia," Pierce growled. "Now. Before I take a chunk out of you, or worse, for what you have done."

Dahlia smirked as she slowly backed away. "It is not my fault the bitch lost our fight. And if she could not handle her punishment, that just proves how very weak she is."

"HOME! NOW!"

She let out a soft snicker as she turned around and disappeared through the trees.

Pierce advanced. "You have taken what you wanted. Now go," he snarled out.

Runi laughed quietly as he shifted to all fours, the others following suit. "Pierce, Pierce, Pierce. Always has to be the hero. Are you angry because of what we did, or are you angry because of who it was?"

Runi lunged at him, but he dodged the blow before moving to stand over Devin's unconscious body. "I. Said. Go."

Cyrus licked his lips. "Do not start something you cannot finish alone, Pierce."

"He is not alone," a fresh voice barked.

Pierce glanced over and saw Zagan and Alastor emerge from the trees. Runi regarded the three of them, and Pierce watched the calculation in his eyes. Six against three. They were all Informants for a reason. Each of them was large and had immense strength. The six of them would likely take himself, Zagan, and Alastor down, but a fight could mean punishment for all of them.

"It is alright," Runi said. "We were finished anyway." Cyrus let out a low growl, but Runi snapped his jaws at him. "I said we were finished. Let us go." The six of them turned around and headed out of the clearing and into the trees.

As soon as they were gone, Pierce shifted to his humanoid form, followed by Zagan and Alastor, and kneeled next to Devin. When he touched her forearm, she made no noise, but at least her eyes opened a fraction. He flicked his gaze to Zagan. "She needs immediate attention. Do you know where my sister is right now? I have not seen her most of the *umbra*, and I need to check on her."

"I think I saw her with Bellona earlier, but it was a little while ago. She seemed fine."

His mind warred between being happy she had seemed okay and irritated that a male had paid enough attention to her to know that. "Alright." He let out a breath. "I am going to take her to the river and clean her up." Approaching footfalls sounded in the distance. Suddenly, Devin's eyes flipped open, and her head jerked to the side. She let out a cry of pain and stilled, her chest heaving. "Do not move, Devin."

"Derrick... No... Not... like... this..." Her voice was barely audible.

Pierce glanced at Zagan. "Stop him." Zagan nodded and took off in that direction. He focused back on Devin. "I am going to take you to the river. Tend to you."

She shook her head but sucked in a sharp breath. It took her a moment to speak. "Lilli. You need... to be with... Lilli. I will... I will be... okay."

"We will take her, Pierce. You get Derrick back to the village and keep him from killing any of them." Yells, and then a howl of anguish, came from somewhere in the trees. "You are the only one he will listen to when he is this angry. He cannot see her like this."

"I know." Pierce let out a harsh curse under his breath. "You and Zagan both live alone. One of you needs to allow her to stay with you tonight. If Derrick catches one glimpse of her like this, not even I can hold him back."

Alastor acknowledged the request. "You have my word. We will tend to her and take care of her this eve." He jerked his head toward the trees. "Go. Before he gets past Zagan."

Pierce regarded Devin. Her eyes had fluttered shut. Hopefully, she had passed out and would remain so, at least until they got her into one of their homes. Both of the males were honorable and wouldn't harm her. Pierce wouldn't have left her with them otherwise. He rose to his feet, dipped his chin to Alastor, then shifted and headed into the trees. Hopefully, he could get a handle on Derrick and keep him away. Swiftly.

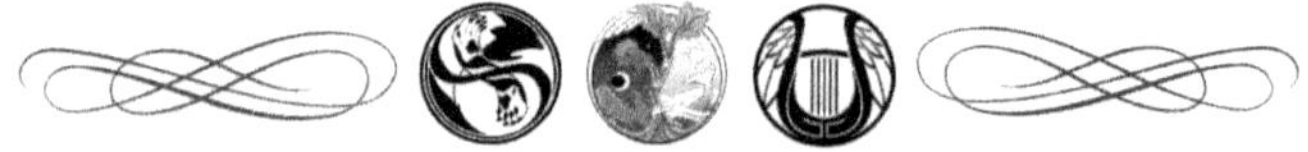

Gavin paced as he waited in the treeline for Parthenia to join him. He hadn't felt fear or pain from her. No anger, either. Nothing but a kind of impatience. And thoughts of him. He smiled to himself. When he sensed someone draw near, he turned toward the staircase. The willow leaves were pushed aside, and a female emerged. Not Parthenia—her sister. Cipriana glanced both ways down the dirt road before she ran across the path and peered around at the trees.

"A marked tree. Marked how?"

Gavin glimpsed around, judged his concealed position, and went back behind a couple more lines of trees to ensure no one could see him if they came upon the scene. Only then did he remove his camouflage. Cipriana jumped back. "You are standing to the right of it. I marked it with my claws. Is Parthenia alright? What is going on?"

Her gaze shifted to the tree on her left, the one he'd left claw marks down the day before, and tilted her head. Cipriana flicked her gaze back at him. "Parthenia is fine. She's just a little detained. No, that isn't the right word. Our other sister hasn't left her side since we joined her for lunch."

"I see." He sighed. "I am sorry for startling you. I had to decide if removing my camouflage or a disembodied voice would be better." He cracked a smile. "Will she not be able to come?"

"I don't know what part of that means." Cipriana let out a slight breath. "I'm honestly not sure. Fantasia doesn't seem inclined to leave. It's why Parthenia asked me to come down."

She likely thought he'd just been hiding before. Her eyes widened with surprise as he covered himself in his camouflage. "My camouflage." He removed it again. "It is an ability all shape shifters come into. If she cannot come…" His chest heaved with a sigh. He had so looked forward to seeing her, and it pained him it didn't seem possible, at least today. He didn't want to go back to the village without seeing her, with this… emptiness inside him. "Would you tell her something for me? Please?"

Cipriana's mouth down-turned and she rolled her eyes. "Let me see if I can finagle something to get her down here. I can't exactly take you up, but I can probably buy you two an hour."

It didn't seem like a good idea to tell her he'd already been up there. Gavin beamed. "Oh. That would be wonderful. Thank you. As long as she is not hurting too badly, and they will not catch her. Thank you."

She blinked, then raised an eyebrow. Oops. She likely hadn't known he knew about Parthenia's wounds. "Um, yeah. She's moving better. A lot better, actually. And I'll make sure she isn't caught."

"I am glad to hear she is improving." He sat down next to the tree he'd marked. "I will wait right here. Thank you, again," he said and threw on his camouflage.

Cipriana nodded. She glanced across the road, then disappeared back to the staircase.

He tried to remain sitting, but he ended up pacing as he'd done before her sister had come down. That she was so near, but he couldn't go toher, made him restless.

After an eon, that was probably only several minutes, Gavin sensed Parthenia draw nearer. Her scent drew closer, and he heard her footsteps crossing the pathway. Stepping out from behind the tree, she came into his sight and his camouflage dropped. "Oh, my love, I missed you." As soon as she'd slipped safely into the trees, he went to her, nuzzling against her.

"I missed you too." Burying her face into the crook of his neck, she sifted her fingers through his fur as she wrapped her arms around him.

He purred. Turning his head enough to lick the side of her throat, he smiled at the shiver that ran up her spine. "Your sister said she could buy us an hour."

Parthenia's brown eyes sparkled. "Then I'll happily take it. I didn't think she would give us any time."

"She did, and I am thrilled. We will not have enough time to go to the treehouse, but there is a lake nearby. Would you like to see it?" It wouldn't be nearly enough time, but they had some time together, and that was all that mattered.

"Yes. That sounds lovely."

He swept his tongue across her skin. "Climb up on me, love. You are feeling better today?" He posed it as a question, but he could feel it from her, too.

"Yes. Much better. I can almost fully extend my wings. I believe I should be able to fly by tomorrow." She pressed a soft kiss to his muzzle, bringing a low rumble out of him, and climbed onto his back with a lot more ease than she had yesterday.

"I am so glad to hear it, beloved. I love watching you fly."

"Mmm, I love the sounds you make. And I certainly enjoy being able to fly as well." She softly stroked his shoulder.

"Your every touch and every kiss brings them out of me." His tail caressed her leg as he trotted toward the lake.

She laid down against his back. He let out another low rumble that turned into a purr.

"Were you able to find out anything about Devin?"

"No, actually. Gabby went to their hut last night, and she was not there. She had not been in the village all *umbra* yesterday. I suppose she could have been there this morning, but I did not see her."

"I hope she didn't find trouble while seeking information."

"As do I." But trouble was unavoidable. Her travels aside, if she hadn't been in the village, hadn't made it home before curfew, then punishment was inevitable. "We should arrive at the lake soon."

"You seem worried."

"I am worried. They punish females much differently than males in my village when they break the laws. Being back in the village by curfew is one law."

"How different?"

He blocked his thoughts as soon as the first image threatened to come into his mind. It was several moments before he spoke, his voice coming out quiet and strained. "If females break the laws, they take them against their will. Always by Markham's Informants, and usually more than one."

Although her fingers clutched his fur, he hardly noticed the faint sting. Neither of them had any words. None were sufficient. That they would harm a female as kind as Devin, any female, in such a way, was abominable. He stroked her leg with his tail, but her emotions, coupled with his own, made speech impossible. They walked in silence until they reached the lake. "Here it is," he whispered.

It took her a minute to climb down, though not because her injuries made it difficult. Parthenia stood there and stared at the lake for a moment. "It's quite peaceful."

He leaned his head against her. "I have always thought so, too. Perhaps we could meet here sometimes, too. Since it is not so far away as the treehouse is."

"Yes. That would..." Her words trailed off.

He nuzzled her softly. "What is it, love?"

She draped an arm over his shoulders and leaned into him. "I just can't stop thinking about Devin. I just... I know we can't be sure, but I keep wondering if something different could've been done. A different decision."

"I am worried about her as well." He sighed. Devin had volunteered to make the journey alone, which Parthenia hadn't objected against despite his suggestion they go too. Not that he blamed her, nor had he failed to seethe sense in it. There were dangers for both him and his mate. Derrick had duties to attend to—and constant scrutiny—as an Informant, and Gabby was with child. Not that he'd spoken to his twin of it, but Devin had said as much when they were at the barrier. The books had told them next to nothing, despite how many they'd gone through. And there were still so many more. "Devin does what she wants. Despite the laws, if she feels what needs doing is important enough, she will do it anyway. At least, that is what Gabby says. Devin does not really talk to me one-on-one."

"I know this is important. For a few of us, all for the same reason. I guess I just never truly thought of all the repercussions."

Turning to face her, Gavin shifted to his humanoid form and took her face in his hands. "We are going to figure this out. We are. It might take some time, but I have hope. I have to."

"There's no doubt in my mind. I just... I feel awful." Parthenia sighed heavily. "I just wish we weren't fighting so many fronts. Or that one of them gave way. Even just a fraction."

"I know, my love. As do I." He kissed her forehead. They would come out on the other side. Figure out how to get past the barrier. Find all the answers they sought, and all of their dreams would become a reality. "This time in our lives is going to be tough to get past. But we have each other every single step of the way. And when we get past it, it will be more wonderful than any dream we could ever have."

She wrapped her arms around his waist, pressing her cheek to his chest. "You're right."

He laid his head on top of hers and moved his hands to her waist. He wanted to wrap his arms around her, but her back and wings might still be tender.

"What did you say to Cipriana?"

As he held her, his tail ran up and down the length of her leg. "Not much, actually. She said you could not get away, that your sister Fantasia would not leave your side. I asked her if she would tell you something for me, and I think my disappointment may have been pretty clear because her next response was, she could probably buy us an hour."

She trailed her fingers through the fur along his back. "Hmm, I certainly didn't expect her to do that. But I'm glad she did."

"Me too. Even if it is just for a short time, it brings me joy to see you and hold you."

"Same. I didn't want to be rude to Fantasia, but I was quite uncertain how to get her to leave."

"It is alright, I understood. If you could not come down, I was just going to ask her if she would tell you I said 'I love you.'"

"I love you, too, Gavin. But I'm certainly glad I got to see you."

He smiled as he brushed his fingertips along her side. "Seeing you during the daytime makes the nighttime easier to get through." Although they would both prefer otherwise, their reality was what it was.

"I thought of something else I would like for our home."

"What is it you would like?"

"A red door. The rest of the house can be white."

It would be a perfect mix of the two of them. The white he liked and her favorite color. "That sounds perfect, my love. Is the door the onlything you want red, though?"

"I think the inside should be different colors. Colors that complement each other. As we do."

He caressed her cheek. "I would like brown somewhere. Like the color of your eyes. What colors would you like?"

"Green." She leaned into his touch. "Like the color of your eyes."

"I think we may have a common theme going here."

"But it's a beautiful one."

"Quite true." He placed a kiss on either side of her mouth. "I love you so much."

"I love you, too. With all my heart. All my soul." She brushed a soft kiss to either side of his mouth, both of his cheeks, and his nose.

He let out a low rumble. "I love every single part of you with every single part of me. Your talons, your legs, your sex that tastes like honey upon my tongue." With a low growl, he brushed a kiss on her jaw, making her moan. "Your stomach, your chest, where you have absolutely perfect breasts." He smirked. "Your arms, back, angelic face, your beautiful hair that I could run my fingers through all *umbra*. Then there are these magnificent wings."

"I love every part of you. Your ears, tail, sex in my mouth, butt. Every part from the top of your head to the tip of your claws. And I love making you purr and growl. Something I look forward to making you do more of."

He let out a quiet rumble in her ear. "I love the sounds you make for me. Your moans and cries of pleasure. I look forward to making you make more of them. And I cannot wait for the *umbra* that my sex can be where only my tongue has been." His hands gently gripped her hips, pulling another magnificent moan from her.

"Goddess, I can't either."

"I wish we had more time so I could turn your thoughts into reality." And that they were in the treehouse with some privacy. "As soon as we can, though, I will bury my face between your legs." He licked up her neck.

"Mmm, me too, my love. And yes, soon we will taste one another again."

Just the thought of having her mouth upon him drew a growl out of his mouth. "You do not know how much I look forward to that." He created a trail of kisses down the side of her throat and shoulder.

She gasped and tilted her head, giving him more access. "Oh? I might."

"Do you think so?" Gavin retraced the pattern up her throat, leaving gentle nibbles against it, before licking down her collarbone.

"Oh, yes. I do." She arched her back.

The rumble in his chest was more like thunder now as he caught her thoughts. How she'd crawl down his body, suck on his neck, stop to pay attention to his nipples. Then rake her nails down his chest until the girth of his sex was primed for her mouth.

He grazed his fangs down the valley between her breasts, then up to the other side of her neck. "Tomorrow, when we have more time, we are going to do everything that both of us are thinking about right now." He'd caress her breasts and sex with her feather, lick her everywhere he could, drive his tongue deep inside her sex until she orgasmed into his mouth. Then he would lap up every drop and repeated it. With each image that pummeled his mind, his cock hardened more and more.

"Oh, gods." Her arousal thickened, nearly saturating the air surrounding them. "Yes, we most definitely are."

"If we had more time, I would drive my tongue inside you right now." He nibbled on her earlobe. "But I fear one taste would make me unable to stop."

She groaned as her head tilted back. "I'd be more than happy to sneak you in."

His eyes darkened with lust at the thought. He didn't need to be home until evening meal. They would have hours. "I will do anything you want. Are you not still healing, though?"

"Mmm, I'm not feeling much at all. Would you like to see?"

"Are you asking me if I want to see a part of your body?" he teased. He brushed the tips of his fingers down her sides next to her breasts.

"Oh, very much."

He gave a soft chuckle against her and stepped back, staring into her eyes. The glow of his green irises reflected on her face. "There is not a single inch of you I do not want to see." He snaked his tongue out across his lips.

She slowly turned around and slid the straps just a little from her shoulders so he could see how much she'd healed. There were still marks, but they weren't nearly as bad as they had been. They looked more like deep scratches. Oh, gods, it still pained him. Just thinking about how they came to be. He pushed those thoughts out of his head. "They look much better. Will it hurt if I touch them?"

"No. It didn't bother me earlier when Fantasia checked them."

Starting at the top and working his way downward, he gave each shoulder a gentle kiss, then stroked it with his tongue. "Your wings look much better, too." He gazed to her right one as the strokes of his tongue traced another of her wounds. "The new feathers are darker."

"They always grow in darker. I didn't realize they'd be that dark, though."

He moved further down her back, slowly covering each wound with his lips. When he got to the small of her back, he was on his knees, his hands on her hips. "No matter whatever happens, at any point in our life, you will always be the most beautiful female in existence to me."

She peered at him over her shoulder. "You will always be the most stunning male to me. Perfect in every way."

Beaming, he cupped her cheek. Getting to his feet, he pulled her into his arms and kissed either side of her mouth. "Should we head back? I do not have to go home until evening meal."

"That sounds like a wonderful idea."

He nuzzled her neck, then shifted so she could climb on his back. She easily mounted him, then laid against him as she had before. He purred as her fingers trailed through his fur and headed off back into the trees. "I love when we travel like this."

"Me too." Her fingers splayed out, letting his fine and soft fur caress each finger individually as she continued to play with it. Her touch felt so magnificent. It relaxed every muscle, calming him. His low, rhythmic vibration continued until they reached the treeline.

"I am going to camouflage now."

"Then I should climb down." Right. Otherwise, it would look like she was floating. Wouldn't that be a sight? Not that anyone would see them. She had snuck him in during the day once before, but they had stayed in the library. This should prove an interesting task.

"I wish you did not have to, but that is a good point. It is a good thing the pads on the bottom of my paws muffle my footsteps." He camouflaged.

"Yes," she said as she climbed down. "Just remember not to speak if someone approaches."

"I know, love. I will wait to say anything until we are in your apothecary, just to be on the safe side." He had gotten good at keeping his mouth shut a long time ago.

"Let us go."

A rumble rose from within him as he nuzzled up against her side. "I will stay right with you." Parthenia started across the path, and he trailed after her. She ascended the staircase, taking them one at a time until they reached the top, where she belted out the notes to open the back door, so to speak. He had to bite back a purr at the sound of her song. It always resonated through him each time he heard it. The boulder slid across, giving them access to the library. Gavin gently nudged her back to let her know he was still with her as he followed.

Keeping her hands clasped together in front of her, she continued forward, only looking back once. She strode down the main aisle and out the primary entrance of the building. They hit the bottom of the stairs when her sister and another female approached her.

"Parthenia!" The second female brightened; her wide autumn browneyes lighting up. Although she looked younger than Cipriana and Parthenia, she was taller than both of them. "We were just finishing the wash. We should be back to your apothecary soon."

"Oh, Fantasia, you know I would love that, but the book request has turned into something more. I must work on that for a few hours."

Cipriana narrowed her eyes at Parthenia. "Has it now?"

"Oh, yes. Very much so. I should be finished by dinnertime. We could get together then."

Fantasia tilted her head and scrunched her nose. "Dinnertime sounds good. I think I need to take a bath before I come back over." She glanced at Cipriana. "And perhaps we should rewash the clothing."

"I'm certain it's fine, Fantasia." Cipriana rested a hand on Fantasia's shoulder. She glowered at Parthenia. "Dinnertime it is. I expect you'll be good and done by then."

"Yes. Of course."

The two females nodded and went on their way. Yeah. Cipriana knew he was right there by Parthenia's side, even if she couldn't see him. Parthenia began walking again, doing everything possible not to draw attention as they made their way to her apothecary.

As soon as they had gotten inside and they locked the door, Gavin busted out laughing while he removed his camouflage. "I am sorry. That was hilarious, though." The look Cipriana had given her.

She chuckled. "I never knew Cipriana could even glare like that. Fantasia, though..." Parthenia shook her head.

"I think my scent is just different. It is not something like anything else smells up here." He shifted to his humanoid form and drew her against him. "Your sister, Fantasia—her eyes lit up when she saw you. I could tell she truly loves you."

Parthenia caressed his biceps. "I love her as well. Though, to be fair, Fantasia's eyes light up whenever we have tea together, or she has a good plate of food in front of her. Of the triplets, she is the most innocent and loving."

"Hopefully, that is a personality she keeps with her throughout her life. At least from my experience, it is very rare."

"Oh, yes. Her other two sisters, Epiphany and Enigma, can be troublesome. Although she's a triplet of those two, Fantasia is nothing like them. Those two are constantly causing issues, so Cipriana and I do what we canto keep Fantasia out of their antics."

"Growing up, Gabby was always the one trying to keep me out of trouble." He led her over to her bedding and laid down, tugging her on top of him. "Why her specifically, though?" She had never really talked at length about her family, but he never tired of her voice.

With her hands atop one another on his chest, Parthenia rested her chin on them. "When the triplets were born, Epiphany and Enigma came first. Fantasia was delivered last, and she was smaller than the other two. She had many issues during her first *penumbras* of life, and most didn't believe she would even make it. Their mother, Echo, had her hands full with Epiphany and Enigma. My father was the one who tended to Fantasia. Often with Cipriana and I by his side. We were quite young, so we could do little to help, but she blossomed in his care. After his passing, Cipriana and I continued todo what we could to take care of Fantasia. You would never know how much she fought to stay in this world."

He gently stroked her back. Her story reminded him again of the difference in their home lives. When young were born in his village with problems, any problems, Markham stole their lives away. Here, they nurtured and cared for them until they were strong enough to survive and thrive. He pushed the thoughts away. "I am sure that brings your father great joy in his afterlife."

"I truly hope so." Parthenia sighed.

He was quiet for a moment. Her thoughts strayed again to Fantasia. He knew every time she pushed for change; she commented about how the laws were outdated. But she wasn't thinking of how it would impact her, but Fantasia. She wanted the female to have a male who would love her. It was still such a strange thing, though not unwanted, to catch snippets of her thoughts. He didn't know it happened when two people mated. Then again, no one had ever taught him anything regarding matings.

"I hope your Elder will listen to you when you go to speak with her." He ran his fingertips gingerly along the back of her neck and shoulder as he stroked the small of her back.

"Me too. I have always considered Vasilia a wise female. While I work on gathering information to show her, I'll figure out how best to side-step those who might prevent me from showing her the facts." Her gaze snapped to the door.

"You locked it when we came inside, love." He flicked the tip of his tongue across the side of her throat. "If there is anything I can do to help with that, though I do not know what it could be, just let me know."

"I have all the information together regarding the loss of lots in The Poppy Field and the drying of The Reflection Pools. Perhaps you can help me transfer that into an easy-to-read chart."

While he certainly shared her artistic hand, something else held his attention. Teasing the silky flesh of her neck with his tongue, he relished in the noises he drew out of her, even more so as she angled her head, giving him more room to work. "If you give me what you have before I go, I can leave it at the treehouse before I head home. Then I can work on it there when I have time."

"I believe we can arrange that." Her fingers skimmed up and down his arm.

A low rumble resounded deep in his chest. "I love it when you touch me. When you moan for me." He stroked her jaw with his tongue as he gripped her waist, the thin material of her dress bunching up in his palms.

"I love making you growl. And the way your hands and tongue feel on me." Her knee brushed his thigh, lighting up his synapses. Her long fingers skated across his broad chest, tracing an unseen pattern all the way to his hip.

"You must love it. I can almost not stop doing it around you. Especially when you are touching me like this." The gods knew he desired more of it. All of it. He peppered kisses and licks down her neck and collarbone. As he caressed her leg with his tail, he trailed his fingers along the small of her back.

Moaning, she dragged her nails over the nuances of his chiseled abdomen. "I absolutely do."

His back arched a little at her touch. "Gods, I love that." It had been days since they'd explored one another sexually. Places they already knew well, but somehow felt brand new at the same time. He could stay like this with her forever, with her laying on top of him.

As he switched sides, so did she. Focusing all of her attention on the other side of his body, she followed the same path she'd taken before. "Oh poppies, I love how you feel." She nipped his ear and then brushed a trail of kisses along his jaw line and to either side of his mouth.

His growl transitioned to a moan. "As do I. Every single perfect inch of you." The tip of his tail caressed the ends of her wings as he pulled her higher up his chest. Her thighs split atop him. Leisurely, he ran his fingers over her legs and taloned feet. He covered her face in kisses and turned his attention back to her neck. "I love how you feel on top of me," he whispered.

Sitting on his hips, she caressed the top of his head and the backs of his ears before nuzzling his cheek with her nose. Her chocolate brown gaze locked on him. They glowed just as they had the first day they'd met. The brightness of his own eyes reflected off her face. It was always like that with them, their eyes connecting and radiating as one, their souls colliding most gloriously. "Mmm, I love how you feel beneath me."

"Then I shall stay beneath you as long as possible." He beamed at her. "My beloved, my love, my mate." He pressed feather kisses all over her face and the side of her throat, where her pulse thrummed to the rhythm of her heart. "I love to kiss you here. I love to feel your heart beating." He placed his hand against her chest, his thumb stroking slowly back and forth. "When I feel it, my heart beats the same as yours."

Parthenia rested her palm over his heart, the steady beat thumping beneath her touch. "I love to listen to yours, too. It is the sweetest lullaby that always fills me with great peace. As our heartbeats sync, I almost always find it impossible not to fall asleep. How could I not? My beloved, my love, my mate." She pressed her forehead to his and brushed a soft kiss across his nose.

He nuzzled her nose with his own. "Would you like to sleep, my love? If not, I could keep you awake."

With her other hand, she stroked the back of his neck. "Mmm, I certainly have no desire to sleep right now."

He let out a soft purr, then licked his lips. "Mmm. Come here." Gripping her hips, he drew her even higher up his body until she sat right below his chin. This was a new angle, one he was completely ready to enjoy. Starting at her left leg, he licked her inner thigh, knee, and talons.

She bit her bottom lip and moaned as her head fell back. Arching her spine, she leaned backward a little. Not only did it give him better access to her thighs and legs, but it also allowed her to reach the tip of his hips with her nails.

A shiver went up his spine, and he growled. Taking the same path, he stopped before he reached her sex. As much as he desired to have her taste flowing down the back of his throat, he wanted to take his time. Nipping her hip, he created a path of licks and kisses to her stomach, and swirled his tongue over her navel as his fingertips danced up and down her sides.

The tips of her wings lightly grazed along his thighs. The plumage barely skimming his fur as she raked her nails up his body. Her hands shifted to her own flesh as she created a trail from her thighs to her neck.

She had him salivating. It wasn't just the way she touched herself, but the images tumbling around her gray matter that he caught. It was almost as if his hands roamed her body, caressing her breasts, those tight pink nipples of hers. A new rumble started in him, deeper and full of lust. Gavin nipped at her other hip, then kissed and licked down her other leg. Fuck, she took his breath away. One day, it would really be his hands all over her body. He stroked her knee with his tongue as he made his way back up. "You are so beautiful."

"You make me feel perfectly exquisite. I wish to show you exactly how." She hung her head back, tracing back down to her breasts. She massaged and kneaded them, letting out a deep, husky moan as her nipples pebbled.

His cock throbbed. The day he could worship her breasts with his own hands and tongue would be a wonderful day indeed. Today, he could worship something else. Gavin adjusted her so her knees rested on the floor on either side of his head. "Do not stop touching yourself." Gripping her hips, he extended his tongue and slowly stroked her sex.

"Oh, goddess," Parthenia cried out. She continued, as he demanded, to touch her own body, molding and reshaping her swollen bosom, even pinching their engorged tips, which made them harden more. And then she lowered her head and the tip of her pink tongue flicked across her nipple.

A desire to see that had just gone through his head. "Oh, gods..." He teased her slit, finding her nub, and swirled his tongue around it. As he did so, he reached down and gripped his cock in his hand, imagining that it was her palm wrapped around it.

Parthenia moaned as she played with those beautiful mounds of hers and ground her sex against his mouth, riding his tongue as he devoured her. Her cry of ecstasy hardened his cock even more. The tips of her wings caressed the inside of his thighs, her feathers dancing across his fur.

Gavin groaned as he watched her, and at her thoughts playing out in his head. His grip moved up and down his thick shaft in unison, with the vision of her hand doing the same. He entered her slick folds, slipping his tongue in and out of her with slow and deliberate maneuvers until her noises became louder. Plunging harder, nipping her nub, he kept his hand at the small of her back to hold her in place against his mouth.

"Come for me, my love. Come for me!" Parthenia screamed in ecstasy. Her thighs clenched as her grip on her breasts tightened. Her head jerked back as she called out his name.

Oh, he came for her. And he came hard. He cried out against her, the two of them pitching over a cliff simultaneously. His orgasm exploded from him in hard jerks. Her release poured over his tongue and down his throat, soliciting a growl from him as he took it all.

The jets of his release between their bodies and his tongue lapping at her sex set off a second release from her. Not as powerful as the first, but enough that she dropped her hands to his arms and dug her nails in as she held on tight.

"That feels so good." The glow of his eyes brightened. He stroked his tongue along her sex. "And you taste too good to stop just yet." Taking her nub in his mouth, Gavin sucked on it hard and slow. Her eyes widened for a second, and another moan escaped. Her grip on his arms didn't shift, only tightened as she dug her nails into him harder.

Small noises he couldn't quite describe vibrated out of him as he suckled at her. All he cared about was getting more of her taste down his throat. He drove his tongue back inside her, his hands encircling her waist. Her taste shorted out every other function of his brain, and all he wanted was to penetrate her sex until she exploded all over him again. He didn't know if their mating link would extend to this, but he couldn't bring himself to part his mouth from her. *Come for me, beloved,* he thought loudly. Who knew? It might work. And, if not, the way he worked her sex with his tongue spoke volumes.

Even if she hadn't heard him, her body did. And it followed his request well. Another orgasm pulsated through her and exploded all around his tongue as her thighs clenched once again. Her nails driving into him harder as she cried out his name.

His cock jerked again. Hot jets spasmed out of him, covering them both. His roar against her vibrated through her sex as he devoured it, being sure to get every single drop of what she gifted him. Sliding his tongue from her, he stroked her inner thighs with slow licks and kisses.

Ragged breaths escaped her as her head fell forward, her nails not yet retracting from his skin. That had been amazing. Explosive. The combination of their scents all over her apothecary smelled divine. Gods, he loved her so much. He purred as he teased the soft skin of her inner thighs with his mouth. Caressing her lower back, he gingerly ran his fingers up and down her spine.

"Mmm. Wow." He chuckled softly.

Her breathing slowly steadied. "I agree."

He nudged his nose at her sex. "You smell…" he growled. "Incredible. Your scent gets so much stronger when—" he flipped his gaze up to her eyes and barely brushed her slit with his tongue, "—we make love." No, it wasn't the complete act, but it was all they had, and they made it work to their full advantage. Not being able to do everything hadn't deterred them too much.

"As does yours. And it's quite intoxicating." Her grip on his arms released.

Gavin tugged her gently down beside him and tucked her against his side. "I made a mess everywhere."

Resting a hand on his chest, her fingers sifted through his fur. "I think it just makes everything smell better." A soft grin spread over her face. "Though I do suppose we'll want to clean up at some point."

"That would probably be a good idea. I would have to clean up anyway before I go back home." He truly hated washing her scent off of him. It was something he wanted on him all the time. And he loathed even the idea of going back to that place. It was a horrid necessity, but they had to maintain the secrecy. Just a little longer.

"When we do, we'll go to The Reflection Pools." She curled up to him a little closer.

"I do not have to leave for a while, love. We have plenty of time." Sure. Plenty. In reality, it wasn't nearly enough. He laid his head on top of hers. Soon, they would figure everything out, and they would never have to part again.

"I know. It just never feels like enough."

"I know. It really does not." He turned her face up so their gazes met, caressing her cheek. "Just keep thinking about our white house with the red door. All the colors inside that complement each other, like we do. With lots of shelves for books, herbs, and spices. A big counter for cooking and baking. A fireplace that we will curl up by during the winter *cycles*. The lake. The trees that we will race through." He nuzzled her nose. "Until we get past this time, and move onto the next, keep our future home in your thoughts. The place where we will live out the rest of our lives together, raise our children together." He brushed a tender kiss across her forehead. "Soon, the dream will be more than a wish. It will be our reality."

"A focal point."

Her thoughts of their future home and children, their little girl with green eyes, filled his heart to bursting. "Exactly, love. I think that is something we can both do."

He pressed his forehead against hers. He couldn't think of that in the village, not when he was anywhere near Markham. The nights would still be difficult without her, without being able to think of her. But he would endure, and soon it wouldn't be necessary anymore. Soon, they would escape and be free—together.

Parthenia yawned and fell asleep, snuggled up in his arms. Images of a white house with a red door and four kids, two boys, and two girls consumed her dreams. A full house bustling with noise and love. Exactly what they wanted. As she slept, he ran his fingers through the silky strands of her hair. The images from her dreams filled him with a peacefulness he was loath to have ended.

Chapter Four

Devin's eyes popped open as she awoke on a pallet that wasn't hers, with scents in her nose that didn't immediately register. She bolted upright into a sitting position and had to bite her tongue not to let out a yelp of pain. Her entire body felt like a herd of spourgiffs had trampled it. Her throat was sore, and she had bandages around her neck and arms. Between her thighs was—She cut off her thought process, forcing herself to take slow, deep breaths. *Push them away... Push them away... All the thoughts... push them away.*

Scanning the room, she took in her surroundings. Zagan's hut. He and Alastor were leaning against the wall on either side of the door that was bolted shut. Both were still asleep in their humanoid forms, arms crossed over their chests. If not for the situation, she could've described the scene as adorable. She couldn't help but smile. Reaching up, she removed the bandages from around her neck and arms with a wince. Ignoring the blood stains on them, she rolled them up and disposed of them in the wastebasket next to her. One of them must have set it there for her. She vaguely remembered throwing up yesterday when—*Nope, not going there.*

Inhaling and exhaling a few more deep breaths, she forced herself to her feet. She didn't know what time it was, but she suspected she'd missed a meeting with Parthenia the other day. At least now she had some things to tell her. She could only hope the knowledge she'd gained would help. Brushing a hand over Alastor's and Zagan's heads, Devin unbolted the door and left the hut. The two males stirred awake behind her, but she didn't stay long enough for them to speak. Ignoring the painful twinges, Devin shifted to all fours and headed across the clearing into the woods. She paid no attention to all the eyes upon her and disregarded Derrick's voice as he called out to her as well. She couldn't speak to him right now.

Burying the pain down deep, Devin picked up her pace and left the village. Hopefully, her brother would get the hint and let her be for now. If she looked at him, saw the emotions cross his face, she may not hold the memories back. And it was imperative that she do so.

Devin headed first to the river to wash, and then to the treehouse. Once she reached it, fresh exhaustion hit her. It felt as though she hadn't slept a single bit. Staring up through the leaves, she tried to muster at least a little energy so she could climb up. Nope. There was no way. Letting out a sigh, she shifted back to her humanoid form and gently lowered herself to the ground. Maybe at least one of them hadn't arrived yet. She knew they both tried to come here and meet daily, if possible. She would just sit here... until—or if—one of them showed.

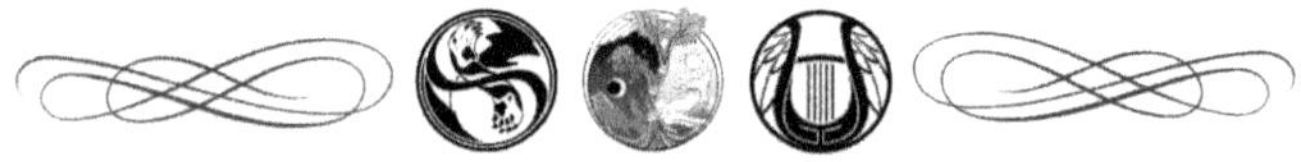

Parthenia's meeting with Vasilia still had her reeling. Especially the last thing the female said to her. 'I know you are doing what you can to help our people. Whatever it is you are trying, keep doing it, and you will find the answers.' What did Vasilia mean? Did the female know she'd snuck out of Pteryrina? Went down to the isle? These thoughts had distracted her so much that she'd completely forgotten to take the invisibility potion before she left. She'd gone down the staircase and into the forest, on automatic pilot, as she flew toward the treehouse. As Parthenia approached, she spotted Devin sitting on the ground at the base of the trunk. The female didn't look all that great. Parthenia slowed, allowing the blades of grass to tickle the underside of her talons. "Devin? Is there... are you..." She swallowed the lump in the back of her throat. "Do you need some help?"

Devin raised her eyes but kept her chin tucked against her chest. "I am alright. But I find I do not have the energy to climb today. I do not know if Gavin is up there or not. If he is—and if it would be alright with you, of course—would you mind seeing if he could help me up there? I have some things to tell you."

Although the female didn't lift her face, the bite marks on Devin were evident. Part of Parthenia wanted to reach out to the female. But she recalled what Gavin had said about how Devin contained her emotions. It didn't seem it would be wise. She could sense his presence in the treehouse already. "Yes. Of course, I'll get him." Parthenia offered a brief nod and flew to the top.

When she landed in the treehouse, Gavin's gaze swung in her direction and his features lit up. He came over from the counter, where he'd worked on the charts, and drew her into his thick arms. After placing a kiss on her neck, his face remained where it was as he breathed in her scent. "What is wrong, love?"

"Devin. She's at the base. She..." Parthenia inhaled a deep breath and let his scent roll through her. That divine aroma of his steadied her nerves, settling her so she could get the words out. "I told her I would get you because she needs help up."

"Of course," he whispered. "I... um, I will be right back." He kissed the side of her throat, shifted, and disappeared down the tree.

For a moment, she considered pacing while she waited, but it would do no good. Instead, she thought back to how they handled her wounds a couple of days ago. They could give Devin the option for the healing potion, though it may not be something she could take. In that case—she sensed it the moment Gavin reached the bottom of the tree, his rage pulsating through her. Shaking off the emotions, Parthenia went straight to the shelves where they kept the herbs. It wasn't her first time making a remedy for pain.

When they reached the top of the tree, she was still mixing the herbs in a jar of water. Gavin stopped halfway inside the treehouse and waited until Devin was back on her feet before climbing the rest of the way in and shifting to his humanoid form. "There is a bedding pallet in the corner," he said. "Please, sit down if you would like. It may be more comfortable."

Devin nodded and slowly crossed the room, easing down into a sitting position with her legs tucked underneath her. A beat passed before she spoke. "So, I found the village where the guilers live. More accurately, someone led me there."

Parthenia's eyebrows furrowed as she continued to mix the herbs. "What's a guiler?" It wasn't a term she'd come across in any of her research. Who accompanied the female? Gavin came over, wrapped his arms around her from behind, and placed a kiss on either side of her neck, then went back to working on the charts.

"Just another species," Devin said. "They look humanoid, but no fur from what I saw, and they have deformities. Misshapen limbs, extra growths, things like that. They can manipulate the elements."

She flicked her gaze to Devin and got a gander at some wounds she hadn't seen. With the way the female had moved across the room, there had to be more. But she couldn't think about that. Having Gavin near her and a task at hand kept her from focusing on the female's injuries. Acknowledging the information, Parthenia returned her attention to the herbal remedy. "I didn't even know anyone could manipulate the elements." Outside of the fae. Gavin reached over, caressed her neck, and gave her shoulder a gentle squeeze. He brushed his hand down her wing before returning to the charts.

"It was lovely to watch what little I saw of it. There was young playing with a ball, but using the air to pass it around." Devin cracked a grin. "Anyway. They granted my companion and I permission to speak to their Elder."

"Your companion?" Gavin asked without looking up from what he was doing.

"Mhm. I met her in another place that someone asked me not to reveal anything about. I assume it extended to the inhabitants of the place."

Parthenia tossed a glance at Gavin and then shifted her gaze to Devin. A place that was protected. Not to be mentioned. Although she wouldn't pose the question, she wondered if it was the hybrid village. She knew one existed; their history books vaguely referenced it, but that was it. Looking back at the herbal mixture, she checked it over before combining it with water and giving it a good stir. "Okay. So, this Elder. They had answers?" Parthenia crossed the room and held the cup out to Devin.

The female stared up at her for a moment before accepting the cup. 'Thank you,' she mouthed, took a drink of it, grimaced, and then took another one. "He had some, yes. Although he said he could not tell me everything he knew, he said he knew many things about the barrier."

"Really?" Gavin posed.

"Yes. He said he is over three-hundred *solaris* of age."

"Wow. I wonder if that's how long all guilers live." Even sirens didn't live that long. Most lived to be one-hundred-fifty. At that moment, it occurred to her Gavin might—nope. She would not think about that. They would have a long, happy life together. A long, long, long life. Parthenia turned back to the mess on the table and cleaned everything up. "Some information is good. That gives us more than we had."

"I have more, I just... I am tired today. I apologize." Devin took another drink.

"You don't have to apologize. It isn't necessary. At all." It was all she could say. It wasn't what she wanted to say, though. Devin had come today. Truly, she should've allowed herself time to heal more. If there was anything she could relate to, it was stubbornness.

Devin gave a slight nod and drank more of the herbal remedy. "So. No, he said, most guilers do not live nearly as long as he has. And he said his purpose here is almost finished. I assumed he knows his life is ending soon." She frowned a little. "He was looking at star charts when we arrived there. And he kept repeating, 'The stars are realigning.' He said change is coming, and it is inevitable. That it was long overdue. I asked him about the barrier and if there was a way to get through it or destroy it." She finished what was in the cup and set it on the floor. "Oh. Do you have parchment and something to write with? I want to write something down for you."

"Parchment? Um, yes." As she repeated the other things in her mind that Devin had stated, she retrieved a piece of parchment and a charcoal pencil. Striding across the room again, Parthenia held out both items. "I feel like there's something in what you've already said, but it's not connecting."

"Not much has connected in my head since I met him, but I remember what he said." Devin took the paper and writing utensil. "He said, 'We do not wish for its destruction. We are ill-prepared for that.' Speaking of the barrier. I do not know the 'we' he was speaking of, though. Then, he said again that the stars are realigning, indicating that it might change soon. So, maybe, whoever the 'we' are, they will be prepared for the barrier's destruction? I do not know." She shook her head. Bending over the paper, she wrote. "I asked him if it might be possible for some to pass through the barrier, and he told me this prophecy. He said that if I knew a siren, they might help with it." A faint smile flitted across her face as she finished writing and read the words aloud before handing the parchment over.

"'Like no other, one so pure; With a touch of gold; That holds the cure; Will one *umbra* return to the fold.' I asked him what it meant in simple terms, but all he told me was, 'She is coming.' I do not know what it means."

Taking the papyrus from Devin's hands, Parthenia read over the prophecy. Was that the term the female had used? Yes, prophecy. Prophecy. Touch of gold. A touch of gold. Parthenia turned back to the shelves and scanned through the books she'd left here. It took her a second to locate the one she searched for. Plucking it from the shelf, she quickly skimmed through the pages. "Touch of gold. I've seen that before."

"Oh. Before he told me the prophecy, he said the key to the barrier is not on the isle and that it has been separate for many *solaris*. That *umbra* at the barrier, you said most require a catalyst or key to both lock and open. According to him, it is nowhere on Prisma Isle." Devin sighed.

"So, *she... she* is coming," Gavin said. "Did he mean some*one*, not some*thing*, is the key to getting through the barrier?"

Devin leaned back against the wall. "Maybe. That was all he said when I asked what the prophecy meant. That sirens have many prophecies and, if I knew one, they might help. I am lucky enough to know one."

Parthenia eyed Devin. "Yes. Everything I've found regarding barriers supports that. But if it's not on the isle..." Shaking the slight panic that threatened to break through, she turned back to the book and flipped a few more pages. "Aha! I knew I'd seen that phrase. 'A siren that is claimed to have a touch of gold has a healing power unlike any other.' A healing power. None of the sirens I know have that." Tapping her chin, she glanced between Devin and Gavin. Somewhere close to when they'd met, she had told him there was speculation of sirens leaving after the war. She refocused on Devin. "Supposedly, after our war with the half-breeds, many sirens left. If this is, in fact, referring to a siren off the isle, then she's going to be unique according to the prophecy he referenced. And if there are other prophecies, I'm not aware of them."

"He said there were many. Are prophecies just not taught?"

"Or were prophecies just another thing that has gotten removed from your records?" her mate asked.

Her gaze swung back to Gavin. "It's possible they were removed. Prophecies give hope for change, but they can also reveal truths about the past that are trying to be hidden."

"Perhaps it is more than a rumor that sirens left after the war, but I cannot think what would bring them here. Unless, perhaps, they know about this place and are just..." Devin shrugged. "... waiting for the right time. It is a female, according to him at least, who holds the key." She rubbed her forehead. "According to him, it is not time for the barrier to be destroyed yet, as it has not fulfilled its purpose. But he suggested that according to the stars, that may change soon. No reference of time, just 'soon.'" She pressed the tips of her fingers to her temples. "My companion mentioned the war, too. Oh. Speaking of my companion again, something she said." Her teal gaze fixated on Parthenia. "You need to be more careful."

"It would have to be female. Males no longer exist." Parthenia frowned and chewed on the inside of her cheek. "Okay. So, a siren with unique healing powers. If she holds the key, then something will bring her here. Maybe it has something to do with whatever is on the other side of the bridge. What if that's what he was talking about?" She thought a minute longer. What Vasilia said to her earlier came back to her mind. She caught sight of the charts Gavin had worked on. The charts, the power, the isle. "If my supposition about the isle losing power is correct, then that could directly relate to why he said we might be ill—" She stopped. Devin's last words finally registered. "Careful? What are you talking about?"

Devin glanced back and forth between them. Her eyes settled on Parthenia. "There have been rumors in the marketplace about a siren being seen around the edges of the forest." A clatter resounded against the floor as Gavin dropped a charcoal pencil. "Nothing concrete, according to her, and rumors are rumors. But some listen to rumors more than others. Just, you should be careful."

Parthenia's eyes widened for a brief second. She reached over to Gavin's arm and squeezed. "She's right. They are just rumors, but I'll be more careful." Like she hadn't been that morning. Okay. And if the rumors were just in the market, she'd be fine. Very few knew about her relationship with Gavin, and sirens didn't go into the market.

"She mentioned nothing about the siren being with someone of another species or being with anyone at all. Only that a siren had been rumored to be seen. I just want you to take care." Devin paused as if her brain shifted directions. "If sirens left the isle after your war, what is to say that male sirens are not on the other side? Maybe there are just no male sirens where you live. And, you may be correct. Maybe something has to happen, or things have to get to a certain point before the barrier can fall. I do not know what could be on the other side either. Perhaps we are being protected from something worse than what we experience here."

Parthenia regarded Devin. "You're right about the males." That had also come as a suggestion between her and Gavin. She'd mentioned it as a possibility why Fagonia pushed so hard to maintain their laws.

Devin peered at Gavin. "I learned some other things from the guiler Elder. The details are not important now, as you two have enough to deal with, and I think this part may be my path alone to take. But I have a bit more hope that one *umbra*, our species will be truly free from him."

Gavin's forehead wrinkled as silence stretched between them. It almost appeared as if he struggled to find the right words. "What does that even mean?"

"I asked him questions about dark magic. It is the only thing that makes sense to me with Markham."

"Dark magic?" She thought back to some things Gavin had mentioned over the last couple of months: how he felt like Markham could see through his camouflage or how some believed the male could read thoughts. Devin's supposition made sense to her. Could that also mean it was the reason for the impact on their village? The issues with pregnancies? Problems with crops?

"The magic," she muttered. It made sense. It was all adding up to one forlorn conclusion. "Like the magic of the isle is draining."

"Markham's power is extensive, but I do not know if it extends any further than our boundaries. As soon as you cross over into our territory, though, it is like evil surrounds you. Over the *solaris*, the feeling has gotten more and more stifling. Almost all-consuming. He leaves the village sometimes, though." Devin shrugged. "I strongly believe that somewhere, the history of our species may be recorded. I have sought to find it but have had no luck so far. It would be ridiculous to think that he is the only leader our species has ever had. There had to have been others before him, who perhaps did not want the pack members to be so ill-educated. We are taught nothing but how to obey and serve him. That cannot be the way it has always been. We are barely surviving now. We would not have made it this long if that were the case."

"His power may not extend beyond your boundaries, but we're going through something similar in Pteryrina. Over the last several *cycles*, we've lost multiple lots of our Poppy Fields, and our Reflection Pools have been slowly drying up over the *solaris*. We used to have a waterfall that flowed continuously and nine pools. The waterfall stopped flowing a few *solaris* ago, and we now only have two pools remaining. Plus, as far as we know, there are no male sirens, and mating outside the species is outlawed. According to what we're taught, that law has been in place since the war with the half-breeds." It didn't seem imperative to mention her and Gavin's other challenges. "If more than our two species are having issues, then it would seem logical it all relates to the magic of the isle. What if that's why the barrier was erected?"

"As you know, mating outside of our species is outlawed as well. Even mating outside of our form causes us to be shunned, but confined to living in the village still. Markham does not allow mixed young to live, only those that come from parents that are the same. Both canines, both felines, etcetera. He views them as abominations. I thought that was just a preference of his. Maybe whatever has happened in the past just bred too much distrust between the species. The youngest child in our village right now is four. Still a nestling but she will be a youngling before too long. There have been no successful pregnancies since then, but there are a couple of currently expectant mothers we are hopeful for." Devin sighed. "This is one of those times where knowing our history would be beneficial." Devin's lips pursed. "If the problems extend beyond our species, you may be right. There are too many coincidences for them not to be connected. What exactly do you mean, though? Do you think someone erected the barrier to preserve what magic remained in our species? Or to keep the evil here from getting out?"

"As these are changes that have occurred, at least for us, in recent *solaris*, and the barrier is believed to have been erected three-hundred-*solaris* ago, it would make more sense that the magic was being preserved or protected. And, since that time, it has become tainted somehow." Parthenia set the book down and scanned the prophecy. "If the siren is supposed to be coming here soon—which could be *umbras, penumbras, cycles*—but if she is the key, or has the key, and it's long overdue, then everything we've been going through should end. And she—whoever she is—may be the trigger."

"If the magic Markham possesses was ever *not* dark, he has certainly tainted it. The guiler I spoke to said that all magic has to have balance, especially dark magic, because of its nature. He said all magic comes at a cost, but the cost is greater with dark magic versus light. No, not light; he called it *natural* magic. He also said that dark magic is used to take life, not give it. And, if it is not used properly, it will rebound on itself. He said his species understands more than most the—how did he word it—the *true cost and true value of magic.* I need to find out if I am correct, that it is dark magic Markham possesses and how he came into possession of it. Perhaps that will aid me in figuring out how to relieve him of it."

"It would certainly explain everything." Parthenia wished the Elder had given them more of an answer with a timeframe. *Soon* was rather open to interpretation. Or that she knew what other prophecies there were that he'd referred to. Or how this Elder even knew of siren prophecies. Although he could've had contact with a siren before the war. No matter what, her Elder had confirmed one thing. "We're moving in the right direction to figure it all out."

"I think so. I travel enough around the isle, perhaps I will meet someone who will give me more. The Elder said he knew more than he could tell me. So, for whatever reason, there were things he could not divulge. At least to a couple of newcomers who happened upon his village." A faint smile crossed Devin's face. "But they are leads, at least. And we know more than we did before."

"Yes. We do," Parthenia admitted. There were still somethings they had to figure out, but they were closer now to complete answers. *Whatever we're doing, even my Elder seems to think we're on the right path*, she thought.

"What do you mean? Did you speak to her? What did she say?" her mate asked.

Oh, poppies! She'd said that aloud. Too late now. Parthenia shook her head. "That's the thing. I was just giving her my daily reports and, as I was leaving, she told me she knew what I was doing to save our people. And that, whatever I was trying to keep doing it and I'd get to the answers."

Gavin frowned. "Do you think she was just letting you know she is supporting you? Or that she knows something she is not telling you, that she wants you to find out on your own?"

"I don't know. I went to ask, but she just smiled at me and sent me on my way." Parthenia dragged a hand across her face. "It could be both. Maybe she knows I'm coming down here and searching for resolutions. Maybe it is her way of showing support." If that was the case, then once she presented her findings and everything Gavin had helped her put together, what would their next actions be?

Gavin wrapped an arm around her waist. "We are going to figure all of this out. I almost have the charts done. When you go home tonight, take them with you and show them to her. See what she says. Then we can go from there." He pressed his forehead to hers. "Remember—difficulty now, but then will come our beautiful future."

Parthenia acknowledged his suggestion. She'd have to watch Fagonia; the female almost always lingered nearby when she gave her reports to Vasilia. She'd been lucky this morning. Fagonia hadn't been around. "I know. One step at a time. We just need to keep looking for information on the barrier. Maybe the prophecies. We have more to go on now." She glanced at Devin.

"I am glad that I could be of help. It is why I did not turnback when I knew my time was running out to get home on time." Gavin's head turned slightly away at Devin's words. "I did not know if, or when, I would get another chance to make that journey and find that information. It was too important. The opportunity presented itself and I knew I had to take it."

Parthenia remained silent, keeping her thoughts to herself. Gavin had told her what would happen, and she could see the proof of it all over the female. "I appreciate what you've done."

"You are very welcome. I hope that, over time, I can find out more," Devin replied.

"I'll keep looking as well. The solutions are there. I know they are." Parthenia sighed. If there were prophecies, there were answers. They just had to be found.

Chapter Five

A couple of days had passed since Devin had spoken to Parthenia and Gavin at the treehouse. She made her way back to the village from her cave when she sensed her brother nearby. Changing direction, she headed to the river. She needed to speak with him, and it wasn't a conversation they could have in the village. It was difficult for them to find the opportunity for discussions at all. He was always busy with *duties* for that demon, the so-called *King* of theirs. Apparently, though, that hadn't been all he'd been up to.

Breaking through the trees, she watched Derrick for a moment. He sat on the bank in his humanoid form with his knees drawn up and his arms draped over them, staring into the water. Obviously deep in thought. He didn't even seem to notice her approach. Shifting to her humanoid form as well, she sat on the grass beside him. Glancing down, she brushed her fingers over the petals of some yellow flowers that someone had planted here, then turned her gaze to him as she mirrored his pose.

"You are an idiot."

Startling a bit, Derrick flicked his gaze at her. He blinked twice. "Excuse me?"

The corner of her mouth lifted as she gazed out at the water. "Did you really think Lillianna was going to talk to you willingly? You are an Informant, Derrick. That you are my brother means little to her. She does not know you."

"You know about that."

"I came across Logan, and I met his mate. She is a lovely female." She peered at him. "The details are not important, so do not ask. I did not know he was even still alive." Devin glared at him, though it wasn't heartfelt. "Thank you *so much* for keeping that to yourself."

"Like I could have risked telling anyone."

"I know." Several moments of silence stretched between them. "You are still an idiot, though."

"Are you going to elaborate on why, exactly?"

"Because. It is not exactly a secret how close I am to Lilli. Despite Ailwin's efforts to not allow her to get close to anyone. Had I known what the plans have been, she could have been out of here a long time ago. How long have you been trying to get her to speak to you, anyway?"

Derrick said nothing for a beat. He ran a hand over the top of his head. "Uh, early *Aphros* or so."

"Three *cycles*? Good gods, Derrick." She shook her head. "Alright. When are you supposed to meet him at the fight club again?"

"Tomorrow."

"Good. Okay. Here is what we are going to do."

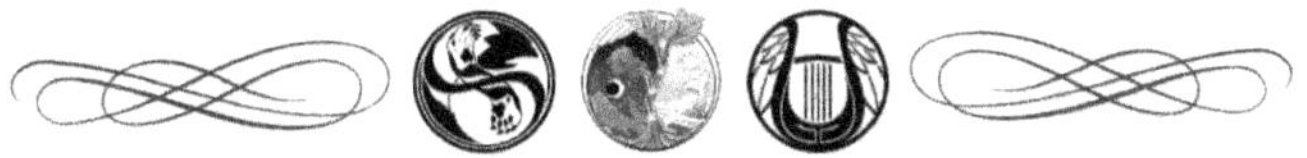

Lillianna awoke early, right before the sun rose. She slept in the front room instead of sharing a room with her sisters. Pierce had his room, but he never slept in it. In fact, he rarely entered it at all. Her father didn't allow her in either of their bedrooms. He always made her sleepout here. Pierce slept near her always, curled up or sitting against the wall, no pallet or bedding. She had asked him why several times, but his only response was it was his preference and he was more comfortable that way. It made no sense to her, but her brother had always done things his way. And it comforted her to have him close. He always did anything he could to protect her.

As she sat upright on her pallet, her foot brushed against something. It was a bouquet of stemless white lilies in a wicker bowl. She beamed. Every year on her day of birth, Pierce left them for her. He was never in the village when she woke to find them, though, and would always brush off her 'thankyou,' only stating that she 'deserved much more than a simple bowl of flowers.' He always said that one day he would make sure she got it.

As Lilli brought the bowl to her nose, she inhaled deeply. They smelled so sweet and made her think of a faraway place full of happiness and peace. A soft sigh left her mouth. One day. Maybe.

Rising to her feet, she held the bowl carefully against her chest. Her sisters were moving about in their room. It wasn't uncommon for Dahlia to be cruel on this day. Any day, really, but especially this one. She saw black fur out of her periphery and turned her head, clutching the bowl tighter.

Dahlia rolled her eyes as she entered the room on all fours. "Get those things out of here. They reek, and Father will be up soon."

That was all her older sister said. No greeting or acknowledgment that it was her day of birth. Dahlia had never uttered a kind word to her. Not once. The female probably never would.

Lilli picked up her basket with a strap on it, carefully set the bowl inside before hanging it around her neck. Without a word to either of her sisters, Lilli left the hut. There was no point. There was nothing worth saying, and nothing that would make a difference. Pierce had remembered her day of birth. That was enough to bring her joy.

As she went about her morning duties, she ignored the ones that did the same to her and quietly greeted the ones that addressed her. Devin was the only one that acknowledged what day it was. It was nice to see her. The female hadn't moved around the village much over the past couple of days. While in the kitchen house together, preparing morning meal, Devin whispered to meet her at the river before afternoon meal. She offered no further details, though, only continued with her kitchen duties as if she'd said nothing. Confused as Lilli was, she didn't bring it up again while they were inside there.

After morning meal, Lilli gave some excuses, and made her way to the river. She didn't know how long it would take Devin to come out here, just that she'd wanted to meet before afternoon meal. It had been a couple of days since she'd bathed, and it was an exceptionally lovely day out. Lilli cleaned herself, then exited the river, laying across the grass in her humanoid form while she waited. Caressing the petals of the flowers Pierce had given her, she hummed to herself. Pretty soon, she sang quietly.

It was a song that her brother had sung to her all the time when she was very young and she'd had nightmares or couldn't sleep. But it had been many years since Pierce had sung anything. The song claimed her as his sunshine, that she made him happy when things were tough, and how he loved her. Her brother was the only one in her family who loved her, the only one who cared.

A shadow fell upon her. She jumped, spun around, shifted into her other form, and bared her teeth with a snarl. Derrick had snuck up on her—and too easily. Her fur stood on edge. She wasn't supposed to be alone with the Informants when Pierce wasn't home. He'd warned her, and they always scared her. Not to mention the ones who harassed her when Pierce wasn't in the village.

"What do you want?" Lilli growled. So what if he was larger and stronger than her? She could take a chunk out of the best of them. And had before, though, it had gotten her into a lot of trouble. But if he wanted to do something to her, she would fight him back. No matter what the eventual outcome would be.

Derrick sat back on his haunches, not moving any closer. "I just want to speak to you. It is important. I did not mean to frighten you, but you have been avoiding me."

"And why should I not?" She backed away from him. "I have nothing to say to you."

"Then just hear me out. Please."

"Why should I? I know Pierce is gone from the village today. What, did you wait until he was gone to come after me? Like the others do? You probably want the same things they do."

Derrick's jaws clenched. "Calm yourself, Lillianna. I did not come here for that. I swear to you, I only came to talk."

"And I should believe you? Why should I listen to anything you have to say?" Out of the corner of her eye, she spotted Devin come through the trees.

"Good gods, Derrick. I told you to wait for me. Look at her. You have her terrified." Devin shook her head and went to Lilli's side. "Everything is alright, Lilli, I promise. My brother would never hurt you. But we need to speak to you."

"About what?" she asked, still casting a wary gaze at the male.

"About your brother."

"What about Pierce?"

"No, your other brother," Devin said.

"I have no other brother."

"Yes, you do. He is but a few *solaris* younger than Pierce. His name is Logan. And he very much wants to meet you."

Lilli froze, searching for a lie in Devin's eyes and voice, but she couldn't find one. Glancing back at Derrick, there was only truth in his face as well. Confusion arose like a tidal wave within her. "That makes no sense. How could I have a brother that I know nothing about? Pierce would have told me."

Derrick's words left him in a rush. "Your father ordered him not to. A couple of *solaris* before your birth, a canine was killed. Logan had angered Markham somehow, I know not how, and was wrongfully accused of the crime. As soon as that happened, your father ordered no mention of him. He was disowned from the family, banished from the pack, and has been hunted down ever since. Logan did not know of your existence or your mother's death until recently, when I found him and told him. Pierce could not risk seeking him out. His only concern has always been your safety."

"But why did he not just tell me? I would have said nothing to anyone."

Devin flicked her gaze to Derrick, then back to Lilli. "Markham has abilities that would have made that impossible. I do not know for sure, but I am far from the only one that suspects he can read minds. If one cannot shield those thoughts, it makes them—and any secrets they may keep—very vulnerable."

"Shielding your thoughts takes a lot of practice," Derrick added. "And Markham does not handle treachery well. Pierce knew you would want to meet Logan. Doing so would be extremely dangerous. But I have spoken to Logan. He lives in a secret place that is well protected, even from Markham. And Logan wants to meet you, and he wants to take you to live in his home. He wants to take you away from all of this and keep you safe." Derrick held up a paw, silencing her. "Yes, I know. Pierce wants that as well. He has always done whatever it took to keep you safe. But I think part of him cannot believe that finding sanctuary in that place is a possibility. He is just doing the best that he can with what he has, and what knowledge the *solaris* have brought to him."

None of this made a bit of sense. Yet in her heart, she recognized it all as the truth. "So, if I meet Logan... if I go to that place he lives in... I do not have to come back here?"

Devin smiled. "No. You would never have to come back here. Never."

"Logan will make sure of it," Derrick said. "And once you are free, I know Pierce will follow."

Lilli sat down hard on the ground, her fur finally settling. Pierce had always done anything and everything to care for her, no matter the cost. No matter how often she'd asked, though, he would give her no details of her birth and mother, or the years before she was old enough for memories to stick. All he'd ever told her was their mother had died in childbirth with her. She wasn't ignorant of the differences in their dynamic compared to other siblings. He cared for her, not as a brother would, but as a father should. Not like *their* father, nor most of the fathers here, but what she imagined a father might. And Pierce would never explain that either, why he took the job for himself, and why their father wouldn't.

She needed answers. And she needed to meet Logan. And if she could truly get free of this place...

"I do not even know what to think right now. I... I feel like I need time to process this, but..." Her gaze fell to the grass as if those green blades offered a solution. There wasn't sufficient time for her to truly think about all of this. She couldn't leave the boundaries. If she made it out without getting caught, it would be a genuine miracle from the gods. "No. I want to go. Now." Her gaze flicked between the two of them. "Can you take me to him?"

"Of course. The few times we have met, this is around the time he has been in the marketplace. We are going to have to camouflage. And we are going to have to run as fast as possible. If Markham senses us leaving..." Derrick's words trickled off. The meaning didn't need to be spoken.

"Well, lucky for us, I am quick." And they would have to be, since her father had demanded she return to their hut soon. Lilli knew why, and if there were any way to avoid that, she would.

"Good. Most of the other Informants are out scouting right now. As long as the felines do not come after us, we should be fine. Camouflage, and stay close. If anyone comes upon us, I want you to run as fast as you can until you find the marketplace. Do not stop for anything."

Devin leaned into Lilli for a moment. "It is going to be fine. We will keep you safe."

Lilli bit her lip. What if she couldn't do this? No... no. She needed to do this. She had to meet her brother. Did she *really* have a chance to be free of this place? If there was even a sliver of a chance that it could be possible, she had to risk it. And if Pierce would come too, it would be worth any danger that might come at them. She had to try. Taking a deep breath, she nodded and camouflaged. "Let us go."

Derrick dipped his chin and camouflaged, Devin following suit. She followed their scents through the trees until she left the boundaries for the very first time. *Oh, wow. The air...the very atmosphere out here...* All she'd ever felt in Métamorphe had been darkness and evil, but *here...* it was like she could breathe properly for the first time in her life. Lilli shook off the sensations as she concentrated on staying close to them. She didn't need to worry, though. Devin remained right by her side. She'd often wondered if the female had some kind of sixth sense or something. Devin always seemed to know when she needed help that no one else could, or would, offer to her.

Once they'd gotten a suitable distance from Métamorphe and they continued to run, Derrick said, "When we arrive, I will get Logan and decide with him where to meet. Do not follow me as I do not want you near the fight ring."

When they reached the marketplace, Lilli shifted to her humanoid form, so she could walk upright on two legs. Devin shifted as well and was the only one of them that removed their camouflage. Were it not for Devin's hand holding hers, Lilli couldn't have moved. Structures larger and more beautiful than anything she'd ever seen, a coalition of magnificent aromas that overwhelmed her senses, a multitude of creatures she'd never seen the like of before. She couldn't put a name to any of it, but it was *wonderful*.

Derrick's whispered words came closer to her ear than she would have liked. He told her to stay camouflaged and not to let go of Devin's hand. After a moment, Devin gave an almost imperceptible nod. His scent moved further away, and her head turned in that direction. Before she even realized what she was doing, she'd taken her hand from Devin's and followed his scent. It wasn't what she was following, though. The same echo she'd always felt in the presence of her family... she felt it here, too. It was her brother. Someone she'd never known about. This was her way to freedom. She couldn't just stand there and wait.

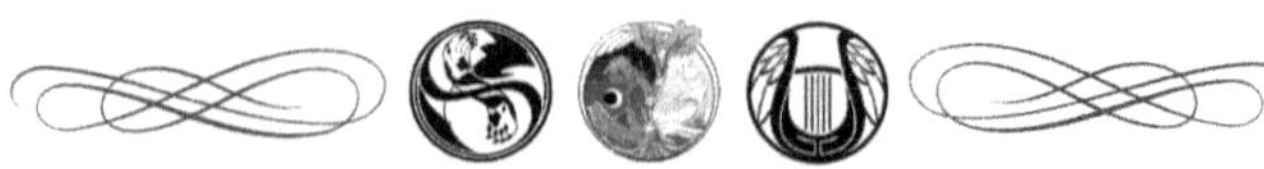

Logan sat at a table in the far corner of the room, as he always had. He watched the small crowd and the fight, much as he'd done every time he came to the ring. His only purpose had been to monitor things as closely as he could. Today, if things finally worked out, it would be different. He would meet his youngest sister. It had him slightly on edge, sending his nerves into overdrive. Despite all Derrick, Pierce, and Devin had told him, he didn't know what to expect of her.

No matter what, he would take her to Migas Village, and she would not return to the hell hole of her birth. His mate had been busy over the last couple of days making preparations in their new home for Lillianna. And the Leo situation had gotten resolved. Truly something that pleased him. He didn't wish to bring his sister to the village with that male walking around, not after what had occurred with his brother's mate. If it hadn't been for Ambrosia's insistence, he would've let his brother kill the male. This was one of those times he wished he had, but he couldn't change it. Shaking the thoughts from his head, Logan swallowed a hard lump in the back of his throat. Gods, Derrick needed to arrive soon.

The door opened and shut, then the male appeared. The two of them acknowledged one another, and Derrick headed his way when the door opened again behind him. He whipped around to see Devin, an annoyed look on her face. Then, a second later, another female appeared as her camouflage dropped. He couldn't see her face from here, but that had to be her. Logan got up and quickly strode in their direction.

"What the—" Derrick cursed. "I thought I told you I wanted neither of you in this place." His voice held a low growl to it as he addressed the female. "I told you to wait."

The female gave an almost imperceptible jerk, then tilted her head way back to look him right in the eyes. She shrugged. "Well, it did not work out that way."

Derrick slapped a hand over his face and rubbed his eyes. He shook his head as Logan appeared behind Devin and... *Lillianna. Gods...*

She stared around in awe. "I kind of like this place." Her gaze landed across the room, beyond the VIP rope, on the fight happening in the cage. "Well, that was stupid. And... yup. He is done. He was just asking to lose."

Logan chuckled. He couldn't help it; she was right. He hadn't quite gotten a full sight of his sister, but he could tell Pierce had taught her over the years. "Many overestimate their abilities."

Lillianna whipped around at his voice. Her jaw dropped as she stared up at him. He towered almost four feet taller than her. "I... I am... Oh, I am so happy to meet you," she said and threw her arms around him.

Oh, gods! She looked so much like their mother. White and light tan fur. Bright amethyst eyes, with a fiery spirit to boot. Just like their mother. Logan hugged her tight to him, trying hard to keep the tears out of his eyes. *He would not cry.* Logan rubbed his eyes and the tears that pricked the corners as he held onto his sister. It was the only way to keep from sobbing. "I am happy to meet you as well, sister."

Devin nudged Derrick. "Come, brother. Let us get refreshments."

"We should get back to the village," Derrick said.

"And I need something to drink. We have some time. Not much, but some. Relax."

The two disappeared, and Lilli took a slight step back from him. He could feel the nerves swirling within her. But he could also feel love; a lot of love for him. "You are tall. Taller than Pierce." She bit her lip. "I do not know if he knows I am here. He has never spoken of you to me."

Logan's mouth curled at the corners. The slight height difference between him and their brother had made for interesting scraps when they were younglings. For this moment, he was glad he'd spoken to Pierce a few days ago. "He could not speak of me to you. It would have risked you both greatly. However, he knows we were to meet. We have spoken."

He sensed her confusion so strongly; it could have been his own. "I have a lot of questions. Where do you live? And... why? Why now, after all of this time?" Before he could answer, a male bumped into her. She startled, snapping her jaws in his direction. He immediately backed up. His hands held up to his chest. Lillianna flushed, so deeply the color showed through her fur. She attempted to utter an apology, but the male left before the words could pass her lips. "Oh gods, I did not mean to do that."

Her emotions hit him like a boulder in the chest. A low growl rumbled in the back of his throat, and his fists clenched as his claws dug into the palms of his hands. Oh, he would make that male pay. Their father should be lucky to count his days, for they were gravely numbered. It took several deep breaths for him to regain control. He gently escorted Lillianna over to a table, out of the way of passersby. "I did not know of your existence." That sounded like a horrible excuse. His sister deserved better. "I was angry for many *solaris*, even once I made a home. It was not until a few *cycles* ago that changed when I met my mate. Soon after, I began coming here hoping to see someone I trusted that would give me information. As soon as I learned of you, I began working on getting you and Pierce out of there."

Her mouth fell open a little as she lifted her gaze to him. Tears welled in the corners of her eyes, and she blinked furiously to hold them at bay. Words fell from her lips in a rush. "I do not want to go back to the village. Nor do I want to be there ever again. I hate it so much. And Pierce cannot always be there. Markham sends him away a lot. I do not know what he does, but when he is gone, and when he is not in our hut, Father... he lets males..."She bit her lip then balled her hands into fists. "No male has ever lain with me. But they do... other things—"She froze when another growl, louder this time, emanated from him.

He was going to burn them all alive. Watch as they writhed in pain and clawed their way in an attempt to escape. Hades, he had to calm down. He couldn't focus right now on what his sister had gone through. Nor the emotions swirling through her. It would never happen again. Logan wrapped Lillianna in his arms and held her close. "You will not go back. You will never return. I have a place where you will be safe, and no harm will ever come to you again. Gods, I am sorry I did not get you sooner." He pressed a kiss to the top of her head.

As a tear fell from her eye, she clung to him, her arms around his neck, getting as close to him as she could. As sorry as he was, he couldn't sense a single bit of blame from her. Only relief. "And Pierce is coming too? I cannot leave him alone there. I do not care so much about Dahlia and Zinnia. Dahlia is cruel, and she hates me. I do not even know why, but she hates me."

"Yes," he reassured her. "Pierce is coming too. He will not be left there." Gods, he didn't want to ask what males had touched her. He would, but not today. Because he would hunt them across the isle. Not a single one would return to Markham, except for their head. And that male would know damn good and well who was taking his Informants down. One by one. Every single one that had harmed his sister. He would save their father for last. That filth would rue the day he dared allow harm to come to Lillianna.

Taking a few deep breaths, stillness washed over her before she sat and took his hand in hers. "There is nothing in the village that is important enough for me to go back for. Can we go to your home? Please?"

As she calmed, his own emotions eased, though he inhaled another deep breath to be on the safe side. "Yes. My mate is eager to meet you. We should say our goodbyes to Devin and Derrick before we leave." Not to mention, he owed Derrick a great thanks. And more.

Lillianna leaned into him as they crossed the room. Devin rose from a stool and gave her a hard hug. "I am going to miss you," she said, then looked up at Logan. "I know you will take care of her. Please tell Pierce that I wish him well. I know I may not see him again."

"I will." Logan acknowledged Devin's request, then turned his attention to Derrick. He reached over and squeezed the male's shoulder. "I owe you a debt." There was only one way he could think to repay him. Leaning closer, he whispered about the location of his cabin, a place that would always be open should the male ever need it. As much as he prayed to the gods that Derrick would take his mate from the village, he feared it wouldn't happen. Once Logan had given him the directions he needed, he straightened. "It is there if you ever require it."

"Thank you. I am sure I will have need of it sooner rather than later." Derrick squeezed Logan's shoulder. "You owe me nothing. I have only done what was right. I wish you happiness, brother."

"You as well, brother."

Derrick glanced at Lillianna. "Take care, little one." She said nothing back to him, only nodded.

Logan hugged Lillianna close to him, tucking her into his side. "Come, Lilli, let us go." With that, he escorted her to the exit and scanned the area before leaving.

Chapter Six

Pierce spent a good majority of the morning running aimlessly back and forth along the eastern edge of the shape shifter boundaries, around the chimera territory, brushed along the marshlands, and circled back again. It was close to midday when he backtracked toward home. As he broke through a portion of the trees into an open space just outside the boundary line of the territory, he heard the distant sound of paws crossing over the ground. He couldn't tell who it was yet, but he sensed two people approach.

Sniffing the air, his ears twitched as he halted completely in his tracks. It took several long minutes before he caught their scents. Derrick and Devina. There was no one else around that he perceived. It should be safe to speak here. Pierce stood there and waited until they came through the trees. They'd come from the direction of the marketplace. Good. This was good. He hadn't expected Devina to be there with Derrick, but it didn't surprise him, either.

He said nothing until they stopped in front of him, almost holding his breath in anticipation. "Is she safe?" he whispered. "Does he have her?"

"She is safe, brother mine," Derrick said. "I had her camouflage and, by the gods' grace, no one came upon us as we left the boundaries. We met with him in the marketplace, and they took a few minutes to get acquainted, said their goodbyes to us, then he took her home. She knows you are following."

Pierce locked his elbows to keep from sagging. He may well drop to the ground if he didn't. "I…" He let out a harsh breath. Gods, there were no words. "For real? This is real?"

"Yes, Pierce. Truly. She is in his safety. I am sure that, by now, she has made it to her new home," Devina replied.

His breathing picked up speed, and he choked up. He blinked several times, refusing to let the tears fully surface. "I do not know what to say. How can I ever thank you? Both of you?"

"By following her and living a good life," Devina answered. "That is how you can thank us."

Pierce inhaled and exhaled a deep breath. "Zinnia… I have to at least try, but…"

"Get to the river, where it flows just outside of the boundaries. If I have to drag her there by the ear, I will make sure she meets you there."

"I may well enjoy seeing that." The three of them shifted to their humanoid forms. Pierce gave Derrick a hard hug, then did the same to Devina. "I should hurry. If my father has not already noticed, I am sure it will not belong before he knows Lilli is not there."

"Derrick, you go along without me, okay? Give me a minute here," Devina instructed.

The male tilted his head, but with a slight dip of his chin, he shifted, and headed through the trees.

Once he was gone from sight, Pierce focused his attention on her. "What is it?" His mouth down-turned as Devina just stood there, chewing on her lip for a moment. "Devin, what?"

"I feel bad saying anything. I feel as if it is not my place, but…"

"By the gods, please tell me."

"It was something Lillianna said. Logan took her over to a table, and I was not trying to eavesdrop, but sometimes I pick up things without meaning to overhear them."

He waited for her to continue. When she didn't, he gestured impatiently with his hand. "And?" Gods, he could only imagine what had come out of Lilli's mouth that would have the female acting like this.

"She said a male had never lain with her."

A deep chill set in, all the way to his bones. His hands clenched into fists and he bit back a growl. It was difficult to keep his claws from digging into his palms, but he suspected his eyes had darkened. His anger, though not directed at her, proved impossible to contain. She had tended to his sister many times. She would know what had been done. Thank the gods she had been there. He didn't know if he would've had the strength to...

"I did not say that to make you angry," she whispered. "I just... if my opinion means anything. It might be a good idea to find someone in the village that she can talk to. If she truly does not understand all that has happened to her. Maybe she just said that, for Logan's sake, I do not know. I heard little." She paused. "If she does not process it in her own time—of course—but if she does not, one *umbra*, it is going to come crashing down upon her." Devin chewed on her bottom lip. "I just worry about her. I hope I did not overstep."

Pierce shook his head as his hands relaxed. "No. It is alright. And I am glad that you told me." He let out a heavy breath. "I will push nothing with her. And that includes talking about any of it. I am sure Logan will not, either. But she will know that we—that all of us—will be there to help her in any way she needs."

"Well, I just thought you should know that. I know that you both will take wonderful care of her. And she is going to be happy there. I can feel it." Devina gave his arm a light squeeze and smiled at him once more. "Alright. Go to the river, and I will have Zinnia meet you there. And good luck."

With that, she shifted to all fours and took off into the trees. Pierce watched her go for a beat before shifting himself and leaving. He had a feeling he knew exactly how this talk was going to go. But he could hope. Either way, he would know soon enough.

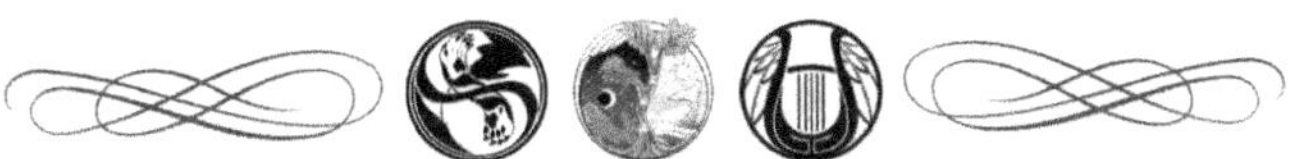

As they approached a treeline that seemed almost like a wall of green, Lilli watched Logan shift to his humanoid form. The branches separated and reformed into an intricately woven archway. It was like magic.

"This is it," Logan said. "Do not be nervous."

She hesitated in front of the archway. Of all the things she'd seen for the first time today, this was the most mesmerizing. "Before today, I had never left the boundaries. Not once." And Logan had promised she would not go back, that she'd seen that place for the last time. She took a deep breath, shifted to her humanoid form, and strolled through the archway. "Today has been very overwhelming." Probably the first of many to come. All new experiences, surroundings, and... family.

Logan followed her, and the archway closed behind them. He tapped her shoulder and pointed to the treeline. "This hides us well. These grounds offer us excellent protection." From where they stood, they saw many hybrids around the clearing and beyond. "You will meet the Elder first, and then I will take you to my home, where my mate awaits your arrival."

Lilli surveyed every bit of the treeline: its endless height and width. So many leaves. Too many to count. "Well protected," she mumbled. But were they protected from their father? From Markham? His Informants? Taking a deep breath, she let it out slowly, then peered around some more. Her eyes widened. There had been so much hustle and bustle in the marketplace, it had been difficult to focus on any one person or thing. Even with the fight she'd seen in the ring, she'd been more focused on the movements the two made, not so much what they were. "I have never seen... There are so many that are not like us." She had seen nothing but shape shifters in the village. Finally, she glanced at him. "I am ready. And I am excited to meet your mate."

"Once Pierce joins us, we will be the only shape shifters here that I know of." Logan strode forward and led her to a hut just off to the right ahead of them.

A male with bright red hair stepped out from the doorway and approached them. With his hands clasped behind his back and his mouth curled at the corners, he acknowledged the two of them. "Greetings, my children."

Logan bowed his head. "Greetings, Santos. May I present my sister, Lillianna?"

Lilli flipped her eyes to Logan, then bowed her head too. This was a male, a male she'd never met, but she didn't feel fear like she thought she would've. It was strange. She was still nervous, though. "G-Greetings," she muttered.

"I am pleased to welcome you to my home, Lillianna." Santos offered her a bow of his head in return. "Shall we go inside to confer?"

"Lilli, you okay with that?" Logan gestured to the hut. "If so, we will go in together."

She said nothing for a moment. Logan was her brother. He wouldn't let anything happen to her. And she didn't get nearly the same vibes from Santos as she did from the males in the village. "If you will go too, then yes. I am okay with that." She regarded the male. It took her a moment to raise her eyes to him. Manners. She must always remember her manners. "Thank you for your welcome."

"Of course, my child. It would be no other way." His yellow gaze flicked between the two of them. "Come, Delenia has tea and sweets awaiting us." Santos headed toward the hut, his talons digging into the ground as he moved.

Logan held his hand out to her. She gently took it, letting him lead her toward the hut. Before they even got inside, her nose twitched. Logan's nose did too. Gods, what was that *incredible* smell?

They reached the doorway, and Santos stepped inside first. Logan gave her hand a squeeze as he led her inside. They had set the front room up with three chairs and a small table covered with a couple of foods she'd never seen before.

Santos sat in one chair and gestured to the other two. "Please, sit."

Lilli eased into the plush cushion, placing her hands in her lap. As much as she wished to relax and enjoy her surroundings, nothing eased the tension from her shoulders or settle the empty feeling in the pit of her stomach. "You have a lovely home," she whispered.

"Thank you, child." Santos nudged a plate of brown balls and small bowls of pudding forward. "You may indulge if you so desire. Delenia will bring forth tea shortly."

Logan sat down next to Lilli. "Thank you, Santos."

A short, blonde female came around and offered a cup of tea to Lilli, Logan, and then Santos last. Logan offered a nod of thanks to the female and sipped at the tea.

"Thank you, Delenia," Santos said.

Lilli smiled a little up at the female. "Thank you." She took a sip of her tea and reached for whatever was on the plate—it smelled *fantastic*—then jerked her hand back. Her father barely let her have meals. He had never allowed her to have anything sweet. Not that they had sweet things in the village, but Pierce had brought them home for her sometimes when he could. She wanted it. The male had said she could have it. But her hand just wouldn't reach the rest of the way.

"It is your choice to partake, child. No judgment shall pass if you decide to take a piece." Santos plucked a nibble from the plate.

Her choice? No one had ever allowed her to make choices. Her father always punished her for wanting to disobey him. But she had made a choice today. A *big* one. Several. She had left the village, met her brother, and decided not to return home. All of those had been her own choices. Lilli hesitantly reached for one sweet. Oh, look, her hand made it to the plate. Picking one up, she brought it close to her mouth, and couldn't stop herself from drawing in the scent of it. Its aroma was intense with a nutty undernote. Gods, it was even better up close. "I have never had it before. What is it called? If I may ask?"

"It is called chocolate. Certainly, a treasured sweet amongst our village." Santos sipped some tea.

She took a small bite and her eyes widened as the creamy taste exploded on her tongue. "Mmm. Oh, wow." She took another bite, bigger this time. "It is very good."

"Yes, it is," Santos replied. "It is one of my favorites. I am certain you will try many new things here."

"Everything about today." She paused. "I have had many new experiences in such a short time. And I look forward to having more. It thrilled me to be allowed to come here. My home—my *old* home—was a very... an unpleasant place."

"I understand. You have had difficulties no child, no person should experience. That will not happen here. I do not allow it."

Lilli frowned. "How..." Her voice trailed off so quietly, it was almost a whisper. "I don't und—how do you know what I have gone through?"

The silence stretched between them. Several moments passed before Santos spoke. "I can see the pain in your eyes. You deserve to know the truth of love. You'll get that here."

Her gaze dropped to her lap. The half-finished chocolate remained in her hand. Lilli blinked a few times when a tear welled in the corner of her eye. She couldn't even say why it appeared. She cleared her throat and lifted her gaze back to him. "I believe I will. It is part of why I wanted to come here. And I... I do not think I would have survived there. Not for much longer." Because she would not have allowed herself to.

Out of the corner of her vision, she saw Logan's forehead wrinkle. He laid a hand on her shoulder.

Santos stood and kneeled down before her. He took her hands in his own and squeezed them. "That is why I granted you sanctuary. You are too precious to those who truly care for you. You will find happiness here."

A tear slipped down her cheek, and she swallowed hard to clear the lump in her throat. "I do not know what happiness feels like," she mumbled.

Santos wiped the wetness from her cheek. "I promise you will. You have brothers who will help you. Females who already love you, though you have not met. Two of them and they will show you the motherly love you have gone without."

Blinking back the tears that threatened to spill over, she squeezed his hands hard in return. "Thank you," she whispered. "Very much. You are very kind. I very much look forward to... to making a life here."

"You will make a wonderful life here." His citrine eyes twinkled. "Trust in your family here. They will take care of you. If you feel as if someone has come against you in a way you do not wish, you may speak tome or any member of your family." He inhaled a deep breath and exhaled slowly. "We have one law in our village. No crime shall be committed against another. It does not matter who committed the crime. I *always* get the truth." His eyes flashed an orangish-red like fire for a mere second. "And the offenders are always imprisoned accordingly."

Lilli gasped. That had been *extraordinary*. A faint smile lifted the corners of her lips, bigger than before. "That is not how things are done where I came from. Not at all. But it is a great comfort to me." She clutched his hands.

"I am happy this comforts you." Slowly, Santos rose to his feet. His gaze shifted to Logan. "I believe Ambrosia has afternoon meal ready for you both." He squeezed Lilli's hands one last time as he returned his attention to her. "I am here should you ever need me."

"Thank you. I will not forget."

"You are quite welcome, child." Releasing her hands, he stepped back and offered a small bow of his head to Logan.

Logan bowed his head and stood. "Thank you, Santos." He held his hand out to Lilli. "Are you ready to see your new home?"

With a slight dip of her chin, Lilli got to her feet. Realizing again she still held the chocolate, she put it in her mouth, chewed slowly, and swallowed. "Yes. I am ready." She took his outstretched hand. "I am ready to go home."

With a warm smile, Logan led her out of the hut.

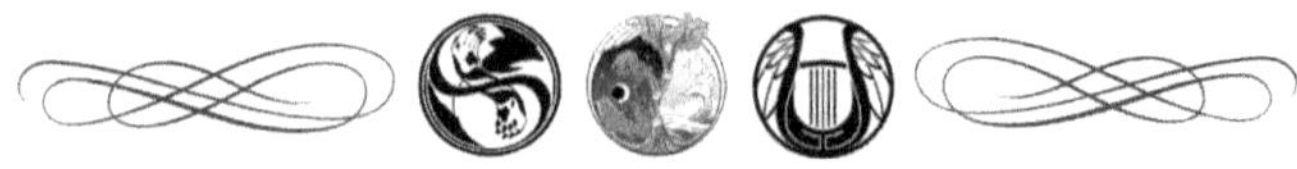

Zinnia was going to die.

No. I will not go with you. I will not leave Father, and I will not leave our sister. I will not leave our king. If you do this... you area traitor, and I will name you as such.

The last words from Zinnia played on repeat in Pierce's gray matter every step of the way back to Migas. No matter what else he tried to think of, the words came full force and played over again and again. He knew she had no genuine desire to stay in Métamorphe. That it was the fear of consequences that kept her in place. But it had still been her choice to make. And she had made it.

If Markham didn't kill Zinnia when she brought him the news, their father or Dahlia would. They would no longer have him to take their anger out on or Lillianna to abuse. Zinnia would be the only alternative. Her heart wasn't black. She was only a pretender out of survival.

Pierce reached the entrance to Migas Village and waited until the archway opened. Crossing the threshold, he shifted to his humanoid form as the archway closed behind him. Then he just stood there. His chest ached. While he had known Zinnia wouldn't come, he'd still held hope. Logan had hoped, too. With a heavy breath, Pierce peered at Santos's hut. Lilli should be hereby now. Zinnia wouldn't come. There was truly nothing left for him back in Métamorphe. He needed to confirm his sanctuary.

He was about to head for the hut when Delenia stepped just outside the doorway. Her gaze settled on him. "He is waiting for you."

"I am sorry?" She indicated the front door of the hut. "Oh. My apologies." Rubbing his chest to ease the ache, Pierce headed across the clearing. He bowed his head in thanks as she led him inside.

"You know the way," Delenia said.

Regarding her briefly, he nodded. "Yes. Thank you." Rubbing at the tightness in his chest once more, he dropped his hands to his sides and strode toward the back room.

When Pierce entered, he saw Santos sitting on the same mat where he had sat during their first meeting. The male inhaled a deep breath and gestured to the mat across from him. "Please, join me, my son."

"Thank you, Santos," Pierce uttered. Crossing the floor, he took a seat on the same mat he had last time, placing his hands on his knees. He would wait until given permission to speak. The male knew why he was here.

A moment passed before Santos spoke again. "State your request."

Pierce frowned a little. The male's voice sounded off, strained, as if he were holding much back. He knew the feeling well. It wasn't his place to ask, though. He cleared his throat. "It has been made known to me that my sister, Lillianna, has gained her safety here. I came to ask if the offer for my sanctuary still stands. I have just come from Métamorphe. Nothing is left for me there, and I would like to be with my family."

Santos's shoulders slumped just a little. He closed his eyes, and after several long minutes, opened them again. "Yes. I granted Lillianna sanctuary. She is currently enjoying afternoon meal with Ambrosia and Logan. The offer for your sanctuary still stands. I would not part you from her."

His body sagged a little, so he locked his elbows, keeping his body from collapsing in relief. To hear it from Derrick and Devina was one thing. To hear it from the Elder's mouth—that she was here, and enjoying a meal with Logan and his mate—was altogether different. "Thank you. So very much. That she is safe..." He cleared his throat and swallowed to clear away the lump that had settled there. "Thank you, Santos. The one rule: I recall it. I will commit no crime against another here."

"I know you will not, Pierce." He cracked a smile. Silence settled across the room before the male uttered another word. "Lillianna would have always been saved."

Pierce didn't reply. The words made little sense to him, yet they did. The minutes dragged on until he wasn't even sure how many had passed. When words finally came, he realized he'd dug his claws into his legs. "Were it not for Derrick finding my brother, I did not know how her safety would come to be. I could see it in her eyes, growing every *umbra*. Soon, it was going to be too late. I did not know how to bring her back from that. I fear that I still do not."

The male stared at him for several moments. "Look at your family. Your *true* family. They will help. They will offer aid, love, and support to young

Lillianna in ways she has not had, as they will do for you. I cannot tell you how, but I can promise you will heal, as will she."

Pierce took time to answer. He didn't know how Lilli was going to heal, how he was going to heal. But he believed what the male spoke. "I will take your advice to heart. And trust in them, honor them and protect them with everything in me. They are all that I have."

"I believe you will. You will make an excellent addition to our community." The hint of a gleam in his eye touched his face. "A mating ceremony is being held two *umbras,* henceforth, for Logan and Ambrosia. Jocasta mentioned perhaps you would join them."

Just at the mention of her name, the corners of his mouth tilted up. "I would be truly honored."

"Then it is settled." Santos bowed his head. "I believe Jocasta has afternoon meal waiting for you in your new home. Delenia will show you the way."

Pierce returned the bow and slowly stood. "Thank you for my sanctuary. And thank you for my sister and brother. I owe my family to you. Itis not something I will ever forget." He inclined his head one last time to Santos and followed Delenia out of the room.

The female said nothing as she led him through the maze of houses until she stopped at one. He dipped his chin in a thank you to her before the female left. Pivoting, he smiled at the house, his home with his mate. He turned his gaze to the house next door. He sensed them inside. Lillianna was in there. He wanted to go to her so badly his feet almost started moving on their own. But, no. She and their brother needed their time to get to know one another. And his mate was waiting for him. Going up the porch stairs, Pierce opened the door and went inside.

Chapter Seven

After leaving Santos's hut, Logan took Lilli to his and his mate's home. He'd only moved a few pieces from the cabin. According to Ambrosia, the dwelling could still come in handy. Logan opened the door for Lilli, letting her in first. She entered hesitantly, and he followed her inside. Her eyes flitted everywhere as she eyeballed everything. She would likely not know the names of much of the furniture, but there would be time for that.

There was a fireplace built into the left wall. A couch and chairs sat around it, with a table in front. To the right was a large square table with six chairs. Enough for everyone in their family and room to grow. His female bustled around in the kitchen just beyond. She was so busy getting afternoon meal ready for their arrival that she hadn't even noticed the door opening. Counters surrounded her on either side, tall cabinets behind her. The sweet savory aroma of fish cooking in the oven wafted to the front door.

"Hello," his sister murmured.

Ambrosia spun around and faced them. Her eyes lit up as she strode to where they stood, her gaze settling on Lilli. Beaming, his mate gripped Lilli's hands and squeezed them. "You must be Lillianna. Gods, I'm so happy to meet you. Logan has talked about you nonstop since he found out about you."

Logan chuckled as he shut the door. "Give her some room to breathe, my love."

Lilli peered back at him. "It is alright." She gazed at Ambrosia. "You are his mate. I am overjoyed to meet you."

His sister initiated a hug, which his mate eagerly returned. Ambrosia shot a brief glare at him, though it wasn't heartfelt. His joy had become her own. Releasing the embrace, the corners of his mate's lips rose. "You may call me Ambrosia or Am. It's what my sister calls me. She can't wait to meet you too, but we thought one of us was enough to start with. Plus, I wanted to give you time to get settled and get a good meal in. I have so much to show you." She stepped back a moment but kept hold of one of Lilli's hands.

Logan leaned down and pressed a kiss to Ambrosia's forehead. "Is there something you need me to work on while you show her around?"

"Would you finish cutting the fruit? The fish should be ready soon."

"Of course." Logan squeezed his sister's shoulder and headed into the kitchen. Out of the corner of his eye, he watched Lilli take it all in, a dozen different emotions coursing through her. But he could sense she was embracing all of them. "It is so easy to breathe here," she blurted out, then gave a soft laugh. "You may call me Lilli. That is what Pierce calls me. I cannot wait to meet your sister, too."

"Lilli it is, then." Ambrosia nodded. "The open-air is necessary for the spourgiffs. I'll show them to you when you're ready. Though, I suppose Jo might get to it first. For now, let me show you around here." She shifted her stance and gestured to the various parts of the home. "Of course, we have the front rooms here with the gathering area, meals, and food prep. The bedrooms are in the back." Ambrosia led Lilli down the hall past the kitchen, where he sliced up a variety of fruit and monitored the fish. With his superior canine hearing, though, he wouldn't have any trouble listening to them. "We moved furniture into your bedroom yesterday, but anything you don't like, we can change out. I wasn't sure what kind of decor you'd prefer, so I left the walls their natural light color."

Lilli's footsteps halted, and nothing but silence stretched between them. "My... *my* room?"

Another moment passed before his mate spoke. "Yes. Your room."

Ambrosia knew little about Métamorphe. Just what information he'd recounted of the village, which wasn't much. But there had been one thing they'd both agreed upon from the very beginning. Lilli would know that she was important, loved, and protected.

He sensed the emotion welling up inside of his sister again. Hades, he could almost smell her tears from here. "I... I have never..." Lilli cleared her throat, and her voice dropped a few octaves, coming out in a hushed tone. "I have never had a room."

Another moment passed, then he heard a soft humming coming from Ambrosia as she comforted his sister. The heartbreak within her for what Lilli must have endured was overwhelming. Logan's hand stilled on the knife, midway through slicing a piece of fruit. After a small stretch of humming to Lilli, Ambrosia said, "You have your own room now, and you always will." Yes. She would. Lilli would always have a place here.

"I do not know what to say," Lilli whispered. "Except... thank you. Thank you."

"You don't need to say anything, but you're quite welcome," Ambrosia replied. "Are you ready to see it?"

"Yes, please. I would love that."

Their footsteps resumed as Ambrosia led her down the hallway, stopping in front of the first bedroom, on the opposite side of the hall as theirs. "Logan and I are right there if you ever need anything. Just ask, and we'll do whatever we can to make it happen."

He sensed the words comforted Lilli. Yes, they'd made a good choice when they'd picked which bedroom to give her. He started slicing the fruit again. It was light in Lilli's room. The sun would shine in through the window as it rose into the sky. The walls were a light-colored wood. There wasn't much in there yet, but they could add more. She could have whatever she wanted. She deserved nothing less. So far, there was a bed, a small table, a dresser, and a lantern to light the room when it got dark. He'd made each piece of furniture with care. They'd all been plain until a few days ago when he'd begun adding intricate carvings of lilies into them.

"Pierce always slept close to me, too. He never slept in his room, and he would not tell me why. But it helped me feel safer." The two females entered Lilli's bedroom, and he heard a barely audible gasp leave her. Awe rolled through her, bringing tears to his eyes. He couldn't stop them from trickling down his own face. "This is... for *me*?" Lilli whispered.

Ambrosia cleared her throat. "Your brother, he made them for you."

Though he heard Lilli choke a sob back, he felt nothing but happiness and pure joy coming from her. "Would it... would it be alright... if I had a moment?"

"Of course." Ambrosia left the room quietly and came down the hall into the kitchen. He hadn't told her everything, but she'd gotten enough to understand the remorse, the happiness, the sadness that he was feeling. They had his sister with them now, and his brother would soon follow. Ambrosia wrapped her arms around him and just held him. His cheek settled against the top of her head as he encircled her in his arms. Despite the physical strength in his body, his mate was the one who held him up. They stood like that for several minutes. Just after he and his mate parted, returning to meal preparation, his sister came into the kitchen, completely composed.

His sister said nothing at first, just went to him and wound her arms around him. "Thank you for giving me a home here with you."

He hugged her tight to his chest and dropped a kiss to the top of her head. "I would have it no other way."

Ambrosia went about setting plates of food on the table, along with the fish, a variety of sliced fruit, and boiled potatoes. She returned to the kitchen and picked up the pot of tea from the counter. "Are you both ready to eat?"

Lilli broke away from him. "Yes, please. It smells wonderful." She glanced back and forth between them. "Will Pierce be here? He did not go back to the village, did he?" A flash of fear consumed her at the thought.

"Pierce will be along." Despite her feelings about Dahlia and Zinnia, it didn't make him pray any less they could get Zinni away from the darkness too. "He went back only to see if he could get Zinnia to leave. We are not hopeful, but she is not as she has been toward you. If he can convince her, she will stay with Pierce and Jocasta. This is a new start for all of us." Logan squeezed Lilli's shoulder.

Though her fear was still present, Lilli leaned into him. "Okay. Though I do not think Zinnia will leave either."

He brought an arm around her shoulders. "Fear not, sister mine. Pierce will get out." Leading her over to the front window, he pointed to the house next door. "And when he does, that is where he will live. I agree with you about Zinnia, but he must try."

Lilli tilted her head. "Wait. Who is Jocasta?"

It didn't surprise him that his brother had said nothing of her existence. Not that he intended to mention it, either. Initially, he thought it best that

Pierce do the introduction. Too late now. Logan cracked a smile. "Pierce's mate and Ambrosia's sister."

"Twin sister," Ambrosia added as she strode up behind them. "She won't be hard to miss." She had taken the pot of tea to the table and placed cups out for each of them.

"Pierce is... He is mated?" Lilli's eyes widened as she let out a gentle laugh. "That makes me ecstatic. I cannot wait to meet her too." Her stomach rumbled. "This smells truly wonderful. May I help with anything?"

"That's kind of you to offer," Ambrosia said. "But it's unnecessary. Though, if you wish to help later, I believe Jo and my mother might need some aid with the ceremony preparation."

Logan stood there, watching them gather at the dining room table. It appeared far more welcoming than it did sitting there, even with the ornate design he'd carved into the wood over these last few days. For the first time, he truly saw all of its possibilities. It was a place where once Pierce joined them here in the village, they would all sit down and eat together. Something he looked forward to.

"I would love to help. What is the ceremony for?"

"A mating ceremony." Logan joined them and pressed a kiss to Ambrosia's forehead as they all sat.

"Possibly two. If my sister and Pierce are mated at the same time." His mate's amber eyes twinkled. "In two *umbras*, our Elder will officially mate us in front of the entire village. It is a celebration that often goes well into the night."

Lilli beamed brightly. "Oh, how exciting! I have never been to a mating ceremony before. There have been a few done in the village, but the festivities get very... well... Pierce has always just told me it would not be a delightful place for me to be in the middle of. I have heard fighting outside of the hut, and not every couple is private in those moments."

Ambrosia stopped with a potato halfway to her mouth. Her eyes widened, and she cocked an eyebrow at Logan. Given what he recalled of those... disasters, it didn't surprise him. He would've done the same thing.

"None of that will happen here. Nearly all couples are private about those affairs," his mate stated. "The only time fighting happens here is in the sparring ring, if you wish to. And there are safeguards in place to ensure injuries are minimal, but training is efficient. Spirits are likely to be passed around, but other than that, dancing, singing. It's a true celebration. Although couples have disappeared well before the party is over."

Logan smirked and shoved some fish into his mouth. Oh, yes, he could absolutely get on board with that.

"I have tried spirits once, but I did not care for them." Lilli bit her lip. "Please do not tell Pierce that. I do not think he would like that." She took a bite of her food. "This is delicious." She took another bite. "I enjoy singing, but I have never danced. And I know how to fight, but I do not really like to. Pierce trained me, but it was more out of necessity."

A soft giggle left Ambrosia's mouth, but Logan's lips tightened. She was far too young to have tried spirits. Even if, in a few years, she would no longer be considered an adolescent. "We will say nothing to Pierce." There were a few things his brother didn't need to know.

"You don't have to spar. Not everyone here does. Even my sister has sparred less. Though I have heard it's similar to watching a dance."

"I might like to watch sometime. The fights I have seen were nothing like what I imagine dancing would be like, though." Lilli peered at Logan. "Thank you. I do not think... no, I know he would not like it. I did not want to try them, but Ev—" Her hand stopped suddenly halfway to her mouth, the bite she'd been about to take momentarily forgotten. By the look in her eyes, she was no longer mentally in this room.

Logan growled. He squeezed the cup in his hand so tightly the wood splintered. Maybe he couldn't see everything that had gone through his sister's head, but he felt her emotions. The name that had nearly come out of her mouth didn't need to be finished. It made him want to kill the bastard allover again. Once he had confirmation Pierce was out of the village, he'd go dig up the fucker's head and deliver it to Markham.

Dropping a piece of fruit, Ambrosia squeezed Lilli's hand. Lilli's eyes snapped up to meet hers. "That will never happen again. No one will force you to do anything you don't wish. You are safe here."

Lilli's amethyst eyes fixated on Ambrosia as his mate spoke. She clenched Ambrosia's hand, inhaling and exhaling a deep breath to ease the trembling that had started. "I feel safe here. It is something I have never truly felt before."

"That's good, because no one would let any harm come to you. We have one law in our village. No crime shall be committed against another. Itis punishable. Santos ensures that happens. If something happens, I don't care what, know that you can come to any of us. Me, Jo, your brothers, even Santos, and we will handle it swiftly."

His sister didn't need to know what had occurred with Leo. It wasn't necessary. But he knew his mate would want to assuage any fears Lilli had all the same. Inhaling a few deep, calming breaths, Logan settled as his sister relaxed. The coming months would be an adjustment for him. He'd grown accustomed to feeling emotions, but it had been a while since he reacted to what he felt from others. Not since—no, he couldn't go there.

"Thank you, Am," Lilli whispered. "A while ago, I stopped telling Pierce when... things would happen. He still walked in on it sometimes, but it is against the laws in the village to retaliate against an Informant. Pierce... he took a lot of punishments for me."

His mate and her twin had spent their lives staying out of the attention of Informants. It had been more for Jocasta's safety than anything. Jocasta had Galenus' ears, while Ambrosia had none of his features.

Ambrosia flicked her eyes to Logan, then back to Lilli. "We believe in justice. And Santos, I know Logan introduced you. He's unique. No one lies to him, ever. He knows when it happens. And the truth always comes out. Even if you don't feel comfortable coming to one of us, then you can always go to him. No matter the sleight, justice will always be served."

"Truly, no one will hurt me here? And, Father..." Lilli focused on Logan. "Will he be able to find me?"

It was good to have his mate so close. At some point, he'd reached out and rested a hand on the small of her back. The contact offered him a sense of serenity, which was exactly what he needed to address Lilli's question. "No. He cannot find you. Ever." Especially after he properly dealt with the male. But he wouldn't tell his sister that.

Lilli blinked back tears, her body sagging in the chair a little. She nodded, unable to speak, as relief poured through her in waves. Her hand shook as she tried to retrieve her cup. She released the clasp she had on Ambrosia's palm and picked up her drink with both hands. Logan rubbed slow circles along his sister's upper back, relaxing her more. Exhaustion flooded her.

"Come, little sister. I think you should rest." Logan squeezed Lilli's shoulder. "I will go check next door for Pierce. We can all have evening meal together."

"Okay. Sleep sounds... really wonderful right now."

Logan helped her up from the chair, and she leaned into him as he led her into her bedroom. He tucked her in, ensuring the bed was comfortable and to her liking. If not, he could change things. He sat there for a moment and watched her drift off to sleep. Once she passed out, he rose to his feet and headed for the door, pausing once again. After all the miscarriages he had witnessed his mother endure, she'd given birth one last time. His brother had taken care of Lilli her whole life. It was time he took over until the day—nope. NOPE. That wasn't ever going to happen. She would never take a mate. He swallowed the lump in the back of his throat and left her bedroom.

Ambrosia had cleaned up. Without saying a single word, she opened her arms to him.

He strode over to her, drew her tight to his chest, and kissed her neck. "Thank you." The gods had truly blessed him when they made her. Nothing needed to be said. She knew what he required and simply held him, giving him strength in ways he never imagined possible.

"I'll keep an ear out while you go check and see if Pierce is back."

Logan brushed a tender kiss across her lips and left the house.

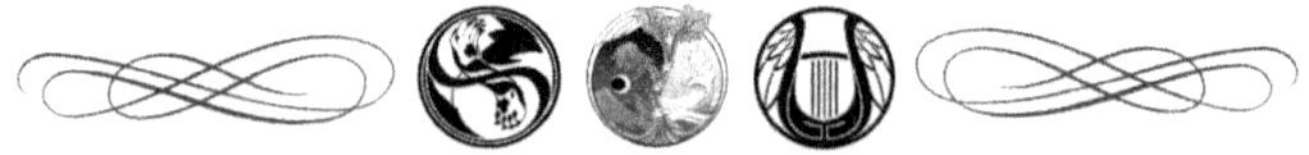

The second the door closed, Jo ran from the kitchen and leaped into Pierce's arms. He gathered her against him. Burying his face in her neck, he breathed her scent in and said nothing. After several minutes, he swept his mouth up her jaw and kissed her hard. "I missed you, my queen," he whispered against her lips.

"I missed you too, my king." Gods, she really loved saying that. And having him here. She couldn't have asked for more. Something seemed a little off, but she didn't want to press. She knew he'd just come from Santos' hut. Sometimes conversations with the male could be off-putting until one had time to process everything. "I have afternoon meal ready if you're hungry."

"I just want to hold you for a minute. If that is alright?"

"Of course." She ran the tips of her fingers along the back of his head. "Whatever you need."

Pierce carried her over to a chair and sat down with her in his lap. Laying his head upon her shoulder, he continued to breathe her scent in as he stroked her back. "My sister Zinnia refused to come."

"Oh, Pierce. I'm so sorry." She knew how much he had prayed his middle sister would come with him. His discourse made sense now. She had been the only other female he had hoped to save. That she'd decided not to come had to be breaking his heart.

He nuzzled more into her neck. "She has sided with them. And she threatened to out me to Markham. It was not an empty threat. He would have me hunted down regardless, but..." His words trailed off. "Her actions are going to get her killed. It is a feeling that has sat deep in my gut since I left her."

Jo continued to rub the back of his head, running her fingers through his fur. It didn't seem like she could do much to comfort him. She didn't know his sister would survive. Not any more than she knew if they would kill the female. "I'm sorry, Pierce. You tried, and you couldn't have done more than that. Regardless of how she responded, you tried. The choice, it still had to be hers."

"I know. I know I did what I could. It just does not feel like enough. But I know there is nothing more I can do. She stayed. Regardless of the consequences, that was her decision to make."

Just like her inability to comfort him. Then again, maybe that wasn't the case. Neither of them truly knew what the future held. Jo stroked his ears and eased back so she could look him in the eyes. "But maybe you did enough. I know what you think will happen, but you don't know for sure Zinnia will lose her life. Maybe she'll survive. Maybe she'll find a way out. Or, maybe, she'll find another path there. No matter what happens, you did what was within your power to do."

Pierce brushed the back of his knuckles across her cheek. "Is it bad of me..." He inhaled and exhaled a deep breath. "Is it bad of me... that I no longer want to think of her? If there comes a time where she reaches out to me, I will do what I can to help her. But unless that happens..." He shook his head. "I am pained by her refusal to leave with me. But, as I told Santos, my life in Métamorphe is in the past. My life here starts today. I have my family here, and all of you are all that I need." He kissed her neck. "Most especially, my queen. At least for now, she has chosen not to be a part of that. I do not want to torture myself over a decision she made."

The ache in his heart that she felt was still the strangest thing, but she'd caught more of his emotions as they'd gotten closer over the last several weeks. "It's not bad of you. There's only so much you can do for someone who isn't willing to help themselves. If she reaches out to you, then we will both help her. I would support you in any decision you made."

He kissed her softly on the lips. "I know you would. That is just one of the many ways you are so wonderful."

She offered him a tender smile. It was just the truth. Even when he doubted himself, she believed he made the best decisions he could. "I think that goes both ways."

Pierce kissed her again. "I will take your word for that, love," he said. "Would you like to eat? If we do not eat, I am going to need something else to occupy my time. I am finding it very hard not to run next door right now."

A slow grin spread across her face. As much as she'd love todo something else, she didn't think there'd be time for that. "Let's eat before the fish gets cold. Besides…" She nuzzled his nose. "Am said Logan plans to come over after they finish afternoon meal, so you two can talk."

"Mmm." A low rumble sounded deep in his chest as they kissed once more, and he pressed his lips to her ears. "Good. It will be good to see him."

"Mmm, you keep messing with my ears, and I'm telling Am to send him later," she teased.

"I cannot help it, my queen. I love them." Helping her up off his lap, he gave her ass a squeeze. "Let us get our food. I would like to feed you."

The dirtiest thought popped into her head. Oh, he had something he could feed to her. Shaking the thought from her mind, she went into the kitchen and collected the tray of filleted fish and vegetables. She gestured to the pitcher on the counter. "Will you grab the tea?"

"Careful, love. If you keep those thoughts up, we will not use this table to eat a meal," Pierce growled. "I will eat something else." He pinched her ass as he passed her and retrieved the tea.

A shiver ran the length of her spine. She stared at him through hooded eyes. "I can't help what comes into my head." She headed for the dining area. "Nor would I want to."

In a few long strides and one smooth move, he had her in his arms, got the tray out of her hands and set it on the intrinsically hand-carved table. "I do not want you to either." Kissing her hard, he plunged his tongue in her mouth. "If you are starving, tell me now, and I will let you go. Otherwise, we are going to put this table to a different use."

Gods, she loved the possessive control he took sometimes. Right then, food seemed so unimportant. "Oh, I'm hungry alright, but not for the fish." Gripping his shoulders, she swept her tongue up the side of his throat and nipped his ear. "Just don't knock it to the floor."

"If I do, I will build us another one." Gripping her ass, he lifted her up and set her on the table.

She'd meant the food, not the furniture. She hadn't given the table a second thought. But the food—oh, good. He had her shirt in his hand, ready to rip it off of her when he picked up the tray and moved it to a chair, then nudged the chair away with his foot. "Now." His tongue snaked across his lips. "How attached are you to this clothing?"

With a gasp, she arched her back and gave him perfect tearing access. She bit her bottom lip and raked her nails along his shoulders and down his arms, pulling a rumble out of him. "I have more where it came from."

Without a word, Pierce gripped her shirt in his hands and ripped it straight down the middle. He took her breast in his mouth, sucking hard. Her nipples pebbled at the tongue lashing, and he used his claws to tear off her skirt. "I cannot wait," he thrust inside her with a deep moan.

Clenching his biceps, she cried out in ecstasy. Oh, gods! Her body was always ready for him. This time was no different. It was going to be hard and passionate like the many times they'd come together. Her head fell back as he pounded into her, setting her body on fire.

He planted his palms on the table as he penetrated her repeatedly, his thrusts so hard and deep the table shook beneath her. "Gods, you are perfect," he growled out as he turned the attention of his mouth to her other breast.

Moaning loudly, she widened her thighs, parted her legs and clutched the back of his ass with her taloned feet. Her back bowed off the table as she dug her nails into his arms more. "Oh, gods. Don't stop, Pierce, don't stop!" Ablaze blasted through her body as he drove into her harder and deeper, throwing her over the edge. Her climax exploded all around him, milking an orgasm out of him so powerful that he squeezed his eyes shut and gripped the edge of the table with his claws. Pierce howled out her name.

Their ragged breaths filled the air as the two of them stilled. She had no words. Nothing, as she focused on steadying her breathing and heartbeat. He leaned his forearms on the table and pressed his forehead to hers. Their bodies still joined. Neither of them had any desire to part from one another. As her chest heaved, her bare breasts brushed up against his chest.

After several moments, Pierce's gaze went to the edge of the table. "I think I broke it."

"It's repairable." With their foreheads together, she brushed a soft kiss across his lips and softened her hold on his arms. "I'm just glad the food survived."

Pierce gave her a quick peck and nuzzled her nose. "Mmm. Mmm." He chuckled. "Well, I did not want all of your hard work to go to waste. I did almost forget to move it, though."

"If you had, well, I can't say I've ever worn food, but it would've been a very interesting take on afternoon meal." She giggled.

A low growl rumbled in his throat. "That gives me some ideas. We may need to find some things that I can lick off of you."

"Mmm, I believe I can arrange that." It had never crossed her mind, but they had all kinds of things that she could get just for that.

"We should eat. And I should allow you to get dressed. Besides how tempting you are,"—he claimed her lips in a languid kiss—"I do not know when Logan is showing up, and this is not a position I want anyone seeing you in but me." His lips lingered against her skin for a moment, then he helped her up and off the table.

Jo couldn't agree more. It was the very reason she and her sister had learned to block their mindlink when needed. Some things just didn't need to be shared. "You get the food on the table and some cups from the kitchen while I go put clothes back on."

He held her against him for a beat, his hands gripping her ass. "If only we were not expecting company." With one more kiss, he nipped her bottom lip, released her, and gave her ass a playful smack. "Clothing. Before I take you again, and do not answer the door when Logan arrives."

"Mmm, as long as he knocks." Family had a tendency to just walk in. Collecting her ripped skirt from the floor, Jo slipped the torn tank from her shoulders. With her clothes in hand, she shook her head and strode down the hallway to their bedroom in the back. She could feel his eyes upon her every step down the hall.

When she returned to the dining room, he'd moved the tray of food from the chair back to the table and was setting the pitcher of tea and two cups on the table. "Do you have plans today?"

"My mother is actually expecting me at her place so we can work on my dress." She hadn't mentioned the mating ceremony to him, but she suspected it had come up with Santos. Right? "For the mating ceremony. Then we're going to work on some preparations. A lot has to be done for the ceremony."

His ruby eyes sparkled. "Santos told me. I said I would be honored. I look forward to being officially mated to you."

Cupping his cheek, she smiled widely. Gods, she loved him. "I am too."

He cupped the back of her head and stroked her ears. Neither of them uttered a word. Pierce leaned down and kissed her, soft and slow. "I love you so much, Jocasta. You have brought such joy to me. A joy that I have never known."

Not once had she ever expected to have a mating ceremony. No mate at all. This male had come like a thief in the night and captured her heart. He'd given her a new family. A female her sister already adored, and she expected she and her mother would as well. Despite the darkness in his own life, he had brought light into hers. "I love you too, Pierce. So much. You brought joy back to me. Something I never thought I'd have again."

"And I am very glad of it. You deserve all the happiness in the world." He nuzzled her nose. Sitting at the table side-by-side, he fed her a bite of the food.

Mmm, that had come out good. "So do you." Jo snagged two small potatoes from the tray, popped one into her mouth, and held the other one out for him to take from her fingers.

He took it from her with his mouth, flicking his tongue against her fingertip, then took a moment to chew and swallow. "Happiness is a strange feeling to me."

She plucked some of the fish and held it out for him as well. This was absolutely the best meal she'd ever had. "I think it's a little strange for both of us. It's been so long; I'd forgotten what it felt like. I suspect it'll take some adjustment, but we have each other to lean on."

"Yes, my queen. We do. I do not remember ever feeling true happiness before. We had some happy moments in our youth, but darkness always overshadowed them." He stared into her eyes and stroked her cheek. "If we... if we ever have young..." Though Pierce tried to keep them buried, she caught a glimpse of doubt and a touch of fear. Not that they lingered at all. "I will not be that male. Not like my father. I will never put another through the things my father put us through. And I will love them so much. They will never doubt my love for them."

Jo leaned into his touch and closed her eyes for a moment. She didn't have the heart to tell him children may not be possible. Hybrid pregnancies were difficult, and some never even occurred. Gods, she prayed, it was something she could give him. She met that powerful gaze of his. "I know you wouldn't. I know you'll make a wonderful father... one *umbra*. You're a wonderful male."

He said nothing, just pressed his forehead to hers. Pulling back slightly, he fed her another forkful of food.

It wasn't necessary for him to say anything. He'd likely felt what crossed her mind. Maybe one day they'd talk about it, but she just couldn't right now. She wanted to enjoy his presence. She picked up more potatoes, ate one herself, and held another out for him. "We've got time, butat some point, we'll want to decide how to decorate the other two bedrooms." She had focused on their bedroom and the main rooms.

He took the bite from her, chewing slowly. Silence stretched between them. Not that anything had to be said for her to know what was on his mind. Neither of those rooms would be for Zinnia. And Lillianna would live with Logan and Ambrosia.

"We will figure it out, love. Together."

Despite another quick peck, she sensed the swirl of emotions he pushed down. It was like they both worked to escape a powerful storm riding on their heels. Chewing a piece of fish, Jo got up from her chair, walked over to his, and climbed into his lap. It didn't seem logical, but somehow, she feltlike they both just needed to hold the other. There was so much they couldn't bring themselves to say.

Pierce laid his head on her shoulder and slipped his arm around her waist. They continued to feed each other in silence. Words didn't seem necessary. She could feel the fears easing from his head. Hers were as well. By the time they finished eating, they had both calmed and relaxed. Everything needed to be cleaned before Logan came over. "I'm just going to wash these real quick and then head over to my mom's."

Pierce slowly stroked her arm as he nuzzled her ears. "Let me take care of it. Spend time with your mother."

"Are you sure?"

"Yes, love. I do not mind. It will help pass the time to keep my hands busy."

"Okay. I'll be back as soon as I can." She pressed another tender kiss to his lips and climbed out of his lap. After showing him how the sink worked, Jo headed to the door, but stopped once she reached it and glanced back over her shoulder. "You should check out our bedroom, too. Your brother helped me set it up."

Chapter Eight

Pierce cleaned up everything from their afternoon meal and rearranged the chairs around the table. They'd gotten moved around a bit. He chuckled to himself, then headed back to find their bedroom. Stopping in the jamb, his eyes fell on every single piece of furniture in the room and their intricate designs. It was impossible not to recognize his brother's work; patterns that were painstakingly carved by a skilled artisan. There was an enormous bed with a nightstand on either side; a small, round table in the corner, with two chairs tucked underneath; a dresser; and a closet. He strolled around the room, running his hand over each hand-carved piece. The woodwork was beautiful and perfectly done.

He spent a few minutes in there, then returned to the front room. His eyes drifted toward his brother's home. Pierce sat at the dining room table, stood, and paced around the house while sitting in another chair every few minutes. Eventually, he settled in the chair closest to the fireplace, rested his hands on his knees, and stared at the door as he waited. It was difficult not to move around. Even harder not to go next door and see his sister, make sure she was alright. But she and Logan needed to have this time to get to know each other.

When he caught Logan's scent, he shot up from the chair. The door opened. "How is she?" Pierce asked when his brother entered the house.

"She is resting." Logan sat on the couch next to him. The male buried his head in his hands for a moment. Digging his elbows into his knees, he glanced at Pierce. "For the first time, she knows she is safe. I can feel it. Everything she went through. I did not tell her about my ability yet."

Pierce cursed and dropped into the cushioned seat, letting out a breath. That his brother had felt that from her; more than that, the male now knew of his failure to fully protect her. "Oh, gods…" As he leaned over into himself, he gripped the back of his head and choked back the tears threatening to escape. "I tried. I did the best that I could to keep her safe. It was never good enough."

Logan clapped a hand on his shoulder. "I know you did, brother. She is safe now. And I will ensure it remains that way."

His brother didn't need to explain what he meant. It wasn't necessary for him to spell it out. Pierce understood perfectly. Markham's true Informants were cruel and cared not who they hurt or killed. They couldn't stand idly by while it continued to happen, not after everything that had happened to their sister. It wasn't just important to the two of them, but to show Lilli life could be joyous.

"I would enjoy assisting you with that. I remember every one of them." Pierce scowled.

"Good. I did not wish to get the list from her."

"No, do not ask her that. There is no need to put her through that. I know who all we seek." He ran his hands over his head.

"Has Jocasta spoken to you about the ceremony?"

"She has not, no. Nothing past that it was occurring. I have had much on my mind, and I did not come back here in the best of spirits." His gaze flicked to Logan. "Zinnia refused to come. And proclaimed she would name me *the traitor that I am.*" At least the grounds were well protected. And Informants didn't visit where Jocasta and Ambrosia worked. They would be safe.

"I feared as much when I did not smell her here. Do you think she will report you right away?"

"I know not. She agreed to give me a few hours. I know the look in her eyes, though, my leaving pained her. I do not know how quickly she will go to Markham."

"Perhaps the return of Evan's head will have him thinking twice before he sends anyone to hunt you."

Pierce gave a brief chuckle. "I wish I could have seen his head get parted from his body. I am sure it was glorious." He shook his head. "You know that will not deter him. Truly, I think nothing does. We will just have to be careful."

"Then when we hunt, we will hunt together and drop a few more heads on his doorstep until he is no longer a threat. I cannot imagine there is nothing out there to defeat him."

"I look forward to it, brother. He will know fully the wrath I could not show in the village. What he has done..." His words trailed off into a snarl. "He is going to pay, as will Father. It is not about revenge for me anymore. I must ensure that Lilli continues to feel safe." As for their king, the male had had something for as long as he could remember. Something that gave him abilities he'd never seen in another. Whether it was because Markham was king of their species or something else altogether, he couldn't have said. "If there is anything, I have no clue what it could be. With each passing *solaris*, it is as if he continues to grow stronger. One can no longer be in his presence without feeling like they are coated in evil. It is unnerving." That didn't even come close to how to describe it.

"Yes, he will. On both accounts. Though..." Logan paused. "I ask you to leave our father to me."

Pierce nodded. He didn't need an explanation why his brother made that request. They both had every right to kill Ailwin, but after all that had been done, he owed his brother that and more. "You may have him with my full blessing. I ask only that you make it... very painful." For every one of Lillianna's screams that their father had caused, he hoped the male was begging for death by the end.

"Do not worry, I have plans for him." Logan paused. "I promised Lilli we would all share evening meal together. The more we include her, the safer and more welcome she will feel."

"Agreed. And that sounds wonderful. It has been too long since we have shared a meal." Pierce eyeballed his brother. "Is she truly alright? I worry over her constantly. She has been through too much. It will ease me not to have to worry so much anymore."

Rubbing the back of his neck, Logan sighed. "It is only her first *umbra* here. It will take time for her fears to truly settle, but Ambrosia was amazing with her. When I took Lilli to lie down, she fell asleep quickly. The three of us have a long road ahead, but we will get through it—together."

The sorrow still refused to leave him. "Yes, we shall, every step of the way. Keep an ear out when she is sleeping. She has nightmares, frequently. They are how I have learned of some names she has refused to give me."

"We both expected she might. Our room is directly across from hers, so we will both stay alert. And she knows you are here if she ever needs you."

"Good. That is... that is good." He took a second before he continued. "It will be strange, not being so near to her. Though I know she needs this, as do you, what little I have slept has been by her side since she came into this world."

"I understand, brother. It would have been the only way to keep her safe. I do not think she understood that when she mentioned it earlier."

"Though I never wished to make her feel overcrowded, there truly was no other way. She may well not remember, but the other Informants have not been the only ones I have had to protect her from." He would never forget waking up to find Dahlia attempting to smother her as an infant. Dahlia had known she wouldn't be able to sneak the child away and had wanted to make it appear as an accident. It had only been the one time he knew of, but Pierce had taken no chances.

"Do you think I should tell her I am an empath? That it may help?"

"I think so, yes. Sometimes, in her fear and anger, she has trouble expressing herself. Knowing you can understand, without her having to put it into words, that could help a great deal."

"Then I will tell her after evening meal." Logan peered at him. "As Zinnia has decided not to leave, perhaps you should set up one bedroom here for Lilli. Then she can stay here whenever she chooses."

A faint smile touched his face, but it didn't quite reach his eyes. He hadn't expected Zinnia to come, but it still pained him she'd chosen to stay there. When she'd told him no, a bad feeling had settled in his gut, one that remained like an ever-present weight. She was going to end up injured or killed for her decision. "I would like to do that." He squeezed Logan's shoulder. "I can never thank you enough, brother. You have already given her more than I could ever. I have failed you both in so many ways. I can never make up for all of it. That you have forgiven me, accepted me again... means more to me than I could ever say."

"I think I am the one who failed you." Logan grimaced. "When I left, I prayed our father would stop trying to get mother pregnant. Every loss... it was so hard on her. She mourned for *umbras* every time."

Pierce said nothing. What could he say? He'd never been able to be there, in any capacity, during those times. No. He'd just left, physically and mentally, while his brother carried the weight of their mother's sorrow.

"Derrick told me what you did for Lilli, her birth, how you brought her back from sickness. I am grateful to you for keeping her safe all these *solaris*. Bringing her here, giving her a bedroom, a home... it does not feel as if it will ever be enough."

"I never should have brought her back to that hell. That is the worst mistake I have ever made. I should have run with her. I should have tried to find you. We could have raised her together." He scratched at his face. "When she came into this world, I was alone with Mother in the hut. Lilli was not breathing. Mother was squeezing my hand so hard I thought my bones would break. She was pleading with me, so I got her breathing again. She gave Lilli her name... then she made me swear never to let her go. After I brought her back and they punished me... that she needed me was the only thing that kept me drawing breath. I am to blame for all of Lilli's pain. It has never been a secret what kind of male Father is. And Lilli looks just like her. It is as if he has been punishing her all these *solaris*. He never wanted her. He only wished to get rid of her without doing the deed himself. You have made her feel true safety; somewhere I have always failed."

Tears rolled down Logan's cheeks, streaking through his dark brown fur. "I know it does not seem like it, but you did the right thing. For all she has suffered, I do not think trying to find me back then would have been much better. I was not in a good place when she was born, and I had no true place to stay. I moved between the villages that would allow me to stay; started a lot of fights."

"But perhaps if I had been there, been with you, I could have helped you through your anger. We could have built a home together. And no male would have ever laid hands on our sister." He could no longer keep his tears at bay, and he wiped at them angrily. "For nearly four *solaris*, I have fought them away, pulled them off of her." With their father glaring at him as if *he* were the one without honor. As if he should have just stood by and allowed their sister to be violated. "It should never have happened. And she should hate me, truly, for being the reason she called that place home."

Logan opened his mouth and snapped it shut. He scrubbed his face and surveyed the room as if he'd sensed another. No one else was here, though, just the two of them. "No matter what we think we should have done, we do not know how the outcome would have been different." The male faced Pierce. "We must stop blaming ourselves. Lilli needs us to be strong for her. That includes no longer beating ourselves up for what happened in the past. No matter how often we consider how things could have been done, we each did what we believed was best. And we cannot change that. All we can do now is look to the future and heal from our past wounds."

The words were hard to swallow, but he knew the truth of them. They couldn't change the past. All they could do, all they *must* do, was move forward from it. "And we must help her heal from hers."

"We will." Logan tilted his head. "When is Lilli's day of birth? If it is soon or has recently occurred, perhaps we can begin with doing something special for her."

"It is—" He let out a slight chuckle. "It is actually today. I left her flowers this morning, as I do every *solaris* on this *umbra*. I would love to do something more special for her, though. What did you have in mind?"

Logan's eyebrows popped. He dragged a hand across his head, sitting in quiet contemplation. "Ambrosia mentioned one hybrid who lives here makes jewelry. We could check with her about a piece for Lilli." He exhaled a deep breath. "During afternoon meal, she let it slip that Evan... he was one Informant. I—we—can tell her that we took care of him. Though, perhaps that is something we should do, anyway."

"I agree with you on both accounts. The jewelry sounds like a wonderful idea. You know how Father was, about personal possessions. No one could have anything unless he allowed it. I think that would make her happy. As for the other..." Pierce couldn't hold the growl back. "He was one of the more determined ones. Knowing he is no longer a threat, it may help, at least some."

"As long as she doesn't ask to see his head." Logan smirked. "Then let us see who we need to speak with and get pointed in the right direction. I do not smell your mate here. Shall we check with mine?"

"Yes, check with Ambrosia. Jocasta is with their mother."

With a curt nod, Logan stood. "I shall return in a few moments."

"Take your time, brother."

His brother squeezed his shoulder one last time before leaving. Pierce followed him, sat on the front step of the house—his home, with Jocasta. After the conversation with Logan, he needed some air. Too many memories, too many emotions, that he'd kept buried for too long. It hadn't been a healthy way to live, however necessary.

Sensing his mate nearing, Pierce lifted his head and turned it in the direction she came from. She approached the houses with another female, each of them carrying a basket in their arms. One was full of fruit, and the other full of flowers. The other female had to be her mother because her features were too similar to both Jocasta and Ambrosia. Glancing at him, Jo gestured for her mother to go on. They parted ways, her mother heading next door, while she approached and sat down next to him.

"You and Logan have a pleasant talk?"

He circled an arm around her waist, tucking her into his side. "Heavy. Difficult. But, yes, I have missed seeing and speaking to him." He dropped a kiss to her neck. "Did you enjoy your time with your mother?"

"Yes. We got a lot of the preparations done."

Beaming, he kissed her neck again. "I cannot wait to mate you properly, my queen."

She rested one hand on his knee and the other on his chest. "I can't either, but I feel the conversation you two had was necessary."

He drew her into his lap. "We both carry guilt and regret for much that was not our fault. Though we did the best we could with what we had, that realization is hard to swallow. But we are going to look forward, not backward. We both—all three of us, rather—have much to heal from."

"I'm glad you're looking forward. It's all I want to do. No matter how difficult. I believe the three of you will heal. You have three wonderful, powerful females looking after you." She leaned up and brushed a soft kiss across his lips.

"And my world in my arms," he said. "I will never let you go. I hope you are alright with that."

"That sounds perfectly wonderful." She nipped his neck.

A deep rumble of satisfaction settled in his chest. "Yes, it does, my love."

"Am told me that Lilli wants to help with preparations for the ceremony. Even with what my mother and I have done, two *umbras* will go by fast."

"That pleases me. I think she will enjoy that. When Logan comes back, we are going to go searching for a gift for her. Today is her day of birth."

"What?" She propped herself up in his lap. "Why didn't you tell me?"

"I am sorry, my love. I did not know she would come today. It was not until Derrick found me on the way back to the village that he told me

Logan had already brought her here. I would have told you sooner had I known she would be here."

"It has been quite an *umbra*." Her eyes lit up. "Oh. That's a good idea. Logan should be out soon. Adara, that's who you're looking for. While you two go see her, I'll go visit with the baker."

Pierce brought her face close to his and licked over her bottom lip. "Not just yet." He took her mouth in a deep kiss, one that left her breathless. "Now, you may go."

She nipped his ear and whispered, "I'm looking forward to having you all to myself later."

"Keep talking like that, my queen, and the baker will have to wait." He gave her ass a squeeze before helping her to her feet.

With a twinkle in her eye, Jo lifted the basket back in her arms. She opened her mouth as the door one house over opened. Logan stepped out and strolled in their direction. "I guess the baker's not waiting."

"Well, Hades. I suppose that just means more anticipation for when I get you into our bed later." He smiled. She had been the best gift life had given him. And now they would get to spend the rest of their lives together. "You do not know how much I love that. Our bed."

"Me too." Her amber eyes sparkled. "Me too. I really do." She acknowledged Logan as she descended the staircase with a bit more swing of her hips.

Gods, that ass of hers. He could literally watch it all day.

Logan snickered. "I interrupt something, brother?"

"Hmm? Oh." He chuckled. "No. She has things to do, as do we. However, I would advise against a visit after evening meal."

"Noted." Logan chortled.

Pierce got up off the porch step. "Alright. Let us get to it. We have a gift to find. Was she still resting when you left?"

"Yes, she was. I think the *umbra* has worn her out. Though, if she wakes while we are gone, both Lyrica and Ambrosia are there. And it appears Jocasta will join them."

"That is good. Being around other females will ease her."

"I agree."

"I have not met those two officially."

His brother cracked a toothy grin at him. "Then I suppose you will meet them soon. The females have started on evening meal."

"I cannot wait. Though I will admit to being nervous." Not something he ever would have thought he'd confess.

"You have nothing to be nervous about. Those two love you simply for what you have done for Jocasta. And I do not mean the incident a few *umbras* ago." Logan started off, and Pierce followed him.

Pierce considered his words for a moment. "You said something similar to that at the cabin. What do you mean?"

Logan blinked a few times, the shock clear on his face. "From what Ambrosia has told me, Jocasta took Galenus' death quite hard. She stopped singing, became furious. Over the *solaris*, with her sparring sessions, she often walked away hurt in some manner, though never as bad as her partner. As a result, she went through many of them. Ambrosia said she has mended her several times. Since you came into her life, she spars less, goes easier in sessions, and has sung again."

Remaining quiet, his brother's words tumbled around his brain. Pierce frowned. How could any of that be his doing? The house they made their way toward wasn't far from their own homes, simply one row up and six houses down. They were almost there when he finally spoke. "I did not think I was good for anybody," he whispered. "I just know that she has saved me."

"You saved her too, brother."

Logan knocked on the door. After a moment, it opened, and a half-humanoid female poked her head out. She had her light brown hair swept-back into a ponytail. The female flicked her champagne-brown eyes between the two of them. "What can I do for you?"

"Good day," Pierce stated, continuing once he confirmed the female as Adara. "We are looking for a gift for our sister. It is her day of birth today. Our mates told us to come here."

"Oh?" The female's face lit up. As she stepped aside, her hooves clicked against the wooden floor. "Come in, come in." They entered the house. The door clapped shut behind them. She headed toward an enormous table in the living room. "What is your sister's name?"

"Lillianna. And she is more beautiful than the flower she was named after."

"A lily. Hmm, let me think." Adara ambled back in their direction and scrutinized both males. "Eye color is unique. Ruby, aquamarine. What color are her eyes?"

"Amethyst," Logan replied.

With one hand on her hip, Adara tapped her chin, and her eyes widened. "Oh! Yes! I have just the thing." She crossed over to her workspace. "You both are getting mated in two *umbras*, are you not?"

Pierce beamed. "Yes, ma'am. And the time cannot pass quickly enough."

"I agree." Logan grinned.

"Where is it? Where is it?" The female muttered as she scanned the various items on her table. A multitude of earrings, necklaces, and rings covered it. Some pieces were in progress, others completed, and others barely assembled. "You are mating the twins, correct?"

Logan tilted his head and glanced at his brother. "Yes, ma'am, we are."

Pierce raised his eyebrow and shrugged. He turned his attention back to the female, watching her as she peered over the scattered pieces. "Our younger sister... she has had a rough go of it. And no one ever allowed her to have any personal possessions. We were hoping to find something truly special for her."

Adara blinked at him, wide-eyed. Her mouth down-turned at the corners. "Everyone should have something of their own. And I have just the thing, if—" she turned back to the table, "I can—aha!" She plucked a necklace from the array of objects. It was a lily on a silver chain. The flower had opal petals and an amethyst bud. The female returned to them and held it out. "I believe this will be perfect. Yes?"

Logan eyed the delicate piece, then nodded.

Pierce took it gently from the female. The center matched exactly the color of Lilli's eyes. "Oh, yes. It is perfect. I think she will love this."

"Wonderful. That thrills me." She turned back toward her table and stopped. "Your pieces for your mates will be ready tomorrow. Come back in the afternoon."

His brother's eyebrows shot up. "Wait, what?"

Pierce was just as confused. They hadn't asked for anything else. "My apologies, ma'am, but what pieces?"

"Well, given the twins' occupation, I intended necklaces. Though, I could make bracelets, if perhaps that suits you both better."

"We ordered nothing. At least, I did not." Logan glimpsed at Pierce.

"Nor did I. I have quickly gotten the impression, though, that matings here differ from where we are from. I admit, we are a bit out of our element."

Adara pinched her chin between her fingers and folded one arm across her body. "Well, I suppose a brief review could not hurt. Mating ceremonies here are social gatherings. We expect the entire village to be there. The pieces I will make for you, you will present to your mates upon the ceremony. After the exchange of promises, of course. As Santos pronounces your official mating status, he will place his hands on each of your wrists, embedding the markings."

Logan just stood there in silence.

"Oh, gods." Why had Jocasta not said anything? "Um... well, thank you. For the overview. I am sure we would have been very surprised on the *umbra* of our mating. When the entire village showed up." Pierce laughed lightly. The brutality of most mating ceremonies in Métamorphe usually led to many retreating into their huts versus bearing witness. And the exchange of promises was definitely not something he'd seen before, either. Completely unexpected. But it was going to be wonderful.

"You are very welcome. Now, return tomorrow. I will have your pieces, then." Adara waved them off as she went back to work at her jewelry table.

Logan exited the house, with Pierce right behind him. It wasn't until they were on the other side of the door and on their way back to their homes that he glanced at Pierce. "Did Jocasta say anything to you about all of this?"

"Nope. Not a single word."

"Ambrosia said nothing to me, either. I noticed a lot of work being done when I returned with Lilli earlier, but I did not expect, well, everyone."

"You and me both, brother. Things changed little in the village regarding matings. A little rougher as time has gone on, in all honesty. I never allowed Lilli to attend one."

"She said as much during afternoon meal." Logan paused for a moment. "I did not even think when Ambrosia said matings here were parties that often went well into the night."

Pierce raised his eyebrow at his brother. "She said that?"

His brother confirmed without saying a word. "Well. This should truly be interesting."

A shit-eating grin fixed on his brother's face. "She did also say mates sometimes sneak away before the celebration ends."

He smirked as the house came into view. "That sounds intriguing. I believe I will have no issue indulging in that."

"Me either, brother."

Chapter Nine

Logan and Pierce ascended the short set of wooden steps to the front porch, and Logan opened the door to his home. The sight before them made Logan stop a few feet beyond the jamb. Pierce didn't make it past the entrance. Ambrosia, Jocasta, Lyrica, and Lilli all worked between the kitchen and dining area laughing.

"I did not!" Jocasta sneered at her sister.

"Yes, you did. I remember it clear as *umbra*. You had wrapped your hands so tightly around the spourgiff the first time it flew into the air that I thought you were going to strangle it." Ambrosia chuckled.

"You were the one that smacked it on the rear. If I hadn't grabbed it around the neck, I would've fallen off."

Tears welled in the corners of Pierce's eyes. She was laughing. Lillianna... was laughing and had the biggest smile on her face. She had never laughed, not like this. Maybe a slight snicker here and there, but never... He couldn't have stopped the quiet sob if he'd tried. Fearful he would fall to his knees; he grabbed onto the doorframe.

Lilli turned her head in their direction. "Pierce!" She ran across the room and jumped into his arms, hugging him hard as one arm wrapped around her. "What on earth? What is wrong? Why are you crying? Has something happened?" He said nothing, and she hopped out of his arms and hugged Logan. "Is he having a stroke?" She peered at the other females. "He has never looked like this before. We may need to call a shaman."

"I think he just..." Logan cleared his throat.

Gods, the emotions rolling off of him had to be choking his brother up. He barely formed words. "You... you laughed." His voice was hardly audible, even to his own ears. "You are laughing and smiling." He had never seen her even a fraction of how happy she was now.

"I do not know. He does look rather sickly," Lyrica jested.

Jocasta smirked. "No, he doesn't. Stop that, Mom." Shaking her head, she ambled out of the kitchen and closed the distance between them. When his mate reached him, he drew her to his side. He needed her close. "Don't listen to her, Lilli. He may simply need a moment."

Lilli glanced at Pierce, and he just nodded, passing the necklace to Logan out of the palm of his hand. He opened his mouth, but no words came out.

"Are you going to be alright, Pierce?" Lilli asked.

With a brief dip of his chin, he glimpsed at Logan gesturing to their sister. He couldn't seem to get his voice to work. Nor could he take his eyes off of their sister. Her smile practically lit up the room.

Logan cleared his throat again. "Lilli, Pierce, and I, we wanted to give you this. It is just something from us to celebrate your day of birth." He held out the necklace Adara had given to them.

Lilli stood there in silence for a beat. He could practically see the thought process flash across her face and through her amethyst eyes. Something she couldn't have before. But they weren't in Métamorphe. They were no longer in that place. The same rules would no longer apply.

"This is for me? It... oh, gods, it is beautiful. I... I love it, truly. Thank you. Both of you." She embraced Logan hard and glanced toward Pierce to do the same, but seemed to think better of it. It was okay, though. If he looked anything like how he felt right now, it surely appeared as if he were about to fall over.

"She has never been like this. Not once. Never," Pierce whispered to his mate as he held her tighter against him.

Lilli's eyes shined. "I am happy."

"I can tell," Pierce said, more tears falling down his cheeks. It was all worth it. To see her like this. Everything he had ever endured was worth it.

Lilli turned her attention back to Logan. "Would you put it on me, please? I really love it. I never want to take it off."

"Yes." Logan took the necklace from Lilli's hands. Stepping behind her, he draped the silver chain around her neck and fastened the clasp. It fell a couple of inches beneath her throat at an appropriate but comfortable length.

Jocasta kept her arm around Pierce's waist, though she said nothing. He hadn't told her everything, but she would know enough from what he'd told her of the village to understand life had been difficult for Lilli. He knew how happy she was that they were both out of that place.

"That is a beautiful necklace," Ambrosia said as she joined Logan. "And it suits you well."

Pierce rubbed his eyes hard, only for more wetness to spillover. Oh, to all the gods and goddesses. He couldn't imagine the impression Ambrosia had of him, let alone Lyrica. First, she'd seen him covered in blood and nearly ripped the throat out of another male, and now he couldn't stop crying.

Lilli wrapped her fingers around the necklace with a soft curl to her lips. "It really is. I love it so much." She lifted her gaze to Logan. "Please do not start crying too. I have never seen him shed a tear. I do not know if I could handle it if you cry too," she teased. Focusing back on Pierce, she squeezed his hand. "It is just a smile, Pierce."

Finally getting himself under control, he cleared his throat, then did it once more for good measure. "It is more than that. So much more." He needed to change the subject before his eyes started leaking again. "The food smells wonderful."

Logan clutched Ambrosia to his side. It was obvious he struggled, trying his hardest not to cry. Between Pierce's tears and Logan's empathic abilities, the emotions going through Logan had to be overwhelming.

"That's probably the stewed apples. Mom makes the best," Jocasta replied.

"To be fair, Lilli helped with that. She's quite good with a knife," Lyrica said as she approached.

"I think she's better than Jo," Ambrosia teased with a shrug.

Lyrica crossed her arms and shot a glare at Jocasta. "Now. Am I allowed to get a good look at my other new son since you refused me earlier?"

"I didn't refuse you. I merely suggested you wait a minute."

Lilli gave both Logan and Pierce a kiss on the cheek before disappearing into the kitchen. His eyes didn't leave his sister. She enjoyed cooking. It had to feel good assisting with the meal.

Refocusing his attention, Pierce dipped his chin low, first to Lyrica, then Ambrosia. "It is an honor to meet you. And meet you officially, Ambrosia." His mouth slanted a little. "I am not covered in blood this time, but I could have done without the tears."

Lyrica raised an eyebrow and glanced between her two daughters. Whatever confusion she had passed as quickly as it arrived. She stood there a moment and studied Pierce, but said nothing.

"Honestly, they both show you're a powerful male," Ambrosia stated.

Peering over her shoulder at Ambrosia, Lyrica nodded in agreement. Instead of saying anything, though, she hugged Pierce as best she could, given he still had Jocasta at his side. "Thank you."

Easing out of Pierce's grip just a little, Jocasta tilted her head and eyed her mother. She flicked her gaze to Ambrosia, who shrugged.

Pierce's eyes widened as he stole a glance at his mate. What was he supposed to do with this? Not just her words, but her embrace. "Thank you?" He patted her shoulder. "For... for what?"

Lyrica inhaled two deep breaths and stepped back. "You gave my daughter back to me. She has been lost for so many *solaris*. The difference I have seen in her these last couple of *cycles* is astounding. I did not know their attribution until she told us of you. I cannot tell you what that means to me."

Pierce didn't speak for a few moments, though several things came to mind that he wanted to say. He swallowed the new lump that had settled in his throat. "If that is true, then you are so very welcome." He dropped his gaze to his mate and stroked her ears. "She has done more for me than I can say. She has made me see things so differently. Given me things I had thought were long lost to me. Filled me in places that I was empty. So much more that I cannot put into words." He lifted his eyes to the female that had birthed the two that had truly saved his and his brother's life. He didn't want to sober the moment even more and hoped he wouldn't anger or upset anyone by bringing it up, but he had to tell Lyrica. "I owe you a thank you as well. For your mate. For what he did for my family, our mother, before he was wrongfully taken from you."

Lyrica simply squeezed his hand. "He was a wonderful male with a big heart. And strong morals." She didn't say she knew what he referred to, but it was in her eyes. She brushed her fingers beneath her eyes and clasped her hands together. "Come now; we have lots of food to get on the table." With that, she strode toward the kitchen.

Flicking her gaze between him and her mother, Jocasta's eyebrows knitted together. Pierce wanted to say more, but Lyrica had effectively cut the conversation off, and he couldn't blame her. To lose your mate was a thought he couldn't even fathom. Kissing the side of Jocasta's throat, he glanced from her to Ambrosia, to Logan. They all shared confusion. "Later. I will tell you all later. Right now, I am starving and wish to share a meal with my family." Holding Jocasta against him, he led her into the kitchen.

Food seemed to get them all moving. Lyrica worked with Lilli to finish up the apples with a dash of cinnamon. They had venison, sweet bread, a variety of vegetables, including carrots, corn, and beans. Plus, fresh milk, tea, or water to drink. With all the plates on the table, they all sat with Logan at one end of the table and Pierce at the other. Lyrica and Lilli sat on one side as the twins sat on the other, each next to their males.

Conversation flowed as food got passed around.

"I must thank you for sending us in the direction you did earlier." Pierce smirked at Jocasta. "Had it not been for Adara explaining some details of the ceremony, Logan and I would have been shocked come the *umbra* of our mating. When the entire village showed up."

Jocasta stifled a laugh. "You can't honestly think I'd have allowed you to be up there without the details. Besides, Adara would have sought the two of you out tomorrow if you hadn't gone to her."

"Actually, she probably would've sent Ina," Ambrosia corrected.

Logan's eyebrows furrowed. "Is there more than what Adara told us?"

"I don't know. Mom, what's left to be done?" Ambrosia asked.

Swallowing the food in her mouth, Lyrica picked up another carrot. "Well, the tables still have to be put out. Someone will prep all the food tomorrow, plus the decor, and we have to finish both of your dresses." She shifted her gaze to Lilli. "And one for you, my dear, if you would prefer."

Pierce almost objected. Their fur made clothing unnecessary. Except he caught a look of hope in his sister's eyes. What she had gone through...her eyes twinkled. "I think she would like that very much."

"Yes. I think I would," Lilli echoed.

"Then you will join us tomorrow. I have the perfect material for you. It will complement your fur well." Lyrica smiled.

"You're in expert hands. Mom's the best seamstress in the entire village," Ambrosia said.

"Oh, posh." Lyrica waved the compliment off. "I am merely well-trained."

The corners of his mouth upturned. "Thank you. I appreciate your kindness."

"The entire village comes out because the complete village contributes. We all do our part. There will be those who work on decorating, some who work on the food, and then others who help with set up," Jocasta explained.

Pierce squeezed his mate's knee and stroked it. No matter how he tried, he couldn't quite find the words to express himself. The sense of community here was strange and unnerving, but welcome. It would take a lot of getting used to, as would a lot of things. "That sounds wonderful. I look forward to finding my place here."

Jocasta's hand covered his. "I'm sure you will. As for tomorrow—" She exchange a glance with her sister.

"Set up," the two stated simultaneously.

Returning her attention to him, Jocasta winked. "I planned to introduce you to Duke, anyway. So I can just take you and Logan together."

"Isn't Rayare in charge of setting up?" Ambrosia questioned.

Jocasta snickered. "Technically, she is, but you know Duke is the one that does all the work. I'm sure he'll be happy to share the duty of table lifting."

Pierce grazed his lips on the back of her hand. "We will be happy to help with whatever needs to be done, my queen." He watched as his sister finished the food on her plate. It pleased him she could eat as much as she liked now. Lilli reached for more, then hesitated. A faraway look appeared in her eyes. The one she got when she flashed back, where the rest of the room vanished, and she disappeared into her memories. Setting his cup down, he slowly pushed the plate of venison across the table closer to her. "Lilli," he mumbled. Her eyes remained locked. She was still somewhere else in her mind. He reached across and clasped her hand. "Lilli." With a slight jump, she returned to the present and peered at him. Pierce kept his voice soft. "You may have more." While he fixed his eyes on Lilli, he noticed the tension in his brother, the way the male's hand disappeared beneath the table. "You may have, however, and as much as you want."

Ambrosia gripped Logan's arm and stroked the inside of his forearm. "Do not deprive yourself, Lilli," Logan said.

Leaning a little closer to her, Lyrica picked up a sweet roll and scooped some apples onto Lilli's plate. "I like to eat until I feel like I might explode."

As she watched more food appear on her plate, Lilli blinked back tears. She offered a faint smile to Lyrica. "I have never eaten that much before," she whispered.

Lyrica clasped Lilli's hand. "I did not either until someone told me I could. You can eat however much you desire, my dear."

Slowly, Lilli's eyes lit up. "Thank you."

Lyrica patted the female's hand and picked up another sweet roll for herself.

After putting more venison onto her plate, Pierce dropped his hand onto his lap, his claws digging into his palm. He focused on the air going in and out of his lungs, trying to keep the rage at their father at bay, for Logan's sake. "What else will we need to assist with, my love? For the ceremony."

With a grip on his forearm under the table, it took Jocasta a bit to answer his question. "Um, tables. Wait, I said that. There's, uh, other places that can always be helped afterward."

"Tables and chairs are always the heavy lifting. Santos handles the altar himself, always has, but I'm sure if help is needed, someone will get one or both of you," Ambrosia added. "Should we go over the specifics of the ceremony itself? Or did Adara tell you everything?"

"She gave us a quick review," Logan answered.

Pierce stroked Jocasta's leg, keeping the motion easy. The contact with her relaxed him more. She was the only thing holding him together. "Yes, but something tells me she did not tell us everything."

Jocasta chuckled. "The ceremony opens with the presentation. Santos will escort Ambrosia and me from his hut out to the clearing to where you and Logan are. He'll then place his hands on our joined hands. At which point, he'll state if we're a good mating or not. Once he says we're a good match, there's the exchange of promises and gifts."

"She told us that, just in not so many words." Pierce still regarded Lilli. As she ate again, albeit a little slower this time, as if she were finally allowing herself to savor it, the pain in his chest settled. Lyrica had been wonderful with her, and Logan had said Ambrosia was as well. He knew his mate would be, too. His earlier conversation with Logan jumped into his mind. How was he going to help her heal? He was a protector, not a healer. He didn't know how to heal anyone; despite what they'd said he'd done for Jocasta.

"I thought the gifts were just for you." Logan raised an eyebrow at Ambrosia.

"No. We have something to give you as well," Ambrosia responded.

Pierce beamed at his mate. "Oh?" He would wear anything she gave to him with honor and pride. "I do not know what our gifts for you two will be. She just told us to return in the afternoon tomorrow."

"She never does. You go to her and she asks maybe two questions. I swear she is psychic or something because she can read anyone and pick out the perfect item. Am and I are supposed to go by after morning meal."

His brother's shoulders sagged. Obviously, the tension had finally eased from the male. Logan refocused his attention between Ambrosia and Jocasta. "Something tells me we are going at different times on purpose."

"Of course we are. Adara would never have us come in at the same time. If you ask her, it ruins the surprise." Ambrosia cracked a toothy grin. "Just don't be late."

"After that, Santos will pronounce us in front of the entire village, and he'll embed our combined initials in our wrists," Jocasta continued.

"A moment I am impatiently waiting for, my queen." Pierce squeezed her thigh, though he remained appropriate, and then grazed his fingers across the soft skin of her knee. He peered at Ambrosia. "We will not be late. She did not ask us much when we were there earlier, either. A couple of questions, then said she had the perfect thing and showed us the necklace."

"It is perfect," Lilli stated, placing her hand over it.

"Adara knows," Jocasta and Ambrosia replied simultaneously.

"The embedding of the initials is the end of the ceremony. At that point, everyone moves over to food, dancing, singing, and so on," Jocasta tacked on.

"Will you teach me how to dance?" Lilli asked, glancing back and forth between Pierce and Logan.

Pierce's eyebrows shot up. "I, well, I do not know how to dance." He eyed his mate. Not that he would ever deny a chance to be close to his mate. "*Everyone* dances?"

Logan's eyes widened. "I do not know, either."

"Not everyone—"

A small smile played on Ambrosia's lips as she cut off her twin. "I suppose it's a good thing we have an excellent teacher. Right. In. This. Room." She crossed her arms and glared at her sister. "Don't give me that look. You dance as good as you sing."

"Do you know how rusty I am?"

"Not since you started singing in the bar again. I think you'd be able to teach us all."

Jocasta let out an exasperated sigh. "Fine. I give."

"Oh, thank you," Lilli said. "And—," She bit her lip. "Do you think you could help me with something tomorrow? I suddenly had an idea, and I do not want to say it aloud because I would like it to be a surprise, but do you think you could help me?"

"We can help you with anything you need," Lyrica chimed in before anyone else could answer.

Lilli thanked her and quietly finished the last few bites on her plate. "After I help with the cleanup, I think I may go lay back down if that is alright. I am still quite tired."

Her comment didn't surprise him in the least. She probably would be for a while. The slow realization that you didn't have to be constantly on your guard would be exhausting for anyone, especially a young female. Pierce's features softened as he regarded his sister. "You do not have to help clean up if you are tired, sister mine. Go ahead. We will take care of all of this."

"But I need to help."

Her voice was soft and hesitant, and Pierce had to clench his fist under the table as his heart broke all over again. "Lilli, I assure you, it is unnecessary. Your rest is more important. Go ahead. Besides, we will need your help with preparations tomorrow. Jocasta said there is still much to be done, and we would appreciate your help." Oh, gods, he hated his father, hated him with a swirling fire that was difficult to swallow. He wanted to move forward and keep the need for revenge from rising back up inside him. But it was so very difficult. Glancing over, he shared a look with Logan. They had agreed he would tell Lilli about his ability after evening meal, but she had been through enough for the day. Perhaps he could tell her in the morning.

Logan gave a slight, almost imperceptible nod. "Pierce is right, Lilli. We can handle this. You should get some rest."

"Are... are you sure?"

"Of course. Here, let me help you to your room." Pierce gave his mate's leg a gentle squeeze, then rose from the table. After helping Lilli up, he led her down the hall to the bedroom she told him was hers. His eyes missed nothing of the furniture as he tucked her into bed. He sat with her until she was sleeping deeply, monitoring the gentle rise and fall of her chest. Eventually, he forced himself out of her room. His family had already cleaned up among themselves. He couldn't look at any of them, and he couldn't have even said why.

"The furniture is beautiful, Logan. What was at the cabin, as well. I am glad you did not stop doing it. It brought me joy to see things again that your hands have created. I missed it." He was rambling. Why was he rambling? And his voice sounded so strange.

"Thank you," Logan replied. He cleared his throat. "It helped me keep my emotions under control. For some time."

Lyrica said her goodbyes to Ambrosia and Jocasta, who quickly returned to cleaning up. She came over to Logan and Pierce and stood between them for a moment. "Do not feel you have to rush into finding where you belong in this community. I am sure you can see we are nothing like Métamorphe. Yes, Galenus told me what it was like when he was there. I know his death separated you both, and that can greatly impact family. Focus on reconnecting. Everything else, it will fall into place."

"Thank you, Lyrica. We are going to try." Pierce's gaze fell to the floor. A moment passed before he could lift his eyes back to Logan and Lyrica. "I prayed for him... afterward. It changes nothing, but I wanted you to know. His loss did not go un-mourned by everyone in the village." His father had beaten and whipped him when the male had discovered what he'd done. There had always been a rivalry between the two. Not that it ever made any sense. Galenus had just been a male with honor, one that wouldn't allow cruelty toward females. Their father had always been the opposite.

"Thank you." Lyrica paused. "I have always believed he watched over us. My daughters have been safe for *solaris*, but it does not mean I do not worry. However, having the two of you here, I now feel he is at peace. And I worry a little less. Eventually, you will worry over her a little less. You both will." She took one of Pierce's hands and Logan's hands within her own and clasped them both. "I will see you both in the morning."

"Yes. We will see you tomorrow. Rest easy." Pierce replied.

"You as well." With that, Lyrica took her leave.

He'd said *later* at their looks of confusion earlier, and he knew Logan would ask him what all of it had been about. He would have thought Logan knew, as close as he'd been to their mother. As much as he'd always been there for her during her losses, when Pierce couldn't. Apparently, it had been something she couldn't talk about, even to him. He would tell Logan and their mates if it was something they wished to know. The full circle of their families and their lives had come.

Both Jocasta and Ambrosia had stood there in silence, in the middle of the clean up, staring at their mother and their mates. It wasn't until the door clapped shut behind Lyrica that either spoke.

Jocasta's gaze swept between Logan and Pierce. "She hasn't spoken about him since he passed."

"I hope I did not bring her any added pain. That was not my intent."

"On the contrary, brother," Logan responded. "I felt comfort coming from her. It was almost as if she had found peace."

Pierce sensed the confusion in his mate, but his brother had to be right. Lyrica hadn't teared up, and she hadn't walked away or even stopped speaking altogether.

"I think you're right. Nothing about that conversation... it wasn't as it's been in the past," Jocasta declared.

"Maybe she's finally healing some herself," Ambrosia added.

"That would be good. Losing a mate..." Pierce's eyes locked on his own mate as he held a hand out to her. "It is not something I can even fathom, not even in thought." He gestured to the couches in the front room. "We should sit. It may change nothing, but you should know the secret that our mother kept."

Jocasta rested her palm against his and they headed into the living room. Logan and Ambrosia followed. He took one chair and tugged Ambrosia onto his lap.

As Pierce sat down, he drew Jocasta into his lap and encircled her waist. He would need his mate close. Recalling his mother was always difficult, and he was loath to release any more tears. "Our father hated him—Galenus—for stupid reasons. Reasons that made no sense to me and would have made no sense to him if he had opened his eyes. But the things he thought he saw, things that were never there, always clouded his vision. Father... Ailwin was always jealous and angry towards him. He thought

Galenus had romantic feelings towards our mother, but anyone who was not blinded by hatred would have known that was not the case. Perhaps there was more to our fathers' relationship with each other, but if so, I do not know what it was."

Curled up against his chest, Jocasta's eyebrows furrowed. Pierce peered down at her. "Your father saved our mother from violence, brutal violence, and more than once. He suffered for it, but it never deterred him. Ailwin cared not and never even entertained the thought of retaliation against the males that attacked her. In his eyes, she asked for it." He growled. "And deserved what she got. I could do nothing less than pray for him after his life was stolen. It made Ailwin angry, but most things did."

Holding Ambrosia close, Logan snarled. "She never told me. I could always sense when something was off, but she refused to talk about it with me."

"She never spoke to me of her... losses. I think she knew what each of us could handle. Not that any of it was ever easy." Their mother had endured too much.

"No, it was not." Logan dropped his head to the crook of his mate's neck.

"Your mother sounds like she was a powerful female," Jocasta said.

Pierce squeezed his brother's shoulder. "She truly was. The strongest female I have ever known." He laid his head on his mate's shoulder, letting her scent fill him. Though he knew he needed to let go of the past and the pain they had all endured, it felt like letting go of his mother. He still, to this day, hadn't said goodbye to her. "Lilli has her spirit. She may not show it much just yet, but it is there. She will learn she can be her true self here, with no repercussions."

Jocasta threaded her fingers through Pierce's. "What was your mother's name?"

He rubbed his thumb back and forth over the back of her hand. "Her name was Sabina." His throat got tight. He hadn't spoken her name since her death.

"That's a beautiful name."

Pierce dropped a kiss on her neck. "It really is. Her heart and soul were even more beautiful than the name she bore. Despite all of her pain, not an *umbra* went by where she did not smile at us, at least once."

"I cannot believe how much Lilli looks like her," Logan commented.

"Me either, brother mine. And her eyes have been that color from birth. They have never changed."

"It took everything in me not to cry the second I saw her," Logan replied.

"I should have prepared you when we spoke at the cabin. I had a feeling it would be emotional. My apologies, brother."

Logan lifted his head from his mate's neck. "Even if you had, seeing her with her name... It would not have made a difference. She loved lilies."

"I remember. It is why every *solaris*, on her day of birth, I would leave Lillianna a bowl of lilies. I could not save our mother, and I cannot bring her back. But I do what I can to keep her close."

With a slight bopping of his head, Logan inhaled a deep breath.

"I miss her smile," Pierce stated. "I saw it on Lilli today. She has never been that happy. Whatever the two of you and your mother did to bring that out of her, I can never thank you enough."

Ambrosia softly chuckled. "I told her tales of all the trouble Jo caused as a child."

"And you really made it all seem worse than it was," Jocasta smirked. "Though I think she came in while mother was admonishing us over something."

"And what might that have been, my queen? I heard something about the spourgiffs. Was it the same tale you told me or another one?"

"Different one."

He laughed. "I can imagine there are quite a few."

"Wait a minute." Ambrosia sat up. "Did you tell him about the one where you almost got clawed?"

"Of course, I did. It's amusing." Jocasta giggled.

In unison, the two of them said, "Unless you were the rescuer." However, Jocasta was a bit more sarcastic with her reply.

Pierce snickered at his brother. This is what they had always been missing throughout their life. A genuine sense of family. He chuckled louder. "I thought it was quite amusing. Though, I said it was probably pretty terrifying." When she'd told him that story, it had been the first time he'd really laughed in a very long time. And the first time he'd admitted to himself that he had thought about young with her. If that was a possibility for him, they would finally have the chance.

"I was terrified, and she wasn't." Glaring at her, Ambrosia jabbed a finger in Jocasta's direction.

"I told you there was nothing to fear, at least on my end. I was going to jump out of the way."

"Just humongous claws." Ambrosia rolled her eyes. "Tell them about the other time."

Logan leaned over Ambrosia's neck. "Oh yes, please do."

"Okay. Admittedly, the first time might have been my fault. But the second time with the spourgiff was her fault. I decided I was going to ride one. Am had been riding them for *solaris*, so she went with me to show me what to do. I got on the spourgiff's back with no problem. As I go to ask her how to hold on—"

"Which I had already told her."

"—no, you didn't." Jocasta raised a hand, silencing her sister. "As I was saying. I go to ask her, and she slaps it on the rear, and the spourgiff just takes off. I threw my arms around its neck and barely kept from falling off."

Pierce tried hard to hold in his mirth, but it was difficult. "You two sound like the two of us when we were young. We got into a lot of trouble ourselves." He chuckled at Logan. "Do you remember when we almost got gored by that deer?"

Logan snickered. "How was I supposed to know it would run right at us?"

Ambrosia shifted to look at him. "Wait, wait. What happened, exactly?"

"We were in the forest when we spotted a deer with these massive horns," Logan said. "I might have suggested we race to see who could get to it first. I really did not think it would charge at us."

Jocasta and Ambrosia both threw their head back in laughter.

Pierce chortled. He had always been slightly faster than Logan. "Oh, come on, brother, you had to know. It was snorting, hooves stomping at the ground. We were just young and stupid, not nearly as experienced enough to be doing that, and thought we could take it down. So, we get ready to run at it, both swearing up and down we are going to be the one to reach it first, and then it lowers its head. And then it charges. We were young and stupid, and that did not deter us. I believe I broke a rib or two, and Logan almost lost an eye."

Logan ran his hands through Ambrosia's hair and played with the ends of her ponytail. "Of course, I knew. But it was a moving object, and it seemed like a much better idea to race toward it than a tree."

Jocasta giggled. "What's a rib or two? They heal."

"Oh, yeah, they heal alright." Ambrosia smirked. "Remind me again, how long did yours take to heal that one time?"

Jocasta glowered at Ambrosia. "Long enough."

The happiness Pierce felt, being able to spend time like this with Logan again, talking and laughing. It was just like old times, but so much better. All of it was enough to make him weep, but he wouldn't do that. He'd had enough of his eyes leaking today. They were going to make this a regular thing, though. He was going to make sure of it. He vowed never to let anyone separate him from his family again. Never again would his brother become lost.

Pierce placed a kiss against the nub in Jocasta's right shoulder blade, then one on her shoulder, overtop of the fading brand, smiling at the shiver that ran down her spine. Hmm, it *was* fading, wasn't it? He was going to have to give her another one. "Oh, I was not worried about my ribs. I was more worried about his eye. And Fa—" He stopped and took a breath. He didn't want to call Ailwin that any longer. "Ailwin was furious, but not over our injuries. Mother was beside herself. She made us swear never to do anything that reckless again, but, of course, we did not listen. Remember the bridge that you swore would hold our weight?"

Soft laughter erupted from Jocasta. "It must've been one weak bridge."

"Mother always made us promise, though she knew we would not listen. And I only miscalculated our combined weight just a little. I had no clue I had gained so much in such a little time." Logan grinned. Pierce might have been faster, but Logan had more muscle and ultimately more weight. It certainly benefited him with fights.

Ambrosia flicked her gaze from Logan to Pierce and back again. "There really is something to this older sibling dynamic."

"You're older by one minute." Jocasta rolled her eyes. "One minute. They're apart by…" She paused and glanced over her shoulder at Pierce. "I just realized you never actually told me."

"Oh, he just thinks he knows everything. You cannot tell him anything." Pierce kept the serious look on his face for all of a fraction of a second before laughter burst from him. He shrugged. "I tried." He kissed Jocasta's shoulder again. "Told you what, love? Oh, we are apart by four *solaris* and…" He paused. "Two *cycles*, I believe?" He raised an eyebrow. "Three? We only got to celebrate our birthdays with our mother when Ailwin was gone from the village, so it was not always on time. I was born in the springtime. Well, it should have been springtime, but according to our mother, the winter would just not go away that *solaris*. I will be in my forty-sixth *solaris* of birth next springtime."

Ambrosia's fingers shot to her mouth as she stifled a chuckle. "Why yes, yes, he does."

"You do realize I am right here," Logan teased his mate with a gentle but firm grip on her hips. He pressed a soft kiss to the side of Ambrosia's throat and shifted his gaze to Pierce. "Three *cycles*. I was born near summertime."

"Yes, I do. If I don't say it to your face, then I won't say it at all." Ambrosia nuzzled her nose against his.

"Oh..." Pierce shook his head a little, then shared a smile with his brother. "Of course. The river outings." It had been difficult, sometimes, to track their birthdays growing up. It wasn't something Ailwin allowed them to bring up. Birthdays—any kind of happiness—was something the male had never allowed.

Shifting her gaze to her twin, Jocasta narrowed her gaze. "Really? Should I tell him some things you said when you first introduced us?"

Ambrosia's amber gaze snapped to Jocasta. The two females both went silent, despite the obvious eye movement.

Logan glanced at Pierce and shrugged.

"Oh, I think you definitely should." Pierce eyeballed their females. "Are you two doing that mindlink thing again? That is not fair," he teased. His hands settled on Jocasta's hips, and he nipped at her ear. He barely suppressed a growl as she readjusted in his lap, rubbing against him. Leaning into her more, he whispered, "If you keep doing that, my queen, we cannot stay much longer."

Jocasta peered at him. "Sorry. It's something we do often. Especially when we're arguing."

"Do not apologize, and I was only teasing. I do not mind." His mate waggled her eyebrows at him.

"Good gods, fine." Ambrosia threw her hands up in the air in exasperation. "But it isn't like I haven't told him any of what you heard."

Turning around, Jocasta regarded Logan. "It really isn't bad. Mostly. She called you an insufferable know-it-all, but apparently, that had more to do with how you met."

Logan chuckled. "Yes, she called me that at our meeting. It was but the next *umbra* before she apologized."

Pierce laughed. "That is funny, but I am sure it was not as bad as our first meeting. I literally ran into her and broke an entire basket of potions."

Jocasta leaned back, snuggling up against his chest. Her gaze flicked to her sister. "Surprise."

Ambrosia's eyes widened. "Wait. You're the one she bumped into?" She gawked at the two of them for a moment and busted out in laughter. It took a second for her fit to settle. She smirked. "Now I know why you were so flustered when you got back."

"And we're done."

Pierce slowly stroked her hips and thighs. "Mmm, flustered, were you? Did I make you flustered?" he jested. "She had me so out of sorts that I could not stay away. I went back the next *umbra* and put my head into the door of Zancle's Rock, looking for her." He saw Logan's eyes practically bulge out of his head. "And no, I do not care it is still against the laws. One look, and I was done for. It just took me a little while to admit it."

Jocasta nibbled on his ear. "And you still fluster me."

Pierce couldn't hold back the growl this time. He vividly remembered watching her perfect rear as she had bent over the counter. As their eyes locked on one another, the surrounding room disappeared, and he had to force himself to remember that his brother and her sister were still here.

"And here I thought I was the reason you put that Ice Moon aside," Ambrosia muttered.

"Sorry, Am. You can't take credit for that one either." She didn't even look at her sister as she spoke. Leaning up, Jocasta whispered in Pierce's ear, "That was all you, too."

Pierce cupped her cheek and rubbed his nose against hers. "I will always be utterly and completely enamored with you, my queen." He pressed a soft kiss to her lips, forcing himself not to devour her mouth. Yes, it had taken him a while to admit how he felt. But he suspected the truth of it was the inability to believe that true happiness would be a possibility for him. That it was something he deserved.

"That's a good thing because I'm quite taken with you, my king." Jocasta didn't waste time. She climbed out of his lap and stood. "Am, Logan, I think it's time we take our leave, but we'll see you for morning meal."

"Absolutely." Pierce tucked her into his side. "We have some...important matters to discuss before we retire for the evening." He pinched her rear, a smirk on his face as she let out a small squeal. "Rest easy, and we will see you in the morning." He picked his mate up in his arms.

Logan and Ambrosia stood. He nodded with a slight chuckle. "You as well, brother."

"Have a good night, you two." Ambrosia smirked as she and Logan walked Jocasta and Pierce out the door.

Chapter Ten

Closing the door, Ambrosia spun around on her heel. She smiled up at Logan. "Finally, I have you all to myself."

"What do you plan to do with me?" He pushed her up against the door and dropped his head in the crook of her neck. His tongue made wet trails along her throat and up her jaw line to her ear.

She ran her hands over his biceps. "Oh, so much."

Logan drew her soft body against his chest and fused their lips together just as Lilli's voice rang out from her bedroom.

"LET ME GO!"

Breaking the kiss, Logan jerked back and snarled, taking a step toward the hallway.

Oh, gods! The words that came out of Lilli's mouth. Her mate's eyes had darkened one other time—when that Informant had gotten too close to the cabin. The obvious rage coursing through him. He was in no state to handle this kind of nightmare. Ambrosia jumped into action and grabbed Logan's arm, yanking him back. "I'll go check on her."

"I am her brother, and I should—"

"Not with the way your eyes look right now. You'll frighten her and only make it worse. Just stay here." Before he could object, she ducked under his arms and strode to Lilli's room. The female had to be awoken gently. Ambrosia opened the door and let herself in. "Lilli?"

"STOP! PLEASE!" Lilli jerked in her sleep. "Do not let him...Father, do not let him... PLEASE!" She jolted again, rolling into the wall with a thump. Her eyes opened, and her head snapped toward the doorway as she froze.

She had helped one female in the village deal with nightmares. The young female had to be handled with care. Ambrosia raised her hands to show she meant no harm. "Lilli, it's just me, Ambrosia. I'd like to come inside if you let me."

Lilli stared at her a few moments longer, then her body shook, and she dissolved into sobs. "I am sorry... I am sorry..."

At least the female recognized where she was now. Ambrosia went to her side and kneeled down next to her. She reached to the nightside table and turned the lantern so soft light filled the room. Wrapping the female in her arms, she stroked the back of her head. "Shh, it's okay. You don't need to apologize. None of it is your fault."

"I did not mean to... Did I... did I... wake you up? I... I am sorry...I am so sorry." Her chest heaved as she tried to draw breath, tears still streaming down her face.

"You don't have to apologize. Whether you woke us up doesn't matter. We're right here for you." She kept a hold of Lilli, continuing to caress the back of her head. Gods, what the female had gone through. How much did Logan know? He'd mentioned earlier Pierce told him she had nightmares, but he never said it would be *those* kinds of nightmares.

Lilli leaned into her chest as she sobbed harder. "He would not... stop... He would not stop... He helped them... do it," she choked out.

Her heart shattered as if a mirror had broken, the shards falling to the floor. It took all the willpower she had not to shed tears for what Lilli had endured. She had to stay strong, offer the comfort and support the female needed. She didn't know who *he* was, but she didn't imagine it was an honorable male. No male with honor would harm a female in that manner. "I'm so sorry, Lilli. I'm so sorry. You didn't deserve that."

Her words came out broken, tears still spilling down her face. "Why does he... hate me? Why did Father... let them... hurt me? I tried... I tried to be... good, I tried... but I did not want... I did not want it... I did not... want it, and he did not care." Still leaning against Ambrosia, she wrapped her arms around herself.

Oh, gods. Ambrosia squeezed her eyes shut to stop the wetness that welled in the corners of her eyes. Lilli's father. Her own father. Pierce and Logan had made it clear in the way they talked exactly how they felt about the male. And the horrible person he had always been. There was no good way to answer that. Regardless of the knowledge she had, there was no true *why*. Ambrosia kept hold of Lilli and rubbed her arms. She didn't want her to hurt herself. "You'll never go back there. You're safe here." No matter how many ways she tried to come up with a *why*, none of them seemed like suitable answers. "You'll never go back."

"What if... he finds me? What if he... finds me? They... they paid him. They gave him... coin. He will... he will... want me back. He will be... looking for me," she sobbed out. "I do not want to go back."

Ambrosia readjusted so she could get Lilli to focus on her face as she spoke. The female needed to know the full gravity of her words. "Listen to me. Your father is a male with no honor. He cannot step foot on these grounds. No one, and I mean no one, will find you here. If they even dare get close, they will have the wrath of the entire village at their feet. You will *never* go back. You'll always be safe here."

"Promise?" Lilli asked, her voice a whisper.

"I promise you *are* safe. You'll never go back. I promise no harm will ever come to you here."

She nodded a little and laid her head down in Ambrosia's lap. "Would it be okay if... would you mind... Would you stay here... for a minute? Just... just a minute?"

Trying not to tear up again, she stroked Lilli's head. "I'll stay here as long as you need me to."

"Thank you, Am. I do not... I do not want to be alone right now. Is Logan okay? I did not make him angry, did I?"

"You could never make him angry." She swallowed the lump in her throat. He hadn't told Lilli. Of all the things not to tell the female. Something that powerful was far too important not to share. Lilli needed to know that. "He would never be upset with you. He just feels things a little more than most."

"Okay. I just... I do not want anyone to be angry at me anymore. My nightmares... they always made him angry—Father. If I woke him up, it made him furious."

She understood more and more why Pierce and Logan hated the male, even why her own father loathed him. "We would never be upset with you. Your nightmares... they're out of your control. I don't care what time of night it is; we will always come to your aid."

Lilli nodded, her breathing steadying a little more. "Thank you."

Ambrosia thought back to when she and her sister were children. There was a lullaby their mother used to sing to them, especially after Jo had a nightmare. It had always soothed them. She opened her mouth and crooned a calming melody, wishing her a peaceful sleep, a life of blessing and finding kindness. It wished for angels to watch over her and keep her safe from all harm.

As she sang, the tension eased from Lilli's body. A steady rise and fall of her breaths occurred, her eyes closed, and before too long, sleep reclaimed the female. Even after Ambrosia finished the lullaby and Lilli returned to dreamland, Ambrosia stayed. She remained there with the fur of Lilli's ears tickling her leg as the female snuggled deeper and she continued stroking Lilli's head. It was a good hour or more before she left the bedroom, ensuring the lantern's light was low but not out completely. Ambrosia left the door cracked ever so slightly as she walked back into the hallway. Every precaution she could take for Lilli. She found her mate sitting in the same chair he had been in before Jo and Pierce had left. His eyes were no longer black. Without saying a word, she simply crawled into his lap and curled up in his arms as silent tears trickled down her cheeks.

How could she tell him what she'd just learned? How could they even talk about this? Ambrosia ran her fingertips over Logan's chest, playing with his fur as her tears continued to roll down her face. He said nothing. Just enveloped her in his powerful arms, laid his head atop of her own, and held her without question. That was the male her mate was. Although his eyes weren't black, the rage was still there. She sensed it sitting right there on the edge.

"You do not have to say anything," Logan whispered.

That was good, because she wasn't certain she could. Though he'd calmed enough for his eyes to turn back, he was still angry. It concerned her. He had to have heard everything. Not that she suspected it would ever change his opinion of his father. Still, what would he do with all of this new knowledge?

At least she could trust one thing. He wouldn't do something stupid and go after the soulless male in the current situation. No way would he risk his life like that. Not when both she and his sister needed him so much. While she could help Lilli, that girl needed the love and support of both of her brothers to get past what had happened to her.

It was like that with all the females she'd helped in the past. Their fathers had cared more about lining their pockets or themselves than their own daughters. Those females had all required love and support that they couldn't ask for in fear of punishment.

Lilli would need constant reminders that she was safe, that her father would never find her. That, even if he did, he'd never get into the village. None of them would give her up without a fight. Just as much as they would need to consistently tell her, she didn't anger or upset them. Ambrosia wiped the wetness from her face.

The problem was Logan's empathic abilities. While he'd understand Lilli's emotions, it was when he would pick up on the images in the female's head that worried her. At least until he could control his body's response. With as easily as he'd gotten triggered earlier, Lilli needed to know. "You have to tell her."

"I know." He sighed. "I just do not know when there would ever be a good time."

"There won't be, but she deserves to know." Gods, she prayed, this was the right move. It might be comforting, but it may also be unnerving. She didn't want Lilli to walk around the house on glass or always be worried that she might upset either of them. Still, if she knew, maybe she'd understand things better.

Logan continued to run his fingers through her hair. "I will talk to her tomorrow."

"Okay." That was good. At least, she hoped it would be. Truth be told, no time was a good time, especially in this situation.

"I want to kill him, Ambrosia. More so than I did before."

She closed her eyes. It didn't surprise her he desired to kill his father. With the way he and Pierce had spoken of the male earlier, and then with this new information regarding what he'd done to Lilli... still, she didn't immediately respond. What was she supposed to say to that? Was she supposed to give him her permission? Not that he was asking. Ambrosia swallowed the lump in the back of her throat. She opened her mouth to say something, but nothing came out.

Instead, she snuggled into him a little deeper. It was all she could do at the moment. Let him know that, regardless of his rage, she still loved him. That would never change. And that was exactly what would help them get through this new stage in their life, and in their relationship. "I know you do," she said, her voice low.

Logan placed a finger beneath her chin and lifted her eyes to his. "I promise you; I will do nothing reckless."

No, he wouldn't, at least not right now. Not that he hadn't done stupid stuff in the past. His regular visits to Belly of the Beast, to the marketplace. But the purpose behind all of that had passed. They were all safe here, and he'd do nothing to jeopardize that. Sitting up a bit in his lap, Ambrosia brushed a soft kiss across his lips. "I know you won't, but thank you for saying it."

The promise meant a lot, but deep down, she knew without a doubt that if the opportunity arose, he'd follow through on his words. He'd go after the male. While part of her wanted him to do so, if only so Lilli could feel safer, the other part was loath to encourage a life to be taken.

"I would do anything to keep all of you safe." He wrapped his arms around her, hugging her tight to his body.

That was what concerned her. Reckless could indirectly counter his desire to keep them all safe. But he was just as new to the village as Lilli was. Maybe over the next couple of days, until their mating ceremony, she could show him—show them both—just how safe Migas was, and that might stifle his need for revenge. Or so she hoped.

Because while he would do whatever it took to keep his family safe, she would too. Even if it put them at odds.

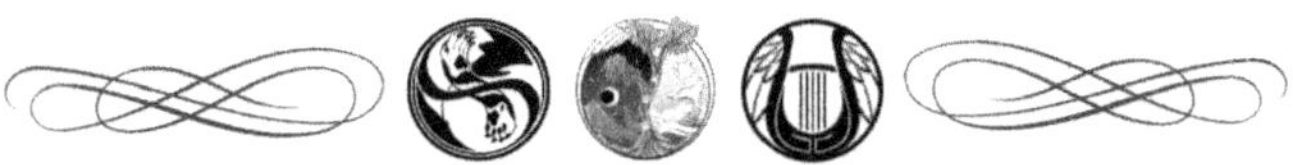

Jocasta collapsed onto Pierce's chest. Both of them breathed raggedly, sweat covering their bodies. They'd gone a few rounds already in their mated bed. Pierce didn't even know he had that many orgasms inside of his body, let alone the different angles the bed provided.

Slowly catching her breath, she rolled off of him onto her side and snuggled up to him. She pressed a tender kiss to his heart. "I'm... beginning...to think... you're trying to make it so..." She paused. "I can't walk tomorrow."

Pierce chuckled and curled his arm around her, stroking the scales over her lower back. He caressed the curve of her rear with his fingertips.

"Mmm, but then I would get to carry you around all *umbra*. I would definitely enjoy that." He lifted her head and kissed her softly. Staring into her eyes, his ruby red eyes glowed brightly for the first time. "I love when you kiss me there. And I love telling you how much that I love you. And showing you."

"I love kissing you there. And I love hearing you say you love me. As much as I love telling you how much I love you, Pierce. But that doesn't mean you can carry me around all *umbra* tomorrow." Reaching up, she caressed his cheek. "I want you to be surprised when you see my dress. I picked it out just for you."

"Hmm, I could wear a blindfold," he teased. "I have excellent senses." He leaned into her touch. "I am going to love anything you wear. But I would not dream of spoiling the surprise."

"That's good, because I think I've been dreaming of it for the last *cycle*. And I really think the look on your face will be far better than I imagine."

"I would never stand in the way of your dreams." He nuzzled her nose with his. "Truly, though, every time I look at you, you take my breath away. From the moment I bumped into you, it has been like that." It still felt so bizarre how much everything had changed since they'd met just a few months ago. They had their own home together, shared a bed together. Sometimes, he worried it had all just been a dream. "I still do not know what I have done to deserve you. I do not know how I got so lucky. You are my everything. There are moments I fear I will wake up and still be back there. That none of this ever really happened."

Gently, she pressed her forehead to his. "Sometimes, I think the same thing. I'm not the same as I was when we met. And I can't figure out how that female deserved you, or what she did to be given someone so wonderful. I don't know if you see that, but you are truly a gift, and I thank the gods we—I—bumped into you."

She was wrong. After the argument he'd gotten into with Derrick, along with his anger, he'd been the one to bump into her. But he wouldn't argue with her. It didn't matter. He wouldn't change a thing. "I am not the same as I was when we met, either. You have changed me, all for the better." He slowly stroked the nape of her neck. "Do you know what I think? I think... that the fates decided we were two very broken beings who needed each other to put each other back together. I may not feel like a gift to anyone, but you believe that of me. And you are a gift to me as well."

Lacing their fingers together, Jocasta closed her eyes. She brushed a soft kiss across his lips. As her eyelids cracked open, those amber orbs of hers were glowing, bright like the sun. A small gasp left her mouth. "You may be right, because I feel pieced back together."

He knew that, with so many mixed parts, she hadn't been sure what would occur to symbolize their mated bond. Though he didn't need to see it to know her heart, he couldn't have asked for anything better. Their eyes, glowing together, lit up the room, washing over the walls in the most exquisite coloring he'd ever seen. "Gods, you are breathtaking," Pierce breathed out. "You have put me back together, too. Before meeting you, I never felt whole. Something was always missing, and there was a darkness inside me with the emptiness. It never went away. Not until you."

Wetness welled in the corners of her eyes as her features brightened. "I love you, Pierce. My love, my mate, my king."

"I love you, Jocasta. My love, my life, my mate, my queen. "He gently brushed the tears from her face as he rolled her beneath him. "I cannot wait to spend every *umbra* for the rest of my life with you." Her head tilted back as he trailed kisses down her jaw and throat. He felt the need rise within her. A calling he would happily answer. A low growl left him as he licked up her neck, nipped her ear, and kneaded her breast. Her body arched beneath his touch. "I need you again."

She stroked the back of his head and caressed his ears. "Then take me. My body is yours."

Pierce let out a rumble of pleasure as he teased her flesh, kissing down her body. Taking his time, he savored every inch of her sweet, perfect skin. He lapped at her ample cleavage, sucking and nipping her puckered nipples. With a gasp, her nails dug into his scalp before he made it any lower. As he licked down her stomach, stopping at her navel, he smirked. "Are you sure you are not too tired, my love?" He brushed the tips of his claws over her hips.

"Not at all," she panted out. Arching into his touch, her legs slid up along his waist, and she gently dragged her talons over the curves of his ass to the small of his back.

Pierce moaned. Gods, what she did to him. Each touch from her talons sent an electric hum down his spine, straight to his cock. Which was throbbing now. Not that he knew how it was even possible for it to get so hard this many times in so short a time. "Gods, I love that." As he settled between her thighs, he propped her legs up over his shoulders. He growled as the scent of her arousal hit him full force. Skimming his claws up her belly and ribcage, he cupped her swollen breasts. She grabbed his wrists, locking them in place against her.

He dipped the tip of his tongue inside her, getting just another small taste, before licking up her slit. Languidly, he reached her nub and sucked it hard into his mouth. The tip of a fang barely nipped it before his tongue swirled around it. Releasing her sex, he lifted his glowing gaze to her. "I am going to devour you."

Keeping his hands in place, her back arched as she massaged her own breasts through his touch. Her nipples pebbled beneath his palms. Her talons curled against his shoulders, biting slightly into his flesh. "Oh, gods, yes, Pierce."

His body pulsated with need. Teasing his tongue inside her, he growled as her taste exploded on his tongue. He slipped it in and out of her in a slow rhythm, his fangs grazing the outside of her plump lips, drawing her closer to that exquisite edge. Removing a hand from his wrist, she clutched at the sheet beneath her body and cried out in ecstasy, a sound that resounded through their entire bedroom.

He would never get enough of her noises or her taste. With a growl that shook the bed and echoed around the room, he swallowed every drop she gave to him, lapping at her until she trembled. With a kiss to her inner thighs, Pierce skimmed his fangs over her hips and swept the tip of his tongue up her belly, before nipping at her ears. When he hovered completely over her, their gazes locked together, his body stilled. Flushed and panting, she parted her lips, her eyes half-open, her hair a mess. She was a goddess in the flesh. Utter perfection. "I love you. So very much."

In these quiet moments, the beating of their hearts synced perfectly. It just showed how truly meant to be they were. Jocasta placed a hand on his chest and took one of his, laying it across her own. "I love you, too. With all my heart, all my soul, and with everything I have. Every part of me belongs to you."

The beat of her heart pulsed beneath his palm, but he could feel it within him, too. He could feel the heat of her skin beneath his own as he stared at her. Those gorgeous amber orbs staring back, infused with want, understanding, and love. She hadn't just healed him. She filled the cracks in his soul, giving him something he hadn't even realized he was missing.

"It was never just fucking with you. Even when I tried to tell myself it was because I had no other choice, it was always more than that. You stole me away from purgatory, and you brought me to paradise. You own me, every part of me. I could never bear to live without you." He kissed her. It was languid and passionate as that undeniable desire built inside of him. He needed her. More than food, more than air, more than anything. "I am yours, and you are mine." As he slid inside her, her name left his mouth in a whisper. He held her body against his own as they joined, their bodies claiming each other.

No other words needed to be said. Not because they couldn't, but because they were two halves coming together as a whole. And nothing was louder than that. She brought his lips to hers. Their tongues danced as their bodies came together in this sacred union. They had desired one another from the second their gazes had first met. Even when they had tried to deny how much they cared, the truth had been there, right at the edge for their taking.

And they had taken it.

As Pierce plunged inside her, her sex sheathed his cock perfectly. Their bodies moved together in flawless rhythm, giving and taking inequal measure. His growls, her cries, and their mutual moans filled the room with unearthly music. Their eyes glowed so brightly it was as if a supernova exploded.

He broke apart, then shattered. She put him back together so they could do it all over again.

Pierce rolled over without leaving the warmth of her body. He held her hips as she straddled him, his cock still rock hard inside her. "Ride me, my queen."

"Yes, my king." Fusing their lips together in a slow dance, she widened her thighs as far as they would go and curled her feet beneath his legs, her talons wrapping around his thighs. She pumped back, each movement unhurried and welcoming.

The light of their union wiped out the darkness of their past. Leaving it all behind as a distant memory. Not to be forgotten, but no longer a part of their future. Together, they wrote something new. A love they would forever celebrate.

As she rocked her body against him, his hips lifting to meet her each time, his hands touched her everywhere he could reach. He couldn't get enough of her, and he never would. Long before this moment between them now, she had found her way into his heart, and into his soul. He couldn't exist without her. And, gods, he would never want to. Holding her against him, he claimed her mouth. When they reached that mutual peak, they came together in perfect unison. As he filled her up and her honey coated him, it was a moment before he drew breath. No sound came from him. Then he let loose an echoing howl that shook the walls that made up their room.

Jocasta pressed a tender kiss to his chest. It would forever be amongst his favorite places for her to kiss him. Her gaze flicked over the walls and her features lit up. It was good to know that, despite the way they shook, they were sturdy. Without moving from his chest, she snuggled close. There were no words to describe what had just transpired between them. It was the most exquisite union. One that made him feel blessed, like he would've never thought possible.

"I love you, Pierce." Joy and the best kind of exhaustion laced her words.

He nuzzled her neck and placed a kiss there as he held her close. A smile beamed across his face, his heart swelling to the point he thought it might burst. "I love you too, Jocasta." Laying his head on top of hers, he curled his tail and settled it over her rear as he gently stroked her skin. "Sleep, my queen. We have much ahead of us."

As she drifted to sleep in his arms, he couldn't remember ever having felt so content, so joyful, or so hopeful about the future. Because he never had. Closing his eyes, he held his queen close as the best sleep of his life took him away.

Chapter Eleven

Logan sighed. His task had taken longer than he'd expected, but it had been a necessary one. The dirt from digging Evan's head up still sat beneath his claws. He would need to clean up before he sat down with his family for morning meal. Though he needed to talk to Lilli first. His conversation with his mate last night told him as much. He couldn't put off telling Lilli about his empathic ability. Not any longer. Logan opened the front door to his home, and his gaze fell to his sister as she stepped into the front room. The door clapped shut behind him. "Good morning, Lilli."

"Good morning, Logan," she whispered. Hesitantly, she shuffled across the room, wrapping her arms around herself. Her amethyst eyes locked onto the floor. "I am sorry for last night," she said, her voice meek. "I know Am said I did not need to be, but I am still sorry."

"You do not need to apologize. Ever." In three long strides, he closed the distance between them and embraced her. Gods, he and Pierce were going to kill every single Informant who had ever dared to lay a hand on their sister. He kissed the top of her head. "If you are up for it, I would like to speak with you. In your room, if that is okay."

"Of course. I…" Her words trailed off, but he didn't need her to finish them. He felt the relief that he wasn't angry wash through her. Hades, he hated she had ever worried about that. "I would like that."

Logan gestured down the hall and gave his mate a brief dip of his chin as they passed by. Once they were in Lilli's bedroom, he did as Ambrosia had suggested and left the door partially cracked. A chair. He should put a chair in here for her. There was enough room. It would be good.

Lilli sat down on the bed and tucked her feet up underneath her. When he just stood there for a minute, she smiled a little at him. "You can sit down with me. It is okay," she stated. "I do not want anyone to feel like they have to be careful... not to make me nervous. Does that make sense?"

"Yes, it does." He wasn't just trying to ensure she was comfortable, but himself as well. He didn't know how she would take what he had to tell her, but he wouldn't hide it from her, either. Swallowing the lump in the back of his throat, he sat down on the bed and leaned forward, digging his elbows into his knees. His eyes flicked to her. "I never want you to think that I am angry with you. Though you have seen me angry, it was not directed at you."

Silence stretched briefly between them. "Last night, Am said you feel things a little more than most people do. I did not know what that meant, but I did not ask her then."

Which he was a little appreciative of. It was better that he explained, so he could answer his sister's questions. "She is right. I am what is called an empath. I can feel your emotions as if they were my own. If a memory strikes you, I feel what happened as if it happened to me."

Her eyes widened, and she gasped. "Oh, gods. So... so last night..." She winced. "Did—" Lilli took a breath, then bit her lip. She inhaled another before fixing her eyes on him. "How much did Pierce tell you?"

"Very little." He paused. "I picked up some when we first met and more during afternoon meal yesterday. And last night..." Logan cleared his throat. He had to keep his emotions in check for her sake. He'd spent years learning to be careful in enormous crowds. Emotions could easily overwhelm him. He seemed to be more susceptible to her and Pierce's feelings. Though, perhaps it had more to do with seeing and speaking to Pierce for the first time in nearly two decades. And meeting Lilli, with how close he used to be to their mother. "We did not want you to think I was angry with you."

"I do not think I really thought you were. It is just, in those moments, it is hard to separate reality from memory." She squeezed his hand. "I am glad that you told me. And I understand why Pierce did not talk about it. He hates himself and thinks he could not keep me safe. He is wrong, though. Were it not for him, it would have been much worse for me."

Logan clasped her hand, reassuring himself this was the right path. "He and I, we both have regrets. Ambrosia reminds me many times that I cannot change the past, but I can affect the future. I try to remind Pierce of that, too." This wasn't the only thing he had to tell her. He and Pierce had agreed; she deserved to know what happened to Evan. He may not have known, but that was one head he was happy had rolled. "Pierce and I, we have spent many *solaris* apart. We slowly remember what the other is capable of." He stopped again, giving himself a moment before he continued. "There is one other thing I wish to tell you."

"What is it?"

While he could draw it out and explain exactly what had occurred, he wouldn't unless she asked him for details. She only needed to know one of her attackers was no more. "Evan, he is dead."

She was quiet, and he could feel it when the realization hit her. "You killed him?"

"Yes. During afternoon meal, you did not say his entire name, but you said enough. I did not know he had harmed you." If he had, he would have taken longer to kill the male. Made it much more painful than it had been.

She sat there quietly, processing. After a beat, the corners of her mouth lifted just a touch. "I am glad." Her arms came around him as she hugged him hard. "Thank you," Lilli whispered. "Even if you did not know when you killed him... thank you."

Gods, at least he could give her something, even if it happened unintentionally. "I would do anything for you, sister mine."

"I know you would." She squeezed him tighter, and then sat back. "I do not want to be sad or scared anymore. While I am angry about a lot of things, I do not want to be angry anymore either. I may have some moments, probably a lot of them. Talking about it may help, but I do not know. I just... I want to be okay."

"Talking through our past pains can be helpful. Just to have someone to listen and to be there. I have spoken with Ambrosia about many things from my past, and it has eased me in ways I did not know possible. I believe the same has happened with Jocasta and Pierce. If that is something you wish to do, any of us will be here for you." He could promise her that. He would keep control of whatever emotions he got from her if she decided she wanted to talk it through with him. They all needed to heal. And they would.

Clutching his hand, she cracked a faint smile. "I would really, truly like that. I do not think that I could talk to Pierce about it. He would, if I asked. I know he would, but he was there for too much. Saw too much. And he took too much pain upon himself. Do you think... would it be too much if, sometime, we...?"

"If that is what you want." He would see her soul restored. See the joy on her face and the light in her eyes every day. He would see her through her pain so she could get to the other side. His sister deserved nothing less. "You can talk to me about whatever you wish."

Lilli embraced him. "Thank you, brother mine." As she sat back, her face beamed with optimism. "You know, you can talk to me, too. I am not so bad to talk to." She nudged him playfully with her elbow.

He chuckled softly. "No, you are not. It has simply been some time since I could talk to anyone. Perhaps I can regale you with tales of our mother. You look so much like her, and she and I were quite close." As much as it might sadden him, he could do that much. Anything else, his sister was far too young to hear. Nor did she require any weight beyond what she already carried.

"I would love that. I would love that very much."

"So would I." Logan stood and pressed a kiss to the top of her head, draping an arm across her shoulders. "Now, let us go to morning meal before it gets cold."

"That sounds like a wonderful idea. I am starving." She leaned into him as he led her toward the long dining room table.

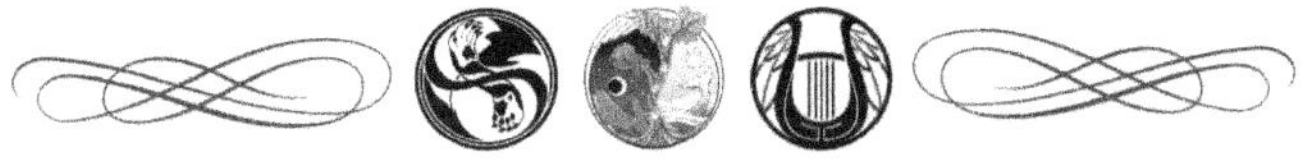

Devin left the village, winding around the tall trees toward the burbling sounds of the nearby river. Stepping through a small underbrush, her gaze fell on Gabby. The female was in her humanoid form, sitting on the bank, staring out at the blue water, her hand over her belly. She had to be around halfway through her pregnancy. Hades, how was Gabby still hiding it? With a shake of her head, Devin moved to the riverbank, shifted to her humanoid form, and sat down next to her friend. Her feet dangled slightly in the water.

"My father has been speaking to Ramsey," Gabby mumbled.

"I know," Devin replied. The context of the conversations didn't need to be spoken aloud. It wasn't like Gembert or Ramsey kept too quiet about it. Even if they had, there was really only one thing two Informant stalked about behind closed doors. Especially when one of them had a son, and one of them had a daughter. They could come to an agreement quick sometimes. Sometimes, it took weeks. Occasionally, it had taken months. It all depended on how quickly the details—the amount of the payment—were all figured out. How much the male son pushed back against the mating.

"I do not know what to do," Gabby whispered. She turned her head away a bit, wiping away a tear.

"You know my answer to that. You know what is going to happen if you stay."

"I know."

Several things would happen. Things that they could avoid if Gabby would just listen to sense. But she also knew Gabby wouldn't leave. No matter the consequences. Not until she could safely get her mother out and ensure that Gavin would come, too. Devin let out a soft sigh. It was a decision that would not end well. For any of them. "How much time do you have?"

"I do not know. Negotiations... they do not seem to be moving rapidly."

"Well, that is something." Silence stretched between them. She knew how Gabby felt about Arman, and knew exactly what it stemmed from, too. "He is not a bad male."

Gabby scoffed. "Do not say things like that to me. You know how I feel about him. What he has done—"

"What they forced him to do. Just like many others here. You know that."

"Gavin almost died because of him."

"I know he did. But Arman did not have a choice. No more than Pierce or Chaz did. Especially Chaz."

"What is that supposed to mean?"

"You know what I mean. Chaz has no control over his mind. He has not, for a very long time."

"And that is supposed to make it okay?"

"No. Of course not. But his choices are not his own. Pierce's choices were for protecting his sister. Arman's are for self-preservation. Just like many others here."

"My father truly hates me. To think of mating me to someone who did those things, to my brother. His son."

Yes, well, Gembert didn't claim his son. Not really. "I wish you would just leave, Gabby."

"I know. But I cannot. Not yet."

A large bout of air expelled from her mouth. "Then you are going to have to resign yourself to what is going to happen. *All* of what is going to happen."

"I am already mated; I cannot..."

The salty scent of Gabby's tears reached Devin. No matter how much the female kept her face turned away, trying to hide them. "If you will not leave, there is nothing you can do about it. If you do not leave... you need to accept what is coming." She was talking about more than the possibility that her father would mate her to another male. If Gabby continued to refuse to leave, as soon as they inevitably discovered her pregnancy, she would lose another young. This time by force.

"I cannot leave my mother here to die. How could I ever do something so selfish?"

"It is not selfish to protect your young, Gabby. Your mother would tell you the same thing. We can save not everyone. Your mother has made her choice. Make yours, not only for yourself but for your mate and your young as well."

"And if I cannot?" Gabby's words came out breathy, almost inaudible.

Devin couldn't immediately respond. She wouldn't say aloud the certainty that would occur regarding the young in Gabby's womb. It didn't need to be said. Devin couldn't have children herself, but she couldn't fathom the choices her friend was making. It wasn't her place to judge, though. She'd tried time and time again to make Gabby see sense, as had Derrick, but to no avail. But the rest... "Then Arman will officially become your mate, probably sooner rather than later. Arman would... he would treat you well. As an Informant especially, he only does what he is told. But he is not a cruel male, and not one to take a female by force. He would treat you... well." It wasn't what any of them involved in the situation would want. Not at all. But if Gabby continued to stay in the village, it was exactly what would eventually happen.

"I need to be alone," Gabby whispered. "Please."

"Of course. I have to, uh, I have to go do some things, anyway. I will see you later. Alright?"

"Sure. Later."

Devin hesitated, then shifted to her animal form and rose to her feet. There were a million things she could say at the moment, but none would make any difference. Gabby, at least for now, was past listening. She'd given up. Hopefully—gods, hopefully—that would change. And soon.

Without another word, Devin turned and walked away from the boundaries. She needed to get to the marketplace.

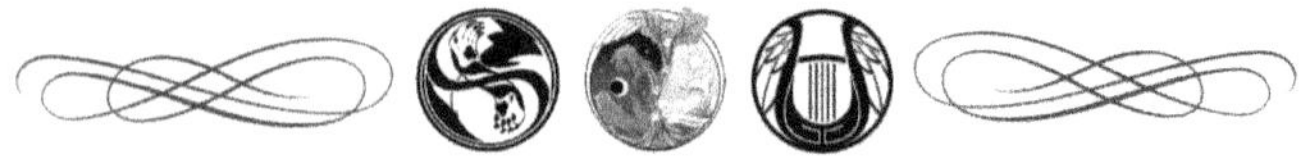

Zinnia finally got up the courage to approach Markham's hut. Nearly a full day had passed since her siblings left the village. She'd made a mistake by waiting so long, but she couldn't wait any longer. Questions were already being asked about where Pierce and Lillianna had gone. Tensions were high, with Evan missing as well. He'd been truly loyal to their King, and his absence didn't bode well.

She bore jagged marks across her cheek from when she'd told her father she did not know of their whereabouts. He knew she wasn't uttering the truth. Earlier, he'd interrupted her meal, giving her one last chance to come clean. She hadn't finished her food. Instead, she'd risen from the spot she sat and headed on all fours across the center of the village. While he'd likely meant for her to tell him, she needed to be the one to tell Markham. That was the right thing to do. She had the information, so she should tell the King.

The closer she got to the doorway of his hut, the more her fur stood on end until she stood right outside. The darkness nearly choked her. But there was no other choice. She had to tell him the truth. It didn't matter that, in her heart of hearts, she didn't wish to betray Pierce. She didn't want to reveal his treachery, that he'd taken Lillianna and joined up with Logan. It was the last thing she wanted to do.

But she had no choice.

Zinnia barely registered the metallic scent lingering in the air as she knocked on the jamb with the back of her paw and requested permission to enter. The coppery stench inside his hut was nothing new or unnatural.

"Zinnia. Enter."

A shudder passed through her. Was it her smell or her thoughts that he reacted to? Did he know? Did he know how much she hated him? Feared him?

"I said 'enter.'"

She pushed the door open and treaded inside slowly.

"Close the door."

After a moment, she eased it shut. He was in his animal form, as he always was, but sitting upright in a chair that she wouldn't call a chair. No, it was more like a throne. It was difficult not to focus on the carvings upon it. Gruesome depictions of murder, punctuated by red paint to signify blood. The carvings made her want to vomit. His giant claws, which were as dark as night, curled over the edges of the arms of his throne. They scraped back, returned to the edges, then scratched along the grain, gouging splinters into the wood. Zinnia clenched her teeth together. His paws were as large as her head, perhaps bigger. And the reddish-black jewel set in the skull of his circlet crown made it appear as if the skull glared at her.

"I already know why you are here. What I wish to know is why you took your time in coming to me."

"I—" Zinnia snapped her jaws shut. No words she could utter would lessen her punishment. The less she said, the better. "I have no excuse. Except that he is my brother, my blood. To see him punished pains me."

"Oh, but it will not be a mere punishment. Punishments seem to have done very little in convincing your brother not to break my laws." Markham reached slightly behind him to a table that was set to his right and brought forth—

Oh, gods. It was ahead separated from its body. It was Evan's. Her stomach recoiled. Markham lazily tossed the head at her. It hit the floor, then rolled until it stopped right in front of her. The dead eyes met her stare. Her stomach lurched again. Gods, she hoped she didn't vomit all over his floor.

"There is no scent of Pierce upon it. It may have been very many *solaris*, but I still remember your brother Logan's scent," Markham growled. "Do you think me stupid? That I do not know what has happened, and where Pierce has gone? That I do not know who he is with?" He let out a wry chuckle. "Yes, I will admit to not knowing their location on the isle, but they are still on the isle. And they are together. Are they not?"

It would do her no good to lie. He already knew the truth, and he knew she knew. "Yes. Pierce has taken Lillianna, and they have gone to wherever Logan is."

Markham cocked his head to the side. "That brings you joy. Whatever opinion you display outwardly, that both your brothers and your sister are safe, brings you joy." Zinnia said nothing, and he cackled. "You do not have to say it. I already know. I can feel it. In you."

A rumbling growl vibrated the walls of his hut as he shoved against the arms of the chair and rose on his hind paws. Zinnia cowered, her body trembling. Even on all fours, he stood two feet taller than she did. Standing fully upright as he was now, he reached ten feet in height, and she was only four.

In her state, she had no chance to get away, or make any attempt to flee. She couldn't have anyway, and it would have heightened her punishment. His paw came toward her. His claws swiped across the entirety of her face. Zinnia fell back, and his claws gouged down her chest. Blood gushed over her and covered the floor. The white and tan of her fur became stained with red, the black darkened. She couldn't even cry out. The force of the blow stole all the breath from her lungs.

He enclosed his fist. It felt as if a vice grip closed around her throat and her heart rapidly slowed. She'd seen this used before on others, she'd never had it used on her. Markham was killing her without even touching her. Her body lifted from the ground. It was actually a relief when he threw her into the side of his hut. The wood splintered and her body slammed down onto the floor. His footsteps shook the ground as he closed the distance between them.

"Get out of my hut, mongrel. I will have you taint my doorway no longer." His paw connected with her side with a loud snap. She yelped. With the wave of a paw, the door swung open, seemingly of its own volition.

Zinnia did not know how she got to her feet, yet she somehow made it outside, though her body dragged. She didn't know how long she heaved herself along the dirt before black fur came into her vision—what remained of it. Her gaze lifted. She barely made out Dahlia's face.

"I told you that you were an idiot." Dahlia sneered. "You should have never gone to speak with him. Pierce became a traitor the moment he even considered leaving the pack."

"Dahlia..." Her voice was weak.

"What? You should have expected nothing less. From him, or from our King."

"Help me, sister," Zinnia pleaded.

"Help yourself." She turned away, then looked back over her shoulder. "You should take the pain like a true shape shifter. You are an embarrassment and a disgrace."

Zinnia collapsed and quickly forced herself back up to her feet. She couldn't stay in the middle of the village, unmoving, with a blood pooling beneath her. In the past, several of the males had descended upon the weak and ripped them apart. Finally reaching the hut, it was blessedly empty. She was prepared to go inside, intent on laying on her pallet. Because if she was going to die, which was how it felt, at least she would die comfortably—a shadow appeared over her shoulder. A low, menacing growl followed.

"You disobeyed me."

Startled, Zinnia squeaked and fell over onto her side with a yelp. She peered at the dark shape behind her, but couldn't quite make out her father's face. His fur was black from the tip of his toes to the tip of his tail, just like Pierce. But his eyes were a silvery gray, so light they were almost white. Ailwin, when angry, was the thing of nightmares.

"I ordered you to stay out of it. Just as I ordered you not to say anything to our King."

"I just wanted to... to do the right thing. You said I had to come clean. I only did... what I thought was right."

"You were to come clean to me. Come clean to me, and *I* would go to our King." Ailwin snarled and put his face right up next to hers. He must have just finished eating something or attacking someone because blood dribbled out of his mouth. A drop hit her eye. Blinking, she winced and let out a bark of pain. "You are a fool, Zinnia," he snarled. "You are a *female*, and it was not your place to go in front of our King. Informant business should be left to the Informants. You should have remembered your place. Your wounds are your own fault. And I hope you perish from them." He rose to his full height and glared at her. "I have but one child. Just the one who has never disappointed me. I renounce the rest of you. Do not cross this threshold ever again. This is no longer your home. I care not where you go." He turned his head away from her. "And I do not want your blood on my floor." Once he'd entered the hut, Ailwin kicked the door shut hard behind him.

As Zinnia did the best she could to rise from the ground again, she couldn't stop the burning tears that coursed down her face.

Chapter Twelve

arkham had sat on his throne for hours with his claws curled over the ends of the arms. Evening meal had passed by now. The door of his hut stood wide open. He didn't need it open, though, to know the emotions that had spread through the village like wildfire. A mixture of anger, confusion, sadness, worry, and fear. Informants had been out scouting since before Zinnia had come to him this morning. It was the procedure when an Informant didn't return home. He would have used his shadows also to look for those who had fled, but they remained tied to his cave. Even Ailwin had gone out looking for his children. Not hoping he'd find them safe. Oh, no. Hoping he would be the one to bring about their demise. The thought brought a smile to his face. Or would have if he did such a thing. It would certainly not happen in his current mood.

He knew where they were. Pierce. Logan. Lillianna. The only place on the isle he couldn't feel the existence of their life force. That cursed hybrid village. The one place he could not find. The one place he could not penetrate. His claws dug into the arms of the chair, scratching over the splintered grain.

The sound of his Informants returning reached him long before they reentered the village. Markham said nothing. They would know to come to him upon their arrival. As they emerged into the clearing—by themselves or in twos, as well as a couple of groups—there wasn't a single member of the village who didn't get out of their way. They were a force to be reckoned with on a good day. With tensions spiraling, the village gave them an even wider birth. They gathered in front of his hut in rows, the felines and canines separate as always. He used to have so many more. Over the years, their lives had ended.

He waited until they all stilled, every pair of eyes trained on him. "Report." After several minutes of silence, it was Ashar who stepped forward. He was a fairly young canine, not too many years out of adolescence. He had no family left. Markham regarded the rest of them. "One so young must speak for all of you?" he sneered. He fixed his gaze back on Ashar. "As you were."

"We have found no sign of them, Your Majesty. We will keep searching until we fulfill our duty, and the order that you have given to us."

"No sign. After all of your searching. Not a single one of you has found them? Oh. Wait. One of you *found* them—at least one of them. They found Logan. Evan. Right before he lost *this*." Reaching to the table on his right, Markham gripped the head with his claws and hurled it at them. They parted quickly down the middle, allowing the head to roll between them and to the center of the clearing. Many of them scrunched their noses up in disgust.

"Is that not a sight you enjoy seeing? I assure you; I do not enjoy the fact that a mongrel who has evaded me for over eighteen *solaris* could get the upper hand on one of you. He was never even one of mine. He did not accept the title that I offered to him. And then he committed a significant form of treachery against me. Yet he was not the one who lost his head."

Pushing himself up off of his throne, he dropped to all fours and strode out of his hut. They all wanted to back away, but none of them dared. He stopped right in front of them, just standing there for a moment. Many of his villagers looked on warily.

In the blink of an eye, he snapped his jaws, closed his mouth around Ashar's head and bit down, clean through the neck. Cracks, snaps, and crunches echoed around the clearing. With a jerk, he ripped the head from the canine's body. Frightened, surprised gasps and screams came from the onlookers in the clearing. Markham relished it all before he spat the remains of the male's head out, letting it join his crumpled body on the ground. Blood spewed everywhere and drizzled down Markham's chin.

After several minutes, he roared. The silence in the village was immediate. He glared down at his Informants. "I want every one of you out at first light," he snarled. "They *will* be found. For every head that is dropped in my village, I will add another one of yours to it." None of his Informants moved or spoke. He nudged Ashar's body with his paw. "Skin and clean him, but save the heart. Clean the head too. He will make a pleasant addition to my hut."

Zinnia wandered through the woods, her feet shuffling through detritus and thick greenery. She did not know where she was going. She had nothing left. Nothing and no one. When she next took stock of her surroundings, she was in a small cave. Her feet must have just led her there. It was her one place of refuge, but she didn't want to stay here, let alone die here. She went inside anyway and retrieved the only thing of precious value she had.

It was a lily flower carved out of wood—the only thing that remained of Logan's creations that their father had burned. She'd saved it for their mother, then hidden it upon Sabina's death.

Using what little capacity she had of her teeth, she wrapped it in a thick cloth, not wanting to get any blood on it. She would hold on to it. Walk until some creature took her down, or she succumbed to her wounds. But she would not go back. There was no point. Her home was gone, and she had ostracized every member of her family that had ever truly loved her. Long ago, her father ordered her to no longer speak of Logan, not to love Lillianna, and then Zinnia denied Pierce his request to leave with him. They all must hate her. Not that she would blame them.

She could only blame herself.

Gods, she was so stupid. Her father was right. She truly was a fool. Why had she not just left with Pierce? Why had she let her fear hold her back? But why not? It was what she'd always done. The dread of what would happen ruled her. Her desire to fit in had always controlled her actions, determining what she did and didn't do.

Zinnia wound her way through the cavernous corridors with the wrapped-up wooden flower tucked as tightly into her mangled jaws as she could get it. As she walked, her heart cried out for her brothers, her soul prayed that they and her sister were safe. She and Logan had used to be so close. Pierce had always wanted to protect her, and she had always refused to let him in. As for Lillianna, they had no hope; not in that place.

She trudged along until the sun set and a chill set into the air. Until her vision all but failed her, and her chest ached from more than just her wounds.

If she was lucky, she wouldn't make it until morning. Not that she could sit still.

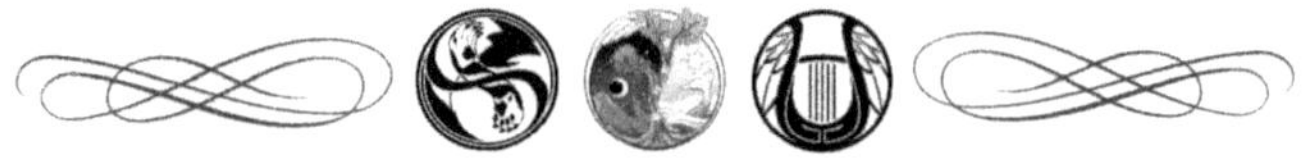

Gavin frowned. They'd searched through books for months and still hadn't found out anything about their sexual issues. He hated to think of it like that, but they couldn't kiss, couldn't really touch each other, and still couldn't have sex. Not that it had deterred them much. They were in the treehouse again. Parthenia leaned against his pecs with a book held in her lap. He only half-paid attention to the written words in front of him.

Parthenia suddenly bolted upright, her eyes moving across the paragraph again. Flipping the page, a single piece of parchment fell out of the tome. Gavin set his book aside as he sat up, dropping a kiss on her shoulder. "What is it, love?"

"I think I found an answer. Though it isn't much of anything." She collected the thin sheet of papyrus that had fallen and carefully unfolded it.

He picked what she'd been reading and eyeballed the words. "Cursed?" He glanced at the yellowed parchment she held. He tried to read it, but he couldn't make out much of the handwriting. "You would think this book could be at least a little more descriptive on that, huh?"

He felt her agreement. Gavin looked back down at the pages of her book. *Sirens took action against a goddess.* What goddess? *As a result, that goddess cursed them.* What curse? Could they break it? How did they break it? It mentioned none of that. Well, that wasn't altogether helpful.

Parthenia read through the letter once, then a second time. It wasn't very long. "Well, this confirms my theory that our history isn't accurate. There's one tome that holds all the answers. Bad news, it's not in the library. Good news. We only have to look for a map to find it."

He ran his finger slowly under the words on the paper as he made them out.

'The truth of the siren history is not protected within these walls. To prevent any information regarding the history, prophecies, and more, Celestimo, the one book with all the answers, we have hidden. If you have found this letter, we separately placed a map amongst the ancient texts that will direct you to Celestimo. Should you locate the map, take precaution, as the journey will not be easy. -A-'

"Ancient texts. That is the section we have been looking in already, yes? It is quite large. How are we supposed to find a map in all of those books?"

"Yeah. That's where we've been scouring. I know we've only gone through a small portion. But this at least limits what we have to look for, instead of having to read through all of them. And at least once we find it, it'll lead us to the tome that's going to detail everything." That was how the letter made it sound, anyway. "Even if we don't know the exact curse, it would explain what we've experienced."

"Yes. Though it is a very mean curse." He nuzzled her neck. "Do you think the book we have to find will tell us how to break it?"

Parthenia's mouth down-turned as she glanced back at the thick, brown leather bound text. "It is mean. I wonder if..." She shook her head. "Well, if it's going to tell us the truth about our history, then I would think so. It would make sense if it gives details about the curse, then it would say how to break it."

Gods, it was difficult to concentrate today. He was catching less of what was on her mind than usual. It unnerved him. Breathing in her scent was the best at clearing the uneasiness that tickled the edges of his senses. He kept his face in the crook of her neck. "Mmm. Well, I certainly hope so. Breaking this curse would be a wonderful thing indeed." He swept his tongue across her soft skin. "What goddess?"

"Nemesis. She's renowned for her curses." Parthenia smirked.

"I know little about the subject. I am just following your lead. That would make sense, though, that it could be her." If he recalled correctly, Nemesis was the Goddess of Revenge. It would just be nice to know the cause. Then it might give them an idea of how to break it.

Parthenia stroked the back of his head. "Is everything okay? I can tell something's bothering you."

"Things are just very tense in the village." That was putting it extremely lightly. "Markham is in a bad mood."

"Oh? Has something outside the normal happened?"

"Mhm. One of his Informants is,"—Gavin made sure he kept the memory of that morning blocked—"dead. Someone killed him. Another one has disappeared with his younger sister."

Parthenia's eyes popped wide. "Good Demeter. That *has* caused some distress in your village. You don't think... will that make things more difficult for you?"

"Probably." He blew out a heavy breath. He hated the idea of spending more time away from her. "At least for a little while. He is... furious. I almost did not get out this morning, but I could not stay there today. I needed to see you." The damn head had almost hit him when it had dropped out of the sky. Thankfully, he'd kept that image out of his mind, though. It was definitely not something his mate needed to see. No.

Parthenia set the parchment down and faced him, straddling his lap. Resting her arms across his broad shoulders, she gingerly ran her fingertips up and down the back of his head. Neither of them had any idea how to get past this, only that they had to.

He nuzzled her throat and stroked the soft down of her wings. Sleep had become almost impossible for him. He knew it was the same for her. Most nights, he was afraid to do so. It took every ounce of willpower to keep his thoughts shielded, to keep them from straying to her. She was all he wanted to think about. But if Markham truly could read thoughts, he couldn't take the chance that any images or thoughts of her would reach the male. "I wish it could be like this always." Gavin bit his tongue. Voicing wishes was painful. They would be together always at some point. That moment just seemed so very far away.

"It will. Soon, my love. We have everything I need to go to, my Elder. And I've been tracking Fagonia's movements. I believe I've found a window for approach; I just need to watch her a little longer to confirm."

"Just promise me you will be careful."

"Of course. I'm extremely careful. I want to ensure I keep coming back to you until we are together for always."

He nestled against her throat, stopping over her pulse point. "Your scent, feeling your heartbeat... it eases me," he murmured.

"As does yours. Just being close to you settles me."

"Just being around you..." He swept his tongue across the smooth column of her throat. "Mmm. So. If we know we are looking for a map, and we know where it is, hopefully, it will not be too difficult to find."

"Mmm, hopefully not. Though if the letter is correct, following the map may prove difficult." Not likely more difficult than what they had already endured. Her fingers skimmed along the nape of his neck. "I'm certain we will overcome any obstacles."

"Together, there is no obstacle that we cannot overcome." He punctuated his words with slow strokes of his tongue, then grazed his fangs down her neck and over her shoulder. "It may be a hard path, but it will be worth it."

A soft moan left her mouth as her head fell back. Her nails grazed the back of his neck a little harder. "Yes, it will. Very worth it."

A quiet growl rumbled deep in his chest. Gods, he loved the little pinpricks as her nails bit into his flesh. "Does that feel good, my love?" He licked down her collarbone.

"Yes, it does. Every part of you feels good." She ran her fingers up and down his spine. "It seems you enjoy it as much as I do."

"Yes, I do. Very much so. Everything you do to me feels amazing." At least what he'd so far felt. One day, they would know every part of each other. He trailed his lips and his tongue lower, stopping before he hit the swell of her breasts. Parting his mouth slightly, his tongue snaked out. Hmm. He couldn't touch them with his hands, just as he couldn't touch her sex. But he could lick her sex. Maybe he could lick these, too. "I want to try something. Would you lay down for me?" If it was something else they couldn't do, he didn't want her getting hurt. But oh, he wanted to know what they felt like in his mouth, against his tongue.

Parthenia raised an eyebrow. She must have caught the images in his head. "Would you like me to remove my shirt first? Or would you like to remove it?"

He growled softly. "I think I would like to remove it." This shirt of hers zipped in the front. It would be easy to take off. Gavin placed a kiss on either side of her mouth before taking the fastener in his hand. He could feel the excitement in her as he peeled the top from her body. The anticipation built as he unzipped the top and revealed her breasts. A low rumble vibrated in his chest. Not that he understood much about clothing, but he liked this one. The way it split in two, only showing the sides of her breasts at first, teasing him. Gavin pushed it off of her shoulders, then licked his lips. "I like this shirt."

"I think it just became my favorite." With her top off, she did as he had previously asked and eased her body to the bedding. Her wings pressed into it first, then her back as her hands came down above her head.

"Mine too. You should *definitely* wear it again." He licked his lips as his gaze trailed over. Gods, she was so beautiful. The way she looked at him, how her arms stretched above her head, lifting her breasts. He couldn't stop the groan as he hovered over her. "I could stare at you every moment for forever and still not get enough." Dropping his head, he extended his tongue and licked over her pale pink buds.

Parthenia gasped, her nipples pebbling. Her body utterly stilled, though he could sense the need within her to grab hold of his shoulders and run her fingers along his arms. Another of those exquisite noises left her as he lashed the tip of her nipple with his tongue.

"I love that sound. And I love licking you here." Gavin caught her gaze and growled as he twirled his tongue around her pert nipple. Oh yes, he was going to take his time exploring every inch of them.

The sound of her moan made his cock twitch. Her hands gripped the back of the bedding. He swirled his tongue around her nipple. Her scent strengthened, pulling another rumble from him. As her back arched, Gavin moaned against her as her creamy flesh pressed more into his mouth. Latching on, he continued to lather her breast with attention. He gripped the edges of the pallet. It was the only thing that would keep him from touching things he couldn't.

"Oh, gods!" Parthenia cried out. Both of her nipples hardened further. She caressed his hip and along his side with her leg, dragging her talons over his butt. Her hold on the bedding tightened, the linen balling up in her fists.

Gods, he loved the feel of her beautiful mounds. He gripped the edges of the pallet firmly, sucking gently, then harder, flicking his tongue against her nipple. Popping her breast out of his mouth, he gently grazed his fangs over it, then took her nipple between his teeth, giving it a slight tug.

She grabbed the bedding harder. A loud moan left her mouth as her taloned feet dug a little deeper against his rear. Her skirt created unique friction as it bunched up between the two of them. He could feel her losing her self-control, and he was barely holding onto the sliver of his that remained.

With a deep growl against her, his eyes lit up. His cock literally throbbed. He skimmed his fangs over her bosom. "Are you going to come already, my beloved? I have not even given the other one any attention yet." He smirked and flicked his tongue over her nipple. Her head fell back as she squeezed her eyes shut and moaned louder. She grabbed hold of his arms and raked her nails over his biceps. Oh, Hades, that had him on the verge of an orgasm already. "Gods..." The glow of his eyes intensified.

Biting her bottom lip, Parthenia dropped her chocolate glowing gaze to his. "Not yet, my love. Though I feel hot. All. Over."

"What do you want? More of this?" He moved to her other breast and slowly stroked it with his tongue, and then captured that hardened peak between his teeth. "Or would you like something else?"

Meeting his eyes, she stared at him as he teased the tight, rosy bud of her nipple with his tongue. She bit her bottom lip. "Oh, I think I'm quite hungry for something else."

Gavin's eyes widened as another image from the book flooded her mind. There was nothing on the page to indicate anything about blood rushing to her head, and it seemed to account for their height difference. "Oh, can we try that?" Gods, he couldn't believe he hadn't thought to try licking her breasts sooner. They were magnificent.

"I believe we should."

"So, I just ..." Licking over her breast once more with another growl, he pushed himself upright and sat back against the wall. "Will this work?"

Parthenia sat up as her tongue snaked across her lips. She got to her feet, undid her skirt, and slid it down her long legs. Using one hand to lean against the wall, she kicked the material free from the bedding. Hades, her sex was very close to his mouth now, and her scent... Parthenia sized him up and crooked her finger as she took a couple of steps back. "Come forward, just a little."

Gavin did exactly as she said. As soon as he was far enough away from the wall that her wings wouldn't hit it, she turned around and backed her ass into his chest. Bending over, she placed one hand on one of his thighs and then the other. Hades, he was panting. "Um, hook your arms... under my thighs."

Gods, he loved it when she told him what to do. "What now, love?"

She didn't verbalize any further instructions, but their bodies quickly got with the program. Before he knew it, he supported the weight of her legs in his arms and she lowered herself, creating a small cocoon with her hair and her lips tightly encircled his throbbing shaft, eliciting a low moan from him. No one had to tell him on what to do next.

It was difficult not to just drive his tongue so deep into her sex and fuck her with it. But he wanted to take his time teasing and tasting her to multiple orgasms. He barely dipped the tip of his tongue into her sex, then slowly licked up her slit.

A groan left her mouth. Hades, this was going to be interesting to enjoy receiving and giving at the same time. Taking him all the way to the back of her throat, Parthenia explored the entire length of his shaft with her tongue.

His head fell back for a moment, a loud rumble emanating out of him. "Gods... Parthenia..." Straightening, he teased his tongue into her slit until he found her nub. He sucked it hard into his mouth as he growled against her.

Vibrations shot down his shaft as she sucked on his length and swirled her tongue around the head of his sex. Her nails dug into his thighs as her talons curled. Oh, gods, he was so close already. She barely had to touch him, and his cock was hard, but this... Every touch, every sensation as she pleasured him sent him to a height he hadn't known existed. His deep growl filled the room, his eyes glowing even brighter. Gripping her legs harder, he had to force himself to keep his rhythm slow, not that he would last much longer.

Parthenia repositioned her arms and raked her nails along his inner thighs. His mate didn't so much as explore his cock with her tongue and teeth as create a suction so hard around his sex, it would make a tornado jealous. The combination of them simultaneously devouring each other was complete torture. But such exquisite torture. With his tongue, he took slow, deep strokes up her slit, teased her entrance, and flicked at her nub.

Her thighs clenched, and her release slammed through her body, flooding his mouth. It tipped him right over the edge. His growl intensifying as he exploded down her throat. He buried his face between her thighs and drove his tongue deep inside her sex. As he took every drop of her orgasm, he didn't want to stop. He wanted more of her in his mouth, wanted to get drunk on her scent. He slipped his tongue in and out of her in a hard, slow rhythm, swept his tongue up her slit, and drove it in deep again.

Swallowing every drop he offered, Parthenia continued to suck and milk him dry. It didn't take long for a second orgasm to pulsate through her, her thighs clenching again as she dug her nails into his legs.

Gavin groaned against her as he licked and sucked at her sex until he took everything she gave him. After one more slow stroke up her slit with his tongue, he lowered her into his lap and leaned back against the wall, panting.

"Holy... poppies..." she said in between breaths. The two of them were breathless. Her body slumped back against his.

"Mhm," he murmured. He wrapped his arms around her waist, holding her against his chest. "That was... incredible."

"Yes... it... was..." Her breathing slowly steadied. She nuzzled her head into the crook of his neck.

With a purr, he laid his head on top of hers, stroking her hip as his lungs found a solid rhythm. Bless that journal she'd found. And there were other positions in it as well. He couldn't wait to try every single one of them. "*You* are incredible." He kissed the top of her head.

"I think I could easily fall asleep right now."

Gavin smiled and dropped another kiss on the top of her head. "Well, as long as we do not sleep too long, we can do that. I have not been sleeping very well. Gabby refuses to leave the village, so I do not expect anyone to come upon us." Falling asleep with her naked in his arms sounded like the perfect idea. As long as his hands didn't wander while they snoozed. That would be a rather unfortunate wake-up call. And it would probably be a good idea if they adjusted, so they were lying down. Less of a chance of any unfortunate accident occurring. He recalled the first time it had happened. The last thing he wanted was for either of them to go flying out of the treehouse.

Gavin laid down on the pallet and pulled her gently down with him, tucking her against his chest with his arm around her waist. He buried his face in her neck and inhaled her scent. "A nap sounds wonderful."

"Mmm." Within a matter of minutes, she snuggled deep and passed out, a steady rise and fall of her chest. The rhythm of his breaths synced up with hers. It took next to no time for sleep to claim him as well.

Chapter Thirteen

Logan and Pierce had spent the entire morning with Duke getting tables and chairs set up. It had taken them just past the afternoon. Once they had finished, Duke sent them on their way. It had seemed an appropriate time to go by and see Adara before they headed home for afternoon meal.

Having both just received the gifts she had created for their mates, Logan eyeballed the intricate details of each piece. They were exquisite. Unlike anything he'd ever seen across the isle. The woman certainly had a keen eye.

His brother flashed a smile at the female. "You have an outstanding talent. And our sister adores her necklace. Thank you for all you have done."

"Oh, thank you. I am glad she loves it. It is quite suitable for her. Now, I do not expect to see you both again until... winter. Yes, winter."

Logan glanced at his brother and raised an eyebrow. Did he know what Adara was talking about? Not if the confused expression on his face was anything to go by. That made two of them. "Winter?"

"Yes. You will have time to come up with your design. No worries."

"Design?" What design? What exactly did they have to do and why? Logan peered over at Pierce again. His brother appeared about as floored as he did. Were *they* expected to come up with something?

"For their day of birth." Adara strode over to her worktable, her hooves clicking against the floor as she walked. She opened one draw after another, searching for something.

"Um... oh, alright," Pierce stated before cocking an eyebrow at him.

"Ah-ha!" she replied and returned with a stack of parchments. "They were born on the Winter Solstice twenty-three *solaris* past. Galenus always cherished them. Like any child, they were his pride and joy. From the first *solaris* of their day of birth, he had multiple designs created for a unique piece each *solaris*. Some were charms he simply added onto a bracelet. I had enough until last *solaris*. As their mates, I presume you will carry on the tradition."

"Um... sure." He would do his best. Logan took what she held out to him and perused the papers. The designs were definitely unique, rough sketches.

She held out a separate stack to Pierce.

Pierce took it and scanned through them. "If it was a tradition that was important to him, I will do all I can to continue it."

"Take the parchment with you. You both have time, and I am always available for consultation. Just remember, I do not repeat pieces."

"Thank you. I am certain we may both seek your advice at some point." If he couldn't come up with something on his own. Though, maybe he would get inspired before then. Not that jewelry was something he excelled at or had ever considered before now.

"It is just not something we are used to," Pierce said. "Thank you again. We should take our leave."

"Oh, yes, of course. You both have a mating ceremony to prepare for." Adara grinned and waved them off. She had some sort of contraption on her head that she'd stated aided her in working with the gemstones. It seemed to have two sets of spectacles, one in front of the other. She flipped the magnifying glasses down and returned to her work table.

Offering a brief nod, Logan opened the door and stepped outside. A tradition. They had been lucky to celebrate their day of birth, let alone have anything as a tradition. He knew things were different here than what he and his brother had grown up with. His gaze flicked back to Pierce as he joined him outside. "Do you think we should do that every *solaris* for Lilli as well?"

"I think so. Yes, I think she would like that." His brother paused for a minute as they started forward. "She seemed okay this morning. Smiling, which is good. But she was quiet. I do not expect her to fully adjust already, of course, but… I suppose I just worry." His brows drew together. "Did she sleep alright?"

"She had a nightmare after you and Jocasta left." Logan gripped the back of his neck. His brother warned him about the nightmares, but it wasn't what he expected. Nor did he expect his reaction. He shook his head. "Ambrosia went in and comforted Lilli. I was… I was in no position to help, but I spoke with her this morning."

Pierce's gaze drifted to the ground. The two of them halting their steps. "I am sorry, Logan. It was something… I did not know… how bad." His ruby gaze remained locked on the dirt floor, shame flooding his features. "I just did not know how to."

"It is okay. I would not have either," he said. Ambrosia had been wonderful. Even with everything it had made his mate feel, he was absolutely grateful to her for last night. "Lilli… she asked to talk to me about it all at some point."

Pierce's eyes popped wide. "If she wishes to speak of it, that is a good thing, right?"

"I think it will be. For both of us. I seem to feel your emotions and hers more intensely." More than he'd ever felt with anyone, except Ambrosia and their mother. Something he was still getting used to; it had never been like this before with his brother.

"How—," Pierce paused. "How bad was it?"

Logan swallowed the lump in his throat as he thought back to the night before. For a brief second, his eyes flashed black. All he'd been able to think about as he felt her pain was murdering Ailwin and the male who'd harmed her. His mate had been right to go in his stead. "If I ever find the male, I will rip him to pieces after I castrate him."

"You will find him. After our mating *umbra*. We will do so to all of them." His brother clapped his shoulder. "Are you… alright, after that? I will never pretend to understand what it is like for you with your ability, but I know how difficult… I know it is difficult."

Alright? He would move forward, but that didn't mean he was alright. Ambrosia's presence eased him, allowing him to be there for her. The chair had taken the brunt of his emotions; the arms had splintered beneath his grip. If anyone noticed it this morning, no one said anything of it. He would fix it in the coming days, after their mating ceremony. "That is not how I would describe it. I am calm, much more so than I was last night.

After Lilli fell back asleep, Ambrosia needed me too much for me not to find a way." Not to mention dropping Evan's head off this morning helped, too.

"I would not blame you for being angry at me."

"I am not angry with you, brother. You protected Lilli as best you could. Ailwin is at fault. And he will not survive. His *umbras* are limited, I assure you." Logan growled. The male would pay beyond measure for what he had done to their mother and to Lilli. The male would burn, and he would never see it coming.

"What we spoke of? Have you taken care of it?"

"Yes, this morning. It is why I was late to morning meal."

"Good." His brother squeezed his shoulder. "Shall we go?"

"Yes."

Without another word, they headed back to the house.

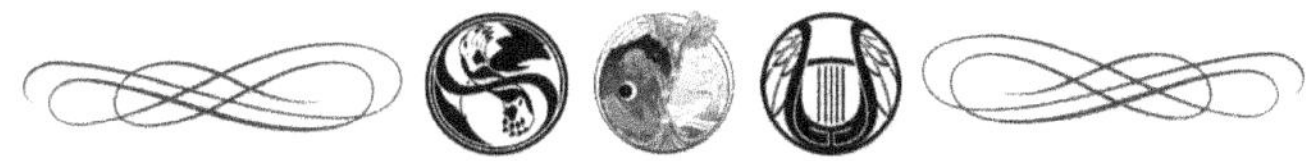

Pierce ascended the porch's short staircase ahead of Logan and entered the house. Stepping inside, he stopped cold. His brother paused in the doorway behind him. Pierce glanced from Jocasta with her hair pulled up into a ponytail, her beautiful pointed canine ears on display to Lilli... in a dress—*Holy Hades.* Inhaling and exhaling a deep breath, his cheeks nearly cracked as a wide smile spread across his face.

Lilli's eyebrows raised. "Beast?"

Ambrosia rolled her eyes at her sister. "Beast is the largest of the spourgiffs. Like seven feet at the shoulder. Nine feet tall."

"Am I in an alternate dimension?" Pierce teased as he crossed the room. He greeted Lyrica and Ambrosia, then gave Lilli a hug. "You are beautiful. The dress suits you well," he whispered in her ear, then kissed the top of her head. Pulling his mate against him, he tucked his face into the crook of her neck and let out a soft growl. "You look amazing, my queen."

"Mmm... thank you." Jocasta stroked the back of his head.

Logan strode over to Lilli and embraced her. "You look beautiful. The dress is fitting." He shifted gears and greeted his mate, whispering something to her.

Lilli smiled shyly. "Thank you both," she said, then returned to helping Lyrica with the slicing. "Nine feet tall? I would like to go see them sometime, Am. Maybe you can teach me how to ride one?"

"I'd love to, Lilli," Ambrosia replied.

"Thank you. It sounds like so much fun. I have never seen one."

Still skimming her fingers through his fur, Jocasta murmured, "Hey, can I talk to you for a second?"

"Of course." He kissed her throat, then led her down the hall. "What is it, love?"

Jocasta said nothing until they were in the back bedroom with the door shut. Not that the distance would likely prevent everyone from overhearing the conversation; they all had superior hearing. "How much does Lilli know about hybrids and Markham's laws?" she asked, keeping her voice low.

Pierce sighed and sat down on the edge of the bed. "Hades. Not as much as she should. And that is my fault." He ran a hand roughly over his head. "They subjected her to so much. I tried to shield her from as much of the bad as I could." He lifted his eyes to her. "What happened?"

Sitting down next to him, his mate caressed his forearm. "You were trying to protect her." A small frown touched her face and her brows drew together. "We were talking about hair, and it came up that I usually wear mine down. She asked why. I didn't exactly know what to tell her. Threw Am and I off for a second, so I just told her what truth I could."

Pierce wrapped his arm around her waist and caressed her hip. Her touch always eased him like nothing else. "I feel like most of the time, I do not know what I am doing. I am navigating in all new waters. With her, especially. I know I do not have to worry so much about her and, because of that, I worry more. She is already doing so much better than I expected, and that brings me joy, but I am terrified. Logan said she had a terrible nightmare last night. The first night I was not with her. Thank the gods for your sister." He shook his head. He was rambling. "My apologies. I should have... I do not know. I should have said something."

Jo leaned into him. "Am told me about it. Not everything. She told me enough that we gave Lilli a chance to raid Am's closet. We are in unfamiliar territory, but we're figuring it out."

Pierce tugged her into his lap and brushed his fingers back and forth across the scales that covered her outer thigh. "Lilli looked so much more comfortable, wearing clothing. Did she enjoy that?"

"It took her a minute, but with some reassurance, she picked out a couple of dresses. I think she still wasn't entirely sure, even when she saw her reflection." Readjusting in his lap, Jocasta draped her legs over his and curled up against him. She cupped his cheek. "I made sure Lilli knew that you and Logan are more of a father to her than the male who gave her life. I told her she's strong, but that sometimes females like me and her need that suit of armor to remind us and to help us show that strength."

He grazed her cheek with the back of his knuckles. "You are so wonderful. Thank you for telling her that." With a soft kiss, he laid his head on top of hers and moved his hand back to her leg. He knew that, no matter what he said, she would never judge him. But he still found it difficult to speak on emotional subjects when looking at someone, when they could see his eyes, the expression in them. His emotion. "I feel guilty for what I am feeling. And then I feel guilty for my guilt. I am so joyful about how she is right now, her joy. I could not be happier seeing her finally get this chance. Despite those moments of fear, sadness. But I suppose I was unprepared for her to not need me so much."

"You've been taking care of her for a long time. Doing it by yourself. And, for the first time, you don't have to. Everything you're feeling makes sense." She rested her hand on his chest, rubbing her thumb across his heart. "She'll always need you. That will never change."

He let out a low rumble. He loved it when she touched him there. She was right. It would take time for things to feel normal for all of them. But the thoughts in his head were still there. "I know she will. It is just, despite what others have said, I do not think of myself as a healer. I am a protector. She does not need a protector so much anymore. You, your mother and sister... I do not know how to explain it. The three of you just have a way with her. You put her at great ease. Logan told me she said she wants to talk to him about the things that happened in the village. It was not something I expected her to want to do. I think it will help her. I understand why she would not want to do so with me, though."

Slowly, Jocasta sat upright. "I know you don't feel like a healer, but you are one. Whether you see it, you've healed me in ways I didn't think I needed. I used to think I was fine. I was living life, but I was just going through the motions. Sparring because it was the only way to get the anger out. Working in the bar because I didn't really have anything else. Don't get me wrong; I love being in the karaoke booth, and I love partying with the fae. But at the end of the night, something was always missing. You made me better, put life back into me. You healed me. No one else. And just because Lilli has different relationships with all of us, it doesn't mean that all you've ever been is her protector."

"Oh, love." He captured her mouth in a slow and deeply passionate kiss, expressing everything he couldn't verbalize. His heart swelled with love and joy. It didn't matter that he disagreed with her assessment. He simply needed her to know that she'd breathed life into him. "You have done all that for me and so much more." He brushed a tender kiss across her lips and pressed his forehead to hers. "With Lilli, I feel as if I could not even do that. I did my best to protect her, and it was never enough. She is safe now, and it had nothing to do with me. I could not save her in the village. She will hold those memories within her forever."

His mate pressed a soft kiss to his nose. "But they won't rule her life. They won't rule the decisions she makes for herself. She's strong enough to overcome them because of what you've done for her."

"What have I done for her? I brought her back there. I made that choice. When I should have hidden us and made us a home elsewhere or looked for Logan instead. It seemed the only choice, though. I knew they would punish me for deserting. But in my heart, I was frightened. I had just watched my mother pass away. I did not know how to raise a child. It was stupid, but I thought that in the village I would have help. Not from Ailwin, not even Dahlia, really. But at least from Zinnia. But no. I took her back there, and she suffered cruelty after cruelty. She survived them all, not because of my strength, but because she is stronger than me."

"What if you had stayed hidden? You don't know that you would've found Logan. Or what if you had? Do you know how your life would be different? How Lilli's life would be different? Do you know if he would've even spoken with you? What if he had turned his back? Walked away? What if you had to keep moving around just to keep the two of you safe? Do you know it would've lasted? That you could've continuously found food? Found warmth during the winter *cycles*? What if you had never been in the market on that *umbra*? What if we never met? Yes, every action has a consequence. Sometimes the outcome is excellent, and sometimes the outcome is horrific. And sometimes, it's neither one and you're surviving until the next decision, the next outcome." She shook her head. "You can 'what if' every decision you've ever made until the end of your life. It won't change what happened in the past, and it will only make you question every decision you have to make in the present and the future."

Hot, burning tears slid down his cheeks, but he made no move to wipe them away. There were so many things that could've occurred if their decisions had been different. If the directions they had taken had altered. "I would not change one thing if it meant that I would never have met you. You are my everything, and I cannot survive without you." He nuzzled her nose. "No, I do not know any of the 'what ifs.' I do not know what would have happened, and that is truly what kills me. I fear that, when this period of change is over and this life becomes her new normal, she will look back on the life that I gave her and hate me for what I put her through, for what I could not save her from. That is not something I could bear." He clutched his mate as he buried his face in the warm curve of her neck. Needing her close, he breathed her scent in deeply. She was the only thing that could ease the ache in his chest.

"Lilli will never hate you. She will never blame you."

Pierce couldn't respond. His throat had closed up and no more words were possible.

Holding him and running her fingers along the back of his head, Jocasta sang softly. It sounded like a lullaby, though it wasn't one he'd ever heard. Not that he had heard any in a very long time. Slowly, his body stilled. The slight tremors that had shaken him eased and the pain in his chest slipped away. His tears dried. He listened to her voice, listened to every word, as it soothed his soul. While she sang, he caressed her spine, his face still buried against her throat, feeling the steady thrum of her heart beat against him. When she'd finished, the song trailing off and ending; he inhaled a deep breath and let it out. "You have the most beautiful voice I have ever heard."

"Thank you," Jocasta whispered. "My father loved to listen to me sing. After he passed, I couldn't find the heart to do it anymore. I only began again after we met." She paused briefly. "Lilli loves you. And that will never change. Everyone in this house does."

"As I love all of you." The more they learned of each other, the more he understood why they'd both been so drawn to one another. Their broken souls were destined to find each other and heal. "I am glad that you started singing again, love. Your voice is too special a gift not to share. I can understand, though, why you could not. After my mother passed… I did not really smile, and I did not laugh at all. Not until I met you. You have taken away the darkness that was inside of me.”

"I'm happy I've been able to see your smile, hear your laugh. I've always known they were there, inside of you. Don't you think Lilli has too? Just as her smile, her laugh, has been inside her.”

"Yes. You are right. About all of it… you are right. It just may take some time for the reality to stay put.” He trailed kisses up her neck to her jawline. "I am sorry for breaking down all over you. I did not intend to.” He brushed a kiss across her lips. "And I am going to talk to Lilli as well. She needs to know there are still dangers, even if they are much further away now. It will not be safe for her to leave the village until those threats against her are eliminated.”

"You don't have to apologize. It'll take some adjustment for all of us. It's one reason Am, and I closed Zancle's Rock and took this time off. And I think that's a good idea. I don't think she's in a hurry to leave, but there's plenty here she can do and a lot of areas to explore.”

"Oh? And I thought you two just took time off because of our upcoming mating,” he teased. "You know we may not leave our home the next *umbra*, right?” A smirk tugged at the corner of his lips.

"Mmm, I like the sound of that.” A soft chuckle left her mouth. "Maybe I should convince Am to keep Zancle's closed for a couple of extra *umbras*.”

He growled. "I like the sound of that even more.”

Lowering her lids, she bit her bottom lip. "Keep growling at me like that, and we won't make it through afternoon meal.”

"Hmm, that sounds so very tempting.” Extending his tongue, he licked her lower lip. "I am hungry for food, but I am hungry for you as well.”

She nipped at his tongue. "Mmm, if only we were at home.”

The rumble in his chest was more intense this time. Oh, gods, how he wanted to be at home. But their family was out in the other room, waiting for them. He had almost forgotten. "Tonight then, my queen.”

"Then you're mine, my king,” she declared, her silky voice heavy with desire.

He couldn't have stopped the moan if he tried. "And you are all mine. We should go out there before I do not let you. All I want to do right now is bend you over this bed and take you." Not that it would be an altogether good idea, no matter how enticing it sounded. There was no telling how insulated the bedroom was. Plus, this wasn't their home, and all of their family was in the kitchen. Not to mention, they weren't exactly quiet.

Jocasta climbed out of his lap. "If I don't get up now, I'll be too tempted to..."

She didn't need to finish her sentence. He'd seen her get dressed this morning. He knew *exactly* what she did and didn't have on. Letting out another growl, he snaked his tongue across his lips and his ruby eyes glowed brightly. "Mmm." Pierce reached out and caressed her shoulder. "I am going to give you another mark tonight." He stood up and drew her against him, sliding his hands over her plump ass. "By the time we make it to our bedroom, I want you naked. Otherwise, your clothing will not survive." Nipping at her ear, he gave her ass a squeeze. Her teeth tugged at her lower lip. "Mmm. Food. Before I cannot let you out of this room." Reluctantly, he released her.

Before she opened the door, she faced him, her amber eyes glowing. "We could always have evening meal at our own home tonight."

Just the thought had another low rumble rolling out of him. They would see their family tomorrow. And, this way, they could have dessert before and after dinner. "I cannot promise we will eat food—right away, anyway—but that sounds like a wonderful idea. You always have the best ideas, love." He kissed the side of her throat. Hand-in-hand, they rejoined their family as the final preparations for afternoon meal took place.

Chapter Fourteen

As he did so often, when he didn't have reason to leave the village, Markham sat on his throne in his hut with the door open. His pitch-black claws curled over the ends of the arms. He sat still this time, though, eyes closed, letting the mental tendrils of his mind wander. It was difficult sometimes to get a bead on many of their thoughts. Occasionally, another learned how to fully shield their mind. But the majority weren't so lucky, and a lot of them couldn't do it very well. When the thoughts were loud, and at the front of the individual's mind, it was as if they were speaking straight to his face. Here, few could protect their secrets.

Some full thoughts reached him, though they were all normal ones, nothing significant. He caught snippets from some. From a few others, their minds appeared completely blank.

Baby... okay...

Markham's head tilted to the side. It had been a female that the thought had come from. Baby. Was there to be a new addition to the village? But why attempt to hide the thoughts? Why, indeed? Unless the union was a forbidden one?

He peered around. His body stayed still, only his eyes moving, allowing them to roam of their own accord over each female he saw in the clearing.

Baby...

His gaze landed on the fully white feline. Gabriella. She headed for the kitchen building as evening meal was in full swing. He took in every detail of her form as she moved across the encampment. There was an almost imperceptible roundness to her belly. Hmm. She spent little time with others here in the village. Though companionship between separate forms was unusual, the canine, Devina, seemed to be her closest friend. And she spent time with the feline, Keres. Perhaps Keres' mate had strayed from her. It was not uncommon for it to occur here in the village. Then again, the female's father was discussing mating terms with Ramsey. Perhaps Arman was to become a father.

As Gabriella reached the kitchen building, his eyes strayed again, landing on Gembert leaving the family hut. He sent out a mental command to the feline. *Come to me, immediately.* The male's footsteps froze in place for a moment before they altered course and strode toward the hut. Going inside, the male stopped just inside the jamb.

"Close it."

Gembert did as he was told, then stood still as he waited.

Several minutes passed before Markham spoke. "Your daughter, Gabriella, appears to be with child. Who is the father?"

Gembert's eyebrows knitted together. "I was not aware of her condition, Your Majesty." A frown creased his forehead as he thought for a moment. "I am unsure who the father could be. She does not spend time with the male felines of the village. However, I have caught the scent of canine upon her before. I assumed it was that female she is close to. Though, it is possible that is not the case." Gembert lowered his head. "My apologies, Your Majesty. My sense of smell is not what it used to be."

Yes, which was why the male remained home most of the time. He was nearing complete uselessness. Markham let out a low, menacing growl. "A canine. You do not say." He tapped his claws in sequence against the arm of his throne. Silence stretched between them.

"What would you have me do, Your Majesty?"

"If this is the truth, and she carries the spawn of another form, it cannot survive. It will be an abomination." Unification diluted the purity of the bloodlines. One could see it in any hybrid, the portions of different forms mixing to make a new whole. *Disgusting.* His brother, that imprudent fool, had welcomed the differences, but they had always repulsed him. Markham rose from his throne and marched over to a shelf in the corner, so tall it almost touched the ceiling. He pulled down a box and opened it, revealing about a dozen vials of clear liquid. Taking one out, he tossed it to Gembert, who caught it in his mouth. "Have her drink this even if you have to shove it down her throat. It will have no effect against any who carry no young within themselves. But it will rectify this situation quickly. Wait until she returns from evening meal. The last of my Informants should be inside the boundaries soon. The traitor will reveal himself, and we will handle him swiftly."

Gembert said nothing, though, with the vial in his mouth, it would have been difficult to do so. He nodded once, then turned and left the hut.

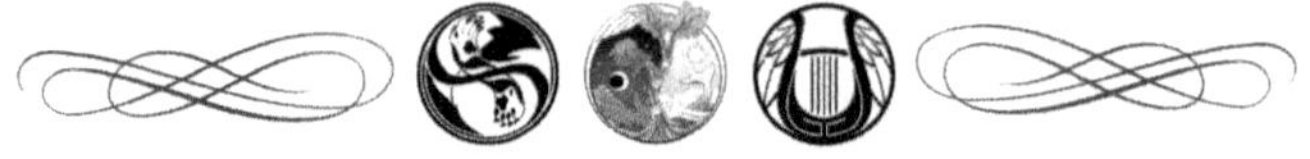

Derrick rolled his shoulders, trying to ease the sudden tension he felt in them. He circled the outside of the larger fighting ring. A sparring session between two adolescent canines had to finish up before he could go eat evening meal. He'd already seen Gabriella go into the kitchen building, though he'd made sure not to appear to be looking at her. He hoped to conclude this before she got done eating. Not that he could sit with her or anything. Even if he wasn't an Informant, the rules didn't permit males and females to dine together. They ate at opposite ends of the dining area. But it would be nice to at least be under the same roof during a meal.

From the corner of his eye, he watched Gembert enter Markham's hut. Several minutes later, the male exited and returned home. Derrick's stomach flip-flopped, but he forced himself to keep his breathing even. It meant nothing. Gembert was still an Informant, even if he wasn't technically active anymore. So, it meant nothing.

"One more round," he called to the two in the ring.

After the session was done and he'd released the two from the ring, he headed to go eat, keeping a normal pace. Though he showed nothing on his face, and kept thoughts of her far from the forefront of his mind, he found her scent immediately. It was a struggle to hold his gaze from her at the opposite end of the room, and even more difficult to prevent his paws from carrying him over to where she sat. Tomorrow. He had no duties tomorrow. They may well be able to steal away. It had been some time.

Gabby left the building, Gavin shortly behind her, before he'd finished eating. Derrick didn't have to see her gaze fall upon him for just a moment to notice it. The corner of his mouth lifted. Tomorrow they could do more than steal secret glances. Perhaps he could take her to the lake again. That was out of the way enough, and others of their species had never discovered there them. It would give them some time alone. They hadn't gone to the treehouse in quite some time. At first, she'd only told him that Gavin needed his privacy, but she'd eventually revealed that he'd found a mate. Of another species. Theirs was a relationship more dangerous than his own with Gabriella. He prayed for the male and whoever his mate was, often.

When the first twinge hit his lower back, he brushed it off. He'd been busy this week and had gone on many scouting trips, even hunted for food to take down venison, several training sess—

Another twinge speared across his lower back, more intense this time. Pain flooded his abdomen. He squeezed his eyes shut, almost choking on his food. As he fought for breath, he dug his claws into the dirt floor. His mate... his mate... her pain... Oh, gods, her pain. Gabby was screaming. He had to goto her. Now. But it would reveal them both. *The baby... no... oh, gods...*

Without another thought, Derrick bolted to his feet and exited the building. He raced across the clearing toward—

A thick chain slammed down on his neck and dropped him to the ground. It yanked tight, holding him in place. A pair of paws pressed down on his spine, another on his hind quarters, the claws digging in. Though he strained against the metal links, he couldn't get free. Tremors swept through the ground. Markham was coming. But he couldn't take his eyes from the hut that Gabby lay within. No one spoke, but he could feel dozens of eyes upon him. As his mate's pain ripped through him again— the emotional so much worse than the physical—his jaws went slack, his chest heaved and he fought to draw air into his lungs.

Another one of Gabby's screams echoed. Or perhaps it wasn't all that loud in reality, as she was in the hut with the door closed. But it echoed in his head, resounding louder than any noise he'd ever heard. He attempted to shut out the pounding of his blood in his ears. It was a struggle to hear anything more than her screams... her pain and anguish. This was so much worse than before.

"What have you done?!" That was Gavin. But what did that mean? What was that supposed to mean? What was he talking about?

"I did what was necessary," Gembert stated.

Derrick fought harder against the chains. *No... oh, gods... Hades, please... no...* Derrick's eyes turned black.

He heard growls. The slam of a body against the wall. More growls. A cry of pain. Grief-stricken sobs, those of his mate, louder than anything.

A howl of despair left him. He felt as though his chest was going to split clean down the middle. He watched Markham cross the rest of the clearing and stop in front of the entrance of Gembert's hut. The door stood open now. Gembert dragged Gavin by the scruff of his neck and tossed him outside.

"Is it finished?" Though he was speaking to Gembert, Markham's gaze never left Gavin.

Derrick didn't hear how Gembert responded. Gavin's yells overrode their words. "This was *you*! You are a *monster*! Curse you to Hades!"

Out of his periphery, he saw his sister, Devina, straining to get to him, but their father held her back. Tears streamed down her face. Their father spoke in hushed tones to her, too quiet for Derrick to hear. After a minute, her body sagged against his.

His eyes fell back to Markham, who stared straight at him. From the corner of his eye, Derrick caught Gavin limping away. The male held up one of his back legs, blood dripping from it. When the King spoke, his voice boomed. There wouldn't be a single villager who didn't hear it, whether they were inside of a hut. "You have a choice to make, Derrick. You can run, as they hunt you down, make one more attempt to save your miserable life before you breathe no more. Or you can stay and gaze upon your *mate* one last time before I kill you where you stand."

Someone removed the chain from his body, and he leaped to his feet. Jaws snapped at his ankles and neck, not quite reaching him but grazing him. He didn't want his mate to watch him die. If he left now, perhaps he could convince her—maybe, finally—to leave too. Perhaps even get her away. He had hoped to spare her from this, but now he had no choice but to be hunted. He had to go. But his feet refused to move. It wasn't until her voice reached him—raw, broken, and shaky—that movement became possible.

"Derrick! Run!"

As his heart shattered into pieces, he sprinted quickly toward the trees. Markham's voice rang out behind him. "Hunt them down and kill them both."

"Gavin, go!" he hollered. They shot off into the thick forest, paws pounding the ground behind them as the chase began. Gavin's speed was slower than normal because of his leg, but, by some miracle, he kept pace with Derrick.

Markham's voice rang out as they left the village behind. "Bring me their hearts. I am hungry."

"River. Jump in," he said to the male, nudging his side to change course. The river emptied into the basin. It was only fifteen miles from there to Logan's cabin. If they could just make it to the river, they stood a chance.

The Informants were closing in behind them, their howls echoing. Branches shook as felines sped through the trees above them. "Faster!" he growled.

"I am going as fast as I can," Gavin snarled back.

They both pushed their speed to their limit, but that hindleg of Gavin's was holding him back. As the river came into view, Derrick altered his direction. "Hold your breath." He shoved Gavin in. Teeth sank into Derrick's side as something slammed hard against him, just as he was about to jump in. A loud snap resounded in his ears as one of his ribs broke. Jerking his head to the side, he gouged his claws down the face of the male that had held him. The male came at him again, and he dug his claws into the male's temples and tore out his jugular. He didn't even know whose blood it was that filled his mouth. Shoving the body aside, Derrick rolled until he hit the river. Taking the biggest gulp of air he could, the water covered him completely, the rush pulling him downstream. He threw his camouflage on and, as he could no longer see him in the water, it appeared Gavin had done the same.

The Informants followed alongside the rolling water for miles until they finally gave up. Perhaps they assumed the two of them had drowned, but he doubted it. He didn't know how long this stretch of river was. He took air when he needed to, but stayed under the water as much as possible, just in case. Camouflage or not, it would be obvious when a body reappeared at the surface. After some time, he rode a white, frothy cascade of water, plunging into a large basin. Derrick shifted to his humanoid form, dredging through the blue pool, and pulled himself onto the shore. A wet spot on the ground about ten feet from him told him Gavin had done the same.

For several minutes, the only noises he heard were the harsh sounds of their heavy breaths. "I have a place where we can go." His voice came out raspy, soft, almost fragile, as though he'd cried for hours. Nope. Not yet. That would come. "It is not mine, but they have given me permission to stay there. If I ever needed to. I am sure they would not mind if you stayed as well."

Silence stretched between them. "No. I have a place to go. I must see my mate. She would not know where to go." Gavin inhaled and exhaled several more times. "I am so very sorry... about your loss."

The male's words came out gravelly. The scent of tears he couldn't see filled the air. He knew the feeling. The sound of movements preceded indents in the grass as Gavin took off. There were only three. His leg must have gotten badly injured, but no blood spots appeared on the ground. At least there was that. Shifting back to all fours, Derrick shook the water from his body and started forward. There was no telling if the Informants would return and follow the river further. If they would find this basin. If they would track his scent, travel to where he headed, and find him. At the moment, though, it was the very last thing he cared about.

It took him maybe fifteen minutes to come upon the cabin. When he reached it, he dropped his camouflage and shifted back to his humanoid form. He didn't quite make it to the porch before he dropped to his knees. His palms hit the dirt. His claws curled, piercing the uneven ground as his chest heaved. Dark spots appeared, wetting the earth. Tears he'd barely held back poured free. Tightly squeezing his eyes shut, he screamed at the top of his lungs. Rage, torment, and heartache painted the sound as he continued to shriek at the separation from his mate. The agony felt like a dagger twisted deep in his chest, leaving an aching void inside of him. The despair from his mate pulsated through him in never ending waves. He wailed for their young, ripped away from them, and for himself. This pain was greater than anything he had ever known. He didn't stop until his voice ran hoarse, his chest lit on fire, and his body shook with tremors he couldn't ease. And then he stayed there, with his forehead pressed to the ground. He sobbed so hard he could no longer see, even if his eyes had opened. Nearly choking on his tears, his lungs constricted. Eventually, his sounds of agony faded away.

It was long past sunset before he rose and dragged himself inside.

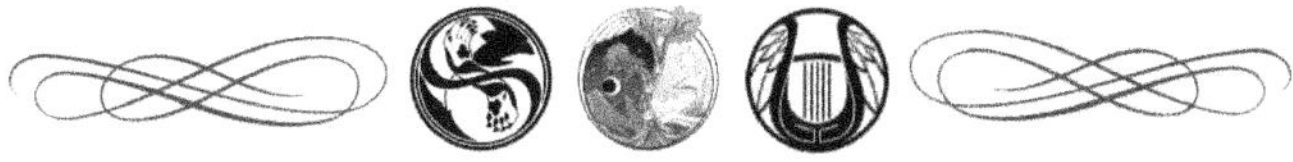

Gavin couldn't track a single thing as he sped as fast as he could to the treehouse. He couldn't focus on anything but what was in his head. Thankfully, his body knew the way because there was no way his mind could have taken him in the right direction. He almost ran into at least a dozen trees, tripping a few times because of his leg. His father had bit deep, all the way to the bone, but at least he wasn't missing a chunk out of it. As he'd pulled himself from the basin, it had still been bleeding. He'd wet some dirt and caked it all around his leg over the wound so he didn't leave a blood trail. It was a shitty job, but it was all he could do at the moment.

His sister's screams and cries rang out in his head. His father's words. The ones he'd heard in his head when Markham had been staring him down outside of the hut. *I know what you have done. I know what law you have broken.*

Markham knew. How on earth did the male know? Why had Markham allowed them the opportunity to run? How had they even gotten away? He'd held his breath so long under the water he'd almost passed out. It was only when his brain had misfired that he'd broken the surface of the river, dragged more air into his lungs, and then held his breath beneath the water again. Thank the gods he could camouflage.

Gavin skidded to a halt, dirt kicking up under his paws as he almost ran into the trunk of the tree. Standing there catching his breath, his gaze lifted way up to the top of the treehouse as he considered for a moment how he would make it up there. At least it was a hind leg and not one of his front ones that had gotten injured. It would be painful and grueling, but he had to force himself up every inch until he made it. There was no other choice. Getting his front paws up on the trunk, Gavin dug his claws in deep and climbed.

An ascent that usually took minutes, took him hours. When he finally pulled himself up into the treehouse, his body shook from the exertion and dripped with sweat. Or tears? Both. It had to be both. The wood beneath his face darkened as the wetness fell upon it. With hazy vision, he barely noticed the pallet in the corner, but somehow dragged himself to it.

Dropping his camouflage, he curled up and faced the wall. His sobs came harder. He shuddered as the ache in his chest intensified, cracking open like a hole in the ground. He didn't want to make a sound. If he released the full weight of his emotions, he'd wail so loudly the entire forest would probably hear him. He brought his paw to his mouth and bit down. Though he tried not to bite too hard, trickles of blood slid down his paw, staining the bedding beneath him, mixing with his tears as he wept.

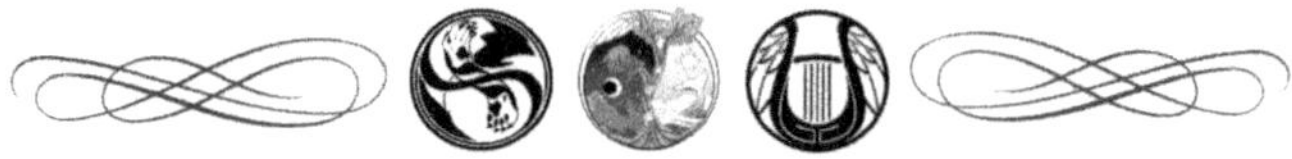

Parthenia hovered by her mate as he lumbered over to the pallet and practically collapsed onto it. Gavin hadn't even looked in her direction when he'd arrived. Maybe it resulted from the invisibility potion. Though she barely remembered taking it, she had done so before she left. The second she'd felt his overwhelming anguish, she'd rushed out of her apothecary. Watching him climb the tree had been brutal.

Not that she could've helped him.

She didn't have the strength to carry him to the top. All she could do was hover nearby the entire trip. Parthenia sat on the edge of the bedding next to him, set the vial aside, and stroked his cheek. His injuries didn't appear as physically bad as the last time. There was something different about this situation. Something she would figure out once she got through to him.

Gavin jerked at her touch, letting out a whimper around the paw clenched in his teeth. But he must've caught her scent. He turned toward her, pushing his face more into her touch. Opening his maw, his paw fell out of it, but no words came. Just a choking sob.

She continued the slow caresses, up and over the top of his head, to his ears and then back. Parthenia swallowed the lump in the back of her throat at the flash of images she got from him. She had an inkling of what happened, but he needed her too much for her to give into the sorrow burrowing in the pit of her stomach. Not even the chill that threatened to travel down her spine was enough to shift her focus away from him. They were safe here. Hidden away from the threats that hunted them.

He kept his eyes open as if he tried to see her, but she didn't think the invisibility potion had worn off yet. Not once did he move from where he laid as she brushed her fingers through his fur. After some time, his sobs quieted, the trembling in his body abated, and his breathing eased. Tears continued slipping silently down his cheeks. She kept her hand on him, never allowing her strokes to cease, even as she readjusted to lie down next to him and wrapped one of her wings around him.

"I'm right here, my love."

"Please do not leave me," he choked out.

"I'm not going anywhere. Not anywhere." Parthenia pressed a tender kiss to his shoulder. She'd stay however long he needed her to be here. Hours, days, however long he required.

He nodded a bit and moved his head, finding the crook of her neck and buried his face in it. She sensed the pain rolling through him as he tried to take in her scent. At some point, his tears slowed, though a few continued to drip down at random.

"She is hurting, and she is alone," he whispered.

Nothing she could say would make anything he was feeling better. They couldn't do anything for Gabby from here. And losing a child, especially a forced loss... *Demeter, please wrap her in your arms.* It seemed minimal that all she could do was pray. But they would've been able to do less for the female if they had killed him or Gabby's mate. "She's a powerful female, and she has Devin. It may not compare to the comfort of you or her mate, but it..." Parthenia swallowed. "It will have to be enough for now." Surely, they wouldn't keep her locked away in the village forever.

"It is not enough," he mumbled. "But he is alive. For now."

"No, it isn't enough, but it will have to do." Trailing her fingers gently along the nape of his neck, her arm remained around him and her wing still blanketed him.

"Perhaps they will find their way back to each other."

It was strange for him to be curled up to her in this form. They were much closer in height this way. But she would hold him and stay with him however he needed her. "I'm sure they will. I can't imagine Devin won't do whatever she can to help." The female had done a lot to help all of them already. It seemed to be what she lived for.

A gentle purr vibrated out of him. "I know she will." He paused. "I saw the look on her face. After I yelled at Markham. Her heart is broken too."

"Devin?" The information didn't surprise her, with everything she'd done for the four of them. The day she'd last seen the female was... gods, she remembered what Gavin had told her happened to females in his village. It had taken every ounce of strength she had not to cry over what the female had endured, just as she was staying strong now for her mate. "She cares for us all. I can't imagine she would be any other way."

"Her best friend and her brother. I know she has been trying so hard to help them. But Gabby, she would not leave. Not even I could... She told me, even if she could convince Derrick, she did not want to leave our mother there. She... they could have hidden, they could have got away, and now..." He sniffled, not even bothering to hold back the fresh tears that sprang forth.

"I'm so sorry, my love." She didn't have the relationship with her mother that they had with theirs. Although she'd always believed there was a different issue. Not that their mother had caused the delay. They couldn't get off the isle yet, and she still sought information on the barrier and more. "We will get her out of there as soon as we can." She would make sure they found a way.

"Okay," he breathed. He snuggled closer to her, careful not to put his weight down on any part of her.

"Rest, my love. I will tend to your leg shortly." She stroked the nape of his neck. He was fighting it, but the burden of his emotions had taken a toll on him. She glanced over her shoulder at the vial she had laid on the nearby floorboards some time ago. She didn't expect he would take it. Not anymore than she had when she'd—

Parthenia tucked those memories away. It wasn't something he needed on his mind. Not with all he already suffered. "I promise I will still be here when you wake." She couldn't leave him. Not like this.

"I love you," he whispered, just moments before sleep claimed him.

"I love you too." Still running her fingers up and down the back of his neck, Parthenia watched the steady rise and fall of his chest. She waited until he was truly deep in respite before she uncurled from his hold. She didn't want the wound on his leg to sit too long. It was going to take a little to get the mud cleaned off. They kept jugs of water here in the treehouse, so she wouldn't have to go far to put a bucket of water and soap together. As she'd brought some of her own items from her apothecary, she could really cleanse it, so it healed well. It was at least one way for her to help him.

Chapter Fifteen

With each female's hand in one of his own, Santos escorted Jocasta and Ambrosia from his hut out to the clearing. Both females had a silver chain bracelet on their wrists. Each bracelet had a multitude of charms attached to it. Neither female outshone the other. Ambrosia had on a silk aquamarine dress with simple spaghetti straps. The skirting flowed with every step she took. She'd swept up her burgundy hair into a bun with small wisps hanging free over her ears. Jocasta donned a strapless ruby-red lace dress. With the hem about mid-thigh, the dress hugged her curves. Like her twin, she also had her hair pinned up away from her face, revealing her pointed wolf-ears.

Both Logan's and Pierce's features brimmed with pure joy as they stared at their females. Santos accompanied Ambrosia and Jocasta forward, a soft grin settling on his face as he handed Jocasta to Pierce, and then Ambrosia to Logan.

Stopping in front of Pierce, Jocasta beamed. "You're stunning."

Their gazes locked on one another as his arms came around her waist, his hand caressing her cheek. "And you are breathtaking. My queen, you light my soul on fire."

"You revived mine, my king." She rested one hand on his biceps and leaned into his touch.

Ambrosia stepped into Logan's open arms. Laying her fingers on his forearm, she gave it a squeeze. "You look very handsome."

"And you are exquisite." He leaned down, pressed a kiss to her cheek, and whispered something in her ear.

Without lingering, Santos walked to the front and stopped at the head of the white archway. The intricate trellises had spades of red roses woven throughout each side panel. He faced the two couples and all of those gathered to witness the joining of the unions. "Any who wish to present themselves for mating, please step forward."

Pierce brought Jocasta's hand to his lips and kissed it, then laced their fingers together and led her forward. Logan and Ambrosia walked next to them; their fingers interlaced together. The four of them came to a halt before him.

"Elder Santos, I wish to take Logan as my mate until the end of our *umbras*," Ambrosia said with a bright smile on her face.

Logan's gaze flicked from Ambrosia to Santos and bowed his head. "Elder Santos, I wish to take Ambrosia as my mate until the end of our *umbras*."

Santos closed the distance between him and them, taking their joined hands within his own. "Ah, yes, this is a good mating. Very good, indeed. I accept your presentation." He released his hold of their hands. "Logan, you may proceed with your promise."

Keeping their fingers threaded together, Logan faced Ambrosia. "The *umbra* I met you, Ambrosia. You made the world around me go quiet and filled it with the most beautiful and the snarkiest voice I had ever heard." He chuckled softly. "I knew then that I had met my match. Not just because you called me out on my crap, but because you stilled everything inside of me. For *solaris*, I had this chaos in my head, soul, and heart, and I accepted it as my fate, that I would simply have to live with it for the rest of my life. Then I caught you. For the first time in a long time, I felt shielded and protected from the darkness that threatened to consume me every *umbra*. You became a beacon of light. Guiding me through the shroud that tried to claim me. Teaching me how to forgive myself. You protected me when I could not protect myself. You let me crumble and then pieced me back together, stronger than I ever was before." He smiled widely. "On this *umbra*, the *umbra* of our mating, I make this vow to you. From this *umbra* until my last, I promise to always stand by your side. I promise to always listen before I react, even when we do not agree. To always support you and encourage you in every endeavor you choose. I will spend the rest of my *umbras* showing you how much I love you and why I feel you have made me the luckiest male on the isle." Pausing a moment, he wiped at the corners of his eyes. "You are my one and only, my love, my heart, my mate, and my shield."

"Ambrosia, you may proceed with your promise," Santos said.

Squeezing Logan's hand, Ambrosia's entire face lit up. "The *umbra* I met you, Logan. You literally saved my life. Despite my snark, you took care of me. Reminded me I wasn't alone. You gave me permission to want something for myself." She brushed the wetness off her cheek. "I'd gotten so used to taking care of everyone else that I'd forgotten what it was like to just think about me. Not only did you let me know it was okay to put myself first, but you became my rock. Someone that was always in my corner, encouraging and cheering me on, even if it was just an everyday part of life. No matter what we were facing, I could always lean on you. And you constantly give me hope, even when I don't think it's possible. You reminded me that no matter how dark things get, we'll always find a way through. I love you more and more with each *umbra*. Some *umbras*, I feel like my heart might explode with how much I love you. But I know if it did, you'd pick me back up and make me whole again." Beaming, she paused. "On this *umbra*, the *umbra* of our mating, I make this vow to you. From this *umbra* until my last, I promise to cherish every *umbra* we have together. To talk to you, so that we make decisions together. I promise to support and protect you, no matter what may come our way. To honor the life we have built. I love you. I promise I will show you every *umbra* just how much." She pressed a kiss to his fingers. "You are my one and only, my love, my heart, my mate, and my rock."

Santos crossed over to Pierce and Jocasta, stopping in front of them. "You may make your request."

Offering a bow of her head, Jocasta smiled brightly. "Elder Santos, I wish to take Pierce as my mate until the end of our *umbras*."

Beaming, Pierce turned his gaze from Jocasta to Santos and bowed his head. "Elder Santos, I wish to take Jocasta as my mate until the end of our *umbras*."

Santos bowed his head to the two of them, then clasped their joined hands within his own. "Ah, yes, this is a good mating. Very good, indeed. I accept your presentation." He released his hold of their hands. "Pierce, you may proceed with your promise."

Pierce turned to Jocasta and placed one hand on the small of her back, the other against her cheek. "Jocasta. The *umbra* I met you in the marketplace... the *umbra I* ran into *you*." He grinned, then cleared his throat, sobering a little. "I was such a different male than the one who stands before you today. My heart was dark from all the cruelty I had seen. Broken by too much heartache. I was angry. Drowning in a sea of guilt, sorrow, and regret. And then I saw you. Even though my mind could not accept it then, my soul knew you. It recognized your soul and knew that we were meant to be. I could not stay away from you, and it pained me every moment we had to be apart. Every *umbra* that I could come to you, be in your presence, hear your voice, feel your touch... you healed me. You put me back together, piece by piece. You took my wounds, the holes in my heart, and you stitched them back together. Took the darkness inside me and washed it away with your light. You have held me through my tears and not looked down on me for shedding them. Witnessed my anger with no judgment in your eyes but a comforting touch that eases me to no end. You have made me want to be a better male than I have ever been, than I ever thought I could be. And you gave me courage that I could not find before, to walk away from a life that was no life to live. You are the most precious gift I could ever have received." He captured her hands, taking them in his own. "On this *umbra*, the *umbra* of our mating, I make this vow to you. From this *umbra* until my last *umbra*, I will not waste one moment of the life gifted to us. I will honor you and cherish you with everything in me. I will protect you always, even if it takes my last breath. And I will spend every *umbra* showing you just how much that I love you. And if the gods wish it and one *umbra* they grace us with young, then I will never be the father that my father was to me. I will be the father that they deserve." He brought her hands to his lips and kissed the back of each one. "You are my one and only, my love, my life, my heart, my mate, and my queen."

"Jocasta, you may proceed with your promise," Santos said.

Tears welled in the corners of Jocasta's eyes. It took her a second to compose herself. With a tiny sniffle, she beamed. "Pierce, the only *umbra* that could compare to today is the *umbra* you barreled into me and into my life. You found an angry, sarcastic, broken female and stitched her back together. Until I met you, I didn't know there was a piece of me missing, that my soul was empty. That my heart no longer felt like it beat. You took the shattered parts of me, and, one by one, you pieced them back together. You replaced my anger with joy. Filled my soul and breathed life back into me. Took my heart in your hands and reminded me I was worthy of being loved. You reminded me I could love someone as deeply as I love you, no matter how much I tried to deny what had always been in my heart. Stood by my side and allowed me to show my strength, even when it made you nervous. You held me without judgment when I was vulnerable and without question. You continuously bring me peace. Through everything, you helped me find the female I was meant to be." She squeezed his hands. "On this *umbra*, the *umbra* of our mating, I make this vow to you. From this *umbra* until my last, no matter the challenges we face, we will face them together. I'll always stand by your side and support you. Always be a listening ear, a shoulder, even if you don't think you need them. I'll spend the rest of my life showing you how much I love you." She lifted his hands and kissed each of his palms. "You are my one and only, my heart, my life, my mate, my other half, and my king."

Pierce's eyes brimmed with tears. He took her face in his hands and brought his lips to hers. The tender and sweet kiss lingered. "I do not know how I ever lived without you," he whispered.

"Nor I, you," she responded and brushed another soft kiss to his lips.

Santos stifled a chuckle. That part was supposed to come later... but it came perfectly for the two of them. "Logan and Pierce, you may present your gifts."

Pierce turned his gaze to where Lillianna and Lyrica sat. Both wiped tears away as Lilli got to her feet and came over to stand before her eldest brother. He leaned down and pressed his forehead to hers as she slipped something into his hand. She did the same with Logan before she returned to her seat.

Pierce faced Jocasta. "Though I did not create this piece, it represents us perfectly. Two as halves, brought together to make a whole. The moon that we shared in spirit when we could not be together in the flesh. The beautiful music we create together. On this *umbra*, the *umbra* of our mating, it is an honor to present this gift to you, my queen." With a slight dip of his chin, he held out his palm and presented it to her. It was a thin chain made of electrum with a circle. A full moon, one-half ruby, the other half amber, rested at the center of the circle. The charm attached to a straight piece of electrum, allowing the moon to spin. It twinkled differently at various angles. A single musical note dangled from the bottom of the circle.

Jocasta's eyes sparkled as tears trickled down her face. "It's perfect. Absolutely perfect." Wiping the wetness from her cheeks, she turned so he could put it on her.

He draped it around her neck and fastened the clasp, then kissed her shoulder over his mating mark. "I love you."

Another smile fell to her lips, and she faced him once again.

While Pierce presented Jocasta with his gift, Logan accepted the necklace from Lillianna and faced Ambrosia. He held out the necklace made from electrum, two intertwined hearts, one made of amber and one made of aquamarine, sitting at the center of a circle. It also spun, revealing a swirl of colors between the two gems. A mountain dangled from the bottom of the circle. "Although this was not created by my hand, it is a perfect representation of the two of us. Not only have our hearts joined, but the love we have for one another is as sturdy as a mountain. On this *umbra*, the *umbra* of our mating, it is an honor to present this gift to you, my love."

Wiping tears from the corners of her eyes, Ambrosia swept her hair back from her shoulders as he draped it around her neck and fastened the clasp. "It's perfect. Absolutely perfect." She smiled up at him. "I love you."

"I love you, too," Logan said.

"Ambrosia and Jocasta, you may present your gifts."

Lyrica stood and pressed her palm to first Jocasta, then Ambrosia, before returning to her seat.

Jocasta's smile brightened as she turned toward Pierce once more, her gaze lifting to his. "I may not have created this piece, but I believe it suits us well. The perfect complement to each other. Our two hearts have come together as one. You, as my king, and I, as your queen." Another small sniffle escaped. "On this *umbra*, the *umbra* of our mating, it's an honor to present this gift to you, my king." With a bow of her head, she opened her palm and held out the bracelet to him. It was a chain link bracelet made from electrum with a rectangular plate in the center. On one side sat an interlocking heart of amber and ruby with *My Queen* inscribed next to it; and on the other side sat an interlocking heart of ruby and amber with *My King* inscribed next to it.

Pierce's smile widened as he gazed down at it. He raised her free palm to his mouth and kissed it. "It is absolutely perfect. I will wear it forever with honor, my queen. It will never leave me." He held his left wrist out for her so she could put it on him.

"I love you, Pierce." She placed a small kiss on the inside of his wrist, then placed the bracelet around his left wrist and fastened the clasp. It fit him perfectly. Jocasta took his hands within her own, and her eyes met his.

Ambrosia offered her mother a brief nod as she turned to Logan with the bracelet in her hand. It was a chain link bracelet made from electrum with a rectangular plate in the center. On one side sat an interlocking heart of amber and aquamarine with *My Rock* inscribed next to it; and on the other side sat an interlocking heart of aquamarine and amber with *My Shield* inscribed next to it. Her gaze met his. "While I didn't make this piece myself, I think it says it all. The strength and armor we provide for each other have created the perfect balance, joining our hearts together as one." With one hand, she wiped at her eyes again. "On this *umbra*, the *umbra* of our mating, it's an honor to present this gift to you, my love, my rock."

The smile on Logan's face widened as she placed the bracelet around his left wrist and fastened the clasp. "I will never take it off, my love. I will wear it forever with great pride."

To complete the ceremony, Santos turned over the right hands of first Pierce and Jocasta, hovered his hands above their wrists, and embedded their combined initials in their skin. Once he finished with them, he walked over to Logan and Ambrosia and, once again, placed his hands above their right wrists and embedded their combined initials in their skin. Santos stepped back to the altar. "It is now my pleasure to announce that from this *umbra* henceforth, you, Pierce and Jocasta, and you, Logan and Ambrosia, shall be recognized as one. You may kiss your mates."

Without hesitation, Logan wrapped an arm around Ambrosia, drew her close, and leaned down, crushing his lips to hers. When the kiss broke, he placed a tender kiss on her nose and nuzzled her throat.

Pierce brought Jocasta's body flush to his, one hand on the small of her back, the other against her cheek. Leaning down until their lips touched, he let out a soft growl. "Mine." And then he kissed her with everything in him. When the kiss broke, he held her against him, his eyes staring deep into hers. "I am yours, and you are mine."

"Always and forever." She stroked the back of his head, and then his ears, and brought his lips to hers one more time.

A low growl came out of him. "I could kiss you every moment for forever and still never get enough," he said. He caressed her canine ears, nuzzled them, placed a kiss against the top of her head, and then kissed her once more. "You are officially my mate, my queen. Nothing and no one can ever part us. Never again."

"Mmm, no, they can't, my king." Her eyes lit up. "Are you ready to head back down the aisle so the ceremonial celebration can get started?"

"I am ready to walk anywhere in the world, my queen, as long as I am walking there with you." He kissed her again, wrapped his arm around her, and led her back down the aisle.

As the couples walked side by side, the entire village threw daffodils at them as a welcome to their new beginning.

Chapter Sixteen

As they reached the end of the aisle, Pierce moved to the side with Jocasta and just held her. It seemed impossible to feel as joyful as he did right now. "I love you so very much, my queen." As he kissed her, he sensed his sister draw near and looked over.

Lilli threw her arms around both of them. "I am so happy for you both. Everything was just so beautiful." She stepped back and wiped at a few more tears.

Still holding his mate against him, he grinned at Lilli. "You look wonderful, sister mine. I am so happy that you were here with us today."

"Me too." Her amethyst gaze swung to Jocasta. "Does this mean I can officially call you my sister now?"

His mate beamed brightly. "Absolutely. Though I already considered you my sister."

"I do too." She embraced them once more and then headed to Logan and Ambrosia. She threw her arms around them, hugging them hard. "I am so happy for you both. So happy I could meet you both, so I could be here with you today."

"I am thrilled you are here with us," Logan stated.

"Me too, Lilli. I'm grateful that we have you here in our lives," Ambrosia said.

"I am grateful to be here, and be a part of this family." She hugged them again. "I do not want to crowd anyone." She grinned at Ambrosia. "Do not say it, I know. But I am also starving. I just wanted to say congratulations."

Ambrosia laughed softly. "Thank you. Go get some food. We'll catch up later."

Pierce flicked his attention back to his mate. "She looks so alive today. You have helped to do that." He kissed her nose and then her lips.

Jocasta caressed the back of his neck, gingerly running her fingers through his fur. "It just gets better from here."

"Yes, it does. Every single *umbra* will get better and better." He stroked her ears and captured her lips, kissing her deeply. A low moan escaped her as she melted into him. It would be interesting to see how long, not just he, but both of them, could hold out before sneaking away.

Someone in front of them cleared their throat.

The kiss released. A small tinge of pink touched Jocasta's cheeks, complementing the flush to her skin exquisitely. "Hi, Mom."

Giving them a quick, tight embrace, she took each of their hands in her own. "Congratulations. I'm so happy for you both."

"Thank you." Jocasta's eyes lit up.

"Yes, thank you, Lyrica," Pierce echoed.

Lyrica lifted Jocasta's hand, the one she had the charm bracelet on. "I am so glad you wore this."

"It was like having him here."

"I believe he was, dear. And I know he would be proud of the male you chose." Lyrica squeezed Pierce's forearm and lowered her voice just a tad. "Four or five, congratulations. Most will go for food first and congratulate you after. After the fifth, you can whisk her away."

Jocasta's eyes widened. She opened her mouth—

"What? How do you think you and your sister came about?" She gave them one last smile and strode over to Logan and Ambrosia.

A low laugh left his mouth. "I really adore your mother. She is a wonderful female." He kissed his mate again, tucking her firmly into his side. His perfect mate; the other half of him. Her bright amber eyes completely captivated him, to such a depth it was a moment before he realized others stood in front of them.

A small line had gathered of about three to four people. They accepted congratulations from each of them. In the end, Duke and Rayare approached with their spirited one-year-old little boy in Duke's arms. While Rayare embraced them both, Duke only gave Jocasta a side-hug.

"Congratulations, you two. It was absolutely beautiful," Rayare commented.

"Guess this means no more sparring sessions," Duke tacked on.

Jocasta giggled. "We spent more time chasing Kayan around than actual sparring." She reached up and squeezed the wiggling little boy's hand, who leaned toward Jocasta and Pierce.

"Although chasing him is still excellent exercise." Duke snickered.

Pierce chuckled. He brought his tail up and tickled Kayan with it. "My mother..." He cleared his throat. "My mother said the same when my brother and I were his age." He beamed. "Your young is beautiful. And thank you both for the congratulations." They clasped palms in a firm handshake.

"Thank you." Duke grinned, the ever-proud father.

Kayan giggled and played grab hands.

"Be careful. He has a tight grip," Rayare said. "You are welcome to chase him around any time."

Pierce smiled. "Thank you. And he is alright." He laughed when Kayan grabbed onto his tail and squeezed. "A tight grip indeed. He is going to grow into a powerful male, like his father." He and Duke had spent little time together, but he already considered the male a friend. Something that had been fairly rare for him until recently.

"I concur with my mate. It will be good practice," Duke said.

"You two are just garnering for a free sitter." Jocasta's amber eyes sparkled. "Not that I think we would ever mind."

Reaching for his son's belly, Duke tickled Kayan, who giggled and squirmed as he let go of Pierce's tail.

Pierce tugged his mate tighter against him. "We would not mind at all. What do you say, Kayan? Would you like to come and hang out with us sometime?"

As if in response, the young gleefully leaned forward and reached out toward Pierce and Jocasta again.

"I will take that as a yes," Rayare replied.

"As would I." Duke glanced at the parting crowd from Ambrosia and Logan. He shook Pierce's hand one last time. "Congratulations again, you two."

"Thanks, Duke."

Beaming, Pierce watched them walk away. It seemed as if it was something he simply couldn't stop doing today, not that he wanted to. "They are lovely people." He leaned down and kissed Jocasta. "That was four or five, right? I may have been counting." He smirked and nipped her lip.

"Yes, it was." No one else came up to them. Just as her mother said, nearly everyone had gone to the tables for food. "I think we can sneak away."

He let out a low growl. "Where would you like to sneak away to, my love? If we end up at home in our bed, we will not make it back to the party. And I would like to dance with my queen."

"The barns worked out *well* for us." An image of the greenhouse entered her mind. "Actually, I have a better idea." She crooked a finger at him, waving him closer. "Especially since I'm not wearing any underwear."

A low rumble left him as his eyes darkened. With a hard, deep kiss, his tongue stroked every part of her tongue and the inside of her mouth. She didn't stop the throaty moan that escaped. "Mmm. I love it when you do not wear any underwear," he mumbled. "When there is nothing between us." He kissed her again as he scooped her up in his arms. "Right now, I wish to carry you. If that is alright with you, my queen? You can tell me where to go."

"I'm quite happy to be in your arms. Head toward the gardens, beyond the houses."

"Whatever my queen demands." His lips connected with hers again, the kiss languid but deep, as he kept one eye on the direction he walked. Running into anyone or anything was the last thing he wanted to do, especially with his mate in his arms.

With one hand, she caressed his cheek, while the other gingerly stroked the nape of his neck. They left all the din behind and wound their way through the maze of houses, past the gardens, and to the large greenhouse. Its glass panels sparkled beneath the sunlight. He reached blindly for the doorknob and carried her inside. Closing it behind them, Pierce leaned back against the door and turned her in his arms. Her legs came around his waist and her arms across the breadth of his shoulders. Cupping her cheek, he just stared into her gaze. "I love you, Jocasta. It is not something I can say enough. I love you so very much."

"As I'll never tire of hearing it or of saying it. I love you more than I thought possible, Pierce. And I'm so grateful to have you in my life."

Both of their eyes lit up. The glow of their combined amber and ruby bathed them in a bright orange light, like fire or the color of arising sun. "As I am so grateful for you, my queen. I never knew my heart was capable of the depth of the love I hold for you." He engaged her in another kiss, his lips and tongue entangling with hers as he carried her over to an empty work table. Sitting her on the edge, her legs remained around his waist. Pierce stroked her ears, the back of her head, then along the nape of her neck. Brushing his lips down her jaw and over the pulse in her throat, he whispered against her, "I am going to worship every inch of you."

Her head angled as she skimmed the top of his shoulders down to his biceps. Tracing the taut lines of his muscles, Jocasta bit her bottom lip. "Then I guess it's a good thing I had half a mind for this dress to be made easy to remove."

"Mmm. A marvelous thing." He swept the tip of his tongue along her throat to her ear, nipping it gently. Despite his desperation to see her bare form, he carefully removed her dress and set it aside. Staring at her gloriously naked form, he lost all breath for a moment. From the glittering pink merfolk scales along her outer thigh where he brushed his thumb to the gray fur of her wolf-ears that he stroked with his fingertips to that brilliant mark of his embedded in her alabaster flesh, every part of her stole the oxygen from his lungs. Cupping her swollen breast, he teased the tight, rosy bud of her nipple. "You take my breath away every time I look at you. I cannot get enough."

Shifting her gaze to his, her fingers continued their dance over his arms. She trailed back up and across his shoulders. One hand skimmed the nape of his neck as her grip around his waist loosened. "I feel the same way every time I look into your eyes. Forever will not be enough."

Beaming, he pressed his lips to hers. Pierce trailed his fingers over the scales on her hip and the small of her back. He traced a path with his mouth from her jaw to her neck as he massaged her breast. To him, she was the perfect beauty, despite her varied forms. They had always fit wonderfully together. He planned to show her, slowly, just how beautiful she was to him.

As much as he took his time, so did she. Not that they needed to explore one another's bodies; they knew each other as well as they knew their own. But they both longed to show each other exactly how flawless they felt about the other. That the gods had designed them for one another. Her fingers sifted through his fur from the top of his head and on down.

"I love how it feels when you touch me." Sliding his hand up her spine, he traced kisses along her collarbone. Her back arched as he wrapped his lips around her breast and lashed the tip of her nipple with his tongue. His fingers brushed over her hip until he reached her leg, dancing over her knee and talons, then wandered back up to her inner thigh.

"Gods, that feels so good." A moan left her mouth as her head fell back. Her grip on his shoulder blades tightened as she continued to trail her fingers over every nuance of his muscles. "I love touching you."

"Then let us not stop." With a growl, he turned his attention to her other breast. He sucked and licked, switching his hold on her. Pierce grazed his claws down her other leg, talons, and inner thigh. Keeping his pace slow, he just barely brushed his knuckles over her sex.

With a soft gasp, her back arched, pressing her breast more into his mouth. Her talons skimmed along the back of his thighs and up over his ass as she rubbed her legs across his hips. The grip she had around his waist loosened, her thighs spreading further apart for him. She gently raked her nails from the middle of his back down to the small of his back and the base of his tail.

A vibration traveled up through his chest. A shiver went down his spine, followed by a moan as he swept his mouth down the valley between her breasts. Grazing his fangs over her stomach, he laid her back fully on the table. Gently, he scraped his claws over her ribcage and sides and brushed his knuckles against her sex. Swirling his tongue around her navel, he nipped at her hips and teased her inner thighs with the tip of his tongue.

"Oh, gods," she cried out. Her thighs clenched, and her talons curled around his ass, digging into him without breaking the skin. She massaged the base of his tail.

Some mixture of a growl and a moan came out of him, one that didn't cease as her exquisite scent filled his nostrils. Gods, he loved how her talons felt. Unable to wait any longer to have her taste in his mouth, he covered her breasts, squeezing and massaging, as he slipped his tongue inside her. The gasp out of her mouth had his senses exploding with delight and satisfaction. He knew every inch of her body, inside and out, but each exploration, touch, and taste was like the first time all over again.

With a loud moan, she raked her fingers up his body until her hands gripped tightly to his biceps. Her back arched as he drove his tongue into her repeatedly. Her talons scraped against his shoulder blades, digging into his skin.

Every scrape, moan, and cries of ecstasy made his cock thicken and his growls louder. As her orgasm gushed over his tongue, he sucked and licked at her sex to get every drop. He could have stayed here all night long, and he wasn't ready to leave it yet. Grazing his claws down her sides and inner thighs, the noises he made vibrated through her sex as he drove his tongue back inside her, harder and deeper, devouring her.

Her taloned feet curled more into his shoulder blades. She cried out his name as another orgasm exploded over his tongue. He didn't waste a single drop as he lapped up everything she gave him.

Pulling his mouth just barely away from her sex, his gaze traveled up her body until their eyes met. He made one slow sweep of his tongue up her slit before he licked his lips. "Mmm. I love it when you scream my name." A smile spread across her face as he moved to hover back over her, worshiping her with his tongue and lips the whole way up. He brushed a soft kiss across her lips, intertwined their hands, and laced their fingers together. Her legs dropped to his hips once more. "I love you so much, my queen."

"I love you as well, so much, my king. So much."

"We will love each other for eternity." He fused their lips together again, the kiss slow and urgent, deep and passionate. As his cock found her sex and he slid inside her, that mixture of a growl and moan came out of him again. She hooked her legs just above his hips, locking them around his waist. Their lips didn't part as he pumped in and out of her with slow, deep strokes. Her hips rose to meet his each time, the rhythm of their bodies in perfect sync.

She ran her hands up and down his body, leaving no part of him untouched. A throaty moan left her as the deep kiss continued, to the point neither could tell where his breath ended, and hers began.

He fisted a palmful of her hair as he skimmed his claws over her soft skin. Their pace stayed the same, slow and torturous. Settling his hands on her sides, he kissed down her jaw, sucked on the side of her throat, and then returned his lips to hers, his orgasm right on the edge. "Come with me, my queen."

Her thighs clenched. As her sex pulsated around him, she cried out his name. They pitched over the edge together in a powerful explosion, the two of them coming together in unison.

As he shook with his release, he pressed his forehead against hers, his sex kicking inside her. The two of them clung to one another as their bodies stilled, their ragged breaths the only noise in the greenhouse. He had no words for how she made him feel each time they came together like this. How she grasped him and cried out his name. It was a few minutes before he could speak. Even when they'd fought their feelings, the quietness spoke their truth. It always would. The sounds they made when they came together said so much, but the peace between them afterward said more. "Gods, how I love you," he confessed.

A soft smile crossed her mouth. "I love you, too, Pierce. More than I ever imagined possible."

He stroked her lips with his thumb and caressed her ears. "I do not know what I ever did to deserve someone so wonderful as you. But if this is a dream, I know it is eternal. There is nothing in this world or beyond it that could ever tear me away from you. You will hold my heart and soul forever."

She leaned into his touch and pressed a soft kiss to his thumb. "If this is a dream, then it's the best kind. One I never want to wake up from. I know this is forever. Nothing could come between us. You have all of me for the rest of our *umbras*."

They'd been gone from the celebration for some time. Not that he knew how much. He chuckled softly. "Our family probably thinks we are not coming back." He nuzzled her nose. "Not that I particularly want to leave where we are or stop gazing at you, especially looking like you are right now." He nipped her lip and gave her another soft kiss. "Should we head back, though?"

"As much as I would love to stay in this nice, quiet corner of ours, Ambrosia will kill me if I ruin the surprise we have planned for you and Logan."

"A surprise, hmm? You are completely spoiling me, my love. It is something I am not used to. I have a feeling, though, I am going to have to get used to it?"

"Oh yes, very much so. Wait until we have a true day of birth celebration." A glint of mischief flickered in her eyes. "I rather enjoy surprising you."

"You surprise me more and more every *umbra*." He pressed a tender kiss to her lips as he pulled her up to sit, withdrew from her warm cocoon, and then reached over to the next table to retrieve her dress. "As breathtaking as you are in your dress, I am a little sad that you have to put it back on."

With a giggle, she took the dress from him, got down from the table, and slipped it on. She turned around. "I promise we won't stay the whole night."

He zipped her dress up and kissed the mark on her shoulder. "We can stay as long as you want, my queen. I have not been to a celebration like this before and, besides,"—he kissed her shoulder again—"I cannot say if we will make it out of our home tomorrow." He nipped her ear as he put his arms around her.

"Mmm, well, it might be a little selfish, but I like the idea of stealing you away for the night so I can have you all to myself." She peered at him over her shoulder. "And staying inside all *umbra* tomorrow sounds like paradise."

"Mmm, that it does." He nuzzled her ears. "You can always be as selfish with me as you want. Having you to myself all night sounds absolutely perfect."

"I'm so glad you agree with me." She threaded her fingers through his. "Shall we rejoin the party?"

"I think so." He kissed her once more, and then led her back to the clearing.

Chapter Seventeen

When Jo and Pierce arrived back at the clearing, the celebration was well into full swing. Several people milled around, chattering; some of the young ran around with ribbons billowing behind them, but most gathered across the multitude of tables that they'd placed around the dancefloor and low stage they had set up. A simple piano, something that hadn't been there before, sat on the platform.

Ambrosia and Logan stood together, side by side, his arm draped across her shoulder, talking to one of the other couples in the village.

Jo's gaze flicked from them to the rich black-colored piano. Exactly as she'd requested.

Pierce glanced at the setup, then back down at her. He caressed her cheek as he turned her face to his. "Is this the surprise you and your sister planned?"

She leaned into his touch. Something she loved to do. "Well, yes, and no. This is mine. The surprise she and I have planned. Let's just say it will make for the best first dance ever."

He kissed her softly. "I will not even try to guess, but I cannot wait for it."

"Mmm, I promise it is something you'll never forget." She gestured to the musical instrument and its bench. "Care to join me?"

"Always, my queen."

No additional words passed between them as she led him to the wooden platform. Stepping onto the stage, the sky's orange, purple, and yellow hues served as their background. Jo didn't miss that several people stopped talking, a hush falling over the village. It was as if they hadn't heard her sing in, well, a really long time. She took a seat at the piano and adjusted her feet to the pedals, then nodded for Pierce to sit next to her.

He settled beside her, angling his body to face her, and placed his hand upon the small of her back. His eyes were only for her.

Resting her fingers against the ivory keys, she glanced one last time to her mate. Her wonderful mate. Flicking her eyes to the piano, everything around them disappeared as she played the opening notes. No one else existed except the two of them. It had often been said between them over the last few days how neither thought they deserved the other, but the fact remained, they did.

Softly, Jo belted out the first line of Plumb's "Don't Deserve You." It was absolutely true. He was the first face she saw when she woke up. The last person she thought of at night. Their initial meeting flashed through her memory. That day in the alley had become their truth. She hadn't stopped thinking about him since then. All those months ago, and he had truly rescued her. They had breathed new life into one another. Now, neither could live without the other.

Getting lost in the music, she coaxed the amazing melody out as she moved into the chorus. Throughout all the vulnerabilities they shared, the issues they faced, they hadn't given up on one another. The first time he held her as she cried came to mind. The way she always seemed to know when he just needed her in his arms. Even when they didn't recognize it was happening, their arms were always open to each other. The words came out of her with everything they meant and everything he meant to her.

Her voice lifted into a powerful aria as she spoke of what they didn't feel they deserved. But they loved each other, anyway. The time they had together, regardless of what they did, would never be enough. They were all each other needed. No matter what happened between them, he would come after her, as she would him. They'd never let the other go.

Her voice softened as she moved into the second verse. Despite the horrors of their past, they'd seen beyond all the darkness and loved each other to the light. Her eyes shined for the first time in years because of him. They pushed forward because of each other. He had given her hope, dreams of their future. Things she never dared to consider before him. He gave her so much. More than she could ever imagine possible.

As she went into the chorus once again, she poured it all out. Told him all she had ever felt over the years and how he changed it in a matter of months. He hadn't just broken her walls; he had put her back together where she no longer needed them. Maybe they'd never fully believe they deserved the other, but it would never stop them from loving one another. The love they gave each other was everything she had ever wanted. One day, they'd find they deserved it. Everything they felt was right there in the words she sang, her voice carrying across the clearing. No matter how they felt about themselves ,their love was enough to withstand it all and bring them into each other's arms repeatedly.

Tears shined in her mate's ruby eyes, but he kept them from falling down his cheeks. When the song ended, he tilted her face toward his and kissed her. "Your voice is the most beautiful voice I have ever heard," he whispered. "I am... speechless. Thank you for singing to me."

She'd sing to him any time he wanted, whenever he needed it. It had given her great joy to put this together. Of all the things she could think to say, only one of them felt perfect. She reached up, caressed his cheek, and pressed her forehead to his. "Thank you for helping me find my voice again."

It was at that point, the explosion of applause broke through, mixed in with a few hoots and hollers. Everyone celebrating the music the two of them had made together because she couldn't have done it without him by her side.

He drew her into his arms as their mouths crashed together. The passion they felt for one another was something neither of them could ever grow tired of. When the kiss broke, he gazed into her eyes. "Do I get to dance with you now?"

Jo glanced over to the bottom of the small staircase where Rayare patiently awaited. Her smile brightened as her gaze found his again. "Yes, you absolutely do."

He kissed her, then got up from the seat and helped her to her feet. Wrapping his arm around her, he led her off the stage. Lilli hovered nearby, a tightness around her eyes.

"Is she okay?" Pierce muttered to her.

Rayare headed up to the stage and toward the piano.

"She has a surprise for us. Mom helped her with it." With the way Lilli looked, she'd guess the female was nervous. She'd been the same way the first time she sat at that piano. She nodded toward the dance floor, where Ambrosia and Logan waited.

Pierce led her out to the dance floor near them and gathered her into his arms. "Is she really…?" His gaze flitted once to Lilli before he focused his attention on Jo.

Didn't that just sum up their relationship perfectly.

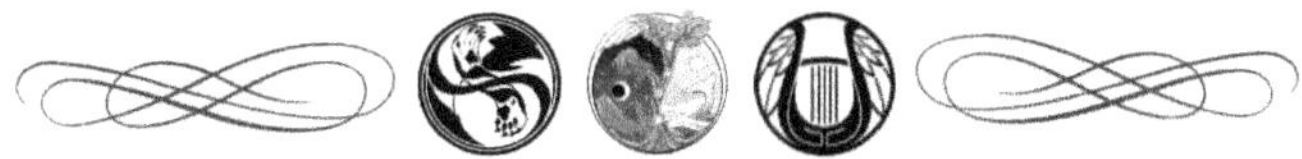

The dark purple silk of Lilli's dress shimmered in the lights as she made her way to the center of the platform. The colors of the fabric appeared to shift from light to dark and back again. Once she found her spot, the swishing of her skirt settled. She opened her mouth, then closed it. Gazing out across the crowd, a fluttery sensation in the pit of her stomach nearly consumed her. She'd done nothing like this before. But then she focused on them—her family. The tension in her body settled some. Not that all the hesitation disappeared from her voice as she spoke.

"Some very special people to me helped me pick this song and practice it for today." She cleared her throat. "Growing up, I did not have many reasons to sing, or to even smile. That all changed just two *umbras* ago on my day of birth, when I was given the best gift that I could not have ever imagined. I was given a family—a genuine family—and a new chance at life." She cleared her throat again. "The gift of a song is so small in comparison, but I am hoping it says all the things I find it difficult to put into words. To my brothers, Pierce and Logan. And to my new sisters, Ambrosia and Jocasta. On this *umbra*, the *umbra* of your mating, this song is my gift to you. I wish the four of you all the happiness in the world."

Lilli stared at her family as the music began, starting out soft and slow. She inhaled and exhaled a deep breath. She trained her eyes on her brothers, standing with their mates, and then she sang. Jo had helped her pick the song: "I Turn to You" by Christina Aguilera.

She felt lost, scared, unable to find any light in the everyday storms, lost all ground, had been losing the will and the strength to fight, and had almost given into eternal darkness.

Pierce had protected her as much as he could over the years. He had fought her battles, defended her countless times, and almost lost his life because of it. Amid the storm, he was both her shield and the source of strength. He'd been there every step of the way, fighting to keep her alive for all these years. Held her and comforted her through her pain. He'd kept her breathing when she didn't think she had the strength to take even one more breath.

Though her relationship with Logan was still brand new, he'd given her an actual home. Things she'd never had. Extended his arms and brought her into the embrace of her new family. Taken her away from the abyss and given her a new lease on life. He'd renewed her faith and given her a brand-new hope that the future ahead of her was bright and full of happiness. He'd inspired her to find courage to speak on the things that, most of the time, were too difficult to even think about.

Lyrica and Ambrosia and Jocasta had loved her and accepted her before they'd even met her. They'd hugged her without her saying she needed one. Brushed her tears away when she couldn't reach a hand up to brush them away herself. Calmed her fears with gentle kindness and understanding. Brought out a bigger smile than had ever been on her face. Helped her find the beauty inside herself that she'd never known was there. And when the nightmare had reared its ugly head, Ambrosia had held her until she calmed, brought safety and peace back to her, and had stayed with her until she was back asleep.

Through the rest of her wonderful life, she knew she could always turn to them for anything. They would love her always, as she would always love them. Through any storm that came her way, they would be her shield. They would shelter her through every downpour of rain. They would be her strength, and she knew without a doubt she could always rely on them. Because of them, she knew she could do anything.

As she hit the last verse before the last chorus, she reached deep down inside of her, belting out the notes with everything she had. Tears streamed down her face, but it didn't stop her from pouring out her soul. It was something she'd never had the courage to do. But now that she'd done so, she never wanted to turn back.

When the song ended, her hands automatically went to her warm cheeks, covering her blush, as everyone in the clearing applauded. Joyous whistles came from Ambrosia. Logan beamed proudly. Pierce and Jocasta both smiled up at her. Pierce wiped at his eyes, then nuzzled his mate's ears and pressed a kiss on top of her head.

Lilli left the stage, her cheeks still burning but with a smile plastered on her features. She wiped the wetness from her face as she went to Lyrica, who took her hands in hers. "Did... did I do okay?" Gods, she hoped they had liked it. She'd done nothing like that before. Not even close.

"My dear, you did beautifully." Lyrica squeezed her hands in reassurance. "They absolutely loved it. I can see it in their faces."

Pierce looked over at Lilli and caught her gaze. He kissed his palm, then placed it over his heart, bowing his head to her, and then laid his cheek on top of Jo's as he held her. Lilli beamed at him, then Logan too, before turning her gaze back to Lyrica. Gods, she couldn't stop smiling. "Thank you, Lyrica. Thank you for everything. I was—" Lilli let out a breath. "Oh, I was so nervous. I have never sung in front of a bunch of people before."

Lyrica patted Lilli's hand and lowered her voice. "It can be quite nerve-wracking. Do not tell Jocasta I said this, but you did better than the very first time she got up there."

Warmth flooded her cheek. "Oh..." Lilli shook her head a little. "She has an exquisite voice." Swallowing the lump in her throat, Lilli's gaze fell briefly to the ground. "I have never done that before. I did not even know I could. My father, he... he did not like it when I sang. But..." She lifted her gaze to Lyrica. "I think—no, I know—I would like to do it again."

"Then it is a good thing you have a family full of musicians. I know. I speak for everyone when I say I would love to hear you sing again." Lyrica grinned. "Shall we find a seat? I believe my daughters have one more thing up their sleeve before we get to join in on the dance floor."

Lilli nodded and followed her to a seat.

Ambrosia grinned as her twin glanced in her direction. Yes, it was time for the last surprise they had planned. She gave Jo a small dip of her chin and signaled for Rayare to begin.

Loudly, the female announced, "We would like to invite all couples to join the newly mated on the dance floor." The last of the sun's rays fell below the horizon. In each corner of the dance floor, red, aquamarine, and amber lights lit up and shined across the ground.

It was absolutely stunning to see the mix of colors together. Just one last touch. She lifted her wrist and found the musical note charm her father had given her and her sister a long time ago. Pressing her fingers tightly together over the amber gemstone, it glowed.

Near to her and Logan, the same jewel lit up. It was the one on her twin's wrist. Notes from the piano filled the air again as several couples joined them on the dance floor.

Smiling up at her mate, Ambrosia took his hands within her own. It wasn't necessary to see that her twin had done the same with Pierce. Simultaneously, in perfect unison, she and her twin belted out the first verse of Jasmine Rae's "When I Found You."

There had been no other song for the two of them to sing together. It spoke perfectly of today, the day they each got to mate their one true love. The warmth, the tears of joy, and the beauty of it all, of watching the dark moments fade beneath the brightness of their love. What they had each found in the male they'd chosen for themselves. Although she sang together with her sister, every word and every lyric she used to serenade Logan.

Ambrosia and Jo broke into the chorus. They each echoed how the world changed when they found their other half. Because they saw one another, they knew one another's truth. They understood it. What they found was safety in one another's arms. It allowed each of them to rediscover themselves. To grow. And become who they were meant to be.

She and her sister entered the second verse. It may not have been her first official dance with her mate, but dancing with Logan, it felt that way every time, especially having officially claimed him as hers before the entire village. Their feet moved a little, but he made her feel like they floated across the sky. Every time. That was how loved she felt. A love she'd never known but would last for all time.

Matching her sister's aria, they belted out the chorus again. Ambrosia thought back to the first time she met Logan. Not everyone could be as lucky as them and literally fall into the arms of their mate. Maybe she didn't know it, but she had found him... waiting for her. Something he didn't seem to realize either. Then again, they'd both been waiting for each other.

And they certainly showed one another exactly what love could be like between two people.

As the song ended, the smile on her face never left. "I love you, Logan, with everything I have."

"I love you, too, Ambrosia." He leaned down and brushed a soft kiss across her lips. "How do you feel about some food... first?"

Ambrosia chuckled. Yeah, her twin and Pierce had pulled their disappearing act not long after the ceremony concluded. Not that she hadn't thought about it herself, but she didn't feel the need to rush right off. There'd be plenty of time to sneak away. "Mmm, it's like you read my mind."

Kissing her again, he wrapped an arm around her and tucked her into his side. "Or we are just on the same page."

"That too." Linking arms, they walked to the table where someone had laid out the food. The spread was vast. All kinds of vegetables, fruits, baked goods, meat covered the table, from kabobs to broiled fish, sweet rolls, miniature cakes, chocolates, stewed apples, and more. For drinks, they had the option of tea, lavender lemonade, and milk. It was all quite enticing. Each of them loaded up a plate, so they'd have plenty of energy to work off and joined her mother and new sister.

Jo and Pierce weren't too far behind them. Those two sat next to Lilli while she and Logan sat next to her mother.

Pierce gave Logan's shoulder a squeeze. "Congratulations, brother mine. And you as well, Ambrosia."

There was so much to celebrate. Their new family gathered together at the table, and an out-pour of joy emanating from all of them. "Thank you. And congratulations to you, too," Ambrosia replied.

"You as well, brother. And to you, Jocasta," Logan said.

All her sister could do was nod. Jo had stuffed a big bite of potato in her mouth. Chewing the bite up, she swallowed. "Thank you. Yes, congratulations."

"Thank you both." Pierce turned his attention to his sister.

To give her new brother-in-law some privacy as he spoke to Lilli, Ambrosia faced her mother, who'd been quiet. Or too focused on eating to say anything. "Everything okay, Mom?"

"Yes. I am just... overjoyed at seeing both you and your sister getting mated today. And it perhaps reminded me a bit... of my mating ceremony."

Taking her mother's hand in her own, she clasped it tight. It probably hadn't been as easy as the woman had made it seem; being there and helping with the dresses. A day she was certain her mother really missed her father. "I love you, Mom." Setting her fork down, Ambrosia hugged the woman.

"I love you, too, sweetheart."

Releasing the embrace, Ambrosia flicked her gaze over to Pierce and Lilli as they parted their own hug. It was nice to feel the warmth being shared by her entire family. The corners of her mouth curled as she saw Pierce slide his arm around Jo and kiss one of her ears before starting on his food.

"It was truly amazing, Lilli. You did such a beautiful job up there," Jo said between bites.

"Thank you, Jo." Lilli's cheeks tinged a light shade of pink; even through her white fur, it was noticeable. "This food is great."

"It is good food," Ambrosia said. It always seemed like that, with any kind of celebration. Usually more so with mating ceremonies. Though this could have been bigger than the last couple. Who had gotten mated last? Duke and Rayare, they'd been the last couple to mate. "I think they went out of their way this time."

Jo canted her head. "I don't think the spread is more than it was the last time we had a mating celebration."

"There was definitely more singing." Ambrosia swung her gaze across each member of her family. Then again, it made the most sense. "But honestly, I wouldn't change any of that. It's rather fitting for our family."

"You two were wonderful. The songs were perfect too. And the lights, oh, they were so beautiful. I did not know a mating celebration could be like this," Lilli said.

"The lights were Adara's doing. She and I have coordinated over the *solaris* and improved them with each celebration." Jo glanced at Pierce. "But they were perfect."

"Everything was perfect, my queen." Pierce kissed Jo's shoulder.

"A lot of our celebrations are like this," Ambrosia tacked on. Most of the time, anyway. Some things they had handled with more sensitivity for their family, given certain circumstances.

"Really?" Logan raised an eyebrow. "What other celebrations?"

Ambrosia peered at her mate. It hadn't occurred to her to be more specific. Of all the things they'd spoken of, he'd told her how little they actually celebrated in Métamorphe. One of the many changes in their new family unit, they would have to get used to around here. "Let me correct myself. Mating celebrations are always more extravagant. That said, we celebrate births, days of births, communal holidays, and such. Each is handled a little differently."

"Do you have big celebrations for the day of birth as well? "Lilli asked, her hand settling over the necklace she wore. "And what on earth is a holiday?"

"Something you will get to celebrate many of, sister mine," Pierce said.

Ambrosia clasped Lilli's hand. "We do yes. A holiday is like a day of birth, except it's an event that holds significance to the entire village."

"Our next holiday is still a couple of *cycles* off, but I promise we'll make sure you know. There is a day of birth celebration in a few *umbras*, though," Jo stated.

Ambrosia frowned. She was typically good at keeping track of birthdays and holidays, always ensuring their family gave a gift. And she was most often the one who took care of it. Had she forgotten a birthday? "Whose day of birth is coming up?"

"Kayan's."

Her eyes widened. No. It couldn't be. "It hasn't been a *solaris* already, has it?" Wow! Had time really flown by that much she hadn't noticed it?

A small chuckle left her twin's mouth. "Yes, it has."

"We must get the young male a gift, love," Pierce said.

"We can certainly do that," Jo replied.

"Perhaps I can make him something." Logan glanced from his brother to her. "He was quite energetic."

Ambrosia laughed. "Yes, he is. Jo knows all about that." She reached for Logan's hand and threaded their fingers together. "And I think that sounds like a grand idea." As they'd both finished their food, this seemed like a great excuse to slip away.

"It is a perfect idea." Pierce smiled at his brother. "Mother often said that we were energetic too at that age. Always getting into trouble, never sitting still." He snickered. "I do not know how they have all that energy in their tiny bodies."

"Try something with wings. Or something that flies. It's his favorite." Finishing the last of her food, Jo leaned against Pierce. "I don't know. I can't tell you how much he loves it when Duke lifts him in the air. Then again, he loves when we chase him, too."

"I believe I can handle that." Logan slipped his arm around her shoulders. His aquamarine eyes met hers and lit up. Gods, staring into those exquisite peepers was like watching the natural ebb and flow of the ocean. It sent shivers down her spine.

"I cannot wait to see what you come up with," Pierce said. He finished his food and settled back in his chair. He flicked his eyes to Lilli. She had finished eating too and was just scanning her surroundings. Focusing back on Jo, the corners of his mouth lifted as he stared down at her, his fingertips moving up and down her arm.

Well, that definitely answered that question. Ambrosia pushed her empty plate forward on the table and got up, with Logan right behind her. "We're going to go back to the dance floor," she called out to their family. They headed toward the dance floor and used it as the distraction to slip away unseen for a little alone time.

Chapter Eighteen

They'd spent hours dancing, mingling, and getting more into the food. Both Pierce and Logan had danced with Lilli. It had been wonderful doing so, another first, and Pierce loved watching the smile never leave his little sister's face. While he swayed with her, his mate borrowed young Kayan as her dance partner.

Afterward, Jocasta had handed the young male off to his mother and rejoined him on the dance floor. It had been a perfect day. There was simply no other way to describe it. While several members of the village still weren't ready for it to end, he was quite ready to have his mate all to himself.

Saying the last goodbye they intended, Jocasta beamed up at him. Despite all the partying, neither of them was anywhere near tired. "Shall we head home, my king?"

Tightening his hold on her, he kissed her. "Mmm. That sounds absolutely perfect, my queen."

"Yes, it does." Threading their fingers together, she started forward, the two of them heading back toward their home.

They hadn't gone far before they heard wings flapping over all the din of the ongoing celebration. Pierce stopped as Jocasta did, shifting his gaze with hers toward the noise. Santos took off toward the trees that hid the entrance. They weren't the only ones that heard it. Several females ushered young away from the clearing. Ambrosia quickly found Lyrica and sent her and Lilli back to the house. "Go. Now."

"What is going on?" Lilli asked, a slight tremble in her voice.

Pierce tracked Santos's movements. A chill went through his body. He couldn't explain it, and he couldn't turn away. Someone was on the other side. Someone he knew. "Lilli, go. Now. Stay with Lyrica, and take Jocasta with you. Go home."

He knew it was difficult for Jocasta to leave his side, but this was one of those moments where it was necessary. With a brief nod, she squeezed his palm, collected her mother, and grabbed Lilli's hand. "Come on, let's go." Ambrosia was just behind them.

Once they were far enough away, Logan's gaze swung in his direction. "Are you getting the same sense I am?"

Pierce didn't even have to ask. "I sense our blood." He didn't know how any of them would have found this location. If it was Zinnia, hopefully, she hadn't come with bad intentions. If it was Dahlia or, gods forbid, Ailwin...Pierce clasped Logan's shoulder. Together, they jogged, practically running, toward the entrance.

Overhead, he heard the buzz of wings. These didn't belong to Santos. Three seiphinx, along with their warriors, raced toward the hidden point of entry. A dark-haired female rushed past them with a bag in hand.

The stone-like figure next to Santos carried a female wolf covered in dark, matted fur. As they moved across the clearing, Pierce's mind slowed down while his body sped up. The copper stench of blood reached him, along with a sweet but bitter scent that was... all wrong. His eyes fell upon the patches of the fur—what he could see of it—but couldn't make out the face. Regardless, he knew. Something inside him just knew. He sprinted across the glade toward them, Logan right on his heels.

"She is gravely wounded, Santos." The female reached into her bag and pulled out a syringe. "I will give her something more traditional for pain, but we will need to tend to her wounds in the medical building immediately."

"Then prepare a bed, Kaylina." His gaze flicked to Logan and Pierce as they approached.

With the shot of medication complete, the black-haired female nodded and bolted from the scene.

Pierce and Logan skidded to a stop. "Zinnia... Zinnia!" She didn't respond, open her eyes, or even twitch. Oh, gods, no... It had happened exactly as he'd feared. His chest heaved, and he couldn't breathe. Digging his claws into his palms, he looked up at Santos as they walked along with him and the warrior that carried her. "Is she alive?"

"She is alive, barely, but she is alive." Santos gave an unspoken order to the warrior, who continued toward the medical building with Zinnia in his arms. Santos turned to Logan and Pierce. "There is nothing for the two of you to do; it is best if you return home. Kaylina and I will tend to her wounds. I will send for you as soon as we can. She carried an item with her."

He held something out in his hand. A wooden lily... Shakily, Logan reached for it.

Pierce felt like his brain shorted out as he stared down at it. Gods, where was his breath? How was this possible? Ailwin had burned them all. Every piece, one by one. He didn't know how long they stood there. Or if there was some kind of exchange of words that he couldn't comprehend. He couldn't seem to get coherent thoughts to pass from his brain to his mouth. Finally, he found his voice again. "Was she followed?"

"She was alone on our borders. Though, to be safe, I have sent our warriors out to the forest to scout."

"There must be something we can do," Logan said. His hand wrapped tightly around the hand-crafted flower.

"You can return to your homes," Santos repeated.

Pierce might have nodded, but he wasn't sure. A twinge barely registered, and he glanced at his hands. Something wet bubbled beneath his claws that remained buried in his palms. He tried to open them, but they refused to obey the simple command. Pierce attempted to thank Santos, but it felt like a barrier had appeared, and he couldn't get anything to come out. He swallowed hard. Then swallowed again. "You will send for us... when you can?" Gods, was that his voice? It didn't even sound like his own.

"Yes." Saying nothing else, Santos turned and headed off toward the medical building.

Both of them just stared at the empty spot. Waiting. He hated waiting. But they were no healers. Neither he nor his brother. Zinnia... she was in expert hands. They just had to trust in that.

He didn't even track leaving. One minute, they were just standing there. The next, they were walking. Where were they walking? Oh, right? Home. He couldn't think. He couldn't breathe. How had she come to be here? He didn't need to ask who had done that to her. He had seen those wounds before on others. Though, those others hadn't made it. Zinnia would make it, though. She just had to.

"Zinni will make it," Logan echoed his thoughts when their feet stopped. Why had they stopped? Oh, yeah. They had returned to their homes. "What do we tell Lilli?"

"I do not know." Where had his voice come from? It still didn't sound like his. "Ensure that she knows Zinnia was alone. That she is still safe. They were never close. Zinnia never spoke against her, but she never spoke for her either. She could not."

Logan rubbed the back of his head, his fur standing on end as his gaze dropped to what he held. "Okay. Yeah. That sounds... yeah."

Pierce eyed the flower. He was still stunned. "She must have hidden it. I do not know. I watched him burn them all. Though I tried to stop him, but..." Their mother had tried to stop him too. Others had held them both back while Ailwin threw each piece, one by one, into a fire that had grown so large it had seemed to reach the sky. He could still smell her tears. Still hear her screams. He shook his head hard. Glancing toward Logan's home, he caught sight of a figure through the window. His mate was inside. They would have stayed together. "Let us go inside, brother. We cannot stay out here waiting all night." It wouldn't do either of them any good.

His brother's eyes shifted to the window. "Right."

He understood. It seemed impossible to get his feet to move, either. But he must. He was the eldest. He had to be strong. Even if his heart froze in heartbreak. Zinnia was in expert hands. She was going to make it. He had to keep reminding himself of that. "Come on." Nodding once at his brother, Pierce started toward the house. Logan followed him. Up the steps. Hand on the doorknob. Opening the door, Pierce released the knob. Why was there blood on it? Oh, his hands. He wiped the handle off with his forearm. Logan came inside, and Pierce shut the door behind him.

Lifting his head, Logan brushed a soft kiss across Ambrosia's shoulder. He wrapped both of his arms around her with the wooden lily still clutched tight in his hand. They'd been waiting for what felt like hours for some information. His brother and Jocasta had disappeared into the back bedroom when they first returned. And they'd rejoined them with Pierce's hands bandaged, not that he recalled when they'd gotten hurt.

Lilli carried two mugs of tea in the room, setting them down on the coffee table. Her gaze fell to the intricately crafted item he held. The last piece of his mother. "What is that?"

He blinked. His body relaxed, but he remained unprepared to answer questions about the flower in his palm. But he wouldn't lie to Lilli either. He swallowed the lump in the back of his throat and revealed the small wooden piece. "It was the first gift I ever made for our mother. Zinnia... uh, it seems she had it with her."

The hours he had spent whittling a broken branch into a perfect replica of a lily flower. Time that would forever remain with him. Not that any of those seconds and minutes played in his mind. The memory of their mother's reaction...that he'd never forgotten.

"It is beautiful," his sister whispered. She rubbed his arm and gave Pierce's shoulder a squeeze in passing as she returned to the kitchen.

He'd been a little worried to see her response. But Lilli was more like their mother than he even realized. She had the female's strength and courage. That was good. If things worked out as he prayed... well, one concern at a time. His gaze flicked to the door. Watching it wouldn't do any good, but he couldn't help himself.

"Are you okay?" Pierce asked Jocasta. "Did you want to change?"

"I'm okay for now."

"Okay." He laid his head on top of hers, his ruby gaze still trained on the door.

Lilli brought two more cups in, while Lyrica brought the last two. She set one on the table, keeping the other in her hand. And Lyrica set another on the table as well.

Ambrosia sat up enough to take one mug. "Thank you, Lilli. This is kind of you."

"Of course. It was the least I could do."

Just as Lyrica was about to sit down, a gentle knock at the door resounded. "I will get it. Stay where you are." She set her mug down, headed around the couch, and opened the door.

Delenia stepped through the doorway. She bowed her head to the family. "I apologize for the intrusion; however, Santos has asked that I deliver an updated status."

Pierce stood quickly, holding Jocasta against his side. "How is she?"

Logan and Ambrosia had both gotten to their feet, too. He had an arm around her shoulders, rubbing up and down her arm. More for his comfort than hers. His brother had asked, so there was no point for him to echo the question, but he desperately needed to know Zinni was okay.

"One wound was infected. They have gotten everything cleaned and bandaged, but they are keeping a close eye on her injuries. She has stabilized; however, they sedated her to give her body time to heal. Santos has asked you to wait until morning to see her," Delenia said.

Pierce's hand gripped the back of the chair as he let out a breath. "She will live?"

"Yes," Delenia replied. "She will live."

"Oh, thank the gods." Logan's shoulders relaxed. Hades, he would never have forgiven himself if she hadn't. Not with how he'd stopped pushing to get her out when he got Lilli and Pierce out. What if she hadn't made it to the village? What if things took a turn for the worse overnight? Hades, he had to stop thinking about that. The female said that Zinnia would live. She would be alright. He rubbed at the tears that welled in the corners of his eyes.

Pierce practically fell back into the chair, his eyes closing as he scrubbed his face. It took him a moment, but he looked back at the female. "Thank you. Thank you very much for letting us know." He inhaled a breath and exhaled slowly. "Did Santos specify a good time or just morning?"

"Wait until after morning meal. She should be awake by then." Delenia bowed her head and took her leave. Lyrica closed the door behind the female.

Dropping into the chair, Logan nodded his head. Morning meal. They could do that. Now that they knew she would be okay. They could wait to see her until then. He dragged a hand across his face, tears rolling down his cheeks. Gods, Zinnia, she was okay.

Pierce scrubbed his hands over his face again as his head fell back. "Thank the gods," he whispered. Jocasta climbed back into Pierce's lap and pressed a soft kiss to his throat as she curled back up to him. He wrapped one arm around her waist, the other over her knee, just holding her. He kissed her lips, and then the top of her head, before laying his cheek against it.

Setting the mug in her hand aside, Ambrosia wrapped her arms around Logan. He just held her close to him, just like his brother. He needed his mate here. To have her close. It was the only way he could silence the emotion boiling up inside of him.

"I am glad she will be okay," Lilli said.

With a heavy sigh, Logan turned his head toward his sister. He felt the tension coming from her. For a moment, he thought it related back to the news, but then Pierce's earlier words replayed in his mind. Lilli and Zinnia didn't have a relationship. He rose to his feet, pressed a kiss to his mate's forehead, and sat down on the couch next to his sister. "Thank you, Lilli. I know this cannot be easy for you, yet you still put Pierce and me first."

She clasped his hand in her own. "You do not need to thank me. I truly would do anything for you two. Just as I know you would for me." She sighed. "It is just..." Her words trailed off.

"Lilli," Pierce coaxed until her gaze focused on him. "We understand. If you do not want to see her in the morning, no one is going to make you."

She said nothing for a moment. "I wish I had the closeness with her, you two do. It would have been nice to feel like I had a sister growing up. But, for whatever reason, it was not there."

"Zinnia could not be her true self in the village, as none of us could. Especially after Mother passed. I hope that being here will change that. Just know that no one is ever going to pressure you into anything or make you do anything that you do not want. Whatever it may be. You make your own choices here."

"Pierce is right, Lilli," Logan said. "We would never ask you to do something you are uncomfortable with. That includes seeing Zinnia in the morning." He squeezed her hand. It would certainly make family meals difficult if they could gain sanctuary for Zinnia, but that would be a discussion for another day. And they would figure it out together. "You decide what is best for you. We support that."

"Thank you, both of you." She paused. "I really am glad she is going to be okay. She is important to the two of you. I know it would have been really hard if..." Her words trailed off, and he sensed there were things she didn't want to say aloud. "You both should know, if Santos allows her to stay... I will be okay with seeing her around, even being around her. I just do not particularly want to go out of my way to see her."

"And that is okay, Lilli," Pierce stated. "You do not have to."

That was good to know. They could figure things out, arrange for her to stay with Pierce and Jocasta, maybe. He didn't want Zinnia living by herself, and that had been the original plan. "That is fine. It is your choice." Logan wrapped an arm around her shoulder and kissed the top of her head. He didn't want to spill her tea.

Lilli set her tea down and hugged him. "I think I may go to bed. It has been a long *umbra*. A very wonderful, but very long *umbra*."

He kissed the top of her head again, embracing her tightly. "All right. Good night, Lilli." His gaze shifted to Lyrica. He opened his mouth—

"I know where everything is." Lyrica turned toward the hallway. "Third drawer from the bottom, correct, Ambrosia?"

"Yes, Mom."

Jocasta raised an eyebrow at her twin.

"Night clothes for her." Ambrosia shrugged. "Don't give me that look. I prepared ahead. I've got some of yours in the back room, too."

"I'm not sure if I should be upset or grateful." Jocasta smirked.

"Grateful. Lilli, there's some in the top left drawer in your room for you if you'd like them."

"Thank you, Am." Lilli made the rounds, telling everyone goodnight and hugging them, before heading down the hallway to her room.

Pierce watched Lilli go, a slight frown on his face. He kissed the top of his mate's head, his thumb stroking her knee. "Are you ready for bed, my queen?"

"Yes, I am."

Logan glanced at his brother. He shared his concerns. Lilli had said she would be okay. He knew she was going to be. They both just hoped she would tell them if that ever changed. Right now, they still had other obstacles to face. His gaze dropped to the table where all the mugs sat. Thank the gods for Lyrica. That female, she was truly special. He picked up two mugs and took them to the kitchen.

"Give me a minute. I will be right behind you, my love," Pierce uttered and collected mugs, following behind him.

Although he didn't pay attention to the females, the sound of Jocasta and Ambrosia's talons against the wooden floor couldn't be mistaken as they disappeared down the empty corridor.

His mate was worried about him. It didn't surprise him. Not that he needed to see it on her lovely features, he felt it coming from her. As he poured the tea and tossed the bags, Logan glanced at his brother. He kept his voice low. "You know Santos will wish to speak with Zinnia before he offers her sanctuary."

Pierce regarded Logan and then washed the first mug out. "Yes, I know. I am worried. I know who the wounds came from. What I do not know is what brought her here. Or how she found this place, alone."

"There are enough rumors around the marketplace for a general direction. Devin found it." While Pierce washed, he dried and put things away. Despite how quietly they spoke, likely the entire household could hear their conversation.

"She did? When?" He shook his head. "Never mind. Some other time." He frowned a little. Logan sensed his concern. Even with as little as he knew her, he'd been able to tell Devin was one of those females; even when she wasn't alright, it wasn't something she made known.

"Ambrosia had a point when we were talking earlier. What if Zinnia came looking for us? It cannot be a coincidence she grabbed the lily." Markham could've easily pursued their sister, used her as bait. Hades, he prayed that wasn't the case.

"Maybe you are right. I hope so. We can ask her tomorrow." His brother paused. "Things were... very difficult, after you had to leave. You two were always so close. And she knew the lily was Mother's favorite. I do not know how she did it. Hid it from him. Afterwards, it was almost as if she shut down. Turned off her emotions. Even more so after Mother died. And Ailwin got worse."

Gods, some days. Logan blew out a heavy breath. It took every ounce of control he could muster not to scrub his face raw. Or charge out of the house and village and hunt their father down. Not that he could change the past. "She was just an adolescent when I left. Maybe she found somewhere she could keep things secret. If she shut down... emotions were never something you could feel in that place."

"That had to have been it. I was in the village as much as I could be, and she never used to leave, that I know of. But my time there dwindled over the *solaris*. Not by choice, though, until I met Jo. I think Zinnia is just... lost. She only ever wanted to do the right thing. I just do not think she knew what that was. Role models there are scarce. She attached herself to Dahlia, tried to be like her. Because that is who Ailwin wanted her to be. She could never bring herself to do the things that Dahlia did, though."

"I truly hope so. If that is the case, then we may convince Santos she would thrive here. If she could never be as cruel as Dahlia, it may be what benefits her." His mate really had rubbed off on him. There he was, trying to resolve issues they didn't even know would be possible yet. "If he gives her sanctuary, I think it would be good if she stayed with you and Jocasta."

His brother's head bobbed in agreement. "I will not uproot Lilli, and she loves living here with you and Ambrosia. But I will not make her uncomfortable either. We have two other bedrooms in our home, and that was the original plan." He was quiet for a minute, staring down into the mug as he washed it. "If Santos turns her away... it will mean her death. If Markham or his Informants find her alive, she will not stay that way. I hope with all my heart that, when Santos speaks with her, she gives him a reason to believe she deserves a chance here. I will speak for her, of course, as I know you will as well. But ultimately, it is what comes out of her mouth that will matter most."

The last thing he wanted to think about was the other possibilities if Santos turned Zinnia away. He couldn't think like that. "There is always my cabin, but I pray it does not come to that." They both did. An Informant had already found the place once. It was a possibility, though. "There is little in our control right now. We simply... we just have to take this one step at a time."

Pierce inhaled a deep breath, exhaling slowly. "One step at a time. I do not think I have ever been very good at that. Then again, I have spent many *solaris* being shut down myself. Jocasta changed all of that. I am glad of it, but the vulnerability can get... overwhelming."

"Yes, it can." Earlier, he'd felt as if he hadn't even been in his own body. "It is as difficult sometimes as the one step at a time. I thank the gods for Ambrosia. She has a way of... freeing my words, as well as my emotions." But it helped him see things he hadn't seen in a long time. Parts of himself he had forgotten existed.

"Jocasta does that for me as well. Before meeting her, the only emotion I had outwardly displayed was anger. I buried everything else. Along with the memories, I refused to think about. I think I lived a lot on auto-pilot. I just went through the motions. She has helped me to remember the male I want to be. The male I can be. For her, I want to be better than even that."

"That is what it is like with Ambrosia. We did not grow up easy, but I know you are right. We can be better males for them. For the future they handed us." Anger had become all he knew after he'd left. It had been the easiest emotion to deal with. Having anything else made him vulnerable when he couldn't afford to have been. Otherwise, he would've made a mistake and not remained alive as long as he had.

"Yes, we can. For our mates and for our sisters as well. Our past will not define our future. Our future is going to be more amazing than we ever thought it could be." Pierce set the last mug down and gave Logan's shoulder a squeeze, then started wiping off the counter.

"That it is, brother. That it is." Finishing up, Logan put the last of the mugs away, ensuring they'd cleaned all six. He checked the wood in the stove and verified it had completely burned out. The cool nights when they would need the heat in the house weren't yet upon them.

Pierce hung the cloth over the edge of the basin of the sink. He turned, scanned everything for a moment, inhaled a breath, and exhaled slowly. His gaze flicked to Logan. "I will see you in the morning, brother mine."

"I will see you in the morning. Have a good rest, brother." Everything seemed in its place. There were no noises coming from outside. The surrounding village had stilled. They had been assured that Zinnia would be okay. The rest of their family was safe under this roof. There was nothing to feel uneasy about. But he needed a minute longer to listen to the calm of the house. Of the village. Then he would join his mate in bed.

Pierce's feet didn't move yet. His brother just stared at him. "Would you like me to stay? Until you are ready to go?"

"No." Logan shook his head. "Go ahead to your mate." It had been a few months since this kind of emotional turmoil had shaken him to his core. His mate had been there for that. His ability had always been at its strongest around his family. The blood connection. That was what their mother used to say.

"Alright. If you are sure?"

"Yes." This was simply one of those things he had to handle alone. No one could do it for him. Not his brother. Nor his mate.

Chapter Nineteen

Parthenia had been up for a few hours, mostly tending to things around the treehouse. She'd done everything possible to be there for her mate when he woke, except for the short time she'd gone to gather some fish. Her mate would need to eat once he awoke. It didn't take her too long to cook the fish at the base of the tree and get the fire out. Despite the dangers, it was safest there. Smoke coming from the treehouse would've drawn more attention. Back at the top, she finished their meal preparation, slicing a few apples and peeling a couple of oranges.

The rumble of Gavin's stomach drew her attention. He didn't rise from the pallet but raised his head for a moment, looking down at his calf. A small smile crossed her face as he settled back down and focused on her working on the fruit.

She placed some of the apple and orange slices on a plate with the fish. Once she had everything together, Parthenia strode over to him and sat down. She caressed his cheek. "Afternoon. I made us some lunch."

Gavin leaned into her touch, his eyes briefly closing. He shifted to his humanoid form, then slowly sat up. Placing a kiss on either side of her mouth, he gently pressed his forehead to hers. "Thank you, my love," he whispered. "For taking care of me."

"I wouldn't have been anywhere else." Nothing could change that. Though she wished she could've done more for him.

"I know. Because you are so wonderful." He kissed her forehead and their gazes met. "I could not have made it through last night without you."

"I will always be here for you. No matter how you need me." She cupped his jaw and stroked his cheek with her thumb. "Always."

He leaned into her touch and cupped her face. "I know you will. As I will always be here for you." He brushed a tender kiss across her palm. "I do not even know how I can think about food right now. But that smells wonderful."

"That's good, because you need to eat. I know it isn't high on your priority list, but it is required for strength." It had certainly been a long night, and his body still had to heal. It required sustenance for that to happen.

"I may not feel like food, but I think my stomach is demanding it." As if to emphasize his words, his stomach rumbled again. "Are you able to stay and eat with me? I am sure you have to return home soon."

"I will stay as long as you need me to." She didn't have anywhere she had to go. Even if she did, she would not leave him until she knew he would be okay for a short period by himself.

"If that were possible, you would never leave." He kissed her cheek and then trailed his nose to the crook of her neck. "I will always need you, beloved." He breathed in deep. "I do not want the food to get cold, but... A minute, I just need..." He inhaled another deep breath.

Okay, he had her there. They still needed a lot of answers. Parthenia trailed her fingers down his neck and along his spine, between his shoulders. "It's okay. Take your time, my love."

He kept his head where it was but arched into her touch, a gentle purr vibrating through him. His chest rose and fell as he took slow, deep breaths. "I am okay. I will be okay. We should eat."

"Okay. I'm going to get my plate really quick then." She had only brought over his plate. She'd given him most of the fish she'd cooked. No way would she eat more than a couple of pieces, if that. She didn't know how much he'd eaten the day before, or any time they couldn't be together. It appeared as if he had lost a little weight. Being apart from one another, especially if it was longer than a day, was a painful ache that threatened to wipe out everything else. Demeter, she couldn't wait until they could get off this isle with his sister and his sister's mate. Soon. That's what she reminded herself of, especially with what had transpired in the last twenty-four hours.

Gavin took a bite of the fish and moaned.

Either it was that good or he was just that hungry. Bringing a second plate over, she started on the fish first. She wasn't certain she'd eaten much of anything yesterday herself. Some days, it was impossible to sneak down. It had gotten easier, as she no longer stayed at her mother's, especially with the invisibility potion. But not all the time. Still, she came down as often as she could. Maybe she could spend nights here with him.

Gavin pulled her gently into his lap and laid his head on her shoulder. He wrapped his arm around her waist and ate one-handed. One day soon, it wouldn't be like this. Soon, it would be more than just a dream. Gavin kissed her shoulder and returned to his food.

With one hand resting on his, they ate in silence. All she had were glimpses from yesterday. His mind had been so scattered she had followed little of anything from the first second she'd felt his pain. Part of her wanted to ask, but she also wished him to eat, too. She trusted he would tell her when he was ready.

He ate all the fish, and then a few pieces of the oranges, chewing slowly with each bite. His thumb rubbed along her hip as he put another orange slice in his mouth. "I was not in the hut when it happened. I was heading back there, though, after evening meal and heard her scream."

She entwined her fingers with his as her eyes popped wide. "Oh, gods."

He gave her hand a gentle squeeze, letting his thumb trail over her fingertips. "When I ran into the hut, she was already..." The words stilled on his tongue. He tried to keep the image out of his mind, but she glimpsed it. Gabby curled up on the floor, blood spilling from between her thighs. "It was... Nothing could stop it." A tear dripped down onto one of the apple slices. "Um..." He cleared his throat. "Our father was just standing there, watching her. I tried to go to her, but he would not let me. By the look in his eyes, I knew what he had done. I asked anyway, though. He said..." Gavin cleared his throat, and another tear fell. "He said he had done what was necessary. It—those words. They froze me. It is one thing to know in your gut, but another to hear it aloud."

Gods. For their father, any parent to purposely—she couldn't even think the word. Her hand lowered with the piece of fruit in her fingers. The emotions she held back yesterday surfaced and she couldn't stop the quiet sob this time. The heartbreak for him, for his sister, a female she considered a sister herself. "I'm so sorry, Gavin. I can't imagine..." It must've been difficult for him to do nothing for Gabby.

Adjusting her in his lap, he gently wiped the wetness from her face. Laying his head on top of hers, he held her against him and ran his fingers through her hair. "He said some things then, but I did not really hear them. There was this ringing in my ears. I do not know how long until I snapped out of it. I tried to attack him. It was stupid, but..."

She didn't think it was stupid. How could he not attack the male? A male with no honor. He deserved nothing less than death for how he'd harmed his children.

Gavin took a slow, deep breath. "He threw me against the wall and then bit me. When he dragged me outside, Markham was there. He asked our father if it was finished. He said that it would not be long. That was when I yelled at Markham. I think I may have actually screamed at him; I am not sure."

Parthenia's eyes widened. Oh, gods, somehow Markham had discovered Gabby's pregnancy. That seemed to answer the questions running through her mind. "I would've screamed too. It's just awful, horrid."

"I wish I could understand, but... I mean, I know his laws. We all know his laws, but there is no reason for them. Nothing makes any sense." He tightened his hold on her. "Markham knows. About us too. I do not, I cannot even fathom how. I was as careful as I could have been. But when he was staring down at me, outside of the hut, I heard words, but not out loud. They were in my head. 'I know what you have done. I know what law you have broken.' While I do not think he knows what you are, somehow, he knows. I could see the truth in his eyes when he was staring at me."

How could his leader have any knowledge of them? Yes, he'd said he didn't know, but it made little sense. Could he have... No, Gavin always bathed before he returned to his village. No one had seen them together in the treehouse. Unless... "If you heard them inside your head, do you think maybe he found out from someone else, even unintentionally?" She didn't know how else it would be possible.

"I do not know. The only one I have told was Gabby, and Devin knows, of course. But, if that is the case, they would never have revealed us on purpose. Unless it was something he caught from a dream of mine, I..." Gavin let out a rough breath. "I cannot make heads or tails of it. Though I thought he might have had suspicions, they have not punished me for anything since... I am so sorry, my love."

Parthenia held onto him for dear life. There was no way he was returning. It would mean his death. She would have to take every precaution, ensure no one found the treehouse. From now on, she would fly through the tops of the trees. It would be the best way to keep him safe. "I will be as careful as ever, so no one will be drawn here to you."

He kissed the top of her head, just holding her against him as he stroked her spine. "Even if... even if he really does not know, and it just seemed that way, I would have a death sentence regardless for attacking my father. He does not do much anymore, at his age, but he still holds the title of Informant in the village. Yet another thing that I do not understand, why Markham gave us the opportunity to run. It makes no sense."

"I don't know." She couldn't follow the male's thought pattern. A random notion popped into her head. He'd told her recently; others had left the village. "Unless he believes you will lead him to others he's seeking." But how? To her knowledge, Gavin didn't know anyone outside of her, Gabby, and Devin. "Do you think he let you go to gain confirmation?"

"Maybe not me. But perhaps Derrick. One of those that left, he was an Informant as well. Two of his sisters disappeared too. Derrick would know him well. As for your question, I suppose that is possible. Or he just wanted to give his Informants a chance to go hunting. He will punish them for not bringing us back." Gavin shrugged. "It could have just been that his attention was diverted. After I heard the words in my head, he turned toward Derrick, and I began moving into the forest. He was being held down and restrained in the clearing. Markham said some things to him. Then he had him released and sent the Informants after us. Perhaps he did not think I would try to run."

"Maybe." She wasn't positive. No matter the reason, she feared what would happen if anyone discovered his location. "Promise me you won't stray far from here. I couldn't... I just... not even for one second."

He took her face into his hands, brushing his thumbs across her cheeks as he stared into her eyes. "I will be as careful as I can, my love. I promise. With the curfew in the village, not even Informants go out at night. Except for the ones that are sent on longer scouting missions, and that puts them far away from here. It will be a good time for me to hunt for food. And I will use my camouflage anytime that I need to leave."

"Thank you." Yes, she would do what she could to spend nights here. Demeter, she couldn't imagine her life without him.

"We will get through this. I know we will. And I will be extra careful."

She knew he didn't want to stay here alone, no more than she wanted him to have to. But they had little choices right now; he couldn't stay indefinitely in Pteryrina either. She needed to return there to keep the heat off of herself that had already come crashing down upon him. "I'll return as many nights as I can. Be here with you as often as possible. I don't... I can't leave you here alone." It would be an impossible feat. She'd spend the time in Pteryrina that she needed to, but if they expected nothing of her, then she would be here. Here with her mate.

"As long as it will not get you into trouble. Your safety must be paramount. The pain of separation..." She watched him swallow back his fear. "It will be temporary until we find the rest of the answers." With one hand against her cheek, he slid his other along the curve of her neck to her pulse point. "I cannot... lose you. I cannot lose you."

Parthenia covered his hand with one of her own. "As I'm no longer in my mother's house, it will be fine. You won't lose me. Ever." If something ever happened, she would fight with everything she had to ensure they had the years they wanted together.

Gavin simply nodded. He kissed her forehead, then either side of her mouth, jaw, and throat as he pulled her back against him. "I would be so lost without you."

"As would I." Before him, she hadn't considered leaving the isle as even a remote possibility. She had believed she would live a life of solitude. That there wasn't any place she truly belonged. Then he'd revealed himself, and everything changed.

He stroked her spine, his tail caressing her wing as he held her. "Focal point. Right? Just for a little while longer."

"Yes. Just a little longer."

Chapter Twenty

Zinnia awakened but didn't immediately open her eyes. She felt groggy, her eyelids heavy. And—*oh, gods*—her chest hurt. She shifted in something soft beneath her body and bit back a wince. Registering a touch upon her, she jerked and yelped. Her eyes popped open as she nearly bolted upright, but—*nope*—that wasn't happening. She realized she was in her humanoid form. When had she shifted? It wasn't how she'd left the village. Taking a slow breath, she surveyed her surroundings while she laid still.

There was a female next to her. Her eyebrows furrowed. She knew there were other species on the isle, but she had seen no other than the ones who'd entered or got brought into the territory. Zinnia had never focused on them, or what happened to them. She'd seen no one like this female and her father had never allowed her out of the boundaries. The female had grayish-colored skin and raven-colored hair. Where on earth had she ended up? She couldn't remember much from before she'd passed out, where she'd been when her vision had conked out on her, or where she had finally dropped.

"Be at ease. You are safe. Some of your injuries have healed, though most are still healing." The female lifted another bandage, gently palpated the wound, and cleaned around it.

Zinnia sucked in a breath, but did her best to lie still. The overwhelming pain was at a level she'd never felt before. Out of curiosity, she wanted to ask what creature the female was, but that might be rude. "Where am I?" She surveyed the surrounding walls—Where was it? "Oh no," she whispered.

The flower. She must have lost it somewhere along the way. Tears welled in her eyes. Her breathing hitched, and she tried to calm herself down. The rapid breaths made her chest ache even more. She had lost it... She'd lost everyone, and it had been all she had left... and she had lost it.

"You are in the medical building of Migas Village. Please calm yourself. I would like to get these changed and food into you before your visitors arrive."

What in Hades' name was Migas Village? And food was—*woo*—with the way her stomach felt right now. That would not happen. Balling her fists around the sheet beneath her, Zinnia inhaled and exhaled slow, shuddering breaths as she tried to stop the trembling. The rest of what the female said finally registered. "V-visitors? What do you mean? There is no one... no one I can imagine that would wish to see me."

"I believe I was told they were your brothers."

Her body stilled, and a ringing started in her ears. As the female removed the bandage from one of her wounds, her lips continued to move, but she couldn't hear a thing that the female said. "I... I am sorry, but... what? Wh—who did you say?"

"I have not formally met them, though I suppose I got caught up in the festivities last night. Logan and Pierce. Are those not your brothers?"

Her mouth opened and snapped shut. Logan and Pierce? How? That was impossible. While she couldn't form words, her head bobbed slightly.

"Now that we have that resolved, may I continue checking your injuries?"

All she could do was nod again.

"Excellent." The female returned to the area along her belly that she'd palpitated before and gently touched it again. "Now, does this hurt?"

Tilting her head down to look where the female was touching, there was nothing in that spot. Strange. No injury had ever healed that quickly on her before. "No," she replied. Come to think of it, her face didn't hurt either. The rest of her chest was a different story, though.

"Good. I have changed the rest of your bandages." The female collected the small basket of discarded wrappings, along with the remaining items, and stood. "I know your stomach may not agree, but I will bring you some bread and tea. You should eat. It will aid with your healing."

"I will try. Th... thank you. For taking care of me." The only one that had ever done so since her mother had passed had been Pierce, and only when she'd let him, which had been rare. Before her mother passed, it had always been her mother or Logan.

The female bowed her head. "I am Kaylina, the shaman of this village. I tend to all who need it."

"My name is Zinnia. It is nice to meet you."

"I shall return momentarily, Zinnia."

Kaylina left the room. There were noises near to where Zinnia was located, but she didn't pay any attention to them. She couldn't really track anything, least of all the million thoughts running through her headright then. Everything that happened in the village—how she had gotten here, the flower, whatever this village was, Logan and Pierce—it was all just too much. Zinnia laid her head back on the pillow and smoothed her hands over the blanket to relax. It might help her chest hurt less, but it seemed an impossible task at the moment.

After a few minutes, Kaylina returned with a small tray. She placed it on a round table close to the bed. "I have butter and apple jam should you hold down the plain bread. As well as some tea." The female set the plate of bread on top of the bedding, within easy reach, and held out the mug.

A sweet, floral aroma with hints of mint and rosemary filled her nose. The scent of the tea brought tears to her eyes, but she blinked them back. She didn't want to cry. It would make the pain worse. Lavender tea. Oh gods, she hadn't had it since her mother had passed away. At least not the way the female had made it. Zinnia had tried, but she'd never quite gotten it to taste right. But this... oh, it smelled... just perfect. She reached up and wiped at her eyes, swallowing hard. "Thank you. This is kind of you."

"You are welcome. Just drink slow. It will be hot."

Zinnia carefully took the mug that was offered. Grasping it in her hands, she brought it to her nose, closed her eyes, and inhaled as deeply as she could. She ignored the stab of pain in her chest that came with it. Just the smell of the liquid brought her right back to the last day she'd had it. Squeezing her eyes shut against more tears, she took a small sip. It tasted just as perfect as it smelled. Looking up at the female, the barest hint of a smile appeared on her face. "I will try to eat some of the bread in a moment. Thank you again."

"I will be in the other room if you need me." Kaylina bowed her head, then left her to her thoughts.

Food was a necessity, but all she wanted to do was sip this tea. It was soothing and was one of the few things that held wonderful memories. Taking another small sip, Zinnia tried to sort through her thoughts, still going a mile a minute. None of this made any sense. She should be dead, not in some strange village with—apparently—her brothers. Maybe she was dreaming. Or maybe she really was dead and, despite the pain and injury, this was some wonderful afterlife she didn't know that she deserved.

A few minutes passed, and she heard a gentle male voice speaking with Kaylina. The conversation didn't last long. Perhaps two or three minutes. Afterward, the usual noises of the building returned.

After she'd sipped a little more of the tea, she glanced over at the bread. She really should try to eat. Ensuring she had a good hold on the mug, Zinnia reached over with her other hand and picked up a piece. Her stomach rolled, but food would probably help. She nibbled off of a corner, then brought the mug back to her nose, inhaling slowly. Letting the scent wash over her, she closed her eyes.

"How are you doing in here?"

Startling a little, she barely kept the tea from spilling. Kaylina stood in the jamb with a ceramic pot covered in various floral arrangements in her hand. Gods, how had the female entered the room so quietly? Zinnia hadn't heard anyone come in. "Oh. Um, okay." At least, nothing was wrong that wasn't to be expected. "I just got lost in my thoughts, I suppose."

"That is acceptable. Would you like more tea?"

"Yes. Please. Um, is there something I might lean back against? To sit up some more?" She didn't think she could sit up unsupported, but it was difficult drinking the tea lying back like this. And she didn't want to stop drinking it.

"Yes, of course." Setting the pot down, the female retrieved an angular pillow. "Here, let me set your mug and plate aside." Placing both on the table, she assisted Zinnia until she got the pillow situated comfortably behind her. Once she was in a more upright position, Kaylina handed the mug back to her and set the plate on the bed.

She breathed slowly through the pain as she accepted the mug. "Thank you." Zinnia paused. "I know I say that a lot. I am just not... used to kindness. It is very much appreciated."

"Hmm, well, you will certainly find it in abundance here." Kaylina glanced out the window; rays of light beamed into the room. "I believe your brothers should be along shortly. Our Elder has stated he will return later to speak with you once you are stronger."

Zinnia tried to wrap her head around all of that, but, once again, not much was tracking. Her brothers. *Oh, gods.* What would she say to them? She could never apologize enough to Pierce. Yet again, her fear had led her to another stupid decision. It was all she had ever done, made idiotic decisions. And Logan... so many years since they'd seen each other. She opened her mouth to speak, but nothing came out. Swallowing hard, she just nodded and took another sip of the tea.

"Would you like more tea before I step out?"

"Yes, please. Maybe... just a little more?"

"Of course. Say when." She poured a little more into the mug.

It was getting close to the top when she spoke. Okay, so maybe more than 'a little more.' "That is good. Thank you."

"You are welcome." Kaylina left the room with the pot in hand.

Zinnia kept both of her hands on the mug as she sipped it. When the level was low enough that she thought she could handle it with one hand and not spill it, she reached over and picked up the bread again. Food. Food was important. It wouldn't be the first time she'd have to ignore her stomach and force food down out of necessity.

It had taken her a bit to get through any part of the food. Zinnia set what remained of the bread back on the table. Her stomach was rolling too much. But the tea was excellent. Yes, the tea was excellent. She brought it to her nose again and breathed in deep before taking another sip. Voices echoing down the hall caught her attention, so she forced herself out of her own head. Turning to look at the open door, she almost dropped her mug. Pierce was actually standing there. He was talking to... what had she said her name was? Kaylina. Tears pricked her eyes. He had actually come, even after all she had said to him. Peering past him at the other figure standing there and—oh, yup, there they were. Zinnia choked back a quiet sob. His fur had changed, but his eyes had not, and his sharp and tangy scent—it was just as she remembered. She put the mug over on the table and tried to push herself up, biting the inside of her cheek as pain speared through her chest. "Logan!"

His feet ate the space across the room, and he stopped at the bed. There were tears in the corners of his eyes. Logan sat on the bed and, as gently as possible, embraced her. "Zinnia."

Both of her arms came around him, clinging to him as hard as she could. The pain didn't matter, and neither did the waterworks. Not compared to how happy she was to see him again.

Pierce stepped into the room and softly shut the door behind him. He leaned back against it with a gentle tilt to his lips.

"Gods, I cannot believe you are here," Logan said.

"Nor can I. I do not know how I even made it. I lost my sight along the way. It is fully back now, though I do not know how."

Logan pulled back slightly. "How are you feeling?"

She sagged back against the pillows, her hand over her bandages. "Hurting. A lot. But it is my fault. My stupidity." She glanced over at Pierce. "Gods, I am so... I am so sorry," she whispered as she openly wept, relief and sorrow flooding her.

Pierce crossed the room and perched carefully on the other side of the bed. He took her hand, giving it a squeeze as he wiped the wetness from her face. "It is alright. I am not angry. I am just so thrilled to see you." He gave her a tender hug.

"I am happy to see you, too. I feel horrible." She shook her head and refocused on Logan. "I never thought I would see you again." She clutched his hand. "I had something with me. I did not really think I had a chance of finding you, but I was going to give it back to you if I did, and it brought me comfort carrying it, but I must have lost it along the way."

A gentle tilt crossed Logan's mouth. "You did not lose it, Zinnia. The Elder here, Santos, saw it with you and gave it to me last night. It is here."

"Oh." She let out a sigh of relief. "Thank the gods, I..." Briefly, she squeezed her eyes shut. She didn't know how much he knew, or what he knew. "I put it in my mouth... that *umbra*. Easy to do in my other form. And it helped keep the emotions off my face. I think, he thought, in his rage, he must have gotten it already. He tore the cabin apart searching for everything." She grew quiet for a moment. Blinked a few tears free. "As soon as... we got word... I told Mother to give it to me. It was really hard to keep my mouth closed the whole time. Once I could, I left the village. I had this cave that I went to when I just needed to be alone. I hid it there. Whenever Father was out of the village, I went back to get it and brought it back to Mother. Ran the woods until I could sense him coming back home. Then I took it back to the cave. Holding it brought her some comfort. She had little."

Pierce's eyes clouded with emotion, but he said nothing.

"I wish I could have saved more," she muttered.

"It is more than I could have asked for. I am glad..." Logan's words trailed off with a heavy breath. "I am glad you could bring Mother some comfort. Leaving was not what I had wanted, but it had been necessary."

"I know it was. You would never have left us if you had any other choice. And despite what *they* say, I know you did not do it, what they accused you of. You would not have. You had no reason to." She squeezed his palm. "It was not I that brought her comfort, though. It was you. Holding that made her feel close to you. She was not the same after."

"Some *umbras*, I still wish I could have done more." Logan's gaze flicked to Pierce. "You do not have to say it."

"No, but you know I am thinking it."

Zinnia's gaze darted back and forth between them. "Are you still carrying that? Both of you, really? You two have always done as much as you could. Too much, sometimes. Logan, you have been in hiding for eighteen *solaris* to protect us. The gods know what you have been through, but I can only imagine. And Pierce, you have been on death's doorstep more than once for the same reason. What more do you think you could have done to protect us?" She shook her head, ignoring the twinge of pain. "No. Stop. Both of you. Neither of you is to blame for any of it. The only ones to blame are still back in that village. And that includes Dahlia."

Logan opened his mouth and snapped it shut. He chuckled. "They are the stronger sex."

She raised her eyebrows. "Excuse me?"

Pierce just stared at her, then let out a laugh and scrubbed his hands over his face. "Yes. Yes, they are. Oh, thank the gods."

She glanced back and forth between them. "I think I may have missed a private joke. I do not know what the two of you are talking about. But what I know—I am really tired of sticking up for that... *bitch*."

"There is much to tell you, sister mine. For both of us." The corners of Logan's eyes wrinkled as he tightened the hold he had on her hand. "I believe we are both just grateful you got away from the village."

She rested a hand over the bandages on her chest. "As am I." Her eyes drifted shut. "I have been such a coward. My entire life, I have been a coward." Zinnia lifted her gaze to the two of them. "I am done. I cannot be that way anymore. With what happened before I left the village…" The look in Dahlia's eyes as she had sneered at her. Their father's anger, the look of death in his expression. The words they had spoken to her. "Things are much clearer for me now than they have been in a very long time. No matter what happens, I can never go back there. I do not want to."

Pierce let out a breath. "I am glad to hear it, sister mine."

"That is good. Very good. I am… it makes me happy to hear that." Logan inhaled and exhaled a deep breath. "Have you been told anything about this village? Here?"

"No. Just the name, and I have never heard of it before. You can tell me in a moment, though. How is Lillianna?" she asked. "I know she must hate me, and I do not blame her. And I will push nothing with her. But I would like to know how she is."

"Lilli is thriving," Logan said. "Happy. There is still much to overcome, but we are all doing everything to help her." He hesitated a moment. "She does not hate you. It may take her some time to know you the way Pierce and I do."

"That is good. So very good. If she does not want to get to know me, I would understand that too. My indifference toward her was for self-preservation, but it was cowardly. She did not deserve that. I stayed away from her to avoid punishment. Pierce did the opposite." She clasped his palm. "Father did not want her to have any attention. Unless it came to… the abuse. I was afraid to endure his anger." Her gaze flicked to Pierce. "What I saw him do to you, and have done to you. I was just afraid. It is not an excuse, but it is the truth." She turned her attention to Logan. "Would you two tell her for me, please? If she would ever like to speak to me… at the absolute very least, I owe her an apology."

Logan glanced at Pierce and then peered back at her. "We will tell her and give her the chance to decide what she would like to do. That is what we told her last night. It is something I intend to stand by." A small smile tugged at the corners of his mouth. "Perhaps one *umbra*, you and she will have a genuine relationship."

"Perhaps. But that will be up to her. I will push nothing with her. And I promise I will not. Now. I have a very serious question."

Pierce's forehead creased. "What would that be, sister mine?"

Her gaze shifted to Logan. "What on earth happened to your fur?" Then she looked at Pierce. "And what on earth are these?" She ran her thumbs over the electrum links wrapped around their wrists. No one had allowed them anything of the kind in the village.

"Oh, well, you missed a celebration yesterday." Pierce beamed. "Yesterday, Logan and I each got mated."

Her eyes widened. "No. Oh, *really*? Oh, my... congratulations. That is wonderful news."

"Thank you, Zinnia."

"The change to the color of my fur is actually because of my mate. It was still black as night when we met. As the anger I carried around left me more and more with each passing *umbra*, the color, well, it became this," Logan answered.

"Well, I think it suits you very well."

"So do I, sister mine. So do I."

She gave his hand a squeeze. Each breath had pain stabbing through her chest again, but she would not ask for anything. She wanted nothing. Each choice had been hers to make, and she needed to suffer through every moment of this until it passed. It was imperative she never forgot what her choices had gotten her. "So. What is this place? You were going to tell me."

A wide smile crossed Logan's face. "Ah, yes. You are in Migas Village, home to the hybrids. This place is well protected, well hidden. Things here are nothing like what we grew up with. It is a genuine community."

"Well. That will take some getting used to," she said. "Hybrid. What is that?"

"What we referred to back in the village as half-breeds," Pierce replied. "Hybrid is the appropriate term."

"Oh, okay. I can remember that. Now. An actual serious question. How well protected and hidden? Markham and Father were extremely angry when I left. I do not know if they will come after me. Though I am sure they think I did not survive, you know how they are. I will not stay here and put any of you in danger if it would bring them here."

"Very. Markham has searched for this place for *solaris*. I do not know of any that have found it or returned to talk about it. Your arrival last night triggered a response, like nothing I have ever seen before."

"I do not really remember anything about it. Well, flickers. But nothing that makes much sense. My senses were not working very well," Zinnia stated. "But my mind works well now. That is a plus, right?"

"It is a plus. What flickers do you recall?"

"Mostly smells. I lost my eyesight sometime—I think—the *umbra* after I left. My left eye was already not working after what Markham did. But somewhere along the journey, I do not really remember when my right one just went black. I could not get my mouth to work, so I could not eat or really drink. I found some kind of water source, but I do not know what it was. Drinking water hurt, so I stopped doing that. I think my plan was to just walk until I stopped moving. Or something took me down. I never planned to go back there. I could not have even if I wanted to. They made that abundantly clear to me." Her shoulders slumped. "But, anyway. The last thing I remember was what felt like grass under my feet. I think the surrounding scents changed, but I cannot put a name on any of them. I heard something." Her mouth down-turned. "Music, maybe? I think that was what it sounded like. But then my legs gave out on me." She shrugged a little. "And then I woke up here this morning. I do not even know how long I have been gone."

While Pierce had spoken little for most of the conversation, Logan sat in silence for a moment. "Zinni, Pierce, and I intend to ask the Elder of this village for sanctuary for you. Something they gave to him, Lilli, and me. Is that something you might want?"

Words momentarily failed her. "Would that mean I would get to stay here?"

"If it is granted, yes," Pierce responded.

If. Okay. "Then yes. I want that. No matter what, I will not go back to Métamorphe. Not after..."She couldn't think about all of it. "I will not go back. And I do not want to spend my life running either. I would love to stay here. With my family." She lifted her gaze to Logan. "I have missed you. Very much."

"I have missed you, too. The Elder will speak with you before he decides. When you do, just be honest with him."

"I will be. I promise."

"If he grants you sanctuary, you will stay with my mate and me. Lilli lives with Logan and his mate."

"Okay. All things considered, that is probably a good idea." Gods, what if Lillianna really hated her? What if she never forgave her? Never wanted to have a relationship with her? She would accept it, of course, but it would hurt.

Logan's gaze lowered a bit. "One step at a time, Zinni. Even with Lilli, that is all you can do; all any of us can do, really."

She didn't answer him at first. Her thoughts momentarily went elsewhere. Lillianna had been just three and had just wanted to play.

Zinnia put her finger up to her lips. "Shh, we have to be quiet, Lilli-bug," she whispered. It was just the two of them and Pierce in the hut, but he was asleep, leaning up against the wall next to Lillianna's pallet. She didn't know where Dahlia and Father had gone, but they weren't here.

Lillianna put a hand over her mouth, stifling a giggle as she bopped her head up and down enthusiastically. "Quiet. I be quiet, Zin-Zin," she replied.

"Okay, good." Zinnia covered her eyes with her hands and counted. She didn't know how long they played. A good hour, at least. "Just one more time, Lilli-bug, okay?" Lilli nodded, and Zinnia covered her eyes once more. "One... two... three... You better hide good, Lilli-bug." Shuffling footsteps across the floor, then another soft giggle from behind the door of her and Dahlia's bedroom. "Four... five... si—"

The door creaked, and their father's acrid scent suddenly registered to her. Oh, gods, she hadn't heard him coming; hadn't heard him enter. She jerked her palms from her eyes as she cowered in the corner. Ailwin's dark eyes drifted from a slumbering Pierce to where Zinnia huddled against the wall to the sliver of Lillianna's form that she could see behind the bedroom door. His nostrils flared and his mouth flattened, filling his features, as usual, with an illogical rage.

Lillianna let out a soft whimper. Crossing the floor, Ailwin pulled his hand back. Two things happened simultaneously. The back of his hand snapped forward, connecting with Zinnia's face with a force that stole all of her breath and slammed her head into the wall. And Lillianna cried out in fear.

"Daddy!"

It didn't matter that her three-year-old self couldn't help it. The word being used regarding their brother only amplified their father's rage. In unison, a loud growl ripped out of Ailwin, rising from deep within him, and Pierce's eyes flipped open, black with fury. Zinnia ducked under her father's arm and bolted out the door. Her cheek throbbed where he'd hit her, her eye already swelling shut. Blood trickled down her cheek as she tripped over the threshold. A loose or broken branch in the siding of their hut must have cut her. She didn't stop to check the wound, though, nor did she stop to look back. She just ran away as the angry yells and snarls filled the hut.

The fight had been a bad one between them. Zinnia hadn't done the right thing then, either. She should have taken Lilli out of the hut. Comforted her and held her. Kept her safe. But, no. She had only run to save herself. She had never spent time with Lilli ever again.

"I may have burned that bridge a long time ago, Logan." Her chin dipped toward her chest as she slumped. "But we will see what happens," she said, to sound positive. "You are the only one that ever called me Zinni. I have missed it."

The corners around his eyes wrinkled. "We should let you rest. Best thing for healing."

"Right. I cannot seem to stomach food, so..." She offered them both a faint tilt of her mouth. "But I am really glad you both came to see me. I am... just glad." Zinnia cleared her throat and blinked back some tears. "Thank you. Come here and hug me before you go."

He leaned across and embraced her gently. "I will come to check on you later."

She squeezed him as tight as she could, then kissed his cheek. "Okay. I love you, Logan."

"I love you, too, Zinni, sister mine." Releasing his hold, he got to his feet.

Pierce leaned over and embraced her just as tenderly. "Get some rest. I will come to check on you later too. And try to eat. Your body needs food."

"I will try. I love you, Pierce." It had been many, many years since she'd said those words to him. She kissed his cheek.

"I love you too, Zinnia." As he got up off the bed, he pressed a soft kiss to the top of her head.

With one last look at her, Logan headed for the door. Pierce gave her hand a squeeze, then followed Logan out. She kept the false smile on her face until they were gone. She listened closely until she no longer heard their footsteps. Then she sagged against the pillows. With an arm draped across her face and a hand on her chest, she let the tears fall. She had tried to hold here motions back for Logan's sake, but she knew she hadn't fully succeeded. Now, though, she didn't think he could feel them from her. Then again, she didn't know how something like what he had worked. Maybe trying to hold them back had done no good. Zinnia made every attempt to keep her breathing slow and steady, not wanting to pull her stitches as the pain rolled through her. She deserved to feel every bit. Caused enough agony to her siblings over the years. She deserved this, at the very least.

Chapter Twenty-One

There was a knock at the door. Lilli watched as Pierce went to answer it. This wasn't his home, but everyone else was busy. Logan was starting a fire, and she worked with the other females preparing afternoon meal. Still, her gaze didn't leave the front door as her brother greeted Santos.

"Greetings, Pierce. May I come in?" Santos asked.

"Of course. My apologies." Pierce opened the door wider and stepped aside. "I am not quite myself today." He glanced over his shoulder. "Logan."

From the kitchen, she wiggled her fingers at Santos as he entered the house. "Good afternoon, Lillianna. I trust all is well."

"Yes, I am well. Thank you." She refocused on the potatoes she was slicing. Her nose wrinkled as Logan kissed the top of her head on his way by. Another round of greetings filled the room.

"May we speak?" Santos questioned.

"Of course. Should we..." Pierce's voice trailed off. "Back bedroom? Or, my home is empty. Or would the front room work fine? Wherever you would prefer, we go."

"Lillianna, will you join us as well?"

Her gaze lifted to the male. Had he addressed her? Maybe she misheard. Except Santos gestured to the front room and walked in that direction, sitting down on the couch. "I am a fair leader. While I understand the two of you," Santos nodded to Pierce and Logan, "wish to speak on Zinnia's behalf, I must consider all sides. My decision impacts all three of you."

Lilli was quiet for a minute as she joined them. She rubbed her hands over her knees. "I... I do not think I am the one to ask. I cannot speak for or against Zinnia. She is a stranger to me. She never acted as if she wanted to know me. I have never felt like her sister. We just lived under the same roof."

"Do you feel that would change? If I gave her sanctuary?" Santos asked.

"Zinnia, she at least wants to apologize to you, Lilli. Though she understands we support any decision you make, whether to hear her out," Logan said.

Her eyebrows knitted together as her gaze dropped to her lap. "Apologize," Lilli mumbled. After a moment, she inhaled and exhaled a deep breath. "This is how I feel. Right or wrong, it is how I feel." She squeezed her knees for a moment, then forced her hands to relax. "I am not close to her. She spent my entire life ignoring me. For whatever reason, she never paid me any attention. Never. Although she knew things that happened to me, she said nothing. She was never cruel to me like our other sister. She was just..." Lilli shrugged. "I know my brothers are close to her. And if they feel as if she should stay here, I want to support that. I want to support them. And I would be okay with her being here. I think I would be okay with being around her. If for no other reason than I know, it would make my brothers happy. They want all four of us to be a family. I think they need that." She peered at her brothers and then stared at her lap as she twisted her fingers together. After a beat, she eyed Santos. "Right now, I do not want to seek her out. I do not want to go out of my way to see her. I do not know if that is ever going to change."

Santos squeezed her shoulder. "Thank you, Lillianna. I appreciate your candor. Please give me a moment with your brothers."

Rising to her feet, she offered a brief dip of her chin to her brothers and Santos. "I think I am going to get some air. Yes. I will just be on the porch." There wasn't more of the conversation that she needed to be apart of; it wasn't her place to decide. Exiting the front door, she sat down on the top step and leaned against the banister. Not much time had passed when the door creaked open and shut. Looking over her shoulder, Santos' yellow eyes focused on her.

She gave him a half-hearted smile, then averted her gaze. "I apologize," she said. "I feel as if I was a little rude in there. How I left."

"You were not rude. It is a difficult topic for you. May I sit with you for a moment?"

"Of course."

Santos sat on the step next to her and clasped his hands in his lap. "You are being very strong, given the current circumstances. Do not feel as if we should not hear your voice."

She didn't feel strong. Lilli took a slow, deep breath. "I just... do not want to upset them. They want for Zinnia to stay here so badly. I do not think I care either way. She never gave me a reason to." Turning away, she pulled her tail over her thighs and ran her fingers through her fur.

"My dear, you could not upset them. They are trying to make the best decision for all involved. That does not negate how you feel about the situation. You are *allowed* to feel however you want."

"I guess I just find it difficult sometimes. Everything made my father angry. Everything..."

"Have you ever noticed how quiet Lyrica is?" Santos asked.

She frowned a little at the change in subject, still staring down at her lap. What did that have to do with anything? "Yes. I have noticed."

"The two of you have much in common."

Lilli's fingers stilled on her tail at his words. Silence stretched between them. She felt like something was trying to connect in her mind, but wouldn't.

"It is difficult to change when something has been instilled in you," Santos continued. "Even when those around you assure you, they will not react negatively. Something to remind yourself of when you find you are repressing your feelings—your father is not here."

She ran her fingers through her fur. "I still feel like he is going to find me," Lilli whispered. She hadn't meant to say it, but she couldn't take it back now. Taking in a deep breath, she blinked a few times when tears welled in the corners of her eyes. "And I feel like the... others will follow."

"You have not toured the premises yet, have you?" Santos posed.

She half-glanced at him. "Not yet. No."

"I believe it is time you do so. If you would like, I would be happy to show you now."

"Really? I would like that if you are not busy. Though I am sure you have a lot of things that take up your time."

"I am never too busy." He rose to his feet. "Simply let your brothers know, and we will go."

"Okay." She stood up and went back inside. Logan and Pierce peered at her as she entered the house. "Hey, um, Santos is going to take me on a tour of the village since I have not seen it yet."

"Of course, Lilli," Pierce said. "Do you want to take something to eat with you?"

"I can eat when I get back. If that is alright?"

"That's perfectly fine," Ambrosia replied. Logan nodded his agreement.

Her eyes brightened. "I will be back later."

"Have fun," Pierce tacked on.

Without another word, she left the house, shutting the door behind her. Santos was still waiting when she stepped back onto the porch. "I am ready to go."

He gestured outward with a wave of his hand. "Then let us go."

Lilli laced her fingers behind her back and followed him. Santos descended the staircase and led her through the maze of houses. "We built the homes here diagonally."

"Was there a reason for that?"

"Oh, yes. Should anyone ever get past our warriors and borders, they should confuse and distract our enemies. We have a safe house where the villagers go if we even suspect an enemy close to our borders."

"Oh. That makes sense. And sounds like the opposite of the way Markham has his village set up." Her eyebrows furrowed. Did that mean... that hadn't happened last night. "So, last night... you did not think Zinnia was an enemy? We all went home, not to the safe house."

"We brought her into the village, sealed the entrance, and our warriors immediately scouted the forest. If they had seen an enemy in any proximity, everyone would have evacuated to the safe house. As for my thoughts, when I saw her, I knew she was not a threat."

"Someone told me she was in a critical condition. And I knew my brothers were anxious." As they walked, she drank in every unique thing she saw. "I do not understand why no one pursued her. Why no one has found any of us. Not even Logan. I did not even know of him before the other *umbra*. But it is just not the way they did things there. No one there may live anywhere else.”

"We are a well-kept secret. Many hybrids, as well as those with unfair laws, have sought refuge with us. You are not the first shape shifters to live here. Markham has spent a lifetime seeking our location, to no avail. It is my duty to ensure it does not happen.” He continued to lead her forward, beyond the houses.

Lilli frowned a little. Logan had said they would be the only ones here. Maybe some had lived there in the past. "Well, I am glad about that. And I am glad to be here. I met no one but a shape shifter until I got here. There were many others in the marketplace, but I did not meet any there.” She paused. "Why does he care so much about finding this place?”

"Because his beliefs do not align with ours. Here, we celebrate differences. Mates come in all shapes, sizes, and species.”

"And he does not celebrate that. He seeks to come after what he does not agree with?” She chewed on her tongue. "Something Jo said makes sense now. I did not know about that. Pierce sheltered me a lot, growing up. As much as he could.”

"Yes. Markham comes after what he does not agree with. If he had his way, he would eradicate those who are ‘others’ on this isle.” Santos raised an eyebrow as they entered the gardens. "What did Jocasta say?”

She stared around in awe at all the fruits and vegetables. There were so many vibrant colors blossoming around them. A variety of different plants, along with a multitude of scents, invaded her nose. "Um... oh, just something about hiding her ears in the marketplace. I did not understand why she would need to. It is beautiful in here.”

"Jocasta is part shape shifter. She is one amongst many that Markham’s Informants hunt. She and her sister were both born here in the village. Our protection is automatic. Though the two of them are safe in the marketplace as well.”

Lilli strolled around, scrutinizing all the various shapes and sizes, row after row. "That is what Pierce was, in the village. An Informant.” She peered over at him. "He is good, though. I know you know that. You would not have let him stay otherwise.” She turned back and leaned over to smell one bloom. "It is strange. I do not know if that is the right word. But, as terrible as Markham is... he was not the one I was really afraid of.”

"Your father?” Santos ambled along by her side.

She stood up and moved through the aisles. "Yes," she muttered. "And... others."

"I am truly sorry, Lillianna. You did not deserve..." His words trailed off and he cleared his throat. "We grow and harvest all of our own food. While we have animals on our land for other sources, we have hunters as well who hunt animals in the forest. Those go into our communal storage for the entire village to share."

Silence stretched briefly between them before they continued forward. "That is a little like things were back there. Nothing grew on the land. Or maybe just nothing was grown. They always brought food back. I spent time in the kitchen sometimes. I like to cook, but we did not have very many options." She stopped, her eyes falling to a bush with green leaves and tiny balls of blue. "I never understood what I did that was so wrong. Though I really tried to be good, but..." She bit her lip. While she didn't wish to discuss her feelings, it was as if the sight of those blueberries drew the words out of her. "I am sorry. You are trying to give me a tour and... I do not have to talk about it. Most of the time, I do not want to even think about it. I just cannot help it."

Santos paused in his steps. "You may talk to me about anything you wish, Lillianna. My door is always open to you." He inhaled and exhaled a deep breath. "Nothing that happened to you is your fault. I do not wish you to think that, ever. The blame lies with Ailwin. The fault is his. Do you understand me?"

Lilli stared at the round things. A tear rolled down her face, slipping through her fur and dropping onto foliage. She blinked fast, sweeping her hand quickly under her eye. "It is... it is hard to believe that," she mumbled. "Really, really hard."

"It takes time to accept what is true when all you have known is different. I know one *umbra* you will. And I will tell you as often as is necessary until you believe it yourself. Ailwin, he is not a male of honor or one who cares for how his children have suffered."

She rubbed up and down her arms, taking a few deep breaths. Settling her nerves, she gathered the courage to speak. "Okay. Thank you." Lilli sent him a small smile over her shoulder, and then moved further down the row. "He likes Dahlia. And I never saw him raise a hand at Zinnia. But he never liked me. Or Pierce. They fought a lot over me. He got hurt a lot."

"Pierce, he did what he could to protect you." Leading them away from the garden, Santos strolled toward a large building covered in glass panels. "It was something he felt was his responsibility. To keep you safe."

"I know," she replied. "He never said so, but I know. I am glad he cares that much for me. But I hated what happened to him. And I could not... do anything." She trailed behind him, entering a glass garden of exquisite blooms, her pace slowing down as she eyed all the fresh flowers.

He didn't stray far from where she walked. "Unfortunately, sometimes our hands are tied. Though we would wish to step in and offer aid, someone or something prevents us from doing so."

"I would have if I could. I was just too hurt to move."

"Oh, my dear." He rested a comforting hand on her shoulder. "I am so sorry." Santos blew out a soft breath. "You will never go through that again."

Hugging herself, Lilli gripped her arms tight, her fingers digging into her own skin. Blinking a tear free, she shut her eyes against the anguish that threatened to consume her. "How long?" she whispered. "Until the pain goes away?"

"It is different for everyone. You will simply think about it a little less every *umbra*, until one *umbra*, you no longer think about it." He paused. "May I give you a hug?"

Her hands squeezed her arms harder as she tried to hold it all back. She opened her mouth, but nothing came out, so she just nodded. Santos embraced her the way one of her brothers would. The tears escaped and spilled down her face, slow at first, then harder, until she sobbed against him. Her body shook. Holding her, he ushered her to a nearby bench, and they both sat. Humming softly, he stroked the back of her head.

She wept harder, as if a dam had broken inside of her. Her chest heaved as she fought to catch her breath, the sobs rolling through her. And all the while, he just sat there and enveloped her in his arms. Amid her tears, something dripped down onto her head. She barely paid it any attention, though; all she could focus on was... the warmth that spread all the way through her. It felt like she was being filled with some kind of intense light... She didn't know any other way to describe it, but it filled her up, from the tips of her canine ears to the end of her long, flowing tail. Her tears slowed and oxygen filled her lungs. The trembling eased. Bit by bit, until she felt like she could really breathe again. Taking the sweet air into her nostrils, she tried to get herself under control.

"Oh, gods," she mumbled. "I... I am sorry. I did not mean..." Her words trailed off, and she bit her lip. Breaking down like this embarrassed her. And it was hard to forget what it had used to cost her. *Used to. No more. No more.* But the memories were still so very painful.

"Never apologize for letting your tears fall. It is cathartic. Something we all must do from time to time. Releasing the pain... it is how we heal."

"I want to heal," she whispered as if she were speaking to herself. "I want to heal." She sat up slowly and wiped her eyes, focusing on keeping her breathing steady. "Even you? What makes your tears fall?" Lilli waved off the question. "Never mind. That was incredibly personal."

He sat in silence for a long moment before he finally spoke. "I am unique. My tears, some I call at will when they are necessary. Some, they fall when I feel another's pain."

She pulled her tail into her lap, staring down at it as she ran her fingers through her fur. "You feel others' pain? Logan told me he could do that with emotions, but he said he could feel some pain, too." She couldn't remember how he'd worded it. She just knew he'd felt the agony she had during her nightmare. And it had been a terrible one. Cyrus always had been.

"So, to speak. Logan is an empath. He feels all emotions, and he can feel what is happening to another person. I cannot feel your emotions. I can only feel it when you are in pain." He adjusted a little on the bench. "My tears are unlike any other. And they can fall when I sense another's pain."

"So, it is more of a physical thing? I am sorry, I am just curious, I guess. There is much I do not know about a lot of things. I think that is how he wanted it, in the village. No one to know anything, but what he wanted them to."

"You are welcome to ask me any question you wish." Santos paused. "Yes. It is a more physical thing. We have a small library here. I will show it to you on our way back if you wish."

Lilli eyed him warily. "Just because I can ask does not mean you have to answer." She glanced up a little and immediately her gaze went back down to her tail. "You do not owe me anything. It is the other way around. You allowed me to stay here, in this beautiful, safe place." She swallowed hard and blinked a few times, then took a few deep breaths.

"This is true. However, here, we encourage curiosity. I would be remiss in my duties if I did not lead by example."

"What is a library?"

"A library is a place where one can obtain knowledge. We outfitted a house for all the books we have. You can read the books there. Some of the younger children gather regularly with a member of the village to read to them. If that does not suit you, you may take a book of your choice back to your home and return it when you have finished."

Books, as in plural. "I have never seen one before. A book. Pierce told me about them. He taught me how to read and write, but we had to do it in the dirt. He used a stick to draw in it. My father did not want me to..." She bit her lip. Her father, like Markham, hadn't wanted her to learn anything. "I would love to see it."

"Then I will happily show it to you. We can go now if you so desire, or we can continue to the barns and stop in the library on our way back."

"I think the library sounds good. Maybe the barns another *umbra*. I am a little tired. But I would like to see the library first."

"Very well." Santos rose to his feet and offered a hand to help her up.

She smiled a little and took his hand, letting go of her tail as she stood. "Thank you."

"You are quite welcome." He led her back toward the houses, leaving the greenhouse and gardens behind. When they approached the last row of houses, he turned to the left and walked until they came upon a house with a bright orange door. "It is never hard to miss."

"That is a beautiful color. And no, I do not think I could miss it." She let out a soft laugh.

Santos ascended the staircase and opened the door. A female voice resounded from the back. As they stepped in, bookcases lined either side of the fireplace. A couch and a couple of chairs occupied the space beyond it. On the other side, where the dining area would be, more bookcases lined the wall. Books filled each one to the brim. A couple of trays of sweet rolls sat on the counter in the kitchen. "The other rooms contain more books. We set up the backroom as a place for reading to the younger children."

Lilli surveyed everything, trying to take it all in. There were so many. "Wow. All these... they are all books? Do they have different things in them?"

"Yes. These are all books. They have many things in them. Some are merely tales written for enjoyment, some contain various histories, while others offer other knowledge, like alchemy or arithmetic."

Strolling over to the nearest shelf, Lilli gently ran her fingertips over the edges of the leather. "What are those?" She cocked an eyebrow at him. "Alchemy and arithmetic?"

"Alchemy is the study of converting or changing one substance into another. Arithmetic deals with numbers and the various ways to understand them."

"Numbers, like counting? I can count some. There was not much use for it there, though." She scanned over the different titles. "What kind of substances?"

"Yes, like counting. And substances like various metals and how one can transform them for uses in medicine or magic."

"All of that is in these?" She reached the end of the shelf and moved to the next one.

"It is some of what is in these, yes. There are many things you can learn. If you wish to know about the structure of different creatures, the multitudes of gems, and how to use or manipulate them. The gardens we visited, you can learn how to cultivate the fruits and vegetables, what kind of flavor they may have. Or the flowers we saw."

It all sounded interesting. "I would like to read about... all of that. But to start, if I wanted to read something that was happy?" Her gaze flicked back in his direction.

Santos tapped his chin. Slowly, the corners of his mouth upturned. "One moment." He headed down the hallway and disappeared into the back room. Several youthful voices resounded the second he entered. She felt a strange pull deep within her to follow him down the corridor, but she stayed put. A few minutes later, he returned with three square books with colorful covers. "I am certain you will read through them quickly, but they all have happy endings. Plus, it will give you a chance to get your bearings with books."

She smiled as she took them from him carefully, studying each cover. "They are pretty. And I can take these home to look at? I will be very careful with them. I promise."

"Yes. You simply bring them back when you have finished. There is a cart in the kitchen they get placed on. Villagers take turns daily, ensuring books are returned to their rightful location."

She clutched the precious items to her chest. "Is that something I might learn to do sometime?"

"If that is what you wish, yes."

"I just... I would like to help with things, if I can. It might help to take my mind off of other things."

"I understand. You can learn to do anything here you like. Everyone helps in different ways; however, you would like to help. Ambrosia can set that up, or if you would prefer, I can handle it."

"Either is fine. Thank you."

"You are quite welcome." Santos gave her a slight bow of his head. "If you are ready, I will escort you home."

"Yes, I am ready. I did not eat yet, and I would really like to look at these."

"Would you like a sweet roll to take with you?" He gestured to the two plates on the kitchen counter.

She eyed them and bit her lip. "I would, but I do not want to get the books dirty."

"Understandable." He strode to the exit and held the door open for her. "Shall we?"

Without speaking another word, she left the library and stepped onto the porch. Ensuring everything closed behind them, Santos descended the staircase.

When they got back to the house, Lilli hesitated at the bottom of the staircase. "Can I give you a hug this time?"

"Yes, you may."

She set the books down carefully on the top step of the porch. Wrapping her arms around him, she gave him a squeeze. "Thank you for today, and just... for everything. Thank you."

"You are very welcome, Lillianna."

Pulling back, she turned to pick up the books. "Goodbye, Santos. I hope you have a good *umbra*." She grinned at him one last time before heading into the house as he walked away.

Ambrosia looked up from the sink. Logan stood next to her, drying dishes and putting them up. "How was your tour with Santos?"

"It was..." She thought back over all that she saw. Despite her episode in the gardens... "I did not see everything, but it was really nice. He showed me the library." She held up the books. "I had not seen books before."

Setting aside the dishrag, Ambrosia's entire face lit up. "The library is one of my favorite places. Do you want to put those in your room while I get you a bowl of stew? I'm sure you're hungry after all of that."

"It was amazing. Yes. I will do that. I am pretty hungry. Did Pierce and Jo go home?"

Logan barely contained the smirk. "Yes, they went home."

"I'm sure we'll see them later," Ambrosia said.

"Not likely," he muttered.

Ambrosia elbowed Logan in the gut. "Go ahead and put those up. I'll get you some food."

"Okay. I will be right back." Lilli went back to her bedroom and set the stories aside on the little table, then picked the top one back up. It had fish on it. Opening it up, she reviewed two pages. The words didn't look very hard, but it had been a long time. She drew in a breath and slowly let it out. Well. She had to start somewhere. Laying it atop the others, she left her room and headed into the dining room.

By the time she returned, Ambrosia had a bowl of stew set out, a plate with two sweet rolls, a cup of tea, and a spoon. Lilli sat down at the table. "This smells fantastic. Thank you."

"You're welcome." Ambrosia returned to the kitchen to finish cleaning up.

"What all did you get to see?" Logan asked.

"The way they set the houses up, and the gardens." Lilli paused. "We were there for a while. He asked if I wanted to see the barns too, but I was getting a little tired. So, he just showed me the library and brought me home." She put a bite of stew in her mouth and chewed thoughtfully.

"Sounds like you got about halfway through. There's still a lot to see. Maybe we can finish the tour tomorrow if you like." Ambrosia wiped down the counter and set the rag aside to dry.

"Perhaps the three of us can plan to go? I have not gotten to see much of the village either," Logan said.

Lilli swallowed the bite in her mouth. "That sounds like fun. We should do that."

"Then we'll do that after morning meal tomorrow." Ambrosia tossed a glance at Logan. "Sound good?"

"Yes, love. It does."

Lilli smiled. "It sounds good to me, too."

Chapter Twenty-Two

Logan ensured Lilli and his mate didn't need any help with evening meal before he headed to the medical building. As expected, Jocasta and Pierce hadn't returned to the house. That was okay. His brother deserved to spend time with his mate. The male had taken care of their family as much as he could over the last eighteen years. It was his turn to render care.

In a much better mood than the first time he'd come here, Logan entered the building with a smile on his face. He nodded to Kaylina and gestured down the hall. "May I go back, please?"

"Yes. Go ahead."

"Thank you." He strode down the long corridor and entered his sister's room. Hades, he still couldn't believe she was here. But he was oh so grateful. "Hi, Zinni."

Her gaze swung away from the window. With a mug of tea in her hands, the corners of her mouth curled as she faced him. "Hey there, brother mine." She lifted the mug to her nose and inhaled. "Oh, it smells exactly how Mother's did. I cannot seem to get enough of it. I think I have peed about a thousand times already."

"They are fairly good with the tea here." It didn't take him over three strides to join her side. He sat on the edge of the bed. Shaking his head, he laughed. "Although I am glad to hear you are enjoying the tea, I could have dealt without the addition of your bathroom habits. Have you eaten anything?"

She gave him an apologetic shrug. "Sorry." She set the mug over on the table. "Um, not much. I ate some this afternoon. Food just is not quite settling well yet. It will, though."

"I suppose that is to be expected. I am certain you will eat food soon. It will help get your energy up and aid with your healing."

"I know. I will try to eat again in a little while. Kaylina said she would bring me evening meal." Her eyebrows furrowed. "I am not used to having food brought to me."

"There are so many things different here. We eat a lot of our meals together, as a family." He couldn't remember the last time that had been done. Their mother had tried, but it hadn't happened as often as it did here.

"Really? Well, that will be new." She paused. "How is that going to work? With Lilli? Have you spoken to her yet?"

"Yes, we did." Gods, he prayed they could build a relationship. If they couldn't, he knew both he and Pierce would stand by their word. "She has no intention of seeking you out, but she will be polite at meals. Our table is big enough that we will seat you either with our mates or on the opposite side of Lyrica. She's my mate's and Pierce's mate's mother. A wonderful female. I think you will like her."

"Okay. Then that is what we will do. But if it ever makes her too uncomfortable, perhaps I can eat elsewhere, Pierce's home maybe. Eating alone would be nothing I am not used to, anyway. You said she is happy and thriving; I wish for her to remain that way. She has not had that, and she deserves it."

"I am sure there will be times we do not all eat together." Logan smirked. "We do not expect Pierce and Jocasta to join us this evening. Come to think of it, they did not join us the other evening either." His brother was happy and that was all that mattered.

She snickered. "Well. I am glad he is so joyous. He seemed deep in thought this morning."

"We were both concerned they would not grant you sanctuary." Not to mention, he suspected their brother attempted to keep his emotions under control for his sake. There had been a lot they had dealt with over the last few days.

"I will admit, I was concerned myself. But Santos seems very fair and kind. I told him I would give him no reason to regret his decision."

"You know, Pierce's home will be your home, too."

"I have not... felt like anywhere was home in a very long time. There was a short period where I did not live with Father and, while that was a little nicer, it still did not feel like a home either."

"Where did you live?"

"I lived with Bennet. It was not a love mating, and it did not last long."

Logan bit back the growl that threatened to escape. *Bennett?* The male had not been amongst his favorites. Few were. Though she could've done worse. "Let me guess. Ailwin."

"Father certainly approved. Bennet wanted me, had the coin that Father wanted. There was no point in saying no, so I did not. And he made it *very* clear that if I became with child, there would be a mating ceremony. I did, there was, so, I moved in with Bennet. It was not too bad, really. A lot less yelling, as long as I did what he said."

"What?" His eyes widened. Had she been with child? By force? If the male was not already dead, he would hill him all over again. Shit. Had he known that... No. No. The outcome would've remained the same.

A moment of silence stretched between them. "Do not give me that look," she finally said. "I did not say no. Things went easier if there was consent. So, I gave it. Well, rather, I said nothing." She paused. "One *umbra*, it had been just two cycles. Bennet got sent on a scouting mission with a few others. He did not return. A few *umbras* later, I was told that I was moving back in with Father. I just assumed death. It would have been the only reason. I was about thir... thirteen *penumbras* when..." Zinnia cleared her throat. "It was a few *umbras* after I moved back in with Father. The pregnancy... did not survive."

Leaning over, Logan dug his elbows into his knees, ran his hands over his head and ears, and gripped the back of his neck tightly. The things the male had spouted... He hadn't cared that the male intended to bring his head back on a stake to Markham, but the second Bennet had uttered one word about his sister, he'd lost it. Despite his injuries, he'd been the one to walk away. Gods, how could he have done that to her? "I am so sorry, Zinni. I did not... gods, I am sorry."

"It is alright," she replied. Placing a finger beneath his chin, she lifted his head until their gazes met. "Do not do that, Logan. I can see it in your eyes right now. It was not your fault. The regret is unnecessary. It is just the way things are there. You know that. I made things as easy on myself as possible.

My life was not nearly so terrible as it is for others." She dropped her hand back to her lap. Her fingers brushed absentmindedly over her belly. "It has been about ten *solaris* now. I was far enough along to know..." Her words trailed off. "It was a girl. I was going to name her Summer."

He couldn't look at her. Maybe he hadn't been directly responsible, but if the male hadn't crossed paths with him and had lived, she would have—fuck. He was doing exactly what he had told Pierce not to do. They couldn't live in 'what ifs.' But he couldn't sit here and not tell her either. His gaze fell to the floor. "He died at my hand."

"What happened?"

"I was staying just outside the chimera borders. Most of the time, I spent my *umbras* there, either helping or fighting alongside them." His eyebrows knitted together tightly as flashes from those long days danced on his brain. "My skills were the only reason they even allowed me access." Shaking the thoughts away, he swallowed the lump at the back of his throat. "I knew I could not stay for long, so I had scouted for land to build. I do not recall how I got delayed that *umbra*, but I did. We crossed one another near to their border. We both dealt equal blows... until he brought you up. The last thing I remember is ripping his throat out. When I came around many *lacunas* later, I was being treated by a chimera."

"What... brought me up? How? If you had not killed him, he would have killed you. I am glad that you won, though I am sorry you got injured. If you had not, we would not be here today." She gave his hand a squeeze. "Do not feel sorry for what you did, Logan. I would much rather have you in my life, my beloved brother, than a mate I did not care for."

The male had known he was losing. Bennet's death had been certain, though perhaps it would have been less brutal if he hadn't uttered one word about the things he had done to Zinnia. It had been no secret in the village how important his mother and sister had been to him. Logan squeezed her hand in return. "He thought he could use you to distract me. He was quite wrong." Something nagged at him as they spoke about this. He didn't imagine any of this was easy for her to hear, let alone to talk about. Yet her emotions gave little away. He flicked his gaze to his sister. How did he ask? He couldn't come right out. If she didn't know, then asking her would certainly ensure she did. He dragged a hand across his face.

"Well. I am glad he could not distract you. Having you back in my life has made me ecstatic." Tightening her hold on his hand, she let out a slow breath. "Logan... I have something that I must tell you. It is something you deserve to know, but it is difficult, and I am sure it will anger you. I asked the Elder for advice. He thinks I should tell you. That it will give you...clarity."

She knew. She knew about his ability. That was the only logical explanation. That's why he sensed less of her emotions. She repressed them. Not that it angered him. Part of him was grateful, and yet it annoyed him, too. Mostly that his siblings felt they had to subdue their emotions around him at all. "I do not think you could anger me, sister mine. No matter what you have to tell me."

Zinnia released the hold she had on his hand and lowered it in her lap. "I never believed that you killed Galenus. Though no one in the village openly expressed it, I never believed it. But I know why he accused you. And why he really offered you the position of Informant. And I know who betrayed you to Markham."

Logan sat there in silence. Did he want to know? Who told Markham about his empathic ability? How did she know? He hadn't even told Pierce the exact reason Markham had offered him the Informant position. The only person who knew was Devin. Because she asked, or he had been in a sharing mood. He wasn't sure why he told her, but he had. "Who?"

"I do not know how she found out, and I knew none of it until after you were gone. It was Dahlia."

"Somehow, that does not surprise me. She was always the kind to use any advantage she could." He shook his head. At least now he knew the truth. But how had Dahlia discovered it? He had been so careful. So very careful at their mother's behest. "Mother always knew I was special. That is what she used to tell me. I did not tell Pierce until we were teenagers about my empathic abilities." None of that was the point. They couldn't change their past. Only focus on the present. He let out a heavy breath as his gaze fixated on his sister. "This is why I feel very little from you right now."

"I do not know who else might know. I was alone with her when she told me." She paused. "The things I feel right now—rather, that I am not allowing myself to feel right now—some of them are very painful. And it is a lot all at once. I will not always hold things back around you. I just... I need time to process things for myself. And I do not want to cause further pain for you." She clasped his hand in hers again. "You are so happy here. A new life, and happily mated. I am overjoyed about it."

"Emotions are always a lot to process. I have to do the same thing when I feel what others feel. I have become better at it, though sometimes I still have moments where I get overwhelmed, but my mate helps me with that. Repressing your emotions... I know you do not want to cause me pain, but I do not want you to harm yourself. And that happens when you hold things in for too long. It is destructive. Process as you need, but do not hold back. Not on my account. That would cause me pain."

"It is what I have done... what I have had to do... for a very long time." Zinnia bit her bottom lip and lifted her gaze to him. "You are sure?"

"Yes. I am certain." He knew firsthand how bad holding everything in could be. It had caused his anger for a long time. It was all he'd allowed himself to feel.

She stared at him for a few minutes—then it was as if a dam had broken inside of her. A well of emotions flooded him as tears streamed down his sister's face. The swirling storm of anger, self-blame, regret, remorse, pain, sorrow, disgust, agony, love, and loss nearly consumed his sister. At the unprecedented wave, he braced himself for the impact of the onslaught of images that would inevitably accompany each. The agony their father and Dahlia had caused the family. All the times Zinnia believed she had done the wrong thing. The filthy acts she allowed the males in the village to do to her. That instead of fighting, she had given into every single bit of it. The feelings she had swallowed and buried. Bennett's torment. What she'd felt for the daughter she'd carried in her womb, followed by her agonizing loss. Losing their mother and him. Refusing to say goodbye. The estrangement from Pierce.

Her chest heaved. "I do not... think... I can... breathe... Oh, gods. This... this hurts." Her words came out between choked sobs as her body physically shook from the torment that ran through her.

Logan embraced her tightly and rubbed his hands up and down her arms as he held her. Although he couldn't stop the tears from falling down his face, he processed the emotions a little better than he had with Lillianna. Thank the gods for that.

Zinnia leaned into him. He didn't know how long they stayed like that until her breathing eased. Although throbbing pain from her injuries wracked her body, he sensed a weight had lifted from her shoulders. For the first time, she had finally allowed herself to grieve… for all of it.

"I did not mean to cry all over you," she murmured.

"That is okay. I clean easily." Logan cracked a smile. Gods, the things she had gone through, and she had suffered alone. He had felt all of it. And much of it had upset him, but he'd controlled his rage and kept it in check. Honestly, it made him feel better about killing Bennet. And reaffirmed his decision to rid the isle of at least one more male. One who would know whose hand he died upon. As for Dahlia—no, he wouldn't kill her. But she would know who took their father's life. He would make certain of it. And if she dared come for his family, he wouldn't hesitate to put the bitch down. He didn't care that she was blood. As far as he was concerned, he only had two sisters. And they were both in this village with their brothers. Where they belonged.

"Well, that is good." Zinnia sighed. "I would have kept her. Summer. If he had allowed me to," she said. "Father wanted no more young in the hut. He did not want to take care of anymore. But he never took care of us. I would have taken care of her even though I did not take care of Lillianna when I should have. I would have taken care of my daughter."

"I know you would have." He continued to hold her. Gods, everything she had kept in over the years… "I know a lot of time has gone by, but perhaps we can hold a vigil. If you would like." He didn't know if she would be up for that. Or if she even wanted the rest of their family to know what she'd been through.

She sniffled, but didn't wipe her tears away. "Maybe. That might be nice. Or… maybe I could plant something for her at the house? At… home. Do you think Pierce and his mate would be okay with that?"

"I think they would be perfectly fine with that." He hadn't thought about that, but he didn't think either of them would oppose. It had been what their mother had always done. And he and Ambrosia had done the same, though up at the cabin. Not that anyone knew about that.

"Okay." She was quiet for a minute. "Things happen how they are supposed to, I think. Even when we do not understand, even when they hurt. Had she lived… I do not think it would have been the greatest life. She would have had cruel experiences that no one should have. She would have had pain inflicted upon her. I would not have been able to stop it. That village is no place for females. It is not a good place to raise young. And

I would have had no good stories to tell her about her father. I could not have told her he was a good male, not without lying." His sister clutched his hand. "Everything... everything has led us here. I would not change that for anything."

"Yes, it has. We can process the pain of the past so we may let it go. And move forward to the future." It was a process. And she had felt it all at once. But sometimes, the bandage had to be ripped off. Not peeled away a little at a time. "Knowing things happened as they should does not make the pain easier to address. Having those who love you around helps. I am glad to have you here, sister mine."

A few more tears rolled through her fur, down her cheeks as the hold she had on Logan's hand tightened. "I am glad to be here with you too, brother mine. So, so very glad. I am not hurting your hand, am I?"

"No. Not at all." He had dealt with worse physical pain over the years. Even the fight with Evan had left him with a couple of injuries. Nothing fatal. His mate had been inside the cabin. And he would have allowed no harm in coming to her.

"Okay. I wanted to be sure." Her eyes crinkled at the corners. "How did you do it? For so long? He never found you. He found others, but never you. When Pierce told me..." Zinnia shook her head. "Whatever you did, I am glad for it."

"I kept moving. I never stayed in one place for too long. Not for ten *solaris*. After I left the chimeras, I located a small hidden clearing about sixty miles from here, and I built a cabin. I have spent the last eight *solaris* there. Only one has come close, and he did not survive."

Once again, silence temporarily greeted him. "I am so sorry, Logan. That must have been... so lonely," she whispered. "I know about Evan. Markham said it was you."

He couldn't help the smile that crossed his face. "Good. I meant for him to." He hugged her close. "I did what I had to do so I could be here."

"And I am so very glad that you are, brother mine. All of my pain was worth it to me to be reunited with you again. We have the chance now to be a genuine family. I do not intend to waste one moment of it. And that includes living in the past. We cannot change it."

He bit back a growl at the pain related memory that flashed in his head from her. Perhaps he didn't think that through all the way. Then again, he couldn't have expected that Markham would throw the head at his sister.

Nor would it stop him and Pierce from adding to the collection. "I am happy that we are reunited, as well. And that you will not live in the past. I love you, sister mine."

"I love you too, brother mine." Brushing the tears from her face, Zinnia sat up. "Please tell me you are creating again. What you made brought beauty into a household that was far from beautiful. I missed seeing them around the hut."

It had been a joy to create all he had. The fact they had a place for him to work here quickly made it feel like this was always where he belonged. "Yes. I am." He hadn't yet started on furniture for her, but he would.

"Good. I am glad to hear it." She slumped, half leaning against the bedding. "I do not know when they will allow me to go home. It will probably be another *umbra* at least, maybe two, before I am comfortable moving around. These are not injuries I have had before. I think Kaylina wants my appetite to return, too. But would you like to show me around when I can leave? Maybe Pierce could come too?"

"It would make sense they wish to see your appetite return. A good sign that you are truly on the mend. Yes, once you can leave, I would love to show you around. I do not think Pierce has seen much of anything here." He'd seen about half of it. The woodworking building had caught his eye, and his mate had laughed at his distraction. It had been a beautiful day. "There are many things to do and get involved in. Gardens, a greenhouse, library, and that is just the beginning."

She raised her eyebrows. "I do not know what a library is, but... gardens? Things grow here?"

"Yes. Things grow here. A library is a place for books." At least, that was what he assumed, since Lilli had brought some back with her. It was one of the few places he hadn't visited yet.

"Books..." She narrowed her eyes. "Oh, wait. Is it that thing? I think Mother had one when we were really young. That had the story in it?" Her face lit up. "I think so, anyway. I remember now, she only brought it out when Father was gone."

"Yes. That is correct. He did not prefer us to learn." Much like Markham. They weren't to be educated. "I have not gone there yet, but Lillianna returned with a few books earlier. She seemed quite happy to have something to read."

Zinnia blinked, incredulous. "She can read? Well, I suspect Pierce probably taught her. So, she is truly happy? She enjoys it here? It will be nice to see a smile on her face."

"Yes. Ambrosia, my mate, is quite wonderful with her. Well, all of them are really. They even helped her pick out clothes. She feels more comfortable in them." It was still an adjustment to him. But they did whatever made her comfortable in her own skin.

"Clothing, really? I cannot imagine wearing any. Although... I suppose I could see how that would make her feel better." His sister's brows furrowed. "Is Pierce really doing alright? I think if I were to ask him, he would just say he was fine, even if he was not. Finding happiness with his mate is one thing and pleases me greatly. But it is not a cure-all. Or perhaps it is. I do not know."

No. It certainly wasn't a "cure-all." Problems still arose in strong matings. Not that he noticed anything out of sorts with his brother. And he refused to mention anything off between him and his mate. They were... dealing. "Jocasta... she has calmed him. And she always seems to know when he just needs her. Or to talk. He and I have been able to speak about many things. There may still be things we all have to talk through, and we will do that."

"I can only imagine." Her mouth tilted ever so slightly. "I look forward to it, though. Even knowing that part of it will be difficult. I have missed the conversations. It will be nice to see you and Pierce close again as well. Growing up, you were attached at the hip. You could have been twins." She snickered.

He chuckled. "Would certainly explain how we both ended up with twins."

Her eyes widened. "Oh. Yes, that it could." She clasped his hand in hers once again. "I am not keeping you from anything, am I? It is wonderful talking with you, but I am sure you have duties at home and with your mate and Lillianna. Evening meal, I suppose, but I do not know what time it is."

"I believe it is getting close to evening meal. Ambrosia and Lilli had begun preparations just before I left."

There was a slight sparkle in her eyes. "You should eat then. I am not going anywhere. I am sure they will bring food in for me again soon, anyway."

She was right. It had been some time since he left. They would expect him back soon.

"Knock, knock. How is my patient?" Kaylina inquired as she stepped into the room with a tray of stew, bread, and more tea.

"It appears you are correct," Logan said.

"So, it would seem." Zinnia's eyes flicked to Kaylina. "Physically, about the same since you last checked on me. Emotionally... Better." She looked back over at the female. "I am going to try harder to eat this evening."

"Well, I have something a bit more solid. But if you can't eat the meat and vegetables in the stew, at least try the liquid. It's better than nothing." Kaylina set the tray down on the table.

"Thank you, Kaylina. I will."

"I will let you eat." Logan hugged Zinnia and dropped a kiss to the top of her head. "And I will check on you in the morning."

"I will see you then. I love you, Logan."

"I love you, too, Zinni." He rose to his feet. This was good. There was still a lot to overcome, but they'd taken a big step. With a brief dip of his chin, he strode to the door and left.

Chapter Twenty-Three

Pierce stood in front of the medical building, unable to make his feet take him inside. Similar to the other day, when he and Logan saw her together. He wasn't sure why he still hesitated the way he did. That was a lie. Of course he was. He'd barely known what to say to Zinnia when they saw her. His thoughts about her rattled back and forth with doubt. Not to mention the way Lilli was feeling about the whole thing.

There used to be a closeness between them, but it was one that had long since dwindled away. A mere two months after his recovery from bringing Lilli back there.

Pierce yanked open the door to their hut and momentarily froze in his footsteps. The smell of fear and blood was even more intense inhere; it literally permeated the air inside. Grunts and growls came from Zinnia's and Dahlia's bedroom. The door wasn't closed. Zinnia was on her hands and knees. Her fingers gripped the edges of her pallet as she fought to hold herself upright. There were two males inside the room as well. One behind her, his claws digging into her hips, and one in front of her, a solid grip on the back of her head. The noises belonged to them. The rest—fear and blood—belonged to her. Punctuated with tears streaming down her cheeks.

Though he couldn't see his own face, he knew his eyes were blacker than they'd been in a very long time. A ferocious snarl left him. He didn't make it halfway across the room before their father exited the bedroom, a coin sack in his hand, and closed the door behind him. He met Pierce face-to-face, wearing a wicked smirk. Father opened his mouth to speak, but before he could utter a word, Pierce slammed him up against the wall.

The fight with Ailwin that had followed had been colossal. So severely Markham had intervened. Thank the gods Lillianna had been with one of the other females of the village.

No matter how many times Pierce had walked in on it, he had always done the same. Attacked. Taken to the ring and punished, or punished by Markham himself.

He squeezed his eyes shut at the memories. None of it had mattered. Not in the end. Zinnia hadn't wanted his protection. There had come a day when she'd followed him into the woods and confronted him. It had been after yet another attack. He'd still been able to smell the blood on her, and beads of crimson still stained his fur.

"Just... please, Pierce. Leave it alone, I am begging you. I cannot continue to watch... as you get beaten—among other things—over something you can do nothing about. It is... itis breaking my heart, Pierce. I give my consent. And I do not tell them no. I am dealing with this how I need to. To get through this. Survive this. That cannot include you interfering. So, please... just stop."

It was the point their relationship had really shattered into a million fucking pieces. He didn't know how to put it back together again. They'd drifted apart, further and further every day, until they no longer spoke. Until they no longer greeted each other when entering the hut. No longer said goodbye when leaving. Eventually, they didn't acknowledge each other at all, and she'd spent most of her free time with Dahlia. Looking at his sister while knowing what their father had forced upon her, the fight had gone out of her when Logan had left and their mother had died; she refused the little aid he could offer—it had been too hard. The shattered remains of his heart and soul couldn't take it.

"You have to think of Lillianna now. Not me. You cannot protect me. Protect her."

And so, that is what he'd done, the best that he could. He'd thrown every bit of energy into their little sister because he'd been unable todo anything for anyone else. And although, in his opinion, he had done little to truly protect her during the first twelve years of her life; she had mostly escaped the violence. Then that had changed as well.

Pierce shook the thoughts away. He didn't want to think about the memories. Never, really, but especially not right now. His sister was in there. She had just survived an ordeal that should have killed her. That they had fully expected to kill her. Instead, by some miracle from the gods, she'd practically ended up on their doorstep. Alive against all odds. She'd turned her back on the village, turned her back on Ailwin and Dahlia—two that he could have never imagined she would have. And she had come to them.

Now he would go to her. And bring her home.

Pierce inhaled and exhaled a deep breath. He forced his feet to move and went inside. Kaylina granted him permission to go back and his feet carried him down the hall to that same room. He stopped in the jamb and stared at his sister. She sat up in bed, her legs tucked under her as she ate. She didn't notice him at first, seeming to be lost in thought. He knew the feeling. Pierce cleared his throat, and she dropped her spoon.

"Hey, sorry." Pierce stepped fully into the room and sat on the end of the bed. "I did not mean to startle you."

"It is alright. I have been up in my thoughts this morning."

"I can understand that."

"Do we need to go, or…?"

"Oh, no. Finish your food. There is no hurry."

She picked up her spoon again. He said nothing while she ate. Didn't know what to say. He hated this distance between them. It would get better. He knew it would. Perhaps they just needed time. "I am glad to see you eating again."

"Yes. Me as well. My appetite came back yesterday evening with full force."

"Good. I am sure that has helped aid in your healing."

"So Kaylina says. And I certainly feel *much* better."

"That is good." Silence stretched between them. Always silence. "I know Logan came back to see you. I…" Pierce sighed. He had come with Logan yesterday morning but had said little then, either. But Logan had come alone as well. He said they'd had a pleasant talk, though his brother hadn't gone into details. Pierce had meant to do the same. "I am sorry that I did not. By myself, I mean. I meant to. We have much to talk about. I just…"

"Pierce, stop it. Look at me."

He flicked his gaze up to her as she took his hand.

"While I appreciate it, an apology is unnecessary. Believe me, I under-stand. It has been many *solaris* since we spoke at all, let alone spoke at length. I take the blame for that upon myself."

"It was not your fault, Zinnia. I know you were doing what you had to do to just get through everything. None of what happened was your fault."

"No more than it was *yours*." Her grip on his hand tightened.

"Yes. So, I have been told. It does not change how I feel about it." Hades, *most* of it, if he was honest with himself. He didn't accept the blame for the actions of Markham, their father, or the other Informants, but everything else... He'd never truly protected anyone. His idea of protection had only ever caused them more emotional pain.

Zinnia withdrew her hand. She placed the spoon and empty bowl on the tray that sat on the table, then reclaimed his hand. "Look. I think things happen how they are supposed to. Even when we do not understand them. Even when they hurt. I said the same to Logan yesterday." She paused. "Some things, I do not think we are supposed to understand them. Some things we must just endure. The pain we go through, the things we survive, that is what can help us find our strength. But we can also find strength in other things. In our family, and in our loved ones. The strength to leave horrible situations, even when they feel normal to us. The strength to stop dwelling on the past, move beyond the heartache, pain, and anger. If we are stuck in the past, if we cannot move past it, how can we ever live in the present? Look to the future?"

Pierce said nothing for a few minutes. The corners of his lips tugged upward. "You are right. When did you become so smart, sister mine?"

She feigned surprise. "Do not be mean, Pierce. I have always been smart. I have just had to act stupid for a very long time."

He chuckled. "I was only teasing. Come on. Let us go home."

"Yes. Home."

He helped her up out of the bed. After she tidied up her dishes and fixed the blanket on her bed, he put his arm around her and led her out of the room. They both bid Kaylina goodbye as they left the medical center.

"Kaylina told me to come back if I have any problems. But honestly, I feel wonderful. Better than I have in a long time."

"I suspect that is because of more than the healing, though."

"Oh, yes." She blew out a soft breath. "Seeing Logan again... I cannot even describe how it makes me feel. I never thought I would ever see him again."

"Nor I. But the fates had something else in store for us. And I thank the gods every *umbra* for it, and my mate." He smiled. "Jocasta is the best thing that has ever happened to me. Most *umbras*, I wonder how I ever came to deserve someone so wonderful."

Her eyes flicked down to the bracelet again, the engraving on his wrist. "I could not even understand the happiness you have found with her. I am so glad about it, though. Whether you believe you do, you truly deserve it. Logan too. I am glad that you both have found it."

He squeezed her shoulder. "You will find it too, Zinnia. One *umbra*, when you are ready." He didn't want to bring up Bennett. Or anything painful. Anything she may not want to speak about. Just as he had decided with Lilli, he would let them bring it up first. "One *umbra*, you will find a *true* mate, one that makes you as happy as Jocasta makes me, and Ambrosia makes Logan."

"Maybe. One *umbra*. I am in no hurry for that, though. Right now, I just want to find my bearings. Process everything." She surveyed their surroundings as they walked. "This place is incredible."

"I have not even seen it all yet. It differs greatly from the village. In more than looks, though. It is like being in a different realm all together sometimes."

"Logan told me some things there are to do here. I look forward to seeing it all."

"Maybe we can see them together. Make an *umbra* of it. Whoever wants to come." He hoped his sisters could mend things, though he also doubted it. But hopefully, Lilli would want to come too. At some point. "Oh, there is no curfew here. You do not need to be home at any certain time."

She raised her eyebrows. "Really? That is different."

"Oh, yes. A lot to get used to. Though, I do not think it would be a good idea to leave the village. At least not..." Not until their father burned to ashes. Until Markham and his Informants were no longer a threat. "Not for a while."

"That, brother mine, will not be an issue. I have no desire to leave this place. Testing fate might be a bit much."

"While I might not put it that way, it would definitely be safer to stay inside the boundaries."

"Duly noted."

His ruby gaze dropped to her. "I know Santos spoke to you. I mean, when he offered you sanctuary. The one law we have here. You are safe here.

No matter what. I want you to know that. No one from the village is going to find you here. And if you never want to leave, you never have to."

"That is hard—harder—to swallow. But I am going to trust in his words, and yours and Logan's."

"Lillianna had the same concerns. But I will tell you as often as you need to hear them. I am sure Logan will as well." All she did was nod. As they ambled along, he pointed out the things he knew about the village. He stopped them when they got in front of his and Logan's homes. "Logan lives in that one, and we live right here next door. I think everyone is over there right now. I can take you inside and show you your room. Logan did your furniture for you."

"He did?"

"Did you think he would have it any other way?" Pierce smirked. "Come on. I know all you have done is rest, but... I mean, if you would like to rest more. Or, Hades, I do not know. But we are all having evening meal tonight, together at Logan's. We would love it if you would join us."

"I think you are trying too hard. But I appreciate it all the same. Let us go in. I would love to see my new home."

With a smile that reached his eyes, he led her inside.

Chapter Twenty-Four

Lilli looked over from the kitchen area as the front door swung open. Her eyes stuck on Zinnia for a minute, who had a wide grin on her face, before flicking to her brother and his mate.

"Just don't think for one second you get them all to yourself," Jo teased.

"Oh, I would never dream of being greedy, my love," Pierce replied.

Lilli couldn't look away from Zinnia. Dinner. It was just dinner. She could do this. For Pierce and Logan, she could do this. She offered a welcomed acknowledgement to Pierce and Jo. "What is that? It smells fantastic."

"We brought apple tarts for dessert," Jo answered.

Lilli leaned into Am as the female gave her a quick side hug. "You get them from Sadiya?" Am asked.

"Of course. She has the best tarts in the village."

"You should probably put them on the counter for later then," Lyrica suggested.

Pierce bit his lip, barely holding back a chuckle, as he led Jo into the kitchen. Moving away from Am, Lilli accepted the basket and set it aside. She embraced her brother and his mate and Pierce kissed the top of her head. Her gaze landed on Zinnia once more.

Lyrica walked over to Zinnia and, with a bright smile, enveloped the female in her arms. "Welcome, welcome."

Out of the corner of her eye, Lilli watched Pierce send an encouraging grin at Zinnia, whose eyebrows had squished together as her eyes widened. Trying not to roll her eyes, Lilli turned away to put the tarts up.

Dinner. Just dinner.

"Um... oh, goodness. Thank you."

"I am so happy to have another daughter. Look at this, I gained two daughters and two sons in less than a *penumbra*," Lyrica boasted.

Jo clapped her hands together. "Okay. What do we need to help with?"

"We've got the kitchen covered. Why don't you help Mom with the place settings?" Am hooked a thumb over her shoulder.

Logan set the tray of fish down in the center of the long table and strode over to Zinnia, exchanging a hug with her. The two of them spoke in hushed tones. While Lilli could have easily heard what they said, she paid no attention.

"Are you alright, sister mine?" Pierce asked.

"I am okay. I promise." She wasn't, not really, but she was going to make herself be.

"Okay." He kissed the top of her head and left the kitchen.

"Lilli, why don't you help me get the vegetables and bread on the table?" Am dipped her chin toward the two platters of food she had picked up earlier.

She could not—*would not*—spend all evening staring at her sister. That would not put her or her brothers at ease. Logan had spoken to her twice, as had Ambrosia. Every time she'd assured them she would be fine—because she wanted to be. It was just dinner. She could do this.

"Of course." Lilli picked up the plate of vegetables and carried it over.

Am grabbed the platters of bread and butter, along with a couple of knives. They had the table completely set, along with cups and three separate jugs. Tea, water, and milk. "Evening meal is served. Let's sit."

As everyone went to sit down, Zinnia put her hand on Logan's arm to stop him. She opened her mouth to speak, then shook her head. "Nevermind." She joined everyone else.

Lilli sat next to Lyrica. Her eyes flicked once again over to Zinnia as she sat on the other side of Lyrica before she forced her eyes away. Everyone started digging in, one platter after another getting passed around. She glanced at her brothers out of the corners of her eyes. Some kind of unspoken exchange happened between the two of them. Ignoring it, Lilli turned her attention to Ambrosia. "I finished those books that Santos gave me. Do you think we could go to the library tomorrow?"

"Of course. We'll go after morning meal. If you like, I can introduce you to Calla while we're there. She's one villager that helps."

"Okay. Thank you, Am. I still cannot believe how many books are there. Santos told me some things that are in them. It all sounded so interesting," Lilli said. Maybe if she just tracked the conversation and focused on eating, she could get through this meal without issue.

"There's a lot you can learn. Several of the villagers here used them for aid," Am responded.

Pierce stacked various items on Jo's plate before his own, as Jo poured them both some tea. Her gaze flicked across the table to Zinnia. "Would you like some tea?"

"That would be nice, thank you." Zinnia turned her attention to Logan and Am. "Your home is beautiful, by the way."

Am shifted her gaze to Zinnia. "Thank you. Nearly all the furniture Logan made himself."

He shrugged it off as he took care of both his and Am's plates. "It only seemed right."

"The furniture really is wonderful, Logan," Zinnia admitted. "As is mine. Pierce told me you made it. Thank you."

"It has been quite some time since I had a family this size." Lyrica bit into a piece of cooked carrot. "Now, you four just need to get to work on some grand young for me."

Pierce nearly choked on his fish. He swallowed the bite in his mouth and smirked. "Well, we are certainly not... *not* trying. Ow." He chuckled when Jo elbowed him in the side.

Logan's eyes widened. His cup nearly fell from his hand. He cleared his throat, reaching for his mate. His eyebrows furrowed as his aquamarine gaze shifted from Lyrica and fixated on Zinnia. "Uh, yes. I have more I am working on."

Jo's mouth fell open. She cleared her throat. "Mom, you just can't blurt things out like that."

Lyrica smirked. "I say what I want, when I want. It is your choice to listen."

"Well, I cannot wait to see more, Logan," Zinnia said. She shifted her gaze back to Lyrica. "Large families can be nice."

Lyrica glanced over at her. "They can be." Then took another bite of fish and muttered, "Sometimes."

"Sometimes," Zinnia echoed, her voice low.

Am sipped some tea from her cup. "We've never had a big family before, Mom. Let's get used to these changes before we think about young."

Her fork clanged against the plate as she stabbed at the vegetables in front of her. Lyrica cracked a smile. "Of course."

Lilli's gaze flitted from one person to the next around the table, skipping Zinnia—what did she know about family—before she took a slow bite of her meal. The tension in the air almost had a palpable scent. She chewed the bite in her mouth and swallowed. "So, um…" She paused. She looked at Pierce, then Logan, then Am. "Do you think I might ride Grace sometime?"

Pierce rolled his shoulders. "Jocasta said Am is the teacher with the spourgiffs."

Pausing with a bite in her mouth, Am turned to Jo. "Think you can handle picking up the order from Kriah tomorrow?"

"Yeah. You two are good." Jo looked to Zinnia. "Why don't you, Pierce, and I take a tour of the village tomorrow after morning meal."

"That would be nice. I have been looking forward to seeing the place," Zinnia responded.

"Yeah, it would," Pierce said. "I have not seen everything myself."

"We'll do that," Jo replied.

Am flipped her gaze back to Lilli. "We'll plan for it tomorrow, then. Either after the library or after afternoon meal."

"Okay." Lilli's eyes dropped to her plate, and she moved the little orange circles around. Something was irritating her, but she couldn't put her finger on it. *Yes, she could. No, she couldn't.* Nope, she was going to be polite. She was going to make it through this meal. For her brothers.

"You will be safe?" Logan asked.

"Of course, we will, love," Am reassured him.

"I will be careful, Logan. I promise." She lifted her gaze to him, offering confirmation, and grabbed another bite, harder than she meant to, her utensil scraping across the bottom of the plate.

Standing, Lyrica picked up one of the empty platters. "Excuse me."

The other remained. "Would you like some help, Lyrica?" Zinnia asked.

"Oh, that is funny," Lilli muttered, then bit her lip hard. *Oh, shoot.* She hadn't even meant for the words to come out of her mouth. Lilli eased her fork to the side. With Lyrica standing, it was easier to see Zinnia. While she could feel the female's eyes burrowing into her, she didn't look away from her plate. "May I be excused for a moment, please?"

"Lillianna," Zinnia said. "If my being here is making you uncomfortable, I can go."

"Oh? Since when did you care about my discomfort?" Lilli dropped her hands in her lap and squeezed her knees. She couldn't do this. She had wanted to do this, thought she could do this, but she couldn't. "I would like to be excused, please."

The table was utterly quiet. The room did not even carry the sounds of the meal.

"Yes, you may," Am stated.

"Thank you," Lilli whispered. "I think I just need a moment." She rose from the table and started toward her bedroom, but Zinnia's voice halted her in her tracks.

"Lillianna, I know you do not wish to speak to me now, but I want you to know that, if you are ever ready, I will listen."

She bit her lip hard. There were so many ways she could respond to that. She chose silence, though. She had already said things she hadn't meant to. Lilli disappeared into her bedroom, shutting the door behind her.

Sitting down on her bed, she drew her knees to her chest and wrapped her arms around them as she stared out the window. A knock on the door caught her attention as it opened just a crack. Am poked her head around the jamb. "Mind if I come in?"

"No, I do not mind."

Stepping into the bedroom, Am shut the door behind her and sat down on the bed. She stroked the back of Lilli's head. "I know this can't be easy on you."

"I am sorry," she said. "It was not my intention to ruin dinner. I thought I would be okay."

"You didn't ruin dinner. And if you're not okay, then I'd just like you to tell us. You don't have to pretend to be okay, for Logan's sake. Or Pierce's." Am continued running her fingers through Lilli's fur, trailing softly down the back of her head.

"I wanted to be okay for them. And I really thought that I would be. But…" Her words trailed off. "I did not mean to say what I said. I did not mean for it to even come out."

"Maybe, but you should never hold something in, just to be polite."

"I just… I did not want to yell during the meal. It would not have been… appropriate. That is why I asked to be excused."

"I understand that, but sometimes you can't predict when that will happen." Am paused a moment, though her fingers didn't still. "Mine and Jo's father died when we were five *solaris* of age. Things were difficult for a long time. She was a bit of a troublemaker and I was constantly bailing her out, saving her skin. I remember this one time; we had just turned sixteen. She thought we should do something wild and crazy. I couldn't talk her out of it, so I went along with it. We'd gone into the marketplace and started chatting up these males. Next thing I know, he's talking about a party somewhere. I told her we shouldn't go, but nothing I said seemed to get through to her. I was so tired of taking care of her, of making sure she got home in one piece, or didn't get herself killed. And I blurted it out. That I was tired of babysitting her. We got into this huge fight. I left and came home, and she didn't return until a few *lacunas* later. We didn't talk for *umbras* after that."

Lilli leaned against her a little. "What happened? I mean, you two made up. You seem like you are very close."

"Jo and I ate polite, silent meals together. Our mother wouldn't have it any other way. Three *umbras* later, during afternoon meal, Jo asked our mother if she could hang out with friends. They were people I didn't care for, and I might have made a sarcastic remark. Which led to another fight and ended with her slapping me. It shocked me, and she felt horrible. But that led to us making up. We tried to see things from the other's perspective for probably the first time. We still get upset with each other from time to time, but that's just part of being siblings." Not once did Am's motherly comfort leave her. "I imagine this is difficult for her, just like it is for you. Even if it's for different reasons."

"I have never had that, a sister. I have two, but I may as well have had none. Not the way…" Lilli shook her head. "I do not care if it is difficult for her," she whispered. "I know I should, but I do not." Lilli bit her lip. "She offered help in there… to someone that she does not even know. When

Iasked her for help, she ignored me. She walked away. I know she did not mean toin there. She was not even speaking to me, but it hurt my feelings."

"I understand that. Something to think about—things are different here than they were in Métamorphe. You got to bring books back from the library that we can return to repeatedly. Maybe things she couldn't do before, she can do now. I know it doesn't make it right, nor does it ease your pain, but it may clarify things."

"I do not think that I need for things to be clarified, anymore than they were back in that village." Lilli paused. "She and Pierce were very different people. They made it clear—very clear—what they wanted to be with me."

Am repositioned herself on the bed so they sat face-to-face. "But that's the thing. You're not in the village anymore. Maybe what was clear back there isn't so clear here. I mean, Pierce changed, right? Is it possible to consider that Zinnia can, too?"

"I do not know." She averted her gaze, dropping it to her lap. "There was not one time—not one time—Pierce saw me getting hurt... where he walked away. She did."

"She ever tell you why?"

"No. She never told me why. She hardly spoke to me. So, I have never asked." A tear threatened to slip free. Lilli blinked rapidly to keep it at bay.

Am gently lifted her chin. "You don't have to go back out there. And I know you don't want to get into a yelling match with her, but you don't want to hold it in either. It isn't healthy. And I want you to be as healthy as possible."

"If I do not hold it in, I am going to do something I have never done before. And it will make all uncomfortable. It might be better... if I just stay in here for now."

"Scream? Yell? Would you believe it can be cathartic?" Am breathed a sigh. "Whether it happens now, or it happens later, it'll happen at some point. Trust me on that. If you want me to go back out there without you, then I will."

"Getting emotional in front of other people can make me... uncomfortable," Lilli said. She knew things were nowhere near the same here as they had been in that village, but it was difficult to forget what had happened when she got emotional *there*. Lilli leaned into Ama little more. "I may come out in a little while. I think... I would just like to sit here, just for a few minutes."

"Okay." Am wrapped her up in her arms, embracing her tightly. "Come out when you're ready."

Lilli hugged her back hard. "Okay. Thank you."

"I'm here for you." Am got to her feet. She squeezed Lilli's shoulder and left the bedroom, shutting the door behind her.

Chapter Twenty-Five

Side by side, hand in hand, Jo and Pierce headed to her mother's house. Of all the things her sister had suggested… It almost seemed cruel. Her mother had a difficult time with her father's death and she had to use the one tool he had used to get the female to speak. It had always worked for her father. Never mind that she hadn't played the song in so long. But something happened during dinner. A couple of them, actually. It was the only way they'd get her mother to talk.

"I think I can make tea. Should I make tea? Or do you think she will want to eat?"

"Maybe start with tea." Jo thought back for a moment, searching her memories. With a heavy sigh, she rubbed her eyes. Yeah, the tea was excellent. That's what her father had done. He had always started the tea, and it was done by the time he finished playing. They'd take a cup into their room, and afterward, her mother would return. Her mood lightened. "Yeah. When it's done, we'll see how she feels at the end. I have to… gods."

Pierce wrapped his arm around her and tucked her into his side. "What is it you have to do, love?" he asked, stroking her hip as they walked.

"Something I haven't done in over eighteen *solaris*." Did she even remember the notes? The lyrics? The melody? Of course she did. How many times had she played that song before her father passed? Too many to count. It had been the first song she performed on stage. Two weeks prior to his death. No. She couldn't think of that. It would be hard enough to get through the song with the memories of her father flooding her. "My father was the one who taught me to play piano."

Her mate held her tighter to him and kissed the top of her head. "Well... he did a wonderful job teaching you. You play the piano perfectly."

"Thank you." She tried to smile, but she couldn't find the strength. Her father had one way to get through to her mother. A way he'd taught to her. Maybe things would be different with her mother if she'd played that song since his passing, but she hadn't been able to bring herself to sing, let alone touch a piano. Jo swallowed to clear the lump in her throat. "He used to play their song. The one they danced to at their ceremony. It was how he got her to open up." Her gaze flicked to the door two houses away from them. The piano he played on, the one she had learned on, it still sat in the living room in her mother's home.

"I see. I can understand how that song would be difficult to hear. And you are going to play it?"

"Yes," Jo said as they approached her mother's home. "It's the only way." Not that she knew whose benefit she said that for; his or her own. It had been her sister's idea, but Ambrosia had been right. Everything she recalled about the song reaffirmed the recommendation. She stared at the wooden door for a moment. Inhaling and exhaling a deep breath, she ascended the staircase with Pierce right beside her. Without knocking, she let herself into the house.

Her mate dropped a kiss to her neck before he headed to the kitchen. As she stood in the foyer, she watched her mate searching through the cabinets. She sensed how helpless he felt. Really, she just needed him here. That was enough. Taking in another deep breath, she turned her attention to the huge, shining black instrument.

"Mom?" Jo ran her fingers along the top of the piano as she strode farther into the living room. Her mother just sat there in her lounge chair, staring at the bright orange flames of the crackling fire. The female hadn't even moved when she and Pierce crossed the threshold. "Mom?"

Her mother's gaze met hers. "Jocasta, when did you..." The sound of Pierce moving around the kitchen drew her attention. Her mother looked back in her direction. "I am sorry. I did not hear the door."

It wasn't important to state she didn't knock. "We wanted to check on you. You didn't really eat and you just kind of left after saying some strange things."

"I know. My apologies. I, uh, I did not mean…" She shook her head.

Turning toward the piano, Jo ran her fingers along the instrument's case. She had so many memories attached to it. "I know you didn't, Mom." She eased down onto the bench and glanced back at her mother. "Are you okay? I mean, you seemed really deep in thought when we came in."

"Just thinking."

"About the past?" Jo lifted the key block and revealed the keys. Exquisite ivory glinted as it nestled beneath her fingers. Her feet easily found the pedals as she stared down. Every note, every chord filled her brain, as if she'd played the song within the last few days, rather than almost two decades before. She peered over her shoulder.

Her mother's gaze returned to the fire's flames. "Yes. It all… it was like… I was there again."

"Like you were where Mom?" Inhaling a deep breath, she focused on the sounds of her mate shuffling about the kitchen as he gathered the materials to make tea.

It was a couple of minutes before her mother answered. "Home."

Home? That made no sense. This was her mother's home. Jo's eyes settled on the shine of the instrument, ready and waiting to bend at her call. She could do this. "But this is your home."

"It is. I was… where I came from. My birthplace."

That was all the encouragement she needed. Jo's fingers caressed the ivory keys as she opened the orchestral of "Everything I Need" by Skylar Grey. Despite all the time that had passed since she last played the song, she still knew every note, every keystroke, as if it had been ingrained in her memory.

Her mother had always been quiet and meek. As she began the first verse, she realized it was quite possible they had more in common than she believed. The female had always said she was an only child, but not once had her mother ever discussed her parents. Had she truly been born somewhere completely opposite of this village? Somewhere that silenced her voice? Convinced her she'd never be good for anyone?

If that was the case, her father had seen beyond the pain and the scars. Kind of like she and Pierce had done with one another. They saw something so much more in each other. She remembered exactly how her father looked whenever her mother came into the room. His whole being just lit up. There was no doubt he saw her mother as a beautiful female, one whom he loved very much. And every day he let her know that.

Her voice didn't falter as her mate entered the room, three mugs of tea in hand. He carefully set one down on the little table next to the chair her mother occupied, ensuring the handle faced outward. The other two he left on the table in front of the couch before he joined her on the bench and encircled his arm around her waist.

Jo broke into the chorus, belting out how her mother was everything her father needed. That she was everything to him. That her mother had become the female she was meant to be. The female he needed. Just as he had been the male for her. Maybe she didn't know what the two of them talked about in their bedroom after he played the song, but the change in her mother had always been clear.

A single tear rolled down her cheek as she started the second verse. Not once could she remember a moment where her mother openly disagreed with her father. But that didn't mean it didn't happen. If her mother ever pushed her father away, he responded by holding on tighter. To let her know he was there to stay. Her mother's voice echoed a line, and another tear trickled down Jo's face.

Her mate wiped the wetness from her cheeks. He stroked her canine ears on the side of her head as his palm settled on her knee. The warmth of his touch encouraged her to continue.

Together, she and her mother harmonized the chorus. This was exactly as she remembered it. Her mother would sit down at the piano beside her father. They'd sing the last of the song together. Tears streamed from her mother's eyes as she sang from the chair she occupied, the wall coming down. This had to be the hardest part. It was for her. How could everything happen for a reason? Be a blessing? Her father's death? What Pierce had endured? What Lilli had suffered? Their family being forced apart? Her mate's as much as hers.

A small smile crossed her face as the words left her mouth, her mother singing along. Maybe in some awful way, the journey was a blessing. All that they'd faced had brought them together. It was the same with her mother. Whatever the female had gone through, she'd been blessed with her father, her, and her sister. And now all the new family they had gained in such a short period. It didn't mean the journey had been easy, but it had led them to each other.

Her mother quietly wept as the last note hovered in the air. "I was not supposed to be alone." A pair of amber eyes that matched her own shifted in her direction as her mother wrapped her arms around herself. "He was supposed to be here with me."

Jo got to her feet, rushed across the room, and hugged her mother. "I know, Mom. I know." She missed her father, too. They all did.

Her mother sobbed in her arms. She didn't know how much time had passed before the female's breathing steadied and she sat up. Not that it mattered. She'd hold the woman for as long as necessary. The dam had broken. That was all she cared about right then. Her mother glanced from her to Pierce and finally stopped on the mug. Wiping at her face, her mother picked up the mug and held it between her hands. She gestured to the couch. "Yes, I lied to you and your sister. We both did. Galenus... he only did as I asked."

Both she and her mate took a seat on the couch, his arms coming around her waist. "Sometimes, keeping the truth to ourselves is easier than speaking the words aloud," Pierce said.

"It can be, yes." Lyrica sipped the tea. "Galenus knew. Though I did not tell him all at once." Lowering the mug, her eyes fell to the dark-colored liquid. "We did not meet in the marketplace, as we told you." Her gaze shifted to Pierce. "I knew who you were the second you walked in the door. And what he had done for your mother."

Leaning into her mate, Jo focused her attention on her mother. Even with what they'd been told, it seemed their families had intertwined for a long time. "How did you two meet?"

"He saved me." More tears streamed down her cheeks. Her mother lifted a hand to stop either of them from moving. "Much like he had done for Sabina."

Pierce tightened his hold on her as his eyes squeezed shut. Her mate scrubbed his hand down his face and shifted his gaze to her mother. "He was a very honorable male. I wish I had known him better. He and Ailwin, my father, did not get along."

"No, they did not. And for good reason." Cleaning up the tears, her mother took another sip of tea. "My family... they lived in the marshlands. We had a small village. It did not even have a name. I was raised much like the females..." Her words trailed off.

In the swamp? She hadn't heard of any hybrids that had ventured that far. If her memory served, it bordered along the chimera territory. Gods, to think that was where her mother had spent a portion of her life. Jo opened her mouth and snapped it shut. No. Her mother would continue when she was ready.

"Do not speak unless spoken to. Be presentable at all times." Her mother paused. "They only allowed us to be mothers. Our opinions, our thoughts, they did not matter. We were property. That was what my father ingrained in my sisters and I." A faint tilt crossed her mother's mouth. "Like you, Jocasta, I had a fire in me. I did not always listen well. It took many... lessons...for me to change."

Though she could feel the sorrow from him, her mate tried to remain positive. "You sound like my mother. She too had that fire... that was difficult to put out. Lilli too." Pierce cocked an eyebrow. "Lessons?"

Jo snuggled closer to her mate. She didn't want to know the answer. Though she suspected she already did. And it broke her heart to think of what her mother had gone through growing up. "Your father, he beat you, didn't he?"

Her mother's lips pursed as she attempted to keep the grimace from her face. "Do not leave a mark on their face. That was the rule." The female's amber eyes dropped to her lap. "By the time I was Lilli's age... that fire... he had sufficiently doused it!"

No wonder her mother never spoke of her parents. Or her life before Migas. So many things made so much more sense with just this bit of knowledge. "Your mother? Your sisters? They didn't..."

"No. My younger brother tried a few times. Only to share in my lesson." Sipping the tea, her shoulders dropped. "The last time Xander helped me was when I escaped."

Wait. What? Jo blinked. "I thought you said Dad saved you."

"He did."

Pierce stroked her thigh. "Do you know what happened to him? Your brother?"

Silence stretched between them—his question going unanswered. Her mother's chest hitched as her eyes shifted back to the crackling fire. "No," she whispered. "I have not left this village since the *umbra* Galenus brought me here."

"How's that possible? The bar—"

"Others in the village helped me with the arrangements." Her mother's chin trembled as all the color drained from her face. "I have not seen or spoken to my family in twenty-five *solaris*."

Pierce said nothing as he focused on her mother. "If you would ever like to know... I would be more than happy to do all I could to find out for you."

The anguish on her mother's face was really getting to her. So much that she and her sister didn't know. How had the woman spent so much time in the village with all the torment swirling inside of her? Her mother slumped further in the chair. "Thank you. Xander..." her words trailed off. "He was the only one I ever cared about."

Jo clutched Pierce's knee. The kind-hearted male he was with that offer; gods, as if she could love him more.

Pierce put his hand over hers and gave it a squeeze. He put a fist over his heart as he bowed his head to her mother. "If you tell me how to find the village, I will see what I can find out." As his warm mug of tea was still full, he nudged it across the table to her. "What happened when you escaped? Who did Galenus save you from?"

"There was a male in our village, Faruk. All the females knew of his cruelties. None ever desired to be his mate. Not that we had much choice. After some time, he came to my father. My two oldest sisters were already mated. It just left Maleya and myself. We were only a *solaris* apart. After..." Her mother let out a faint whimper as her eyes began watering again. She sniffled and wiped her face before she continued. "After he inspected us, Faruk decided on me. He and my father spent most of the *umbra*... negotiating." She glanced over at them and visibly swallowed hard. "Xander helped me escape the village the next *umbra*. But it did not stop them. Faruk and my father... they came after me. I do not know where in the forest we were. Faruk, when they found me, he did not wish to wait until we got back to the village. Galenus..." More tears rolled down her face as her eyes swung back to the fireplace, whose dancing glow opposed the mood of the conversation. "I am uncertain of the details. All I remember... I no longer felt him atop me. At some point, something covered me, and someone picked me up off the ground and brought me here."

Oh, gods. Jo squeezed her eyes shut as she cried, listening to what her mother had gone through. She understood why the female had chosen not to tell her and her sister this story before. Why she'd kept it to herself. Why her father comforted her mother many times over the few years they had been together. Blinking more tears free, she leaned into her mate more. "I'm so sorry, Mom."

"It was a long time ago," her mother whispered. "I do not think about it often. Now and then, something triggers it. Pulls me back to those silent meals. And I remember, all over again. Galenus... he had a way to still them. Bring me back to the present."

"May I have permission to hug you?" Pierce asked. Her eyes shot open. That wasn't something she ever expected him to ask.

Her mother's amber gaze swung from the fire to Pierce. They had hugged twice since they met. Slowly, she nodded and set the mug in her hands on the nearby table.

He lowered his head and kissed Jo, then gently shifted her out of his arms. Moving over to where her mother was, he hugged her mother the way he would've embraced his own.

Her mother quietly sobbed in her mate's arms. "Thank you," she whispered.

"That is unnecessary," he murmured in her hair. "You are a wonderful female. You did not deserve..." He cleared his throat. "I think my mother would have loved you."

"I think I would have loved her too," her mother replied as her tears slowed.

Pierce pulled back. "Would you like something to eat?"

"Perhaps something small. I am quite tired and I would like to rest."

Jo did her best to clean up her face. "Do you want me to draw you a bath, Mom?"

"Yes. I think that would be nice."

"Okay. I can do that."

Her mate stood and enveloped her in his arms, kissed her softly, and then disappeared into the kitchen. After quickly embracing her mother, Jo headed down the hall. It wouldn't take too long to get a good hot bath going. She sensed Pierce moving around the kitchen to throw something together.

After getting her mother settled into the bath and ensuring she didn't need help with anything, Jo returned to her mate. She came up and wrapped her arms around Pierce's waist. That had been hard to hear. What her mother had gone through. The truth about how her parents met.

Everything she'd ever faced with her mother made so much sense. Her mother had never raised her voice, never yelled, and when she cried, she always did it in private.

Pierce stopped what he was doing immediately and brought her against him. Pulling a chair over closer, he sat down and tugged her into his lap. He held her tight, running his fingers up and down her back.

She curled up to him as best she could in the chair. Inhaling deeply, she let his touch soothe her. "How am I supposed to tell Ambrosia all of that?"

"Gently," he replied. He cleared his throat. "Probably... privately, would be good. If you would like, I could help you. Or, at least be there with you while you tell her. I understand much of what your mother went through. Logan and my sisters do as well. Unfortunately, too many do."

"Yes. I don't think... I can't imagine telling her this without you. It would probably be best if Logan is there, too. For her." She couldn't have sat and listened to everything from her mother without him by her side. It had been difficult to hear. Even without details, her mother had given enough to understand the sorrows she'd endured.

"I will always be right by your side, my queen." He tilted her head up and brushed a soft kiss across her lips.

Gods, he was truly an amazing male. Every day, he made her feel a little stronger. "Would you be opposed to staying here tonight? I just... I don't want to leave her alone."

"Of course not, love." He grazed his knuckles over her cheek. "If Logan needs me to help break up the battlefield, he knows where to find me. We will stay right here."

"I'm sure that isn't the case." She cupped his jaw, stroking her thumb along his face. If something had gone wrong, she suspected her sister would have reached out. Or at least, more than whatever was already weighing on her twin. She could feel this small nagging in the back of her mind, but there hadn't been time to dig into it.

Pierce leaned into her touch as he stared into her eyes. "Somehow, I think you are right. But then, you are always right." He caressed the nape of her neck. "I am so very lucky to have you."

"I don't know about that." Her lips pulled back. "I'm lucky too. No, I'm grateful. Very grateful to have you."

"How can you not know..." He shook his head. "No. I am so very lucky, and so very grateful, to have you. Without you—Jocasta, my queen—I am truly nothing. Before I met you, I had no more spirit left. You brought me back to life. You did that."

She bit her bottom lip. Maybe she should've clarified. "I know what we've done for one another. I know how much our souls needed each other." Nuzzling her nose against his, she kissed him. "But I don't think I'm always right."

He snorted. "And why do you say that?"

"Because there are many things I'm still figuring out. And no one's perfect. Even if we're perfect for each other." She loved him more than she thought possible. And she expected their love would only grow as they got older.

"We will figure them all out together."

"You two remind me so much of Galenus and myself."

Jo looked at her mother over Pierce's shoulder. "I'm afraid to ask how."

"Just the way you are with one another."

"Thank you," Pierce said. "Even though I did not know him well, I always thought of him as the father that I wish I had."

"He told me he tried a few times to get you, your siblings, and Sabina out of there. It killed him the number of times he failed." Her mother ventured farther into the kitchen.

"Really? I didn't know he said anything about the village." Her father hadn't ever mentioned it around her or her twin.

"Just with me. He didn't want you or your sister to go looking for it. He believed the less you knew, the less you'd be curious."

Pierce was quiet for a moment. "She wanted to go. She wanted us safe... away from that. But she refused to leave one of her young there, and Dahlia... she would not leave Ailwin. She tried to get Logan and me to take Zinnia and go with Galenus, but we would not leave her behind."

Her mother walked over and rested a gentle hand on Pierce's shoulder. "I am certain the decisions she made were difficult, but she did what she could, given the circumstances. Though, I fully believe they are looking down on us, happy that all of you are out and thriving."

Jo reached up and took her mother's other hand in her own. "I think you're right, Mom. I think they're both at peace." Though her mate didn't reply, the acrid scent of his heartbreak reached her nose as she felt how much it hurt to think about his mother, and what the female's life had been like. Just as it saddened her to recall her father. "Mom, will you give us a few minutes? And we'll bring the food out."

"Of course." Her mother left the kitchen and returned to her chair in the living room.

Enveloping Pierce, Jo stroked the back of his head and ran her fingers through the fur at the base of his ears. As he buried his face in the crook of her neck, he inhaled deeply. His hot breath tickled her skin.

"I miss her," he whispered. "I miss her very much."

She continued comforting him. While she couldn't see it, she sensed the tear that slipped free. "I know you do." It was a feeling she understood well. They had both lost someone they loved. But her mother had a point. And by all the gods, she really hoped it was true. That, even though they were gone, they looked down, watching them in peace.

"Even when she was sad and in pain, she always had a smile for us. She was smiling at me as she left. And I think she is smiling now. I think they both are. And I think it would make them happy, to see all of us happy."

"Me too." She hugged him a little tighter and pressed a kiss to the side of his throat. Despite everything they'd gone through, they were joyous.

As they soothed one another, time stretched between them. Eventually, Pierce leaned back, nuzzled her nose, and then kissed her lips. "I love you, my queen."

"I love you too, my king." There were no words that could thank him enough for being here with her. He'd sat there by her side as she'd played, helping her get the song out. It wasn't the first time, nor would it be the last. They'd gotten each other through the tough moments and thrived in the happy ones.

He pressed his lips to hers; the kiss lingering a little longer this time. "We should get the food in there and eat."

"Mmm, yes, we should." Hmm, she'd never had a male in her bedroom before. It seemed wrong to think like that. Except there were so many ways she could make use of having one here for the first time. Biting her bottom lip, Jo climbed off of his lap.

Barely holding a growl back, her mate stood and dragged her against his chest. "You are tempting me to want to skip our meal, love." With a gentle kiss, he nipped her lower lip and stepped back.

"Mmm, I can't seem to help myself." Actually, she could think of a couple of places they could—okay, she needed to stop that line of thought.

Right now. She checked on the stew he'd thrown together and gave it a quick taste. Searching for the right herb, Jo sprinkled it in and tasted it again. Much better.

He came up behind her and gently gripped her hips. He pulled her ass back against him, leaned over, and nibbled on the tip of her ear. "Neither can I."

With a small gasp and a slight arch of her back, she grazed her nails along the nape of his neck. "Then, after my mother goes to bed, we may just have to do something about it."

A rumble sounded deep in his chest as he rocked that thick, rigid length of his against her. "Mmm, now that does sound intriguing." He dropped his lips to her neck and sucked lightly. "I am being mean and I am not even sorry."

A soft moan left her lips. Jo ground her ass against him a little more. Even with clothes on, that very male part of him felt exquisite. The material created wonderful friction, allowing her to tease him just as easily. Not that she thought it was mean. *Not. At. All.* In fact, she kind of enjoyed it. "Mmm, I think we should get the food out and get her to bed—quickly."

He groaned as he got harder against her, his grip on her hips tightening. "Hades. As quickly as possible."

She reached for a small stack of bowls, scooped stew in each of the three, and selected a few spoons. With two bowls in hand, she glanced over her shoulder at her mate, giving him her best *come hither* look. "Don't worry. I'll go first." Leaving the kitchen, she intentionally gave her hips a little extra swing as she marched toward the living room. Yes, she knew exactly what her ass did to him. Among other things.

Pierce chuckled low, picking up the last bowl and spoon. With his tail wrapped as casually as possible around his front, covering all the appropriate areas, he followed her. Jo handed one bowl of stew to her mother and sat on the couch with her own in hand.

"Thank you," her mother said. As she started eating, her eyes returned to the warmth of the fireplace.

Pierce kept his tail in his lap as he sat to her right. He draped his arm over the back of the couch and stroked her shoulder. Being careful not to spill his stew, he ate one-handed. A smirk crossed his face. "I hope that the stew tastes okay."

"It is very good."

Jo paused with a bite midway to her mouth and peered at her mate. Slowly, she took the bite, chewed, and swallowed it. As soon as she finished, she licked the spoon, giving it a nice flick with the tip of her tongue. "Mhm, very good." It saddened her a touch that they'd forgotten to bring tarts with them. Guess they'd have to enjoy the ones at home tomorrow night. Not that she required them to torture her mate. This meal and utensil worked just fine.

His spoon froze somewhere between his mouth and his bowl. His jaw dropped open. Licking his lips, he moved his hand lower and stroked his fingers along her collar bone.

She sucked just a little on the metal implement before she returned to eating her stew. They'd have to make sure the dishes were up before... Although, they could save them for after. That could be a fun way to clean up. She knew *exactly* what he was thinking about each time she sucked on her spoon. It was precisely what she was thinking about, too. He didn't take his eyes off of her as she teased him with every bite, but still he ate.

Her mother didn't pay them much attention as she ate in silence, staring at the fire. It didn't take long for her to finish her meal. She got to her feet. "That was good. Just what I needed. I believe I will head to bed. I am quite tired."

"You sure, Mom?"

"Yes." She headed to the kitchen, left her dishes in the sink, and disappeared down the hall.

"Good night," Pierce called out to her mother. As soon as the bedroom door clicked shut, he set their bowls on the table and hauled her into his lap so she straddled him. "I will put everything up in a minute." Their lips crashed together in a slow and deep kiss.

She rose on her knees and encircled her arms around his neck. Her tongue swept along the inside of his mouth with a soft moan. Gods, she loved kissing him. It was something she'd never get enough of. Well, one amongst many things with him.

He slid one hand to her nape and the other to her ass, grabbing and squeezing her cheek. Her moan intensified. Jo sucked on his tongue, pulling a groan from him. The dishes might just have to wait. His taste was all too consuming, and she was nowhere near ready for even a slight break.

Grazing her fingers along the back of his ears, she skimmed her nails down his neck and spine. She pressed in closer until their bodies were flush against one another. Pierce growled, gripping her ass harder. He kissed and licked down the side of her throat. With a soft groan, she tilted her head, giving him more access. Sliding his hand under the thin material of her shirt, he palmed her breast.

"I need you out of these clothes," he rumbled. "Now."

Gods, he could rip the damn things for all she cared. She had more in her old bedroom. They'd make it there eventually, but right now, with how hot she burned, she didn't care about moving. She nipped at his ear. All she wanted was to feel him buried deep inside of her. And there was one sure fire way to get him there quickly. "Then perhaps you should remove them."

With a grunt, he sucked on her neck. He tore her shirt and shoved her skirt up around her waist. Gripping her bare ass, he returned his attention to her breast. "Get on my cock," he demanded.

She bit her bottom lip and stifled her outcry. Gods, she was so hot. His bossing her around just turned her on more. Moving her hips back, she reached between them, and wrapped her fingers around his shaft before sliding him deep inside her sex.

"Hades," he barked out. His head fell back, and he grasped the back of the couch, making sure not to dig his claws in.

She held onto his shoulders, using them to anchor herself as her hips slowly rocked against his. A loud rumble rolled out of him. Readjusting her knees, she split her thighs wider, taking him in deeper. All the way to her core. Unable to stifle it this time, she cried out, "Oh, gods!"

"Oh, fuck yes, that is perfect."

The sounds he made with the slow, steady rhythm she maintained sent a blast of heat through her body. She scored her nails over his shoulders and biceps as she changed angles. "Oh, fuck," Jo cried out. The readjustment opened her up further and allowed her to take him deeper within her body.

A guttural moan left him as the couch creaked against his grip. "I love it when you talk like that, my queen." He lashed the tip of her nipple with his tongue, capturing her swollen breast in his mouth.

Gods, with the anguish of the earlier conversation, the two of them needed to be reminded how alive they were. Jo dug her nails into his skin, clinging to his broad shoulders as she increased her pace. A blissful explosion sat right there at the edge. "Oh, gods. Come with me, my king. Come with me."

On a growl, the two of them pitched over the cliff together. He came so hard his head fell back against the couch. "Fuck…" he hissed out, his eyes glowing bright. Their gazes locked on one another. The desire she sensed for him to have her in his mouth was a roar that sent another blast of heat straight through her. Fuck, yes, she wanted that, too. Pierce gripped her hips, lifted her so she stood on the couch, and hooked one leg over his shoulder. "Grab on," he instructed, before burying his face between her thighs.

The rasp of his tongue had Jo crying out his name. Clutching his shoulders with her calf, she raked her talons across the bulging muscles of his back. His growl vibrated through every inch of her. Her head fell back, the room no longer lit by the dying fire, but the combination of their glowing eyes. A beautiful swirl of amber and ruby.

He sucked and licked the moist, warm folds between her thighs, driving his tongue deeper inside her. Wrapping an arm around her waist, his thumb stroked her nub. Rubbing it hard and fast, he swept his tongue up her slit. Their gazes met. That exquisite amber and ruby vortex brightened. "Come in my mouth," he growled. With their eyes fixed on another, he drove his tongue back inside her.

Gods, he looked sexy as all get out. The constant growls, his demands, how he dominated her and moved her—she loved all of it. It had her womanly center pulsating with pleasure, taking next to nothing to throw her over the edge. As she cried out her mate's name, her body did exactly as he demanded.

His bellow vibrated through her sex as he devoured her, not wasting a single drop. When he'd taken every bit of her orgasm, he slid his tongue from her and licked up her inner thighs. "You are so incredibly beautiful." His tongue trailed slowly up her slit. "I love when you say my name when you come for me."

"I will never tire of calling it out." She grinned widely, a wicked gleam in her eyes. "But I think it's your turn."

Fair was fair.

He let out a low rumble. His erection thickened. "You may do *anything* you want to me, my queen."

Jo slipped the torn shirt from her body and tossed it aside, paying no mind to where it landed. Unhooking her leg from his shoulder, she kissed the top of his head and grazed her nails along the nape of his neck as she climbed down from the couch. When her feet hit the floor, she gave the table a gentle push and continued skimming her nails and tongue across the contours of his body. She took her sweet time getting to his cock. That spoon had gotten sucked on with great purpose.

Not that he let her get too low before he lifted her chin and smirked. "Take your skirt off first. Slowly."

Taking the same path back up, she gave him a deep kiss and sucked on his tongue. If he wanted a show, she'd happily give him one. "If you insist." She nipped his bottom lip and pivoted on her heel. It pleased her to tease him, taking her time unbuttoning and unzipping the skirt. Especially as she dragged it over her hips, then purposely stuck her ass out as she tugged it down the length of her legs.

His breaths almost came out in pants. "Oh, sweet gods in the heavens." She knew she was torturing him, but he absolutely loved it. He squeezed her ass. Leaning over, he nipped at one cheek, then the next. He trailed his tongue over the merfolk scales on her lower back, then up her spine as she straightened. "Mmm... I could keep my tongue against you all night long, my queen. You are exquisite."

Jo kicked the skirt aside and faced him. "But then, when would I get *my* dessert? Hmm?" She didn't waste time dropping to her knees. It wouldn't stop the slow torture, but she was ready to be between his legs. Reaching up, she dragged her nails down his thighs, licked up one inner thigh, and then the other.

Pierce groaned and leaned back more against the couch, spreading his arms wide over the back of it. He snaked his tongue out across his lips as he stared at her. "Absolutely, *any* time you want, my queen."

"I like that answer, my king." Sliding her hands around to his ass, she gripped tight and took his entire length in her mouth. She sucked along his shaft and popped the tip of his erection out of her mouth, then repeated the process.

"Oh, gods!" he moaned. He gripped the back of the couch so hard the ripping of fabric filled the surrounding air. Yup, they were replacing the couch. She did it again, pulling a deep rumble out of him. "Holy... Hades... Jocasta," he growled. "Fuck, show me how much you love my cock, my queen."

Oh, she was going to show him all right. She gently grazed her teeth along his length. Popping his erection from her mouth, she slowly licked back up. When she encircled her lips around his engorged flesh, a slight growl vibrated in the back of her throat as she sucked on his cock. Her fingers traced over his ass cheeks to his tail.

The couch protested, groaning against Pierce's hold as it tightened. One hand went to the back of her head. His growl was enormous as he came deep down her throat. And then she kept sucking. He couldn't speak over the sounds coming out of his mouth, his head falling back, a louder rip filling the air as he dug his claws in.

Her fingertips trailed along his tail, then to his ass as she continued to suck. It had been oh so long since she'd had this flavor of dessert. She fully intended to make the most of it before she rode him again. Heightening every sensation, she raked her nails across his thighs. His swollen head hit the back of her throat, another growl vibrating through her.

"Hades, do not sto—" His words were cut off by another groan. He fisted her hair as she milked him dry, refusing to stop until she'd taken every drop.

Jo swept her tongue across her lips and crawled back up his body. Straddling his thighs, she dipped her head into the crook of his neck and brushed a kiss across the side of his throat. "Yum." She nipped at his ear and growled. "Best dessert ever."

"Hades, I love your growl." She rolled her hips against him, her sex slipping against his cock. He fused their lips together. Pierce reached between them and lifted her up, crying out as he buried himself deep inside her.

"Oh, gods." A shiver ran down her spine. Pressing close to him, she rocked against him. Her movements started slowly, and she quickly found a steady rhythm. Gripping the back of his neck, Jo drew her mate into an unforgiving, passionate kiss.

Pushing his hips up into hers, he moaned against her as the friction increased, her nails digging into his nape. "Fuck... yes," he groaned. He plunged his tongue back inside her mouth, their tongues entangling. One hand gripped her ass while the other caressed her ears.

Gods, she loved the things he did. Switching the angle, she picked up the pace and dug her nails into his shoulders, biting into his flesh. With her breasts up against his chest and their tongues battling, her entire body was on fire as she increased the rhythm more. "Fuck!"

Pierce stood up with her, withdrew, and turned her around. Positioning her on her knees, he placed her hands on the back of the couch and gripped her hips, thrusting deep inside of her, all the way to the hilt. With a growl, he bit down on her shoulder, sinking his fangs into her flesh without breaking the skin. Pulling his hips back until his cock was just barely still inside her, he penetrated, easing back inside of her.

Gripping the back of the couch hard, she ground her ass against him, easily meeting his slow thrusts. Her head tilted back, giving him better access to her shoulder. Gods, she loved how it felt when he marked her, repeatedly claiming her as his. It was a reminder, a display that she belonged to him. But the slow, gentle thrusts were complete torture with the friction it generated between the two of them.

He smoothed his large palm down her arm, intertwining their fingers together. "Hades, you feel so good, love." Maintaining a steady rhythm, Pierce pistoned in and out of her.

Tightening her grip on his just a little, she moaned. "Gods, so do you." Adjusting her knees ever so slightly, she lifted her ass in the air a bit more, grinding into him. It shouldn't be possible to take him any deeper. Somehow, the shift not only had his shaft deeper inside her, but the swollen head brushing against her g-spot with every thrust. "Oh, gods, faster."

Pierce let out a loud moan. Gripping the back of the couch hard, he picked up his pace. He turned her face toward his and fused their lips together. His long fingers swept over her bare flesh, reaching her deeper heat as he stroked her nub, matching the pace of his thrusts.

Their tongues danced as their bodies melted together. A storm swirled inside of her, gathering speed with each touch, each stroke, each penetration. That crescendo almost seemed out of reach. She couldn't say what coaxed her over that edge, but she found the most exquisite release. Her thighs clenched as she exploded in spasms all around his cock. Jo growled against his mouth as her body released.

He jerked inside of her, his orgasm filling her. Her mate trailed kisses down her jaw and neck, then over her shoulder and the mark he'd left there. "Mmm, I love your growl, my queen."

"I didn't even realize I had one in me. I've never done that before."

"Well, you must never stop using it. It... does things to me." He nipped her ear.

"Oh, I would *never* stop using it. I love what it does to you."

He let out a low rumble and swept the tongue across the side of her throat. "Good." He kissed her slowly, then leaned his forehead against hers.

"We never got the dishes into the kitchen. But I am so very okay with what we did instead. Although we owe your mother a new couch."

"Me, too. And, yeah, I kind of noticed the couch. I don't think she'll miss that. Guess it's a good thing we can pick up furniture in the woodworking building." She pressed a soft kiss to his nose. "We should get the kitchen cleaned up."

"I will take care of it tomorrow. Or we could just switch her couch with ours. And you are right, we probably should." He dropped a kiss to her nape and groaned as he pulled out of her.

A shiver ran down her spine. Good gods. She sat down on the couch. "You can take care of it while I'm at the bar."

He dropped next to her. Saying nothing for a moment, his eyes widened ever so slightly. "You have to go to the bar tomorrow?"

Jo crawled back into his lap and wrapped her arms around his neck. "Hey, I'll be fine. I'll have Bruce and Jacques there, and Ambrosia will join me later in the afternoon."

"I know." His hands encircled her waist. "I guess…" His shoulders tensed. "Nerves." It was more than that, though. Not only did she feel the fear within him, she heard his heartbeat race. "You carry my scent on you. And Markham will be hunting me by now. He does not allow Informants to walk away from his pack."

"It'll be fine. Shape shifters don't come into the bar. Our crowd is satyrs, some hybrids here, merfolk and a few others. And the only other place I'll be going is to get our order from Kriah." Despite the precautions she'd taken her entire life, it didn't seem to satisfy him. Not that she blamed him. She pressed her forehead against his. "Would it make you feel better if you went with me as far as you could? Saw me most of the way there?" It wasn't like the village was that far from the marketplace. She knew he would go all the way with her, but that would be too dangerous.

"When you go to Kriah's, will you please take Bruce or Jacques with you? Maybe they can even walk you back far enough to meet me, and I can walk home with you," he suggested.

"Bruce or Jacques always go with me to Kriah's." She'd never gone to Mystique Herbs by herself. Shape shifter hybrid. Enough said. As for the trip home… maybe? "I'll see if Bruce will walk me back at the end of the night. He likes you, so I don't think he'd have a problem with that."

"Thank you. That would make me feel better." He held her tight against him and gingerly ran his fingertips over the merfolk scales on her hip.

She wiggled to get more comfortable. If they stayed like this for too long, she'd fall asleep. Why hadn't she thought to have this conversation with him before? They'd both known the day would come when she'd return to work. Still, she should've known he'd be concerned. Whatever it took to settle his fears, she'd handle it. It would get easier as the days went by. A few minutes passed before either of them spoke.

"Would you like me to take care of the cleanup so we can go to bed?" he asked. "It will not take long. I do not want to leave it until morning."

"Yes, please. I'm going to go to the bathroom and wash up really quick."

Kissing her once more, he nuzzled her ears, and then helped her off his lap.

Maybe she didn't know what had happened back at her sister's yet, but despite the nagging feeling, Am hadn't reached out. Nodding to herself, Jo collected her clothes and left the living room while Pierce handled the dishes. They would be fine.

All of them would.

They had to be.

Chapter Twenty-Six

Down the hallway, a soft click resounded as a door creaked open. Zinnia looked up in time to see Lillianna enter the room. Her sister stood frozen in the entrance to the corridor. Zinnia offered a polite smile and returned to clearing the dishes. No one had touched Lillianna's plate, so it still satin the same spot.

Logan adjusted the logs in the hearth, trying to get a fire going. Ambrosia picked up a couple of apple tarts from the basket and gave Zinnia's shoulder a squeeze. "Thank you for cleaning up."

Zinnia offered her a small nod. Out of her periphery, she watched Lillianna walk back into the dining room and pull her plate to another spot across the table before sitting down. "It is no problem. Spend time with your mate." She glanced at Logan. Refocusing on Ambrosia, Zinnia lowered her voice. "You make him joyful. It is heartwarming to see."

"It's quite mutual." Ambrosia's entire face lit up as she headed into the front room, where warmth radiated from the fireplace. Logan sat in a large plush chair, and Ambrosia curled up in his lap. Zinnia continued moving around the table and counters while she cleaned up as Lillianna ate her food, not taking her eyes away from her plate once. As her sister finished the last bite, Zinnia placed an apple tart on a plate and slid it across the table, pushing it toward her.

Lillianna lifted her gaze. "What?"

"Would it be okay if I sit?"

Lillianna shrugged. "It is not up to me what you do."

"Right now, it absolutely is. If you do not want me to sit, I will not sit. I know you do not want to hear anything that I have to say, and that you have no wish to talk to me or be around me. But as we are going to be around each other, probably frequently... I thought that, perhaps, you could try to listen. And I will do the same."

Silence stretched between them for a moment. "Why do you even care? Why are you acting like you care?"

Zinnia sighed and eased into a chair. She kept her voice gentle as she spoke. "I have always cared." Lillianna rolled her eyes. "It may be difficult to believe, and I understand why, but it is the truth. I have always cared for you. I was just never allowed to show it."

"Pierce showed it. He always showed it."

"And they always punished him for it."

"You can't interfere. They need this," Ambrosia whispered. Were it not for her canine hearing, Zinnia wouldn't have caught the words, soft as they were.

Lillianna's face screwed up, as though she bit her tongue. "You do not have to tell me about that. I know what he suffered, and I hated it. I hated every bit. And he did it all for..." Her words trailed off and her lips pursed.

"Because he wanted to protect you. Our brother is a protector. Both of them are. They are fierce fighters, who love deeply. As are you. I used to be like that a very long time ago. Over the *solaris*... I lost that part of myself."

Her sister glared at her. "Is that supposed to make me feel sorry for you?"

"No, not at all." Zinnia opened her mouth to say something else, but Lillianna cut her off.

"You never spoke up for me. Not one time." Her sister's voice trembled slightly and tears sprang to the corners of Lillianna's eyes. "You did none of the things that Pierce did for me. Or Devina. Not once did you act like my sister, or even acted like you wanted to be. You never made sure I ate when Pierce was not home. Never wiped my tears from my face. Or hugged me when I needed one. Nor did you help me go back to sleep when the nightmares woke me up. Or cleaned me up after..." She bit her tongue again. "You never even really spoke to me. You even tried not to look at me." She tilted her head. "But you looked at me that one time, did you not?"

Zinnia tried hard to hold back the tears, but it might not work. At least not much longer. She knew exactly what time Lillianna spoke about. "Yes," she whispered. "Yes, I did."

"And what did you see? Huh? What did you hear? Was I happy, Zinnia? Or was I begging you for help?"

"Deep breaths, love," Ambrosia murmured in Logan's ear. "I know this is painful, but they need to get this out. Between them."

Zinnia squeezed her eyes shut tight, but it didn't stop the memory from surfacing in her mind.

Her sister's screams and pleas reached her, even from outside the hut. Even from halfway across the clearing. Zinnia wouldn't have come back to the hut at all if her father hadn't ordered her to do so. But it was midday, and he'd made it clear she was to be back in the hut.

Shifting to her humanoid form, she entered the hut and closed the front door quietly behind her. The sounds her almost-thirteen-year-old sister made pounded in her ears. In the past, she would have to force tears back at those noises. But she didn't cry anymore. Her heart and soul might still crack and break, but there was barely any left of either to shatter. She stood where she was and clasped her hands in front of her, staring down at the floor as her father exited the bedroom.

"Zin—" Though her head stayed lowered, Zinnia's eyes snapped up as Lillianna's voice cut off abruptly. Their eyes met through the doorway. "Hel— Help me! Please!"

Zinnia couldn't tear her eyes away from those amethyst ones, but she forced her mouth to stay closed. If she said anything—anything at all—against what was occurring to Lillianna... what was coming for her would be worse. So much worse.

The bedroom door slammed shut. Lillianna continued screaming. Their father crossed the room, the bag of coin in his hand jingling with each stride. He gripped her chin, jerking her head up so her eyes met his. "Did you hear what I said? Runi's hut. Now."

Zinnia took several deep breaths, then another one for good measure, before she lifted her gaze across the table at Lillianna. "It has been...a very long time since I have done the right thing. In any aspect of my life." Her eyes dropped to her lap. "When Logan had to leave, I lost a huge part of myself. When our mother died... everything that was left inside of me broke. And then Pierce was gone, and you with him, and—"

"What are you talking about?"

Zinnia's gaze snapped to her sister's face. Had Pierce never told her? How could that be? "Um, I think that might be something you should ask our brother about."

"I am asking you. What do you mean, he was gone and me with him?"

All Zinnia could do for a minute was stare across the table at her sister. *Oh, gods, forgive me.* "When you were born... you would not survive. Pierce took you away for a little while, so that you could."

"I do not understand," Lillianna replied. "How was he allowed to do that?"

Zinnia let out a heavy sigh. "He was not."

"But..."

"It was our mother's dying wish for you to live. Pierce made sure that happened. And when he returned with you... he paid dearly for it."

Silence stretched between them. Confusion danced across Lillianna's amethyst stare. "What was wrong with me?"

The memory surfaced before Zinnia could stop it, not that the recollection was necessary for her to remember every moment.

Zinnia sat silently at the top corner of the pallet, gently stroking her mother's head as she labored. Pierce had only gotten home from the latest scouting mission early that morning. Their father hadn't allowed their mother to leave the hut once her labor had started. Both of Aradia's granddaughters, Iridessa and Cassandra, tried to come in over the past couple of days to give medical attention, but their father had refused them entry. Now, it was too late. If she made it through the actual delivery, it would be a miracle. If she didn't... they would have to do what needed to be done to get their sister out safely.

"It is not even supposed to fucking be here yet," her father growled.

"I know... Ailwin..." her mother spoke softly while struggling to breathe—too soft—and so weak already. "But this... is one thing... that we... cannot control." The female rasped between her words, taking in as deep a breath as she could. She was pale and sweating, her body shaking. And she'd already bled badly for quite some time. "Whether... or not... it is time... she is coming... now."

Pierce moved around their father and kneeled down beside their mother, draping another blanket over her. Their father's glare was so intense it could have lit the hut itself on fire. He tried to grab a hold of Pierce's arm, but Pierce jerked it out of the way as he finished adjusting the blanket.

"I am going nowhere," he said, a low snarl permeating histone.

"Sabina is fine. She can do this on her own," their father snapped.

Pierce didn't even look at him as he spoke. "And yet, she is not going to."

"Get the fuck aw—"

Pierce's eyes turned black, full of fury, as he glared at their father. He let out a deep roar, his jaw clenched tight. "I am not leaving her side. When Logan, Dahlia, and Zinnia were born, I was there with her. I am damn sure not leaving now. If you want to risk losing them both, keep at it. Otherwise, you can get the fuck out of the hut." Their mother shakily caressed Pierce's cheek. He immediately turned his gaze back to hers. One of his hands covered hers. "Just breathe, Mother. It will be... it will be over soon. Just breathe."

Their father barked out a few more strings of curses and demands, and several more choice names and words directed at their mother, all of which went ignored. He crossed the room and gripped Zinnia by the scruff of the neck, jerked her up off the floor and forced her outside. The door slammed so hard behind them that the whole hut rattled. Pierce's yells followed them for a few steps as their father forced her across the clearing. He wouldn't follow, though. They had spoken quietly beforehand, before their father had returned to the hut. No matter what, she'd made him promise he wouldn't leave their mother, not even for a moment. Both of them had already known she wouldn't make it.

Logan hadn't moved from his position, his face tucked into the crook of Ambrosia's neck, his arms tight around her waist. Zinnia didn't know how much he knew, how many of the details Pierce might have told him. But he was about to learn them. At least, as much as she could say aloud. She wiped away the wetness from her eyes before they fell. "You came earlier than expected, by quite a bit. I could not be there for the actual delivery, but from what I was told later on, you were not breathing." She peered at Lillianna, who said nothing, so she continued. "In the village, when young are born sickly, they do not survive. It is Markham's law. Pierce would never have allowed that to happen. Even if our mother had not asked it of him, he would never have allowed that."

"So, when I was born... I was going to be..." Lillianna's words trailed off.

Zinnia shook her head. No way in hell was she going to tell her what had occurred. Those details would never leave her lips, not to her little sister.

"But you were not. The important part is that Pierce saved your life. He did not care what it cost him. He took you away and made sure you survived."

"How did he get out of the village with me?"

She didn't need this one to play out in her head either, to recall every detail. But the memories came like a tidal wave that she couldn't stop.

Their father had ordered her to stay away from the hut, but Zinnia couldn't help herself. Not when she sensed the shift. The pregnancy was no more. Now she sensed new shared blood.

Dahlia rolled her eyes as Zinnia moved past her. "It is just a new baby. Stop being such an idiot, Zinnia. If Father said to stay away, then you need to stay away." A smirk grew on her older sister's face. "Maybe Sabina does not even want you there."

Zinnia ignored her and continued on. She dared to at least go to the door of the hut. She wanted to see their mother, see if she was okay. Maybe they'd been wrong. And it hadn't been that much blood. Maybe their mother had made it through.

The acrid stench of copper overwhelmed her more and more the closer she got. Pierce and their father yelled at each other.

"Give her to me, Pierce! NOW!"

"NO! Stay the fuck away from me, or so help me..." Pierce growled out. "You are not getting her, and NEITHER IS HE!"

Zinnia's hand covered her mouth as the sound of vicious snarls filled the hut. Jaws snapped, finding purchase in flesh, though she couldn't have said whose. And then a howl of pain came from their father.

A door banged open across the clearing and the ground trembled. Looking over her shoulder, Zinnia watched as Markham left his hut and marched across the ground on all fours. Oh, gods...

She almost didn't get out of the way before the door of their hut burst open. Pierce shot out, crimson covering him. The carrier she'd made for their sister was in his mouth. Pierce didn't stop, and she barely caught the sound of a young's whimper before he disappeared into the woods. Their father stumbled out of the hut, his hand half-severed from his wrist, the wound hemorrhaging blood onto the ground.

Zinnia wiped away more tears. "By sheer force of will."

Lillianna said nothing for a few minutes. "So... where did he take me?"

"Now that, I do not know. To my knowledge, he has told no one. We heard nothing of him, or saw either of you, for about a *cycle*. That was not for lack of trying on Markham and Father's part. They sent Informants out daily to search. But nobody could find you two. When he brought you back, you were as healthy as could be." She flicked her gaze momentarily into the next room. Logan ran his hands up and down Ambrosia's arms as they continued listening in. Zinnia focused back on Lillianna.

A moment passed before her sister spoke. "Why did he bring me back there?"

Zinnia let out a slow breath. "He has never given me exact reasons. But I am sure it was several things." She paused. "At the time you were born, Logan had been in hiding for about two *solaris*. No one that I know of had ever successfully hidden from Markham before. Not forever. Maybe he thought it was only a matter of time before they found him. I do not know. What I know, though, is it was very difficult, and painful, and lonely for Logan to stay away, stay hidden. To do that with a young, well, young need shelter, steady food, and things that I cannot imagine they could guarantee had he not returned with you. When he did so, and after his... punishment... I was forbidden certain things. So, I did not get the chance to speak to him. But I did it secretly when I could, and he spoke in his sleep. Besides wanting to ensure that you had what you needed, he came back for me. Dahlia too."

"But Dahlia hates him."

"At one point she did not. Her heart just hardened a lot quicker than ours did. She has always had a darkness in her, though. She is the only one of us that is truly like our father."

Out of the corner of her eye, she watched Logan lift his head and chance a look in their direction. She knew it wasn't to interfere, but to remind her that he was there if she needed help from him. They had hidden a lot from Lillianna. Maybe it was time they trusted she was old enough to hear the truth. Zinnia caught his gaze and managed a small smile. She nodded at the chair next to her, letting him know he could come over if he wanted to.

"She is cruel. Like he is," Lillianna replied.

"Yes, she is."

"Why did you have to see him secretly? Was he not in our hut?"

"No. Father did not allow him inside for a while. He did not return to our hut until he had fully healed. Neither did you. Derrick took care of him until he was well. They put you in the nursery with the orphaned young. Father would not allow me to see you. And Dahlia did not want to."

Lillianna blinked a few times when tears pricked the corners of her eyes. "Why have they always hated me?"

"Because their hearts are not capable of love."

"What... what does that mean? Surely, Father loved our mother? Were they not mated?"

"In a manner of speaking."

Logan kissed Ambrosia's forehead and her lips before he helped her to her feet and stood. He strode across the room, covering the short distance in a few strides, dropped a kiss to Lillianna's forehead, and then Zinnia's head and joined them at the table. "Mating in Métamorphe is not like what you have seen with Ambrosia and I, or Pierce and Jocasta. They did not occur because of love. For most, they were arranged. Ailwin did not love our mother, but she loved us. She considered each of us a gift." The chair's legs scraped the wooden floor as he sat. "She loved every single one of us with all her heart."

"What does it mean,"—Lillianna whispered—"when you say they arranged it?" Though the question left her sister's mouth, Zinnia saw the realization in the female's eyes. She answered the question anyway.

"Mother did not choose to mate our father. She was forced. Like Father was trying to do with you. And... like he did with me."

Lillianna's mouth down-turned. "But you never acted like you did not like Bennet."

Lillianna had only been about six then. And Zinnia had already been so docile. She blinked a few times. It was getting harder to swallow her tears, but she would keep it together the best that she could. "I did not openly show a lot of things that I felt. Doing so brought about punishments, ones that I was far too afraid to receive. Father wanted things to be a certain way. I learned quickly that going against what he wanted was not very smart for my wellbeing."

"So... when you got mated to Bennett..."

"It was not because I wanted to." Zinnia shot a glance at Logan and bit her lip. She truly didn't know how much he knew. Focusing back on Lillianna, Zinnia hesitantly reached her hand across the table. Though it shocked her, her sister actually took it. "You are not the only one who Father got paid for. Except, things went just a little different with me."

Logan balled up his fists, but not to where his claws pierced his skin. He inhaled and exhaled a deep breath. Slowly, his fingers unfurled. "There were very few males that were good, even when I lived in the village. Ailwin, he made decisions that lined his pocket and pleased Markham. No other reason." He rested a hand on Zinnia's shoulder and squeezed.

Zinnia clasped his hand tighter than she intended. Hopefully, it wasn't too hard, but she felt as if she was about to break in two. Speaking about this to Lillianna was more difficult than it had been when she had done so with Logan.

"So, Father..." Lillianna's words trailed off.

"Father allowed just one thing with me that he never allowed with you. And I became with child." Zinnia's eyes shut briefly. She steadied her breathing, in and out, and lifted her gaze to her sister. "That was Father's rule. Give me the coin; do whatever you wish. But, if she gets pregnant, she is your responsibility. That is why I lived with Bennett until he...died. Then I had to move back in with Father."

"But, you—no, you have never had a child."

Zinnia took another bout of oxygen into her lungs and blew it out. "Father... wanted no more young in the hut. So, he took her away." Her grip on her brother's hand tightened. The gentle pressure from his palm gave her the strength and support to continue. "I was only about three *cycles* along when..."

"Why would he allow that with you, but not with me?" Lillianna asked.

"Because you have a fire inside of you," Zinnia murmured. The tears trickled down her cheeks. "Mother had it as well. I used to have it inside of me. Over the *solaris*, mine went out. Everything about myself—my true self—I buried it deep down inside. It was the only way I knew how to survive under our father's roof. I stopped doing anything that would anger him. No matter what that was. I became someone ruled by their fear." She gave Lillianna's hand a squeeze. "They could not extinguish that fire inside of you. And no male in Métamorphe wanted a female for a mate who could not be put in their place. They told Father many times they would not mate you. You had a voice, and a spirit, that would not be silenced. So, he did not allow that because... you getting pregnant was not a fight that was worth it to him. Not when he had me."

A tear dripped down into Lillianna's lap and she dropped her gaze for a moment before looking back up at Zinnia. "I am really sorry," she mumbled. "I never knew that you knew what it felt like when..." She visibly swallowed. "You were never mean to me, but I just thought... I thought you hated me."

"Oh, sweet sister mine..." Zinnia shook her head. "I never hated you. I have *always* loved you so much. But I did not know how to be there for you. I did not know how to save you. I could not even save myself." She went quiet for a minute. "May I hug you? I have not hugged you in thirteen very long *solaris*."

Lillianna frowned. "What... I do not remember you ever..."

Zinnia traced invisible lines on the floor when Lillianna shuffled up behind her and flung her tiny arms around her neck. She barely bit back the laughter that bubbled up inside her. Turning her head, she grinned at her three-year-old sister and scooped her into her lap, embracing her. "Are you being silly, Lilli-bug?"

Lillianna nodded, a wide smile on her face. "Can we pway?" she whispered. "I wanna pway a game."

Zinnia tilted her head and thought for a moment. She didn't know where Dahlia and their father had gone, but they weren't there. They should be gone for a while. "I think we can do that. What about hide and seek?"

Lillianna's head bopped up and down. "Yeah, yeah!"

"Alright." She put her finger up to her lips. "Shh, we have to be quiet, Lilli-bug." Pierce had passed out into an exhausted sleep, but, not only that, she didn't know when their father would return, and it would not go well for them if he caught them having fun of any kind.

Lillianna put a hand over her mouth, stifling a giggle. "Quiet. I be quiet, Zin-Zin."

"Okay, good," she kept her voice low.

Shaking the memories away, Zinnia wept, but pushed forward. "Pierce was sleeping. He had not slept in three *umbras*, maybe four. Father and Dahlia were gone. You wanted to play. So, I played with you." The corners of her lips curled up ever so slightly. "Hide and seek. Just in the hut, so..." She shrugged a little. "But we always had fun playing it. I was not expecting Father to be back for a while. I guess we were enjoying ourselves so much, I did not hear him return. He got so furious..." If she parted the fur on her cheek, the scar was faint but still visible. And it was not the only one. Fur was a wonderful thing. "It was the... the last time..." She swallowed the lump in the back of her throat. "Then Father and Pierce got in a... a horrible fight." Tears continued to trickle, darkening her light-colored fur.

"I should have taken you out of the hut with me. Not left you there for that. I am so, so very sorry."

Lillianna said nothing as she quietly cried. After what feltlike several long minutes, she got up from her chair and strolled around the table. Enveloping her arms around Zinnia's neck, she hugged her as hard as she could.

Unable to hold back, completely breaking down, Zinnia returned the embrace with everything in her.

Logan had sat there in silence, but at that point he stood, stepped around Zinnia's chair, and encircled both of his sisters in his powerful arms. They each wrapped an arm around him too and squeezed. The three of them stayed like that for quite some time, just cherishing one another.

"Oh, I have never gotten to hug both of you simultaneously," Zinnia said. "It is so very nice. Now we just need Pierce here." She laughed softly. They would see him tomorrow, though.

Logan's mouth upturned at the corners. "Hey Zinni, if you would like, you could stay here tonight. We have an extra bedroom in the back. Then we can all have morning meal together. Would that be okay with you, Lillianna?"

"That would be okay with me."

Zinnia's smile widened. "That sounds wonderful. Thank you, Logan."

Logan kissed the top of each of their heads. "I am going to check on my mate, but I will be back in a few minutes."

Zinnia beamed at him, still hugging Lillianna close to her. "Take your time, brother mine. I think we are okay here."

He nodded, left the dining area, and disappeared down the hall.

They stayed like that a few minutes longer before Lillianna sat back and wiped at her eyes. Zinnia did the same, but kept a gentle hold on her hand. "She gave you your name. Mother did."

Lillianna lifted her gaze to her. "Really?"

With a brief dip of her chin, a tilt of her lips crossed Zinnia's face. "Mhm. Lilies were her absolute favorite flower. Particularly the white ones." She paused. "Pierce and I only spoke about her the one time in the village, after she passed. I had asked your name."

"He did not speak about her very much to me. And never when Father was around. I asked, but he could not seem to find very many words. Why just the one time?"

"Mother is a bit of a difficult topic for him. She was such a wonderful female. But there are a lot of sad memories there. And, at that point, Pierce and I had grown further apart. I hope now we can talk about her more." She clasped her sister's hand gently. "But he told me her last words were naming you." She smiled. "You look just like her. He never said so, but I think the particular flowers he brought you every *solaris* on your birthday was his way of sharing her with you when he could not share words."

The corners of Lillianna's mouth tugged upward. "They were always fresh. Even though we grew nothing in the village. They always made me feel better."

"I know they did. A bit of sunshine in a dark place, huh?" A sudden thought struck her. "Would you like to plant some with me? I asked Logan if he thought Pierce would mind if I planted something... for Summer. He said he did not think Pierce would mind. Maybe we could do it together?"

Lillianna frowned a little. "Was Summer your...?"

"She would have been. Yes."

"I would love to plant them with you. If Pierce and Jo do not mind. But I do not think that they will."

"Come on. Let us go sit on the couch." Lillianna nodded, and they both got up. Draping an arm across her shoulder, Zinnia led her sister into the living room. They sat on the couch side by side, and she tucked Lillianna against her. "I remember a song that Mother used to sing to us when we were very young. It was her favorite song. Would you like to hear it?"

"Yes, please."

This, right here, was something they could never have had back in that place. Their father had made sure of that. But they had it now. Her sister laid her head on her shoulder, letting out a soft sigh as she started stroking the back of Lillianna's head.

Zinnia's gaze drifted toward the flames crackling in the fireplace. "I'll Keep You Safe" by Sleeping At Last. It had been their mother's absolute favorite song to sing to them. Sometimes at the river, during walks through the forest, in the middle of the night when their father had passed out from drinking too many spirits and it was safe to sneak away from his bed. Zinnia's mind returned to the last time she had heard their mother sing the song. During her labor with Lillianna, before Ailwin had returned to the hut, during a brief lull in the pain, their mother had held both of her hands out to her and Pierce and whisper-sang the words. Zinnia's own words were almost as soft as she sang.

Sabina had sung of keeping them safe. That the weight of the world might be at their fingertips, but they shouldn't be afraid of it. They were bound to make mistakes but, no matter how many they made, she would always keep them safe. That they could do absolutely anything they wanted in their lives and create beautiful things. They would rewrite the darkness and discover all the secrets of the world around them. They would unearth their creativity and build masterpieces more beautifully than anything she'd ever seen. And no matter what they ever encountered, she would always be there, keeping them and their hearts safe through every single bit of it.

Logan never returned, but Zinnia suspected that after a conversation like that, he had just needed his mate. Somewhere during the song, her tears flowed down her cheeks. She never stopped stroking Lillianna's head. Her sister's breathing slowed and deepened, bit by bit, until she fell asleep. Zinnia sang the song through twice. When she'd finished it for the second time, she stayed right where she was, holding Lillianna against her. She stared into the orange blaze, letting many years of unshed anguish escape.

Chapter Twenty-Seven

When Pierce and Jocasta left Lyrica's in the morning, she'd still been in bed. He worried for the female. At least she'd eaten the evening before, though. He nuzzled his mate's ears as they walked. Last night had been difficult. He almost growled just thinking about it, but he bit it back.

"It is still fairly early. Should I check on Zinnia before we go for morning meal?" It would have been her first night in the home. Gods, she would have spent it alone. He felt bad, but Lyrica needed someone; what Jocasta had done for her had been necessary. And his mate needed him; he would have been nowhere else but right with her.

"Yes. I think we should." Jocasta held his hand a little tighter, her thoughts on her mother. What the female had gone through—not just to escape, but to lose her mate as well—it was an unimaginable loss. One no one ever truly got over. That wasn't something he *ever* wanted to think about.

Jocasta hadn't heard from her sister. Hopefully, that was a good thing. She'd told him she'd tried to check in last night through their mindlink, but Ambrosia had locked her out. They should definitely check on Zinnia, but Ambrosia, too, if she was up.

Pierce tucked Jocasta into his side and rubbed her arm as he dropped a kiss to her head. Even when he'd gone to beg Zinnia to come with him to Migas, he hadn't expected her to come. Then she hadn't. Then she'd shown up like she had. Now she was here. What was she feeling? Especially after how dinner had gone last night. Gods, hopefully, she was alright.

They hadn't been close in a very long time, but he still cared about her very much. Now that they reunited, maybe they could mend the broken bridges together.

They got to the house and Pierce frowned a bit as they went inside. He didn't sense anyone else there, nor did he catch anyone's scent. "I will be right back."

"Okay."

He gave her another kiss on the head before heading down the hall. It didn't take him long to confirm what he'd sensed, and he returned to the entrance in less than a minute, trying not to panic. "She is not here and her bed has not been slept in. I do not think Lilli would have been okay with her staying there, but I want to check there first. Perhaps she... went for a walk or something?" That seemed logical, right? Nope, not really.

"Maybe." His mate gently smoothed a hand over his forearm. Her touch immediately calmed him, easing the panic and thundering of his heart. He was still worried, but definitely not in full-blown panic anymore. It boggled his mind what just a simple touch from her could do for him. "Maybe she stayed there, just talking to Am or Logan."

Leaning down, he brushed a soft kiss across her lips. "Alright. Um, next door first." If Zinnia wasn't there, well, they'd scour the village until they found her.

"Yeah. Next door first."

With a dip of his chin, he gave her another kiss and tucked her back into his side as they left their house. In next to no time, they headed up the front porch steps of his brother's home. Pierce froze with his hand on the knob. What? Huh. Maybe she had... Letting himself in with Jocasta right behind him, he halted in his steps. He couldn't move. Zinnia half-sat, half-laid against the arm of the couch. She was wide awake, staring into the empty fireplace. By the looks of it, the flames had gone out hours ago. Her cheeks appeared puffy—had she been crying? But all of that, none of it, was what shocked him into stillness. Lilli—barely noticeable between Zinnia and the back of the couch. Curled up to her. Fast asleep. What in Hades' name had they missed? Zinnia didn't seem to notice them enter the house. He eyed his mate. "I do not know what to do," he whispered.

It seemed she didn't either. He sensed it surprised her as well. "Gentle hand," Jocasta replied, her voice low.

His gaze drifted back to Zinnia. Maybe he could do something...something he'd told his mate he hadn't done in years. Talk to his sister. Just as he had with his brother. Maybe. Could he? Could they? Talk? He'd barely said anything to her at the medical center. They'd spoken a little on the way back to the house, but the really important words hadn't come yet. Then dinner last night. Pierce peered at his mate. "Okay," he whispered. "I will, um..." He gripped the back of his neck. "Yeah. Would you mind making some tea? It looks like she might need some?" That shouldn't have been a question, but it was the way it had come out.

"Of course." Jocasta gave his hand a squeeze of encouragement and kissed the inside of his palm before she strode into the kitchen.

It took a moment for Pierce to cross the front room toward the couch. He didn't know the true reason for the hesitation. Well, maybe he did. He just didn't want to think about it. They'd been through a lot—too much—and had to do it virtually alone when they should have been able to lean on each other. Would they really be able to fully mend that bridge? Time. That was what they needed. Time.

Reaching the couch, he gently touched Zinnia's shoulder. She jumped. Lilli stirred slightly, but didn't wake. Pierce jerked his hand back. "Hey, sorry." He kneeled down on the floor next to her. Neither of them uttered a word for a minute, but she at least turned her attention to him. He kept his voice low as he spoke. "I kind of want to ask what we missed."

Zinnia inhaled and exhaled a slow breath. "She came out of her room. She ate. I wanted to at least try to speak to her. She was angry. Furious. But I mean... I understood." Silence stretched between them. Her gaze drifted back to the fireplace, and it wasn't until he reached over and took her hand that she refocused on him. "She... she knows."

A chill swept down his spine. "Knows what?"

"Everything."

"As in?"

"I am sorry, Pierce. I did not... I never imagined you would not have told her. About her birth."

Oh, gods. He closed his eyes briefly. He had always meant to, but, in the village, deep conversations hadn't really been possible. Not to mention the topics had been so very painful. Hades, he had barely taught her how to read. They only ever had stolen moments for that. Lilli caught on quickly enough, but they'd never gotten beyond the basics.

He felt his mate's gaze flick to him and glanced over at her in the kitchen. A smile faltered across his face. Despite how hard he tried, he couldn't seem to pull one to the forefront. He shifted his eyes to his sister. "I would have. Since we have been here. But she has not asked. I have not wanted to bring up painful subjects that she might not be ready to talk about."

"I know. She was not angry. At all, actually. There was sadness—on both ends—but once I started talking and she was listening... *everything* spilled out."

Pierce just stared at his sister. "So, she... she *knows*." His eyebrows furrowed together as he let out a breath.

"Yes. She knows about me. All of it. And she knows that, though it was the way it was back there, she was never alone in how she felt."

He knew his mate wasn't intentionally eavesdropping, except with her extensive canine hearing, she couldn't really help but listen. A faint gasp exploded from her. He hadn't come close to telling her everything, but she had enough information. Gods, he just wanted to hug his sister, but he didn't want to wake Lilli up. "Are you okay?" he asked as Jocasta entered the room with a couple of mugs of tea.

"Oh, yes. I mean, I will be. In time. Logan came in on the conversation later. I know it was difficult for him." Zinnia offered Jocasta a tender tilt of her mouth. "Thank you."

Lifting his gaze to his mate, he caressed her cheek. "Thank you, love."

"You're quite welcome." She set two mugs on the table closest to the chair and held the other out for Zinnia. Once Zinnia had taken ahold of it, his mate sat in the plush chair opposite the one they often occupied.

Zinnia took a careful sip. "Ambrosia went to bed at some point, and he followed her in there. Lilli and I talked a little more." She smiled. "She let me hug her."

"I can see that." He was still a little floored by it.

"Thirteen *solaris*. That is way too long to go without a hug. Eighteen is even longer."

"I know." Happiness radiated from him. "Not anymore, right?"

"No. Definitely not anymore."

"I am..." He let out a contented sigh. "That makes me glad. I was worried about you two."

She clasped his hand. "We were okay. We decided we would like to plant some lilies. White ones. For Mother and..." Her words trailed off. "If you two do not mind, of course?" Zinnia glanced from him to his mate.

Pierce's throat closed up for a moment. He knew who the 'and' was. He shook his head. "Of course, we do not mind."

"I think lilies would be lovely in the yard," Jocasta said.

"You are very kind. Both of you. I do not d—"

Pierce shook his head. "No. Do not go there, sister mine. Whatever it is you think you do not deserve, you are wrong. You do."

Zinnia acknowledged his words. "I sang her the song."

He raised an eyebrow. "First off—you *sang*?" Gods, he couldn't remember the last time. "Wait, the song, *the* song?" It was so difficult not to allow the heartache in right now. He hadn't heard that song in over sixteen years.

Zinnia tightened her hold on his hand. "It was her favorite. And it seemed like the right time for Lilli to hear it. She fell asleep to it. I just... spent all night crying and thinking."

His mate rested a comforting hand on his shoulder. He laced their fingers together and kissed the inside of her wrist. She was his anchor, his haven. Always there for him in whatever way he required, no matter how big or small. After a moment, Pierce glanced back at his mate. "Mother's favorite. The last time I heard it... the *umbra* Lilli was..." He cleared his throat. "The *umbra* she was born."

His mate turned her attention from him to his sister. "Maybe one *umbra* you can teach it to me."

"I would love to." Lilli stirred and Zinnia glanced at her as their little sister opened her eyes. "Hey there, sleepyhead."

"Hey." She rubbed her eyes as she sat up slowly and peered from Zinnia to Jocasta to Pierce. Her eyes flicked back to Zinnia. "I... I did not mean to fall asleep here. Did we sleep here all night?"

"It was perfectly fine. I did not mind one bit." She kissed the top of Lilli's head.

Lilli said nothing as her focus returned to him. He stared at her, unsure of what to say. Her eyes sparkled. Suddenly, she climbed over Zinnia's legs, threw her arms around him, and hugged him hard.

Pierce's throat closed up, and a tear welled in the corner of his eye. He couldn't utter a single thing. He just didn't have any words. Couldn't even really explain the sudden onslaught of emotion. So, he just returned the embrace.

Zinnia got up off the couch and sat on the arm of the chair Jocasta occupied. Her voice lowered. Not that it would do much, but she did it all the same. "Thank you."

Lilli did not move, so neither did he. He kept his arms tightly around her, holding her close as his mate and his sister spoke.

Jocasta's eyebrows furrowed, and she leaned closer to Zinnia. "For what?"

"For everything you have done for him. Brought back out of him. He was so lost for so long. More lost than me in some ways." Zinnia peered over at him and Lilli, then beamed at his mate. "You brought him back."

"We saved each other," Jocasta declared.

Zinnia squeezed his mate's hand. "She will always have a special place in his heart. More than Logan and I ever will." She grinned. "He is going to make such a wonderful father one *umbra*. Logan too. They have that chance now. It will be... very good."

"Yes, he will. They both will."

Lilli finally drew back and stared at him. She kissed his cheek, then got up and headed for the kitchen. "I am going to start breakfast."

Be careful. Do not burn yourself. The warnings were there, but his throat wasn't working. He just sat there, watching her. She didn't blame him. A hug like that... No. She didn't blame him. He blinked a tear back.

"I think I will go help her." Zinnia joined Lilli in the kitchen.

His mate kneeled down in front of him. She rested one hand on his forearm and made slow strokes with her thumb while she gently caressed the nape of his neck.

His gaze shifted from the kitchen to her as he ran his fingers across her ears. Pierce leaned his forehead against hers, letting the calmness of her touch wash over him. Gods, there had been so many emotions in these last few days, but so much happiness, too. Not that he was knocking it, but it would take a lot of getting used to. Being so happy all the time. Here, he and his siblings had found a home and family. He and Jocasta had officially claimed each other. He would never forget a single moment of their ceremony, the words they'd spoken to each other, her song to him, dancing with her for the first time. Although he was no dancer, he couldn't wait to do it again. Pierce nuzzled her nose and kissed her softly. "I love you."

"I love you too." With her lips still pressed against his, joy spread over her face.

They had dealt with a lot, but it didn't change the outcome. They had all come out on the other side of all the horrors they'd endured. There was still more that had to be handled, but by each other's side, they could do anything. And he couldn't wait to see what the future held for them.

Chapter Twenty-Eight

As Pierce's paws pounded across the ground, he did something he'd never done willingly—he let the memories in. Every one. Lilli's screams. Her blood. The scents of the males that had become an ever-present stench in their hut. Every nightmare she had faced for the evil that had happened to her. Zinnia's wails when their father forced her child from her, the only time she had allowed herself tears, to fight, to break. The times he had come across Devina amid an assault. Their broken bodies. His inability to help, to stop the monsters from what they did. Pain. So much pain. And the information that they just received from Zagan and Alastor, that Derrick had had a child ripped from him and his mate as well. He let it all flow through him, permitting his anger to grow, then surge. Within a couple of miles, he knew his eyes were pitch black.

By the look in Logan's eyes, his brother welcomed the emotions that rolled through him. A fresh scent appeared on the wind, and Logan shifted his direction. With a growl, his paws thundered against the lush forest floor, kicking up dirt and grass with each step.

Pierce was right with him, neck-and-neck, as they sped toward an oncoming clearing. Upon entering it, he saw Cyrus standing right in the center, completely unmoving. Not even his tail twitched as Logan charged right at him, his claws prepared to rip a chunk out of whatever part of the male he struck first. Pierce didn't have time to follow suit. A dark brown form launched off a nearby branch, landing straight on his back. Claws dug in and held. He heard snarls, growls, a sickening pop, and clashing as

Logan and Cyrus tore into one another, but he couldn't focus on what was happening with them. Not with an attacker on his own back.

Catapulting his body into the air, Pierce rolled. He tried to land on his back, throwing his full weight on the male, but it didn't pan out that way. Set dug in harder. With a jerk, he forced Pierce to the ground on his side. He bucked hard, trying to throw the male off of him, but the male's claws dragged to the base of his tail. Jaws clamped down on the scruff of his neck. He jerked hard, finally landing on his back and crushing the smaller male beneath him. It was enough to get the male's jaws to release, at least.

Wrenching his head around, Pierce closed his own jaws around Set's muzzle and yanked. Set's claws released from his back as he threw the male away from him. The pain would be great later, but he felt nothing now. Too much rage coursed through him, overriding everything else.

Set hit the ground with a thud, but immediately jumped to his feet. Pierce tracked every movement he made as they countered each other. They both lunged simultaneously. He latched onto one of the male's legs, clenching his fangs together hard. A loud crack rang out, followed by a yelping bark as he flung Set aside. He circled, waiting for the male to get up. Pierce wanted him to fight, the pain to be great, and the male's death to be slow. "Come on, Set," he snarled. "You are not finished yet, are you? Such a disappointment. Come on. *Fight me.* I am rather enjoying the taste of your blood in my mouth."

Getting to his feet with one leg held in the air, the male roared. As Pierce leaped toward him, Set dropped to his side, sliding beneath Pierce's body at just the right moment. The male clamped his teeth onto a meaty part and wrenched Pierce to the ground. Not that he noticed anything. Just his fury. Pierce twisted around, snapping his jaws, trying to make purchase. Set struck him, blood gushing from the back of his neck. He clamped down on one of Set's back legs this time, teeth to bone, and jerked as hard as he could. A sickening pop bounced around him. Set's jaws released, a cry of anguish leaving him, as a good two-thirds of the male's leg came off in his mouth. Pierce spit it out and got to his feet, circling him slowly. "Is that all you have got?" He laughed. "But I am not done with you yet."

Out of the corner of his eye, Pierce saw Cyrus fly several feet back, his ear detaching from his head. Flipping his body around, the male lunged at Logan, dropping his head down and biting hard into Logan's hindquarters. He kicked out at Logan's face as the claws of his front paws found his belly.

Clamping his jaws onto Cyrus's tail, Logan yanked him back and slammed him into the closest tree. With his maw still on the male's tail, he swung him in the other direction and hurled him into a large, distorted trunk. Snaps resounded as something broke. Releasing his hold on the male's tail, Logan clawed at Cyrus's belly, digging deep, blood spurting everywhere. He pressed his paw down on the male's dick and glowered, his eyes still black. "Are you afraid yet?"

Cyrus said nothing, unmoving. Likely, his spine had broken.

Set pathetically tried to drag his body away. Pierce latched onto his other hind leg, bit down hard, and snapped the bone clean in half. To his remaining front leg, he did the same. The howls of pain Set made brought him great pleasure. Hearing his brother's words, he glanced over and chuckled. "Of course he is. Even I can smell it. You are going to take away his favorite toy."

"Do not kill me. Please, I beg of you." Set's words came out weak, tense, laced with anguish.

A maniacal laugh left his mouth as he put his face right up to Set's. "I have no sympathy for rapists. And look at that, it appears my brother does not either." Walking around to his side, Pierce put his front paws down on the male's back. He pushed down, impaling Set's back until the spine snapped and the male lay still. He may not have been moving, but he hadn't died just yet.

"Make sure that you watch what my brother does. I would not want you to miss a moment of it, because you are next," Pierce hissed in Set's ear. Grabbing onto that piece of flesh, he jerked the male's head up, so he stared across the clearing, straight at Logan and Cyrus.

"I will never be afraid of you, Logan," Cyrus growled weakly. "You may take my breath and stop my heart from beating, but you will never take my face from her nightmares."

Logan dug harder into the male's groin. "You may say the words, but your emotions give you away, Cyrus. I can feel your fear. And it pleases me." In one fell swoop, he tore the male's dick from his body and then got up close to Cyrus's face. "Perhaps Markham should have warned you of my ability." Logan latched onto his throat and ripped it open.

Maybe Cyrus hadn't been afraid at first, but it eventually found him. Fear always found a way in. Stepping off of Set's mangled body, Pierce flipped him over onto his back, his remaining legs flopping around. He could see the reflection of his eyes in Set's, still fully black. "You are going to stare into my eyes as I take your last breath," he snarled. Without tearing his gaze away, he swiped at the male's chest and neck, digging deep, that vital red liquid spraying all over and around him. Even after the life left the male's face, he still struck the male. It wasn't enough. None of it was enough .And he couldn't stop.

He didn't want to see what was in his head anymore, what he had pulled from to fuel his anger, the memories he had welcomed with open arms, the images that haunted his every nightmare, the scents that had become as familiar to him as the very air he breathed. But he couldn't quite seem to push them away just yet. All of Lilli's spilled blood and injuries, the attacks he hadn't prevented, every loss of his mother's. Not once had he been by her side. He'd caught the whiff of copper and, before he'd even known he was doing it, he'd charged through the forest. Running away. No, it had always been Logan. Always Logan with her, holding her and comforting her through every loss. When she planted a flower for each one, he hadn't joined them to say goodbye. When Logan had left and the losses continued, Pierce had gotten her to the river at her request, then waited only as long as it took for Zinnia to sneak away and stay with her. Their mother had never blamed him, but he'd never stopped hating himself for it. With Zinnia, it had been the same. But, by that time, they'd no longer spoken to one another in any regard.

At some point, he severed the last tether of the head to the body. Another swipe of his claws had it rolling across the ground. It was the absent head, his claws connecting with the dirt, that finally broke his mind away from where it had gone. His eyes followed the path the head took, the direction it careened, as his chest heaved. He couldn't see his back. His face and the entirety of his neck burned. His eyes fell on his brother, sitting on his hind legs, just staring at the spongy green grass.

"Logan." Pierce tried to take a step, weaved, and fell back onto his hip. His body shook as the pain registered. "Fuck," he hissed. The metallic taste of Set's blood nearly had bile rising in the back of his throat. Agony hit him in waves and he retched, though nothing came up. "Logan. Are you alright?"

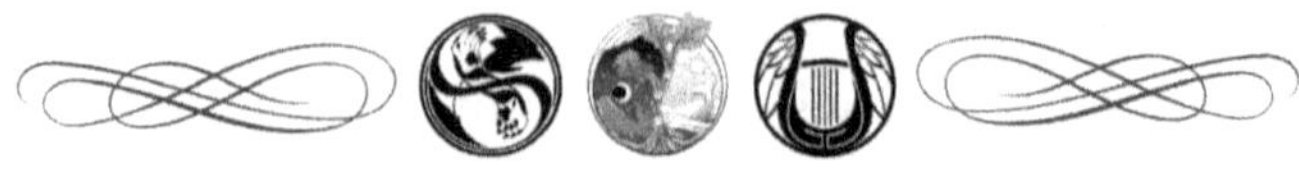

Standing over the sink with a mixing bowl, Jo lifted her eyes to the front door as it opened. She'd just put sweet rolls in. But for the last hour, she and her twin had done whatever they could to occupy their minds. Wherever their mates had gone and done, well, they had their suspicions. She glowered at the empty space she was positive her mate now occupied, even though she couldn't see him.

Pierce cleared his throat. "Um, before I drop this—my camouflage—it is, um... not great."

Her grip tightened on the bowl in her hand. "Drop it, right the fuck now, or I'm throwing this bowl at your head!"

The door quietly clicked shut. Logan appeared as he removed his camouflage and limped one step to the right.

Becoming visible, a grimace crossed her mate's face. The bowl fell from her hand, clattering into the sink. "What *the* fuck, Pierce?"

He winced. "That is, um, not all."

Those were the last words he was ever going to speak. Her shoulders tensed as she balled up her fists. Oh, she was going to kill him. "All of it. Right now. And then you can sit the fuck down so my sister and I can get a good assessment."

The front door opened again, and her twin stopped in the jamb. "Oh, fuck. Seriously?!" Ambrosia glared at Logan. "By all the gods, Logan, you better not have gone to that damn fight ring again."

Pierce cringed. "Please do not hit me, love." He sighed and slowly turned around, bracing himself.

She scrubbed a hand down her face. It was the only way to keep the string of cuss words back. Inhaling a deep breath, she walked over to the dining table and yanked out a chair. "Sit."

Logan looked at his own mate. "It was not the fight ring, I promise you."

"That doesn't mean much at the moment." Ambrosia scowled and pointed to a chair as she practically slammed the door shut.

"Yes, love." Logan made his way over without hesitation and flinched as he sat down.

Pierce moved as quickly as his body permitted him to, straddling the proffered piece of furniture. Gritting his teeth against a groan, he sat. He rested his palms on his knees. "It was not the fight ring. But if it means anything, we came out better."

Jo and Ambrosia took up opposite positions, their backs to one another, as they each assessed the damage to their males individually. The two of them had a conversation via their mindlink.

A few of these will need to be stitched up. How are Logan's wounds?

It looks the same on his chest. Good gods, what the fuck did they—

Straightening up, Jo paused. "The only way you fared better is if—"

"—oh, fuck no!" she and her twin spouted simultaneously.

"You were hunting, weren't you?" Ambrosia asked.

"With good reason, my love. We simply want to ensure our family remains safe," Logan replied.

"I call bullshit." Jo glanced over her shoulder at her sister. "I'll start working on the pain medication and get some stuff to clean the wounds." She stepped around the chair her mate took residence in and headed toward the kitchen. "Don't even think about moving."

"I am not moving, my queen. He is right, though. Yes, we were hunting, but it *was* for good reason. Today, there are two less breathing air that harmed our sisters. And two less to return to that village to harm more females. And I will be fine without pain medication. I have had such injuries before."

Jo halted in her tracks, faced her mate, and gave him the evil eye. While he had the good sense to stay put, his response to pain medication was completely unacceptable. "We will discuss the first part later. But the pain medication is *not* negotiable. You will fucking take it if I have to shove it down your throat myself. We clear?"

"Yes, my queen," he stated.

"I'm so glad we agree."

Logan snickered and winced.

"It's great that you think that's fucking funny. Snicker again and I'm gonna put Jo's sparring skills to use," Ambrosia remarked.

"No more laughing, my love."

Jo disappeared into the kitchen and collected the herbs she needed, along with a big pot and rags to clean the wounds. "Am, do you have enough dressing over there?"

"We should be good. Enough for the larger of their wounds. Though, maybe it would work better if we just wrap them completely in gauze. For fuck's sake, I hope it was worth it," Ambrosia uttered. "If you're smart, you keep that thought to yourself. We both know how the two of you felt by the end."

Logan said nothing. Just kept his trap shut.

Pierce hung his head with a grimace.

Good. Maybe these two assholes had learned their fucking lesson. Gods, this was a mess. It took her a few minutes to get the herbs mixed in with water for the pain. She brought over two cups, handed one to Pierce and one to Logan. Just in case her mate protested again, Jo's amber gaze locked on him as she spoke. "Drink." There wouldn't be any chance of a misunderstanding. Returning to the kitchen, she gathered whatever supplies she and her twin required to clean the wounds that their mates hadn't thoroughly rinsed out.

He took a drink and almost gagged. "Hades, this tastes awful."

Without saying a word, she shot daggers at him. Like she cared how shitty it tasted. He'd drink every fucking drop and enjoy it.

"Sorry, love. It is wonderful. And I will drink all of it. I swear." He swallowed more.

"You better," Jo muttered. Her sister got lucky, which just meant Logan had been through this before. He drank the concoction without complaining once. She half-glanced at her twin.

Shaking her head, Ambrosia crossed her arms. "You did a shitty job cleaning your wounds."

"We did as best we could, focusing more on the blood than anything," Logan said.

With a large pot of soapy water and a stack of washcloths, Jo came back into the dining area. Setting the container down, she held out a couple of rags to her sister. "I'm going to start with the ones closest to your tail."

"Yes, my queen." Her mate was quiet for a moment. "If it means anything, I *am* sorry that I returned to you looking this way. It was not our intention. They were just very skilled."

What was she supposed to say about that? She didn't feel bad for him. He'd actively left the village. Hadn't they just addressed his concerns regarding his scent all over her? And he pulls this shit? How the fuck could he do this? It didn't matter that they'd gotten mated only a week ago.

She wet the cloth and, as gently as she could, worked on cleansing the wounds closest to his tail. "It doesn't. You went *searching* for them, Pierce. I mean, for fuck's sake, is *that* supposed to make me feel better? It wasn't like you were defending the village or just defending yourself because they happened upon you. No, you actively went out and sought them."

"Don't think your silence is helping you any. You promised you wouldn't get into any more fights *unless* you were defending yourself. Evan... he was an exception. This isn't. The two of you, gods, we should kick your asses ourselves," Ambrosia claimed.

Logan sighed. "I am sorry, my love. It was not a promise I meant to break. I just... I could not sit around doing nothing with those who hurt our sisters out there."

"That better not be your way of saying this is going to be a regular thing."

"No," Logan replied. "I believe we have both learned our lesson."

It was difficult not to pay attention to the conversation between her sister and brother-in-law. But it certainly kept her from screaming like a mad-woman at her mate.

"Yes. It was a lesson well learned, on my end as well, my queen," Pierce added.

The door flung open. Jo peered over her shoulder, catching the wide-eyed look on her mate's face out of the corner of her eye.

Zinnia's eyes were dark as she stood there. She glimpsed over the visible wounds and then crossed her arms over her chest. "What in the actual fuck is wrong with you two?" They both opened their mouths, but she shook her head slowly, causing them both to snap their mouths shut. "You do not even have to say it. If this is what it appears, I know *exactly* what this was."

Jo returned to cleaning out the wound just above her mate's tail. "This one will have to be stitched." She glanced at Zinnia. "They won't be doing this again."

"No, they won't," Ambrosia echoed.

Zinnia nodded at them both and leaned back against the door, her arms still crossed.

"I am sorry, my queen," Pierce said, then sighed. He looked back over at his sister. "I cannot stand that they breathe after what they have done. I want them all dead."

"And we need you both alive!" Zinnia yelled.

Her mate's ruby gaze fell to the floor. Shame coloring his features. "It will not happen again."

Another moment passed before Zinnia spoke. "I am sorry. I did not mean to yell. And I should not have intruded. I just had to... I wanted to make sure you were both okay." Dropping a hand to her hip, she pinched the bridge of her nose. "*Hades*, what were you two thinking?"

"They weren't." Her sister-in-law could scream at Logan and Pierce all she wanted. Jo supported it. Might holler a few more times herself, until that shit sunk the fuck in. "Look, we get it. All of us." Her eyes swung over to her twin. "But Zinnia's right. If it's this bad this time, what happens the next time? Or the time after that? One of them, you don't come home. And we *all* need you. Both of you. And, Pierce, I swear to the gods, if you die on me, I'll bring you back to life so I can kick your ass myself."

Ambrosia's head bobbed in agreement as she lifted her gaze to Logan. "No more going out searching for fights."

"No more," Logan repeated. "I am sorry, my love."

"I know you are, but this is enough. Beyond enough." Her twin moved to the injuries along Logan's belly.

Zinnia just stared at them both. "I was on death's door when I found you two again," she kept her voice low. "And Lillianna..." She closed her eyes briefly. "We have all come back together. And you have both found such wonderful mates that love you more than anything in this world. You have been given a gift of a new life from the gods—this family, this community—such as we have never known. And you almost threw it all away. For what? Revenge? Did you think this was what *any* of us would want? Or were you just letting your anger think for you?"

"That is exactly it. My anger was all I could think of." Pierce sighed. "I get it."

"Do you?"

"Yes." He glanced up at Zinnia, then back down at the floor. Reaching behind him on his good side, he stroked Jo's knee. "I am truly sorry. And I give my word I will not go looking for any more fights." He gently squeezed her knee and then moved his arm back to his thigh. "I would welcome the ass kicking, my queen, were that to occur. But I will not allow it to. My word. I swear."

Jo got in front of him. "That's good, because I can't live without you." Swallowing the lump in the back of her throat, she focused on the wounds covering his face. It wasn't much. The injuries on his back still had to be finished, but she would deal with them in a moment. Right now, she needed something that didn't make her want to cry, scream, and punch her mate at the same time.

Logan winced, then flicked his gaze to his sister. "I am sorry, Zinni. You *both* have my word." His eyes shifted to Ambrosia. "I will not seek any more fights."

"Good. Now, the two of you just have to figure out what you're going to say to Lilli," Ambrosia asserted.

"Thank you," Zinnia said. "Both of you. I understand the anger. I truly do. But the possibility that—" She shook her head. "No. It is not worth it. You both know Lillianna would say the same."

"I know. I am sorry." Pierce stroked Jo's cheek. "I cannot live without you either, my queen. Please believe that I am truly sorry."

"Though I would hug the two of you, I think it best to save that for another time." Zinnia glanced at Ambrosia and Jo. "Is there anything I can do before I go back next door? I do not know when your mother wished to head home. But I will stay there to keep an ear out for Lillianna until she wakes, so that you can finish here. I can try to get her out of the house early tomorrow as well. The less she sees of the wounds..." She smirked. "Perhaps I can find enough to occupy our time, make an *umbra* of it. Give you two at least some time to heal."

Pressing a kiss to the inside of Pierce's palm, Jo cracked a faint smile at Zinnia. "Thank you, but I think we've got it covered. I won't say I'm a pro, but Am has stitched me up. I don't know how many times, but enough to get this down."

"Five," Ambrosia answered. She turned toward Zinnia ."Actually, when Lilli wakes up from her nap, why don't you and Mom take her somewhere in the village for a couple of *lacunas?* Mom enjoys spending time with you both and it'll give us time to finish patching them up, and less likely she'll see their injuries."

"Alright. We will do that then." Zinnia bobbed her head once and then left the house.

"I deserve anything else you have to say to me, my queen. I know it was stupid," Pierce admitted.

Logan's eyes focused on her twin. He watched as she moved between his legs and tended to the claw marks along his chest. "Ambrosia—"

"Just don't. Right now, I want to get you patched up. We'll discuss it later."

"I think—" Her nose twitched. What the— "Shit!" Jo tossed the washcloth on the table and darted into the kitchen. In her fury, though less angry than when he arrived, she forgot the sweet rolls. She grabbed a couple of towels and retrieved the rolls from the oven. Well, she hadn't burned them. That was something. Maybe just a little crispy. Jo set the tray aside for the rolls to cool and returned to Pierce. Threading her fingers together, she gripped the back of her neck. "I'm gonna finish stitching up your back."

"Okay," he said. "I wish there was more I could say. Besides, I am sorry."

She thought she had known everything she intended to say; yell, scream, ask, all the above. Words evaded her as she cleaned and stitched the last cut on his back. Yes, she understood why he'd done it. Why he'd purposely gone out and sought Informants. But that didn't mean she understood all of it. "I just don't get why you didn't talk to me about this. Beforehand."

"I did not want to worry you. Or for you to tell me no. I did not think you would have agreed to it. Even if you understood it. But it was something I felt I needed to do. I am used to making my own decisions, despite the consequences. But I always seem to make the wrong choices in protecting the ones that I love. You are my mate. I should not have..." He sighed. "I also did not think I would get this injured. Not from one opponent, anyway. My anger, my cockiness... it got in the way." Pierce paused. "I am not good at talking about... difficult things. I know that is something that I need to change."

Stitching the last laceration, she picked up a new wet cloth and stepped around to face him. It was going to be the easiest way to get to the hunk that had gotten ripped from his side. All she could do with that was clean it and bandage it. "We have to figure out how to talk to each other, especially about the difficult things. Your decisions impact me, just as mine impact you. You're not invisible. But you're right about one thing. I would've told you no, and then I would've told you to talk to your sisters and see what they thought." Straightening, her eyes met his. "You can't get revenge on everyone that has ever caused harm to our family, whether it was before we got together or after. Otherwise, where does it end? When does it become enough?" Her lips pinched together as she tried to get her frustration under control. "The desire for revenge will eat you alive, chew you up, and then spit you back out just to do it all over again."

"I do not know how to deal with my anger any other way," Pierce said. "Talking about things there, it was just not done. They expected us to swallow it, bury it, and move on. But I know we are not there anymore. I know I need to change that. I know I need to get better."

She took a piece of gauze and taped it along his side. It would need to be changed tomorrow if it still bled. Probably a good idea to change it later before he fell asleep for the night. Peering over his shoulder, she checked on her twin's progress. The apology was written all over Logan's features, but Ambrosia was too pissed to hear it. Jo reached over and wet another cloth to clean up Pierce's face. "Look, I know a lot has changed for us in a short amount of time." Three months. In that timeframe, he had left everything he knew behind and they had mated; it could discombobulate anyone. "I don't expect you to change overnight. You've had to live your life one way for a long time, so it'll take time to adjust. To fully accept that what you couldn't do there, you can do here. That this—us—will always be a safe space."

"I am going to try. For you, for us, and for them. I am going to try." He brought her empty hand to his lips and pressed a kiss over their engraved initials on her wrist. "I love you, my queen."

"And I love you, my king. And trying, that's all I ask." Her gaze dropped to those chest wounds. The ones up top just needed to be cleaned. She could easily access those. It was the lower ones, the ones close to his abdomen, that the chair blocked. His back had definitely been the worst of it. "I hate to do this, but you're going to have to get up and turn so I can get to the last of your injuries. Then you can rest." And, hopefully by that point, her sister and Logan would finish, too.

He nodded a little, inhaled a couple of deep breaths, then braced himself on the table as he slowly stood from his chair. It was a good thing they were sturdy. He wasn't entirely steady on his feet. "Do you need me to sit back down? I cannot lean back if I sit back down in the chair. Perhaps this would be best?"

"Just sit sideways, unless you don't think you'll get to your feet again." If that was the case, well, at least his height would come in handy.

"I am not... entirely sure, to be honest. Just so you know." Pierce used his other hand to grip the back of the chair and slowly lowered himself down into it sideways with a grunt. He kept his one arm on the table so it wouldn't get in her way, but returned the other to his thigh. He watched her as she got back to work. "I am not used to my wounds being tended to."

"Did you tend to your own wounds?" She went about gently brushing the soapy, wet towel along the ones at the top of his chest. They looked worse than they were.

"No," he mumbled. "A few times. If they were terrible. Most of the time, I could clean them and nothing more."

Her hand stopped. It certainly explained a few things. She had never commented on it, but she'd noticed the scars beneath his fur. She felt them any time she ran her hands across his body. It truly showed how little Markham cared for his people. Not that she didn't know it already, but still. It made her even more grateful he was out of there. "Normally, Kaylina or Santos tend to the wounded. It simply depends on the severity. Although, given the circumstances, it's probably best that Am and I handle this. Not that I suspect either would've uttered one word regarding your injuries."

"Did that count? What we did? We were not supposed to commit a crime against another. Or does that just mean against the ones that live here? We were not defending ourselves. They may have been hunting me—us—but we sought them out."

"Not according to the laws of the village. It's against anyone who lives here in the village, even if it wasn't within our bounds, unless provoked or defending yourself." Like Leo, but she didn't say that. Nope. She wasn't ready to think or talk about that. "They weren't members of our village. Whether you sought them out would be a moot point." Hopefully, her twin got the hint about that, too. Although, from what she'd already heard, it may not matter much. Her sister still had said nothing, and Logan's focus remained on Ambrosia.

"Okay. I am sorry that you felt all of that from me. I am not proud of feeling that way."

"Honestly, I was more afraid that—at that moment—it was going to get you killed. And, judging from your wounds, if you'd had your wits about you, half of this damage wouldn't have happened." She started a gentle cleanse on the lacerations above his abdomen. "Especially the ones on your back. If I had to guess, I'd say your opponent was smaller than you and went with a tactical advantage to take you down." It wasn't until she and Am had compared notes, then recognized that both of their mates had survived, that either of them got pissed off. Actually, that was putting it mildly. They'd both been livid.

"Yes, he was smaller than me. The one I faced. He had visions. If I had been in my right mind, he probably would not have gotten the upper hand. He leaped off of a tree into the clearing, landed on my back, and then would not let go. He bit my side when he threw himself on the ground and slid underneath me."

"Like I said. Tactical advantage." It hadn't been hard to identify. It was a move she had pulled herself a time or two. Of course, that was in sparring sessions. This... gods, *this*. This was different. On a whole other level. Her gaze flicked over to her twin and Logan. Her sister had been way more pissed off than she was and still appeared to be furious. It had taken some teeth pulling, but she'd finally figured out why. Gods, they definitely *could not* do this again. He'd promised he wouldn't, and she believed him. "Last one." Jo refocused her attention on the last claw strike. She'd tended to all the rest: the ones on his back, the front and back of his neck, his face, and now his chest.

"I felt none of it when it was happening. Most of them are so far gone, they feel no pain." Pierce exhaled a soft breath. "I know I have said it, but I will say it again. Never again, I swear. I will not fight unless it is to defend myself or a loved one."

"That's good because if you do, I promise you haven't seen just how enraged I can get." As she finished with the last wound, she realized it really only needed to be washed. "This doesn't actually need stitches. That's good. I'm sure you're ready to rest. You need help to the bedroom?"

He nodded. "I feel as though I could sleep for a *penumbra*."

"I'm sure you do. After we get you in bed, I'll grab the ointment from the bathroom. It will keep the sutures from scarring." She set the cloth in her hand aside and held out her palm to help him up.

Pierce opened his mouth, then snapped it shut again. Taking her hand, he pressed a kiss to the side of her throat as he used the table to stand up out of the chair.

A small smile tugged at the corners of her mouth. Maybe he wasn't as hard-headed as his brother. Idiotic, maybe, but not hard-headed. She waited, letting him take as long as he required to get to his feet.

He squeezed her hand before they headed to their bedroom, steadying himself against the wall as they started down the hall. The closer they got, the more the exhaustion pulled at him. "Will it be alright if I lay down while you put the ointment on me?"

"Yes. That's fine. It'll be easier that way, anyway."

"Okay." It took several minutes and some maneuvering, but as he finally laid down on his stomach, he groaned and shut his eyes. One of his arms hung off the side. "This feels fantastic."

She snickered. Yeah, she bet it did. "I'll be right back." Leaving their bedroom, she jogged down the corridor to the bathroom to collect the ointment.

"Ambrosia, I—"

"Don't *even* bother to apologize, Logan. You've said it before and it obviously doesn't mean shit."

Jo paused mid-reach and peered around the jamb. She hadn't expected her brother-in-law and sister to say anything to one another. Apparently, that wasn't the case.

"Ambrosia, please. I am truly sorry."

"Okay. You're sorry. Does that mean if, given the chance, you wouldn't go out and do it again? You don't have to answer. I already know the answer's *no!*" Ambrosia snapped. "You went hunting, Logan! Hunting! With no regard for your life. And maybe, if this was the first time, I could... I could deal with that, but this is the *third*. You're always sorry afterward. Except it doesn't change!"

This might be a good time to return to her and Pierce's bedroom. It would be rude to intrude. If Ambrosia needed to talk, she'd be there, willing to listen. With the ointment in hand, Jo made her way back to their room at the end of the hall, shut the door most of the way behind her, and climbed up on her side of the bed. She didn't really need to point out that they were fighting. No doubt Pierce heard it as well as she did. "This, uh, this might be a little cold, but it'll help tremendously," Jo said, keeping her voice low.

Her mated tried not to move as she spread the salve on him. He let out another groan. "Feels great, actually. Though your touch feels a million times better. Might fall asleep on you."

"You are right. If I had to do this over, I would take the same actions. The more I learned of what happened to both of my sisters in my absence, the more I—" Logan started.

"No. No. No. You do *not* get to use them as an excuse again. Because that's why you kept going back to Belly of the Beast after the first fight. I even offered for you to use Zancle's. You declined it, saying that you couldn't take that chance, but you were *already* taking a chance. Every damn *umbra* you went out there. And even now!" Ambrosia screamed.

Sensing her mate tense up, Jo got off the bed and shut their bedroom door all the way. While it seemed neither of them wanted to utter a word about her sister and brother-in-law's argument, easing that wooden slab shut would help some. "Sleep will be good for you. Once I'm done with this, I'm going to clean up everything at the table. We'll probably want to change the bandage on your side later."

"Okay. Remind me when I am fully coherent that I owe you something extremely special, my queen."

"I told you why I could not use Zancle's. I would not put you at risk like that," Logan retorted.

"Oh, but it's okay for you to put yourself at risk? That's bullshit and you know it. I need you here, and I can't even trust that you'll think about that before you run off and do something like this again. I've bandaged you and stitched you back together. Lilli *doesn't* need to see you like this. Stay here for the next couple of *umbras*. Maybe by then, you'll come to your senses."

Jo heard the simple sound of her twin's talons click against the wooden floor as she crossed the foyer, and then the front door slammed shut. Shit. That sounded beyond bad. Grimacing, Jo stood there at her bedroom entrance for a minute. Shaking what had just happened from her head, she returned to her spot on the bed and continued rubbing ointment on her mate's back. What was the last thing he had said? Um, right? "Okay, but it's unnecessary. We take care of each other. That's how a relationship works."

"Just because it may not be necessary does not mean I do not want to do it." Getting his arms underneath him, Pierce let out a grunt as he attempted to push himself up. "I should take that to him. The ointment."

"No, you need to rest." Not to mention, he was in no position to do much of anything or even hit some places that Logan wouldn't be able to reach. "I'll take care of it."

Pierce hovered for a moment, and then slowly lowered himself back onto the mattress. "Alright," he practically whispered. "Thank you, love."

"You're welcome." It was what family was for. Well, what they were supposed to be for, anyway. "I love you." Jo pressed a gentle kiss to the back of his head and climbed off the bed. "Go to sleep, my king. I'll be around when you wake up."

He reached over blindly and found her hand, bringing it to his mouth and kissing her wrist over their entwined initials. "I love you too, my queen." He gave her hand a squeeze before releasing it.

Standing there, she just stared at him. "They'll be fine." Both of them had clearly heard the argument. Loud and clear. With a small nod, Jo left their bedroom, cracking the door on her way out into the hallway.

"Ambrosia... uh..." Logan's words trailed off.

"It's okay. I know." Stepping back into the dining room, she held up the ointment that she'd used. "Let me get this on your face and chest. It'll keep everything from scarring up."

He let out a heavy sigh. "I deserve the scars."

"No, you don't." Neither of them did. They already both carried so much weight in emotional scars. The physical didn't need to match.

"Yes, I do." He paused. "She was right. I got angry that all this time, I was not there to help my sisters... or even be there for Pierce. I feel as if I let them all down."

"You can't change what happened." Without arguing further with him over the ointment, she walked over to the chair where he still sat and put some on his face. When he again tried to stop her, she shot him a look, and he stopped. "Going out and trying to make up for the *solaris* you've lost won't do anything but eventually get you killed. The two of you got lucky today."

"Is that what you think? That I am trying to make up for the *solaris* I lost?"

"I think both of you, in your own way, are trying to make up for a lot with your sisters. Because you can't let the past go." Her hand halted briefly, hovering over his cheek. There she was, lecturing him on letting go of what had happened, and it wasn't something she'd done herself. She hadn't forgiven... Jo glanced toward her and her mate's bedroom. Maybe it was time that changed. Clearing the thoughts from her head, she focused on her brother-in-law. "All you can do now is to be in the present and concentrate on your future."

Another sigh left him. "Ambrosia does not trust me."

"Give her an *umbra* to cool down, and I'll work with Zinnia and my mother to get Lilli out of the house tomorrow. Then you can talk to Am. But you need to be honest with her." Altering direction, Jo coated the lacerations on his chest.

Logan offered her a faint tilt of his mouth. "Thank you, Jocasta. More and more, I see why my brother fell in love with you."

"He couldn't resist my charm," she teased. It was certainly much more than that, but she didn't think she needed to further explain it. Instead, she got salve on the places that her sister had stitched. "Alright. You're done. Why don't I get you settled in Zinnia's—"

"The couch is fine. I will not put my sister out."

Yep. Stubborn ran on Pierce's side of the family, too. Her sister had already ignored each request she made to their mindlink. Hopefully, she was right about one night being enough. "Okay. Fine. I'll talk to Zinnia and see if she's okay crashing over there tonight. That way, you can rest properly."

"Thank you for understanding."

Maybe she did, but that didn't mean she wouldn't support her sister with whatever came of this argument. Still, she prayed they would overcome it. They all deserved happiness.

Chapter Twenty-Nine

Jo hadn't taken this path in nearly a month-and-a-half. The last time she'd visited the basin, which hadn't occurred since—she shook her head, cutting the thought off. Last night, as she laid in Pierce's arms, she'd decided she was ready to go back. She'd been ready a couple of days before, but he'd still been healing from the injuries he'd gotten a week earlier, and she couldn't face this alone. Not that she wanted to enter through the basin. No. This time, they'd trek to the top and take the waterfall. It was the only way she thought she could get in it again. And it was too important not to return. At the bottom of the path, her amber gaze swung from the plunge pool to the frothy cascade of water to the rocky outcropping. That was their destination. Inhaling a deep breath, she glanced at her mate. "We'll take this to the top."

"You lead, my queen." He gave her hand a gentle squeeze and brought it to his lips, brushing a kiss over her knuckles. "I will be right here with you."

Jo stared at the dirt path. *It doesn't go to the basin,* she reminded herself. The top of the waterfall wasn't any easier, just for a different reason. But she didn't want this place tainted. It held too many wonderful memories. Loving memories. With her father, sister, and mate. She swallowed the lump in the back of her throat and tightened the grip on his palm as she started up the trail. Several years had passed since she'd gone to the top.

Pierce let her choose their pace. With their fingers laced together, she didn't give any attention to the sun-dappled trees they passed. Neither of them spoke as they traveled farther up the dirt trail. Her thoughts were heavy. So were his.

"I ever tell you how we found this place?" The joyous memories were easier to think of. Even if they led to unhappy ones. She could deal with the good and get to the bad. They were unavoidable, but she didn't want to think about them. Not just yet. There was a lot he didn't know. There was a lot she didn't know, too. But she was ready to bear it all, and so was he. Perhaps today would be the day for words, and together, they could find the strength to utter them.

His thumb stroked over the back of her hand. "No, I do not believe so."

"My father found it before Am and I were even one. I learned to swim before I could walk." She snickered. "I remember the first time I ever gave him a panic attack. He and Am were down in the basin, and I had made my way to the top of the waterfall. When I got there, I called out 'Daddy!' The look on his face."

He chuckled softly. "He must have been terrified. Did you jump?"

"Oh, he was, and yes, I did. I jumped, and he rushed over to where I came up, scooped me up in his arms, and held me for a few minutes. Then told me not to scare him like that again." A faint giggle bubbled up from her.

"But that was not the last time, I am sure. You were an adventurer." He nudged a stick out of her path with his foot as they walked. Although her mate didn't point them out, she noticed his ruby eyes continuously scanning for loose roots. He seemed concerned she might trip and lose her footing.

"No. It wasn't. Just the first of many." She'd never considered herself an adventurer, but perhaps she was in her own way. Jo followed the path as it veered off and leveled out. The rushing water of the river crashing below resounded, though they still had perhaps a half a mile to go.

"Logan and I were the same way. Zinnia too, for a while. We gave our mother many panic attacks when we were young. But I think a part of her encouraged it."

"Like the time you told us about the deer." Jo tilted her head as her eyebrows furrowed. "You know, I think my father did, too. He kept bringing us back here. I even remember the time he jumped with us. He only did it once. I asked him about it. His response to me was, 'Canines were not meant to jump into water from great heights.'"

"She told us she did not want to stifle our adventure. She just wanted us to be careful. Losing us... it was her greatest fear."

Jo bit her bottom lip and canted her head at him. "How do you feel about jumping in with me?"

Her mate raised an eyebrow. "That is not something I have done before. Your father was right. We are not made for that." Pierce snorted. "But if you would wish me to, I would love to do so."

"I would." She didn't think she'd have the courage to do it without him. The height never bothered her, but the last time she'd made that jump... Her steps slowed as the shimmering blue water came into view. "I haven't made this jump in a long time."

Pierce stopped her and turned her to face him. He stroked her hip and cupped her cheek. "You know I am with you through anything and everything, my queen. If this is something you need me for, then I will gladly do it with you."

Jo leaned into his touch, covering his hand with her own. She didn't believe she could get into the water any other way. But she desperately wanted to return, to overcome the thoughts that haunted her. The things she'd refused to talk about. "Three *umbras* before my father left. That's the last time I made this jump." The basin had been easier to deal with after his death. Then that had gotten ruined. Too much pain. Too much death. For both of them. And it was time they *both* allowed themselves to move past it.

Pierce brushed a soft kiss across her lips. "We will make this jump together, my love. Just as we will make them throughout the rest of our lives." Together, they would bring happiness back to this place. Wash away the terrible memories, and return it to what it had been before. A place full of cheerful memories of her father. And the place where their love blossomed.

Her gaze lifted to his. She could see the affirmation in those bright ruby eyes of his. "Together."

He kissed her again, then wrapped his arm around.

Jo inhaled and exhaled another deep breath as they continued forward. The rushing falls reached her ears. The faint hint of salt hit her nostrils. She'd always preferred it to the harsh ocean waters. Nothing would make her go out there. "I've missed this place." The chirping birds. The woodsy scent of the forest.

"It is very peaceful." He held her closer to him as they inched toward the edge. "I think terrible memories have stolen a lot of both of our peace. Perhaps this is the first step to taking it back?"

The harmony they'd found within one another had cracked. Could this be as he suggested? A step to reclaiming it? Was that why she'd decided the waterfall was the way they had to take to the pool below? Instead of just climbing in like they used to do? Even if it meant sharing things he didn't know. Yeah. A way to take it all back. "I think it might be."

He lowered his head and kissed her, lingering for a moment. "Then let us take the plunge, my queen."

Gods, she loved this male. A little more every day. Even when she didn't think it was possible. She'd left her backpack and top at the bottom. For this trip, she'd gone with a swimsuit, something she hadn't done in years, and skimpy shorts. It was appropriate. Her gaze shifted to the boulder she'd always jumped from and then back to him. "I'm ready, my king."

As they climbed up onto the boulder, he lifted her up into his arms. "Shall we, my queen?"

She didn't expect him to pick her up. But she supposed it would be easier this way. Jo kissed him once more. "Let's."

He tightened his hold against her and leaped.

The free fall felt like it lasted longer than it actually did. The time they were airborne before they hit the water was freeing. In the arms of her mate, the male she loved with all her heart, a male who had rescued her in more ways than one. Then they hit the pool. It was a good thing the closest part of the waterfall was about twenty feet deep.

Their bodies rose to the surface and Pierce gathered her in his arms as his head broke through. He opened his mouth to speak, but his words got lost as he stared down at her. Hair plastered around her face, water dripping down her neck and over her arms, an exhilarated expression in her eyes. She felt it, all the love he had for her, in every part of his heart and soul.

Jo brushed her hair away from her cheeks and stroked the back of his head as they bobbed there in the water. Good gods, that was amazing. It was exactly what she needed. What they needed. To wipe the horrific memories away. Just to jump in, feet first. She fused their mouths together in a passion kiss.

He caressed the merfolk scales around her back and hips. "How did that feel, my queen?"

"Liberating." It was the only way to describe it. That one plunge made her feel lighter. As if some of the weight she'd carried on her shoulders over the year had left her. It wasn't the end all to every memory she had here at the waterfall and basin, but it was the first of new, joyful memories.

"That makes me happy to hear that." He kissed her again, deeper this time.

A quiet moan left her as her body warmed beneath him. It wasn't the reason for this trip. They hadn't spoken about the last thing that happened here. She had refused to speak of it. To think about it. Leo had gotten punished. The end. Except it hadn't brought her back to the basin. This was a way to wipe out the sorrow and bring forth the joy.

He growled softly and moved them toward the shore. Heat radiated from his body. Despite the desire she could feel burning through him, Pierce broke the kiss and rested his forehead against hers. "I am glad you wanted me to come here with you today."

"I couldn't have done it without you." She drank in the sensation of his fingers running along her spine. That feeling was something she'd never tire of, one that she found quite relaxing.

"You will always have me, my queen." He nuzzled her nose.

"I brought some food along for us. Something to munch on."

"That was a good idea. Means we will not have to worry about leaving for any reason."

"Nope. We have *lacunas* here." She'd even gotten someone to cover her at the bar tonight. And that had been difficult. She didn't like anyone touching her equipment. It was stuff she had mostly put together herself, with a little help, but it seemed like a good idea.

"I love the sound of that, my queen." Pierce brushed a kiss across her lips as they reached the shore. He helped her to a large patch of green grass, laid down, and held his arm out for her. "What made you choose today? To come back here?"

Lowering her body, she curled up on his chest so she could better hear his heartbeat. He let out a contented sigh. "I don't know. It was just something that told me it was time. To put it all behind us."

His fingers trailed over her side and the scales on her hip as he held her. "I think you are right. I had a thought when we were at your mother's place, after Zinnia arrived here. There are many things about me, my past, that I have not told you. And while many of them are very painful, I do not want there to be anything we do not know about each other."

Had that been what set her down that path of memories? The warnings she'd ignored? Maybe. "I'll always listen."

"I know you will. So will I."

Staring out at the sparkling water and how the sun's rays glistened, she thought back to that morning, the one she hadn't thought about since it happened. The way the water had restricted her movement and tightened around her body. Her focus had been so much on the restraint of her arms, she had paid little mind to what he'd done to her ankles. Just that Leo had stopped her from going anywhere. A shudder passed through her as she leaned into her mate. A tear rolled down her cheek. "I don't like to think about that *umbra*. What could've happened."

Pierce's claws scraped against the ground. He gently wiped her tear away, and then returned to caressing her hip and lower belly, his touch unhurried. "I know you do not. What he wanted to do... I knew. I know many like him. He has no honor. And you did not deserve that. I am glad that I got here in time, though I wish I had been quicker."

"I wish I had listened earlier." She sighed. The statement may not have made much sense to him, but it had been her stubbornness. Not that she blamed herself entirely. She didn't know what would've occurred if he hadn't been in her life at all. "Leo was my sparring partner for two *solaris*." Jo paused. The question didn't have to be asked. She knew what he wanted clarified. "Yes, those first bruises you saw came from him. I didn't..." This was harder than she thought. "It wasn't the first time I ended up with bruises during one of our sparring sessions. A few *cycles* before that, I'd gotten a black eye. Ambrosia was so mad at me. She tried to tell me then. She had her suspicions, and I didn't listen."

The rise and fall of his chest remained steady as his fingers continued their gentle strokes. "You cannot blame yourself for his actions. Nothing you did or said made him do what he did. Nothing you could have done or said would have deterred him either. Some just have that inside of themselves."

"I just... I never thought... I mean, two *solaris*, I thought I knew him." And she hadn't. She hadn't known him at all. He had hidden it well. If Pierce hadn't shown up when he had—that's what got her. A fresh tear slid free. What would've happened? And she had been helpless to stop it.

So many things could've gone wrong. They hadn't, but they could've. And the signs had been there. The number of times she ended up with bruises. One on her thigh. Multiple times, she had them on her arms. The black eye. And she had overlooked it all, chalking it up to a normal result of sparring.

Pierce tightened his hold on her. "There are some in this world who are just very good at hiding their true selves. They can hide it from everyone, even those they are closest to. They will hide it away for self-preservation, or until they can get what they want. Nothing about you changed him, love. I suspect he was always that way. Just an excellent actor. Where I come from, some of us had to hide the goodness in ourselves, not the evil. They rejoiced evil, welcomed it with open arms. Were he a shape shifter, he probably would have done rather well there."

She wiped at the wetness on her face. It hadn't occurred to her how much it still bothered her. How much she blamed herself for not seeing the truth. For not listening to those who tried to warn her. Ambrosia. Bruce. They had all seen it and she hadn't. Jo swallowed hard and replayed Pierce's words in her head. If Leo had always been that way, how had others seen through the façade and she hadn't? There was one experience she had with Leo that explained all that. She couldn't line up the two versions because they were opposites. But maybe that had been part of the mask. Lifting one knee up and resting it on Pierce's thigh, she focused on the steady thrum of his heart. The combination of that strong beat and his stroking of her ears relaxed her. "Like you had to hide your goodness?"

One hand remained on her ears as he stroked her thigh. He placed soft kisses on her cheeks and then laid his head back on the grass. "Yes," he said. "I did things there that I am not proud of. That I dislike thinking about. And still feel guilt over. But they were necessary, to keep as much of my true self hidden as I could."

There should be no reason for him to feel like that. He had to protect himself. And his family. She opened her mouth and stopped. It was exactly what she'd done, wasn't it? It didn't make it any less true. What would've happened if he hadn't kept himself safe? They may not be together. That... that would be gut wrenching. "I'm glad you did what you did. No matter what you did, because it made it so you could be here with me."

"I know what I did was necessary, but that does not lessen the guilt any." He sighed. "There is a fighting ring in the village. When a male had done something, Markham deemed wrong, he would often put them in the ring with Informants. Usually two, sometimes three. They had to fight until they could no longer stand. They made me many times inflict harm against those who, to my knowledge, had truly done nothing to deserve it. At least, nothing that would lead me to believe that they did. I tried to do minor damage without arousing suspicion, but that does not change that I still caused injury. I still drew their blood."

Jo sifted her fingers through his fur as she listened. She sensed how much it bothered him. That he hated having to be in that position. And maybe, under normal circumstances, they had done nothing wrong, but she knew that didn't matter. With Markham in charge, nothing in the shape shifter village was normal. "That you feel guilty over it shows what kind of male you are. Not to mention, you had little choice."

"Were it not for my mother and my siblings, I would have refused him. I know what consequences that would have brought. I tried to makeup for what I had to do for him in other ways. Ways that were reckless and dangerous."

"Oh? How so?" As she continued creating trails along his fur with her fingertips, a calm settled deep inside of him.

"There had always been rumors of Markham's powers to read minds. I learned to shield my mind as quickly as I could growing up. Hid information from him over the *solaris*. Spoke many lies. If I found shape shifter hybrids while out scouting, I helped to fake their deaths and reported to Markham that they had perished. Two Informants died by my hand during those times, and I helped three hybrids go further into hiding to remain undetected. At least, to my knowledge, they have. If Markham discovered them, their executions were public. I feigned interest in females that were being sought after by vicious males within the pack. Derrick's sister was one of them. If I was present in the village, she remained untouched. It was the least I could do for him, after what he did for Logan."

That explained how they'd kept their relationship a secret for as long as they had. All that he'd done to help other hybrids warmed her heart. Not to mention how he protected females. But she didn't understand the last part. She knew they had accused Logan of something, but she had never questioned what, exactly. Maybe what Derrick had done had something to do with that. "What did he do?"

"In my eyes, Derrick saved his life. When they falsely accused Logan of a crime, he was absent from the village. Markham banished him from the pack and our father disowned him. With Markham, banishment equals death. He issued immediate orders to hunt Logan down and execute him. I tried to leave, to find Logan and let him know, but my father would not allow me, our sisters, or our mother to leave. Derrick did. He told me later that he had found Logan and told him what had happened. Told him to go into hiding. I would like to think that, even if he had not, Logan would still be here. But I do not know."

So many of them had looked out for one another. It sounded a bit like what her mother had described with her father, at least without going into details. The thing was, they could never know what would've occurred if they hadn't taken certain actions. "I see why you've always considered him one of your friends."

"Yes. Though we grew apart over the *solaris*, I still consider him one of my closest friends. A brother. And his sister, she took care of Lilli when I could not."

"It's good that you had people to help you." She pressed a soft kiss to his chest. "I suspect it helped you emotionally, even if you didn't know it."

He stroked her spine and nuzzled her ears. The one part identifying her shape shifter genes. What she'd hidden almost her whole life. The day they'd met flickered across her mind. When she'd revealed her pointed, furry ears. Even then, she'd known she could trust him. And now, every time his fingers or touch came across her ears, she felt seen and treasured. How could he doubt any part of who he was when she saw it so clearly?

"Maybe. I have not thought about it like that. I could not put much thought into emotions there. There were times they slipped out. Mostly anger. Rarely sadness. I learned quickly how dangerous emotions were."

"I imagine there was a lot you couldn't do there. Especially, allow your emotions to be shown. They can be a tool to be used against you."

"That is true. And they were." The fur of his cheek tickled the tips of her ears. "Sometimes it was Markham. Sometimes it was my father."

Gods, one she expected, the other, not so much. Though, as she thought back on some conversations she'd heard between him and Logan, the one with her mother about her father and his father, maybe it shouldn't have surprised her. She returned to gently caressing his chest, running her fingers through his fur. "You should never have had to endure that."

His fingers lazily trailed up and down her spine. "Please do not stop doing that," he stated. "Your hand upon me, it helps." He was quiet for a few moments. "It was not what I endured that was so painful. I could take that. I would have taken more."

He didn't have to say anything else. She knew he'd gone through a lot to protect his sisters. And sometimes, he hadn't been able to. She understood that had to be difficult. Something he blamed himself for, even if it wasn't his fault. Pressing another kiss to his chest, she traced patterns across his skin. "Your sisters."

"Yes. My mother too." His mouth pressed in displeasure. "Not all my sisters, though. Not Dahlia. She was always his favorite." There was no jealousy or anger in his tone, just resignation. "She is just like him. He enjoys causing pain. And if it gave him coin, that was just a bonus. She finds humor in it. I tried to protect Zinnia. Until she made me promise to leave things alone. She could not handle suffering through what she did if I kept getting punished for intervening. So, I focused on Lilli. I did what I could for her. It was never enough."

Gods, what the females in his family had gone through. It made sense why her mother connected so quickly with Zinnia and Lilli, though. "I'm certain she knows you tried as hard as you could to protect her."

"I hope she does. Though she hated I got punished as well. She never said so, but the look in her eyes... I know it broke her heart each time. I did not want to cause her further pain, but I had to do something. My mother was gone. Zinnia did not want my aid. Things were already so horrible for her. I needed her to know that someone cared for her enough to..." A tear rolled down his cheek. "There came a point, after a terrible one, where she stopped telling me when it would happen. I would still see sometimes, but only if I was in the village and heard... or if I walked in on it. I would come home and Devina would be tending to her. Or she would pretend to be asleep, though I could smell her tears and blood." Another tear slid down his face.

Jo brushed the wetness away with her thumb and cupped his cheek. The heartache he felt for what his sister had suffered. Sorrow that he couldn't prevent it from happening. Guilt that it had happened at all. That he couldn't protect her. Honestly, she didn't know what she could even say. There wasn't anything she could think of that would assuage any of what he felt. She pressed her lips to his chest, over his heart. "As much as you were trying to protect her, she wanted to protect you."

He leaned into her hand. "She may not think so, but she is stronger than me. She has a spirit like our mother did. Zinnia gave in to what was happening to her and did not fight it. I cannot fault her or blame her for that. Fighting the ways of the pack changed nothing, and she dealt with the reality the way she needed to. But Lilli... even when her strength weakened, and she came so close to giving up, she never stopped fighting. She drew blood and left marks on many. She has been my little warrior since the *umbra* she was born."

Jo beamed at him. Did he even realize the way he'd spoken of Lilli? Probably not. But it confirmed everything she ever saw in him. "You're going to make a wonderful father one *umbra*."

He kissed the top of her head. "I hope so. The only role model I had growing up was not even my own. I truly hope that, when that *umbra* comes, I will be a good one."

"I believe you will." With all her heart, she did. Although the idea of pregnancy frightened her, she knew he'd be there by her side throughout everything. And when they had young, he would be an amazing father, a wonderful partner to raise them with. "Who did you have as a role model?"

"Your father."

It almost seemed like kismet that they'd bumped into one another. He had always said he didn't know her father very well. Though, whatever time they spent around one another obviously had an influence. "What's a memory you have of him?"

His eyes lit up. "The first time I remember him saving my mother." Pierce paused. "I was young. Just five. I do not really remember. But Logan was very little. I was taking a walk with her in the woods when three males from the village came upon us. They harassed her, and then worse. She was mated. They should not have been allowed to even touch her without permission. But they told her Ailwin had given them permission to do so. I tried to fight them off; bit one, but he threw me into a tree. I heard a snap, and the pain was so great I could not move. Later, they realized I had broken my leg. They came very close to..." His words trailed off, and he visibly swallowed. "It was hard to focus on what happened next. But I remember a lot of growling, and the sounds of fighting. My mother crawled over to me and held me against her, kept my head tucked away so I would not see. When she allowed me to look up again, your father stood over us. He had blood all over him, but he picked me up and held me, then helped her to her feet. He walked us all the way back to the village. When my father saw us entering the clearing, he was furious. He jerked my mother away from your father and confronted him. Told your father that it was not his place, and demanded that he put me down." Pierce gave her a toothy grin. "Your father gave him a glare the likes of which I had never seen. I still remember the words he spoke. He said, 'It is unfortunate that you are their father. As long as I am around, your family will always know that someone is there to protect them.' And then he carried me off to the shaman's hut and ensured they tended to my leg before taking me home."

She could see the image clear as day and heard her father's husky voice as he said the words. That deep baritone that she loved to listen to for hours. "He really was one of the best males."

"He truly was. I aspired to be like him. It brings me joy still that he was there for my mother as much as he could be. She was very young when she had me, only sixteen. They had sold her to my father. Her brother had died before I was born. I do not know the details, though, she never told me. Ailwin did not allow her to have friends. At least, none that I ever met. I think, were it not for Galenus, she would have been alone."

Good gods, sixteen. She was still causing trouble at sixteen. No way would she have ever been prepared to be a mother. And that father of his... gods. The more she learned, the more she was grateful her father had been there as much as he could've been for Pierce's family. Her father had always put others before himself. He'd even done as much in Migas. He'd helped wherever aid was required. "I'm glad you guys had him." It was nice to hear things about her father. Although she missed him, hearing stories in some small way, it felt like he was still here with her.

"Me too. I wish I had gotten to know him better, but my father hated him so much. Truthfully, I think he was afraid of him. They fought often, in and out of the fighting ring in the village. My father could never take him down unless he had help."

She didn't know how his father physically compared to her own. Though if his and Logan's height and size were anything to go by, she could see why. Her father had been quite tall, a mountain of a male. "I think he would be proud of the male you've become." She was certainly quite proud. "I think he'd even be okay with you as my mate."

"Gods, I hope so. My father instilled nothing in me but fear and anger. I never wanted to be anything like him. He was just someone to endure.

Galenus, he showed me what a male was supposed to be like. How a male was supposed to treat his family, treat others. He made it well-known that, despite it being fairly normal in the village, the dynamic of my household was not normal at all." Pierce turned his head, his gaze meeting hers. "My mother…" There was a gleam in his eye. "She would have loved you. I know she would have."

She beamed at him. All she had to know about his mother was his memories. Not that it changed her opinion any. "I would've loved her too." They would've been a family full of powerful females. Each in their own unique way. A small chuckle left her mouth. It occurred to her that, if they had come to the village years ago, she and her sister would've been quite young, perhaps not even a twinkle in her father's eye. Despite the losses and struggles they'd faced; they had found one another. Although she knew he missed his mother as much as she missed her father, maybe things had happened the way they were supposed to.

He brushed the back of his knuckles across her cheek. "I love your laugh. Even the small ones. What were you thinking just now?"

"How strange it would've been if we had grown up together."

"That would have been strange, yes. I wonder if we still would have ended up together. But I think so. While I wish a lot of things had happened differently… a lot of things… if your father had gotten us out of the village, Lilli would not be here. She fought so hard to come into this world, and to stay in this world. I could not imagine her not being here."

"I think we would've too. It would've certainly been interesting to see him interrogate you and question your intentions with his daughter." She giggled. "But that's true. Lilli wouldn't be here and our family wouldn't be complete without her."

"Oh, yes, very interesting. Considering my intentions upon meeting you were not very honorable." He snickered. "I never told Lilli. About her birth. I should have, but the memories are so painful. That first dinner we had, after we went to your mother's, Zinnia ended up letting something slip and…" He shrugged. "I feel bad that it did not come from me." His fingers trailed up and down her spine. "I feel bad that a lot of things with her have not come from me. The painful memories kept me from talking about the happy ones."

"That happens. Even when we don't mean for it to, the awful memories have a tendency to override the wonderful memories." She glanced out toward the basin. They had laid here long enough; her suit and shorts had mostly dried. Staring at the small ripples the water created from the falls, it reminded her how easy it was to disturb someone's peace. If allowed. And this place, it had been full of wonderful memories. Those first looks they shared when he came out of the trees. The day he held her as she cried and then made love to her for the first time. The time they had spent nearly all day together. None of that included the memories she had with her father and sister here. "We can't let the terrible memories take away the good ones. I think it just takes time to get there. But we will. And maybe, some things she still doesn't know, you'll be able to talk to her about."

"You are right, my queen. Letting the terrible memories override the good ones, it made me wallow in them. Focus on the sadness. I do not want to do that, not anymore. I have so much to be happy about, thankful for." He nuzzled her ears and kissed the top of her head. "I think I will be able to. Now that things do not have to be hidden, and we can openly express our emotions. I want to tell her stories about our mother. About Logan and Zinnia and I when we were young. I want her to know how strong she is to have endured all she has and still have a smile on her face." He pulled her fully onto his chest. Starting at her ears, he stroked up and down her back. He stared into her eyes and kissed her softly. "You are so wonderful. I hope you know that."

"Mmm, I do. But sometimes, it's nice to be reminded." She brushed a kiss across his lips and caressed the nape of his neck.

He let out a low rumble. "I will remind you every single *umbra*, my queen."

"You're pretty amazing yourself. And I agree. The terrible memories, they don't get power anymore. Neither does Leo. Neither does Markham. They don't get that power. We hold it." This was their place. No one could take that away from them.

He pressed his forehead to hers and cupped her cheek. "I am sure the terrible memories will still find their moments where they sneak in, but I know you will always be here with me, to make them go away again."

"Yes, I will, my king. I will always be here." She placed a tender kiss on the tip of his nose.

"As I will always be here for you." Pierce sat up and adjusted her so she straddled his lap. Staring into her eyes, he let out a sigh. "There is something that I must do, but I do not feel right doing it without telling you first."

Oh, she didn't like this look. Her immediate thought was no; whatever it was, the answer was no. He didn't have to do it. Resting her hands on his shoulders, she bit the inside of her cheek. She could hear him out. Whatever he thought he had to do, she could listen. She could do that. "Okay?"

Pierce inhaled and exhaled a deep breath. "I have told you that some mourned your father. But only that. I have not told you the details of his death, and while I would if you wished for them, I would prefer not to. But..." His words trailed off. "After I learned of his death, and as soon as I could leave the village, I found where he lay. I gave him a proper ceremony." Her mate paused. "I did what was proper with his ashes. And I hid them. I must retrieve them. For you, your sister, and your mother."

She had no words. Tears formed in the corners of her eyes, though she tried not to cry. They hadn't even learned of his death for days after he'd left the village. When they had, they didn't have his body, his ashes... not that it had stopped them from celebrating his life and mourning his loss. The three of them had planted an apple tree along the forest edge for him. As for what had happened; over the years, all she ever had was suspicions based on rumors she heard of Métamorphe. Nothing concrete. It would make no difference if he confirmed her beliefs now. Nor would it offer any comfort. But her father's ashes, a proper ceremony... Jo blinked, and she choked out a sob. There had to be only one reason he was telling her. "How close? How close do you have to get?"

He cupped her face in his hands and gently wiped at her tears. "There is a hidden cave full of tunnels that Logan and I used to play in when we were little. But there is only one entrance. It is not in the village. But it is inside the boundaries."

Her throat tightened and her lungs constricted. Not in the village, but inside the boundaries. It was on the tip of her tongue to tell him no. It wasn't worth it. They had mourned her father's death. Then she thought of her mother and sister. Silently, she wept. Did it make her selfish? Not to want to risk her mate's life so they could give her father a proper send-off? They had said their goodbyes. Hadn't they? It had been over a month since Pierce had left Métamorphe. What if he came across Informants? Or worse, Markham? Gods, she was so conflicted. What if he took a spourgiff?

No, Santos would never agree to that. Maybe he could take Duke with him? He was a half-troll. No. He had young to consider. It left only one option. Otherwise, she said no. "You take Logan with you. And he has to tell Ambrosia first. And you come back. You come back to me in one piece." Tears streamed down her face. Not because she was thinking of her father, but because she feared what might happen. She was terrified he would go for something simple and he wouldn't return. That she would have to live her worst nightmare.

He brought her face to his and kissed her hard. Taking her hand, he placed it over his heart and covered it with his own, and rested his other hand on her chest. "On my honor, as a male and as your mate, not even Hades himself could keep me from coming back to you, my queen. I swear to you I will return. I will speak to Logan and ensure he speaks to Ambrosia first. But I ask that you do not tell your mother. I warred with myself about telling you; I did not want to give you false hope. But it will be dangerous and I could not go without you knowing. It would be cruel to give Lyrica that hope before she holds him in her hands again."

"I won't say anything to her," she whispered. It was all she could do. She was grateful he told her, even if still frightened her. Her father had said he would come back. No, this would *not* be the same. It would *not* end the same. Pierce would return to her. "If you get close and it looks like you can't, then please don't risk it. I need you here with me."

He lifted her hand to his lips, kissing her knuckles. "I promise." Gathering her into his arms, he held her tightly against him. "I know you are scared, but I will be as careful as possible. And I will come home to you. I just..." He shook his head. "He does not deserve to be there. He deserves to be with his family. And the three of you deserve to have him back."

He would be careful. He would come home to her. She repeated that in her head like a mantra as she buried her face in the crook of his neck. No. Her father's ashes didn't belong there. But she needed the male in her arms more. She prayed to the gods that somewhere her father understood that, and would protect her mate from above.

He didn't let her go. Nothing would assuage her fears of the possibility of him not returning. Not until he actually returned.

It was quite some time before she relaxed. She trusted him. Trusted that he would be as safe as possible. That he would come back to her. And if he had to talk to Logan, who had to talk to Ambrosia, it would be a couple of *umbras*, at least, before this even happened. When he left, she would know, and he would return. He promised he would come back. Nothing would keep him away from her. She had to believe that. Her racing heart finally settled to a steady rhythm. Her nerves calmed. She found safety in his arms and he would do everything possible to ensure that never ended.

Pierce leaned back just enough to look her in the eyes, his thumb stroking her cheek. "I love you, my queen."

"I love you, too, my king." She sat up and kissed him, pouring all of her love and concern into the depth of the kiss. He slid his hands to the back of her head, caressing her ears. When their lips parted, their gazes locked on one another. "I need you inside me now."

With a flash of his ruby red eyes, he growled, laid her down on the grass, and hovered over her. Pulling down the stretchy material of her swimsuit top, he took the tight rosy bud of her nipple between his teeth, sucking vigorously.

Oh, gods! Yes. She moaned as her back arched and she lifted her hips to get the rest of her clothes off. He could shred it for all she cared.

Capturing her breast in his mouth, Pierce quickly stripped her. Stretching one of her legs up, he dropped to his knees and slid deep inside her. "Fuck, yes," he barked out. Her other leg came around his waist as he took deep, unhurried strokes in and out of her.

"Yes!" Her talons curled, scraping against his ass as she lifted her hips, meeting his. Fuck. The way his girth filled her to the hilt nearly drove her insane with pleasure. Jo grabbed onto his biceps and raked her nails up and down, dragging her fingers through his fur. Each touch heightening the sensations, setting her synapses on fire.

Growling, he slid his hand to the apex of her thighs. His long fingers rubbed her nub, matching his rhythm as he pistoned in and out of her, setting her synapses on fire.

"Oh, gods! Don't stop!" Her thighs clenched as she continued to meet him, thrust for thrust. Digging her nails harder into his forearms, half-moons denting in his flesh beneath her touch, she grazed his ass with her taloned feet. The pressure building inside of her.

"Not stopping, my queen. Come hard for me."

Tightening her grip on his waist, she met each stroke of his shaft, thrust for thrust, and cried out his name as she pitched over the edge. An orgasm pulsated through her body, exploding all around him. Holding her against him, he roared out her name as he came deep into her sex. Then, with her still in his arms, he slid his warm and powerful hands to her ass and sat up so she now straddled him. He fused their lips together in a vigorous kiss.

Draping her arms across his broad shoulders, she stroked her fingers along his spine as their tongues entangled. Gods, he felt amazing. His nimble fingers flexed, digging into her taut cheeks. With his cock still buried deep inside her, every inch of her body throbbed, humming from their perfect union.

Pierce let out a low rumble. "Mmm. I love you so much, Jocasta. Everything about you." He trailed kisses along her jaw, nuzzling the crook of her neck and stroking it with his tongue. "I love you."

Her head fell back with a soft moan as she trailed a nonexistent pattern across the breadth of his thick shoulders, over his biceps, and then started all over. As if she hadn't explored his body a million times already. "I love you too, Pierce. How we fit together. It's perfect. I love you, with every part of me."

He licked the side of her throat as he leaned her back ever so slightly, skimming his lips and tongue down the valley between her breasts. "Mmm, you are perfect, my queen." As he hardened inside of her, his hips thrusted upward in a slow, yet steady rhythm, edging her closer to a breaking point.

Gods, no matter how many times they came together, she couldn't get enough. Taking her time to re-familiarize herself with the dips and curves of his body, she anchored her legs around his waist, lowered her hips, rocking against him. She relished the silkiness of his fur beneath her palms. A faint gasp left her mouth.

"I love the sounds you make for me." Latching onto her breast, he sucked on it and twirled his tongue around her nipple. A rumble deep in his throat vibrated against her.

"Oh, gods!" A shiver swept down her spine and she moaned. "I love your growl." Her fingers continued to roam over his bunched muscles. Every nerve ending in her body registered each movement he made. Each stroke of his rigid length had her body burning hotter and hotter. The sensations were so heightened. Much more than any other time, their bodies had come together.

Trailing his tongue across the apex, he captured her swollen breast in his mouth. The rhythm of his hips increased, but only slightly. "Are you going to come for me again, my queen?" He flicked the tip of his tongue across her nipple. His grip on her ass tightened as his fingers curved around her shoulder, drawing them closer together.

Each thrust came a little faster and a little harder, wiping away the memories that had threatened to steal this place from them. The fire in her body being stoked was like a volcano ready to burst. Her talons scraped against his ass as she raked her nails down his back, digging in with a bit more force. Her climax was right there on the edge. "Gods, yes!"

"Hades! Do you want to come on my cock, or do you want to come in my mouth?" he growled.

That was all it took to send her soaring over the cliff. Her inner walls clenched around him as another release slammed through her body, stronger than the one she had before. Her nails dug into him, as did her talons.

Her mate roared as his orgasm exploded out of him, his cock jerking and twitching inside of her, his release filling her and spilling over. Through ragged breaths, they stayed joined as their mutual release drew to an end. Neither uttered a single word as a comfortable silence passed between them. Not that either of them needed to say anything. Pierce pulled out of her and laid back on the grass, keeping her on top of him. Panting heavily, he caressed her spine.

Her fingers lazily stroked his chest, over his heart, as her labored breathing slowly steadied. They had both needed that. To feel each other close, inside one another's soul, as they connected in the most intimate way possible. It hadn't been just to wipe away the impressions from the last time they'd been here, but to remind them of everything they had to live for.

He nuzzled her ears. "Mmm. Incredible, my queen. Always incredible."

"It was amazing, my king." She pressed a soft kiss to his chest as the feeling of utter contentment washed over them both. She would never grow tired of this. Every glorious moment she spent with him. There was still a road ahead of them to be traveled, but they would take each step at each other's side. "As always." Her stomach rumbled in response to the moment between them. She let out a short laugh. "I think we worked up an appetite."

With a small chuckle, he kissed her ears. "I am certainly starving." He tilted her head up, staring into her eyes. "Do you feel better now? About this place? Though I hope you know, if you ever need to speak more about it, I will listen. I will always listen to you."

"I do. We have too many wonderful memories here for me to let him take it from us." She brushed a soft kiss across his lips. "But if I need to talk about it more, I promise I will."

"I am glad to hear it, my love." A slow smile spread across his face. "Let us eat."

Chapter Thirty

In the treehouse, Gavin listened intently as the Informants' voices carried on the breeze outside.

"So what if he *is* up there?" Bardin called up. "We have better things to do than look for a runaway."

"The King wants him," Caith replied. "That is good enough for me."

"He will not be up there," Hunter said. There was a slight rustle of leaves as the male lounged against a branch. "Too close to the boundaries. It would be suicidal for him to hide here."

"And yet, I am going to check, anyway. If we do not, and someone finds him here later? Whose head will it be?"

"That would be his. It would be his head," Hunter answered.

"It is just an old treehouse, Caith," Bardin uttered. "Likely a hangout spot for some of the younger ones. Hunter is right. This close to the boundaries? He is being hunted. No one is that idiotic."

Keeping his breath as quiet as possible, Gavin swallowed hard as he inched across the floor in his humanoid form, his claws retracted so they made no noise. Fully camouflaged, he tried to see if there was a way for him to sneak out a window. The three Informants were on the side of the door, so a window was the best option. If it had just been Bardin, the situation would be different. The male might be an Informant, but he'd never seemed fond of Markham. But Caith and Hunter were both brutal when they wanted to be, and they always seemed to enjoy it.

He inhaled and exhaled silent, deep breaths, trying to stay calm. If his mate sensed his fear or stress—no, she couldn't arrive now. She couldn't get close. It would be bad enough they could catch her scent if they came any nearer.

"Caith. Let us go. I have somewhere I need to be. This is the last thing I wish to spend my time on," Hunter said.

"Do you think I care if you get your dick wet?"

"Markham instructed us to stay together. I am not sitting outside the brothel while you have sex, Hunter," Bardin asserted.

"So, go to the marketplace. Get something pretty for Keres. I will not tell on you."

"His scent is all over this area," Caith argued. "He may not be an Informant, but he will still bring a prize if we bring him back to Markham."

"Of course, his scent is all over the area," Hunter commented. "It has not been that long since we chased them out."

"A *penumbra*-and-a-half," Caith grumbled. "More than long enough for the scent to have dissipated if he did not frequent the area."

"If Markham wanted him so badly, why did he let him go?" Bardin posed.

"You know exactly why. You know what he is searching for. Or who, rather," Caith added.

"For the love of all the gods," Hunter mumbled. "Come on, Caith. Let this go today, and I will put in a word for you at the brothel. Perhaps they will let you inside again."

"After last time?" He chuckled low. "Yeah, I doubt they will ever let me inside the door again. That *was* a lot of fun, though."

"It was disgusting, is what it was," Hunter remarked. "Coming from me, that is definitely saying something," he scoffed. "Whatever. I am leaving. Do whatever you wish. I have a... date of sorts I would prefer not to miss."

"I do not know how either of you does *that*," Bardin countered.

"What? *Fuck* random females?" Caith laughed.

Hunter gave a slight chortle. "Not everyone can find *true love* in Métamorphe like you did, Bardin. Some of us prefer variety, and certain proclivities that are difficult to find elsewhere. Though I prefer them willing, unlike Caith here, I will certainly pass on the love thing. There is not a female in this world who would be better off finding that with me. But, anyway. I am off. Both of you do as you wish. We can rendezvous at the usual spot before curfew."

Gavin sensed two of them leaving, but Caith lingered for far longer than he was comfortable with. Though just a minute or two had passed, it felt like an eternity. Before he left, the male paced, his claws scraping against the bark as he leaped between a couple of branches. Outside of the natural sounds, stillness surrounded Gavin in the treehouse, but he could only hear his heart pounding in his ears. He sank to the floor, sliding down the wall, and brought a hand up to cover his face, while the other rested against his chest, feeling the tremors. *Shit. Deep breath. Deep breath.* Holy Hades, that had been close. Too close.

Maybe he shouldn't have stayed here. Perhaps he should have taken Derrick up on following him to the cabin. He might have met Parthenia and led her to the cabin. It was too late now. He had nowhere else to go.

He would just have to be as alert and more careful than ever before. It would be fine. Everything would be fine. They'd left without actually coming up to investigate—this time. *Shit.* He had to settle his heart, which was now beating like a drum. Thank Hades, Parthenia hadn't been here when they'd gotten close. *So close. Shit.*

"Gavin?" Parthenia called out as she stepped into the treehouse.

His chest still heaving, he didn't remove his camouflage as he moved across the floor. He gently pulled her onto his lap, burying his face in the sweet-smelling curve of her neck. Gavin inhaled and exhaled deep breaths, drawing in her scent. His breathing steadied. The pounding of his heartbeat eased. Slowly, the tremors that had wracked his body faded. "Right here. I am,"—he swallowed—"right here, love."

"What's wrong? What happened?" She wrapped her arms around him, her fingers gently caressing the back of his head.

A soft purr rose out of him. He nuzzled deeper into her neck, tightening his hold around her a bit. "Informants. Three. Close, they were really close."

Her feathers ruffled as her body tensed, a signal of unease. "How close is close? As in... the treehouse itself? The base of the tree? A lower branch?"

"One on the ground, two in the trees; a lower branch, same side as the door. They... they caught my scent. One wanted to come investigate further, to come into the treehouse. I was going to go out the window if he did, but they ended up leaving instead." He dropped his camouflage.

"That's… that's really close." She glanced over her shoulder before turning her attention back to him. "You don't think they'll come back, do you?"

Adjusting, he crossed his legs and settled her more in his lap. Running his fingers through her hair, he felt the feathery texture of her wings with his tail. He didn't think Bardin or Hunter would. Neither of them seemed interested. But Caith… "I… I do not know," Gavin said. "I want to say no, but one, maybe. It is possible."

"I don't like this. They didn't see you this time, but if they come back… There has to be…" Her words trailed off.

He didn't like it either. Not even a little. "I will just be as careful as possible. As careful as I can be." It was all he could do. It wasn't like he could stay with her in Pteryrina. They had already played with fire when he spent time with her there; almost every time he'd been there, someone had smelled him.

"Okay, careful is good." Parthenia returned to brushing her fingers along the nape of his neck. "And… I don't know, maybe there are other things we can do too. Things that might throw them off your scent."

"Maybe." His neck arched into her touch. Hades, nothing else eased him like she did, like her touch did, her scent, just her presence. "What about a cleansing potion? Or…" Was there even something they could use that could cleanse his scent enough? They would need a lot, whatever they used. He couldn't stay in the treehouse all the time. He had to get food and water regularly. And it would take a lot, too, to cleanse his scent from the treehouse itself. He sighed. "Mud, maybe? That can mask a scent." That could get messy. Small price to pay. Gavin shook his head a little.

Her brow wrinkled as she bit her bottom lip. After a moment, her eyes lit up. "Maybe if I put some wards in the surrounding trees. And then limit how often you go out for food, and when you do, use the cleansing potion before you return. Plus, I'll make a new ward for the treehouse too."

All good ideas. He already went out only once a day for food, but he could go out less. He wasn't unfamiliar with not having very much to eat. And he wouldn't ask her to bring him food. That could draw too much attention. Gavin smiled. "That sounds good, love. Thank you." He placed a soft kiss on her neck, his lips lingering for a moment. "I think if it were not for the protection charm you already placed here… he might have come up here. Caith. Two of them left. They did not really seem interested, but he lingered, just pacing for a couple of minutes. I could hear him outside, in the trees. But he did not come up here, even after the other two were gone."

"Still, we'll take extra steps. I'll bring food here. That way, there's less reason for you to hunt. Less of a chance they come across your scent again. I hate the idea of trapping you here, but at least... at least until we find a way off." Keeping her arms draped across his shoulders, Parthenia snuggled against him, breathing in his scent.

His purr deepened as she continued to stroke the back of his neck. Without a word, he gently lifted her, the feel of her weight familiar in his arms, and carried her to the pallet. Lying down, he pressed her to his chest, relishing the soft feel of her skin as he nestled his face into her neck. "As much as I might not like it, it is better to be trapped here for the time being and be safe. It is not forever." He licked at her neck, and with each touch, his fingers gently caressed her spine and the delicate tips of her wings. "Are you sure about the food? I do not want too much attention drawn to you." Her people watched her, too, closely. She'd said so more than once. "I do not want you in any danger."

"I won't be. They won't think twice about it as I take things to my apothecary. And I can take spices and herbs from my garden." Beaming brightly, she ran her fingers up and down his arm. "It'll be fine."

He wrapped his tail around her leg. "Okay. I just..." There were so many ways to finish that sentence. "We are going to be okay, right? We are going to be fine—and be free—soon, right?" Even if it wasn't true—because neither of them knew how long it would take to get off the isle and find true freedom, nor did either of them know what they would encounter until that time came—he just needed to hear the words from her. The Informants, as close as they'd been, had shaken him to his core. He didn't like it.

With a slight tilt of her chin, she met his gaze, her eyes locked on his. "We'll be fine. We'll get off this isle, just like we want, with your sister and her mate along with us. And we'll have a white house with a red door, like we've always dreamed." She pressed a kiss on both sides of his mouth. "I promise."

Gavin inhaled and exhaled a deep breath as he kept his gaze on hers. The images filled his head—everything they dreamed of for their home together—his sister and her mate with them, and the young they had dreamed of.

With the back of his knuckles, he gently stroked her cheek. "Yes, just like we have always dreamed." He smiled and kissed both sides of her mouth, then pressed his forehead to hers. "Thank you."

"Anytime, my love."

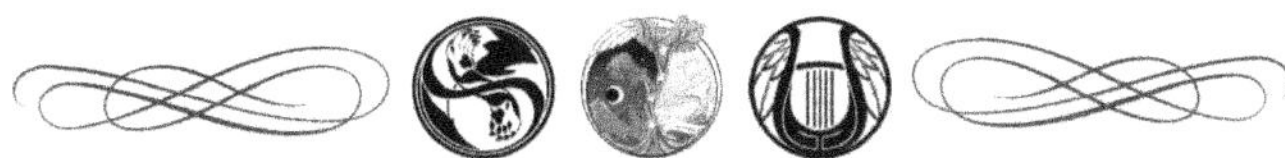

Pierce threw his camouflage on before he left Migas. He traveled around the marketplace and across the isle to between the chimera and fairy territories. Keeping to the fae border, he followed Lyrica's directions into the marshlands. He didn't have to go too far into them before he caught sight of the first hut. As he neared the small village, he paused on the outskirts, watching. He shed his camouflage and then passed through the trees, the crunch of leaves underfoot accompanying his transformation into his humanoid form.

Perhaps fifteen huts dotted the landscape, their weathered appearance a stark reminder of the structures he'd left behind in Métamorphe. Only a few people were visible. Each one who saw him averted their eyes. Great, this was going to be easy to get information out of anyone. He couldn't leave until he did, though.

Regardless of how many people he approached, he remained unheard, with nobody willing to speak to him. As the last person in the tiny clearing disappeared into a hut, he let out a huff of frustration. As he approached the first house, ready to knock, the wind changed direction, carrying with it a scent, and he knew his search was over. Frowning a bit, he turned his head and stared back into the trees. He'd only caught a whiff, but it was undeniably female. Pierce took a few steps toward it, then stopped, gazing at the landscape with a puzzled look. He saw nothing move aside from the expected swaying of the trees and the flight of birds. With the layout of the land here, though, it was difficult to tell. The dark greenery of the land was dense; barely any light made it through the trees. But he sensed eyes upon him, though he wasn't getting anything sinister about them.

Instinct drew him farther into the topiary. He crouched, listening intently to the sounds of the forest, his body tense. Nothing. But he caught the scent again, stronger than before. "I will not harm you," he whispered.

He didn't want it to carry back into the huts of the village. "I seek only some information. You can come out, or not; it is up to you. I came only to ask a few questions. I mean no one any harm."

After several long moments, he felt a sort of *knock* in his mind. He shook his head to clear it. He was accustomed to the feeling of someone probing his mind, yet this attempt lacked the malicious intent that accompanied Markham's intrusions. Not that it was enough for him to drop his mental shields. "Alright," he said, his voice quieter now. "Can I come to you? Do that again—once for yes, twice for no." After several longer moments, he felt another mental knock.

Pierce said nothing, just nodded and stood back up. Led by the smell, he found his way to a hidden nook within a cluster of trees a short distance from the village. It took him no time to see the female kneeling with her hand on her extraordinarily rounded belly. About five-feet-tall, maybe a couple of inches over, wavy, ash-colored hair that went all the way down her back, and light-colored skin. The trees concealed her easily because of the drab hues of her garments.

He crouched back down slowly, his eyes never leaving her, ensuring she saw his every move. "I am going to stay right here," he kept his voice low, "but I am going to camouflage, so I am not seen. Alright?" Once she nodded, he did exactly as he stated. "I will not ask you what you are hiding from; it is not my business. I come seeking information about a male named Xander. His sister, Lyrica, used to live in this village, though she has not been here for many *solaris*."

"I know of whom you speak," her tone meek. "I was a child when he was... taken. They made an example of him."

He sighed heavily; the sound echoing the discomfort he felt about the direction the conversation had taken. "What happened to him? Does he still live?"

She shook her head. "I will give you details; however, you must take me with you."

Shit. Definitely not the news he wanted to bring Lyrica. He scrubbed a hand over his face and then looked back at the female. Crouching in the trees, she spoke softly, avoiding his gaze, especially when she addressed him. He really didn't need to ask questions. "I can do that if you truly need to leave this place. You must know, though, that it could be very dangerous. I am hunted outside of my village. Are you in danger here?"

Her hand rested on her belly. Dropping her gaze to the rather obvious young growing inside of her, she inhaled and exhaled a deep breath. "It is not safe here for us. It is worth the risk."

"Say no more. Come quickly. I prefer to stay camouflaged while traveling, but I will protect you if it comes to that. Do you require help in your condition? Usually, I travel in my other form, but I can stay in this one too."

"I cannot walk fast if that is what you are asking." Her gaze lowered. "I do not look it. However, I have perhaps six to eight *penumbras* left."

"Quick and fast is what we are going to need in this situation." He thought for a moment. No, Jo wasn't the type of female prone to jealousy, but he still hated not being able to ask her first. They could do nothing to help it now. And, with as far along as she was, she didn't need to travel on foot all that way, anyway. "Would you consider allowing me to carry you? I would like to get us out of danger, and back to the village I live in as quickly as possible."

"I apologize; however, I do not know what you are."

"The apology is unnecessary. My species is called shape shifter. I have the form that you saw, and I also have,"—he removed his camouflage, waited a second so as not to startle her, and then shifted to his animal form—"this one." Judging by what he could make out from her size, kneeling as she was, he would still be at least a foot taller than her, if not more than that in this form, when she stood. He pulled his camouflage back on. "If you would consent to my carrying you, and it would make you more comfortable, I can carry you on my back."

"Varilliah," a male hollered across the village.

Her muscles clenched, and she swiftly maneuvered herself out of the alcove. "On your back is fine. We must go now."

His eyes darkened slightly. Yeah, he didn't like that voice. He liked even less the way she tensed at the sound of it. Removing his camouflage, he turned to face her, the forest floor crunching beneath him as he crouched down. "Get on, lean forward to brace yourself, and grab on wherever you feel most comfortable. You will not harm me if you grab my neck."

She glanced over her shoulder. The male strode through the village rather quickly. With some difficulty, she climbed onto his back, carefully maneuvering around her rounded belly. The female leaned forward, stretching as far as she could, and grabbed hold of his thick fur. "Please go. Go now."

Pierce stood up carefully and took off into the forest. He wanted to run, but he didn't want to jostle her. They moved much quicker than they would have had she been on foot, though. He didn't need to ask why she was fleeing. The male in her life, whoever he was, had clearly instilled a deep fear in her. "No matter what happens, I will not allow you to be taken back there. Alright?"

"Thank you," she whispered. "If you hear hooves, they have followed us."

With a sharp jerk of his head, he continued on. Just moments later, he heard the thunderous drumming of hooves on the earth. Gods, he wished he could speed up. At his top speed, she might not keep holding on to him. He didn't want to spook her, but as the sound grew nearer, he knew there wouldn't end up being a choice but to confront him. "I am going to have to stop. Stay low and do not let go of me. Just keep in mind that you are not going back there. I will allow no one to take you anywhere against your will."

"I will." His nostrils flared at the sharp, salty scent of tears that the breeze carried. "He will not let me go without a fight."

"I figured as much. But that is alright, because neither will I." Pierce slowed his pace so as not to jostle her. As he came to a full stop, he faced the direction the male had come from. It had been a long time since he'd forced his eyes to turn black, but it wasn't altogether difficult. He could smell the fear radiating from the female, which made him see red. A scent that had become a constant in Métamorphe. He'd not been able to do much then, but he could now.

Varilliah hunkered down to him as close as she could with her belly. Her fingers tightened on his fur, but he barely registered it. He stood still as the male approached. He was alone, riding on the back of a creature similar to that of a deer. By the looks of it, standing upright, he would be close to Pierce's shoulders in this form. Dark blue eyes and scales, blue-black hair, and bulging muscles. It wasn't hard to see how the male would overpower her. "If you enjoy breathing, you will turn around and head back the way you came."

"Return my property, shape shifter. *She* is of no concern to you." The male pointed at her.

Shaking against him, Varilliah pressed her face into his fur, a near-silent whimper of terror barely reaching his ears. He was all too familiar with those mannerisms, and coupled with the rest, all he saw in his head were flashes of his sisters and mother. He let out a low growl. "You have no property here. She is no longer *your* concern; she is now *mine*. Turn around and head back the way you came. I will not tell you again."

"Since when has Markham concerned himself with hybrids?" the male hissed. "Last I checked, Informant, he has no business with us, which includes *her*."

He had to be smart about this. Markham hadn't been able to read his mind, nor had this female been able to get in. If this male had that ability, he wouldn't be able to do it either. He really didn't want to get into a fight, especially not with the female on his back. And he didn't want to put her down, as that would only leave her exposed.

Pierce let a gleeful smirk spread across his face. "So, you are familiar with my mark. Good. Then you will know I did not get it for fun. It means something. And apparently, you know exactly what that is. What my King wants with her is none of your business. If you know of him, then you know what he is capable of. Let her go. I am sure you can find another female to *amuse yourself* with." Despite the churning in his gut, he maintained a composed expression.

A shudder passed through the female's body as the male hissed. "I hope he enjoys his new playtoy. For however long she lasts." With a scowl etched on his face, he turned the hooved creature around and, kicking up dust, vanished.

Pierce stood perfectly still until the male disappeared, and the rhythmic drumming of hooves faded away. Gods, he'd hated that exchange. Hated saying those words. Her overwhelming fear damn near broke his heart. He turned his body around, a small sigh escaping his lips, and started forward. "I am sorry I had to frighten you like that," he mumbled. "Varilliah, is it? I am not taking you to any male, for any purpose. I no longer live in the shape shifter village. The village I live in, which I am taking you to, is a well-guarded place of refuge. It is not within my power to grant sanctuary, but the Elder, Santos, is a wonderful male. If for any reason he does not give you sanctuary, I know somewhere safe I can take you, where you and your young will be cared for. I do not see Santos saying no to you, though."

Her muscles loosened, and she exhaled deeply, her whole-body sagging with relief. The air filled with a subtle yet unmistakable scent of fresh tears. "Thank you," she croaked. "Gods, thank you."

"You do not need to thank me, but you are welcome. My family was raised much the same as you seem to have been. My brother, two sisters, and I were lucky to have escaped the ultimate fate of our village. Our mother... was not so lucky. The village I am taking you to is a wonderful place. They would take care of you there. Though I seriously doubt it will happen, on the off-chance Santos says no, I know a good female who would be overjoyed to provide for you and your young. Either way, you have nothing to worry about." So long as they didn't run into anyone, they would be fine. Camouflaging would do no good with her on his back. She would appear to be floating midair, and that would bring just as much attention. He'd just stick to the trees as much as possible, and pray to the gods no one saw them.

"Yes, my name is Varilliah. You may call me Arilla." Relaxing a bit more, her tears ebbed. "May I ask yours?"

"My name is Pierce." They could no longer hide among the trees. He'd have to take them over open land now. If he cut in a diagonal behind the marketplace, though, it shouldn't take too long. "Will you be alright if I go a little faster?" He tried to be as gentle as he could, but felt the soft kicks of her young against his back. Something he'd had difficulty ignoring, though he'd tried to. That he had no familial ties to her was the only way it was possible.

"Yes, I think that will be alright."

Pierce increased his velocity, stayed vigilant, and hoped to get a heads-up on any unwanted company. "You said you would give me details? Of Xander?"

"Yes. It had been an *umbra* since Pello and Faruk had left. One of the other males went and sought them out. He returned with news of their deaths. It angered Faruk's family. They demanded a life from Lyrica's family as payment. Her family offered Xander. They tied him to the pole in the center of the clearing. And beat him with sticks, stones, anything they could get their hands on, until he breathed no more."

Pierce swallowed the growl that threatened to escape his throat. Hades, he hoped Lyrica didn't need the details. The male had gone through a lot in his attempt to save his sister from horrific abuse. It was several minutes before he spoke. "Thank you for telling me." He knew Lyrica had said all she'd ever cared about was her brother, but he thought, just in case... "Do you have knowledge of Xander's mother and other sisters?"

"Yes. Their mother passed away a few *solaris* ago. Not long after, the youngest got mated. The two oldest still live with their mates, and all three have children of their own. They all remain in the village."

"Thank you." They continued silently on their way back to Migas, the crunch of their footsteps the only sound. She would need help, but with his mate's aid, he could arrange all of that.

Chapter Thirty-One

Pierce figured that with Jocasta busy in the kitchen, now would be an opportune time to talk to his brother. As much as his mate wanted what he had to retrieve, he'd sworn not to go without Logan. He wouldn't break that vow, so hopefully, Logan would be on board. But would Ambrosia? Pierce kissed Jocasta's neck and then kissed her wrist over their embedded initials. "I will be back soon, my queen." After leaving the house, Pierce started next door. Logan sat on a rocking chair on the porch, so he sat down on the top step, leaning against the railing. It had been just over a week since they'd gone hunting. Since that conversation. Not that either of them had brought it up again. Not that he wanted to think of it all, but he'd promised Logan he would be there if he wanted to talk about it. What he and Ambrosia had gone through, what they had lost. "Are you well, brother mine?"

Logan's gaze drifted to him. "Yeah. Ambrosia, she just... she had a rough night."

Pierce said nothing for a minute. "Would you like to talk about it? Or... anything?"

Logan stroked his chin. "No, but thank you, brother. Was there something you had on your mind?"

"You are welcome. And there was, but if this is a bad time, I can wait. I was going to ask if you wanted to go get something with me. But it will be dangerous, and Jocasta has made me swear not to go without you. Provided your mate agrees as well. Perhaps another time may be best."

"I do not think there will be a better time. And if it is important, we should not wait."

There was no way to put this simply, so he should just come out with it. "I gave Galenus a proper ceremony when he died. I want to retrieve his ashes, for his mate, and for both of ours."

For a moment, Logan sat there, the silence broken only by his own breath. With a weighty sigh, he stood up and peered into the doorway. "Ambrosia, can you join me outside for a minute, love?"

"Sure." Her talons made a harsh noise against the wood floor, then she stepped out onto the front porch. Her gaze flicked between him and his brother. "What's going on? Is it my sister? Is she okay?"

"She's fine. Come here and join me." Logan gestured to his lap. She took a seat. "Pierce has a request and something to share."

"Oh, okay."

Pierce faced them both and put his hands on his knees. "This is about your father." Despite his best efforts, he couldn't seem to start beyond that, which always happened. Before he knew it, his mouth had opened, and the words spilled out. "I have spoken with my mate, once with your mother present, about what your father meant to me. I did not know him well, not as well as I would have liked to. But growing up, he was a role model where I had no other. He protected our mother and us when others would not. If the circumstances had allowed, he would have taken us away from there." Pierce paused. "The *umbra* that he died—after I learned of what had happened, and as soon as I could sneak out of the village—I found where he lay. I gave him a proper ceremony, as well as I could. There was no less that I could have done for him. After I had done what was traditional with his ashes, I hid them. Doing so—" No, he wouldn't say that; that wasn't necessary. Neither Ambrosia nor his brother needed to know what had happened once Ailwin had discovered what he'd done. "I was only doing the right thing and, like most things that occurred there, it was something I had to bury deep in my memory. It was something that I had not thought of for a very long time. I never knew he had ever had young, nor that he had even found a mate. Not until the *umbra* I met Jocasta. Since then, time has passed so swiftly. So much has happened in such a short time. I have no excuse for not mentioning it until now, except that it just did not cross my mind. But I wish to make it right. It will be more dangerous to do so, and cannot happen without your blessing, as my mate has made me promise not to go without Logan. But I would like to bring him home. For my mate, you, and your mother."

Ambrosia sat there in Logan's lap and stared at him as he spoke. With a worried frown, she twisted the soft cotton of her shirt between her fingers. Silence stretched between them. Her gaze dropped to her lap. "How close to the village?"

"Not close. But it is inside the boundaries." He flicked his gaze to Logan. "The tunneled cave we used to play in." Pierce glanced back at Ambrosia. "There is only one entrance, and it is well hidden. As our sisters and I have not been gone from there for very long, and a couple of others have escaped since as well, if we make the trip during the *umbra*, there would be very few Informants in the village, if any. There is a curfew there, though. At night, everyone would be present." He could see it in her eyes. It was on the tip of her tongue to say no.

"We will take every precaution necessary," Logan said as he slipped a finger beneath her chin and lifted her eyes to his.

Turning her attention back to Pierce, Ambrosia visibly swallowed. "Jo has already given her blessing?"

"Yes. She has. I also promised her that if we got close, but it appeared we would not be successful, that we would not continue. That we would return home instead. I asked her for only one thing. Do not tell your mother until—unless—we succeed. I feel as though it would be too cruel to give her that hope before reuniting them again. Even if it is only in that form."

Ambrosia sat there for a moment, then offered him a small dip of her chin. "Okay. Yes. I'm fine with that. And I won't say anything to my mother. She had a hard enough time with his loss as it is. I wouldn't... yeah."

"Okay. We do not have to go today. But I am ready whenever you are, Logan."

"We will go first thing tomorrow after morning meal. I think that would be best," his brother suggested.

"Agreed," Ambrosia said. "I don't think there's enough time left in the *umbra* for it to be a safe trip. Although you both run faster than Jo and I do. I know you always slow your pace to match ours when we're heading toward the marketplace."

"Tomorrow is good. It will give us plenty of time as well." Pierce pushed off the step, then reached over to squeeze his brother's shoulder, a gesture of comfort. "I am going to go let my mate know."

"Okay." Logan nodded. "Tomorrow then."

"I will see you then." Pierce gave a slight bow of his head to Ambrosia, then headed home. When he got back inside, he went to his mate in the kitchen, wrapped his arms around her, and dropped a kiss on her neck. "We are going to go tomorrow," he mumbled.

"Tomorrow. Wow, that's..." Jocasta inhaled and exhaled a deep breath and leaned into him a bit.

He gently nuzzled her ears, then spun her around to face him, his gaze locked on hers. "Everything is going to be fine. We are going to be smart, take every precaution, and we are going to come home. I swear to you."

"I know you will. It doesn't mean I'm any less nervous."

"I know, my queen." He placed a soft kiss on her forehead. "We are going to go after morning meal. It will be the best time for us to go. With few informants and little chance of our crossing Markham. We are going to be safe, and all of my promises I made to you stand."

"I know. Just don't be surprised if you show up and I'm pacing, or champing at the bit, or baking up a storm." Her breath hitched as she let out a heavy sigh. A tempest of worry, fear, and anxiety brewed within her. "I know everything we've talked about and that you'll be safe up here." She tapped her head. "But trying to convince my heart, it's not as easy."

Pierce bent and kissed her neck, then placed a kiss right above her heart. "I know. I wish I could do more to reassure you." He moved his hand from her waist to cover her mating necklace. "I will always come back to you, my queen. Even when it is difficult to believe, I will come back to you. We will run full speed tomorrow and be back as soon as we can. I pray it will be a successful trip."

Looking up at him, the corners of her mouth curled into a subtle smile as a tear trickled down her cheek. "I do too. It would be good for us to really say goodbye."

He kissed her ears, wiping away the tears that streamed from her eyes before finally kissing her lips. "I pray we can bring that to you. To all three of you." He brushed another kiss across her lips. "We will think good thoughts, my queen, and spend the rest of this *umbra* just me and you. How does that sound?"

"Like paradise."

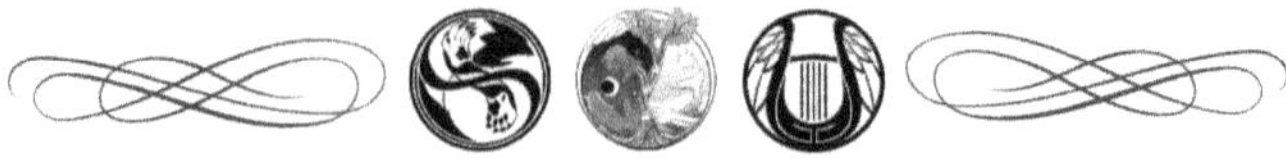

As the front door closed, Lyrica looked up in unison with her daughters, Zinnia, and Lillianna. Those two stood at the counter with her as they prepared a meal together while her daughters occupied the dining room table. Her own expression likely echoed their strained ones.

Pierce smiled at Jocasta as she and Ambrosia rose from the table. He nodded his head once and then crossed the room with Logan until they stood in front of her. Lyrica stared as the two brothers kneeled on the floor at her feet and bowed their heads. Pierce lifted his hand and opened it without a word. In his palm, he presented her with a slightly dirtied, amethyst-colored satchel.

"What is..." Her words trailed off as she caught full sight of what was in the satchel. Could it be? She gasped, her vision blurring as tears, salty and warm, traced a path down her cheeks. Hesitantly, she reached for the hand-stitched pouch and shakily accepted it. Her mate. Her mate had returned home.

With his head still bowed, Pierce lowered his hand. "Close to nineteen *solaris* ago, I laid your mate and the father of your children, Galenus, to rest. In the best way that I could. His friend, our mother, helped him away in an offering instead of laying him to rest in the proper way. On this *umbra*, we humbly return his remains into your hands. And I would offer my deepest apologies that it was not sooner."

There were no words to express her gratitude. It didn't matter that it had taken such a long time. Her mate's spirit had remained with her. But at least... at least now, they could truly lay him to rest. As she clutched the satchel, her tears still flowed silently, each drop a tiny echo of her sorrow. For a moment, she could almost feel the warmth of her mate's embrace. The day he left the village played in her mind. They had spoken at great length regarding Markham's invitation. He assured her he would be as careful as possible, but that if their daughters could know every part of their heritage, then it was a chance that had to be taken. Lyrica's throat burned, a silent sob escaping as the weight of her grief settled. There were so many things she could say, but only one felt right. "Thank you. Thank you for bringing him home."

"You are most welcome." Pierce lifted his gaze to her. "He did not deserve to be there. We wanted him to be where he belonged." He bowed his head and rose to his feet.

Lyrica glanced at the two females that had recently been added to her family. Lillianna peered at them in question, but Zinnia didn't seem surprised in the least. Her eyes showed happiness and relief.

Then she turned her attention to both of her new sons-in-law. Logan followed suit, dipping his chin and rising to his feet. Both males crossed the room and dropped to their knees in front of their respective mates. Remaining in the kitchen, Lyrica watched as each male consoled her weeping daughters. While Logan soothed Ambrosia similarly to how Pierce reassured Jocasta, there were differences, too. Each male drew their mate into their lap and ran their fingers through their mate's hair. That was the similarities ended.

A single tear escaped her eye, reflecting a lifetime of sorrow as she remembered Galenus's absence. The actions Pierce and Logan had taken reminded her of exactly how Galenus would quiet the ache in her heart. He'd often held her close. Given how much he towered over her, it hadn't been difficult. A mountain of a male who had the gentlest touch. She believed with all of her heart that these two males were the same way with her twin daughters.

It would have thrilled her mate to call these two males' family. Each of them treated both of her daughters with such kindness. That didn't even include what Pierce had done to put the light back in Jocasta. And Logan, what he'd done for Ambrosia. Lyrica wiped at the tears that continued to streak her face.

Zinnia reached across the counter and clasped her hand. Lyrica stood there thinking back over the years she had with her mate. It hadn't been long enough. Still, through all the memories, one thing remained consistent. Not just the love Galenus had held for her, but the love he held for their children. Her gaze lifted to where her daughters sat, each with their mate. The day they'd gotten mated, she was certain she'd felt Galenus's spirit there. It had been a moment to remember. A joyous occasion.

Her mind once again drifted to the day they found out Galenus had died. The day he'd left, when she'd felt the life leave him, she'd doubled over in pain. Her body had felt as if it had been ripped in two, a brutal and sudden agony. She had struggled to control her tears, to get to her feet, but she'd had two young daughters to care for. Somehow, she'd tended them until two days later. It had taken that long for the news to travel, confirming his death. It was a day she'd never forget. The anguish that she had felt equaled the scream that had ripped from her throat that day. Antonia had delivered the news. The female had even attempted to comfort her as she broke down. After the devastating news, it was a week before she could find the strength to leave her bed and begin the day. All she could do was watch each of her family members as she thought back to the worst day of her life.

Lillianna set mugs of tea in front of everyone. At some point, Pierce and Jocasta and Logan and Ambrosia had moved from the dining room to the chairs in the living room. Zinnia remained in the kitchen with her.

She didn't know how much time had passed since Logan and Pierce had first returned, but her quiet sobs had settled. Lyrica strode over to the couch and sat down in the middle. She set the satchel in her lap and stretched out a hand to each of her daughters. While she didn't wish to take them from their mates, she needed them close. "Come, *ta morá mou.*"

It had been quite some time since she'd used those words to call her daughters to her side. Something Galenus had taught her. Her wonderful mate—a male who'd given her everything and more.

Jocasta was the first to join her on the couch, taking up a seat next to her as Ambrosia sat on the other side of her. Lyrica wrapped her arms around her daughters, taking in the sweet scent of their hair as she inhaled and exhaled deeply. She glanced over her shoulder at Zinnia and Lillianna and gestured for the two to join them.

Leaving Pierce and Logan on the floor by the large lounge chairs, Zinnia and Lillianna each took a seat on the couch.

"When my mate, Galenus... when we first received confirmation, I was in no position to hold a proper ceremony. Although we did..." She offered a motherly smile first to Pierce, then to Logan. "I believe we can give him the goodbye he deserved. All of us. His family." She blinked, attempting to stop the tears that were threatening to escape. "I think there is no better place than Mosina Falls. I may never have gone with you girls, but he always told me everything whenever you returned. The joy on his face... it is something I will always treasure."

"It would honor us to be there for that," Pierce said. "Thank you."

Lillianna looked from Zinnia to Pierce to Logan. "He meant a lot to you, right?"

"Yes, he did," Logan replied. "He was the one who taught Pierce and me what it meant to be a male. One your family could turn to." His gaze fell on Lyrica, and then his mate. "I agree. It would be our honor."

Jocasta glanced up at her. "Mosina Falls was his favorite place."

"It was his favorite place because you girls loved it so much," Lyrica commented. She peered around the room, her gaze stopping on every person's face at one point. Her chin trembled as she struggled to keep the tears at bay. Losing Galenus had broken her in half. She still felt the sharp pang of grief, a constant reminder of her lost love, even after all this time. But seeing their family together like this... it reminded her of her mate's legacy, and that meant the world to her. "Everything he ever did was for the people he cared about."

Zinnia smiled softly. "Thank you for including us. It would be an honor to be there."

"I would have it no other way." It would be exactly as her mate would've wanted it. A celebration of his life with the ones he loved and sacrificed for, all together. That's exactly what they would do. They'd give him a proper send-off and remember all the good and all the love he gave them. The legacy he'd created for his family.

Chapter Thirty-Two

Lyrica glanced from Zinnia and Lillianna, who took up the middle of their group alongside her, to the surrounding forest. It had been a quiet trip to the waterfall, as well as her first time there. Lyrica had lived in the village for over twenty years, and not once had she left. She drank in the scenery as they made their trek to Mosina Falls. The forest was more beautiful with all of its greenery and massive trees than she ever imagined. She felt like a young person seeing things for the first time. Although she didn't know how much further they had to travel, she understood why they'd come here so often. "It is quite peaceful out here."

Zinnia gave her shoulder a squeeze, a moment of shared silent understanding. Lyrica glanced back at the female, then offered a slight tilt of her mouth at each person, stopping last with Lillianna, whose hand she currently held.

"It is truly lovely," Zinna said.

"I see why you two always spend so much time out here," Lyrica commented. Despite their reason for the trip, it didn't sadden her—at least not in the way she expected. Her mate might not physically be with her any longer, but his spirit always appeared in her time of need. She still carried him in her heart.

From the front, Jocasta peered back at her. "Wait until we get to the top. You can see so much from there."

"I imagine it is just as wondrous." Her gaze passed over everyone. Her family. Maybe they hadn't known it, but Galenus had given her more than they ever dreamed possible. She'd missed having a noisy house. Although her two daughters had created enough by themselves over the years, it didn't compare to how full her heart was now.

Pierce held Jocasta's hand as they led the group up the path. With their fingers intertwined, he stroked the back of her hand as he dropped a kiss on her head.

Jocasta stared at Pierce with a secret smile. "You're right, Mom. It is pretty wondrous."

"I wish I had come out here at least once with the three of you." Lyrica drank in the sight of her family once again. "Though perhaps we can make new memories together as a family."

"I like the sound of that, Mom," Ambrosia spoke up from behind them.

"That sounds like a lot of fun," Lillianna said, her amethyst eyes positively sparkling. "It is really beautiful out here."

Lyrica nodded as they continued their way toward the top. "I think so too, Lilli. What do you think, Zinnia?" The stories they had regaled about the waterfall and the basin over the years Galenus had taken their daughters; she could add to them. A new experience would be nice. It had been quite some time since she had dared to try anything new. Come to think of it, not since she'd opened Zancle's Rock. Her daughters had only taken it over in the last six years. Perhaps something new could be good.

Zinnia beamed. "I think that sounds truly wonderful."

As they approached the top, Jocasta slowed her pace and glanced back at her. Lyrica's gaze flicked to the distinct faces, starting with Ambrosia and ending with Pierce. Galenus was the common factor among them all. Two families that had come together as one. Logan, Pierce, and Zinnia had known him before she, her daughters, and Lillianna came into the picture. A slow smile spread over Jocasta's face, and a tear of joy came to her eye. Jocasta looked once again at her. "We're here."

Lyrica's gaze lifted as she stared out across the treeline. They could see much of their surroundings from here. It wasn't the prime point of the forest, but that had no impact on the peace she felt. The first time they'd mourned Galenus, it had been traditional. This time, they needed to do it differently. She'd insisted that those who wore clothes wore something of color. She gave Lilli's hand a squeeze and eyed her daughters and their mates.

"You never truly say goodbye to your mate, no matter when they pass from this world. Everything you share, it lives on inside of your memories, your never-ending love, and your young. I look at you, Ambrosia, and you, Jocasta, and I see so much of Galenus in you. His fire. His strength. Even his adventurous side." She turned her attention to Logan and Pierce. "I know how much you both respected him. I can see elements of his teachings coming across in the two of you. He'd be proud of the males you've both become." She swung her eyes to Zinnia. "You remind me a lot of me, but I see him too. I see it in the way you take care of me, your siblings, this family. Even in the way you take care of yourself. I believe you take after your mother more than you know." She gazed at Lillianna with affection. "You may not have known my mate, but I can see the lessons he taught your brothers passed on to you. You always try to help, even when you aren't sure there is much to do. Sometimes, just being there is all that one needs."

Lillianna smiled at her. "I wish I had gotten to know him. I can tell, just by the love all of you have for him, how special he was."

"He truly was." Lyrica paused, the silence amplifying the beat of her heart. "The *umbra* he died, a part of me broke. You cannot prepare for the *umbra* you lose your mate, no matter if you have had *solaris* or a lifetime together. It never feels like it is enough. I know why he went to Métamorphe that *umbra*." It had been about so much more than assuring their daughters could know every part of their heritage. His plan, if it was all for show as he'd expected, had been to try one last time to get Sabina and her family out. Her gaze flicked from Pierce to Logan. She still recalled one of the many conversations they'd had about those two males. Though her heart was heavy, her lips still curved upward slightly. Her gaze shifted once again to Lilli. "He remained true to his beliefs to the very end. I would love to share stories about him with you. He and your mother were friends, even before she was given to Ailwin."

"Really?" Lillianna's eyes shone. "I would love to hear stories about him. Both of them."

Pierce reached out and gave Lillianna's hand a brief squeeze. "I did not know how long they had been friends," he said. "He was always just there. In any way that he could be."

"There were only a few *solaris* between the two of them in age. He once told me that, from the moment they met, she became a sister to him. They spoke and played together whenever they could as children. That changed once she became mated, but he never stopped being there for her." Pausing, Lyrica silently cleared her throat. She hadn't spoken of her mate in so long or shared any of the tidbits her own daughters would've loved to hear as the years went on. It had been... difficult to speak of him. "I may not have known your mother, but I can see it went both ways."

As Jocasta teared up, Pierce rubbed his hand gingerly up and down her arm, holding her against him. "She never said so aloud, but I know she cared for him too, as a brother. Her own brother died before my birth."

"She had a brother?" Lillianna asked.

"Yes, an older one, though I know little about him." Pierce's gaze dropped to the satchel in Lyrica's hands. "That *umbra*, she tucked that into my hand before I left the village. She knew what I was leaving to do, and that the... I could not observe the usual traditions."

Lyrica's amber eyes dropped to the handstitched bag—the significance wasn't lost on her. It took several moments for her to sort through her memories. Conversations she hadn't thought about in so long. Slowly, she lifted her eyes, a soft sheen to them. "Lincoln. That was her brother's name. They had been a trio, the three of them." She swallowed the lump in her throat, the taste of her sadness bitter, and pushed through the sorrow that felt like a lead weight on her shoulders. "Galenus always told me he, Lincoln, and Sabina had caused a lot of trouble over the *solaris*. I recall something about a fire that had gone awry." Lyrica chuckled ever so quietly. She remembered the difficulty her mate had speaking of the night Sabina had been given to Ailwin. They had killed Lincoln. And that was all it had taken for him to despise Ailwin.

"I think the troublemaking might have run in the family." Pierce cracked a sly grin. "She told a few stories about him, but very few. And never around Ailwin. I never heard her speak his name."

"Our families have been intertwined for a long time. I imagine it was difficult for her. It took Galenus almost a *solaris* here before he spoke to me about his past." Lyrica closed her eyes, lifted her face toward the sun, and inhaled the warm, fragrant air, exhaling slowly. Once she had a sense of which way the breeze was blowing, she opened her eyes and peered around at her family.

"I could spend all *umbra* talking about Galenus and telling you the stories he told me." Her eyes teared up just a little. "If only so I could delay saying goodbye." Her chest felt constricted as she once more focused on the satchel. "I know we will one *umbra* meet again. Until that *umbra*, may your memory be eternal."

Zinnia came forward and put her arm around Lyrica's shoulders. "We can speak of him every *umbra* if you would like," she said. "I would love to hear more stories about him, and our mother, and our uncle. Saying goodbye in this way does not mean he is gone. I know they are still with us. I can feel them sometimes, watching over all of us." Her eyes drifted across everyone in their family. "They will live on forever in our hearts, in our memories. All the things that they taught us, we can pass down when the *umbra* comes."

"You are quite right, my dear." There were many stories she could tell them. The time Lincoln and Galenus nearly fell out of a tree. Or how the three of them often raced through the forest and Sabina always won. The number of times they tried to scare one another. So much to share. She wasn't truly saying goodbye to her mate, her other half, her one true love. One day, they would be together again. Just as they had brought him home to her, she would see him again on the other side. "I am ready."

"Take your time." Zinnia gave her shoulder a gentle squeeze, stepped back a little, and stood next to Logan.

Lyrica drew closer to the water and kneeled down, the satchel pressed to her chest as she heard the gentle lapping of the water against the edge. She watched the direction the water flowed, stared at it as it churned and bubbled over the rocks and sediment, and rushed over the cliff into a pool below. Her plan had been to set his ashes free in the water. That was what she had always believed he wanted, but as her gaze tracked the rolling water, she realized that was only part of what he wished for. It was the reason she had checked the direction of the wind. Her male, her mate. Her wonderful, loving mate. Even after all these years, he still whispered in her ear. A small smile crept onto her face as she tenderly opened the satchel and drizzled out his ashes. Just as she suspected, the wind swooped in and carried his remains off. Though not all of them, but just enough. She tracked the wind as far as she could. Not that it was difficult to discern the direction it carried them toward. "Staying true until the very end."

Peering back at her family, Lyrica took stock of those gathered. They still had a road ahead of them. It was the only reason she believed her body continued through the motions. Not only so she could see Jocasta and

Ambrosia through certain stages of their lives, but so she could be there for Sabina's children as well. At least through a new generation.

Still holding Jocasta against him, Pierce watched the wind carry the ashes away, a smile on his face. Silent tears streaked down Jocasta's cheeks. Pierce pressed a kiss to the top of her head as he gently wiped her tears.

Lillianna moved over next to Ambrosia, clasped her hand within her own, then reached up high to give Logan's shoulder a squeeze.

Galenus and Sabina were both here with them today. And their presence was powerful.

After a few minutes, Zinnia kneeled down on the grass next to her and extended her arm. She let her fingers trail into the water where some of his ashes had been swept away. "Thank you, Galenus," she whispered. "For the little girl, I was at seven."

Without hesitation, Lyrica wrapped an arm around Zinnia's shoulder. Zinnia hugged her in return, reaching up to wipe a tear away before it fell.

There were no words. Nothing needed to be said. They were two healing females that the most wonderful male had saved. A male whose presence she had felt from the second her feet hit the floor that morning. He'd been by her side, walking along, as they traveled to the waterfall he'd loved so much. So many wonderful memories flooded her mind during the trip. Even more as she spoke of him and talked to their children and Sabina's children. Their families truly intertwined a very long time ago.

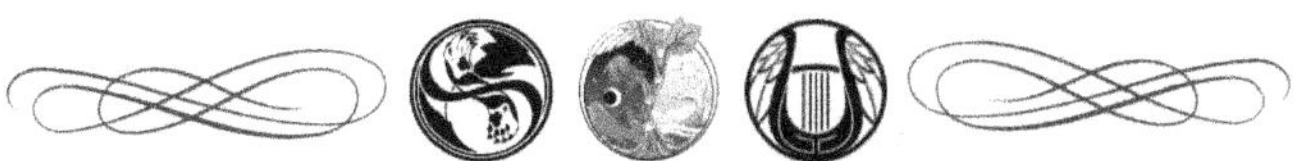

Jo and Pierce had spoken about doing this once or twice, but hadn't actually acted on it. She wasn't due at the bar for a few hours, and everyone had been blissfully out of the house, as well as her sister's. Ambrosia was already at work, Lilli and Zinnia were in the gardens, and Logan was in the woodworking building. Which was where her mate was returning from now. So, she'd done something she hadn't in quite some time. Stripped out of her clothes, laid them across the couch, pulled on her camouflage, and waited.

Pierce entered their home and froze in the doorway. He glanced around, his gaze falling on the couch where her jeans and top were. A slow smirk crossed his face. She never left her clothing lying around their home. Only in their bedroom or the bathroom, and that never lasted long. "My queen?" he called out as he closed the door behind him.

Jo stood up from the chair she occupied and the corners of her lips tugged wide as she approached her mate. "I thought we'd play a game, my king."

His smirk widened, a low growl rolling out of him. "Mmm. I see. Just any old game? Or a specific one?" he teased. He took a step toward where she stood. "Do you want me to chase you, my queen?"

"Oh, it's a *very* specific one," she replied as she altered her direction so that she danced around him toward the exit. It wouldn't take much for him to catch her at all. Even in his current form, he had speed on her, but that wasn't the point. "Do you remember the game I told you I liked to play? Camouflage tag?"

Though he couldn't see her, he turned toward her. Not that he needed to see her to garner that information. "I certainly remember. I have *very much* been looking forward to playing that with you." Licking his lips, he pulled on his own camouflage. "Are we playing that now? Do I get a prize when I catch you?"

"Oh yes. It'll be a prize I'm certain neither of us will ever forget." She already had a rough path mapped out in her head. And she'd tried her hardest to block him from seeing anything in her mind. After all, it should be a surprise. Backing up to the door, she turned the knob and opened it. "Are you ready?"

She sensed it took everything in him not to reach out and tug her into his arms. "I am always ready for you, my queen."

As she'd left the door open, it didn't take more than a matter of seconds for it to close. She sensed him shift to his animal form.

"Should I give you a head start?"

She slowly backed up toward the stairs. "Where would the fun be if you caught me too soon?"

"Oh, I can think of plenty of fun to be had after I catch you." He chuckled.

Of that, she was certain. Hmm, what would be a good count? Five minutes might be too much, and one minute wouldn't be enough. She descended the staircase. "I think three minutes should be perfect."

"So, I have to wait three whole minutes before I come after you? How will I stand the anticipation?"

"I'm sure you'll find a way," she taunted, and then took off. Her plan had been simple. With where their home was situated, if she darted between the houses, she could easily cut across to the training center. While there were likely to be a few people there this time of day, at least there wouldn't be any classes with children.

She sensed how antsy he was as he counted down the minutes before following her. When she reached the training center, it was harder to get inside than she'd expected. She had to be careful as she opened the door, and it wasn't just because of the desires her mate had for her. It wasn't like ghosts would open it. It was all about timing. Jo got the door open without incident, or drawing attention to herself. Once she was inside, she headed for the staircase and ascended the steps to the second floor. Those rooms were the most likely to be unoccupied. Perfect. Jo slid into the third room on the right.

When Pierce reached the training center, she sensed as he shifted to his humanoid form. It took him several minutes to get inside. As intently as she listened for his footsteps, she heard nothing, but she felt his excitement. They'd had sex publicly dozens of times—at the basin, in the barn, and on their kitchen table, in full view of the window. This felt different somehow. A whole new kind of thrill. She stifled a giggle as she heard him enter the room. It wouldn't take much for him to find her, but that had been the point.

Pierce dashed across the room, the air thick with anticipation, and stopped just inches from where she leaned against the wall. Although they couldn't see one another, they both sensed exactly how the other moved. He spun her around so she faced the wall, took her wrists in one of his hands, and raised them above her head. His cock pressed against her ass, and she couldn't help but arch against it. She bit back a small moan. Dropping his head, he dragged his tongue up her neck and nipped her ear. Gods, she loved when he did that.

"It did not take me very long to find you, my queen." With a low growl, he slipped his hand between her thighs and grazed his fingers against her sex. Jo gasped. "Should I let you try again?"

"Mmm, maybe I should try again. Although this certainly provides an excellent challenge. Not only do we have to remain unseen, but we can't be loud either," she whispered as she drove her ass further back against his cock.

"Hmm, I agree. Such an interesting challenge." Pierce stroked her sex harder, dipping two fingers just inside her. She had to bite back another moan. Gods, she wanted more. He nipped at her ear and sucked on her neck. "Mmm, so wet for me already. I *was* supposed to get a prize for catching you. So, I think I know exactly how I can keep my mouth quiet. The question is, can you do the same?"

A groan slipped out at his question. "Mmm, that definitely sounds like a challenge, my king." She rocked her hips and ground against his fingers.

A soft growl escaped him. Slipping his fingers out of her sex, he slowly rubbed her juices over her nub. "Mmm. Let us see how you do then." Releasing her wrists, he planted her palms against the wall and used his knee to spread her legs a little more. He settled onto the floor, placing his back against the wall as he faced her. Running his hands up her legs, he gently gripped her waist. He pressed tender kisses across her stomach, hips, and inner thighs. "Hm. I wonder, can you stay still and quiet?"

He was asking for a lot. She didn't know that she had *that* much control. It took a lot of effort just to stay quiet. Neither of them had ever been good at that. One of the many reasons she'd always been grateful their bedroom was soundproof. Pierce stroked his tongue slowly up her slit. As her talons scraped against the wooden floor, her hold on the wall tightened; her knuckles turning white.

It was a *lot* more difficult to stand still than she imagined possible, especially as he slid his tongue deep inside her, exploring her sex. She just bit back a moan, which only threatened to get louder as he licked up her slit and took her clit in his mouth, sucking hard and slow. Oh, gods. She got a flash of an idea in his head—he wanted to take her right to the brink of an orgasm, and then it would be her turn to chase him. A low rumble escaped her mouth and he let out a soft growl against her sex. Her grasp on the wall tightened, and she gasped, her head snapping back. The image of hooking her leg over his shoulder and riding his tongue entered her mind.

Pierce executed the silent demand without fail and drove his tongue harder into her, keeping his pace torturously slow. Deep, languid strokes of his tongue, hard sucks and gentle nips at her nub, had him growling against her sex. Her talons curled against his back as she lost control of her body. She rocked her hips ever so slightly, riding his tongue. "Fuck," she whispered. Gods, the way this felt. How easily they could get caught, especially as they both barely held onto their camouflage and struggled to keep their voices low.

Keeping his grip on her ass, he moved one hand between her thighs and slid two fingers deep inside her, teasing the inner walls of her sex. He nipped at her nub and sucked on it hard, assaulting it with his lips and tongue. Oh, gods. She couldn't stop the swing of her hips as she increased her pace, grinding vigorously against the combination of his fingers and tongue. Her talons scraped across his back and her nails dug further into the wall. A growled moan left her mouth as she went flying over the sweet edge.

Removing his fingers quickly, Pierce shoved his tongue into her sex, not letting a single drop of her release spill as it flooded his mouth. As he licked her clean, he raised his hand and slid his fingers into her mouth, growling against her sex as she tasted herself off his fingers. When he'd thoroughly cleaned off her sex and thighs, he kissed and swept his tongue up her body as he rose from the floor. Still moving his fingers slowly in and out of her mouth as she lathered them, he sucked on her breasts, then her neck, and nipped at her ear. "Now it is your turn to chase me, my queen," he growled low.

As the words left his mouth, he moved away from her, then disappeared from the room. Jo knew—the both of them hungered for more. She still sensed the desire and need from him, no matter how many rooms she chased him through. Only one thing resonated in her head as she went after him.

There was a certain convenience in their height difference. She intended to take full advantage of it once she caught him. Not that she hurried as she chased him. She pursued him through a multitude of rooms. Each time she passed through a doorway, his fingers would graze over her ass, hips, or breasts. With each touch from him, she took a moment to caress exactly where his fingers had gone, heightening both of their arousal each time.

Not once had she ever claimed to play fair. She wanted him panting for her by the time they got to the last room.

He halted at the top of the stairs and waited only so long as it took her to reach him. Then he skated into the first room on the right. Their ultimate stop. Stepping into the room, Jo shut the door and locked it. The heady scent of his arousal filled the room, mixing exquisitely with hers. She sensed the desperation he felt to have his cock in her mouth or her sex. Unhurriedly, Jo closed the distance between them, where he leaned against the wall in a corner. "Should we see how well you can stay still, my king?" she asked, a sultry tone in her voice.

A low growl rolled out of him. "We can certainly try, my queen. I cannot say I will succeed very well, though."

"Oh, I don't expect you to." Reaching out to him, she punctuated each word with a gentle caress of her fingers, creating a trail down the top half of his body. Her touch inched further and further south. She figured he might last, well, maybe as long as she did, or less. What she predicted would happen—she'd start by stroking the length of his cock, and then she'd wrap her mouth around it as she grabbed his ass. Before he came, he'd flip them around and slam into her from behind.

Pierce grazed his claws over her ass, his other hand going to the back of her head. Fisting a handful of her hair, he licked over her lips. "Get your mouth on my cock, my queen."

She moaned. Gods, she loved it when he got rough with her. Even more so when he got demanding. Dragging her nails down his inner thighs, she wrapped her hand around his shaft and stroked it. A deep rumble resonated in his chest, then shifted to a moan as she covered his cock with her mouth. She wrapped her other hand around his balls and squeezed.

"Fuck," he growled out. "Suck my cock, my queen. Show me how much you want my cum."

Tingles ran down her spine. Gods, she loved his noises. She skimmed her fingers back over his thighs to his hips and gripped tight onto his ass as her head bobbed up and down his length.

"Fuck yes," he groaned, his head falling back against the wall.

Slathering his cock with her tongue, she sucked on his shaft until the head of his cock popped out of her mouth. Then she started over, going down until the tip of his dick hit the back of her throat. A rumble reverberated up the back of her throat, vibrating up his erection.

With a moan, his hold on her hair tightened, and he drove his dick in and out of her mouth. "Fuck, Jocasta... suck my cock."

While he never needed to take over, she loved when he couldn't control himself. Digging her nails into his ass with one hand, she returned the other to his balls. She gave them a gentle tug as her tongue swirled around his shaft, sucking hard on his cock. Another growl left her mouth as she squeezed his balls.

Unable to hold the orgasm back, he exploded, his release pouring down her throat. "Fuck," he barked. She swallowed every drop. Once she'd taken every bit, he did exactly what she'd thought about a few minutes earlier. Pulling out of her mouth, he flipped them around and planted her hands on the wall in front of her. With one hand on the wall and the other gripping her hip, he growled out her name as he slammed into her from behind.

"Oh, gods!" she cried out. As much as she'd tried to keep her voice down, she hadn't been able to stop the noise, especially as he pistoned in and out of her. Unable to hold back a moan, Jo rocked her hips as she met him thrust for thrust.

How she kept her camouflage on as he pounded into her repeatedly, she didn't know. Not that it was something she gave much thought to, either. His growls didn't cease as he slid a hand back up into her hair. His fingers tangled in her silky locks. Angling her head, he grazed his fangs over her neck. Another moan left her mouth. "Always so tight."

Well, at least she'd locked the door behind them when she'd come in here. There was a strong possibility someone would hear them, but at least no one would walk in on them. Not that they'd see anything if they did. The hand at her hip slid down and hooked behind her knee, pulling it up. The change in position allowed him to go deeper into her. His cock slammed into her with each hard thrust. She cried out, her fingers curling against the wall.

"Fuck," he rasped out as his pace increased. "Come for me," he demanded. Their pelvises met together once more as he sent her careening again, gushing all over his shaft. "Fuck, you feel so good. I love when you come all over me." He didn't stop pounding in and out of her, another release of his own sitting right on the edge. His thrusts came harder and faster until she came again, exploding all over his length. Her sex clenched hard around his cock, yanking an orgasm out of him.

While she didn't lose her camouflage, she certainly couldn't stop the moan that left her mouth. Or how she cried out in ecstasy. With heavy pants, she rocked her hips back against him as they rode out their mutual releases together. "Oh, gods…"

Footsteps echoed along the staircase as someone headed toward the room they occupied. She glanced over her shoulder and bit her tongue to silence her heavy breathing. Pierce licked over her lips as he caressed her ears. "We are going to have to stay silent, my love," he whispered and fused their lips together in a slow, deep kiss.

Arching her back, Jo wrapped her hand around his neck as she swept her tongue along the inside of his mouth, grazing over his fangs. Quiet was going to be even more difficult than it had been before. With his hardened cock still buried deep inside of her, she continued to rock her hips against him. This wasn't unusual for them. That someone might have heard them meant they really had to be quiet. Even with the door locked.

The kiss deepened as he ground his dick into her core. And he didn't stop there, or make things easier for her. As one hand massaged her breast, the other hand moved between her thighs, its touch feather-light. He panted into the kiss, stroked her soaking wet slit with his fingers and rubbed her nub as he pistoned harder into her. Swinging her hips back, she met him thrust for thrust, his balls slapping up against her. Jo nipped his bottom lip as she barely bit back a moan and dug her nails into the nape of his neck. Oh, gods. Lacing her fingers through his, she connected their hands on her breast and tightened their joined grip. It got more difficult to stay quiet, especially as another orgasm sat on the cusp for her again.

He rubbed faster at her nub as he rocked harder. "Fuck," he breathed out against her lips.

Jo tightened their joined grip on her breast even more. Fuck was right. "Come with me," she whispered. A whimper slipped through and she bit her bottom lip as the inner walls of her sex clenched. A massive bought of ecstasy slammed through her body. He came right along with her, his own release tremendous. Pierce moaned as her back arched and she threw her other hand out against the wall. Jo had no clue whether the person who checked on the noise had left or not, but she didn't really care either.

His moan trailed off into a growl as his release poured into her. "Fuck." As they rode out their mutual orgasm together, he nibbled on her ear and brushed a kiss over her lips. "One more. I need you in my mouth again."

One more. After that last one, she wasn't sure if she had another. But there wasn't time to question it. Her mate pulled out of her, sat down on the floor, laid back, and tugged her to straddle his mouth. He moaned against her sex as he licked up her slit and nipped at her nub. "Ride my tongue." His fingers clutched her thighs as he lapped at her ravenously, like he'd been starving for an eon, and she was the only thing that could take his hunger away.

The noises he made as he assaulted her sex, along with the demand, sent another blast of heat to her core. Oh, gods. Pierce's hold on her thighs brought another moan out of her. She gripped the wall, spreading her thighs a bit as she rocked her hips against his tongue. His growl vibrated through her sex and she spread her thighs further apart. Driving his tongue as deep inside her as he could, he devoured her hard and fast, sucking at her nub, and rumbled against her. His fingertips caressed up her legs, creating a trail from the merfolk scales along her lower back until he reached her breasts, where he tweaked her nipples, and then repeated the path.

Gripping the wall tighter, her head arched as she rocked against his tongue harder and faster. "Oh, gods…" Tingles shot down her spine as her body thrummed with pleasure and gushed out into his mouth. His growl against her was deeper this time. He lapped hard at her sex, not letting a single drop of her release spill.

"Mmm." Pierce nuzzled her sex. "You always taste so fucking good, my queen."

"Mmm, I could say the same about you, my king." Ragged breaths escaped her lips as she leaned against the cold stone wall. Somehow, she still had her camouflage pulled on. Small favors. It took a moment for her to climb off him. "You might have to carry me."

"Are your legs a little shaky?" he teased. "You know I never have a single problem carrying you."

She laughed softly and glanced over at the windows of the room. Well, there wasn't anyone hanging around at least. "Best camouflage tag ever."

Chuckling a bit, he got up off the floor. Wrapping an arm around her waist, he lifted her up into his arms. "Absolutely. I think that just became my favorite game ever." He brushed a kiss across her lips. "Definitely want to play that again. Soon."

She hooked her arms around his neck. While she probably could've walked, she enjoyed him carrying her as much as he enjoyed it. Oh yeah.

It was definitely something they'd be playing again. "Mmm, anytime you want."

"I like the sound of that." He smiled. "Should we play here again next time, or pick somewhere new?" Glancing out the windows of the room, he ensured there was still no one out in the hall before he shifted her to one arm long enough to unlock and open the door.

"Oh, I think we should definitely pick somewhere new. Switch it up. You know, keep the romance alive." She giggled. Not something she ever thought they'd have a problem with doing. Still, it certainly made it fun if they didn't do the same thing.

"Keep the romance alive, huh?" He lowered his voice as he carried her through the hallway toward the stairs. "Switching it up sounds fun. Do I get to pick the place next time?"

"Hmm, I think that would only be fair." Jo kept her voice as quiet as possible. Maybe no one had caught them this time, but they didn't need to draw unwanted attention to themselves. Even if they had on their camouflage, their voices could carry if they spoke too loudly.

He stroked her hip as he whisked her down the stairs. "I can think of so many possibilities."

Tilting her head, she considered the images that flashed through his mind. "A few of those might be challenging."

"The bigger the challenge, the more the fun, right?" he said, a smirk in his tone. He lightly pinched her ass, letting out a silent chuckle.

Her fingers grazed along the nape of his neck. "It certainly can be."

His neck arched at her touch. "I look forward to *playing the game* in every one of them." Placing a soft kiss on her neck, he nudged the front door open and stepped outside with her.

"So do I." It would be a lot of fun, no matter where they played the game. The challenge would be how many places they could get away with being unseen, and were there other places where they had to stay quiet?

"I wonder how many times we will play before someone catches us."

"That's an excellent question. I suppose the only way we'll find out is if we play again." What would they do *if* they got caught? She giggled. There wasn't any way of knowing until it happened.

He growled softly against her neck. "I am already looking forward to it. Next time, I may make you work extra hard to stay quiet."

"Mmm, that sounds like a challenge." Who would have to work harder to stay quiet? She could have fun, making it more difficult for him to check his growls.

Chapter Thirty-Three

Panting heavily, Logan brushed a kiss across Ambrosia's lips. Hades, he loved her so much. He nuzzled her nose and caressed her cheek with the back of his hand. "I will get the shower started for us, my love."

"Thank... you," she said between ragged breaths and vaguely waved a hand toward her legs.

He chuckled. Yes, he'd definitely left her more than satisfied. Walking immediately had become impossible. And it had been perfectly wonderful, especially as the house remained empty. Pressing a tender kiss to her forehead, he climbed out of their mated bed and left their bedroom. Stepping into the hallway, Logan disappeared into the bathroom. Not that he wanted to wash away the remnants of what he and his mate had just done, but his sister didn't need to return to find either of them in that state. He busied himself getting the shower going and noticed the bar of soap needed to be replaced. Alright. He could take care of that.

Ambling over to the cabinet, he kneeled down and opened the doors. His height often made it difficult for him to do some of the easier things around their home. Although he couldn't really see what he was looking for, he had a rough idea of where they should be. Logan reached into the far back and frowned. That didn't feel like soap. The lining was soft and it was squishy. His nose twitched as the unpleasant smell wafted towards him. No—it couldn't be. Tightening his grip on it, he yanked the pouch out and nearly fell back on his ass.

As he rose to his feet, he stared at the tiny bag. He didn't have to open it to smell the herbs. Its aroma carried from the second he retrieved the item. He even knew what they were and what they did. Why would they be here, though? And who would take them? Neither of his sisters would've had a need for them. Which could only mean—

"What's taking..." Ambrosia's words trailed off as she appeared in the doorjamb. "Where did you get those?"

Logan glanced over at his mate. The love of his life. No. No. It couldn't be, but her reaction said it all. "Have you been taking these?"

"You don't need to worry about that." With the pouch now in her possession, she spun on her heel and walked away, the sound of her footsteps echoing behind her.

No. No. *She had not been taking herbs to prevent pregnancy. She did not say just that.* The words themselves hadn't come out of her mouth, but they didn't have to. Not after that response. He swallowed the lump that formed in the back of his throat, then, with a heavy heart, he followed her into their bedroom. "I am your mate! These are conversations we should have before either of us decides these things."

"It isn't your body that's impacted! Why should you have a say in it?" Ambrosia stormed over to the dresser, yanked open a drawer, and dug out some clothes.

Dumbfounded by her words, he stood there and watched as she got dressed, throwing on a pair of pants and a top. It didn't take a genius to figure out why she'd been taking the herbs. "This is because of Carrick... right? Because we lost him?"

"*We* didn't lose him. I did. It was my body. And it's still my body. My choice." She glowered at him.

"You know damn well that it was not your fault, but that does not mean we are not both impacted by this decision, Ambrosia!" He wasn't trying to get upset with her, but how could he not? She'd lied to him; not just that, she'd hidden this from him. While he'd known for some time that the miscarriage had caused her a lot of emotional pain, he didn't expect she'd go out and purposely try to prevent them from becoming pregnant again. Not without talking to him first.

She whirled on him. "Oh! So, what you're saying is I'm not allowed to decide? Because while you'd like to think you're impacted... you aren't! You're not the one who has to carry it in your body. You're not the one that gets attached, and then has to deal with the loss, knowing you're the one that failed!" By the time the last word left her mouth, tears had sprung to her eyes and rolled down her cheeks.

Logan gripped the back of his neck. He hated seeing his mate cry. But they never spoke of Carrick. They never once talked about what happened, even though he'd been there by her side. And now this. He shook his head. "You did not fail. I do not blame you. Not for that. But this…" He didn't get it. How could she hide this? With a sigh, he crossed his arms. As much as he didn't want to ask for more information, he had to know. "How long have you been taking them, Ambrosia?"

"It doesn't matter." She slammed the open drawer shut.

"Yes, it does." It mattered a lot. But, Hades, her refusal to give him an actual timeframe told him all he needed to know. Not that he could stop himself from asking again. "How long?"

Ambrosia visibly ground her jaw. "Since before our mating ceremony."

That wasn't the answer he expected. No, he thought maybe after, but not before. They'd gotten officially mated a month ago. And they'd lost Carrick back in the spring. Hades, it didn't feel like much time had passed at all. Of course, that was a weight they both still carried with them. Not that it was something anyone ever really got over. Nor was it something they openly spoke about. There was a long time between those events. Nearly three months. His eyes narrowed. "How long before, Ambrosia?"

"That isn't important." Without another word, she shoved past him and stormed into the hallway, heading toward the kitchen.

Not important. She couldn't be serious? Logan chased after her. "How can you even say that? Every time I lied to you about the fight ring or getting into a fight, you said something. Even a few *penumbras* ago, you had the nerve to ask how *you* were supposed to trust *me*? And now, I find out you have been using these herbs behind my back for possibly *cycles*?"

Stopping mid-step, she spun on the back of her heel and pointed a finger at him. "First, you've come home bruised and beaten nearly every single time! And the last time, you might as well have been the walking dead with the way you looked. Second, you kept promising *not* to go back. *Not* to get into any more fights. And you broke that promise repeatedly! Not once have I ever said I wouldn't take these. Not once have I lied to you about them."

"No! Instead, you hid them from me! If you believed for one second any of the bullshit you just uttered, then you would not have kept this from me. We would have discussed this." At that point, he didn't know which was worse. Breaking his promise to her, or her hiding the truth from him? Despite everything they'd said to one another on the day of their mating, this was actually how they started it.

Logan rubbed his forehead. A throbbing ache built behind his eyes. There was more light streaming into the house. Maybe that was the cause. Not that he knew why. He glanced around and his gaze stopped at the open front door.

Lillianna stood there, wide-eyed, as she stared at both of them, clutching a basket of vegetables to her chest. "Excuse me," she whispered and left the house, the front door closing silently behind her.

"Damn it." He practically jogged across the room as he went after his sister. Although he and Ambrosia had argued before, it hadn't ever been anything like this. And they always tried to protect Lilli from it. Logan wrenched the door open. His sister wasn't too far off. If he left, he could catch up with her. From what had transpired, he wouldn't get any further with his mate. Not at the moment. He peered over his shoulder at Ambrosia. "You may not see it, but that you hid this from me for *cycles* does not make it better than lying."

Shaking his head, he stormed out, slamming the door shut. Maybe he couldn't fix the problem right then with his mate, but he could at least address the one that had just occurred with his sister.

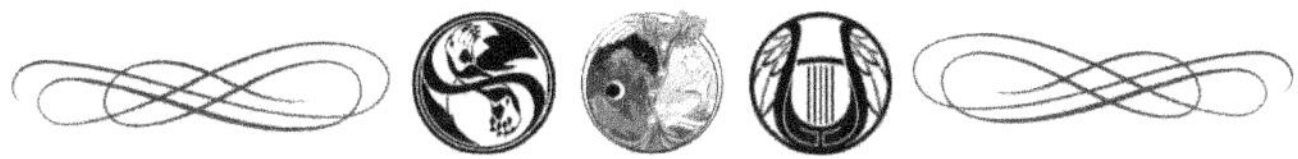

"What in Hades' name is wrong with you, Gabriella?"

"There is nothing wrong with me, Gavin. Why, because I want to do everything I can to save our moth—"

"She will not leave," he hissed out. Hades, it was hard to keep his voice down. "She will *never* leave, Gabby. Never."

"You do not know that."

"*Yes.* I do. I know that. Because we are almost three decades old and she has not once stepped foot outside that village. Even *thinking* of leaving Father? How can you honestly think—"

"I have to!" She glared as he shushed her. He watched his sister cross her arms after she took a deep breath, the scent of pine needles filling the air. "I have to. I have to believe that she can be free. Somehow. Some way."

"And what else will you sacrifice before you realize how naïve you are being?"

Tears welled in the corners of her eyes. "That... is *not* fair."

"Oh, is it not?"

Her hands clenched into fists, but quickly released. The fire in her emerald green eyes flickered, a fire that had dwindled more and more over the years. "I cannot just leave her there. *You* did not. They *forced* you out."

"Yes, *forced out.* With your mate. Right after you lost your twins." More tears sprang to her eyes. He couldn't help but feel like he was being cruel, but she *had* to see sense. She just had to. His sister opened her mouth, but he spoke over her. "You have your mate back now. You know I am safe." As safe as he could be. With what Parthenia had done—bringing him cleansing potion regularly, and the wards in the surrounding trees, as well as the protection ward inside the treehouse itself—no more Informants had come near in the past few weeks. He prayed to the gods regularly, as did his mate, that his good fortune continued. "Knowing what our mother's fate will be, it breaks my heart into too many pieces to count. It does. But there is nothing we can do for her. You need to accept that, as I have. It is best—" Gavin inhaled and exhaled a deep breath. "You need to go stay with Derrick out at the cabin and *never* go back. Never return to that accursed abyss. Because the next time—if you do not become with child again, and it is not another young you lose—the next time, it will be you. Or they will track you and find Derrick. Then what? Is it worth the loss? The sacrifice? How much more are you willing to give for someone who will give nothing themselves?"

"I can get her to leave," her voice broke. "I know I can."

Gavin shook his head slowly, as if in disbelief. "Then you are more naïve than I thought you were. By all the gods, Gabby, our mother, gave up a long time ago. Probably before we were even born."

"That is not true, Gavin, I—"

"Cannot save everyone. Hades, you are just like Devin. The both of you—" He cut his words off, barely holding back a curse. "You will not save our mother; you are going to get yourself killed. That is what you are going to do." He scrubbed his hands over his face. "This will probably be the last time we ever see one another," he said into his palms.

Gabby sighed, the sound echoing slightly in the small space as she walked across the wooden floor, settled onto the pallet, and hugged her knees. Folding her arms across her chest, she rested them on her knees. "You are not usually so negative."

"Circumstances have a way of pulling that out occasionally. I keep the positivity for my mate. I have little left for anyone else."

"How is she?"

"Good. She is doing well."

He didn't go into much detail. Of how difficult all of it was. Confined to the treehouse for his own protection. Only able to see his mate when she could leave Pteryrina. The restrictions the curse put upon them. The constant danger they both faced. Knowing with absolute certainty he would never see his mother again. Or that he no longer held a single doubt that his own father would rip out his throat if they ever came face-to-face again. The danger his sister put herself in, insisting on her foolish quest to save someone who refused to be saved. And—if he were truly honest with himself—anger. He was angry with his sister. She could be with her mate, be with him constantly. Never had to be parted from one another or worry if the other was safe and well or in danger. And even after everything they had lost, she decided not to do so. She insisted on returning to the place that had given them nothing but maltreatment and abuse, mostly at the hands of their father. A place that had stolen three young from her and her mate, for a reason that was just so *stupid*. The first miscarriage had been no one's fault, but still. Jealousy. He was jealous. Jealous of what his sister had at her fingertips, but basically threw away.

Gavin cleared his throat. "I think you should go."

Turning her head, she stared up at him, the emotion barely contained on her face. But he knew if their mindlink was open, it would have been a tidal wave. "Really. Alright. I thought... we could visit for a while. It may be some time before I can return—"

"Do not return, Gabby."

Her mouth opened, then closed. Fresh wetness shone in her eyes and she blinked a few times. Tried to speak again, but no words came out.

"Returning here will just put the both of us in more danger," he declared. "Informants have already come near once. I cannot risk it again. Not as often as my mate comes to me."

It seemed like forever before she spoke, and it wasn't until she was fully on her feet that she did. "Fine." With that one word, his sister crossed the floor swiftly, camouflaging when she reached the entrance. "I love you."

He opened his mouth to say it back to her, but she was gone before he could get one more word out. It was probably for the best. He'd said enough. More than enough. And had broken her heart. Not that he'd take any of it back.

Chapter Thirty-Four

Unsuccessfully getting another pair of pants to button, Jo removed them and went back to the closet. Gods, had she gained weight? Without noticing? It was possible. It had been a couple of months since she'd sparred or chased Kayan around. Well, she'd have to exercise somehow around the village. Maybe run or something. It would not do for her to gain weight. Hmm, what could she wear instead of jeans? Oh! She returned the pair of jeans in her hand to the closet and exchanged them for a light blue hi-low dress with a halter top. That would work.

Once she'd finished changing, she left the bedroom and headed down the hallway. Pierce had been working on afternoon meal. It wasn't often that he figured out meals on his own. If they ate alone, just the two of them, they prepared meals together, but she had been tired today. As she crossed the threshold into the kitchen, the overpowering stench of fish filled her nostrils. A hand shot to her mouth. "Oh, gods!" She spun on her heel and ran straight for the bathroom. Sweet rolls were good going down, not so much coming up. She slammed the bathroom door behind her and just got to the toilet in time.

Less than a minute later, Pierce was in the bathroom, kneeling down behind her, and holding her hair back. "I am sorry, love."

Another round of upchucking, and she fumbled to flush the toilet. Jo took a second to make sure nothing else intended to come up. Not that she thought she had anything left to throw up. She was pretty certain she'd just vomited the sweet rolls she'd had after morning meal, as well as—oh, gods. Nope, there went the tea she had an hour ago.

Worry swept through Pierce in droves. He rubbed circles along her back, still holding her hair away from her face so she wouldn't get any vomit on it.

This time, when she flushed the toilet, she was positive nothing remained. She had completely evacuated everything she had eaten in the last couple of hours. Sluggishly, she sat up and leaned against her mate. Before she spoke, she took shallow breaths, making sure the last of the sickness had passed, leaving a lingering sour smell. "Fish... has to go."

"Okay," he replied. He nudged the door closed with his foot to stifle the smell. He wouldn't get up off the floor until she was ready to, as well. "I am sorry," he stated. "I must have cooked it wrong. Would you like some water? Or can I take you to the bedroom while I get rid of it? I do not want to leave you on the bathroom floor."

"Water. That would be good." Yeah. She could handle that. And she really wanted to get this vomit taste out of her mouth.

He reached up to the bathroom sink, easily filled the cup that sat on the counter two-thirds full before shutting the faucet off and holding it out to her. "Are you alright? Are you getting sick?"

She took a sip of water and waited before taking another. "I don't know. Maybe. I don't get sick often. Maybe something from earlier just didn't agree with me."

He ran his hands up and down her arms. "I do not want to leave you here in the bathroom, but I will go get rid of the fish. Maybe they have not eaten next door yet."

Whatever it was, she no longer felt like she had to throw up. Her stomach had settled. Probably because there was nothing left in it. Her stomach rumbled.

"Are you... hungry now?" he bemused.

"Actually, yes." Yeah, it was strange, but she didn't want to put too much thought into what had caused the retching. "Help me up, and I'll wait in the bedroom while you get rid of it. And then open the front window." Just the thought of it made her sick to her stomach. On the plus side, she didn't feel like she had to throw up again.

"Okay. I made some potatoes, and there is a salad and some fruit. We can make something else if you would like." Pierce got her to her feet and kept his arm around her waist. Their bedroom was down the hall from the bathroom, so she'd only have to smell it for a moment. Opening the door, he carried her to their room. "I will... I will be back in a moment." He dropped a kiss on her neck, left the bedroom, and shut the door behind him.

The rest of what he'd mentioned had her salivating at the mouth. It all sounded good. She continued to work on the water while he dealt with the unfriendly food. She sensed it when he opened the window, then picked up the tray and headed outside with it.

Jo stared at the closet door as she sipped the water. Her mind ran through her symptoms. She easily explained it as something not sitting right, but it didn't make all that much sense. Her gaze shifted to the door, back to the closet and her jeans. Her pants had gotten a little tighter in the last couple of weeks. She stood and walked over to the mirror on the wall. Staring at the way the dress hung, she chewed on the inside of her cheek. Had her breasts gotten bigger? The dress hung just a little differently. And now this. Could she—no. Nope. Not possible. It was just something she ate. That's all it was; nothing else.

"I gave it to Logan," Pierce said as he opened their bedroom door. Crossing the room, he wrapped his arms around her from behind, dropped his head to her neck, and nuzzled it. "Are you feeling any better, my queen?"

Jo stared at her reflection a second longer and plastered a smile on her face. "Yeah. A lot." *Just something I ate*, she reminded herself again. It was the only *valid* explanation. No other possibilities.

"Mmm. Good. I am glad. We should go to the kitchen and eat. If you are still hungry after, we can make something else."

A shiver ran down her spine. Curling her hand around his neck, she stroked along his nape and beamed up at him. "Yes. Food sounds fantastic right now."

He growled softly. "Mmm. Okay. Food." Pierce took a step back and laced his fingers with hers. "Let us go eat."

Mmm, she loved his growls. She could feel it all the way to her toes. But, food first. She was hungry. Jo strode with him back to the kitchen. Fish stench gone. Good, everything else smelled quite divine. A nice variety of sweet fruits: cherries, strawberries, and blackberries. They would go well with the potatoes.

Realizing the front door was still open, Pierce chuckled and went to close it. He pulled out a chair for her, then retrieved the rest of the food from the kitchen. "I would hold you in my lap while we eat, but we may not end up eating if we do."

"Food first." She was too hungry to even consider—Jo blinked. That had *never* happened. The number of times they'd had sex around a meal, they had always wanted each other first. Food second. Gods, she definitely had to have a bug or something. Whatever it was, part of it had already passed. Surely, the rest would follow in a couple of days.

"Whatever you want." He set everything on the table and poured them both some water to drink. As he put food on the plates, he sat down beside her, his fingers gently brushing against her skin.

Jo got into the fruit as soon as the bowl hit the table. A small moan escaped her as she bit into the juicy strawberry. Pierce let out a rumble. Okay. She probably should've controlled the moan, but the sweet strawberry was bursting with flavor, making it hard to contain herself. "These are superb. You pick them fresh?"

"Um, oh, yes, this morning."

"You chose a great batch." She noticed how much pickier he'd gotten selecting food lately, but didn't put any focus on the thought. She took a bite of another and held one out for him.

"I tried to find the best ones for you." He bit into the strawberry and offered her one.

Jo bit into the piece he held out, taking nearly the whole thing in one bite. Then she reached over and picked up a few cherries and blackberries to add to what was in her mouth. It was oh-so-good. At this rate, if she kept eating the sweet fruit, she'd taste like sugar. But it had become all she wanted.

Pierce ate the mashed potatoes. He pushed the plates of fruit closer to her. She sensed how much it pleased him that, despite getting ill, she at least had an appetite.

"Mmm, thank you." Jo continued munching on the fruit. "Oh, will you go by my mom's house later? The last of my dresses are still in my old bedroom." She may need them. She'd have to decide on an exercise regimen, but until the weight came off, she could wear dresses to work.

"Mhm, of course." His eyes raked over her slowly. "Are they anything like this one?"

She paused with a blackberry halfway to her mouth. A small, seductive smile played upon her lips as she gazed at him. "Oh, yes, they are." She popped the blackberry into her mouth.

He let out a low growl. "Good."

Jo scooped up some potatoes from her plate onto a spoon and licked it clean. His spoonful of mashed potatoes stopped halfway to his mouth as he watched her. "You're definitely going to see me in more of them." She wasn't quite full yet, but at that moment, all she could think about was slipping off her underwear and crawling into his lap.

"I like the dresses you wear. They are very..." His gaze lingered on her cleavage as a guttural sound emanated from deep within his chest.

"Appealing?" she finished for him. She fingered the musical note that hung from the necklace he'd given her on the day of their mating. It sat perfectly in the dip between her breasts. Most of her clothes revealed it. This dress didn't cling to her form, but it accentuated certain areas of her body. Just the way she liked it. Jo scooped another spoonful of mashed potatoes into her mouth. She knew *exactly* what she was doing. Her body already hummed just from his growls and the way he stared at her.

"Very appealing." His tongue snaked out across his lips. His eyes moved from her breasts to her mouth as her tongue stroked over the spoon again.

"Better than my jeans?" She finished the last of the potatoes on her plate and returned her fingers to the fruit, which apparently she'd already eaten most of. How had that happened? She didn't think she'd eaten that much.

"I love anything you wear. The dresses, though, there is something about them." Reaching over to her collarbone, he trailed a finger down to the valley between her breasts. "I am trying very hard to let you finish eating."

As another shudder passed through her body, the last cherry remained all but forgotten. "Then I guess it's a good thing I'm done."

Pierce dropped his spoon on his plate and shoved all the dishes to the side. He lifted her up, the cold table a contrast to her warm skin, and with a sigh, he tugged at her panties, ripping them in two. He nestled his face between her thighs and growled as his tongue found her sex.

"Oh, gods!" she cried out. A few hours ago, it had just been her breasts that were sensitive. Lately, it seemed she felt everything over her entire body.

His mouth didn't move as his tongue stroked her slit. He eased her back onto the table, arranging her legs over his shoulders as he hiked up her skirt.

Pulling the top down, he covered her breasts and groaned against her as his tongue stroked deeper.

Her nipples were already hard beneath his palms. She grabbed onto his arms and cried out his name. It took very little for her to orgasm these days. She'd gone from around three releases to nearly five or six in one round for them. Not that she minded the change in their sexual intimacy. *Not in the least.* Her talons grazed his shoulder blades as her thighs clenched from the eruption that passed through her body.

A vibration traveled through her sex as her orgasm coated his tongue. Not that Pierce stopped. A shiver snaked up her spine as the quivering in her sex made her body tingle. The slippery satin feel of his tongue had her lifting her hips. She dug her nails into his arms harder as she flew over the cliff. "Fuck."

His growl intensified, a sound that seemed to vibrate through the air as he devoured her without a second thought.

"Oh, gods! Don't stop! Pierce, don't stop!" The sensation of his tongue moving against her wet core ignited a frenzy of signals in her brain. There was no edge to the third burst of pleasure that pulsed through her body. It quickly followed the last one as the inner walls of her sex contracted and more of her release flooded his mouth.

He nearly roared against her as he swallowed every drop, then stood up. She sensed how close his own release sat and exactly how much he desired to be inside of her that very second. He gripped the far edge of the table tightly as he slid deep inside her, moaning her name as his climax quickly overtook him.

As another release set off for her, a visible shudder rolled through his body. With each delicate thrust, he moved in and out of her. Gods, the friction created by the slow pace teed her up all over again. Jo reached across, clasping the far side of the table, her legs locking around his arms while lifting her hips. Her talons scraped across his sides.

His cock swelled inside of her, their hips meeting repeatedly. The tip of his shaft stroked her core with each thrust. His claws gripped the edge of the table as he pistoned harder into her without his pace picking up speed.

Her back arched with the sensations rippling through her. With every noise that emanated from him, and every movement he made, it didn't take long at all for her sex to clamp around his length. Waves of pleasure, more massive than the last few she had, gushed all over him. "Fuck."

His hips locked in place as he exploded deep in her core. "Fuck," he growled out, the sound echoing, transforming into a howl. This orgasm was so powerful it sent a prolonged shudder throughout his body, its intensity lasting longer than the last. As he gripped the edge of the table harder, a sharp crack echoed in the room.

Ragged breaths left her mouth as one last shiver passed through her body. She couldn't find words to describe how that felt. Her hands still clutched the table above her head. That was also apparently now broken. Hadn't they replaced this table twice before?

His breath left him in pants. Pierce leaned over, pressed his forehead to hers, and nuzzled her nose. "Mmm. Wow."

"Uh huh." It was all she could say to agree because she absolutely, one-hundred percent, did. She released her hold on the table, stroked the nape of his neck, and brushed a loving kiss across his lips.

His neck arched up against her touch and he let out a low rumble. He released the table, then gently tucked one hand under her neck as he caressed her ears.

"Mmm. I love when you do that." She continued stroking the nape of his neck, trailing her fingers over the back of his head and ears. Never enough.

"I cannot help myself. I love them." His lips curled. "Gods, I have been craving you." Even now, after he'd already orgasmed twice, she sensed his body humming. In her presence, his body was almost constantly sexually charged. Not that she'd ever complain.

"I don't think I'll ever get enough of you." They had certainly spent a lot of time between the sheets over the last few weeks. After she came home from work, before she left, sometimes before morning meal. It might explain why Zinnia spent so little time here with them anymore. A smile crossed her face. She could still feel every part of him.

"I will never get enough of you, my queen." He kissed her deeply as he wrapped his arms around her, taking her with him so she straddled his lap as he sat down. He remained within her, but she felt his reluctance to leave, and she didn't object in the slightest. A shudder ran through him, followed by a low growl, and he began stroking her spine, holding her close before bursting into laughter. "I think we made a bit more of a mess this time."

With her fingers caressing his back, Jo glanced over her shoulder. Not only did the table have a fresh new crack in it, but they'd scattered the dishes and spilled food all over the floor. "Wow. Uh, that we did." Her gaze returned to him, and she noticed the open window, through which a gentle breeze was flowing. Her eyes widened as a hand shot to her mouth, covering a snicker. "We might have given a show too."

He glanced over at the window and chuckled. "Well, you told me to open it."

"Just to air the house out." It kind of got forgotten amid things. "Do you think anybody heard?" Not that it would've been the first time. Her mother had given them a knowing look when they'd spent the night at her house.

"Oh, possibly. Especially if their window was open, like it usually is." He chortled. "At least I remembered to shut the front door when we came back in here. I left it open when I came back inside."

Her eyes bulged out of her head. "Yeah. That's definitely a good thing. I'm sure the last thing you want is for people to see me half naked." At least her dress tied at the back of her neck. Easy to put on and easy to take off. And it had survived.

"No, definitely not." With a kiss to her neck, Pierce re-tied the top of her dress for her. Just in case. Family didn't always knock. "I am extremely content like this. But perhaps we should clean up? I am going to have to get us another new table as well. Or, at the very least, learn how to repair them."

She giggled. "I'd say we should stop breaking them, but I kind of enjoy being splayed out on the table for you."

"You are my favorite meal, my queen."

Yeah, they definitely needed to clean up. She may even need a quick shower. "Yes, we should clean up. I kind of want some more fruit before I have to go to work."

He kissed her, languid and deep, then reluctantly pulled out of her and helped her off of his lap. "I will get some more fruit ready for you as well."

"Thank you, love. I'm going to check my dress and grab fresh underwear before I get in the shower." Her eyes sparkled.

"I will try my hardest not to join you. I know you do not want to be late. If I did, you would probably be very late." He smirked.

She bit her tongue. The official opening time for the bar was sunset, but that didn't mean there wasn't work to do beforehand. Gods, the image he had in his mind. Yum! She slowly backed down the hall. "Mmm, there's always later." With a twinkle in her eyes, she turned and disappeared down the hallway with an extra swing in her hips.

Chapter Thirty-Five

Camouflaged and on all fours, Pierce paced back and forth between the trees of their normal meeting spot. If Jocasta didn't get here soon—like, in the next minute or two—however dangerous it was, he was running the rest of the way and finding her. It was all he'd been able to do to keep from going to the marketplace as it was. He'd felt it each time the nausea and dizziness had hit her, and now it didn't even feel like she was even awake. She shouldn't have gone into work tonight. However well she'd felt before she'd left, whatever illness ailed her hadn't passed yet.

He couldn't stop pacing as he waited for her to show up. Gods, he hated waiting.

His ears pricked up as he heard someone draw near. The footfalls didn't belong to his mate, but he sensed and smelled her close by. He halted in his tracks as they approached. A nine-foot form came through the trees. His camouflage forgotten, Pierce's heart seemed to stop, then break apart, a silent explosion in his chest. He could tell Jocasta was okay, but that didn't stop the worry from slamming into him so hard he almost fell into the tree next to him. Bruce carried her.

He never wanted another male's hands upon her, holding her, or touching her. He barely bit back the growl as it surfaced. No, Bruce had been helping her. That was all. He wouldn't have carried her if it wasn't necessary. She hadn't felt up for the trek. Shifting to his humanoid form, Pierce rushed forward and gently took her from Bruce. "What has happened?"

"We stopped when she did not feel well. I thought we might end up with more stops if it continued, so I convinced her to let me carry her," he said.

Pierce held her close, feeling the steady rhythm of her heart as she nestled against his chest. "Thank you for helping her. I should get her home."

Bruce nodded. "Ambrosia told her to take tomorrow off. She will make arrangements in the morning to cover the booth." He grimaced. "Perhaps, do not tell Jo that."

"Ah, no. I will try not to. I will try to convince her not to return until she is fully well," Pierce replied. "Thank you again."

"You are welcome," Bruce responded, and then took off deeper into the forest.

Jocasta stirred ever so slightly and buried her face a bit more into the crook of Pierce's neck. "Mmm, Pierce. You smell yummy."

A primal growl escaped him before he could stop it, a purely instinctive reaction. A shudder went through her. He felt it through every inch of his body as he turned to go. "You should have stayed home from work today."

"I was fine when I left."

"Bruce said Ambrosia told you to take tomorrow off. Perhaps you should take a few *umbras*. Just to be on the safe side." His thumbs moved rhythmically as he caressed her arm and knee while holding her.

"Tomorrow is one thing, but I'm not leaving Demetrius to run my booth and have to worry about a mess when I get back."

He remembered she'd been cleaning up crumbs for weeks. She'd spoken of it many times, particularly about the collection of cups he'd left behind. Just two days ago, she'd found one still there, hidden behind everything. He quite agreed with his mate; the male was disgusting and had no respect for her equipment. "Your health is more important than anything, my queen."

"You didn't see the pigsty I had to clean up last time," she muttered. "I'll make a deal with you. I'll go see Kaylina in the morning. If she says a few *umbras*, then I'll take a few *umbras*."

He chewed his tongue for a moment. Despite her desire not to, she was being reasonable and making a compromise. It was one he could deal with. "Alright. Though I would prefer you to go sooner rather than later. I just..." He sighed. It was really late. She wouldn't want to run to Kaylina all because she'd thrown up a few times. No matter whether he felt it was a valid reason. "I have been anxious this evening. I came very close to coming to the marketplace." So very close, he'd been out the door at least once before he'd even realized.

"I'm sorry. I probably should've come home sooner, but I thought I could just push through it. The last thing I want is to worry you."

"It is alright, my queen, I just..." His words trailed off and he took a moment to compose himself. "If you are ill, I want to be there to take care of you. I did not like being so far away." And it really wasn't that far away. They had just decided that his staying away from anywhere public was the safest option. Markham wouldn't stop hunting him, and he and Logan had already pushed their luck with his Informants. He let out a heavy breath. "I know it is late. As it is not an emergency..." Though he felt like it was, his mind knew it really wasn't. She had a bug; that was all. She just needed to rest and it would pass. "Morning. First thing. Please? Would you like me to go with you?"

"I'll go first thing in the morning. Promise. I'll be okay going alone."

He wasn't getting much from her, in her thoughts and emotions. But he could tell she didn't want him to go with her. She didn't want him to worry so much about her. But he couldn't help it. "I know you would be okay with going alone. But if you want me to, you know I would." He gave her a soft kiss on the forehead. "You will tell me if you change your mind?"

"If I do, you'll be the first to know."

"Alright." He kissed the top of her head. They spent most of the trek back to the village in silence. Reaching the archway, he didn't pause as it parted for them, and he carried her inside toward their home. Pierce held her with one arm so he could open the door, then brought her inside. "Do you want me to start the shower for you, love?"

"Yes, please." She stroked the nape of his neck and brushed her lips across his jawline. "How would you feel about joining me?"

Strange. She'd spent the evening throwing up more than once, and now she was ready to go again. As her arousal flowed through her and into him, his body ceased to allow much thought. He growled, his eyes flashing. "Are you sure you feel up to that?" Joining her in the shower would cause only one thing. His hand grazed her ass before giving it a playful squeeze.

Raking her nails across his chest, her own eyes flashed, and she rumbled softly at him. "Oh, very much so, my king."

That nap she'd had on the way to their meeting spot must have helped tremendously. The only thing on her mind now was continuing where they'd left off earlier. "Hades, that growl of yours!" As their lips met in a deep kiss, his hand on her neck, they moved toward the hall. He bumped into the table and opened one eye, not stopping the kiss for a moment, as he made his way to the bathroom.

With a decisive kick, Jocasta shut the door behind them as the kiss deepened. Her fingers danced on his neck as their tongues tangled, and the other hand traced the warm line of his spine. He impatiently turned her, his hands gripping her arms, and pressed her against the rough wood of the door. Pulling at her clothes, he tore the dress and underwear from her body. All he cared about was getting the fabric off of her in any way possible. There didn't need to be anything between them.

The scent of her sexual need, her heat, was like bolts of lightning straight to his cock. "I need you," he demanded and plunged his tongue deeper into her mouth. Fuck, would they even make it into the actual shower?

Jocasta moaned, her breath hitching in the heated moment of the kiss, her legs coiling around his waist while her dress and underwear pooled on the floor. Their tongues reengaged as her nails dug into his shoulder blades.

"Nails. Harder." Gripping his shaft, he angled her just right and lowered her down onto it, moaning her name as her sex sheathed every inch of his cock. "Fuck," he barked out.

Her nails bit into his shoulders as he moved her up and down his length, her talons digging into his ass. "Fuck... more..."

"Not... stopping," he panted. His kisses trailed down her jaw and neck as he sucked and licked at her skin. Her scent made every one of his synapses light up and crackle, his eyes glowing brightly. But he kept his rhythm slow, his cock stroking her core as he rocked into her. "Mmm. Mine."

She tilted her head back, giving him more access. He sensed her hyper-sensitivity. Her hips met his, but with his hands on her ass, he controlled the pace. The pressure built slowly inside both of them. Jocasta gripped his shoulder blades tighter and bit his shoulder as a powerful orgasm slammed through her body, the inner walls of her sex clamping around his cock.

His release punched out of him, and he let out a roar that quickly changed to a howl. One hand slapped hard on the bathroom door, the hinges rattling, as his cock continued to jerk and twitch inside of her.

As her nails dug in just a little harder, Jocasta moaned, the sound echoing in the close space. Another climax pulsed through her, following the first as the inner walls of her sex contracted around his cock a second time. As her body stilled, she pulled her teeth from his shoulder, then let her head fall against his chest, her breath coming in ragged gasps.

He leaned his forehead against the door as he tried to catch his breath. Once he finally did, he softly nuzzled her ears before tracing kisses down her neck. "You have to do that again." Gripping her ass firmly, he carried her over to the shower and flipped the water on.

She lifted her head, and her eyes widened. There were marks in his skin. Slight punctures where she'd sunk her teeth into him. Given his fur, they wouldn't be easily noticeable to the naked eye, but she was up close and personal. "Um…" A smile fell on her lips. "Hmm, you may be right. I *need* to do that again."

"Yes, you do, my queen. The way it felt…" With a low growl, his eyes flashed. Checking the temperature of the water, he carefully stepped in with her and shut the curtain. The hard wall pressed against her as he kissed her, his tongue skillfully nudging her lips apart.

She nipped and sucked on his tongue as it found hers, contracting the inner walls of her sex around his cock, still buried deep inside of her. Raking her nails along his back, she grazed his ass with her talons.

The shudder her talons always sent through him was more intense than usual. His back arched into her nails. He moaned loudly into the kiss and deepened it more, drawing a growl out of her. With one hand gripping her ass, he put the other on the shower wall and rocked his hips into her. She continued to contract the inner walls of her sex.

"Fuck, yes," Pierce groaned. Leaning her back slightly, he avidly latched onto her breast, alternating between sucking and licking it as he swayed with her. He wanted to go harder, faster, but his body refused. It wasn't the first time this had occurred either; lately, he hadn't been able to pick up his pace at all. Hades, maybe something was wrong with him. The walls of her sex clamped down on his shaft harder, pulling another growl out of him. Gods, he was going to come again any moment. He ran his tongue across her nipple, savoring the taste. "Come with me, my queen."

With a slight bow of her back, she threw her hands up against the rough texture of the wall. Her thighs clenched and her talons tightened their grip on his ass.

His deep growl reverberated as she reached her peak on his shaft, her sex gripping his cock tightly and intensifying his climax. Leaving her breast, his mouth closed over her shoulder. Though his teeth grazed over her skin, he didn't bite down. It had been a while since he'd actually done that; the last mark he'd given her had faded weeks ago. Not that his love for her was in any way diminished. He *desired* to mark her. He just couldn't get his teeth into the program.

It took a moment for her to move her hands from the wall to his shoulders. She pressed a kiss to the place she had bitten him earlier, then brushed one across his cheek through heavy pants.

His chest vibrated with a low rumble in response. With his chest still heaving, he gently licked her shoulder and then nuzzled her neck. "Mmm, I do not want to pull out of you," he got out between breaths. "But shower, sleep, you need rest." Her energy had already depleted.

"If the water wouldn't get cold, I could just sleep right here." She smirked. "But there's always tomorrow. You'll have me here all *umbra* long."

"I love the sound of that." He stroked her lips with his in a slow kiss, groaning as he pulled out of her and set her on her feet. As her talons found purchase on the floor, she held onto his arm for a moment. As she inhaled and exhaled a deep breath, the water pressure in the shower suddenly shifted. He frowned as her dizziness hit him full force. Keeping a good hold on her, he reached over and shut the water off. "You are dizzy again. The shower can wait. I am taking you to bed."

She opened her mouth, then closed it again. "Okay."

Pierce scooped her up into his arms, carefully stepped out of the shower, and set her down on the toilet lid while he got a towel. He wrapped it around her and grabbed another one for himself. "I will get a shower ready for you in the morning when you wake, and make tea for you before you leave."

"Okay. Thank you."

He finished drying off and hung up his towel, then kneeled down to dry her off as well. "Do you want to wear anything to bed tonight, love?" Though he loved it the best when she curled up against him naked, she would likely get no sleep if she did that tonight. Considering how hard it was for him to keep his hands off of her, it was best not to tempt him.

"I probably should."

He nodded, then wrapped the towel snugly around her and held her, the scent of the fabric filling his senses. He would take care of it later. Zinnia still didn't sleep well most nights, and he didn't want them to run into her out in the hall with Jocasta naked. He exited the bathroom, carried her down the hall into their bedroom, and closed the door behind them. Laying her carefully on the bed, he went to the dresser and retrieved one of her nightgowns. Not even tracking what color it was or what it looked like, he brought it over to her.

She slipped the towel from her body and easily stood on her own. The dizzy spell had passed. As she raised her arms to pull the nightgown on over her head, his gaze zeroed in on her belly—the change that had come over it, however slight it was. Jocasta looked up at him. Their gazes met.

An icy wave washed over him. He felt colder than he had ever felt before. And he sensed her—Pierce mentally shook himself. It was a bug. That was all it was. There was no way it—Pierce gave himself another mental shake. She was just ill. In the morning, the shaman would tell her what she needed to do for the sickness to pass. With his gaze leaving hers, he laid down on his side of the bed and propped up on one elbow. He just stared at her, no words coming to him. He couldn't feel much of anything from her, just tiny snippets of fear. She never held back emotions from him. He couldn't remember a time she'd ever done so. "I should go with you in the morning."

She lowered herself onto the bed and, without looking at him, rolled over to her side and curled up to him. "I'm okay going by myself."

He said nothing at first, then stretched his arm out so she could lay her head upon it. His other hand gently caressed her ears before sliding down to the sensitive nape of her neck. "I know you will be okay, love." He continued a slow path over her shoulder. "You truly do not want me to come?"

"No," she whispered. "I don't." She wasn't looking at him as she uttered the words.

His fingers stiffened, an icy dread gripping his very core. It took him a moment before he could move his hand again. "Okay." It was all he said as he tugged her more against him. He ran his hand down her side and over her hip. Leaning his head back against the wall, he stared up at the ceiling. She gently caressed his fur, her hand resting on his chest over his pounding heart. It wasn't difficult to tell she was trying to comfort him as much as he was trying to comfort her.

A million thoughts went through his head—the last several weeks and her symptoms. He shut them all down, slammed a steel trap down on every single one of them, refusing to let any of the thoughts fully form. He just held and stroked her. Her fingers stilled for only a moment before she returned to caressing his chest. Everything was fine. Everything was going to be fine. She would find out what was wrong in the morning and he would take care of her and help her get well again.

It was a while before Jocasta fell asleep. Her caresses, and her hand over his heart as sleep claimed her, soothed him. Whatever thoughts tried to push their way in, he kept locked down tight. He didn't want to think right now. Just wanted to hold his mate. She was ill, so she was resting. That was the important thing. He focused, listening to her breaths, and the subtle thump of her heart against his body. Sleep completely eluded him.

They had absolutely *nothing* to worry about.

Chapter Thirty-Six

Parthenia peeked back out of the small sliver of the door to her apothecary. She'd kept it partially cracked so she could watch Fagonia. It had taken months to gather all the material she planned to present to her Elder. Gavin had spent so much time helping her, and she'd finally been ready as of a few days ago. But she had to wait for the right moment, so there was no chance that Fagonia interrupted or prevented her from sharing everything she'd learned over the last few years.

She'd seen the female disappear into the library a few minutes ago. Usually, Fagonia only went in there when she was looking for her. Waiting a little longer to ensure the female didn't come back out wouldn't hurt. Although she had grown tired of just sitting there staring out of the opening. But she'd never put a window in her door that she could look through. Besides, people would eventually realize they were being watched. It wasn't like they had many sirens living here any longer.

Their everyday suffering was part of the problem. She couldn't stand by and do nothing anymore. Her people—her sisters—they deserved better; they deserved a chance to thrive and to be happy. Parthenia chewed on the inside of her cheek as she checked again for movement. Nothing. The female hadn't left the library. Huh, interesting. Well, she could look into it a bit more later. For now, she had to take this opportunity while it presented itself.

Getting to her feet, she collected the stack of parchment containing all the documentation that she and Gavin had gathered. Without a second to waste, she left her apothecary and quickly made her way toward Demeter's Temple. While they all lived in houses on the far side of Pteryrina, the Elder lived and worked out of a small building close to the Temple and the main gates. While she'd been there multiple times to deliver regular updates on the levels of The Reflection Pools and The Poppy Fields, none of that compared to this moment.

In a matter of minutes, she could very well end up altering the course of the sirens. And she truly hoped she'd be successful. Parthenia didn't bother to offer acknowledgement to the two guards standing at the closed gates as she passed by them. But she didn't walk as if she were in a hurry to get to the Elder's dwelling. That was the key. Her stroll had to appear natural, as if she was just going for one of her daily meetings with the female.

Parthenia approached the Elder's hut and knocked on the green door, which was offset by the dark brown shade that covered the house along with the inlay of golden borders. Three sacred colors of Demeter. The entire building was the only true color in all of Pteryrina, except for The Poppy Fields and The Reflection Pools. Parthenia waited until the female granted her permission to enter before she opened the door, shut it behind her, and stepped into the main room. Offering the Elder a smile, she bowed her head. "Elder Vasilia, thank you for agreeing to see me."

"Of course, child. To what do I owe this visit?" Vasilia stated from the kitchen.

The front room was where they usually met. And it had always been quite comfortable. It was a large open space that comprised two couches set on either side of a long coffee table on one side of the room. On the other side, three chairs sat around a small round table. Just beyond that was the kitchen, with an enormous counter separating it from the receiving area. Parthenia gestured to the nearby table. "May we sit?"

"Yes, of course." With a plate of sliced plums, the Elder crossed over to the circular table, the sounds of the kitchen fading behind her. Her gaze flickered toward Parthenia as she set the plate down, the clatter echoing in the room. "Would you like some tea?"

"Thank you. That would be lovely." She didn't know what the previous Elders had been like, but she'd always respected Vasilia. The female always had motherly tendencies. At least, what she believed a mother should be like. Her own mother never quite fit the description. But she'd seen how Echo treated her children. It was very different.

Parthenia took a seat at the table. Letting out a quick breath, she rubbed her hands down the skirt of her dress. Her mate could probably feel the tension in her body, and they were miles apart. Something they'd been able to do for quite some time. This was something they both needed. And it would help her species in the long run, too. She watched as the Elder returned with two cups and a ready pot of tea.

Once Vasilia had everything set, the female sat down. "Now. Tell me what is on your mind."

"As you know, I've been monitoring The Reflection Pools and The Poppy Fields. I've conducted a multitude of tests consistently, looking for some kind of change in their chemical makeup. And nothing has altered." Parthenia placed the stack of parchment in her hands on the table. "Based on my findings... I think the issue is magical. If I'm right, that means the cause is linked to something going on with the isle itself."

The Elder's eyebrows knitted together as she picked up the documentation between her slightly withered fingers and scanned through it all. "How do you believe this is possible? We have had nothing to do with the land for over a century."

"I know, but look at how our people have been impacted. It isn't just The Reflection Pools and The Poppy Fields. There's been a decline in births; more females born than males. Plus, we've seen a change in our crops. I've tested the nutrients, the levels of metal particles. Although we have shifted the crops and planted in new areas, nothing has been resolved. This has been an ongoing problem for decades. I believe—if we don't do something, if we don't alter our laws, our current course—we'll lead ourselves into extinction."

Vasilia lifted her gaze momentarily to Parthenia. "You realize that changing a law of such magnitude would need to go before all those of voting age?"

"Yes, and I'm prepared for that." She had one last play to push the Elder to a call for action. One she'd kind of pointed out, but maybe she needed to be a bit more direct about it. "Think about it like this. Only females remain. Although two of us have hit mating age, and others will shortly follow, it'll be impossible for our species to grow if we cannot find mates. Pregnancies still require a male counterpart. While our bodies may adjust our reproduction abilities as the *solaris* go on, it's only supposition that will happen."

Sifting through the pages presented, Vasilia leaned forward and piled them all back together. She tucked a loose strand of her fine, tawny hair back behind her ear. "I will go through this and consider everything you have stated. Allow me two *umbras* to decide."

Two days? Okay. Not what she had hoped for, but it was better than being outright turned down. On the bright side, she'd been able to make her case and offer as much information as she could to the Elder. Parthenia slowly nodded. "Thank you, Elder Vasilia."

"You are welcome. Now, how about we enjoy some tea before you rush off?"

"I'd like that." Though it made her wonder—how had the female known she planned to take off? Yeah, she wanted to get to Gavin as quickly as possible and share the good news, but the only person who knew about him was Cipriana. Right?

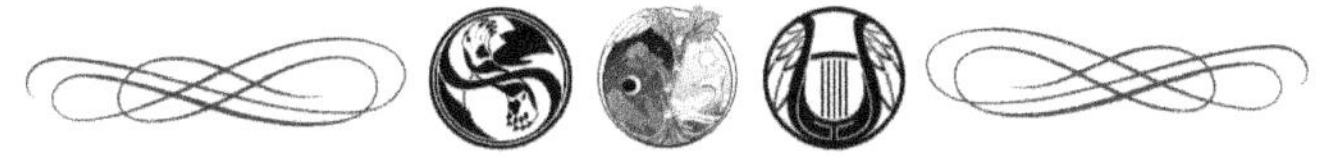

"I love the way your fur has changed," Jocasta said.

The way the sun's rays streamed through their bedroom window showed how his fur had gone from jet black to a deep reddish-brown. Pierce turned his head, a gentle smile gracing his lips, as he stroked her ears softly. "I had not even realized a change until you first said something." He brushed a tender kiss across her lips.

She reached her hand to his neck, and held her lips against his, soft and lingering. "You don't see it unless you're in the sun."

His hand went to her hip, and he almost rolled her beneath him. But she needed a shower so she could go see Kaylina. He gave her another tender kiss. "I am glad it pleases you, my queen."

"Mmm. There isn't much about you that doesn't please me." She ran her fingers up and down the nape of his neck.

A smirk crossed his face as his neck arched up into her touch. "Not much, huh?"

She moved her hand to his jaw and caressed his cheek with her thumb. "Not. At. All."

It was on the tip of his tongue to ask her again if she wanted him to go with her this morning. He wanted to go with her, to be with her, no matter what the issue ended up being. Even if there were a possibility of something, that shouldn't be a possibility. No, it was impossible. And it was *not* that. But Jocasta had been adamant the night before. For whatever reason she refused to share with him, she wanted to go alone. He nuzzled his nose against hers and stroked her lips with his, barely holding back a growl. "Should I start your shower? So, I can make you some tea?"

"Yeah. Shower."

"Okay, love." He kissed her again and was about to move off the bed, but his lips hovered over hers. He didn't want to move away from her, couldn't pull his body away from hers. His cock twitched. His mouth parted, and he took several deep breaths. Licked his lips. With a groan, he forced himself off the bed and out the door, down the hall, and into the bathroom. Flipping the water on, he checked the temperature and ensured it was just right before heading to the kitchen. Zinnia's bedroom door was open. Not that she was in there. She wasn't in the living room or kitchen either. His sister must already be at Logan's for morning meal. She really had spent barely any time here lately. How long had it been since she'd been here regularly? He couldn't even put a finger on it. Pierce started a fire and filled the teapot while he waited for the stove to heat.

He sensed it when, after a minute, Jocasta slowly got out of bed. Hades—he'd barely touched her and she was turned on. As she moved about their bedroom, he could hear the light scratching of her talons against the wooden floor, a familiar sound. The smell of tears, briny and sharp, permeated the kitchen. He felt pricks of her emotions, fear and sadness, because she was holding back from him—he froze in motion. The tea-bag he held lingered over the mug he'd set out for her to use. His body tried to force him down the hall to the bedroom, where his mate was. But she didn't want to talk about whatever was bothering her, what had been on her mind, what was scaring her. She wanted to do this—whatever *this* was—without him. While his mind wanted to respect her decision, however much he hated it, his body had other ideas. He'd gotten halfway across the room, intent on getting to his mate, before he realized and grabbed onto the wall. The tea-bag remained in his hand. Curling his claws into the palm of his hand, he turned around and returned to the kitchen.

Sixty-seven. Sixty-seven. Sixty-seven. That I know about. He slammed the door in his head shut, locked it, and refused to let any more of *that* nightmare in.

Pierce got the tea going for her. Then he leaned against the kitchen counter and stared out the window. It was all he could do to keep his mind quiet. Focus on nothing, not even the gentle sounds of Jocasta's movements around the house as she showered and dressed. He barely noticed the passage of time until his mate wrapped her arms around his waist. She had her hair pinned up and wore a lavender-colored dress, much like the one she'd worn the day before.

His arms encircled her, and he gave her a soft kiss on her ear before he laid his head against hers. It was a struggle to keep his mind empty against the memories that were trying to invade—*NO.* He refused to think of them. *This* was not the same thing. *This* was not the same situation. Jocasta was absolutely *not*—she was not. His mate was just ill; sick with some kind of bug. Kaylina would tell her what to do, and he would do it. He would take care of his mate and help her get better again. That was the end. He kissed the top of her head. "I made your tea. When will you head over?"

"As soon as I finish the tea."

He still couldn't catch her thoughts or most of her emotions, but he sensed she didn't want to let go of him. Not just yet. She just needed to stand there in his arms a little longer before she drank her tea. He lazily skimmed his fingers down her spine as they held onto one another. She could hold on to him for as long as she needed to. If the tea got cold, well, he would just make some more.

He wasn't sure exactly how long they stood like that. Not long enough for the tea to get cold, but surely long enough for it to be lukewarm. Which was okay. His mate never minded drinking it that way. She didn't move to the table, or sit in a chair in the living room, or even sit on the bench of the piano. She stood in the kitchen and drank it.

He leaned back against the counter as she did so. Held her hand in one of his, stroked his thumb over her fingers and the back of her hand. Just staring down at her—his beautiful, kind, wonderful, perfect, caring, spirited queen. Why did he feel like there was a void growing between them? They had moved past all of that at the basin, when they'd spilled their darkest thoughts. All the unhappiness that had disturbed their peace. They'd decided they would not allow it to destroy their joy any longer. Yet here they were, barely talking. They hadn't made love before getting up like they usually did. And they were keeping things, fears, from each other. Again. Why?

Pierce opened his mouth, then snapped it shut. She'd finished her tea. "I am going to go next door. While you are gone." *Ask me to go,* he silently begged. *Ask me to go, please.*

Jocasta's gaze shifted to the floor. "I, uh, I'm gonna wash up the dishes, then go. It should be half an hour at most. Then I'll join everyone."

"It is just your mug." He had drunk no tea. Or eaten because he would eat at Logan and Ambrosia's. He hadn't eaten hardly anything since yesterday's morning meal, actually. Afternoon meal had been—nope. He couldn't go there right now, not when they had places to be. During evening meal last night, he'd been too worried to eat much. "Let me take care of it while you go. Then I will head next door."

"Are you sure?"

"Yes, of course, my queen." He brought her hand to his lips and kissed her wrist. He wanted to pull her hard into his arms and—the height of the counter created some interesting possibilities. Good gods, how was this even on his mind right now? He couldn't help it; she smelled incredible. "I do not mind at all."

Jocasta hugged him, threaded their fingers together, and brushed her lips across their joined hands. It seemed like they were both keeping their thoughts and feelings from one another. Doing whatever they could to be strong for each other. But he couldn't help but think they were going about this all the wrong way. "I love you, Pierce, my king. It'll be fine. We're going to be fine."

All he could do for a moment was nod. He took her face in his hands, feeling the smoothness of her skin as he caressed her cheeks, and then looked deep into her gorgeous amber eyes. "I love you too, Jocasta, my queen." No matter what. No matter what, they would get through it. They would find a way. Pierce kissed her forehead, his lips lingering for a moment. If he kissed her lips right now, he might not stop. "I love you so much."

She placed her hand over his. "It'll be fine," she repeated.

"I know," he whispered. He pressed another kiss to her forehead. "I love you, my queen. I will see you soon."

"I love you too." She lifted her gaze to his for a moment, then turned and headed for the door. She paused on her way out. "I'll be back as soon as I can."

To stop himself from following her, he gripped the rough counter tightly behind him. "Soon. I will see you next door."

She walked out of the house. He watched her through the window as she stopped on the front porch and stood there for a minute. She glanced over her shoulder, faced the door, and hesitated. Whatever had crossed her mind, he didn't get. Instead, he stared at her as she descended the staircase and took off toward the medical building.

Stab. Stab. Stab. Honest to gods, it felt like someone stabbed him in the chest. Hades, he wanted to go with her, but she didn't want him to. Right. This would not make the next half hour go any quicker. Pierce rolled his shoulders, trying unsuccessfully to rid the tension from his body. He cleaned up the kitchen, left the house, and headed next door.

When he got to Logan's porch, he heard everyone inside. Moving around. Talking. Laughing. His mood was dark. He didn't want to take that inside to his family. He sat down on the top step. Leaning on his knees, he put his head in his hands.

After a minute, the door opened and his brother stepped out onto the porch. Logan sat down on the step next to him and squeezed his shoulder. Right. No way Logan wouldn't have sensed his emotions, even from inside the house. "Care to talk about it?"

He didn't look up, keeping his head in his hands. "Jocasta has not been feeling well lately. She just went to see Kaylina. But she did not want me to go," Pierce mumbled.

"Did she tell you why?"

"No. Just that... she would be okay going by herself. And when I pressed, she said she did not want me to come." *Sixty-seven.* He shut that down hard and scrubbed his face. "She just has a bug. Kaylina will know what to do to help her feel better. She will be fine. Fine."

"Are you trying to convince me? Or are you trying to convince yourself?"

Oh, himself. Definitely himself. Because *nothing* about this situation was fine. A sideways glance at his brother was all it took for Pierce to bury his face in his hands, his shoulders shaking. "I do not even think it is possible for me to..." His words trailed off. "And we have not... discussed it, but..." He gripped his neck. "No. No. She is just ill. I am sure of it." Because he *had* to be sure of it. Had to *make* himself be sure of it. It was the only thing he could handle.

"And if she is not?"

He couldn't say anything for a moment. The truth of the matter was—whether they wanted to believe it—it *was* a possibility. Oh, gods, he felt sick. Each gasp was a desperate prayer, a fight against the crushing weight threatening to steal the air from his lungs. "I do not know," he whispered. "I... I cannot..." If she was... Pierce tried, but he couldn't get air into his lungs. It was a damn good thing he was sitting down.

His brother gripped his shoulder tightly. "They are stronger than we are, brother. Sometimes, they can hear news we are nowhere near ready for."

A cold sweat prickled his skin as his breath hitched, each inhale a struggle against the suffocating dread. Where the fuck was all the air? "So, you think... maybe good... that I did not go this morning?" He dragged his hand down his face. Maybe if he rattled his brain cells, his organs would start working properly.

Logan cleared his throat.

Hades, he was being selfish. He couldn't imagine how difficult this was for his brother to talk about after what had happened with him and Ambrosia.

"If the shaman does not say it is a bug, would you be ready to hear that?" Logan asked.

He almost didn't hear the words his brother spoke. The only sound he could discern was the deafening thud of his own heart. If it wasn't a bug—which, of course, it was, but *if* it was not—was he ready to hear that? *Sixty-seven.* He squeezed his eyes shut. "I want to say yes, but..." Pierce swallowed past the ache in his throat. "No," he whispered.

"Then maybe it is good she went alone."

"I should be there. It should not be like this. I am supposed to be strong for her. She should not be doing this alone." But she had wanted to.

"There are several ways we can be strong for our mates. Even if it means we have to step back." Logan rubbed his eyes. "So, be strong for her when she returns from her checkup."

Pierce didn't miss how his brother rubbed his own eyes, but, gods, with everything that thundered through him right now—not to mention the subject—it had to be a miracle Logan could sit this close to him at all.

Taking in a few shallow breaths to calm himself, he rolled his shoulders, focused on steadying his racing heart and the churning sensation that pulsed through him. "Yes. I cannot be like this when she gets back. I will…" His words trailed off. Pierce's voice lowered. "Everything is going to be fine. She will be fine. We will be fine." His fingers briefly gripped the bridge of his nose. "Okay. I should eat; I need to eat. I have barely eaten lately. Is there anything that needs to be done inside?"

"They were setting the table and finishing up."

"Okay, alright." Pierce lifted his gaze, staring out across the way. Jocasta would come back, and she would tell him that everything was fine, that she just had a bug, and the illness would pass soon. Everything would go back to normal. Right. How much longer would he be able to convince himself of that? He turned his head and looked at Logan. "Thank you, brother," he mumbled.

Logan simply dipped his chin in acknowledgement. It took a moment before he stood and went back inside. Pierce got up and followed him in.

Pierce just stood there in the doorway. He couldn't seem to move. Someone gently took him by the arm, steered him to the table, and into a chair. He barely noticed what was happening until a plate full of food appeared in front of him. He glanced up at Zinnia, who knitted her eyebrows together.

"Eat," his sister said.

He just nodded. He suddenly couldn't seem to get his voice to work. She put a fork in his hand and filled a cup for him. He didn't track what liquid went inside it.

"Eat," she repeated.

With another small nod, Pierce started eating, slowly at first, but as the first bite hit his stomach, he barely held back a moan and he practically shoveled the food into his mouth. Hades, he was starving. He'd really had barely any food lately. Not that he could say why.

"When was the last time you ate well?" Zinnia asked. He didn't answer her, as his mouth was full of food. She just shook her head and walked away.

Chapter Thirty-Seven

Jo stared at the door to the medical building. She had spent the last couple of days doing everything possible to keep her emotions at bay, to keep her thoughts away. The last thing either she or Pierce needed was to feel her fear, her concerns. What she thought this *bug* was and gods, she still hoped she was wrong.

Was she going about this all wrong? Should she have had him come with her? Who was she trying to protect? Him? Her? They were supposed to lean on each other, weren't they? Was that why it felt all wrong? It would have been smart to have him come with her; except they had never actually talked about *it* as a possibility. It was always in passing. Never a reality that either of them considered. And now that it stared them both in the face...

Gods, please don't let it be *that*. She and Kaylina had the conversation that had been necessary when she turned sixteen. Facts. Statistics. All of it. For every part of her. Merfolk. Siren. Shape shifter. The chances. Those facts and statistics had tugged consistently at the back of her mind. No, it was better this way.

With a deep breath, she steeled her resolve, and entered the building.

"Hi, Jocasta." Kaylina's mouth curled at the corners. "Are you feeling okay?"

Nope. Not at all. She shouldn't have convinced herself it was better if Pierce wasn't here, but she had decided. And it wasn't without reason. "Um, that's actually what I came to talk to you about."

"Well, come on back. We will get you settled and you can tell me your symptoms." Kaylina gestured down the hallway.

Her mouth was dry despite the tea she had finished not that long ago. Jo followed the female to one of the back rooms. Her gaze fell on the bedding, then across some tools the female kept, and herbs, and so on. Gods, she was really here—in a room. There was no turning back now.

Kaylina approached the chairs near the small table and gestured toward one with a nod. "Have a seat. Tell me what you have been feeling."

Right. She took up one chair as the door was closed. Her symptoms. All of them. "I, uh, I've been feeling a little off lately. Threw up a few times yesterday and had a couple of dizzy spells. My appetite has been, well, kind of all over the place. Plus, I've gained some weight, and my, uh, my breasts are a tad bigger, and I seem to be hypersensitive... all over." She hadn't meant to spit it all out like that, but she had to get it out. If she didn't, she might not include everything.

"Okay. When did the vomiting and dizzy spells start?"

"Uh, yesterday." She had felt slightly nauseous over the last few weeks, but she hadn't thrown up like she did the day before. And there definitely hadn't been any dizzy spells.

"When did you notice the weight gain?" Kaylina sat in the chair across from her.

"Well, yesterday, but my jeans had gotten a little snug before then. Maybe a *penumbra* ago." At least that was the first time they had felt a bit on the tighter side.

"What about your breasts? The hypersensitivity?"

Gods, she had to think. Her gaze fell on her hands. When had she first seen it? Paid attention to it? She didn't know. It had been after the basin, when she and Pierce had talked. Laid it all out. But they hadn't, had they? They had discussed Leo, Pierce's past, and her father's ashes. But they completely skirted the possibility of *this*. She had told him he would be a good father and that had been the end. Anytime they talked about it, it was always in passing. Gods, she had meant to. How had they managed not to talk about it? She never thought of it as a possibility. Had he? Had he considered it? In more than just passing? She blinked, and the salty sting of a tear rolled down her cheek. Damn. How had that... Jo wiped her face. "I, um, a few *penumbras* ago. I think."

Kaylina held out a square linen to her. "Is it possible you could be pregnant?"

With the tissue clutched in her hands, she stared at it. She didn't want to think about that word. The short answer was yes. They hadn't exactly been safe from day one. But she didn't think it would ever be possible for her. Not with her mixed species. "I, uh..." She hiccupped a quiet sob. Not that she understood why she was even crying. Wiping her face, she opened her mouth, but the words caught in her throat, refusing to come out. Why was this so hard?

Standing up, Kaylina strode over and took Jo's hands in her own. "It is all right. We will check and go from there. Yes?"

Jo just nodded. It was all she could do. Gods, she should've let Pierce come. He had wanted to, but she kept pushing him away. She didn't want him to sense her concern or fear, or to worry. Over something they hadn't ever discussed. The statistics had been that constant nagging feeling overriding everything. Was that why she had never brought it up?

"Inhale and exhale. Take a deep breath with me."

She took a deep, shuddering breath, trying to compose herself and squash the tears. With her tears still clinging to her cheeks, she took another shaky inhale and exhale. And another. And another. She wiped the tears from her face. "I'm okay."

"Change into a gown and I will return in a few moments." The female gave Jo's hands a quick squeeze and left the room.

Right. The gown. Her gaze flicked to the pink gown that barely covered anything. Normally she wouldn't mind changing into it, but what if it was that? What if Kaylina's thought process was right? Then what?

She didn't know.

She could do this. Pierce needed her to be strong. For him, she could be. Chewing on the inside of her cheek, Jo got to her feet and quickly changed from her dress to the practically nothing-there pink gown. Then she walked to the bed and sat on the edge. Maybe this differed from all her other checkups, but she had been through some of this before.

The door opened and Kaylina returned with a small tray of instruments. "I would like to check your pulse and blood pressure first."

Still sitting up, Jo gave the female a brief acknowledgement. Easy enough. She could handle that. It was the other tools that worried her a little. She hadn't ever seen that glowing blue disc before. What was that?

What was it supposed to do? She nearly jumped when Kaylina's fingers settled upon the inside of her wrist. What was she—oh, right—her pulse.

"Eighty-five. This is good. Now, I am going to check your blood pressure."

This one she knew. The little air thing. It took a couple of tries for Kaylina either to get it to work or she was double-checking something. She wasn't quite certain. All she knew, it took longer than usual.

"Your blood pressure is a little low. Would explain your dizzy spells."

Oh. Simple enough. As she thought back on it, she hadn't eaten an evening meal last night. She had made a couple of attempts to go to the kitchen for something, then the smell hit and sent her running to the bathroom. Maybe that was why she got dizzy both times last night.

Setting the instrument aside, Kaylina retrieved the glowing blue disc. "Lie back. I am going to place this against your lower belly here. It may be cool, but it will allow me to see your uterus."

Right. Okay. She could do this. Slowly, she lowered herself onto the bed, the sheets cool against her skin. The female had been right. The blue disc was a bit on the cold side. She focused her attention on the ceiling above her. Stared at the crevices and counted the lines, noting the way they crisscrossed.

"Congratulations, Jocasta. You are pregnant. From what I see, I would say about six *penumbras*. Would you like to hear the heartbeat?"

"Huh?" What had she said? Had she said—no... no, it wasn't possible. It wasn't. They weren't—they hadn't—and now...

"The heartbeat. Would you like to hear it?"

A rather loud racing *thump, thump, thump, thump* filled the air. She must've nodded or said something. She didn't recall having said anything. Tears rolled down her cheeks at the sound. "It's so—" Jo swallowed the lump in her throat. "So fast."

"That is normal. They are growing and their hearts beat much faster than ours."

"So... so, it's okay?"

"Yes. The baby looks perfectly healthy." Kaylina's lips upturned as she removed the glowing blue disc from Jo's belly. "In a few *penumbras*, you will see an image of the baby for yourself. In the meantime, there are a few things I would like you to adjust."

It was okay. Healthy. Then why was she crying again? Jo wiped at her face and replayed the female's words in her head as she sat up. "Um, okay. Adjust. I can... I can do that." Yeah. She could do that.

"Limit your caffeine intake. If you are taking hot showers or baths, make them lukewarm. They attribute to your dizziness. Also, make sure you get plenty to eat and drink, and lots of rest. No fresh—"

"Don't even say it." Nope. She couldn't even think about it.

Kaylina chuckled. "Very well. I will give you some herbs that will help with your vomiting. It is perfectly normal at this stage, but I always like to take extra precautions. I am also going to give you a supplement. The baby requires a lot of your nutrients as it grows."

Doable. It all sounded doable. Easy to adjust. Take some herbs and remove a few things from her diet. Oh, and avoid hot showers. Minor adjustments. Tugging the gown closed as much as possible, she chewed on the inside of her cheek. "Can I, um, ask you something?"

"Of course."

Oh, how did she put this? Delicately? Straight forward? She sighed. "Is it normal for mates to... be really active? Sexually?"

The female let out a soft laugh. "Yes. Your hormones are increasing, which often makes your scent more noticeable."

Well, that was good to know. Explained why they couldn't keep their hands off each other. Not that it clarified—no, she wouldn't ask about that. Something told her that was between her and Pierce. Good gods, they had made a—she couldn't even think of the term yet.

Six weeks. Could something go wrong? She had heard the heartbeat, and it sounded strong, but it could change, right? How many females in the village had faced that? Gods, how was she supposed to tell Pierce? Jo frowned. "These changes—they'll... they'll help, right?"

Reaching over, Kaylina squeezed her hand. "Yes. We will take every precaution necessary to see you through the next four and a half *cycles*."

Right—four and a half *cycles*. Eighteen weeks. That was a long time to get through. A lot could happen between now and then. Every precaution, she repeated in her head. There had to be a good way to tell him. Not just blurt it out. Oh, gods. They were eating breakfast with everyone. She definitely could not tell him in front of their entire family. But he would ask. Of course he would. He had been so worried about her last night. And that had just been throwing up. How would he react when she told him this?

Okay, she had options. The last time they had spoken in private was in the back bedroom. No, that wouldn't do. Nearly everyone in their family had extensive hearing. Their entire conversation would be heard. She knew Ambrosia had heard them last time. The lullaby had been her idea. Jocasta dragged a weary hand down her face. She'd find another way.

Maybe when they got home. They had all day together, right? Yeah. Then she could say, oh, hey, remember that thing we haven't talked about? Well, it's kind of here. Gods, how was she supposed to tell him when she couldn't even say it in her own head?

Time. She couldn't wait forever, but she could at least wrap her own head around it. Maybe while she did that, she could... yeah. Something special. She could make it into something special.

She liked that idea.

"Jocasta? Did you hear me?"

"What? Sorry. No."

"I am going to get your herbs mixed while you get dressed."

"Okay. Thank you," Jo said. Herbs. Right. Okay. She had a plan, which was good. She watched as Kaylina left the room, taking all her tools with her, and then got to her feet. Yeah, a plan was good. Even if it was only partial.

Writing a song was out of the question, but she could certainly make something. Who could she get to help her? What would she make? Biting her bottom lip, she changed out of the gown and back into her own clothes, then sat in a chair patiently. Oh gods, what if he didn't want it? Or what if he freaked out? Jo bounced her knee anxiously as she gripped the tense muscles at the back of her neck. It would be alright. They'd figure it all out.

As she waited, she pulled her dress a little tighter, and her eyes dropped to her small belly. It wasn't much, but it was there. Part of her wanted to touch her belly, rest a hand on it, but what if it hurt the—nope. She would not take that chance. She let the dress fall loose just as the door opened.

Kaylina stepped back in and set two different pouches on the table. She pointed to the purple pouch. "This is your nutrient supplement. Drink this with breakfast. And this other one is to help with your nausea. You are going to drink this twice an *umbra*. For today, lunch and just before bed.

Tomorrow, when you first wake up and just before bed, and then continue that way going forward. Okay?"

"Sounds good."

"Excellent. Now, I am making an appointment for you in three *umbras*. I would like to check your blood pressure again."

She picked up the pouches. Wait, did that mean...? "Um, do I need to take off of work?"

"Today and tomorrow and we will discuss again at your next appointment."

Oh, gods. That would mean that for two days Demetrius would have his greasy paws all over her stuff. It was to get her blood pressure back to normal. That was needed for the—nope, she still couldn't say it. Okay. Two days. She could handle two days. With the pouches in hand, she got to her feet and followed Kaylina back to the front. "Okay. First thing in a few *umbras*. I'll see you then."

"Come back if you need to. Any time of night, Jocasta."

She stopped with her hand on the door. Right. Just like—she couldn't think like that. Healthy. That was how she needed to think. Healthy. "Okay." Without another word, she left.

She had watched. Those forty-two females who had come out happy, only to be saddened within a matter of weeks. She didn't know whether she would be among them. Healthy—it was healthy, she reminded herself once again. It didn't mean she could look at her belly or even touch it. Eventually, it would be inevitable. Right? Eventually, she'd be able to... it was their—nope, still couldn't think it, let alone say it. She didn't know how, but somehow, they'd get through this.

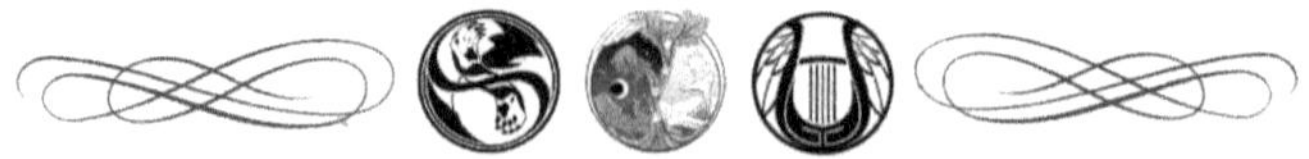

Pierce hadn't said a word throughout morning meal. When he finished his food, he didn't track who picked up his plate and utensils and took them to the sink. He sat staring at the table; the silence amplifying the stillness. Not much conversation had gone on with any of them. Lilli had been quiet, but she hadn't seemed upset or anything. Tension had never sat well with her, and there was certainly plenty of that. Logan was upset, though he didn't outwardly show it. It wasn't hard to tell, though.

He sensed it when his mate returned to their home. First, she entered their bedroom, lingering for a moment to gaze upon the rumpled sheets of their bed. Then she left and came over here. Jocasta ascended the stairs to the porch and paused at the door, her hand hesitating on the knob before she came inside.

As soon as the door closed behind her, Pierce pushed back from the table and practically bolted across the room. He hardly noticed Zinnia startled or comforted Lilli. He reached for his mate and wrapped his arms around her, their embrace a silent moment as no one else stirred. In her hands, she clutched a purple pouch. Those smells—the steel door in his head slammed shut again. He lowered his voice. Not that it would help with their family's excellent hearing, but he did it anyway. "What did she say?"

"I'm fine. Just a little low blood pressure. She gave me some herbs for everything."

He stroked her ears, searching her eyes. Just a little low blood pressure. She was fine. Everything was fine. Was there more to it? Part of him knew that there was. The other part refused to acknowledge it. He dropped a kiss on her forehead, his lips lingering. If it was more, would he be okay? Hades, with the way he'd felt all morning? He didn't have an answer for that, not one that made him feel good about himself. He leaned back and stared into her amber gaze. "That is all she said?" A loud clatter echoed from behind him, causing him to swiftly glance over his shoulder.

Zinnia had gotten out of her chair and set her plate on the kitchen counter. "Please excuse me. I promised to help in the gardens today." She headed to the front door, pausing with her hand on the knob. "Lilli, would you like to join me?" His youngest sister didn't vocalize a response, just offered a silent yes, and left her plate on the counter before the two exited the house.

Ambrosia didn't even bother excusing herself. She just stood up and disappeared down the hallway.

With a heavy sigh, Logan collected his and his mate's plates and trailed after her.

And just like that, the room was empty.

Jocasta averted her gaze to the floor. Without lifting her eyes, she said, "She, uh, she wants me to take today and tomorrow off and see me back in three *umbras*. Some diet changes and, uh, no more hot showers or baths."

He could have frozen water with a single touch right now, with the chill that swept through him. Swept through him and held. There was more. Oh yes, there was more. But she wasn't telling him. Because he couldn't get it together. The vow they'd made at the basin—he couldn't do it. He couldn't think of *that*. The possibility that—*nope*. No. Surely, if—no. It was several moments before he spoke. "Okay." He stole a quick kiss on her head, because she was refusing to make eye contact, and then moved to the table, fixing her a plate. Pierce sat it in front of a chair, then cleaned up.

The emotions swirling within her were a tempest he felt, hard to understand amid the chaos of both their feelings. Jocasta's fingers clutched the bag of herbs in her hand. She got a glass of water and then headed to the empty table. "Did you eat?"

"Yes, Zinnia made me."

Though he had his back turned to her, he felt her eyes upon him, and every move she made. Jocasta removed one of the proportioned pouches from the larger one, and mixed it with water.

How many times had his mother taken those herbs? Hundreds? Thousands? Not that they'd helped much. She'd still gotten so sick most of the time that she could barely consume food. And then *that day* would come. She would be gone from the hut, and Logan with her. He stayed far away from the hut for the day because all he could smell was the bl—

A chill ran through him, and he slammed the door shut once more, but then another one swung inward. Zinnia's screams as Ailwin—*NOPE.* Slam. Lilli—he slammed that one shut even harder. He couldn't do it. Couldn't stare those memories in the face. Couldn't face *that* reality. He cleaned up the counters and washed the dishes. It wasn't *that*. It couldn't be *that*. She would tell him if—wouldn't she? All he felt from her, when he got anything at all, was fear. His mental state wasn't helping a single bit, either. But he couldn't do it. He almost peered over his shoulder, but if he did, he would crack. Pierce opened his mouth, then snapped it shut. He couldn't do it. Couldn't talk about it. Not even if Logan wasn't down the hall right now. Maybe... maybe it was too late, if it was *that*—which, of course, it wasn't. But *if* it was... maybe... That would make sense.

"What should we do today, love?"

Jocasta stared at the cup of mix and the food. She hadn't quite touched any of it yet. She picked up the cup but hesitated before drinking any of it. "Hmm." She paused, the silence of the moment hanging heavy around them. "What if we feed the spourgiffs?"

The memory of the first time she had shown him the spourgiffs came into his head and he smiled a little. What had seemed like impending doom had turned into hope. They had spent time there, conversed, spoken briefly about his mother and her father, made love against the wall and—oh, Hades, if... Oh, *no*, they couldn't do that. They had already... *so many* times, and—no. No way, absolutely not, not if... No. He mentally shook himself. Not until he was sure. If she would even tell him. But they could feed the creatures. They could do that. That could be fun. "Yes. We could do that. If that is what you wish to do, my queen, that is what we will do." He clamped down hard on his thoughts and his fears. They stayed down this time, and he glimpsed over his shoulder at her.

"Yeah. That would be nice." With a quick look, Jocasta saw the empty table, and the quiet made the space feel vast.

As he finished the dishes, he would steal glances at her. She was eating, but not even a third of her plate was gone. But the drink with the herbs was gone. Pierce cleared his throat and joined her in the dining room. "You need to eat, too." He got closer to the table and—the gods must truly hate him. It was timed perfectly. A gentle breeze found its way in through the open window, ruffling her hair as he held the chair. Her scent—a mix of sweetness and spice—suddenly filled his senses. His eyes flashed, and he was immediately hard as stone. He snarled with lust, his grip on the chair tightening. It took everything in him to force his hands to release their hold. He had broken their own furniture, but he wouldn't break Logan and Ambrosia's. The sensations, the need, pulsed through him. As he pivoted, he darted into the kitchen, immediately pressing his body against the cool counter. "Shit," he hissed out. He turned the cold water on, splashed it over his face, and scrubbed hard. "When you finish eating, we can go. See the spourgiffs. Feed them. Yes. Um. Go ahead. Finish eating, love."

She readjusted in the chair, her thighs rubbing against each other. Oh, Hades, he could feel it, as if they were his own. Her sex practically called out to him. His lips parted as he panted. Fuck, his throat was parched. Oh, good, the water was still on. He splashed more on his face, drank some from his hands, and shut the water off.

"Pierce..." She paused. Gods, he could feel how much she wanted him. The ache in her already. "I'm..."

Losing it—nope, that was him. He was completely mentally losing his shit right now. He needed to be inside her, buried deep in her core, but if—*if*—oh, no, nope, can't do that. They couldn't do that. Pierce dragged his hands down his face. "We should go. Are you ready to go? Feed them?" Feed my mouth with your—He barely bit back a growl. "Um."

Jocasta's feet carried her across the room. She stepped into the kitchen. His desire intensified with every step she took toward him. He needed to be inside her more than he required air in his lungs. Which seemed to escape him at the moment. But... *if*... He couldn't. They couldn't. Another shudder passed through him. His body's need and the threatening reality in his head were throwing blows. He dug his claws so deep into his palms that he felt a sharp pain. With his closed fists pressed against his forehead, he leaned over in thought. Tried to take deep breaths. He opened his mouth. The words got stuck. It was like his brain short-circuited. Fuck, he had to get out of this house. Where were they? Logan and Ambrosia's. This wasn't even their house. They had to leave here before—

Jocasta paced the length of the kitchen. "Pierce... I'm..." Her words trailed off. "Not what we thought. I'm... six *penumbras*... healthy. I'm... we're healthy."

His blood pounded in his ears. *Six... penumbras... six... penumbras... six... penumbras.* Oh, look, the world was tilting. He barely registered a thud. The back of his head throbbed. Why was he looking at the ceiling?

"Pierce!" Jocasta kneeled down beside him and checked the back of his head, but he didn't feel any blood.

As he desperately searched for her face, his vision blurred. His lungs tightened. He couldn't breathe. *Six. Penumbras.* Something wet poured down his face. He couldn't hold it back anymore—the overwhelming fear—as it rushed through him in torrents. No, he couldn't let her feel all of this from him; it wasn't good for the... the... *Oh, gods. Oh, gods. Oh, gods.* His hand shook as he tried to find hers.

Jocasta grabbed his hand and squeezed hard as she sobbed. He didn't squeeze her hand back—couldn't—just let her squeeze his. What if he squeezed too hard? He couldn't track anything going through her mind.

He couldn't get his body to move as she laid her head on his chest. No, he had to stay still—despite the trembling in his body that had to stop—what if he moved the wrong way? *Sixty-seven* that he knew about. *Sixty-seven.* What were the odds? Not good. Not good at all. He couldn't... no... no... not her... not his queen. He had lost so many brothers and sisters that he hadn't been able to bring himself to say goodbye to them. Lost his mother. Zinnia had lost her daughter. Lilli had not been—then he'd almost not been able to... Logan and Ambrosia. What if—fuck, no, not her. Not his mate. Not theirs... theirs... He couldn't even think *that* word right now.

Gods, one of them needed to say something. But how could he expect her to say something when he couldn't? Gods, why had they never talked about this? Actually, discussed it. Both sides. So many losses. Oh gods, she was scared. Terrified. She was crying. He had to pull himself together. *Right. Now.* His mate, his queen, she needed him. He had to *pull. Himself. Together.* Pierce squeezed his eyes shut and focused on the steady rhythm of her heartbeat against him. Strong. Strong heartbeat. What she had said before finally registered. *Healthy. Healthy. Healthy.* He repeated it over and over in his head, trying desperately to ignore the 'for now' that stabbed at the back of his brain. *Deep breaths. Deep. Breaths.* He brought his trembling hand to her head, his fingers lingering as he caressed her ears. Tears continued to stream down his cheeks. Pierce feared moving, so he just flicked his eyes toward her, staring at her, as his hand brushed gently down her ears. "Jo," he whispered. It was all he could get out.

"I'm so sorry... I just couldn't... if she... and I thought... and then she did..."

"Shh." Fuck, his voice was so shaky. "No... no sorry." Gods, what if she had taken him with her? If he had been there for *that*, he would probably be worse than he was now. No, *probably* about it. Or maybe it would have helped. He would never know. Pierce kept up the gentle caresses of her ears. His mate needed him, and he needed to stop breaking in half. "Healthy?" His voice cracked.

Jocasta sniffled as she choked back her sobs. Tears still silently fell down her face. "Yes," she mumbled.

"Healthy," he whispered, trying to blink back a fresh wave of tears. *For now.* Nope—he couldn't let the memories in. They had to stay locked away. He was barely handling this. *Get it together.* "Okay. Healthy. Good."

Fuck, he couldn't even form sentences. "Both? You, and...?" He still couldn't say it.

"Yes," she replied, her voice hoarse. "She really said low blood pressure. And she, uh, another bag of herbs."

He couldn't nod his head, couldn't jostle her. One wrong move—that was all it would take. The words went through his head, but only some of them came out. *More herbs,* "For?" *What do we do for your,* "Blood pressure?" Fuck, this was not getting it together. Pierce brushed his fingers over her ears.

"The herbs are help with the throwing up. Blood pressure..." Her words trailed off. "No hot showers or baths. Limit caffeine. And..." She paused. "Meals. Regularly, lots to drink, and rest. She'll check it again in a few *umbras.*"

He shook harder, and with a decisive movement, he removed his hand from her head. He didn't want to, but he wouldn't take his other hand away from her. His hand clenched into a fist and couldn't release. "Okay." He could do this, couldn't he? Yes, absolutely. Whatever it took. She needed him. She needed him. Their—couldn't say it—but *it* needed him too. Oh gods. Why couldn't he get it together? "Okay. Got it. Got it. Okay." *When do you take the,* "Herbs? When?" His hand released. His fingers moved through her hair and brushed against the delicate curve of her ear. A few days. A few days. Fuck, he wanted to be there. To go with her. Would it be possible for him to do it? She shouldn't have gone alone today. Shouldn't have felt like she had to. Why couldn't he—*calm down, Pierce. Calm down. Healthy. Both... healthy. Both are healthy. Oh, gods.*

Her tears, which had been flowing freely, had ceased, even though she stayed nestled against his chest. Both of them did what was necessary to get their emotions under control—to remain steady. "Afternoon meal and before bed tonight. Then starting tomorrow, first thing and before bed. The ones..." She visibly swallowed. "Um, the ones I took earlier, every *umbra* with morning meal."

"Write it down. I gotta write it down," he whispered. Oh, an actual sentence.

"Heartbeat. It sounded like this," she muttered.

Heartbeat. He froze at the word. Momentarily got a ringing in his ears, but it didn't stick around. "Like...?" he muttered. Oh, gods, he had to stop shaking. But at least it was closer to a tremble now.

"I heard the heartbeat. It was fast. Kaylina... She said it was normal. Maybe when I go back... you can go with me?"

"I want to," he replied, his voice low as he fought back more tears. "I want to." He returned to stroking her ears. "But I do not know if I can." Hades, he hadn't meant to say that, not aloud, let alone think it. "I am so sorry. I..." As his shoulders tightened, the beads of sweat on his forehead prickled and grew. He couldn't tell her the truth, explain why, or even bring those memories to the forefront of his mind. "Sorry... so sorry..." Gods, he was so— "Afraid. So... gods... cannot... lose..." He clamped down hard on his tongue. If he couldn't get the words out, at least he could get them off the floor. "I want to go with you." But could he? It would make it more real. How could it be more real than this? Would he even be able to handle it? How could he not? This was his mate, and she was... It was their...

"You should."

He opened his mouth, but nothing came out. Silence stretched between them before he finally uttered one word, "Okay." He drew in a deep breath, and it seemed like a full hour before he could slowly, painfully, lift himself from the floor. Oh, gods, what if he moved her wrong, or too fast, or the wrong way? But they couldn't stay on the floor. She was supposed to be resting, not lying on the floor. He wasn't sure how, but somehow, he scooped her into his arms. As soon as he stood, he leaned back against the counter with her. He stood still for a minute or two, the world tilting around him until the dizziness subsided. His head throbbed with a dull ache. Not that it mattered now. "I should take you home."

He sensed that part of her didn't want to go home. They'd planned to feed Grace and Beast. But he could also sense she no longer felt up to the task. Any more than he did. Even in his arms, she just felt emotionally drained. "Okay." Yeah, home. Where she could rest. Eat some more food soon. She hadn't finished the plate he'd made.

"Okay. I just need a minute. One minute." Pierce took a few more deep breaths, feeling the air fill his lungs before letting it go. He couldn't do this—let the emotions and memories overtake everything. He had to take care of his mate. She needed him to take care of her and their—deep breath. His steps were unhurried and even as he carried her across the room. He stopped so she could pick up the pouch of herbs, then kept his pace just as easy as he went to the door. How many times had he held her in one arm to open a door? But he couldn't do that now; what if his dizziness came back, and he fell, or, gods forbid, dropped her? "Can you get the door, love?"

"Yes." Without issue, Jocasta turned the knob and the door swung inward. His mind was so preoccupied that he couldn't grasp any of her thoughts.

He went through the doorway and turned around so she could shut the door. Tracked every careful step all the way back to their porch. As she opened the door, he gave it a gentle nudge, closing it quietly behind them. Down the hall. Into their bedroom. He laid her down on the bed, stood there for a minute, and sat down on the floor. Put his head in his hands. "I am sorry, love," he said. "I wish I could say…" He swallowed hard. "Say why, but I cannot." There was no way he could explain it. "Better. I will get better." But would he? He had to. For her. For it. For them.

"We'll figure it out."

Pierce leaned his head against the bed and felt for her warm hand. If he lost—no. He couldn't think of that. He would just… There were things he could do to help. Those he would do. Focus on Kaylina's instructions and take care of her. Whatever she needed.

Jocasta took his hand, but she didn't have the energy to squeeze it or thread their fingers together. He could feel her love for him. But she felt depleted. It wasn't a sensation he liked any more than she did. She should feel energized, warm, especially now. He wanted things to be like they had been before—before she knew, before she told him.

"Will you lay down with me?"

A strange feeling washed over him, and he couldn't identify it. He couldn't understand this, and it made perfect sense. They had slept together, lain together, been in each other's arms, and made love every day and night since he'd come here. Every single day and night. And he was afraid to get up on the bed and lay down with his mate. Healthy—*they* were healthy. So why… Well, he knew why. Because that moment would come, like it always did. Sixty-nine—almost seventy—times in the seventy-three pregnancies he knew of in his family. One had been forced, and he had brought Lilli back. He almost hadn't been able to, but he had somehow managed it. He couldn't get that number out of his head. Six weeks. Just six weeks. *So* much could go wrong.

With his free hand, Pierce gripped his knee. His mate needed him. He might have nodded in response to her question, but he wasn't sure.

Slipping his hand out of hers, he got up off the floor and headed to his side of the bed. Lying down on the bed, he moved as slowly as he could, something he'd never done around her.

His movements were so careful, as though she was a delicate glass sculpture, vulnerable to any touch. It was utterly ridiculous, but he couldn't help it. Emotion, fear, and dread had smothered the fire that had burned between them.

He wanted to roll toward her, but what if he moved wrong and jostled the bed? Pull her into his arms, but what if he tugged her too hard or the wrong way? Hold her close, but what if he held her too tight? Stroke her, kiss her, just simply touch her. But that would lead to things they couldn't do, things that could trigger... He wanted that back, what they'd had just... yesterday? Was that it? It felt like years. Like eons had stretched between them. Because the news was going to come. That day would come.

Pierce turned his head and stared at her. There were a million things he wanted to say about this dream, this wonderful thing that they had both wanted. Right? But they had never talked about it. Not really. Why had they never talked about it, like it could be a reality? Because he'd never thought it could be. Had she? Something would happen; he would do something wrong, or it would just be done.

He couldn't do anything to move her closer. He stared only at her. In that moment, lying on her side, peering back at him, he knew she saw it, just as he did—the mountain that had moved in. How had it happened? How had a divide, a silent chasm, come between them? How had they ended up with this immovable space? She reached across the bed for his hand.

His hand clasped hers with utmost care, as gentle as a feather, but he stopped there. He desperately wanted to do more, but he couldn't. And he hated it. He had to silence these feelings or soften them somehow. Their fear wasn't supposed to rule them and take their peace away, not anymore. But it held onto him with an iron fist, and he didn't know how to make it let go.

If she had any more tears to cry, he imagined she would have. But she had nothing left to give. She was empty. And tired. It made his heart break, made him want to weep, but he had nothing left either. He felt so far away from her; further than he actually was, further than he'd ever been, even when there had been miles of physical distance between them.

Eventually, she fell asleep. Pure, utter exhaustion could do that. It could drag one down, even when one thought it couldn't.

Chapter Thirty-Eight

It had been a few days since her last visit. As she reached for the doorknob, Jo turned to Pierce, her heart pounding, and cast a last glance over her shoulder. He hadn't budged from that chair since she sat down—no, that wasn't accurate. He had carried her to the table. The same thing he had done for the past two days. When he carried her, it wasn't as he had done in the past. Not close to him. No, he carried her stiffly, focused more on where they were going than her. As if one wrong move...

Her shoulders slumped. Nothing she'd tried had convinced him to join her on this visit. He had been—still was—a ball of tension around her. Another seventeen and a half weeks to go. Gods, she prayed, something changed in him. This wouldn't be good for either of them. "Okay. I'll be fine. I'll, uh, I'll return shortly."

Nothing. He said nothing, just nodded.

Jo opened the door and left the house. She thought the first day had been rough. He made sure she ate, took the herbs as instructed, and carried her wherever she needed to go. Bathroom, check. Living room, check. Dining table, check. It seemed he was an attentive mate to his—nope, she still couldn't think about it—but it was in his manner. He was stiff when he carried her around. The one time she had gotten to her own two feet and hugged him from behind, as she had often done, he froze. Just stood there.

He didn't take her hand, didn't wrap his arms around her, none of it. Even when they lay in bed, he joined her, lying down slowly and only holding her hand. His touch had been minimal. Since the morning of her last appointment, come to think of it. They had always made love regularly, but the last month had been more than normal. Morning, afternoon, night. But not since the day of her first appointment.

She shook her head, a slight frown creasing her brow. Something had been going on in his mind. She had sensed it. It had been more than just her own fear over the weeks still to come. Whether *this* would even survive the next seventeen-and-a-half weeks that she had left to go. Whatever it was, she hadn't broken through. But she wouldn't give up. There was a way. Maybe once she made him... Well, she hadn't come up with anything for that yet either. Maybe once she did, she would get through.

Jo stopped in front of the medical building and stared at the door again. It hadn't changed, but part of her still dreaded going in, especially now that she knew. She sighed. Kaylina was just going to check her blood pressure. And hopefully give her permission to return to work. Otherwise, she'd go stir-crazy without something to do. Gods, if she had to, she'd help in other areas around the village. Something to occupy her time.

She entered the building and flashed a half-hearted smile to Kaylina. "Good morning."

"Good morning, Jocasta. How are you feeling today?"

Confused about her mate. A little afraid she would still lose... Worried about how it would impact her and her mate if *that* happened. She said none of that. "Well, I'm not throwing up anymore. Still nauseous from time to time. Other than that, I feel good." Mostly good.

"Excellent. Come on back and we will check your blood pressure."

Following the female, she bit her bottom lip. Her intention, her deepest hope, was to have Pierce hear the reassuring thump of a heartbeat. It would be good for them. She kind of needed to hear it again herself. It would certainly help. Maybe silence, some of the fear rattling her nerves. "Do you, uh, I mean, is it possible... could I hear the heartbeat again?"

"Of course. This is your appointment. We can do whatever you wish."

"Thank you. I appreciate it." Good, this was good. As much as she hated being in that gown, she'd take that over not doing everything possible to calm herself. To relax.

Kaylina gestured to the room. "Get changed and I will be back momentarily."

Acknowledging the request, she stepped into the same room she had been in a few days back and closed the door. She quickly changed from her dress to the gown and sat on the bed. Her gaze roamed the empty room. The table with two chairs. A couple of light-colored cabinets. The warm yellow of the walls. Nothing in here settled her nerves. Gods, she needed Pierce here with her.

Dragging a hand across her tired face, the memory of her last appointment resurfaced. No matter how many times he had asked, she had been adamant about going alone. And here she was, alone again. Had she started a chain reaction? One she couldn't take back? No. No. That couldn't be it. For two days, she had told him to join her on this visit. Insisted, practically begged.

When she had first said something... when he had been on the kitchen floor in her sister and Logan's house, she thought, well, she thought he would go. What had changed? What had happened? Had she said something to make him think she didn't want him here? Didn't need him here? Or was it something else? Something she couldn't pull from him. Something she couldn't sense.

She brushed away the wetness beneath her eyes. There was a way through. Whatever barrier had come between them, there was a way through. The only thing that mattered was finding it, and that was all she knew. She could do that. She was strong enough to do that.

The door to the room opened and Kaylina stepped in with a tray of instruments—same as before. At least she knew what most of them did this time. The female walked over and sat down next to Jo. "Blood pressure first. And tell me no more dizzy spells?"

"No, none." Everything the female had previously instructed; she had followed. No more hot showers. Not that taking them had been easy. All she kept seeing was the last shower she and Pierce had shared. Now he got her into the bathroom. It almost seemed pointless to go without underwear anymore. She'd even put a pair on this morning. And it felt... strange. Like she was purposely covering up. Before, she only wore them when she went to the marketplace. For the first time in her life, she felt like she had to wear them all the time. As if she had a reason to be ashamed of her ever-changing body.

She barely paid attention as Kaylina checked her blood pressure and then her pulse. All she could think about was her clothes. How little they covered. Even her dresses. Maybe they didn't hug her curves, at least not the ones she had worn recently, but they all showed skin. Did she...? Should she...? She wouldn't even know where to begin.

Had Kaylina said something? Gods, she needed to focus. "Hmm?" Jo questioned.

"Your blood pressure is good, as is your pulse. Lay back, please."

"Oh, right. I'm sorry." She eased her body back onto the bedding.

The female placed the bright blue disc against her belly. After a moment, a loud thump echoed again through the room, just like the one she had heard before. A fresh set of tears trickled down her face. It was a beautiful sound. Still so fast. She couldn't believe a heart could beat that fast. "Is it... still good? Still okay?"

"Yes. Still perfectly healthy. Your baby has a strong heart."

Jo swallowed to wet her parched throat. That's good. Great—a strong heart. Then maybe she wouldn't—gods, she didn't want to think about that. But she couldn't help it. So many of them. Maybe if she knew, she could prevent it. "Kaylina... is there, um, I mean, something I can do, so I don't...?"

The female grabbed her hand and squeezed it hard. "Listen to me. You are already doing everything you are supposed to do to ensure your baby stays healthy. I can give you a few more adjustments if that would put you at ease."

"Yes, please. Anything. I just... I can't..." Gods, she couldn't lose it. She just couldn't. Pierce was having a hard enough time with this. If she lost it... Jo choked back a sob.

"It is perfectly acceptable to be nervous, Jocasta. Even scared, but you cannot let that drive you. As long as you take care of yourself, your body will do the rest."

Take care of herself. Okay, she could do that. Right? Yes. Whatever extra precautions she could take, she would do. Even if she had to stay in the village. She wouldn't like it, but she could do it. She had to, for both of them. "Okay. That's something I can do."

"Good. Now, go ahead, sit up, and we will discuss your next steps."

Slowly, she sat up. She hadn't even realized the female had removed the disc and its heartbeat no longer filled the room. Inhaling another deep breath, Jo wiped at her face. "What else... what can I do?"

"Keep your stress levels low."

"Does that mean no work?" Her job didn't stress her out unless Demetrius took over, but she could figure out a way around that. Even if she had to accept him taking over for her on a semi-permanent basis.

"How about you limit it to eight *lacunas* per *umbra*? I know your *umbras* can often be longer, but I believe a shorter schedule will be beneficial."

Jo blinked. Really, she could go back to work? She hadn't expected that. Although they had said they would discuss it, she actually expected not to be returning. This was good. It would be something else to focus on. Something she loved—music—eight hours. She'd take it. "Shorter *umbra*. I can do that."

"Being around family is an excellent way to keep stress low. As is sex regularly."

Family. A memory from a few days back played in her mind. In less than a minute, the entire house had nearly emptied. Zinnia and Lillianna had gone off to the gardens. Her sister and Logan had disappeared into their bedroom. Her mother hadn't even been there. Right. Family. And Pierce couldn't even—no, she couldn't think about that again.

Jo lowered her gaze to her hands. "Anything else?"

"Places that you find relaxing. Or activities you enjoy."

"That I can do." There were a few places around the village she liked to visit. It would be a way to stay busy and keep her stress low. Maybe the other two things would follow soon. She had to get through to Pierce first. That would help.

"Good. Keep taking your herbs as I have instructed and I will see you again in two *penumbras*."

"Two *penumbras*?"

"Well, you are nearly past the first term. Most things that go wrong occur within the first eight *penumbras*. For right now, every two *penumbras*. Once you get past the second term, we will visit every *penumbra*. However, if you feel off for any reason, come see me."

For a moment, she just sat there. Did that mean—no, she hadn't said it would be smooth. Just that they usually went wrong in the first eight weeks. Implementing everything they had discussed would be her course of action, and it would prove beneficial. "Okay. Two *penumbras*."

"Yes, now get dressed. I will see you out in a moment." With that, Kaylina stood and left the room, her instruments in hand.

As Jo redressed, she fidgeted with the musical note attached to the chain around her neck. There had to be something she could give Pierce. Something that would snap him out of his stupor. But what? Obviously, it had to be something that, well, *it* needed. They needed a lot of things. It had to be something small. Something that could be passed down. Her gaze fell on the musical note between her fingers. A small smile settled on her face—Adara. She could get an idea from her; the female always knew the right gift.

That was it. That was who she needed to see.

Adara would have the answer.

Jo opened the door and met Kaylina in the hallway. She'd go see Adara as soon as she left.

"There is one other thing I would like you to do. Have a stool or chair in your booth at work. Stay off your feet as much as possible when you are there."

"Okay. That's easy enough." She didn't think her sister would take issue with that. There was plenty of room in her booth for a stool.

"Excellent. I will see you in two *penumbras* unless you need me before then. Day or night, do you understand?"

"I do. Thank you." Jo nodded one last time to Kaylina before she exited the medical building. She stopped just on the other side of the door and stood there as various hybrids walked in each direction. Some coming and others going. Everyone had some tasks that they handled, some part of the village they helped with. As part of the money earned by Zancle's went to the village, that was her and Ambrosia's part. If she couldn't work at the bar, there had to be some way she could contribute around the village. Maybe she could give music lessons. It was a thought.

For now, she could go back to work. Not that she had any idea how Pierce would take the news. With a heavy sigh, she started toward Adara's house. What would it need? Clothes, but she didn't want to make that. Jewelry was definitely out. Way too early for that. Maybe something to hold its attention. Like something that had been passed down through their family. Her father had always made sure they gave her and Ambrosia something special for their day of birth. Wait, a second—the first thing he'd ever given them.

It had been... a rattle. That's it! That's what she could make. Jewels in the handle to represent her and Pierce and their names engraved in the rattle itself, with room for its name. Once they knew what it was and had chosen one. Oh gods, if they even got there.

Strong heartbeat. Strong heartbeat. It was going to become her fucking mantra at this rate. She had to stay positive. As she desperately tried to find her strength, Jo rubbed her arms anxiously, biting her lip. Somehow, she had to find it inside of herself to stay strong for her mate and their—

Swallowing the lump in the back of her throat, Jo zigzagged through the maze of houses until she reached Adara's. She knocked on the door.

The rhythmic thump of hooves echoed against the hardwood floor on the other side. After a minute, the door swung wide. "Jocasta. How are you this morning?"

"I'm good." At least it was mostly true. "Hey, um, Adara, I was hoping I could get your help with a... trinket of sorts." It was the best way to describe it. She'd have to tell the female exactly what it was, but she didn't want to do it standing outside. It was bad enough that members of the village had probably seen her go into the medical building twice now.

"Oh, yes, of course. Please, come in."

"Thank you." She stepped into the front room and glanced over at the female's work table. So many pieces—such a wide variety of bracelets, rings, and necklaces. There were even a couple of... were those jewelry boxes? That's new. She didn't recall those the last time she had visited.

The door closed and Adara came further into the room. "Do you know what you are seeking?"

"Well..." How did she explain this without mentioning *it*? She chewed on the inside of her cheek. A direct approach would work best. "I want to make a rattle. I just... I've done nothing like this before, so I was kind of hoping you could help guide me."

Adara's eyes widened as a broad smile crossed her face. "Oh, yes, absolutely. I can definitely help you make a rattle. It may take us several *umbras*, if that is alright with you, of course."

"Several *umbras*?" She supposed that made sense. They would need to cut or whittle it down, sand it, and paint it before adding any of the extras. Or so she assumed from what she had seen with the other woodwork. Not to mention the inside for sound. There wasn't any other choice. "I'm good with that, but do you think we could work on it at your shop? I want to surprise Pierce."

The female excitedly clapped her hands together. "Oh, yes. We can absolutely do that. I love surprises!"

Jo grinned for what felt like the first time in a few days. Gods, she loved them too. Happy surprises, though. She hadn't determined which one *it* was. Weren't they supposed to be wonderful surprises? Joyful? She wasn't certain she was there yet. Then again, it didn't feel like her mate was, either. Something she prayed changed for them both soon. "Thank you. I appreciate it."

"If you can, we could get started today. I was going to have some breakfast and then head off. We could head there together?"

"Oh, wow. I, uh..." She really didn't want to turn the female down, but she hadn't expected to start so soon. Although, it might be a good idea. She could still sit while they worked. And morning meal, well, it would be a good time to tell Pierce about work. And the new restrictions. Would this count as work? Hmm, it might. "Yeah. That sounds good."

"I would recommend you change clothes as well."

"Really? I can't... my pants don't... well, they don't button." She had gotten them over her ass and zipped up part of the way, but no matter how hard she tried or which ones she had pulled on, none of them buttoned.

"Easy fix." Adara strode over to her work table, picked up a small pile of string, and held it out to Jo.

Accepting the proffered string, she raised an eyebrow. "That's it?"

"Yes, loop it through the hole and tie it off, then loop it around the button. You will need to wear a top long enough to cover it, of course, but it will give you some more time in jeans."

How come she hadn't thought of that? It was simple and easy to do. At least until her belly got bigger. Did she have any tops long enough? Hmm, maybe a few, but not very many. She really only needed them to last long enough for her to make the rattle. Then once she surprised Pierce with it, she could go back to dresses. Sounded like a plan in her head. One that she hoped snapped her mate out of his daze so they could actually celebrate this and worry a little less. "Thank you. I didn't know that."

"Enough of the females around here do it. So, shall we meet after breakfast?"

"A *lacuna*? If that works for you." It would give her time to talk to Pierce, eat, and change clothes.

"That is fine."

"Okay. I'll see you soon." With the string in her hand, she smiled once again at the female and left the house. Pausing on the other side of the door, her gaze fell to the string. Such a small hack. Maybe her mother knew of a few others. Not that she was ready to tell their family yet. No, she and Pierce needed to fully wrap their heads around it all first. Though her sister and Logan probably already knew. It wasn't exactly like she and Pierce had had that conversation in the privacy of their own home. She sighed and headed home.

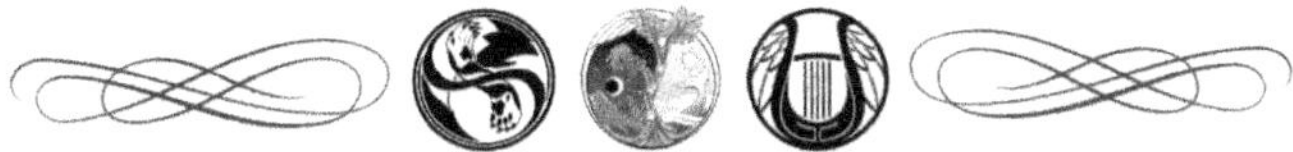

Pierce leaned against the kitchen counter, tracing invisible patterns in the grain, when Jocasta returned. Not quite at the window, because his expression wasn't anything he wanted their family to see if they peered over here. He didn't turn to look at her as she entered their home, closing the door behind her. He'd shut his thoughts down a while ago, so his mind was blissfully blank. At least, it appeared that way. He could handle the euphoric vacancy. What he couldn't handle was everything else that tried to shove its way in. Nope—didn't want to deal with that. Or think about how this appointment had taken longer than the last one had. "You were gone for a while." Gods, is that really what his voice sounded like right now? He cleared his throat. It had been days since she had told him—*nope.* He couldn't even handle thinking about *it.* How was he going to make himself okay with this? Whatever ended up happening, his mate needed him. And he couldn't even make himself look at her. But they could get through it. They had dealt with a lot in a short period. They could; they could handle this.

"Yeah. Sorry about that. I was talking to Adara after my appointment. Guess I was at her place longer than I thought." She started for the kitchen, her pace slowing as she got closer. "I'm okay, Pierce. We're okay."

Okay, that was good. It hadn't just been the appointment that had caused her to be gone *fifty-seven minutes and eighteen seconds.* What *wasn't* good, not good *at all,* was the tension that started up, moved in, and increased the closer she got to him. Gods, all he wanted to do was fucking hold her, his mate, his queen, like he used to. Just days ago. Literally days ago. But if she wrapped her arms around him again, he couldn't... he couldn't feel *that*. Hades, it was not an *it*, it was—

He had to stop this, had to get over this, had to do *something*, anything. Anything that was normal. Not that he could even tell her why he was so afraid. He was *so* afraid—afraid of losing her, afraid of losing *it*. He should just talk to her. Just tell her. But how could he do that when he refused to let the words even form in his own head? Because with the words came images, and he just couldn't. It was good he was leaning on the counter. She was okay. She had said 'we.' *They* were okay. Okay was good. *Okay, for now.* "I am glad. That it went well."

"Yeah, uh, everything's returned to normal. My blood pressure is where it should be and Kaylina let me listen to the heartbeat again. She said it was a strong heartbeat." She paused. "Even said I could go back to work with some restrictions."

Strong heartbeat. Strong heartbeat. Strong heartbeat. That was good. That was great. But she was only six weeks. Things could change. Things could always change. They usually did. He reached his hand up and rubbed his forehead. *Work?* Had she said *work*? Work, where she wouldn't be resting; where she would walk back and forth from the village to the marketplace every day she went. Where she would be around the hustle and bustle of the marketplace, of the bar. So many people. So many more things could go wrong, could happen. Where the smells could make her sick, and where he couldn't be there. Not like he was really *here* now, though. *Stop it, Pierce, stop it, stop it, stop it.* "Do you think that is really the best idea?" He really needed to get his voice back to normal, at least. Fuck.

She finally stepped foot into the kitchen and leaned against the counter opposite him. "It'll be fine. I won't be there as long as I am now, and I'll have a stool put in the booth like Kaylina requested, so I'm not standing for *lacunas* on end. I'll even put my evening meal order in early with Jacques. And probably a couple of other snack items in between. Some normalcy will be good."

Normalcy. What the fuck was normal? He couldn't even find the concept in his own head right now. All he could see up there in that fucked-up organ of his was something happening—with her there, and him stuck here. He squeezed his eyes shut. It was a few minutes before he opened his eyes and spoke. "And this... this is what you want? What you want to do?"

Closing the distance, she reached out and rested her hand on his arm. "Yes. I would like to go back. I love what I do. If I couldn't, then I'd find something around the village to do. I can't... I've never sat still. I enjoy being active."

His body froze. When had her touch become like ice? It was the only thing that would calm him down. Even when she'd gotten pissed off at him. Hades, he wanted to light himself on fire right now. Maybe that would wake him the fuck up. Oh, gods, she smelled good. Oh, so good. His eyes darkened, and he closed his eyes. He took shallow breaths through his mouth. In one half of his brain, he wanted her as close to him as she could be. But in the other half, the complete opposite, he couldn't stand being this close to her. It was like the two sides of his brain were literally throwing blows at each other. A dull pounding throbbed in his temple, and he pinched the bridge of his nose, trying to stop it. He wanted her—his body craved her—but he couldn't have her; he couldn't chance it, no way. Words, he needed, words. But they would not be the right words. He couldn't find the right words. The words that would take them back to how they'd been, the words to put her at ease like he should do, the words to get past this headfuck. "I will not tell you I am okay with it. But I will not tell you no. If it is something you truly wish to do... I will not tell you no."

Her hand dropped from his arm. With a heavy sigh, she crossed her arms, went back to the counter opposite him, and leaned against it. Her gaze fell to the floor. "What if we do a test run? I've got a project to work on Adara with over the next several *umbras*. I'll go to the bar afterward and leave when the kitchen closes down. If... if it's too much for either of us, then I'll relinquish my booth to Demetrius."

He would never be okay with it. He knew he wouldn't. But he was going to have to at least *appear* to be. Going back to work—however much he hated it, however much it scared him—would make her happy. She deserved to be happy. Deserved more than he was giving her. Deserved everything. He didn't see this headfuck going anywhere, anytime soon. The least he could do was... Well, fuck, he had to do something. "A test run," he muttered. "Okay."

A moment passed as she stood there, nervously biting her bottom lip. "Okay." She paused. "Have you eaten yet?"

He frowned. Had he? He hadn't stopped moving since she left, not until he'd sensed her returning to the house. But had he actually stopped to eat? "I, um, I actually do not know. Which means it would probably be a good idea."

"Then we can enjoy morning meal together before I meet back up with Adara."

Normal. This was normal. Sort of. Not completely, but close enough. "Okay. I will make us something." He pushed off the counter and moved around the kitchen, his feet softly padding against the wooden floor. Eating a meal together was good. That was something, at least. Something—that was it. He needed to find something he could do in the village. Something to help—his place. And... he had nothing. But he had to find something. He had been here long enough, done some things, helped here and there, but nothing consistent. Find something—a routine, something to keep his mind occupied so the bad thoughts didn't sneak in again. So that, maybe, he wasn't constantly thinking about how worried and afraid he was for his mate and their—

He was just making things worse for her. If he could just *appear* okay, maybe that would help.

"Why don't I dice some potatoes to go with it?"

His feet stopped for a second, but he forced them to get moving again. Keep moving—the more moving, the less thinking. "It is alright. I have got it. You should sit. Rest."

"Okay. I guess I'll, uh, go change. Adara thought my jeans would be more appropriate for our project." Jocasta turned and disappeared down the hallway.

Once she'd left the room, he gripped the edge of the counter. Honestly, he wanted to bang his head against it. Maybe a crack in his skull would help. Pierce groaned. He knew what he should do right now. He should go down the hall and lay it all out to his mate. Like he should have done at the basin; when he'd told her everything else. Instead, *this* was the one thing he'd left out. Why the fuck had he left this out? Why had they not talked about *this?* If they had, would he be like this now? Probably. But at least she'd understand. He'd never know, because he'd refused to think of it, even when he'd laid out the rest of his pain. Talking. Talking was supposed to be good. Yup, that is what he should have done. Instead, he pushed off the counter and began preparing his mate a meal.

Was this going to be their new normal? Until it came? Would it change afterward? Truthfully, he didn't know. Neither did she. Not once in the five months they had been together had they even discussed this as a possibility. He hadn't brought it up, and neither had she. The salty scent of tears reached his nose. It halted his footsteps. But he forced himself to move and finished preparing morning meal. Sweet rolls she had taught him to make in the oven. All the same fruit she had eaten the other morning, cut up on a plate for her. Going to get them was one thing he'd done while she was gone. It had helped to focus on something. He readied the herbs she was supposed to take with morning meal.

Pierce leaned against the counter. Maybe he couldn't say *all the* words. But he couldn't leave it like this. He couldn't stand this. It was hurting her too much. And it was hurting him, too. Maybe it wouldn't help, but he strode down the hallway, anyway. The door was cracked open. Oh, Hades, her sweet aroma was like a punch to his gut and his cock, but he swallowed it all, along with the growl. Pierce leaned against the icy wall, scrubbing his sleep-filled eyes. "Can we just…" He cleared his throat. "Just… stay there for a minute, and… can I say something?"

He sensed where she stood in their bedroom—in front of the closet, clutching a blouse in her hands. "Please," she croaked out. It didn't even sound like her, but he felt how much his actions were breaking her and how much she didn't understand. Neither of them knew how to fix it.

He swallowed hard, feeling the tension in his throat. Maybe not all the words, but he had to give her something. His voice was hushed, and it seemed to carry the weight of unspoken sorrows. "I do not want to be this way… act this way. You do not deserve it, not at all. I want to tell you why. But I cannot. I cannot put it into words. Not… not yet." It hurt too much. Far, far too much. All he could think about was *that day* coming… and what if… it took her with it? He squeezed his eyes shut, feeling the sting of tears as they threatened to spill over. Put his hand against the doorjamb. He was dying to go inside their bedroom. But all that would happen was more of that automatic freezing his body wouldn't stop doing. He didn't think she could take any more of that. "Time. I just need… I hope that time is all I need. And I am so, so very sorry. And I love you very much." He cleared his throat. "I should go check on the food."

But he didn't move. Not yet. He sensed the tears gathering in the corners of her eyes and silently spilling over, tracing slow paths down her cheeks.

He wasn't making this any easier on her—that the only way they could speak to one another was with a barrier between them.

"I love you too. If you need time, I can give you time. That's... I can do that."

"I wish I did not need it," he whispered. "You should... I hope you know that. I want you. I will always want you." He just hoped—prayed—she would always want him. He knew it was there—the mountain between them, the cracks and the fissures that were turning into a vast hole he didn't know how to fill back up. What he had created. What he had done. "I want us back, but..." He didn't know how to take another step further than this. How to deal with the memories, pull the words out of his head. Move past it. Be with his mate again. Be the male that she needed. He swiped at the one tear that had escaped. "I will be in the kitchen, my queen." He pushed off the wall and disappeared back down the hall.

Chapter Thirty-Nine

"I have news," Parthenia announced as her talons hit the edge of the treehouse.

Gavin stood next to the entrance, waiting for her. As soon as he embraced her, he held her, nestling his face in her neck, savoring the soft smell of her. Parthenia stroked the nape of his neck and he purred. The last couple of months had been hard, being apart. For once, she felt like her arrival brought good news. A chance for them to be together on a more permanent basis, even if it was in this treehouse. At least until they could get off the isle.

After several minutes, he nuzzled her neck and flicked his eyes to hers. "News. What news, love?"

"My Elder, she listened. She's convened a meeting between the sirens to reconsider the law and..." Her words trailed off. This should be good news. This *was* good news. A chance for her species' laws to be changed. For at least one of them to be in less danger because of their relationship. It was the second part of the announcement she didn't like. And one she didn't think he would either. The other species' Elders. They wouldn't leave any out. "... choose ambassadors to visit with the other species' Elders."

Gavin said nothing for a minute. He stroked her wing. "Who did they choose?"

"None... yet. We'll be meeting over the coming *umbras* to discuss the law and select ambassadors. Gavin..." She bit her bottom lip. This was the part she hated. With so few of them, it didn't leave many options. Six. Six options that included her. "My love..." She didn't know how to tell him. "I am... I could... they could decide upon me as one ambassador."

He squeezed his eyes shut tight. His chin trembled as she felt the inner turmoil rising within him. It took a minute for him to gain control. Opening his eyes, Gavin stared into hers. His hand moved from her wing to her cheek. "You cannot go in front of Markham," he whispered.

"There are—" She knew that. It wasn't an option. Gavin's scent was all over her. The suspicion that had caused injuries to him months earlier would be—no. Although Gavin was no longer in the village, a meeting with Markham... Parthenia shook her head. "There are others who may go. That they may select, like my mother and Fagonia, but I can't allow that. I may not intend to stay, but my sisters..." They needed this for just a chance of a future. "We won't know for a couple of *umbras*. If I'm elected, we will figure it out. Avoid meeting with Markham."

"Is that even possible? I cannot imagine your Elder would allow that." Gavin pressed his lips to her forehead. Neither of them wanted to think about what they had already lost. They didn't want to lose each other. "Okay. Alright." His eyes, filled with unspoken words, flicked back to hers. "I do not want to think about it today. Not that part. In a couple of *umbras*, when we know for sure, we will deal with it then." He placed a kiss on both sides of her mouth.

She gingerly ran her fingers up and down his neck. Another purr rose out of him. "I have some other news." This was much better. Not that it was the map. That would've been the best news. There was still a row of books to go through, but they were close.

He slid his other hand to the small of her back, his thumb caressing her cheek as he tugged her closer to him. "Such a beautiful smile. What is your other news, love?"

"I found some more information about the curse. Not how to break it, but it confirms a lot of our suspicions." As much as she would've preferred to find the map, she'd take anything that brought them a step closer.

"Oh?" He raised an eyebrow. "Well, that is good. One step at a time, right?" Leaving her cheek, his hand found hers and he intertwined their fingers, leading her to the pallet. As he sat down, he urged her sideways onto his lap. "What did you find?"

"A siren went against the goddess and she's the one that cursed us. It has everything to do with why we can't... why we're limited the way we are.

However..." Her eyes lit up. "There's a prophecy about how to break it, but it wasn't in the book." She groaned just a little. "I've always known sirens are manipulative and secretive, but book jumping—it's just a little—" A sudden, forceful breeze swept through the treehouse, interrupting her mid-sentence. She glanced toward the entrance, her heart pounding in her chest. "What the—"

Gavin's gaze focused in the same direction. His nose twitched at the aroma, and his ears perked up, listening intently. "That did not seem normal." He gently lifted her, then shifted forms, and crawled on all fours toward the opening. Poking his head out, he surveyed their surroundings.

There was definitely a shift in the air. A rather subtle change in the scent. Saltier. More earthy. Lighter, even this high up. Parthenia got to her feet. Her feathers ruffled. That hadn't been just a normal breeze that had come through. The sun was close to setting, and it hadn't been her first time in the treehouse this late. This was something else altogether. Could it be? Her gaze flipped to the parchment she'd left here with the prophecy Devin had written.

His nose twitched again. Whipping his head around, he focused on her. "Is that *sea air*?" He'd only been near the sea the day they'd gone to the barrier. "You do not think..." Gavin crossed the room and eyed the parchment, then stared at her. Silence stretched between them. His eyebrows squished together. "Do you feel like going on a little adventure?"

She grabbed the vials of invisibility potion she'd left here in response. "It would be irresponsible of us not to check." They'd been waiting for this for months. Constantly searching for answers. Dealing with all kinds of situations and enduring pain. If this was what they'd been waiting for, they had to take this one step at a time, just like everything else. She slipped the knapsack from her shoulders that she'd almost forgotten about.

Gavin leaned up and licked her neck. "Race you down the tree?"

"I thought you'd never ask." Beaming, she clutched the vials tight in her hands, darted around him to the entrance, and dove into the air, taking flight. It didn't take long for her feet to touch the ground.

Her mate rubbed his body against her side. "You almost beat me this time, love."

"One *umbra*." Parthenia tucked a vial into the back pocket of the skirt she'd elected for her trip there. One of the good things that had occurred over the last couple of months, she'd perfected the potion, so it included everything on their person. Plus, they lasted a little longer now. She un-corked the other vial, knocked it back, and placed the empty vial in her other pocket. The last time they'd taken a trip toward the bridge, it had taken a few hours. "Same route as last time?"

"Yes, my love. I will follow your scent and stay close. Unless you would like to ride me?" he said, a smirk in his tone. "We would move more quickly that way, if you are alright with my running."

Oh, she'd like to ride him alright. She bit her bottom lip and shook the thought away. Despite where her mind had gone, he ran faster than she flew. And time was of the essence. "Yes. I think that would be best." With both of them invisible, she'd have to feel her way to climb onto his back, but she could handle that.

With her hand resting on his shoulder, he crouched down. He waited until she was firmly in place on his back, letting out a low rumble as she got situated, before standing back up. "If we run into anyone." He paused. "I need you to do something for me. I need you to fly away. Alright?"

Parthenia tensed. Oh, she knew who he meant all right. The idea of leaving him alone didn't sit well with her. The camouflage may prevent him from being seen, but if anyone came near, they would catch his scent. If that happened, she could land in a nearby tree to ensure he was safe. "Yes. I can... I can do that."

"Thank you." Gavin wrapped his tail gently around her leg. "Hold on tight. You can grip wherever you need to. It will not hurt me." Every time she'd ridden on his back, he'd been walking, not running. While her wings would keep her from plummeting to the earth, a fall would still be unpleasant.

She locked her legs around him, gripping him as tightly as she could, and dug in her talons. Best to be on the safe side. Leaning forward, she sifted her fingers into his fur and grabbed a hold just above his shoulders. A deep purr rumbled out of him. With her wings tucked in tight, she adjusted herself to minimize the impact of the wind. "Ready."

Gavin gradually picked up his speed, easing into it. His precision was perfect as he moved through the forest. Trees and bushes whizzed by as he darted through the thicket. She'd seen him run before, anytime they raced up the tree, but this was so different. They were on the ground, but it almost felt like flying. It was fun, utterly freeing. At this rate, they'd be there in no time.

It only took them a little over an hour to reach the treeline they'd gone to with Devin previously. Gavin slowed his steps before stopping completely. "Oh, gods."

"Shh." The fog was completely gone, but that wasn't the only thing she noticed. A couple of guards stood near the entryway of the bridge they'd walked on before. Well, guards and another male with dark hair and an olive complexion. The barrier was down, but there was no way they were getting across the bridge. Not even to see what was on the other side.

Crouched low and hidden within the trees, she could smell the salty air as they stared across the beach at the guards. Golden armor. Exquisite weapons. Humanoid in appearance.

Gavin whispered in her ear, "What are they?"

She was about to open her mouth and answer when more filed out from somewhere nearby. At this angle, she couldn't say for sure from where, but there was no doubt regarding their species. "Dragon-shifters," she kept her voice low.

"I thought they must be, but..." His words trailed off. About half of the group of dragon-shifters that had filed out stayed outside of wherever they'd come from, while the rest continued on to the bridge where the two guards and the unarmored male stood. "I wonder what is over there," he murmured. "Where did they come out of?" When they'd come here last time, they hadn't poked around to investigate further, only gone to look at the bridge before leaving.

"I don't know. Let's keep watching, though," she said, her voice soft. She'd wait until they left to take the other invisibility potion. The male by the bridge wasn't really saying anything, but studying the bridge? Possibly the water. More than likely, they were searching for some answers they themselves had sought.

Nothing much happened for a while. Suddenly, there was a great *whoosh* of air and... a siren with blue feathers emerged from wherever the others had come from and soared for the bridge. "Blue?" Gavin whispered.

"What the—?" Parthenia leaned a little closer to her mate, trying to get a better look. That was definitely a siren. She knew her own species. But none of them had blue feathers, or feathers of a color other than brown. How was that possible?

"Do you think she... I mean, the one in the prophecy..." Gavin's whispers trailed off again when another dragon-shifter emerged. This female wasn't walking or flying, though, more like floating on a sort of cloud. More of the guards followed, and they were leading another creature. One that had shackles on. Back at the bridge, the other male who had been there was bowing to the blue siren.

Parthenia turned over the prophecy in her head. What kept striking her were the first words, 'Like no other.' That siren wasn't like any other siren. Blue feathers. Blue hair. They weren't close enough to see the color of her eyes or hear anything being said, but getting any closer would be way too risky. Especially with more dragon-shifters appearing. "It's possible."

The three, besides the guards, appeared to be speaking amongst themselves. Then the siren began gesturing to the bridge. "The engravings," he whispered.

Her mate had a point. They were referring to what they assumed represented each species on the isle. They'd identified at least two, each of their own. The rest? Maybe the meeting her Elder had called could prove useful.

How long should they stay? Invisible or not, this was risky. It might be better to come back another time, but they couldn't leave now. What if the barrier closed again? All they could do was stand here and watch.

They continued to track what was going on. After a little longer, one guard took away the shackled creature. The three continued to speak. It would be nice to hear what was being said, but that would be too dangerous. Way too dangerous. The blue siren took to the skies again.

"How long do you think it is wise to linger here?" Gavin asked.

"I think we've seen all we will." Sitting up, Parthenia peered at the sky to see if she could follow the path the siren took. The female disappeared rather quickly into the treeline. If they got anything more, it wouldn't be until morning. There was one good thing. The barrier had opened. And the blue siren. She was the key—she had to be. "We should return to the treehouse."

"Closer and closer." Though she couldn't see him, she could hear his smile. It wouldn't be much longer before they could leave this place behind for good. They could both feel it. It was coming. But how long would the barrier stay open? What else would they face before their freedom finally came? "Take the other potion and I will race us home."

Parthenia removed the other potion from her back pocket, drank it, and tucked the empty vial away. Yes. They were definitely getting closer. Demeter, soon, they could finally leave. Perhaps they should check back in the morning. She had a feeling, as long as the blue siren stayed on the isle, the barrier would remain open. The question was, how long would the dragon-shifters guard it for?

The run back to the treehouse was virtually silent. Once they got back to the tree, he crouched down to let her climb off of his back, then leaned into her for a moment. She stroked the top of his head as they remained at the base of the tree. "I'm going to stay here tonight." Joy poured out of him and he nuzzled her neck. The meeting they expected her to attend tomorrow could take hours, or even a couple of days. It depended on how much disagreement occurred. "Do you think we should go back in the morning?"

"I think we should. We may learn more. Maybe the guards will have left as well, and we can see what lies on the other side." He ran his tongue along the smooth skin of her neck. "Will they miss you tonight? I do not want you to get in trouble."

"No. They didn't even notice I left." Never mind the fact that she no longer spoke to her mother. And Fagonia hardly sought her out anymore for any reason. Something had changed with the female in the last month. As for the bridge, she wasn't sure the guards would be gone. But they could hope.

"Okay. I just wanted to be sure." He brushed his muzzle across her neck. "Let us go up, love."

Parthenia nudged him with her hip. "I'd race you, but how would we know who won?" She was still invisible. No telling how long the potion would last. Probably not much longer.

"Well, you have not beaten me yet," he teased.

A giggle escaped her mouth. "But you can't catch what you can't see." It didn't mean he couldn't hear her as she launched into the air toward the top.

Parthenia laughed as she heard the leaves bustle, which meant her mate surpassed her to the top of the treehouse. By the time she got inside, she spotted him lazing about on the pallet. The potion finally wore off as she lay down on top of him. "That was fun."

He stroked her cheek with the back of his knuckles. "Very. I love racing you."

"Me too," Parthenia said. Demeter, the barrier, had truly fallen. She had found out more about the curse. They were close. Really close to having everything they'd dreamed of, which meant soon they would leave this place. It had been—no, it hadn't been home since her father passed. Gavin was her home. And that meant that wherever he was, that was home. Anywhere in the universe would be home if they were together. "Could you imagine being able to race around a lake? Or through a forest?" She leaned into his touch ever so slightly.

"Right now? Absolutely." He cupped her cheek, his thumb gently tracing the curve of her face. "Soon, my beloved. So soon. Our dream comes closer to reality every *umbra*."

Closing her eyes, she leaned more into his gentle touch. "Yes, it does."

The rest of the evening and into the night passed blissfully. They talked about their dreams that would soon be more than dreams, held each other in their arms, and made love the best way that they could, despite their limitations. Parthenia fell asleep on Gavin's chest, both of them drifting away into one of the most peaceful slumbers they'd ever had in their lives.

When morning came, Gavin nuzzled her neck as he stroked her wing. Gently, she stirred. Poppies, was it morning already? The sun was streaming into the treehouse. She wasn't quite ready to move. She was comfortable right where she lay. "Mmm, just a little longer."

"As long as you want, my love. There is no hurry." He trailed his fingers up and down her spine as she curled more against his chest. "I rather love where you are right now."

"Me too. You're the best pillow I've ever had." Not that they had all morning. She had to get back for the meeting her Elder had called. She had no choice. And she definitely wanted to check the barrier, as close as they could get, before then. But she was oh, so comfortable.

"Mmm. Well, you can use me for a pillow anytime you want." Neither of them moved. "We will go whenever you are ready. I can eat when I return."

"Mmm. I think I'll come back after the meeting then and use you as a pillow again." She always slept better, curled up on him. Something they'd been doing since he'd moved into the treehouse on a more permanent basis. Still, it had been one of the most peaceful nights of sleep. Less of their worries to weigh them down and more of their future within their grasp.

"I already cannot wait. That was the best sleep I have ever had."

"Definitely the best sleep in a long time."

Gavin brushed a kiss across her neck, and then just lay there, completely content. Neither of them was in a hurry for her to leave his arms. The next few days would be nerve-wracking, but they would just have to do their best not to worry until—or if—there was a reason to. Right now, his arms around her, his heartbeat beneath her, kept all of her fears at bay.

Demeter, as much as she loved where she was, they needed to get moving. It would take them at least an hour to get to the barrier, plus an hour back. The meeting was due to start just after lunch. She kissed his chest. "I don't wish to, but I'm getting up."

He grumbled, his warm breath on her skin as he licked her neck. "Okay, love. I will behave." Smirking, Gavin removed his arms from around her.

She groaned low. He was playing with fire. Trying to tempt her. Letting out a soft breath, she climbed off of him. He turned on his side and propped himself up on one elbow as he watched her. Going to her knapsack, she pulled out a change of clothes. Much like the clothes she'd worn the day before, a denim skirt and tank top that zipped in the front.

"That is a shame. Necessary, but such a shame," Gavin bemoaned.

She paused, the tank top halfway on, considering whether to tease him one last time before finishing getting dressed. But then they'd never get out the door. She glanced over her shoulder as she zipped the tank up. "I promise, love, as soon as we are off the isle and wherever we make a new home, I will walk around as often as you wish me to be naked."

"I love the sound of that. So very much." When she had fully dressed, he got up off the pallet and shifted to all fours. "Are you ready, love?"

"Let me just grab a couple of vials." She crossed the room and stared at the remaining vials left. Only four remained. She'd have to make more. A quick glance over the table let her know everything she needed was already here. Okay, good. She snagged two, tucked them in her back pocket, and headed toward the entrance. She paused long enough to stroke Gavin's head before she leaped out of the treehouse.

After a moment, he headed down the treehouse himself. He leaped about a dozen feet from the bottom and landed with a thud. As graceful as his landing was, it was louder than necessary. Still, she loved to watch him move. She didn't bother going to the ground this time. Instead, she lowered herself directly onto his back.

A deep rumble resonated within his chest. "I should probably be quieter. Being around you just excites me." Gavin smiled over his shoulder at her before camouflaging.

"I think we should be okay here." She stroked his head. Demeter, she loved feeling his fur beneath her fingers. Taking one vial from her pocket, she gulped the potion and tucked it back where it belonged. Just as she had the day before, she sank her fingers into his fur, folded her wings tight, and leaned forward. "Shall we?"

"Absolutely." Wrapping his tail around her leg as he did every time she rode atop him, he took off through the trees, taking the same pathway they had yesterday.

It took just as long for them to get there as it had previously. Her grip was firm as Gavin sped through the forest, dodging trees and bushes along the way. When they arrived at the spot they'd watched from yesterday, the scenario was a little different. The female that had floated down now paced back and forth. Guards still surrounded the entryway to the bridge. Coming from across the other side were the blue siren and the male who had been studying it. Parthenia sat up. The barrier was still open. No sign it had closed and opened again.

"They made it across the bridge. And back with no problems, by the look of it," he whispered.

"If everything we have learned is correct, she likely has the key on her person," she responded, her voice low. The three spoke, well, sort of. It appeared the siren leaned against the bridge. And the other two talked. Her eyesight wasn't as good during the day as it was at night. They looked more like blobs this far away. But they dared not get closer.

"I wonder what it might be? It does not look like she carries anything on her person. Could she herself be the key, or would it have to be an object?" He paused. "She could have hidden it somewhere by now as well."

"I suppose. Though it would be an object. Often, they are small, and they do not have to look like a key." Poppies, she wished she could see better. There was something going on between the one female and the male, but she couldn't say for sure. "I don't see as well during the day. Can you tell what they're doing?"

"They just appear to be talking right now. She does not appear to like the siren very much."

"I'm not surprised. From what I've gathered, we may share the sky, but they still think we are inferior to them."

The dragon-shifter female went back to her guards, then returned to the other two. The siren moved off the bridge as the dragon-shifter female began doing something with the male's neck. He tilted his head. "He wears a collar. The dragon-shifter is doing something to it, but I have seen nothing before like what is going on with her hands. They have an odd golden glow to them."

Golden glow? Collar? "It is the same male who was studying the bridge last night, correct?"

"Yes, the same male." He tilted his head in the other direction. "The siren is irritated too. I do not think she likes the dragon very much either. I wish I could hear what they are saying. Though it is best we not get any closer. I cannot imagine they would appreciate being spied upon."

"No. We are close enough." As long as the trio didn't come in their direction, they'd be fine. It was a suitable spot. All they needed to do was see, for now. Though if the others came closer, then they could hear some of what they said.

"She is still just, I really do not know what she is doing. Why would he be wearing a collar?"

"I don't know. Maybe it's a device of some sort?" They had things like that for their warriors. Weapons. Items that they had built for protection or to cause damage.

"I do not know either. I have seen nothing quite like it before. Similar. It does not appear to be comfortable, so I would not call it jewelry. Markham has used chains before, and shackles." She sensed when his gaze focused on her. "Not on me. But I have seen it a few times. When he has been angry."

Shackles?! She had to bite her tongue to keep the words from leaving her mouth. She didn't like that idea. Not one bit. Demeter, she had never been more thrilled for him to be out of that village. Even if the circumstances hadn't been preferable. "I'm glad not on you."

"Me too." He paused. "Um, they appear to be ready to leave. They are getting clothing out, and..." His whispers trailed off, and she sensed a wince from him.

Softly, she caressed his shoulder. She didn't know what he was seeing. Whatever it was, it bothered him. "What is it? Are they changing?"

Though her touch soothed him, a shiver still ran through his body. He lifted his head and rubbed it against her. "The male. He has scars on his back. Scars like..." His whispers trailed off again. "But yes. They are changing."

He didn't have to finish the statement. Though her wounds had healed, she knew the chilling image would forever haunt his thoughts. She continued to caress his shoulder. "Interesting."

"If they are leaving, we may want to do so as well. They may come this way."

"I agree," she said. "If nothing else, if they are moving farther inward, then the barrier will not close soon." That much she knew.

"That would make sense." Gavin raised himself up off the ground, careful not to dislodge her. He waited while she took the second potion and tightened her grip back upon him, then he took off back through the trees.

They zigzagged through the forest as they returned to the treehouse, following the same path back. That the barrier was still down. This was good. And if the trio was going farther into the isle, it gave them time to figure out how to take advantage of this. And get off the isle permanently.

When they reached the treehouse, she left his back and he climbed the tree. Still processing everything they'd witnessed, Parthenia took a little extra time to get to the top. Over the last several months, they had gotten small glimpses of light, but this was the brightest it had ever been. She landed at the top of the entrance and beamed as he removed his camouflage.

With a shift, he strode across the floor and enveloped her in a warm embrace. He stared down at her for a few minutes. So close. They were much closer than they'd ever been. If only they could leave now, but there were still things they needed to accomplish before they could do that. At the very least, they didn't want to spend the rest of their lives unable to have sex. Unable to have children. That was a dream of theirs they weren't prepared to give up. But this... Escape was at their fingertips. "I love you."

"I love you too." She snuggled into his arms. Yes, she'd have to leave within the hour, but she didn't want to think about that right now. This was the first real glimmer they'd had in months. All she wanted to do was revel in that. There were still answers they needed, and they'd have a limited time to get them, but they were so close she could taste it.

To Be Continued...

In Book Three
Rebel Tides

Rebel Tides

Thalasia glanced over her shoulder at the humanoid-creature. It resembled a human, except for the magic it seemed to possess and the pint-sized, bony wings protruding from its back. At least it couldn't fly with those things. She turned and ran out of the forest toward the beach. None of this had been what she'd searched for since her arrival.

All she had to find—stepping out of the edge of the forest, her eyes fell upon a bridge about fifty feet in front of her. *Finally!* The bridge from her vision swarmed ahead. Now, she just had to—a swoosh of air came up behind her, lifted her in the air, and slammed her backside down on the ground.

Fuck! Her left wing burned as grains of sand made their way into the gaping hole in her appendage. Thalasia pushed up on her hands and spotted the humanoid-creature fast approaching. She got on her feet. He could manipulate the air. Well, she could too.

In more ways than one.

Tired of running, she opened her mouth and sang. Her angelic voice carried across the wind and soothed the anger the creature compelled. Her song didn't require words, just the melody. As she closed the distance between her and the humanoid, her aria stilled the wild wind and its manipulator.

She placed one hand at the nape of its neck and reached for the dagger tucked into the belt of her pants. With one swift move, she removed the blade from its hiding place and thrust it into the creature's gut.

It grunted as black blood spewed from its wound, and then it dropped to the ground with a thud.

Her heart pounded beneath her chest. The last of the tune left her lips. Thalasia leaned over, yanked her dagger from its body, and wiped it clean using her pants. There was no time to waste.

She didn't know how many of those things had followed her. Returning the dagger to its rightful spot, she took off for the bridge.

Her talons dug into the gritty white grains as she ran toward freedom. It took longer to reach the bridge than if she could've flown. Damn arrow had taken a small chunk out of her wing. It'd be useless for the next day.

With the bridge a few feet away, Thalasia stopped. The first board of the wooden overpass had some sort of weird engraving. Studying the image, she walked closer and looked across it. Well, half the bridge. Fog gathered somewhere around the middle, a good thirty yards ahead. Still, each board had a different engraving, although after so many, they began repeating. One caught her eye.

Five or six panels in—she noticed a familiar lyre.

Her ears prickled. She peered over her shoulder. This was the bridge in her vision. As for what she'd just seen, there was no time to contemplate it.

Thalasia started across the bridge. Half-way across, the fog grabbed her and yanked her through some invisible field. The barrier rippled outward as it carried her forward and tossed her out the other side. Her legs and arms flailed for a moment until she face-planted and landed in more white sand.

With a small groan, she pushed up on her arms and faced the shield that had been there. It billowed out in an iridescent wave.

What the hell?

Her pulse quickened. Where in Good Demeter had she ended up? Another realm? Getting to her feet, Thalasia scanned her surroundings. A tall cliff stood a few feet away. Behind her, the waves crashed into one another as the sun set below the horizon.

Nothing about this flight—her mind's eye opened and tossed her against the jagged rock of the towering cliff-side.

In her head, the scenery changed. The beachy sand disappeared and, in its stead, she saw overgrown grass and a forest full of thick, tall trees. The surrounding woods were so lush she almost missed the dark-haired person with green wings that ran by. Not that she noticed the face. Or the eyes. But something about this person... it seemed familiar.

Thalasia gasped as the vision left her head and practically threw her back to the pebbly sands beneath her feet. She leaned against the rugged seaside cliff and closed her eyes to settle her thundering heartbeat.

Man, things really needed to get easier.

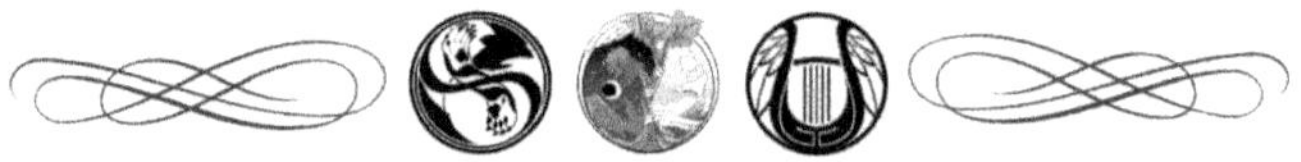

Winding her way through the clouds, Aurelia easily spotted the source of the disturbance. A substantial tear shimmered an iridescent rainbow over the beach, near the foot of the Stairway to Heaven—the bridge that once permitted the earthbound species to rise above the clouds to visit the draconic cities. She watched intently as a strange creature exited the gateway. Her vision zeroed in on the blue-feathered woman as she dug her talons into the white sands.

A nasty snarl curled her lips, exposing her fangs. She rushed to the beach, her amethyst scales shedding in a flurry of gold particles and white sand. Only a few of her draconic features remained—her menacing reptilian eyes rimmed by dark purple scales with a powerful glow and her fearsome fangs. Just enough to strike fear into this exotic newcomer.

"What have you done?" Aurelia demanded.

The girl's distant, glossed over stare cooled the dragoness's rage, depriving it of its potency as she watched the other woman collapse. She caught her by the arm, careful not to dig her gilded nails into the female's flesh, and she held the woman steady until she found her balance. Whoever she was, this girl was cursed with a terrible affliction.

She possessed the sight.

"Easy. I've got you," Aurelia murmured. The remnants of her rage dissipated, releasing on the tails of her power as she reverted to her human form. No eyes, no scales. Just flesh and bone.

Aurelia's gaze drifted to the girl's wounded wing. She clasped two of the metal talons in her teeth, her fingertips emitting a warm, golden energy that brushed the wound, smearing it with enriched stardust.

The dazed bird-girl recoiled, a hiss escaping her lips as she returned to herself. Aurelia's magic must have brought her back to reality from... wherever her far-off stare had taken her.

Wincing, the girl attempted to pull away. "What're you doing?"

"Tending your wound," Aurelia said around the jewelry clamped between her fangs as she maneuvered the appendage gently, inspecting for further damage and mobility as the medicine did its job.

Once, she allowed the female to back away while she replaced her talons on the appropriate fingers. "What did you see?" Aurelia pressed. "Better yet, what attacked you?" She scanned the beach but found no signs of the attacker, only a few drops of the woman's blood staining the sand a brilliant scarlet. Her opponent, or opponents, must still be on the other side.

Crossing her arms, the bird-girl narrowed her silver eyes and sneered. "Doesn't matter. It's dead."

Aurelia's rage threatened to reignite at the other woman's nonchalant response. "Oh, it matters," she growled through clenched teeth, forcing herself to take a deep breath before continuing. "If it has friends, they might come through. That pathway"—She gestured toward the open bridge—"isn't closing. There has to be a reason." She fought to keep her emotions in check as the full weight of the situation settled. Nothing like this had ever happened before—not to her knowledge. Once she resolved this situation with the bird-girl, she'd need to consult Seru—and his library.

"Seeing as I've never been here before, I couldn't tell you." The girls smirked and started down the beach, her talons kicking up tiny grains of sand with each step.

The bird-girl paused and glanced over her shoulder. "I can tell you it's one of those things on Candescent Isle. At least, I believe that's what they called it."

"Never heard of it." For all she knew, the girl had made up the names and places. Aurelia used her magic to reappear in the woman's path, forcing her to an abrupt halt. "If you think you're going to walk or fly away, you're wrong. The longer that gate remains open, the more unstable the magic in this realm becomes. And when that happens, even your fortunes aren't going to save you."

Frowning, the girl rolled her eyes. "I'm assuming you live here, or at least near here. Seeing as it would cause some issues, don't you think it would be prudent to figure out how to close it? And sweetheart, if you don't have the answers, then I'm sure there's someone here who does."

Aurelia wrinkled her nose at the suggestion. "Only earthbound live on the ground, bird. The only reason I'm here is to ensure your disturbance doesn't lead to more trouble." So, the woman didn't know how to close the portal... did that mean she wasn't the one who opened it? Aurelia's brows knitted together, still refusing to yield to the stranger.

As her internal questions led to more questions, Aurelia's frustration mounted. *Someone who does...* A thought occurred to her. "Enoch!"

In an instant, Aurelia shifted and took to the skies.

Rising to her feet, Thalasia partially extended her left wing but didn't get more than a quarter of its full length. She grimaced at the spot where she'd lost a few feathers. Stupid creature had caught her with an arrow and knocked her to the ground.

The cave seemed massive. She could easily see an extensive tunnel beyond her current location. Big enough to live in. It wouldn't be ideal, but after her interaction with the dragon-shifter a few hours ago, it was better than the alternative.

Aside from the crackling fire, the moon provided the only other light in the cave. Thalasia squeezed the muscle in her shoulder one last time and glanced back out at the night sky. Her gaze fell to the bridge she'd spent hours watching. Yes, she'd left the creature's remains on the other side, so at some point someone would discover it. That didn't mean the broken barrier was her fault. How could it be?

Maybe she wasn't like every other siren, but she didn't possess the power to break a barrier. At least she didn't think so. Even if she wasn't normal by siren standards, this couldn't be her fault. No matter what the dragon-girl had insinuated, no one could blame her.

This wasn't the time to fret over something so coincidental. Thalasia stretched out on her makeshift nest of sticks and moss. It would suffice for the night. She had to rest for her wing to heal. By morning, it would be restored, and then she'd be ready to continue her search.

Something landed with a thud at her feet, startling her from the slumber she hadn't begun. Metal against stone soon followed.

Thalasia cracked open an eye and shifted her gaze toward the noise. A human-looking creature with spiky black hair, dark eyes, black-rimmed glasses, and shackles half-stood at the end of her bed.

The dragoness returned with a small gilded army at her back, their golden armor reflecting the flames of the dwindling campfire. Another group emerged from the darkened tunnel, each boasting the finest weapons she'd ever seen. They'd cut off every exit.

"I'll have whatever *catalyst* you used to open the barrier, blue bird." It was no longer a request, but a demand. The dragon-shifter held out a taloned hand, expecting full compliance.

What in Demeter's name? Thalasia jerked upright. She crossed her arms and frowned. *Catalyst?* "What part of 'I didn't open the damn thing' didn't you comprehend? Are you just that stupid? Or was that information too much for your brain to handle?"

"According to the expert here"—The dragon-girl nodded to the nearby creature, who still scrambled in the dirt, his lips to the ground as if he was grateful to be alive—"you're lying. Enoch! Quit your groveling and get on with it," the girl reprimanded, delivering a swift kick to his backside.

He stumbled forth, nearly landing in Thalasia's lap. "P-pardon me, young lady ..." He offered a forced smile. It didn't take long for his black eyes to be drawn to the chain adorning her neck and glistening in the firelight. "The matriarch requests to borrow your—" he gestured toward the golden necklace.

Good Demeter, of all the creatures to run into, she had to find the darkest of them. Her silver eyes lit up the cavern as she narrowed her gaze at the dragon-girl. Gods, dragon-shifters really had a way about them. Thalasia stood and offered a hand to the human-like creature at her feet, then refocused her attention on the so-called matriarch. Bitch was more like it. "I don't give a shit who the hell you think you are. No one deserves to be treated like dirt."

The dragon-shifter's lips tugged into a toothy sneer. She chuckled. "He might appear harmless to you now, but Enoch is no saint, I assure you. He could live a thousand lifetimes and never escape the weight of his sins. Remove those shackles and see how your kindness serves you, siren."

"It might surprise you how far kindness will get you. I don't know you. Nor have you bothered to try asking for anything. While I appreciate the aid you gave my wing, it'll heal on its own." Thalasia snorted. "I don't tolerate bullies, and obviously you've got some kind of stick up your ass."

She crossed her arms again and drank in the full sight of the army dragon-girl brought along with her. "Case in point, you seem to think me, a single siren, is pretty dangerous. Instead of trying to ask for my help, you brought an army along. How far do you think that'll get you?"

Enoch winced at her biting remark. "Never wise to piss off the queen," he whispered, leaning in as he offered the advice.

Dragon-girl inclined her chin, meeting Thalasia's silvery glare with her violet one. "Anyone who recklessly jumps through realms are dangerous. I won't allow you, your flock, or any other to bring your troubles to my door. Funny, I don't recall you knocking or requesting passage through our lands last we spoke, either. You stormed off, leaving your problems to be dealt with by others. As you're within my lands, that responsibility falls to me and my people. I assure you, there's no trouble in being prepared when dealing with someone as charming as you," the dragon-shifter proclaimed.

Thalasia raised an eyebrow. Her flock? Had she landed somewhere near the home of the sirens? A place she'd never set foot in before. This was news to her. Then again, she didn't exactly know where she'd ended up to begin with. Her lips curled into a small smile. "One: I don't know what flock you're talking about. Two: I didn't storm off, I walked away... from you. I've spent the last few hours watching the bridge. Three: I didn't recklessly jump. The fog grabbed me and tossed me here. It didn't exactly give me a choice. Now, if you want to figure out what happened, I'd be happy to talk to your so-called expert." She shifted her gaze toward Enoch, who still hovered nearby. "Without your army. Unless you're incapable of acting like an adult."

"If you've been watching, then I'm sure by now you've realized the situation isn't going anywhere." The dragon-girl's violet eyes twinkled for a moment. She let out a heated breath and turned to the men behind her. "Half of you wait outside; the rest go guard the bridge." The dragon-shifter proceeded to those across from her. "You lot, retreat to the end of the tunnel and no further."

The towering men and women shuffled uneasily.

"I said OUT!" the dragon-shifter roared, stirring them into action.

Enoch nearly jumped out of his skin before retreating closer to the siren.

As the last of the elite guard filed out, the dragon-shifter focused on Thalasia. "Make no mistake, if you try anything, I'm more than capable of subduing you myself. As I'm sure your new *friend* here will tell you."

Enoch took the moment's silence to steal a glance at Thalasia, never quite allowing the necklace she wore out of his sight.

Reaching up, Thalasia stroked the back of Enoch's head, much like a mother comforting her child. She didn't know them, but the situation had to be de-escalated, and he was staring at her just a little too much. Specifically, the gold chain around her neck. The trinket itself remained hidden beneath her tank top. It held no power that anyone should sense, so it made no sense why his attention was so focused on it. No matter, it belonged to her mother, and she would protect it at all costs. "I'm aware that it isn't closing the way it should. How long has the barrier been in place?"

Enoch relaxed into her tender touch. He cleared his throat before replying, his voice low and raspy. "Mm... about three-hundred years, give or take."

Dragon-girl's violet eyes flicked from him to Thalasia.

He swallowed and then proceeded. "The barrier was erected after the Great War, when the species diverged and the last of the witches perished. Both sirens and dragons came here, taking to the skies, while others remained on the ground. An interspecies war broke out among the sirens about a hundred years after the Great War. Shortly afterward, the barrier appeared."

Thalasia blinked. Continuing to stroke Enoch's head, her gaze shifted past the dragon-girl toward the bridge. She had seen multiple engravings on the panels. Looking back at Enoch, she raised an eyebrow. "Do you know who built the barrier? Or how they did it?"

Enoch tilted his head. "There are many theories. The most common states it was erected to keep something out. To preserve the utopia herein."

The dragon-shifter snorted.

"The dragons despised the guilers, grew weary of their abuse of magic and... experimentation." Enoch's words dripped with sourness. "The silver queen... the previous matriarch."

He sat up, reached into the remnants of the fire, and retrieved a stick with which to sketch out his scene, the wooden point scratching out the epic battle in the ashes. "She's said to be the one who put an end to the last enchantress, burning her—and her bird—alive for their treachery..."

Catching a slight change in his demeanor as his story abruptly ended, Thalasia's stance stiffened, so she didn't roll her eyes. Good Demeter, this matriarch needed a serious attitude adjustment. Replaying Enoch's story in her mind, she glanced over her shoulder at the night sky and turned back to him. It certainly explained a few things. "I'm going to assume the theories remain unproven. If we don't know what caused the barrier in the first place, then we have no way of knowing what would've broken it. That said, the best way to figure out what happened is to find out how and who built it. Wouldn't you agree?"

To that matter, it also seemed she now had a name for the creature she'd killed earlier. "And that thing I fought on the other side; would it be safe to presume that's a guiler?"

Enoch pushed his thick-rimmed glasses up his nose with a nod, black smudges appearing where his fingers touched. "Most barriers require a catalyst, or a key to be opened and closed." He briefly glanced at the dragon-shifter before allowing his eyes to drift back to Thalasia's necklace. "When the matriarch appeared demanding answers, naturally I thought you were the only possibility. But it appears she may have... jumped to a few hasty conclusions before gathering all the facts."

He shifted uncomfortably, like an animal awaiting another lashing. When it didn't come, he continued. "Either you, lovely siren, or that fallen guiler must possess an item that allowed the barrier to reopen. Did you see anything of that sort? It needn't be remarkable or extraordinary. Perhaps you noticed the guiler enacting a chant, spell, or magic which may have led to the bridge?"

His words made perfect sense to her. Everything she'd learned about magical barriers indicated the item could be small or even insignificant. Thalasia frowned. "I can't say I noticed anything with the guiler, but he had magic. Air magic. Every one of them I saw on Candescent Isle had magic. I thought it was strange because I've seen no human with magic, not that they were entirely human either." That wasn't entirely true, but they didn't look like witches or warlocks. And she certainly refused to share more than was necessary with these folks.

Otherwise, they could cause further unwanted problems.

About the Authors

Author of the Love's Worth Series, **Brigit Rosé,** lives in a world of romance. She has taken her life experience and made it into one endless love story. When she's not writing, she's singing loudly and off-key, hanging out with friends, or playing with her 2 fur babies. She can usually be found with a kiss in one hand and a twist of line in the other, exactly the stories she likes to read and write. If you'd like to know more about Brigit, you can find out more on her website: https://kbfennerrose.com

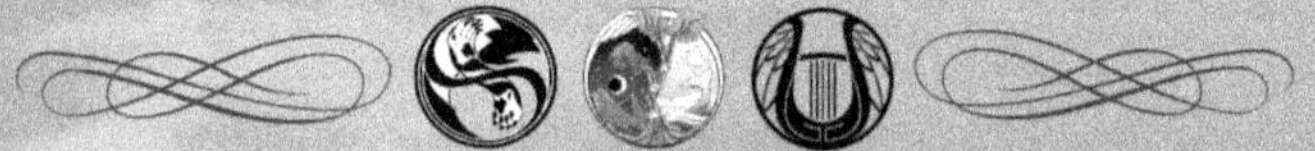

Nikki Haras has had a passion for writing since she was a small child. She will use whatever means necessary to get the words down that swirl inside her head, bleeding ink onto the page and breathing life into the characters who demand to tell their stories. When she's not immersing herself in her fantasy worlds, she's a full-time mom of three children and three fur babies, but you can usually always find her with a cup of coffee in one hand and a pen tucked into her messy bun. Always plotting the next amazing scene, fantastic new story, or immersive fantasy world to bring to life. To find out more about Nikki Haras and her upcoming book releases, you can find her on Facebook.

Other Works by Brigit Rosé

Love's Worth Series
UnHinged
ReIgnited
The Lucent Chronicles
Grace's Beast
Shattered Wonderland
The Mystic Chronicles
Detached
Standalone
Savage Seas
The Arcarean Academy
Wicked Ground

Under Krys Fenner

Co-authored

Prisma Isle Series
Perfectly Reckless
Chaotic Tranquility
Rebel Tides
Prisma Isle Puzzle & Coloring Book

Coming soon